How to Cyberbully Your Teacher

How to Cyberbully Your Teacher

A Non-Fiction Narrative

by

Daniel Curzon

l'Aleph

Daniel Curzon

How to Cyberbully Your Teacher

Published by *l'Aleph* – Sweden – www.l-aleph.com

l'Aleph is a Wisehouse Imprint.

ISBN 978-91-7637-575-4

Oh, what a tangled web we weave,
When first we practice to deceive.
                    — Sir Walter Scott

How much of this "novel" actually happened?
. . . Too much.

This book is dedicated to
Jerry Rosco
for his many contributions
and kindnesses over the years.

He was in the Non-Faculty Dining Room when he first heard of "The Problem." (You dare not call it the Faculty Dining Room, it should be noted, because that implied that faculty might have a room (or even want a room) for themselves where they might — the elitist bastards! — *actually want* to get away from students.)

"Okay, I'll bite. What does it say about me?" he asked Spike Burns, the chair of the English Department. They were at a small table near the window of the so-called Lowe-Rankin Dining Experience (named after two chefs who had died in an unfortunate tainted tofu double poisoning several years earlier).

"Believe me, you don't want to know," Spike replied. Spike (Spencer) was a man in his sixties, going on ninety, always impeccably dressed, with pure white shirts and pale neckties, rather ancient and pink overall as a presence. He wore oversize horn-rimmed glasses and was a strange combination of school politician and absolute cynic. He was buttering a floury roll and just about to leave, taking the roll with him for a snack later.

"It can't be that bad. *Can* it?" Nathaniel asked.

"Look up yourself," Spike said, a glimmer of something close to satisfaction in his smallish, windowed eyes. But then that was always true of Spike.

"I can't bend over that far anymore — to look up myself," Nathaniel joked.

Spike didn't laugh. Maybe it was too "gay" for Spike, who was something of a mystery to Nathaniel. He talked a lot, but he was one of those people who never reveal a scrap of information about their private lives. But he knew all the dirt in the department and beyond in the wondrous kingdom called Shite College.

"I just wouldn't look at the website if I were you." These were Spike's parting words.

"*That* bad?"

Now I'll have to look at it, Nathaniel told himself. What have I got to fear? I'm an excellent teacher — colorful. Sure, I say things that are a bit direct sometimes, but it's a breath of fresh air around this place.

Right? Besides, I'm just trying to maintain academic standards. Anyone with half a brain would agree about the parody of higher education that we're all engaged in at this place. *Right?*

Yeah, right.

Nathaniel went to a computer in the library and summoned up the website via the INFORMATION section of the college's webpage. The Alliance of Students and several other organizations on campus had promotional links directing users to use it:

TEACHERSONPARADE.com.

All in all, the website was quite elaborate, with a special SPEAK OUT LOUD section for discussion of campus issues. You also could read REVIEWS OF THE DAY to see who were the latest teachers to be put up for "review," and there were even two sections called TIP OF THE TOP and THE PITS, where teachers were ranked by their cumulative scores as the best or the worst at Shite College.

Nathaniel found his name right in the middle of THE PITS. This website just started, for god's sake, and already I'm . . . He looked at it more closely, his throat dry. His eyes were burning too. When he checked, he saw that there were only six reviews of him. How could whoever was running the website put up top and bottom lists based on so few reviews?

He steeled himself and "looked up himself" and read the top review:

> Dr. Tack he no good. He not ethnic! He racist. He no pass students from my couhtry. I hate him. i hope he die i hope college administers gouge out his eyes and discpline him very soon.

I'm not ethnic? Everybody's ethnic! Only apparently some were more ethnic than others on this animal farm.

It was like having the wind knocked out of you. Followed by a flush of anger. Your English is about as far from college-level writing as it is possible to be, and so *I'm* a racist? Nathaniel despised the simplicities of both the Right and the Left and thus could give no allegiance to either. He didn't want people to be mean to others, but it was WAY beyond that — all around him at his college he felt the coils of Political Correctness about "minorities" of a particularly one-sided view of reality, and, my, had his students learned to jump on that bandwagon as soon as they got off the boat. It wasn't that all of them were bad. It was that you had to say *none* of them were. The first million or so were charming, or cute, or even sad and welcome. The rest of the FOURTEEN MILLION in one decade alone weren't. Xenophobia, my ass! Nathaniel didn't like crowds — it didn't matter what color they were. He was on the front lines and knew more about the subject than most people did. It wasn't pretty, especially when it came to "minorities'" view of gay rights. Gay *what*? They could use a dose of Political Correctness themselves!

He forced himself to be calm. We are delighted to have members of the Third World like you here at Shite College. You are but one small example of the many delights of our Beauty of Diversity Program, and, no, your shit doesn't stink. Yeah, Diversity, that self-serving version of Paper/Scissors/Rock, in which Female trumps Male, Minority trumps Majority, Race trumps Everything. Nathaniel knew that life was pretty much a Darwinian struggle, and that included squabbling among the self-serving varieties of the human species. He just didn't want to be one of the ones to bite the dust in the competition. He was already being severely tested in the Galapagos called Shite College.

> He read another review:

> Nathaniel Tack think he a brilliant and clever man, but he not. He have a lot to learn from his students, but he to far gone to save. Avoid his classes and maybe Administration will have no choice but to be rid of him. He evil, evil man. Then students will do well here & have much deserve college success!

Well. Double well! He looked it over again. Am I so desperate I need to find writing errors to protect my ego? Ego, my dick. They're trying to get me fired — even though every single evaluation I've ever had from my colleagues has been laudatory! I should learn from my students? Students learn and teachers teach, for god's sake! How old-fashioned to think so!

Gulp!

Nathaniel checked down at the bottom of the review. No name of the reviewer. Age: 20. Sex: Female. Class Taken: English 101. Grade Received: W. Grade Point Average: 4.0.

So she didn't even finish the class. Fuck her! He looked at the review again, trying to figure out who had written it. Was it that young Burmese woman with the pierced eyebrow and the lisp, the Asian feminist? She'd sat all but scowling at him for two weeks and then dropped. Was this her revenge because he had written "Jane Austen was not exactly a Wymyn's Liberation Pioneer as you say in your essay." The Lisping Feminist — yeah, fuck her too. Two weeks do not a class make!

But maybe it wasn't her. It was anonymous, so it could be anybody. He looked up Spike Burns's reviews. There weren't any. None. How could that be? He looked up Gilda LaMatresse, the head of the Wymyn's Studies Program. She had six reviews too, all raves. She was on TIP OF THE TOP as one of the outstanding teachers. He'd observed Gilda teaching one time. It was all that touchy-feeling, self-esteemy crap, women sitting around in a circle congratulating each other on their Collective Feminine Strength and the need to overcome their genital oppression. How tired.

He read the next one:

> Dr. Nathaniel Tack is an arrogant bastard who will not survive
> the righteousness of Student Power!!! He'll be kicked out of
> here within a year if some of us have our way!!!!!!! — Hackers
> United

Even the hackers had a union now? He stopped reading the reviews because he was breathing too hard. I need to exercise, he told himself. I also need to be thirty again, slim and sexy, and — Jesus H. Christ, this hate-site was serious! *Very*!

He left the school's library and headed across campus toward the faculty parking lot. Shite College (named after nineteenth-century Irish founder/philanthropist Boylan T. Shite) in the amazing city of Santa Francesca (named after the lesbian sister of St. Francis) looked like nothing so much as an old whore, spreading her less-than-beauteous parts across a hill and half of almost prime real estate, settled into her special corner of the city, ready day or night, to service her customers, who slogged up the various steep staircases to prod the old gal in one orifice or the other, hoping to get An Education or at least A Degree and get the hell out of there before they came down with something permanent. Miss Shite as she was known, unaffectionately, spread her veined and leathery, tired, old snatch for one and all and barely noticed as they hopped on and off. Hell, what's one more fuck at my age, she thought as she entered the twenty-first century.

Although at Shite College it was considered very important to be Devoted and

Committed to Students, it must be said that the students weren't especially devoted to Shite College, almost all of them there because they couldn't get in anywhere else. They had either done so badly in high school (and in America that meant *really* badly), were foreign students, or were so screwed up psychologically that they malfunctioned in an educational environment. Needless to say, Shite had done outreach to homeless shelters, mental institutions, even prisons, all to promote its multiple SUCCESS!!! programs. (The capitals were real. Only the SUCCESS wasn't.) Of course, there were *some* decent students there as well, Nathaniel had to admit, including some of the foreign ones.

He just wished *he* wasn't there. He certainly had not gotten a Ph. D. in a hard graduate program in the Midwest and published scholarly articles, plays, and fiction in order to spend his days putting commas and semi-colons, to say nothing of idioms, coherence and sanity, into students' remedial papers. And those were on the good days! The school had more than its fair share of the deranged, the weird, and the frightening — and that was just on the faculty.

Nathaniel had come to Shite College twenty years earlier through a series of misfortunes, bad choices, and historical forces over which he had no control. He was now a man close to sixty years of age though, lucky for him, he had always looked younger than he was, say forty-five, with very bright blue eyes in an American (half Irish, half hillbilly) face. Alas, now he was beginning to beef up, his chest expanding along with his waistline, his formerly brown hair, mustache, and eyebrows in need of a Loving Care tune-up every month or so to keep them from revealing the dying little gray thistles underneath. To stave off the inevitable, he'd had liposuction on his chest, love-handles, and belly. Then a little surgery on his double chin, leaving a scar that was only noticeable . . . when you looked at it. At least the wattles didn't wattle quite so much. Now he was thinking of getting laser treatments for the brown spots that were beginning to appear on the backs of his hands and near his right temple. He would have had the treatments already, for such was his vanity, but he couldn't afford them on his professor's salary. My, what life does to you before it kicks you out, he sighed.

His office in the Horace D. Fellon Building was an eight-by-eight cubicle he shared with three other people, two of them part-timers — with no ceiling. Some of the flimsy partitions didn't go all the way to the walls, so it was possible for people to go into other offices without a key if you could just get into your own. Not that you would want to. You could already overhear almost everything that was said up and down the length of t for trying." This from an economics teacher with a particularly loud voice. "Did you feed the ferals under Bungalow 122?" This from Louise Beeze, also known as the Cat Lady, former eligibility coordinator in the English Department, and now forgetting to comb her hair and spending her every spare moment feeding feral cats up one side and down the other of the goddamned campus.

Just as Nathaniel got to his office he noticed a flyer thumb-tacked to the felt bulletin board where he and his office mates posted their class schedules and office hours.

He read through the rest of the flyer. Phrases flew out at him like hornets:

> You need never step into the classroom
> To know what your getting!
> Don't waist time on bad classes!
> Its your educashun! You paid for it.
> Students are customers!
> Get whats coming to you!

They're wearing out the exclamation point, though certainly not the apostrophe, Nathaniel thought. And students were customers? Since when? The students were buying their grades? The customer is always right? You don't like the F you're getting? Could I interest you in an A? And on top of it, tuition at Shite College was incredibly cheap. Compared to the other colleges in the area it was a downright steal. And if it came to deserving, who should 'scape whipping at this place? Including me!

As soon as his office hour began, a student came to see him. It was Mr. Mustapha from his Plays and Novels class. He thought Mr. Mustapha liked him. At least he smiled a lot during class and nodded when Nathaniel said things. And this was his third office visit.

"What can I do for you, Mr. Mustapha?" Nathaniel said. See, I'm nice to my students! I even address them formally.

Mr. Mustapha sat in the brown plastic chair next to Nathaniel's desk. He was in his late teens, vaguely Middle-Eastern with big black eyes, American born, his English excellent. His parents were wealthy and he was going to Yale the next semester, he'd said. He was just killing time taking a creative writing class until he got over a bout of Crohn's disease that kept him dyspeptic and toilet-bound much of the time.

"Have you seen it?" he asked Nathaniel.

"Seen what?" Coyness had its place. No use advertising the damned website.

"Teachersonparade."

"What's that?"

"It's this cool website where you can review your teachers."

"Really?"

"You haven't seen it?"

"No. Tell me about it."

Mr. Mustapha's black eyes got even bigger as he leaned closer. He had narrow shoulders, Nathaniel noticed. I'm so glad I'm not attracted to men his age. There's already enough to worry about in this old world. But Mr. Mustapha probably thinks I want his skinny body. Nathaniel got up and made sure the door to his office was open. Accusations of harassment against the faculty seemed to be growing more common semester by semester. There'd even been a memo from some campus office or other about it.

"You're on it, Dr. Tack," Mr. Mustapha said.

"Am I? What does it say?"

Mr. Mustapha hesitated. "Oh, I wouldn't pay too much attention to it." He smiled what he thought was a secret smile.

"I won't. Did you want to discuss your play about the giant who has Crohn's disease?"

"I've written another couple of pages. It's hard going." He took out the pages and placed them on Nathaniel's desk. They were in pencil with lots of words crossed out and new ones written in.

Nathaniel cast his eye across the first page.

"Want me to go out for a few minutes while you read it?" Mr. Mustapha asked.

"No, that's all right. Just give me a minute or so. You can give me a more polished version later. Possible?" Nathaniel hinted.

"I'm sorry it's so messy."

"No problem. I live to serve my beloved students here at Shite."

Mr. Mustapha smiled appropriately.

Nathaniel began to read the dialogue, which was pretty good. Mr. Mustapha had talent. Maybe the Crohn's disease was a blessing in disguise. He'd have to stay close to a toilet. That way he'd stay home and write more. God has His ways.

"You really don't know about the website?" Mr. Mustapha interrupted.

Nathaniel looked up from the manuscript. "Is there something you want to tell me?"

"I don't believe it, because I've seen you teach. You're a very good teacher."

Nathaniel smiled, a pinched one. "Thank you."

"I'm not just saying that for the grade. I'm going to major in chemical engineering."

"I didn't think you were just saying it."

Mr. Mustapha looked down at his shoes. "I don't know if I should say this or not."

"What's that?"

"Maybe I'd better not."

Nathaniel put down the manuscript. "Okay, you've got my full attention. What is it you don't want to say?"

Mr. Mustapha looked like he was having a stomach cramp. He even rubbed his abdomen, and a small belch came out. "Excuse me."

"You're excused." Nathaniel sat back in his swivel chair, waiting.

"I ran into somebody in the student cafeteria yesterday."

"Yes?"

"He noticed that I was writing something for your class. He saw your name on the assignment sheet."

Nathaniel waited.

"He said, 'I know all about that Tack. He's an asshole. He doesn't help the students succeed.'" Mr. Mustapha paused. "I'm just quoting him. It's not what I think."

"I understand."

"He asked me if I had sent in a review of you yet, and I said I hadn't. Then he said, 'Well, *I* have! And I haven't even been in that fucker's class!'"

At first Nathaniel didn't take in what was being said to him. "How could he send in a review of me if he's never had me?"

"I guess you can send in reviews just by pretending to be in a class."

"Say that again."

"You can put down any information about yourself that you want to. But it doesn't have to be true." Mr. Mustapha hastened to add: "Not that I'd ever do something like that."

"You mean to tell me that nobody *verifies* the actual enrollment of the student reviewing a teacher?"

"I don't believe so. You can put down any age or sex you want. Or any grade point average, even if it's made up."

"Or any other lie you feel like putting down, is that what you're saying?"

"At first I didn't think anybody would lie until I ran into this guy in the cafeteria, who said he's sent in three or four reviews of you."

Nathaniel's armpits began to percolate. The swivel chair was hurting his back. "I see. What did this person look like, the one who sent in these multiple reviews of me?"

"In his late thirties, I'd say. Dreadlocks — only he was white. Yeah, blond, knotted dreadlocks and a little goatee — under his lip, not on his chin. He said he's been around here for a few years and he's heard students complain that you're too hard."

"*Am* I too hard?" Nathaniel asked.

"Not at all," Mr. Mustapha said.

That's it because it's a creative writing class, Nathaniel thought, and you have to be dead to get less than a B. "Maybe I should take your scene and read it more carefully," he said to the student. "I'm having a hard time concentrating right now."

"Of course."

"I'll bring it to class."

"That would be great."

"Do you think you could identify this student with the dreadlocks if you saw him again?"

"I'm not sure. Why?"

Mmm, Mr. Mustapha was backing off already, the overly cautious bastard. "In case this website goes any further. Would you say the students are using it to pick classes for next semester?"

"Some are."

"A lot?"

"Yeah, I'd say so."

Nathaniel smiled at Mr. Mustapha. "Well, thank you for the information. It hadn't crossed my mind that someone could write reviews of teachers they haven't even had. Ain't modern technology grand."

The student left, smiling one of those fake is-there-anything-I-can-do-to-improve-my-grade smiles? Extra work maybe?

Yeah, what I need from you is more bad work, class. For god's sake just give me something competent in the first place and not in pencil! But Mr. Mustapha wasn't so bad. Naw, he was all right.

When Nathaniel went to his afternoon 101 class, he was a little early. Some of the students were looking at copies of the school newspaper when he arrived. Nobody ever read that rag. So why today? He could see some of them smirking together, though he pretended not to notice. He wouldn't give them the satisfaction of asking if there was a news story about the website. There were about fifteen of them there, most of them "minorities." Actually he was the "minority" now where he lived – a double one. He was white and he was gay. The school was 81% "minority," a term one was supposed to use with reverence. Language had broken down like almost everything else! He looked at his watch. He couldn't look at a clock in the classroom because there wasn't one. He'd made the mistake of sending in a request to the Office of Repairs. Never a good idea. Usually no one from that office paid any attention to requests whatsoever, but this time somebody had come and taken the clock away. Seven weeks ago. Now there was just a wire sticking out of the wall. Down the hall most of the signs indicating CLASSROOM had been vandalized into ASSROOM and ASSPOO. That is when they hadn't been destroyed entirely. Morons. College, my ass. *My* assroom!

Nathaniel looked at his class roll. Someone was always absent. Two or three were always late. Always. Or they'd take a break even though the class had no break. Had it always been like this, and he just couldn't remember? Or were the students really that much worse now? The attention span of gnats. Was he just getting old and grumpy? No, there were articles all the time. "My Students Have Fallen and Can't Get Up," "Tide of Remedial Classes Overwhelms Budget."

"Let's begin, Nathaniel said, meaning they should put the newspapers away. "Let's talk about diction. You never know. You might need it sometime." He noticed Mr. Bhatangsombatuisit in the back continuing to read the student newspaper. Should he stop the class and wait? Should he say something? "Let us begin class!" he said, aiming the words at Mr. Bhatangsombatuisit. "Have you ever misused a word? Has anyone ever laughed at you because you did? Perhaps what you said was a malapropism." He found a tiny piece of chalk, the only one on the ledge, and wrote the word *malapropism* on the blackboard, which was actually green. When he turned back, Mr. Bhatangsombatuisit was putting the newspaper away. Good. No need for a scene today, Nathaniel told himself. Last semester had been especially bad — he'd had to kick a snot out of class

16

because the student had refused to take off his Walkman and kept snapping his body to the music he was listening to. Oh, what a cruel tyrant I am!

He caught the eye of Mr. Bhatangsombatuisit — a Thai or maybe Malaysian? Sweet kid. D-minus. His last paper had had these memorable single-spaced sentences:

> Connotation's are commonly used even when we get older. . .
> Connotations are words that we all get used to. . . . Slangs are
> also a nonstandard vocabulary consisting typically of arbitrary
> . . . . Many languages are dialectal. . . . Puns in comedy clubs
> makes the show funny and itneresting. The comedians gets the
> audience to laugh by saying puns.

All his papers had sentences like that, except, that is, for the paper written out of class. Somehow that had magically turned into a Pulitzer Prize winner, with phrases like "The population explosion defies the hegemony of any one particular nation and calls for a trans-global, perhaps, eventually, a trans-galactic network of policies: agrarian, economic, and bio-ethical." Yeah sure, Mr. Bhatangsombatuisit, you wrote that. Or just possibly some relative wrote it for you? Or you copied it from somewhere, despite your denial? I'm sorry, you are not writing English 101. Hello! It's called *University*-Level Reading and Writing, and I am not going to pass you. Sorry. I just can't.

Nathaniel looked at Mr. Bhatangsombatuisit again. There was something in the eyes, the hint of a smile at the lips. Of course! Mr. Bhatangsombatuisit had written that first review on the website! Maybe the first two. The little prick. From persecution *of* the "minority" to persecution *by* the "minority."

Most of the Mayflowers were terrified of being called "racist." Nathaniel called the white teachers *Mayflowers*, even though most of them weren't Anglo-Saxon Protestants, more likely had peasant Irish ancestors like himself, or German, Dutch, Polish, even Lithuanian Jews. Jews on the *Mayflower*, for God's sake. Oh no, they were all White now, and White was bad. It was some kind of Neo-Puritan guilt mongering, now everywhere. "Thou hast sinned in thy heart most grievously, Goody Sucker. White People have no problems! Nor does it matter what you or your ancestors had to put up with, for thou hast White Privilege." Yeah, I get to teach at fucking Shite College, Nathaniel thought.

Yeah, Hillbilly Privilege and Gay Privilege — Nathaniel had those too.

He was dining out with Marty, his lover of seventeen years. They liked this restaurant near Nathaniel's condo. Marty had his own apartment, but they slept over at each other's places a couple of times a week. Less now. Hell, it had been seventeen years. Anyway, the restaurant they liked was cozy, old-fashioned, with middle-aged Italian waiters, off-white curlicue wedding cake decor. Early Mussolini, Nathaniel called it.

"Why don't you just forget about it?" Marty was saying. "You've got tenure now. The website can't hurt you."

"It can *too* hurt me. I can feel the pressure already to ease up on my grading. I'm thinking about giving Mr. Bhatangsombatuisit a C."

"Who?"

"A student."

"Oh, give him the C. He probably had a hard time getting here."

Nathaniel put down his fork and shook his head. Sometimes Marty exasperated him. What did he know about the problem, processing more immigrants than they could handle, more immigrants than the US had ever had — ever! Marty wasn't a college teacher. He was a librarian. Not even that really. A library technician. Most of his patrons no doubt didn't know the difference since Marty did all the things a librarian was supposed to do: checked out books, showed people where things were located, sat at his computer a lot, cleaned up the bloody needles from the addicts who used the restroom at his branch to shoot up in. Tonight he was in his "liberal" mood. They took turns, although they both considered themselves "ex-liberals." Often Marty railed against the library's patrons, especially on those days when somebody deposited human excrement in the Book Return again. But, no, tonight Marty was being "liberal," most likely just to get Nathaniel going.

Marty was also looking very handsome tonight — those sad, sad baby browns, the dark beard, dark hair, cut very short (almost Marine boot camp short), the few leftover acne scars on his cheeks well hidden under the beard, the substantial nose (not overdone) apparently free of methamphetamines at the moment, a checkered yellow shirt from Lands' End, and enjoying the hell out of his salad with Thousand Island dressing. Discount cards were great, since they both hated to cook.

"You don't seem to understand that this website can be used to undermine the entire grading system, the entire power relationship between student and teacher."

Marty chewed on that, or maybe it was just on the salad. "Do you suppose Socrates gave grades?"

"Socrates wasn't teaching at Shite College." Nathaniel pressed on. He liked arguing, as long as he was winning. Was he winning? "It's nothing less than the fall of Western civilization."

"I thought *we* were that," Marty said, gesturing at the two of them. Homosexuals.

"That goes without saying," Nathaniel agreed, smiling. "But if students can bad mouth teachers and interfere with the enrollment in their classes, they suddenly have a tremendous tool to wield power with."

"I wish I had a tremendous tool," Marty said.

Oh, Jesus, not that again. Marty was always going on about the need for a bigger sex organ when he was perfectly normal. "Do you want to hear about this hate site or not?"

"I got this video that shows how you can add three inches to your penis size."

Nathaniel shrugged. "I'll bet.

"No, it sounds good. And the results look great."

"They showed a before-and-after penis?"

"It involves cutting a cord at the base or something."

Nathaniel cringed. "Please! I'm eating." He took a bite of bread.

"They say it doesn't hurt at all. They use a laser or something."

"No one is touching my cord! Now about this website —"

"It's not for you. It's for me," Marty said. "Why are you so resistant? You've had all that liposuction and whatnot on yourself. I've never had anything!"

Nathaniel put a finger up to his chin to cover the scar there. "Because you're perfect the way you are, luv."

"Bullshit."

The waiter brought their entrees, and Marty tore into his steak tartar. "God, this is good tonight. I might really get that operation, you know."

"You are *not* getting your penis lengthened without a written permit from your boyfriend. And that's final!"

Marty laughed. "We'll see. The next time I come over to your place I may surprise you with a poke from a porn star — me."

"Size doesn't really matter that much," Nathaniel said, and he meant it. "We've done all right all these years. Haven't we?" Maybe not of late, but in the past, he thought.

"I guess," Marty said, taking a sip of his Coke. At least he didn't drink anymore. Yeah, he was on crystal meth most of the time, but at least he didn't drink alcohol. And the marijuana was down to two or three times a week. Maybe.

"We're doing just fine," Nathaniel said, reaching out and patting Marty's hand, but quickly. He was far out the closet at school and yet he still always had a quickening of breath whenever he thought the waiters or the other diners might see him touching another man in an intimate way. He'd tried to get rid of the Bad Old Days, but they still lived on in his head. Old scars are the worst. Once in a while he and Marty held hands in the gay neighborhood where Marty lived, yet it was always a strain for Nathaniel. And even there, he could tell, such behavior was merely indulged, never ignored, and certainly — don't kid yourself — disliked by most non-gay people.

"Yeah, we're doing just fine," Marty agreed, patting Nathaniel's hand back.

Actually they weren't doing all that fine. They didn't fight as much as they used to. But their sex life had pretty much dried up. Whether it was going to fly away altogether remained to be seen. It had been months — six months and two days. But who was counting? They had always had an open relationship. Sex was sex. Love was different. They didn't live together. They didn't mix their money. God forbid! They didn't even qualify as "domestic partners," that quaint term. All they had was seventeen years of good sex, bad sex, fighting, traveling, talking on the telephone, dining out in greasy spoons, dining in, fighting, supporting each other through bad drugs deals and then methadone for Marty, depression for Nathaniel, especially during ten of those years because of his part-timer status at Shite, togetherness, loneliness, hatred, boredom, annoyance, laughs, dining out in better places, disappointments, thinking about breaking up, Marty hooking up for a time with somebody emotionally and lying about it, Nathaniel trying to find somebody else and not being able to.

This was Love, wasn't it? Wasn't this the way it was for all people, really, whether gay or straight or whatever, under all the ads and all the hype? A mixed bag. But a mixed bag was better than no bag at all. God, I want to be in Love! I am so goddamned ordinary! Nathaniel thought, digging his fingernails into the palm of his hand as he took a sip of his Merlot.

"Why don't you think about retiring?" Marty said. "Then you wouldn't have to worry about no stinking website."

"You know I can't retire. I can never retire."

"If you want it bad enough, you'll find a way."

"Easy for you to say." Marty would probably be able to retire before he would, and he was fourteen years younger! "I got caught."

"Yeah, yeah," Marty said in that dismissive way he sometimes had.

"I did!"

Marty rolled his eyes. "They gave the teaching jobs to women and blacks — any woman, any black over any white male. Your job, yeah, yeah."

"Oh, shut up."

"You shut up."

They both shut up. For a minute.

"Gay didn't count," Nathaniel went on.

"Yeah, yeah. I know — it counted *against* you."

"Well, it did!"

This was maddening. Marty usually agreed with him on this topic, but for some reason tonight he was being a prick.

He glared at Marty. "Affirmative Fucking Action —"

"— has ruined your life."

They both laughed.

"But it hasn't made me bitter," Nathaniel smirked.

Marty scratched at an itch at the top of his beard. "Would you be against Affirmative Action if gays got it?"

"Absolutely not!"

They both laughed again.

"See."

"I'm joking, I'm joking! Of course I would be against it. It is true evil. I can never retire because I don't have enough years in."

"Because they gave your job to the approved minorities, I know, I know."

"I'm sorry it's so boring. It just happens to affect my whole life. Excuse me."

"Get another job."

"Sure, at fifty-nine. I'll become a ballet dancer. I hear they're hiring."

"You can't dance very well."

"Well, let's have Affirmative Action for the dance-impaired then."

The busboy came over and refilled their water glasses. He was a twin, in his twenties, broad-faced, with bad posture.

"Do you think the busboy's sexy?" Marty asked when the twin was gone.

"Not especially. Why?"

Marty glanced the busboy's way. "Oh, I could give him some affirmative action. The two of them, him and his brother."

Nathaniel laughed. "You slut."

"Do you think they're South Americans?"

"Probably Mexicans."

Nathaniel looked over at the busboy. "I have this new theory," he began.

"Oh, no, save me," Marty said.

"Hey, listen. It's something you don't hear every day."

Marty pulled on his ears. "Okay, I'm all ears." His ears were sort of big, actually.

"I think people's attitude toward immigrants, especially illegal ones, is based on whether they're sexually attracted to them or not."

"I thought it was whether they can work cheap or not."

"That's a given." Nathaniel grinned. "But on top of that it's whether you want to fuck them or not."

Marty didn't say anything.

Nathaniel finished his salad. "You don't think this is profound?"

"Not particularly."

"You want to stop them at the border, or make them go back, depending on whether they give you a hard-on or not."

Marty mulled that over. "What about women's reactions? They don't get hard-ons — or so I've heard."

Nathaniel didn't hesitate. "Whether the immigrants make them wet or not."

"So it's not really a problem of wetbacks but wetbottoms?"

"And hard-ons. Have you seen how many *Mayflower* men are hooked up with Asian women in this city?"

"It's about getting an Alpha male."

"And getting a feminine fuck. If I were a straight man I'd want some pussy too that wouldn't bite me all the time."

"Stereotype!"

"*Bullshit* it is! Besides, lots of people *are* stereotypes, political correctness notwithstanding. I can't get the Asian women in my classes — the foreign-born ones — to say boo."

"If they could hear you!" Marty said, shaking his head.

"It's the truth. You just can't say it. I *hate* not being able to say it!"

"Maybe that's why they have Teachersonparade."

"Screw you."

"Well, if you have all these negative feelings . . ."

"Listen, Marty, I see what I see, and nobody is going to tell me what I do or don't, what I should or shouldn't notice. I also bend over backwards, as a matter of fact, to give "minorities," including blacks and women, every benefit of the doubt. I've passed more than my share of people who shouldn't even be near a college, let alone waltzing off with a certificate of higher education. Have I shown you the latest set of papers I just got?"

"Do I have to look at them?"

"The writing on the hate site is just as illiterate."

"Yeah, yeah."

Nathaniel threw down his napkin and looked away.

Marty stopped eating as well. "I'm just saying that if you don't want people to write bad stuff about you, then don't say bad stuff about them."

"I bite my tongue a lot and don't even write it out. I hint."

"They still pick up on it. They're not *that* dumb."

"They don't write well! They don't speak well! How can I pass them? American education is in a total toilet! This isn't teaching. It's a monstrosity. In a quiz today in my 102 somebody wrote, and I quote: 'William Shakespeare was borne — with an *e*, mind you — from 1564 to 1616.'"

"At least they got his years right, yes?"

"Shit!" Nathaniel said.

He turned his head and noticed that other patrons were staring at them.

After Marty didn't come over to spend the night, Nathaniel thought about going out for sex but changed his mind and went to his computer instead. It was dusty and had almost no megahertz. His cat, Slacker, was dozing on the keyboard, and he shooed her away, or tried to. She didn't want to leave and lifted her small, striped head at him as if to say, Make me. "Oopsey daisy!" he said, lifting her down to the floor. "Bitch." Slacker wandered off and started scratching the sofa in the living room. "I hear that!" Nathaniel yelled. But he didn't go in to stop her.

He went online to Teachersonparade.com. Now there were ten reviews of him. One of them was actually positive:

> Don't believe what you read here about Dr. TACK. He is real
> cool and will give you a rough time, but you'll lkearn. I did.
> His Plays and Novels is first-rate.
>
> A good man, honest teacher.

Well, thank you. I'm glad you "lkearned" something from me. Was it a review by Mr. Mustapha?

Nathaniel skimmed the other reviews. Another one wasn't that bad, called him "cheerful and funny." That's me all over, Miss Congeniality. Whoa! He didn't like feminizing himself. The world did enough of that to gay men, and it wasn't true of him.

Now he was even lower down in THE PITS, second from the bottom. Only Tadd Dryer was lower Oh, god, Tadd Dryer was a rotten teacher! Am I like *him*? A little Hitler with a Napoleon complex, or maybe the other way around? A prissy, Republican straight man with a thin voice, divorced, obsessed with Christ and William Empson. Like our students know from Seven Types of Fucking Ambiguity! Tadd still taught the subjunctive mood, for heaven's sake. Nathaniel could hear him right through the thin wall in the next office: "If I were to reconsider your grade, Miss Kong . . ." "Were you to peruse Mr. Empson's valuable book, Mr. Yip . . ." Yipes! God, only tired old Tadd Washer-Dryer, the Christian next door, was lower than he was!

Nathaniel suddenly had a brainstorm. Yes, yes, yes. He went to the section that said:

DO YOU WISH TO REVIEW THIS TEACHER?

I do, I do. He looked at his grade-point average again. How many reviews had come from his real students and how many had come from that dreaded dreadlocked cyberfuck in the cafeteria that Mr. Mustapha had told him about? All right, you want to play dirty, I'll play dirty. He wrote a review of himself:

> Dr. Nathaniel Tack is an outstanding instructor, the best I've
> ever had. Taught me everything I need to know to be a
> complete human being. I recommend him highly.

Why not? Nathaniel looked down at the places where information about the reviewer was to be placed: Age? He typed in 21. Sex: Female. Then he changed it to Male. Major: Astrophysics. (yeah, in Heaven, after I leave Shite College). Grade Point Average: 4.0. And the grade for the teacher? Why a great big A of course!

He pressed the Send button. In no time at all a new page came up:

> SUCESS! Your review has been posted.

And sure enough there it was! Even his grade point average had gone up. I'm a fucking SUCESS even though the webmaster who made this abomination is an illiterate bastard who should have his fingernails pulled out.

I should stop with just one review, Nathaniel told himself. No, this is too good to pass up! He wrote more:

> Dr. Nathaniel Tack he good. i like him very much. he kind to
> people from my country. take him please. you learn much. he
> polish much your punctuation

> I have a Ph. D. from Oxford University, and I recently took
> Nathaniel Tack's Plays and Novels course. He is a genius, who

will give you tips on writing that will stand you in good stead for your entire life. I told my friend, the Queen of England, that she should give a knighthood to this man, and she is considering it.

Too much? Surely not.

I have had many teachers in my eighty-seven years of life, yet none has meant more to me than Dr. Nathaniel Tack, who I can say with complete assurance is no less than a god among men.

Nathaniel had to stop typing he was laughing so hard. What a bunch of shit this website was if he could send these in, no questions asked. He pushed the Send button again. And again he was a SUCESS!

That afternoon he ran into Charlotte Wiggley in the Meeting Room of the English Department xeroxing some materials for a class. A tiny woman in her forties, she had a bad habit of jabbing her index finger into your stomach as she talked, so Nathaniel kept his distance. She also talked much too fast and was "perky" beyond belief, probably some kind of thyroid condition. On certain days she seemed to be troubled with white pimples on her throat and had recently been hit by a bus and was wearing a metal brace to steady her jaw. How terrible. But Charlotte was the kind of person who *would* get hit by a bus.

"Have you seen the new website?" he asked her.

Charlotte's brace made her bite down hard on her words and thus hard to understand. "Zomeone told me, but I haven't zeen it." She put more paper into the xerox machine.

"It's not whether the teachers look at," Nathaniel said. "It's whether the *students* are looking at it."

"Zits free speech," Charlotte said. "Want a cuppy of my handout?"

How could he refuse? He was going to need allies, he knew that. He took the piece of paper she held out. It was for Charlotte's course called — guess what —"Dress Up for Success," and gave information to "indigent women" on how to spruce up for job interviews.

"Does this work?" Nathaniel asked gingerly, waving the handout. He'd seen the women who came to her class: bag ladies, drug addicts.

"Zits great. My ztudents come in very poorly dressed, through no fault of zeir own. Zeir welfare checks simply don't cover clothing. And by the end of the term, we have a fazion zhow with a runway and everyzing."

"Really?"

"Zits marvelous." Charlotte looked ecstatic.

This was so Shite College. It wasn't enough to help homeless women. You had to make them parade down a fashion runway as if they were in Paris. It wasn't Paris. It was Parody. He wondered if they took their shopping carts with them when they strolled down the runway. But of course laughing at this was not permitted.

"Aren't you going to look at the website?" he asked her.

"Zey can say what zey like."

"No, they can't."

"Free speech!" Charlotte scooped up the xeroxed copies in her arms.

"Not if it's full of lies. And hate!"

"Zey zay I talk too fast. And I zuppose I do!" She laughed.

He wanted to rattle her mouth brace.

"People who aren't even students can review teachers," he said, an edge coming into his voice.

"Free speech, Nathaniel!"

"It's not free speech to review teachers you've never had!"

"Zits the only hope of the poor," Charlotte said, suddenly solemn. "Zee you, Nathaniel!" She hurried out of the room to her class, arms full of handouts.

He and Charlotte had been friends, sort of, a few years earlier. At least they'd had lunch together. But, no, he didn't even like her when he liked her.

He hung around the Meeting Room. He needed some support from somebody!

After a few minutes little Tadd Dryer came in for coffee. "Is this damn thing broken again?" he said, fiddling with the coffee maker. You were supposed to pay a quarter per cup, but everybody knew that Tadd never did.

"Someone spilled coffee all over. But I think it's at least working."

"How you doing, Nathaniel? Found Christ yet?"

"Not yet. And yourself?"

'He's always here in my heart."

'Must be a comfort." Nathaniel was pretty sure that Tadd did not approve of the Queer Next Door — little jabs now and again, nothing blatant. He could live with it.

"How are your students in 101 this semester? Mine are unbelievably bad," Tadd grumbled.

Ah, an ally! Not the ideal one you wanted, of course, but a start. "I've complained to the ESL Department about how many they pass," Nathaniel said. "I've been on the Standards Committee for three years. I'm doing my part."

"They won't listen. Save your breath," Tadd said, blotting the spilled coffee and then throwing down the recycled brown napkin in disgust. "Screw it!" he said.

"Before you go," Nathaniel jumped in.

"Yes?"

"Have you heard about the new website, about teachers?"

Tadd hesitated. "A little."

"Have you looked at it?"

"No."

Should he tell Tadd that he was at the bottom of THE PITS? Maybe not. "There's some pretty rough stuff on there."

"I don't look at it, Nathaniel."

"It could affect enrollment. Your Shakespeare class usually has trouble with enrollment, doesn't it?"

"Don't give in to it. It'll go away. Turn the other cheek."

"I don't think so. Students can have their way with teachers on this thing."

"In time the culprits will be punished for their ways."

No, they won't! Nathaniel thought. They need attending to *now*, not in some Final Exam in the Big Bang Nowhere.

"In any case, I know I am a fine teacher," Tadd said piously.

Maybe *you* shouldn't look at the site, Nathaniel thought. You'll kill yourself and then go to Hell for it. Wait! Am I in as much denial as little Tadd here? No, I teach good! as my students would say. I do! Most of my colleagues are such bleeding-heart suckers or else hopeless throwbacks like Tadd. What about somewhere in between, please!

"I hope that's fixed the next time I come in here," Tadd said, pointing at the coffee machine.

But *you* won't fix it! You won't even tell Gladys to fix it. You'll just huff off and let somebody else do it, like you always do. No, Tadd Dryer couldn't change if he read the website twenty-four-seven from now until the Last Judgment, which evidently he believed in literally.

Jesus, I need your help! Who can I get to fight this thing? Nathaniel thought.

Jesus didn't answer, but Arlene Buboe-Pitsky came in to the Meeting Room. She was angling to be the next chair of the department, maybe even a dean. Her husband, Max, was already a dean of something. Yes, Arlene and Max Buboe-Pitsky, the Polish power couple on campus — or trying to be. Arlene could have been any age, between thirty-five and seventy, with one of those heavily powdered granite faces that never sag and hennaed red hair that looked great, and never moved. She was worth a try. "How you doing, Arlene?" he asked.

"Finished the exit exam for Pre-Pre-Reading for Readers," she said. "We've nailed it this time. My experimental class is already reading at seventh grade level!"

"Sounds great, Arlene." God, he was glad he didn't have to teach the remedial classes any longer, the ones actually *called* "remedial," the ones way down at the end of the Great Chain of Being: "Pre-Literate Tactics in Our Changing World," "Reading for the Non-Reader." Eeek!

"Have you seen this new awful website that everybody's talking about?" Nathaniel probed.

Arlene's face went even whiter, and she almost dropped the book she was about to copy pages from. "I don't want to know what's on it. So please don't tell me!"

Her reaction held promise. "It's —"

"I don't want to know, Nathaniel." She was almost shaking. "Did you look up me?"

"Hey, I'm gay," he joked.

She didn't get it. Good thing. She's probably accuse him of sexual harassment. She was one of those riding that hobbyhorse for all it was worth. She'd even put a note on Dylan Tante's class observation report that he needed to watch himself because he had made a joke about a tampon. Yeah, everyone knows that tampons are not funny; they're *serious*. Maybe Arlene wasn't the way to go after all.

"Somebody was telling me the kinds of comments that are there, and I prefer not to be told, that's all!"

"I wasn't planning to quote them to you." But maybe I should? he thought.

Arlene xeroxed a page of the book and stood there patting her hard hair. He wondered what she used to make it so firm.

"See you around," he said when she left.

But Arlene didn't answer him.

So what was on the website that was she so adamant about *not* seeing?

He sauntered over to the library and commandeered a computer. This time he looked around him to see if anybody was watching. What was he afraid of? Am I going to do something I shouldn't? He summoned up Teachersonparade.com. It was scary how fast it came up. He went right to Arlene Buboe-Pitsky:

> Mrs. Buboe-Pitsky is Old and Ugly!!
>
> She can barel;y hold the chalk anymore.
>
> Nice but dull overall. You can do better than her.

If *you* don't know about it, then it's not here, is that right, Arlene? Confucius say: "Person who stick head in ground leave butt up to get fucked."

Maybe he should send in a review of Arlene too? Tempting.

He looked up Charlotte Wiggley. There were five reviews, every one saying that she was a dedicated teacher but that she talked too fast. She probably can't stop talking too fast if she wants to. Another review of her came in as he was reading. This one said:

> Look like evil-devil in jaw brace. I hope gone soon. I no can
> understand her now even more than befor. May drop. goodbye.

What if he sent in a review of Charlotte Wiggley? He wasn't a student; hadn't even seen her teach, just heard rumors, caught a glimpse of her now and then in a classroom with the door open. Of course he had seen her evil-devil jaw brace.

It's *free speech*, after all, Charlotte. (*He he* !)

He went back to her vitals at the top. She had an M.A. from State. It figured. She had placed a Teacher's Statement in a box provided at the top:

> I welcome the chance for my students to evaluate me, both as a human being and as your teacher. I am as committed to improving myself as I hope you all are to improving yourselfs.

Yourselfs? Maybe Charlotte should look at the website if only to proofread what she'd put there. God, what a pussy! He began his review:

> Ms. Wiggley is a lovely person. Too bad. That is not Enough.
> And is her jaw brace dressing for SUCESS?

He gave her a C and sent it in. Maybe she'd take the site more seriously if she saw how it could be abused. Take that! . . . Hey, no wonder the students wanted this site.

He looked up his own reviews again. The webmaster had put a note at the top of his name:

> *The webmaster has deteccted a misuse of this site and feels some these reveiws were likely send in by Dr. Tack himself and so they've been removed. This site is for STUDENTS only!

Sure enough the ones he'd sent in were gone and his grade point average was back in THE PITS.

How does he know whether *I* sent them in or not? Nathaniel seethed. The webmaster is just guessing! I sent four in together, like I thought you wouldn't notice! Eat my cookies, Sherlock! Have you removed the reviews from the cyberfuck who was never my student? Not on your life. You couldn't tell a fake review from a legitimate one if it jumped off the screen and ate your face.

Couldn't he tell that Nathaniel wasn't the only one misusing the site? Who was this webmaster anyway? Why was he doing this? There was an e-mail address right at the bottom, though no name: pancake@ earthlink.com. He took his time writing and polishing what he'd say. He wound up with:

> I remember this webmaster from several of my classes. He stuck in my mind because, as we sat in our circle and discussed our aspirations in life, he gave such eloquent expression to his wish that one day people would be tolerant of pedophiles like himself and that eventually he would find wholeness working at a children's nursery school. Although I was not able to provide this student the recom-mendation he requested, I do wish him well and hope that he will one day conquer his aphasia and achieve the bachelor's degree in Nazi Studies at an accredited college he likewise has expressed such a desire to attain.

Nathaniel pressed the Send button. See how it feels, Mr. Academick Suck-cess! It wouldn't appear on the website, but maybe the man would get the point — anyone could destroy a reputation this way. You want free speech, I'll give you free speech, Pancake!

He graded some papers in the library, looking up every now and again at the view outside the large windows. Shite College did have a nice new library and wonderful views: the foggy, green hillsides of Santa Francesca. I must find something valuable in this place, he reminded himself, or I'm going to go nuts.

When he checked the website an hour and half later, the webmaster had put another emendation near Nathaniel's name:

> *Apparently Dr. Tack has no end of rantings. He has acused this webmaster of various and sundae crimes. We will see what action can be taken to stop this kind of behavior by faculty members against student who are only trying to get their educashun.

You're going to stop me from sending an e-mail that merely points out what you're doing to faculty members? You are a total jerk!

But a dangerous jerk, Nathaniel knew now.

He went back to the home page of the site and looked for information on the webmaster. Ah, there it was! There was a small picture of him down in the far left corner. He looked to be a nerd in his mid-twenties with a long, horsey face and little hole of a mouth, like a cat butt. And a dirty blond. Dirty rotten blond! He had some kind of "do" on the top of his head that was perhaps two-toned. Orange and blond? It was hard to tell from the tiny photo. He was identified only as YOUR WEBMASTER.

There was also a statement:

> I have never had a particularly easy time in school, due largely to teachers who did not undrestand that some students have diffrent learning stiles. I flunked out of first collage I ever attented and then worked for a while in the business sector later I decided to return to collage and thought Shite would be somewhere to which I could resumb my educashun. So I enrolled in summer school, thinking to get back into my educashun by taking Beginning Piano. I had to share the piano with another student and the teacher wouod not give me the individual attention that is promised in the catelogue and that I paid $33 for! When I asked for help, she was rude. Thats when I decided to start this website so that students never again will have to set foot into a classroom without knowing what they are getting. This site is run by students for students!! Take an active role in your own educashun. Your fat lies in your own hands.

I guess he means "fate," not "fat." Too bad your spell-check doesn't lie in your own hands, Nathaniel thought.

So it was some disgruntled loser who had started this abomination. This dropout was going to tell teachers how to teach! After all, he'd paid a whopping $33 for his God-given right to pass. If he played the piano the way he spelled, no wonder the teacher was rude.

Nathaniel searched for more information. Know your enemy. Actually the webmaster's *name* was nowhere to be found. Wasn't there a way to trace websites back to the person or organization running them? He thought so, only he didn't know how to do it. His computer skills were not as good as they might be, not as good, alas, as those of Your Webmaster. The fucker. Well, he'd probably had help. Surely his real name wasn't "Pancake," was it?

Nathaniel suddenly remembered there was something called WHOITZ or WHATIS. WHOIS — that was it! He got off Teachersonparade and searched for WHOIS. Okay, let's trace this educational basket case back to his roots.

And sure enough, there it was! Teachersonparade.com

It listed the address as 31 Albert Einstein Street in Santa Francesca. With a telephone number. The name given was Dude Lather. Could that be his real name? It sounded like some gay lubricant that Marty would buy. Could Your Webmaster possibly be gay? Impossible. Gays spell better than that.

Nathaniel copied down the name, address, and telephone number and went back to Teachersonparade. He was going to put in a Teacher's Statement. He didn't want anything to do with this site, but maybe he could destroy it before it got out of hand. And it certainly was going to get out of hand; that was obvious.

His Teacher's Statement read:

> This website is set up so stupidly that anyone can write reviews on it and these can be taken as truth all over the world. Complaints from interested parties should go to the webmaster:
>
> Dude Lather/31 Albert Einstein Street/Santa Francesca/94115
>
> 415-555-1244 or pancake@earthlink.com

Exposed at last! Nathaniel smiled. Would a mother really call her child *Dude?* It had to be a nickname. Did I ever have a student named Lather? I don't think so. I've had a lot of odd names: Jinah Jones, Jesus Tang, Tyeesha Songbird came to mind. But I think I'd remember Dude Lather. Dwayne Blather? That sounded vaguely familiar. But the horsey face in the photo didn't ring a bell. Nathaniel was good as both names and faces. It was a source of pride for him to remember them.

Time will reveal all, he told himself. Will the real Dude Lather please stand up!

He checked back to see what was up on Teachersonparade. He noticed that a new disclaimer about the site's "standards" had appeared:

> We will not except reviews that are racist, sexist, homophobic, or show other signs of arrested develoipment.

Well, aren't you *P.C.*! Nathaniel thought. Eat me!

He was still ahead of Tadd Dryer on THE PITS list. There was a new review of him, two in fact:

> Nathan Tack should die of Aids. He teaches that homosexuality is okay. He seems normal when you first encounter him, but deep inside he is just another fruit, a mental case. Take his class at your own risk. Better yet skip him and take Tadd Dryer. Your system will stand the shock better.

How cruel! Worse than little Tadd Dryer!

The other review read:

> where i came from n. tack would be killed . . .goddamn queer

Wasn't that a threat? Why was it still there, especially if Your Webmaster now had a stated policy of refusing "homophobic" reviews? Maybe he didn't consider killing queers homophobic? Just something normal out of Cuba or Bosnia or Mississippi maybe. You know — "ethic cleansing."

I knew it would descend to this, Nathaniel thought, pleased to be proven right — and beginning to be frightened.

When the call came from the Vice-Chancellor's office, he began to get a little hope back. Maybe at last the Administration was beginning to wake up to the monster that had been created in their midst? And wait until they heard about the homophobic reviews!

He sat waiting in her outer office while she finished some other business. It was in Nimbus Hall, recently renamed Chief Sitting Bull Hall, one of the oldest buildings on campus. It had a certain Fifties charm — if old brown linoleum and rain stains on the walls and the vandalized sign (into Shitting Bull Hall) could be called charming. (How long before the protest march about this "defaming" of our fallen Native American Founding Fathers?) Most of the Administrators had offices there, probably because of the views.

Vice-Chancellor Lung welcomed him into her office after fifteen minutes. "Sorry keep you waiting," she said insincerely. He had never seen her before and noticed that she was tall for a Chinese woman and not unpleasant to look at, the teeth a little prominent. She was wearing a black blouse and black skirt and a sweater with some kind of Chinese lettering as decoration. "Please take seat," Lung ordered. The accent was as heavy as Charlie Chan's (yes, it was), only at Shite it was considered impolite and "racist" to notice. You could notice German or French accents You could notice Canadian, British, Irish, New York, or Southern accents, just never *Asian* accents. More of the Politically Correct Bullshit *Denial* filling the place. Well, he noticed hers, and nobody was going to tell him he didn't!

Lung was not smiling, now why was that?

"I'm from English," Nathaniel said, not knowing whether he was to start.

"I know that," she snapped.

Hmm.

"Come to my attention you expose student's identification," she went on in her heavily accented way that you weren't supposed to notice, even though she was very hard to understand.

"I did what?"

She looked down at her desk, where there were some notes. He noticed that her desk was as clean as a carcass after vultures. "Student named Drew A. Lather has filed complaint against you for revealing private information." Her cold eyes found Nathaniel's hot ones.

"I did no such thing," he protested. What was going on here! He should have known that the sport coat he was sporting was too heavy for October. He felt himself beginning to sweat.

"Explain, please," Lung Woman said. The teeth came out from under the upper lip.

She wasn't handling this very well. Maybe the rumors were true about her. She was barely competent, had very poor English skills, and only had the job because of political pressure. A previous Chancellor had tried to get rid of her, but her cronies in the "Asian and Pacific Islands Community," as it was known, had lobbied, and lobbied hard with all sorts of threats (at the top of their lungs?) that Lung must not go or there would be hell to pay.

"What have I supposedly done?" he heard himself say, a smile cracking his face. What could she do to him? Suspend him? Get around tenure somehow and fire his butt?

"According to report I receive, you give student's personal information to Internet."

"I don't know what you're talking about." He set his face.

She set hers. "Didn't you put Drew Lather's name, address, and phone in Teacher's Statement?" She smiled victoriously at him, one eye drooping.

My god, she's a fucking Dragon Lady! "What I put there is public information," he said.

She looked surprised. "How get you this information?"

How get I this information? "I get this information from a place that tells who runs websites. Are you aware of the existence of Teachersonparade?"

"Shite College have no connection with website," she announced.

"I beg your pardon?"

"It run by student, not by college."

"Pardon me again, but I accessed the website from the Information section of the school's website."

"Have no connection with college!" Lung was adamant.

"The Alliance of Students, the Komputer Klub, and the Inter-Proactive Council of Campus Entities all have links to it — and not just links — ones that sing its praises and encourage students to use it. There are flyers everywhere."

"Website have no connection to college!"

Uh oh. So this is where the Administration was going with this.

She seemed to think she had won. "Will overlook what you did when you remove private information from Teacher's Statement," she said. Great big gracious smile.

Nathaniel felt like he was swimming in his own sweat. But he soldiered on. "I'm afraid I can't do that, Vice-Chancellor Lung."

Her eyes opened very wide. "What are you saying . . . ?" She seemed to be searching her notes for his name.

"Nathaniel Tack of the English Department," he helped her out. "What I put up for my Teacher's Statement is merely information about the webmaster, who happens to be using the names of Shite College and its faculty as he sees fit. What gives him the right to put our names up there without permission, making the entire world think that Teachersonparade is somehow an *official* part of this college, especially when you say it is not? I merely let the world know who is running the website, information available to anyone who cares to check."

"Our college have no connection to website."

"I understand that's what you are maintaining, but the fact of the matter is it very much looks like the college is not only sponsoring but *recommending* the website. And are you aware that you don't even have to be a student to write a review of a teacher?"

"College have no connection."

"Then why has the college allowed flyers urging students to use the inaccurate information — and name-calling — on the website to be posted all over campus?"

"Have not allowed!" she protested.

"But the school has! There are three flyers for Teachersonparade in the hallway outside your office."

"Never see," she said.

"Come, I'll show you," he said, getting up from the chair.

"No need."

"You really should see the flyers. They are stamped Shite College Approved, I believe."

"No connection with college. We do not endorse."

She wouldn't budge.

"I'll get one of the flyers from the wall." He took a step.

"No need!"

"Have you seen them?"

"School approve many flyers, Mr. Tack. "

"Are you telling me the school approves any flyer that anyone wants to put up?"

"Unless not approved."

"Some are approved, but some are not. Which are which?"

"Administration approves flyers that wise for school. Good for staff."

Where had this woman come from, one of Chairman Mao's re-education camps? "Who approved the flyer for Teachersonparade, may I ask? Do you think it's *good* for the school to allow the faculty to be trashed anonymously?"

"Who trashed?"

"Several people including Yours Truly."

"Who's *that?*"

She wasn't joking. "Including *me*. There are two recent reviews that say I should die of AIDS and that I'm a 'goddamn queer.'"

She looked at him oddly. "You goddamn queer?"

"Yes. Me 'goddamn queer.'" Stop this! he screamed in his head. With her no-doubt-sterling-gay-rights background in her native land, he doubted that she deeply resented homophobia.

"Have talked to chair?"

"Yes, he knows about it."

"Complaints go through him or her."

"What good is that kind of complaint?" he said. "The forms used on this campus have five copies that go to every conceivable office — and nowhere."

She was done with him, he could tell. She must have another appointment. "So you will apologize to student, in written form, and I will forward to him. You will re-move private information from website." She nodded like they were both agreed on this.

"There seems to be a communication problem here, and it's not on my side," Nathaniel dared. "I'm not apologizing to anyone over this, and I'm not removing the information about the webmaster either."

It took a long time to come. ". . . I see. Perhaps your paycheck will be withheld until you comply?"

"What!?"

"It just a question, Mr. Tack."

"Why is it students have so many rights, but the faculty has almost none? I can't give a plus or minus grade or post student names or Social Security numbers next to grades, but people can spew venom at teachers, anonymously, when the teachers are just doing their job. I can't write anonymous reviews of *students*. But they can – and they don't even have to be students!"

"Faculty must comply with all reasonable demands," she said. "That all for now."

God, most of his Asian students were nice and hard-working, homophobic of course, but at least quiet about it, but this bitch was . . .

"This isn't the end of this," Nathaniel said.

She looked him dead in the eye. "College no connection with website, Mr. Tack!"

Could that woman really withhold his paycheck? She wouldn't dare. *Would* she? Nathaniel had seen worse on that campus.

Because students were parking in the faculty lots and not getting tickets from the campus police, he was ten minutes late for his office hour when he couldn't find a parking space. Mr. Early was waiting for him outside his office in Fellon Hall.

Oh, no! Nathaniel cringed. Mr. Early was one of the smart students but a pain. He was in his Plays and Novels course and always contradicted Nathaniel when he made suggestions on student work discussed in class. "Well, *I* liked it!" Or "It spoke to *me*." "No, *I* don't agree that description is all that necessary in fiction."

Yes, praise was necessary Nathaniel understood, and he would praise when a compliment was warranted, but in general the students were too easily pleased with their work.

"I was just about to post a warning on your door," said Mr. Early.

Nathaniel had his key in the lock. "I beg your pardon?"

"I've been waiting ten minutes."

"Did you say *warning*?" Should he explain about the parking or say nothing? He motioned Mr. Early into the office. He was tall, well-built, perhaps twenty-one or so, wearing a white knitted cap pulled down over his ears. His brow was the most noticeable part of his face — it was large and stuck out, and the eyebrows were full, like dark brown caterpillars. He had his father's snotty eyes, Lucifer's. He took off his jacket and said, "Is there somewhere where I can hang this?"

Nathaniel was surprised. Usually students didn't bother to take off their coats. "There's a hook over there by my office mate's desk. I don't think she'll mind."

Mr. Early hung up his jacket but left on his knitted cap and came back — only he didn't sit down, even though Nathaniel had seated himself at his desk. Mr. Early, he noticed, had tattoos all over his arms: scorpions and obscenities all the way up to the shoulders, even some on his knuckles. So the display of these was the reason for the jacket removal. Read me: Fuck You.

"What can I do for you. Mr. Early?" Nathaniel said. He would ignore what this strapping young man's "warning" might have been.

"Let me begin by saying that I have enjoyed your class . . ."

"Thank you."

"Lately, though, I have begun to change my mind a bit."

"What a shame. What seems to be the trouble?" Nathaniel knew what the trouble was. He was just playing the game.

"The B you gave me on my chapter last week."

"Oh, yes. Did you get a B?" Nathaniel made the gesture of getting his grade book out of his briefcase. He opened it to the proper page. "I see that the one short chapter is the only work you've given me so far this semester."

"Well, I intended to give you more, but now I'm not so sure."

"And why is that? I believe three complete scenes of some kind are required in the course."

"So you say."

My, Mr. Early was confident. His deodorant was also a little old.

"I'm not sure I can turn in any more assignments under these circumstances."

"And what circumstances are those exactly?"

"I think you know."

"Enlighten me, Mr. Early. Why don't you have a seat?"

He sat, reluctantly. "I really believe my chapter was better than a B. My father is a published writer, and he was quite impressed with it."

Perhaps you should take the course from your father, Nathaniel started to say. No, he would not give in to snottiness although provoked. "It was a first draft, was it not?"

"I guess I shouldn't have told you that." Mr. Early moved his arm, and a scorpion quivered on his biceps.

"I suspect I might have figured that out in any case," Nathaniel said, trying to smile.

"I've never gotten a B before."

"In your whole life?"

"Never."

It was probably true. There was something intimidating about Mr. Early that no doubt had served him well in his short life.

"What would you like to happen?" Nathaniel asked.

"You gave me a B for my mid-term grade besides. I didn't come to see you about it before, however."

Nathaniel looked hard at the young man. "Am I not correct that you hadn't turned in a single assignment by the mid-term?"

"Yes, but I thought we discussed that after class."

"We did. And that's why I gave you the B even though I'd seen nothing of your work." (And heard nothing but your wrong-headed comments in class, asshole.)

"I fully intend to give you the assignments, professor."

"I'm sure you do. It's just that I haven't actually seen very many. I thought, under the circumstances, a B was rather generous. It showed faith on my part, did it not?"

"Oh, it did, did it?" Mr. Early was glaring at him. This was most unusual. College students didn't act like this. Not yet anyway!

"Are you aware of how you're coming off?" Nathaniel asked.

"What do you mean?"

"You're being quite rude, it seems to me." (Now tell me it's "free speech" to be rude!)

"Really?" Mr. Early seemed surprised. "Perhaps you're just used to having your butt kissed."

A hot poker ran through Nathaniel's spine. "There are many things I could say right now, Mr. Early, but all I will say is that the approach you are using is not the most effective one for achieving your purpose."

"And what is my purpose?"

"You want me to tell you what your purpose is?"

The young man was tugging on the edges of his cap. There might be a little nervousness showing, but not much.

"Well, first off, you were pissed off because I was late, even though I was late because I couldn't find a spot in the faculty lots — any of them."

"You could leave earlier," he dared. "That's what you tell us so that we're not late."

Nathaniel bit his lower lip. It hurt. He sucked in some air. That hurt too. "Then you told me that you were about to post a *warning* on my door. Let me guess what that warning was . . . No, you tell me."

"I was just kidding."

"Were you?"

Mr. Early glared at him full face. "Not really. I was going to put up a note saying that the professor shouldn't be late, especially when he's so adamant that his students not be late to class."

"Is that a *warning*? Is that the right word? Are you in the habit of issuing *warnings* to people?"

Mr. Early's body language was not good. "I guess I'm in the habit of doing whatever the teacher wants, whether I want to or not."

"Bosses of course let you do exactly what you want. Perhaps you shouldn't be in school if you're so unhappy."

"Perhaps." Mr. Early flipped a little smile in Nathaniel's direction. "But then again maybe . . ."

"Then maybe what?"

The young man drew in a big breath. "I don't know quite how to say this."

"You're articulate, Mr. Early. Speak away. . . . But do think first."

"I'm not stupid."

"I didn't say you were."

"Are you aware of the Teachersonparade website?"

"Vaguely."

"Quite a few students are using it."

"So I've heard."

"It's good to have more than mere word of mouth about teachers, don't you think?"

"Depends on the accuracy of the information."

"I do like your class. I want you to know that. You're a very lively teacher. Most of them are duds."

Nathaniel kept mum.

"Okay," Mr. Early jumped in, "here's what I've been wondering. Let me run it by you."

Nathaniel looked at his own hands and noticed that he was gripping a pencil much too hard, his knuckles discolored, although not tattooed.

"I'd hate to see you get more bad reviews, professor. I think you have about fifteen now."

"Do I? "

"You're at the very bottom."

"Am I? How kind of you to let me know. So I can mend my ways, is that it?"

Mr. Early smirked. "Do you know that one person can go on that site and leave a bunch of reviews for one teacher?"

"Really? I thought the webmaster was supposed to be alert and remove those."

"Not if you just wait a day or so between reviews."

"You sound well learned in the world's false subtleties."

It was Mr. Early's turn to keep mum.

"It's from Shakespeare," Nathaniel explained.

"Or Machiavelli?"

"Interesting. What are you saying to me, Mr. Early?"

"Just an observation."

"Nothing more?"

Another student had come and was waiting for him.

"Just this." What amazing nerve this kid had. He wasn't even blinking. "Professor Tack, I'd very much hate to see you trashed on the site anymore than you have been already. Wouldn't you? You might never get off the part called The Pits."

Nathaniel was fighting his anger, gripping the pencil so hard he thought he might break it in two. "What are you plans for your future education, Mr. Early?"

"To transfer to a university."

"In what?"

"Maybe creative writing."

"And so a B, you think, would hurt you? Is that it?"

"I was going to ask you for a recommendation, but I don't think you appreciate my work."

Nathaniel stroked his own throat, then the scar under his chin. "I'm not sure I've seen enough of it to judge."

"I can hand in some more. I'm working on something right now."

Can't wait, Nathaniel thought.

"It's quite good. It's angry."

"But controlled anger, right?"

"I know you believe that writers should control their output, but I think too often people self-censor far too much."

"Do you?"

"They're too bland."

"I agree that can happen. People also quite often indulge themselves. I wouldn't want you to indulge yourself, Mr. Early."

"It seems to me that I am in control of what I write, pretty much."

Including what you write about me on the website? Is that what you mean? Nathaniel cursed. "So where do we stand, Mr. Early?"

"I don't know, professor. Why don't you tell me — I'm sure you will."

What a snot! "You seem to think very well of yourself, for such a very young man," Nathaniel said.

"I'm just looking out for my future."

"I see. Do you see life as a Darwinian struggle, the survival of the fittest?"

"I think so. Kill or be killed."

"I've heard that some mammals survived the various cataclysms and the dinosaurs by staying out of the way, pretty much. They went on to triumph."

"Did they?" Mr. Early said blandly.

"I really don't know what else to say to you, Mr. Early. But I'm not going to change you grade to an A, if that's what you think."

"That isn't why I came by."

Yeah, right. "No?"

"I can live with a B if I have to."

"It's not written in stone. You do have some time to turn in more material. Good material."

"I don't think I want to do that now."

"Meaning?"

"I don't want to be pressured to grind out material. I am an artist, not a . . ." He couldn't quite say what he wasn't.

Nathaniel threw the pencil into the air and let it fall onto his desk. He shook his head in exasperation, but he kept his voice under control. "Do what you have to do," he said.

"Do you think of yourself as Jesus and me as Judas?" Mr. Early scoffed. The kid was smart!

"Only on some days," Nathaniel answered.

"I'm sorry this conference didn't go very well, professor."

"Yes, I feel the same."

"Good day, sir." Mr. Early got up and got his jacket and left.

Nathaniel, his face burning, got up to call in the next student. "How are you doing, Miss Stickleback?" he said, not looking at her.

He watched Mr. Early putting on his jacket down where the room curved toward the exit. He's going to write me up royally on the website, Nathaniel realized. And how many times? What a clever bastard. When future anthropologists discovered Early Man preserved in some river bed or other they would notice the tattoos, the large forehead — and the even larger asshole.

"Yo."

"Yo yourself." It was his son, Jimmy. "Good to hear from you. I was just about to call you about something."

"Yes."

"Still a virgin?" You want your child to do well.

Jimmy laughed. "I am. Not for lack of trying, though."

"You're too nice. Girls always go for the bad boys. You'll do well down the road." Jimmy was seventeen, a junior, six-four and built like a lumberjack. He was good looking, no doubt about it. Nathaniel had seen women and girls checking him out when he visited up in Oregon. Big blue eyes. Still boyish and liking to rough house. Deep voice. Into video games and computers. Did pretty well in school. Had had two girlfriends already, but "nice" girls. Yeah, Jimmy was your typical all-American boy child of a totally gay father and totally lesbian mother.

"How's your mom?" Nathaniel was always very careful to ask. He and Diana really had nothing in common except this child they had concocted — engineered? — what was the word? — that they had thought long about, planned carefully, and created with the help of a midwife and an eyedropper.

"She's good. So is Lana."

"Tell them I said hello." Lana was the mother's somewhat prim lover.

"Yo."

"What's with the *yo*, Yimmy?" Nathaniel called him Yimmy sometimes. It was from the *Exorcist*, the head-spinning Hell child talking like the priest's mother or something. Nathaniel had had a novel published on the same day as the *Exorcist*, but it was "gay" and — guess what — somehow it didn't become a bestseller or a movie. Not that he cared about bestsellers. But you do want your novel children to do well too.

There was a pause. "So what were you going to call me about?" Jimmy asked. He wasn't always the best conversationalist.

Nathaniel was determined that he'd have better communication with his son that his father had had with him, damn it. "Well, it's turned real cold out here in Bad Axe. Er . . . now here's your mother." No small talk. No big talk either. So sad. Life was very sad at its core, and that's why you had to keep goosing it. "I need some help with computers," Nathaniel said.

"I'm your man."

"My thought too." Jimmy had conquered every video game he had every tried, and he'd tried more than Coxey's army, as his hillbilly mother would have said. He'd even fixed Nathaniel's A drive when it was stuck and he'd been sure he'd have to get a new computer. "How many courses have you taken in that stuff now?"

"I'm on my third. What do you need?"

"Can you send a virus to somebody?"

"Whoa! That's heavy. You serious?"

"Are viruses illegal?"

"I'd say so."

"I always wondered why somebody would send a virus. It seems so mean. But now I want a virus of my own."

"Any particular virus? I could get in trouble."

"Somebody has insulted your biological parent, Yimmy, and something must be done about it," Nathaniel joked.

"I'm not exactly a hacker."

"There are good hackers and bad hackers, just like good witches and bad witches. There's this awful website that needs to be taken out."

"Cool."

"I want something to eat its insides out."

"What kind of website?"

Jimmy might go and read what was on it about him. "Just some website."

"You want me to target a certain website, not just a general virus?"

"That's what morality means, my boy. Love your friends, kill your enemies, or at least their websites."

"I thought it was 'love your enemies.'"

"And actually the Biblical text is 'love your enemas.'"

"Dad!"

"The text got corrupted over the centuries, like so many other things."

"Actually I'm dating a Christian girl."

"Really? No wonder you're not getting any."

"Dad!"

"Son!"

"You're right. She said I have sex appeal, but she doesn't believe in sex before marriage."

"What if she gets married and finds out that her husband likes to strangle her when he comes?"

"Dad!"

"If she'd tried him out before tying the knot, she might not have become so tied up legally, so to speak, if you know what I mean."

"How's Marty?"

"Fine. Why are you calling?"

"Can't I just call for no reason?"

"Of course you can. So what's the reason you're calling?"

Pause. "I have a . . . rash."

"I thought you weren't getting any."

"Just oral sex. That's all she'll let me do to her."

"This is the Christian girl we're talking about?"

"Her and Mona. Mona goes to West High."

"There's always a Mona. So what you're telling me is that you think you might have a venereal disease?"

"Do you think I could have?"

Hmm. Who was he, Nathaniel thought, to lecture on venereal virtue? That might even be a spot of cum, his own, on his corduroy jacket. "So what you're telling me is that you're a technical virgin but you've stuck your tongue into at least two girls?"

"Dad!"

"Just clarifying. Do you realize that I didn't have sex until I was twenty-five years old?"

"No way."

"Thanks to the Pope. And I suppose, the way the world counts, technically I'm still a virgin. I didn't even know what masturbation was until I was twenty-one. I've made up for lost time, though."

"Should I really know all this?"

"You shall not have a Victorian childhood, the way I did."

"How did you live through it?"

Nathaniel laughed. "Who said it was living? What kind of rash is it?"

"Red. Is there another kind?"

"Haven't you heard of the notorious Purple Rash of Papua New Guinea?"

"Really?"

"That's to scare you into celibacy. Have you told your mother about your rash?"

"I can't."

"I understand. Any pustules?"

"God, no!"

"Chancre sores?"

"Eek, what are those?"

"Noticeable eruptions." Nathaniel smiled. Jimmy said "Eek!" just like Nathaniel did.

"Do moles count?"

"Not unless they're festering."

"Dad!"

"Well, you asked. Have you seen a doctor?"

"No."

"You're sure it's not just jock itch?"

"It could be. I sweat a lot. I'm on the track team, did I tell you?"

"Congratulations. That's all it is most likely."

"There might be something on my tongue too."

"Show it to me."

"On the phone?"

"Where are you calling from?"

"My room."

"Is there a mirror?"

"On the inside of the closet door."

"Is your mother or Lana home yet?"

"No."

"I thought not. Open the closet door. Open all closet doors!"

"What?"

"A joke. Is your closet door open?"

"Just a minute."

Nathaniel waited.

"It's open."

"Stick out your tongue and examine it."

"Ukay."

"What do you see?"

"Widges?"

"Ridges?"

"Uh huh. Cwacks and widges."

"Sounds like you inherited my tongue. Do you see any unusual bumps or lesions?"

"Wassa lesion?"

"A morbid change in texture or functioning of an organ."

"Dad!"

"Keep looking."

"If you say so."

"Look on the underside too."

"All right. *Ahh.*"

"Don't gag."

Nathaniel pictured his son probing the tongue. God, who'd want to be a dentist!

"It wontay up."

"What?"

"It won't stay up. The tongue."

"Make it."

"I don't see anything."

"You got Cruex?"

"For my tongue?"

"For the other place. Why don't you buy some. You get an allowance, right?"

"Yes."

"And if it's not gone in a day, go see a doctor. Do you have a family doctor?"

"I guess. The one who delivered me?"

"I guess. Don't be embarrassed. Just make an appointment. Or ask the track coach. Is there a nurse at school?"

"No way am I asking her!"

"All right. Just don't be ashamed to have it checked out somewhere. Now I *am* a doctor — the kind that doesn't *help* people, as somebody once defined the Doctor of Philosophy. I want you to promise you'll have it looked at if the rash doesn't go away by tomorrow."

"Okay. Do you really want me to send a virus to some website?"

"If I can't stop it any other way. Let's keep in touch on this, all right? Just don't get any viruses on yourself, okay, Yimmy?"

"Sorry, got to go, Dad," Jimmy said. "Mom's home. And I haven't fed Rusty."

"Okay. Take care of yourself."

"Bye." Jimmy hung up.

Nathaniel kept the receiver next to his ear for a little while even though there was nobody there.

Ah, fatherhood.

He went to his computer to check on his latest reviews and to see if the homophobic ones had been removed by the webmaster. Sure enough, he had a brand new nasty review:

> Of all my host of teachers, Nathaniel Tack is the least able to accommodate those in his charge. It is a shame that a man with his talents, though these talents are certainly not on the highest stratum of humanity and what it is capable of, he evidences only the superficial attributes of the educated male of Western Civilization, only to squander even these when he could put them to better use in applying his so-called enlightened perspective to the very real needs of those he is entrusted to help. It is with great sorrow that I must assign him a failing grade.

"Female" was checked, but it was Mr. Early no doubt. He'd even given his Major as "Bio-Dynamics," whatever Darwinian thing that was.

Elegantly written too. The prick! I'm just supposed to sit here and wait for the other nasty reviews to come? Can't people see it's because I gave him a B! There's no way for me to go online and explain the real situation. Not that you would want to! The son of a bitch!

Indeed just then another review came in on Reviews of the Day:

> I must take exception to the previous review of Dr. Nathaniel Tack. I have had him for several classes, and he is hard-working, dedicated teacher. It's not his fault that he is incompetent. God knows, he tries! He often makes mistakes in speaking and asserts his opinions over those of mere students, but the man means well, and I for one think he should be commended for expending energy far beyond his innate capacity. You could do far worse with a teacher.

This reviewer gave him a C. More subtle damning with faint praise. This was also Early's work — the reference to "asserting his opinions over mere students" was the give-away. Wasn't it? Do I not let my students express their opinions? Nathaniel suddenly worried. Of course I do! God, all opinions weren't equal. Some were quite wrong. Early always complimented the other students on their work. It seemed to Nathaniel that he was mustering support for his own work, if it ever came in. The compliments made the faces light up temporarily, but still he could tell the class didn't like Early, made faces and eye-contact with Nathaniel when he was giving his opinions. Not that popularity is the measure of a man. Clearly not of a teacher. In fact, there was a disjuncture between too much popularity and telling the truth — that had to be true, didn't it? — both as a writer and as a teacher. It was the core of Nathaniel's view of the universe. If you weren't honest, you were nothing. What else was there to believe in, if not that?

But it didn't seem to be playing very well on the website.

The homophobic reviews were still there, hoping he died of AIDS. So much for the promises of the webmaster!

Nathaniel was going up the ramp (to the Johnnie Cochran Arts Building, no less) for a class when he noticed five or six Black male students standing below making comments to passing female students. He knew it would be best just to keep on going, but he couldn't un-hear what they were saying: "You be one fine bitch!" "Whatcha be doin', Momma?" "Come over here, girl, and let me show you somethin.'"

They were big and mean-looking, with baggy clothes and head-bands and in-your-face Bad Attitude for days. They'd been hanging out near the ramp for weeks now. Most of the girls just tucked in their heads and kept on walking.

This was a job for Superman!

But Nathaniel knew he wasn't Superman. Maybe a dean could do something. He could perhaps kill two birds with one stone. It would be delicate, because the culprits bothering the female students were black, and Black was Beautiful, even when it was Ugly. You could even hear their voices coming through the windows into the classrooms, yet nobody had the balls to say anything to them. Heavens! It might be "racist" to stop these Bad-Asses from acting like animals. It didn't mean all blacks were like this; it didn't mean there hadn't been discrimination in the Bad Old Days – but by God that was old, old news, and this was now — and yet you could be fired if you mentioned it. After all, they were part of the goddamn Beauty of Diversity. Making lewd comments was clearly a blessing to Shite College and the world. Fuck them. They hated "faggots" too.

Nathaniel found a piece of paper in the Foreign Languages Department office and began to scribble a quick note to the appropriate dean. He wondered how "Foreign Language" had been left untouched in the P.C. Cultural Revolution that had swept over them in recent years. Someone might actually be "foreign"? Impossible! Surely the Second (But Equal) Languages Department would be more fitting!

And it was the Dean of Student Rights — didn't that say it all? The Alliance of Students had engineered that change of terminology in the last six months. What a piece of work they were, about twenty of them, rabid about STUDENT THIS and STUDENT THAT. They had a whole agenda and seemed to believe that they were the rebirth of student activism of the 1960s, and they were. Only now it was the remedial version.

And the Dean of Student Rights was in their pocket, he'd heard. Dean Deane was her name. Daphne Deane. A dumpy, plain woman in her late forties. He'd seen her image on various campus mailings. Rumored to be a lesbian. From Prickeley City across the bay from Santa Francesca. Oh, my god, not another one of those. So predictable. Mind-numbing. They never met an endangered inchworm they didn't love.

He wrote a note anyway:

Dear Dean Deane,

Certain students are yelling things at other students near the ramp that leads to Arts. Can you perhaps check this out and put a stop to it before it gets completely out of hand? The noise is disrupting classes. As for another matter, did your office approve the flyers for Teachersonparade.com? I hope not. Perhaps you can inform me of what the school's role has been in the dissemination of information about the use of this website?

After five days he had heard nothing from the dean. And his paycheck was delayed too. The Payroll Office explained it as a "temporary snafu."

I'm not going to take this, Nathaniel thought. There is no respect for the faculty around this place. The number of assaults on teachers by students has risen, keeps rising, to say nothing of gratuitous discourtesy. In the hallway he'd talked to Nona Dwibble, the former chair of English, about the Black students on the ramp, and she'd said that she'd been hassled herself when she called something to the hasslers from her classroom window. And Nona Dwibble was your basic sixty-year-old, former nun in a wheelchair type. "Cool it, honky bitch!" they'd said. Needless to say, Nona was very upset, but she was having hydraulic problems with her wheelchair and hadn't done anything yet.

So Nathaniel took matters into his own hands and wrote Dean Daphne Deane yet another note. He even sped a copy off to the Chancellor:

To Whom It May Concern:

Please advise as to the exact relationship and support of Teachersonparade by the Administration of this college. I thank you in advance for your speedy attention to my inquiry.

He heard nothing from either one. Probably wouldn't touch it because it involved RACE — wrongs committed by "minorities." Impossible! Shut up! Shut up!

He dared a message on Dean Deane's answering machine. Very polite.

There was no return call.

He called and asked to speak to the Chancellor.

The Chancellor was out of town, at a fund-raiser for Shite College. No, the secretary wasn't sure when he would be back. Yes, she'd take a message. Except that she couldn't seem to understand his name and kept calling him "Spaniel Track."

He gave up.

But not for long. This situation would not stand! It was an outrage. It was a catastrophe. It was . . . it was . . .

Still, he couldn't get a single person with some power to do something about it.

Miss Blutwurst from his day 101 came to see him in his office hour the next Wednesday. She was a pretty girl of perhaps twenty years of age, blonde, tall, with a definite Lutheran cast to her blue eyes and sharp nose. She was wearing a book bag on her back, which stuck out too far and probably hit other people as she hurried around campus.

"Yes, Miss Blutwurst?" Nathaniel said.

She beat around the proverbial for a couple of minutes, wondering how she could do better than the C she was getting in 101. Then, almost as if an after-thought, as she stood to leave, she looked down at him and said, "By the way, Professor, I understand you have some bad reviews on that website." She paused to let that fully sink in.

"*Moi?*" Nathaniel smiled.

She hesitated, then said, "I could, perhaps, help you out, Professor."

"I beg your pardon?" No, this couldn't be happening too!

"You know, like, I scratch yours if you scratch mine." She colored a bit as she made the offer, but she definitely had made the offer.

Nathaniel blushed as well.

"I mean, it's really a pity you have so many bad reviews and you're so low down in the ratings, like, you know . . ." She shrugged, a girlish one.

"What are you saying, Miss Blutwurst?"

"Oh, never mind. I wasn't serious. Well, I have to get to class now."

She adjusted her book bag and combed down her Lutheran hair with a free hand. "I think you've really, like, helped me today," she added with a big toothsome grin.

And she was gone, and another student came in to replace her.

But Nathaniel couldn't get himself to focus on the new student. Miss Blutwurst had something better than mere sex to offer — sex that she knew very well he didn't want from her anyway. She could *grade* him! And her grade would matter more than his grade of her would matter. Her grade would go on a website and be read by hundreds, thousands, and affect the one-sided way he was perceived by the world, even affect enrollment, whereas his grade of her would hardly affect her life at all. She'd pass, and she knew it. Only she wanted a B. What was it she'd said? "I'll scratch the website if you'll scratch a B in your grade book, for little ole me? Why, the little "Lutheran-cunt" was too good a word for the likes of her! And the worst part was that Nathaniel had almost been tempted by the offer.

He ran into Guy Mountain in the courtyard of the Helen C. Keller Visual Arts Building as he was buying a quick lunch from the Roach Coach — the food van, which sold soggy bagels and less-than-crisp bacon, lettuce, and tomato sandwiches, and Chihuahua (or something close.) He didn't have time to go to the *Non*-Faculty Dining Room and settled on a diet Pepsi and a dry raisin scone. He could see his face in the grimy windows of the food van: My god, his hair was thin on top, and did it look dyed!? Loving Care didn't seem to be making Medium Brown anymore, and he'd had to use Ash Brown. I'm not really an Ash Brown kind of fella, he told himself, making a face. Oh, Jesus, was he beginning to look painted? Entirely too *Death in Venice*? Were people laughing at him behind his Von Aschen*bach*?

"You're looking good!" Guy Mountain said.

"Can I talk to you about something important that's taking place on this campus?"

"Sure."

Guy was a man who spent hours counseling his students in the Humanities Department, which was a sub-section of the English Department, and seemed exhausted all the time. He was also enormous and hulking with a pitted nose, long page-boy hair, and some kind of growths on his hands. The Hunchback of Notre Dame crossed with a bloodhound, only not as good looking. He was actually married — somehow — and had a little Mountain or two at home. A sweetheart.

"Thanks for the compliment. I needed it," Nathaniel said. Still, he wasn't going to tell Guy Mountain that he looked good. He searched for something nice to say. "I bet you're working hard as usual."

"I'm teaching an extra course. My mother had some unexpected expenses that I'm helping her with. She has to have a transplant. Something very private."

"I'm sorry to hear that." Nathaniel paused appropriately. "Have you seen this hate website that's been set up?"

But Guy seemed to want to discuss his mother's site instead. "I'm very worried about her future bowel problems." He had already unwrapped his hoagie and was chewing like mad next to the Roach Coach. Guy wasn't his most attractive with barbecue sauce on his front teeth. "Want to sit and chat?" Nathaniel asked. (They'd get beyond the motherly bowels to the hate if it killed him.)

"I have a class, but, sure, a few minutes," Guy said. Ah, maybe here was an ally at last in the fight against Cyber Evil.

They sat at a bench in one of the campus courtyards. It was a sharply sunny day, the sunlight hurting Nathaniel's eyes. He had forgotten his sunglasses and wanted to get back inside his office as soon as he could. Am I part vampire? he wondered. But Guy Mountain needed to be schmoozed right then and there.

"Is your mother very ill?"

"Unfortunately, yes."

"If you'd rather not talk about it, I understand," Nathaniel feinted.

"It's a little hard to talk about, but, as I tell my students, people need to share their feelings more. We're all bottled up in this country."

"Really?" Nathaniel said vaguely. Bottled up, in America? *Pul-leeze*! There was apparently nothing that people wouldn't "share" about themselves — and on national television to boot!

"Mom needs major surgery. And soon."

"No."

Guy swallowed some more hoagie. "Needs her lower plumbing completely restored."

Do we really have to go *there*?! "Have you seen the website I mentioned, Guy?"

Guy's subject wasn't ready to be changed yet. "She's not working, shall we say, in that area anymore. But Mom's gotten so big it's difficult to operate. Four hundred and twenty-five pounds now, the poor thing."

"I'm sure she'll recover," Nathaniel said hurriedly. "Have you seen the review website?"

"Oh, yes, I think it's a great idea," Guy said.

Hmm.

"Have you seen what's on it? I looked at it again this morning. There's a review of Nona Dwibble calling her a 'fasceest, raceest Beetch.' Spelled wrong, of course."

"There are bound to be some excesses, but overall I think it's a great idea for students to evaluate their teachers. Don't you?"

"We get evaluated by our students every three years — and they are real students, not phantom ones. That's plenty. Are you aware that fake students are sending in reviews?" Nathaniel thought it politic not to mention that he had been one of the early phantoms.

"I doubt that happens very much," Guy said.

"How many fake reviews would it take to convince you?" Nathaniel said, trying to keep the edge out of his voice.

"I believe teachers might improve based on student feedback." He had barbecue sauce all over his big, thick, chapped lips. And what in the hell *were* those growths on his hands? Syphilis chancres?

"Have you ever seen yourself on video?" Nathaniel suddenly asked. "Teaching, I mean?" He wondered what kind of mountain Guy's mother looked like.

"No. Why?"

"Oh, just a thought."

I'd better not say it, free speech or not, Nathaniel told himself. Would you continue teaching if you could see the way you look? No, I don't mean that. Yes, I do! Oh God, I have a cruel eye. And I definitely never should "share."

Fortunately, Guy didn't seem to be reading his mind.

"A student once wrote that I needed to enunciate more carefully — in an official review this was — and I took that to heart, and I've been a better teacher ever since."

How peachy. "What if somebody told you to have your growths burned off, would you oblige?" Nathaniel started to say. Instead, he said, "What if somebody told you to enunciate *less*? Would you do that?"

"I don't think that was my shortcoming, Nathaniel."

"The website gives too much power to students to influence their grades. That's the essence of the problem. For instance, this girl from my night class was just in —"

"It's better here than the last place I taught," Guy interrupted. "At Santa Maria Pinta student evaluations count 90% toward tenure."

"You're kidding."

"I got only 79 % and had to leave."

"You can't be serious!"

"Completely serious. So at Shite we're actually much better off."

"I'm sorry to hear you say this, Guy. I was hoping for some help shutting the site down."

"I don't think it should be shut down. It can be very useful if it's properly used."

"But it's not *being* properly used. That's my point."

"Yeah, I heard you weren't doing too well on the site." Guy took the head off his hoagie.

"There are also some downright homophobic reviews on there."

Guy finished chewing. "I'm sure they don't mean it. So I wouldn't get too sensitive about those, if I were you," he said.

"But you're not me. And you're not gay."

"You wouldn't want to have a chip on your shoulder about it, I'm sure."

"I don't think I *do* have a chip on my shoulder about it." Nathaniel put down his unfinished scone. "But something tells me that if it said black teachers 'should die of sickle cell anemia' and 'where I come from niggers are shot' I bet we'd have some action about the website."

"I don't think the situations are comparable. I'm not with you on this one," Guy said, getting up from the bench.

Yeah, because queers don't count!

"I'm sorry to hear that," Nathaniel said, getting up as well. Sweetheart? Where did I get the idea Guy was a sweetheart?

"Goodbye, Nathaniel. See you around. I've got to go pick up my mother."

Nathaniel waved, despite himself. Goodbye, Mr. Chip on my Shoulder. And best of luck on your mother's transplanted anus! . . . I'm sorry. I'm sorry.

The *hell* I'm sorry! Good luck *picking up* your four-hundred-and-twenty-five-pound mother. Hope you find that ass donor in time!

"How's it going?" Marty wondered. They were on the phone together, Marty at the library, Nathaniel in his condo. In the late afternoon.

"Not that well, actually." Nathaniel was still in his pajamas, sitting on the sofa. His day off. He picked at some cat hairs. There were more on the Oriental rug. Slacker was outside, getting hit by a car or killing something. He called her the "prowling purr-vert" sometimes.

"I thought you were going to see a dean or something about it."

"I can't get anyone in the Administration to acknowledge the problem. Not a soul. They've learned that if they don't do anything most people simply give up."

"The most effective warfare, all in all." Marty sounded sniffly, like he'd just snorted some meth.

"The faculty is worthless too. Any suggestions?" Marty was much better with people than he was. He was very well liked at the library. He complained about his co-workers and the conditions, but apparently he kept his criticisms close to the vest. "I can use some help about now, Marty. Nobody seems to see it as much as a threat as I do."

"Yeah. I looked up your reviews. They don't seem to like you very much."

"Thanks."

"Well, *I* like you!"

"I feel all warm and fuzzy."

"I sent in a review of you, from here."

"Really? . . . I hope it was good."

"It was. I spent some time on it. It was slow around here."

"And what did you say exactly?"

"That you were good in bed."

"You didn't!"

"I said that I had observed you teaching and that you were an excellent teacher."

"So you lied for your honey, huh?"

"I've seen you teach lots of times — remember I used to pick you up for dinner after class."

"I'd forgotten. But you're still not my student."

"I was! That time your creative class didn't have enough enrolled and you signed me up."

"During those awful days when the state decided to charge three times as much for people with degrees. They thought they'd make more money, and it almost cost me the class."

"But your honey came riding to the rescue." Sniffle, sniffle. Oh, god, Marty was sniffing speed at work.

"He did. And I thank him for it."

"You're very well spoken, and you have a nice rapport in the classroom. I don't understand why your reviews aren't better."

"Because only the disgruntled ones bother to write in! How many of your patrons say what a great job you're doing checking out their books?"

"We get candy and cookies sometimes."

"I can't accept bribes."

"I don't accept bribes!"

"Sorry!" Still, he knew that Marty sometimes canceled library fines for certain people he liked, including himself.

"I sympathize," Marty went on. He was speaking so low it was hard to hear him. He was probably in the back room taking a longer-than-usual break. His boss had called him on it before. "I've seen some of the papers you get. Pathetic. You're perfectly right. Our Chief of Branches has a so-called Master's degree from State and you should see the memos she sends out. Illiterate."

"Why don't you correct them in red and send them back?"

"She'd transfer me to an even crummier branch than this one."

"Do it anonymously, like my students."

"She might be able to trace it back to me."

"I wonder if there's some way to trace back the homophobic reviews I got. I find myself suspecting every student I come across."

"What about other faculty? Do you suppose *they're* sending in reviews?"

"Who knows." Nathaniel suddenly felt a chill. Outside the window of his living room he could see that it was a drab, overcast day. "I should get dressed," he urged himself. But why bother? He felt the stubble on his chin.

"Got to hang up soon," Marty said.

"What if it's true, Marty."

"What?"

"That I'm a terrible teacher." Nathaniel was having an epiphany, or at least half an epiphany. "Maybe I shouldn't even be teaching."

"Nonsense." Marty's voice grew concerned. "Now don't get depressed again, okay? You're a wonderful, funny teacher."

"You're just saying that."

"I've seen you in the classroom. It's not your fault the students are so incompetent. Sorry, I've got to go. Cowboy is getting peach juice all over the pages of a book."

"Who?"

"One of the creeps who comes here in a cowboy hat and spurs. Mr. John Q. Public. The same thing, more or less, you face with your students at Shite."

"The world is falling apart, Marty, and we queers have got to save it!"

"I've got to go!"

"At least you don't have to read Cowboy's papers," Nathaniel said.

"No, just sop up his peach juice and kick him out until the next time."

"Can't you ban him?"

"We are 'to rent our service to our customers— for "render our service"— as the Chief of Branches would put it. Got to go. My boss is breathing down my neck these days. Now don't be depressed. Get dressed. Go for a drive. Have an orgasm!"

"Is that an offer?"

Marty paused. "I've got to see my sister tonight. She needs some advice about getting a new job."

"No problem." Marty was very close to his older sister.

"Don't get depressed, okay? You are a terrific person, and I love you very much."

"But can I save the world for education?" Nathaniel joked.

"You're a damned good teacher, better than most of the ones I had in college." Marty had gone to State. Hmm.

"Thank you, Mr. Dent. I needed that. Love you."

"Love you too!"

They hung up, and Nathaniel forced himself get off the sofa and get dressed.

He got a stack of 102 papers out of his briefcase and grabbed the lap desk he liked to use. I'll start with the best papers, he encouraged himself, or what are usually the best — Mr. Dong's. Mr. Dong was a young man who gone to the best school in the city and wrote well when he put his mind to it. But his papers were growing sloppier, being turned in later and later as he became more and more acclimated to American life. Welcome to America, Mr. Dong!

Nathaniel got out his green marking pen. He'd stopped using red because some study or other had said that "red is intimidating to students." Okay. Whatever, as Jimmy would say. This time Mr. Dong's paper was quite fine, and he'd written it himself. Nathaniel made sure of that by requiring two rough drafts of all papers written out of class. Good for you, Mr. Dong. B+.

But the next paper in the stack began with:

> "Have you ever experienced the interruption of sweet relationship between you and your lover because both of you are gay? If you have, as I'm sure is true, you may have felt depressing, stressing, and pounding. By soon, facing the facts must insist on understanding everything its relationship, believing in who you are. Even thought you are type of homosexual person; it does not mean you have no love, truly love, not just dirty sex. I once wished I were a girl, so both of us could get marry and spend the rest of our lives together, forever. Totally, we were wrong. We just had some sort of strong friendship that

we ever had before. Oh, my goodness, I was not a gay! Nonetheless, I am convinced that there is no such thing as a cute gay guy. I mean every one of them is too gay, too fat or too ugly. What is the purpose? I am so sick of it."

Good grief, somebody had passed this person out of 101! Nathaniel threw the essay on the floor. "Unclean! Unclean!" he yelled. He pushed the lap desk off his lap and covered his eyes with his hands and began rubbing the eyeballs with his palms. I can't stand this anymore. I can't correct another one of these. University Level? Second Semester? The Study of Literature Through Literary Analysis? What universe, never mind university, was he living in? Okay, I could keep on going when I could correct these monstrosities and gradually ease the students into a Withdrawal. They never got better when they were this bad to begin with. He'd wind up with a small class, but at least the remaining ones were fairly competent. Now, with the website, he had to worry about revenge for not passing the ones like this. And he might be pressured into passing them!

"I'm going out to have sex," he said to Slacker, who had come in from outside. She had some grass seeds on her forehead, but nothing dead, or alive, in her mouth. She ignored him and curled up in her cat bed on his bed and pretended to go to sleep.

He changed his clothes again, this time getting into one set of his Sex Clothes. These consisted of worn Levi's, black boots, a blackish-brown corduroy jacket, and a faded baseball cap. He touched up his mustache with some left-over hair color from his Darker Days and wetted down his hair with water from the bathroom faucet and checked himself in the mirror. He looked pretty good. He was actually handsome. Yeah, he'd suck that guy in the mirror off! If he could reach. But no masturbation. Masturbation meant you couldn't get anybody else, meant loneliness.

He checked outside to see what the weather was like. It was late afternoon and getting dark already. Good. The night-tripping fairies would be setting out on their appointed rounds very soon. An ejaculation or two in the right place at the right time, or even the wrong place, could certainly take the edge off a stack of lousy papers and a hateful website.

It is a truth *not* universally acknowledged, Nathaniel felt, that men have more sperm than they know what to do with. It turns them cranky, vicious, deceptive, and several other unpleasant things, and all because they don't get that spunk out nearly often enough to suit their very real and very carnal needs. Unlike poor straight men (sorry but you chose to be straight) gay men, it should be noted, have managed to overcome this situation by neither raping nor pledging their troth but instead by seeking out accommodating partners in all sorts of creative arenas.

Thus it was that Nathaniel came to the forested park, with the moon-lit ocean just across the way. He could hear the waves rimming the shore in the near-distance. The cypresses and high weeds and abundant grasses provided perfect trysting spots for those in the mood to tryst. There, off the beaten path, many a happy man had been beaten off.

He and Marty had an open relationship. Indeed, that's why they were still together. This was just sex. Sex didn't matter. Except when you couldn't get it. Sex wasn't love.

But, oh brother, I love you when you do that!

It was werewolf weather, the fog hovering chest high, billowing among the trees and bushes as he made his way through the dwindling light. The street lamps on the perimeter hadn't come on yet, and he strolled through the underbrush, alert for Victims. Willing Victims, of course. Also alert for the police, who sent out patrols from time to time to stop men from having sex. Nobody else but men having sex ever came there, but the police felt obliged to stop it. Meanwhile, over in the parking lot near the ocean, men and women were fucking in their cars and making out on the beach. Undisturbed. Fuck the cops! Sperm will out!

"What are you goin' up there for?" a voice suddenly accosted Nathaniel, who was on the cobblestone stairway that crossed over to another section of the park. The voice startled him, because the men who came here usually kept very quiet, except for some queen who stumbled in by mistake every now and again. Who was calling to him?

"Don't go up there!"

Nathaniel cupped his hand over his eyes to see better. He said nothing.

"There are queers up there!"

"Screw you!" Nathaniel heard himself say. "Go home. Nobody's bothering you."

"Fuck you, you fruit!" the voice said.

Should you argue that you weren't a fruit?

The street lamps had just come on. The guy was drunk, staggering in the street. He was tall and beefy. Why was he so mad? Had he just witnessed a blow job and he wasn't getting any at home?

"Fuck you!" Nathaniel yelled.

"Come down here and I'll fight you!" came the surly response.

"I'd rather have a blow job," Nathaniel replied, under his breath. He kept moving up the staircase. The Stairway to Heaven.

Jesus, isn't there enough grief in the world without denying a man a little physical relief with his peers?

He waited at the top of the stairs to see if Loudmouth was coming his way. I don't need a fistfight right now. Anytime, but if you want to fight, asshole, I'll fight you. Only I'll do it by running you over with my car. But Nathaniel had parked several blocks away, because the police patrols had stopped and looked at him sitting in his car a few times in the past when he'd parked closer.

Here and there were male couples sporting — and that was a four-way over by the wooden fence. Safely sexual. If I didn't come here, I wouldn't get any exercise at all, he reminded himself. He trod the untrodden paths beside the springs of cum.

Someone touched his crotch. Felt. Then moved away.

Well, pardon me, if my hard-on didn't measure up.

Actually, it wasn't much of a hard-on, he realized. He was one of those men whose penises tended to shrivel when not employed but become regular ring-a-ding lingams when properly nurtured.

He waited. All good things come to those who wait. Fools, rush in where angels fear to tread.

But then: He who hesitates is lost, right?

He trod some more. He felt his own penis. It wasn't getting as excited as it usually did on such occasions. Oh, my god, it's age! No!

Of course. The tired old blood wasn't manning the station the way it used to. Oh, dear. If you couldn't have free, anonymous, carefree, utterly meaningless sex, what was left? Low-cal sherbet just didn't cut it.

He watched as two men kissed in the shadows beside an old tree stump, their hands busy. He wanted to join them, and sometimes he did. But tonight he was feeling self-conscious about his un-aroused state.

"Well, it's a *little* aroused," he pep-talked to himself.

He leaned back against a far part of the wooden fence and listened to the ocean through the slats. Above him he could see stars and planets doing nothing, just being. Why can't we be such as these, he smiled. They toil not, neither do they spin, and yet even Guy Mountain in all his glory is not arrayed like one of these.

As he looked down, someone was kneeling in the fog in front of him. It was difficult to make out the figure, but it didn't seem to be a werewolf, or even one of the raccoons that lived in the park and came out at night. It was a man in his graying forties in a sailor's pea coat, with a pleasant if unremarkable face. He was gently rubbing his lips with his fingertips and looking Nathaniel's way. No smile. None was needed.

Nathaniel took the few steps necessary to bring his needs to the eager, receptive vacuum of the wonderful, sucking stranger. Warm lips came together, that rush of happy, coursing blood, the springing to life, creating life in the old dog yet, and Nathaniel closed his eyes and caressed the bent gentleman's head that went to work and made life — oh yes indeed! — entirely worth living.

He hadn't done anything more about the website and felt stymied, but he hadn't called Jimmy back. He couldn't really ask his child to send a virus, could he? Starve a cold, send a virus? Damn. Most people didn't do anything about anything. But you're not most people, Nathaniel reminded himself. Am I powerless? Most people are powerless. The Black male students were still hassling the females on the ramp. Had race trumped everything once again? It wasn't "racist" to stop what these creeps were doing! What cowards people could be!

When he ran into Spike Burns, his chair, in the men's room on the fifth floor of the building, he knew something was wrong even before Spike stopped peeing and zipped up his fly. "Gladys and I have been doing the scheduling for next semester and the enrollment in your classes is way down. What's going on, Nathaniel?"

Nathaniel waited. He was still a little pee shy, though not as bad as he used to be. "Seriously?"

Spike wasn't smiling. "You have or two people in each section, and that's all. Usually by this time they're full."

"Am I the only one?"

"Tadd Dryer's are bad too."

"I guess we're The Pits," Nathaniel said, stepping up to the urinal.

"Do you think it's that website?"

"Evil reigns in the land."

"Isn't there something you can do to get the enrollment up?"

"I can give everybody an A."

"Short of that."

"I don't know." He turned and watched Spike washing his hands. The institutional soap penetrated the air like atomic waste. "What happens if I don't get enrollment?"

"It's never happened before, to a full-timer. The part-timers we just let go."

"I know, Spike. I was a part-timer, once upon a part-time. It was not pretty. You never knew if you were going to eat or not."

"Yeah, yeah," Spike waved his hand. "This makes it so complicated!"

"Sorry," Nathaniel said lamely.

"And yet some sections are over-filled."

"The easy graders?"

Spike thought about it. "Probably."

Nathaniel was pretending to pee. He wished Spike would go away, but he was washing his hands so hard he looked like he was expecting cholera. Come to think of it, the stains on the bathroom's sinks were pretty frightening. The school by this time of the term was always more soiled-looking that usual, with "things" left on the floor of the cubicles and toothpaste puddles and pubic hairs in the porcelain basins. One wants to pick and choose the pubic hairs one interacts with, *n'est pas*? Nathaniel thought.

"Is it possible I could have no classes next semester?"

"You could always bump somebody else."

"No doubt *that* would go over well."

"Maybe it's just a computer glitch. That happens sometimes. The enrollment doesn't show up in the proper places." Spike was drying his hands on the coarse, recycled paper from the dispenser. He gave himself a quick once-over in the cracked mirror. "Got to go. Got a meeting," he said.

"Let's talk about this," Nathaniel said.

Finally he peed, just as somebody came in and started flossing. Yuck, there was also something called Too Much Hygiene!

He zipped up his pants and made himself look in the mirror. It was bright daylight, and he'd found that the demi-light of his own bathroom was much more flattering. Here it was like the john of an airplane: every sin you had ever committed was etched there in your face: every pitiful zit, every unshaven patch on your neck, every raddled capillary rising to the surface around your nose. Glory to be to God for dappled things! No, the horror, the horror!

In the parking lot behind Arts he spotted a ticket on his windshield. Shit! He had parked "out of space." He had parked out of space because students or other non-faculty were parked in what should have been faculty spaces in the faculty parking lot. This happened every term and the Administration wouldn't use the campus police to block the malefactors from parking there in the first place. Also those handicapped spaces — six of them — sitting there empty. Empty ninety-nine percent of the time. Shit! Surely someone could figure out a better system than this. King Louis the Fucking Fourteenth didn't have as many empty parking spaces as the handicapped did!

And who was that coming toward him? Oh, no, it was a former student, Mr. Loo from years ago. Was he still on the campus? He was an older man in his seventies, always in a suit. From Hong Kong, a rabid anti-Communist, wasn't he? Or was that somebody else? Nathaniel grabbed the ticket off the windshield and resisted the impulse to tear it to shreds and started to get into his car quickly to avoid Mr. Loo.

But Mr. Loo saw him and even crossed over. Nathaniel prepared a face to meet the faces that you meet. "Hello there! he said, steeling himself for some harangue or request.

"Dr. Tack, correct?" Mr. Loo said, pointing his finger.

"That's right."

"I had you eight years ago."

"Yes, you looked familiar. Nice to see you." Nathaniel tried to scramble onto the front seat.

"You were an excellent teacher."

Nathaniel stood upright. "I was?"

"Teach me much."

"I did?"

Mr. Loo was all smiles. "Now I have good job, thanks to you. I do writing for my company. Chinese medicines."

"How wonderful," Nathaniel said. With a proofreader, I hope. It would be very bad to misspell that order for tiger bone. Sorry, I shouldn't be grading him now, not here. But the English *is* a little broken. Better Broken English 101 than having to dial #1 for Chinese, the way you now had to dial #2 for Spanish. Whatever happened to the *Unum* in *E Pluribus Unum*?

"You very kind, very good teacher," Mr. Loo said. It almost seemed as if he wanted to pat Nathaniel on the shoulder to confirm what he was saying.

God, I'm so judgmental, Nathaniel winced. "I'm very happy for you . . . it's Mr. Loo, right?"

"You remembered my name!" Now Mr. Loo was three steps from bliss because Nathaniel had remembered him. My, my, why couldn't Americans have this attitude toward their teachers! If you could only get the best parts of each culture all together in one package instead of the way it was!

"I must go now," Mr. Loo said, heading across the parking lot. "Very nice to see you." He bowed his head slightly.

What a prince, Nathaniel thought. How generous. And he has nothing to gain from me now, so the compliment is sincere. Hmm. He's not re-enrolling next semester, is he? No! He's just being nice. Should I ask him to go on Teachersonparade and give me a good review?

How humiliating. Out on the streets, in every parking lot, begging for a compliment. "Please, sir, just one tiny handout of a review, to insure my enrollment so I can feed my poor starving child, who is named Slacker. Oh, please, sir! Just one kind review!"

That night he noticed a flyer for Teachersonparade.com outside his classroom, right next to the ASSPOO sign. In fact, there were two. They were a new variation of the first flyer:

WHAT ARE YOU WAITING FOR?

YOUR WEBSITE "FIND OUT THE TRUTH

ABOUT YOU'RE TEACHERS!

USE COMPUTERS ON CAMPUS.

GATHERING WITH FREE PIZZA ON CAMPUS MALL

It gave the next Friday's date.

What did that mean — they'd have computers set up so that students could review teachers on the spot? If the college wasn't supporting this site, then why was it permitting its computers and its mall to be used?

Nathaniel wandered down the hallway among the milling Diversity, noting more flyers attached to the walls. School rules forbade attaching posters anywhere except on the official notice boards, and then only if approved, but people violated the regulations all the time. There were two more Teachersonparade flyers on the doors at the end of the hallway. Both of them had his name scrawled in red ink across the top. He looked around to see who was watching but then tore the flyers off the doors, his heart beating horribly. Yes, someone had written "Nathaniel Tack" and "Check Him Out" by hand and placed them on the doors for more exposure.

He crumpled up the flyers in his fists and looked for a trash container. But there hadn't been a trash container in the hallway for months. He'd caught the so-called Maintenance Crew sleeping and socializing in their lounge on the fourth floor plenty of times, yet somehow they could never seem to get a trash container, once they cleaned it, back in less than two months. All in all, maintenance didn't seem to "maintain" much of anything. So, like today, there were usually candy wrappers and spilled coffee stains in the classrooms and hallways, to say nothing of the scotch tape and bits of former flyers festooning the walls like the guts of some public project. I must not despair, Nathaniel warned himself.

He checked out the almost-empty classroom that he taught in most of the time. Someone had placed flyers in there as well, again with Nathaniel's name scrawled at the top in red ink. One of the flyers was attached to the front of the instructor's desk, as if perhaps the teacher wouldn't see it but the classes would. There was even a flyer on the broken television set mounted overhead. If I weren't a trusting soul, I'd say that somebody has it in for me.

He removed the ones from his classroom, straining for the one on the television, just before his students began to appear for class, including Miss Blutwurst of the Offer He Almost Couldn't Refuse. She didn't make as much eye contact with him as she had before their "conference." Just as well. He looked at the squashed balls of paper lying in the corner where he had placed them, feeling a combination of guilt and rage.

He didn't think he taught particularly well that day either, the flyers a distracting reminder that anyone could say anything about him without accountability and without hearing his side or seeing the students' work. Mr. Vulcovich hinted in one of his questions about the existence of the website, but Nathaniel chose not to bite.

His evening class the next night was better. The students were generally better, or at least interested in literature. This was his favorite class. Was it all right to have a favorite class anymore, or was that injuring the self-fucking-esteem of the others? Parents had favorites too, even if they weren't supposed to. Nathaniel knew that, because he'd been his mother's favorite, making him a favorite target of his resentful much older half-brother from his mother's first marriage. Thanks, Mom! No, you can forget the past, Nathaniel told himself. You can have a happy childhood even after fifty, it you just try! Look on the bright side: Mr. Early wasn't attending the class anymore. The lying reviews he was writing every day or so kept coming in, however.

I want sex. I want Marty. I don't want Marty. I do want Marty. I want sex, hot, wild, promiscuous sex with innumerable partners in the darkest reaches of anonymous night! You can't have drugs, you can over-do alcohol, my last book didn't sell very well. For god's sake, let me self-medicate this ache in my loins and my heart!

He taught the class, on Finding Your Voice, and he could tell it went well. Mr. Ulluababa from Uganda, or wherever, seemed especially pleased with what Nathaniel had to say: Write about what you know. Do you know some world that others don't? Share it with your reader! Mr. Ulluababa was writing about financial schemes run out of African countries and was afraid that his American readers might not understand his novel. Never fear, Mr. Ulluababa, you have our complete attention. Mr. Ulluababa had also once mentioned that there were no gay people in Uganda.

"Very nice presentation," Mr. Ulluababa said as he handed in a chapter.

Do you mean for one of those rarities, a gay person? But, no, — Nathaniel said to himself — teaching is not a performance. Only of course teaching was. And I give very nice "performances," as any number of my colleagues' class observations have noted over the years. Only I won't give away grades the way I'll give away my mind and body for the Cause! (What was the Cause now? An educated electorate? Oh, how old-fashioned! Get with the times, buddy. Give in. It will stop hurting if you just give in!)

I wish I smoked, Nathaniel thought, gathering his notes into his briefcase and heading down the back staircase. It might be nice just to sit on one of the stone benches in the little courtyard beside the Health Clinic and draw nicotine into myself and feel satisfied with my "performance." Of course he didn't smoke and someone had been assaulted and robbed there earlier in the semester, so maybe just some frivolous sex somewhere? Of course AIDS was always a possibility still, although it you kept your dirty ways out of your own and others' butt holes you were probably okay.

He spotted what he took to be Dean Calvin Visigoth having a smoke in the very courtyard he had considered for himself. He seen the dean there before, but he didn't really know him, had merely seen him at campus functions. He was a strangely shaped man who resembled a fat leprechaun, or maybe it was a reptilian-eyed Tweedledee that he looked like. He had a large head with a bad comb-over and goofy-looking teeth that badly needed cleaning. Smoker's teeth. He always wore a dark blue blazer — either the same one or a series of identical ones, it was hard to tell.—but they were all too tight on him. Yet despite the man's appearance, he was always spoken about on campus with diffidence, perhaps even with fear. He'd had somebody in the Photography Department fired for dating a student. This was during one of the contract negotiations when the dean was trying to get leverage for a pay cut for the faculty. This was strange indeed since at least two senior Administrators were married to their former students. I guess they got grandfathered in, Nathaniel thought.

He was going to pass the dean without acknowledgment, the way he had for years, and keep on avoiding the petty politics of Shite College, except that something told him that this particular fight about the website wasn't petty and had to be won.

"Good evening, Dean Visigoth," he said, like a con man.

"How do you do." Up close the dean's head was bathed in cigarette smoke. He waved it away ostentatiously.

"I'm Nathaniel Tack of the English Department."

"Yes, I know," said the dean. Knowingly. He had dark, intelligent eyes.

"I don't believe I've spoken to you in the twenty years I've been here."

"Cigarette?" the dean offered.

"No, thank you."

"My one vice," the dean admitted.

"I guess we're all entitled to one," Nathaniel said. Of course mine is homosexual sex in the bushes, Your Highness. Any problem with that?

"Is there some particular reason for stopping tonight, Mr. Tack?" A slight wind was blowing the comb-over out of its place and leaving a wide part in the dean's hair. Yes, it was true his teeth were yellowed and gnarly. And yet somehow he had married the prettiest administrator at the school, hadn't he — the Eurasian beauty who had been a Miss Universe contestant at one time, before she had finished her Master's and come to Shite? She had kept her original name, Heidi Ho, wasn't it? Dean Calvin Visigoth and Heidi Ho were a testament to what the college was all about.

"I was wondering if any of you in the Administration have made any plans to do something about the so-called review website. I've written to the Chancellor and to Dean

Deane, but so far I haven't had a reply."

"What kind of a reply were you expecting? The school doesn't really have anything to do with the website."

"I think it does," Nathaniel said, more sharply than he intended. "To anyone looking at it, it would seem to be a reliable source of information about the faculty of this school."

"It's run by a student organization, but there is no official connection to the school. Our lawyers have assured us of that."

Oh, I see. "Have you looked at what's actually on it?"

"Not very much, no. It's for the use of students, I believe."

"It accuses almost everybody of racism. Nona Dwibble, for instance. She is about as far from a racist as one can be. I read one today that says Chester Austen-Dryden hates his Japanese students and prefers his Filipino students. There are plenty more besides. In fact, anyone who maintains *standards* is labeled a racist. That's supposed to stop us all dead in our tracks."

"It seems to me that the website represents a clear example of free speech. It may not be pleasant, but it's protected by the Constitution of the United States. Just as your free speech is protected as a teacher, is it not, Dr. Tack?"

"I doubt that I could accuse a student in class of being a racist against *white* people without hearing about it and probably having to go before a tribunal of some kind. Or maybe my paycheck would be held up! Through a snafu, so-called."

The dean looked a bit annoyed. "We tolerate a great deal of diversity of opinion around this campus, it seems to me, Dr. Tack."

"No we don't! It's all one way, all numbingly P.C. I don't mean it has to be politically conservative. By no means. To me that's just as brain dead as the other kind, but it's simply not true that all free speech — about many things — is tolerated around this campus. If I put up a website for faculty where they could write nasty reviews of students and linked it to the school's website through various clubs, do you think that would be tolerated?"

"It might be."

Can you say "bullshit" to a dean? "If it even *hinted* at the same kinds of insults that are being leveled at teachers, it would be shut down in five minutes." It was a struggle to keep his voice from rising.

But something had to be done here, by god!

But the dean was likewise angry, Nathaniel could tell. "I'm sorry you don't care for the site, Dr. Tack. I assure you that it won't be used in any kind of official way for promotions or firings."

"Not yet anyway."

The dean hesitated. "When I became the club's faculty moderator, I did it because nobody else on this campus seemed to have the guts to do it."

"Excuse me, did I understand that correctly?" he asked. "*You* are the faculty moderator for this website?" Nathaniel could smell the cigarette smoke getting into his clothes. It smelled like brimstone.

"I continue to teach one class a year, History 12, to keep my oar in, so to speak," the dean explained. "So I agreed to endorse the First Amendment Club."

"That's the club that runs the site?"

"Pretty much. I believe there are ten or so students involved. Enough for a quorum."

"And yet you say the college is not involved even though you, a dean, have helped it to function?" (Keep your goddamn oar out of me!)

"It's as a faculty member that I endorse it, not as an administrator. Surely you, Dr. Tack, especially as a published novelist and playwright — isn't that correct? — cannot object to free speech? And gay material, am I correct, isn't that what you write?"

Nathaniel felt a little flustered. The cigarette smoke was burning his eyeballs. "That's not only what I write. I've written about being a father too."

"Really?"

Of course you wouldn't know because you and most of the other people around this place haven't read a word I've written. You can't be bothered. Screw you, Dean Visigoth and the hordes you rode in on!

"I believe you are a provocative writer, if what I hear is true, and even some of the things you say in class are rather strong, are they not?"

Nathaniel regained his composure. "I imagine to some they are, but at least everyone who hears them knows that I said them. They aren't anonymous."

"I believe those running the website feel that they have too much to lose if their comments about teachers are not anonymous. Retaliation in grades and such, you see." What a fucking Leprechaun he was!

"To say nothing of retaliation in a court of law for libel? Students now have more power than teachers because their grades carry more weight."

"I doubt that, Dr. Tack." The dean gave a little contemptuous laugh as he stubbed out his butt. "Libel is very difficult to prove, I believe. Again I paraphrase the school's lawyers."

"Some students are sending in multiple reviews of the same teacher, destroying their reputations. One person can do it over and over. You can't tell me this is *right*!"

"I'm sure that's also a rarity, Nathaniel," the dean said patronizingly. "I've got to be going. My wife, Heidi, is picking me up in the parking lot. I'm probably already late. Will you excuse me?"

Nathaniel wanted to say more, much more. But how could he insist that the dean stay there and hash this out? There wasn't even an invitation to come to his office and discuss it more. Okay, go off and ride your Heidi Ho! Free speech, my ass! Yeah, Benjamin Franklin and Thomas Jefferson framed the Constitution so that some honest, hard-working ex-nun in a wheelchair could be called a "fasceest, raceest Beetch" on the Internet!

Am I the only one this bothered by this website? was Nathaniel's first thought the next morning when he awoke. It has little to do with actually improving teaching and seems more for mean-spirited revenge than anything else. But maybe the faculty members actually enjoy wearing an electronic Scarlet Review to expose their so-called sins to the world. Nona Dwibble, missing the S&M delights of her nunnery, is now forced to wear FRB on her wheelchair, required to confess "Yes, I am a fasceest, raceest Beetch!" publicly on the campus mall. Followed by stones and whipping. Perhaps it soothed her troubled Catholic soul. Was nothing either good or bad except that thinking made it so? Who said that? Vlad the Impaler?

Slacker was sleeping between his legs. Yeah, this cat is the only thing between my legs, Nathaniel thought grumpily. He had not gone out for sex after class, the conversation with Dean Visigoth dispiriting him too much. Along with impotence, or whatever you called half a hard-on — half-harded impotence? Dynamic professor-writer Nathaniel Tack suffered a case of Mild Impotence at his favorite sex area last evening. He is resting comfortably, his dick in a splint, at his HMO.

I wonder if Viagra would work? he thought, flipping his soft penis with a finger. I'm only fifty-nine. I think my father was humping my mother long after he was that age. At least until they had retired back to the hamlet in Illinois — in the middle of nowhere, surrounded by flat plains and Good Midwest Farm People with an average IQ of 66. Or was it the nearby highway that was 66? Whatever it was, it was best not to speculate on the sex life of your parents. They might even — eek! — have kept photographs! He remembered his mother saying plaintively, in her eighties just before she died, that she just wanted "a little arm-lovin'" now and again from his father. His father was far gone into depression by then, so Nathaniel doubted that she got much "arm-lovin.'" Just the inevitable wait for the body to decline, the broken hip, and Agamemnon dead.

I wonder what Jimmy would think of my sex life, Nathaniel mused. I suppose he thinks Marty and I are monogamous, like his mother and Lana. Or do those two have lesbian bed death already? It's been three years for this lover, hasn't it? Maybe they'll be lucky — four years before they cuddle themselves into lesbian boredom. Oh hell, let 'em be! Nathaniel chastised himself. If I could only cease to think. A mind is a terrible thing — never mind wasting one!

He jumped out of bed like a tot and got dressed, fed the cat, fed himself, and went to school even though he had no classes that day. I am on a Quest for Good! he told himself. He went to his office and prepared a general letter to the faculty, typed out laboriously on the ancient typewriter he shared with his office mates. Soon his students would say, "Professor, what was a *typewriter*? And did you ever use one yourself?" "Yes, boys and girls, back in the old days we had such things. Consider yourselves fortunate that you can trash your teachers online much faster now."

His letter said this:

To Whom It May Concern

It has come to the attention of this committee that the following review has been posted about you on Teacherson-parade.com, which purports to give reliable information about the faculty at this college. Would you say that this review of you reflects one of the following? Check the appropriate letter:

A) The review is completely true.

B) The review is partially true. Which parts?

C) The review is mostly false. Which parts?

D) The review is a bunch of lies.

E) Comments:

—The Committee on Truth

Yes, the "Committee on Truth" — that was good. He wasn't a real committee, just one person, but it sounded more important this way. It also resonated with the carved words on Shite's Caesar Chavez Science Building: THE TRUTH SHALL MAKE YOU FREE. It also sounded like something from the French Revolution or the Alliance of Students: "The Committee on Truth has examined this matter and has determined that you are indeed guilty of thinking an ill-thought about an Approved Group or indeed Any Student (Free Speech being permitted to the Student Body but even Free Thought being *forbidden* to the Faculty) and thus are to be guillotined at high noon on the mall during the Pizza Party and Faculty Purge on Wednesday next."

I'll give you a taste of your own guillotine!

He xeroxed twenty-five copies of the form in the Department's Meeting Room and would have handed some to faculty he saw coming and going, but he didn't have the reviews ready yet.

He went to the library and, with trepidation, went online to the college's website. Nothing had changed. There were huge prompts from the same campus organizations to use the site. The ALLIANCE OF STUDENTS had even added a pep talk.

He clicked a couple of keys and was on Teachersonparade.com in no time at all. He didn't want to check his own reviews, but he thought he owed that much to the Committee on Truth, for, if he was going to thrust their unflattering reviews into the faces of other faculty members, he ought to thrust some more into his own. The reviews sent in by the cyberbully who had never been in his class were still there, as were Mr. Early's, which seemed to be up to about five now. The homophobic reviews seemed to be gone. There were two surprising reviews of him from the day before:

> Students, ignore the vicious reviews that have been appearing here about Dr. Tack. They are very wrong. I had Dr. Tack for English 101 and he was hard but fair. I got a C from him, that's all I deserved. I didn't turn in a whole paper and he still past me. It is not true what dumb things are being said about him here. Dr. Nathaniel Tack is a lively and ihjspiring teacher. He is well versed in the tools of writing and i personally recommend his coarse highly. He will tell you what he thinks, not jjst what you want to hear. Take him and see for yourself.

He will teach you about Finding Your Voice and even some punctuation.

Well. How nice, even with the errors. These two reviews had pulled him off the bottom of THE PITS, and he was in the middle again. Gilda LaMatresse was now lower than he was, and she had been on TIP OF THE TOP the other times he'd checked. The Fickle Middle Finger of the Internet.

Maybe this site isn't so terrible all in all, Nathaniel thought. What am I thinking! How easily we accustom ourselves to being terrorized. Of course it's terrible. I'm sitting here hoping my approval score will go up because somebody arbitrarily chooses to give me a crumb or not. I will not submit to this. I cannot and will not recant! Stuff your Diet of Wurms in your own pre-literate mouths, whoever the fuck you are!

He looked up Gilda LaMattresse's reviews. She'd obviously pissed some people off in recent weeks:

> Ms. LaMatresse is a mess, a tall, lanky drink of water with a heighth complex. I was expecting more than I'm getting. She is nice but I feel under-stimulated and all we do is "discuss, discuss, discuss."

With a D from this under-stimulated malcontent.

There were seven other reviews, obviously from the same person, only the webmaster hadn't noticed or didn't care. They all more or less said the following:

> LaMatress doesn't like men in her classes. Her Wymyn feel threatened by a real man. Try to contradict some of the "received feminist wisdom" and see what you get. Bad grades. Hate to be a party pooper, but them's the facts. Avoid hopping on Lamattresse's gravy train, and save your cajones.

My, this was offensive! (*He, he.*) Even though it was this one guy who no doubt had dragged Gilda into THE PITS with him, it probably was more accurate than the ones that praised her to the skies. Or the truth lay somewhere between this macho pig and the Feminist Sanctimony of Ms. Gilda LaMattresse.

He printed out the seven nastiest reviews of Gilda and attached two of them to the Committee on Truth form and fought the gloating in his breast. Let's see how Gilda reacts when presented with these for her edification and delight. Question: Are a man's *cajones* in danger in your classes, Ms. M? Now be careful what you say. It could get UGGILY!

He looked up Guy Mountain's reviews. He had just two:

> I love Mr. Mountain he speaks clearly and gave me extra time on my papers. He always finds time to advice his students, and looks tired but his sould is great. Take Mr. Mountain!!!!!

Take him where? I have been to the Mountain and I have seen his fat mother!

The other review had more possibilities for the Committee on Truth:

Mountain is a disgrace to the teaching profession; he is fat, UGLY, with hideous growths on the backs of his hands. Whenever he writes on the blackboard I feel like I am watching Bigfoot teaching the class. He stiffles discussion and ramrods his own agenda about conspiracy theories on his unwilling victims.

And I didn't even write this one, Nathaniel thought. He printed it out. How thoughtful of the webmaster to make it so easy to gather the proof.

He also found a one about Arlene Buboe-Pitsky:

Mrs. Buboe-Pitsky has fake hair and bad breath. she grades papersby throweing them in the steps. Top. step get A. Bottom step get F. I get B from privious teacher, Mr. Laidamour, who is gone now. I hope Administration eliminate Mrs. Buboee-Pitsky soon.

By firing squad or lethal injection?

Yes, let's see what old Hard Hair, Queen of Denial (would-be Dean of Denial?) has to say when she gets this one put in front of her, whether she wants to see it or not.

He noticed that there was even a review of Dean Visigoth. So you could review Administrators as well? How delightful!

The lone review said:

Dean Visigoth goes out of his way to ensure the sound education of the student body of our college. I respect this man greatly.

It sounded like something the dean had written about himself. And of course there was nothing to stop him from doing that — except integrity. What, *that* old thing!?

What if *I* write a review of the good dean? Nathaniel thought. Just one. An ironic one? Go for it!

I like Dean becuz he not make students be quiet in the halls he loves our free speech!! We park in faculty lots and he not care! He also have Beeutiful Wife, Miss Universe. Miss Heidi. God bless them both. I love Shite!!!!

Was it too much? Would the dean notice the allusions to their talk? Naw. And what if he did? The website was open to one and all to use — and *so* unconnected to the school! How do you like *my* Free Speech, you student-ass kisser! Now what grade to give him? An A of course! What could be better than an A — because I am an Archetypal Shite Alumn*i*. *Sic!*

Nathaniel sent in the review. It was a SUCESS! Dude Lather *still* couldn't spell to save his soul. And there were hundreds of reviews by now. Hadn't anybody complained about the illiteracy displayed everywhere on the site? What was wrong with the world? Am I just too overly sensitive about criticism? About literacy? *That* old thing!

Should he review Tadd Dryer? *That* old thing! No, that would be too cruel. But perhaps a copy of what's already here? No, if the man ever saw his reviews, he might stop believing in His Own Personal Republican, and what else did he have?

Instead, he looked up Vice Chancellor Lung's reviews. She had three, the first of which said:

> Bad woman, Mrs. Lung. She is bought and paid for. Her sister
> judge also bad. Bad fanmiy.

What did this mean? Bad family? Bad *fanny*? Her fanny had seemed all right to him when she had questioned him about revealing the webmaster's "personal information." But then he hadn't really looked at it that well. So far she had not fixed the "unfortunate, unintended snafu" about his paycheck that she had finally mentioned in a note to him. She hadn't gotten around to it because she was suffering from bad fanny?

Her other two reviews were also dismissive, commenting on her accent and nepotism about a niece. "Well, she must be guilty! After all, I read it here on Teacherson-parade.com!" Nathaniel said, printing it out. Let's see how the Administrators feel when it's *them* that are getting skewered! How do you like this Thomas Paine in the butt, huh?

He had sent copies of their bad reviews in the campus mail to ten different people. And he admitted to a certain apprehension once he had done it. Maybe the people who had sent unfair reviews of teachers felt the same, but the way the website was set up there was no taking back what one sent forth into cyberspace. Sort of like Yahweh with lightning bolts and plagues.

While waiting for responses, Nathaniel decided to visit the SPEAK OUT LOUD section of the website. But first he couldn't resist looking to see where he stood in THE PITS. He was still right there in the middle. He didn't bother to read the reviews, but he had the most of anybody. He noticed also that his Teacher's Statement about Dude Lather had simply disappeared. Hmm. Should he send it in again?

On SPEAK OUT LOUD you could follow the thread on different topics, such as Campus Facilities, Transfers, Student Government, and the like. The usual stuff. However, there was also a discussion thread devoted to Teachersonparade.

He took a breath and jumped in and began reading:

> i love beeing able to tell my tewachers what I really think of
> them, and not haveing to kiss their smutty buttholes

Said one discussant.

Do you think teachers don't have less-than-pleasant thoughts about our students? Nathaniel wondered. Not me, of course. Well, the teachers don't say them either. And we certainly don't write them. That's what civilization means, Smut-Butt!

Another said:

> The review website is meant to provide a true service, yet are

there not now a lot of gratuitous insults and inappropriate comments getting on there? Just Asking.

Well, Just Asking, now that you ask, there are indeed a growing number of graffiti-like tags posing as "reviews." Build it and they will cum. And little old me didn't even have to write most of them! Was there ever anything human meant for good that hasn't been corrupted by somebody by day two?

There were other "discussions," almost all of them singing the praises of the website and how it provided a "valuable resource" for information. Under a banner proclaiming the website's mainstream acceptance (WE HAVE ARIVVED!!!), the webmaster had even put up a link to an article in a legitimate newspaper, in Jerusalem no less, that said the following: "There is now a website available where students and others can find valuable sharing of information so that students get only the best education and educators."

Whoa! The reviews tended to be either mash notes or payback, very few of them well considered, governed solely by emotion and written by whoever in a fit of pique or gratitude about a grade, to say nothing of revealing an utter throwback in grammar, syntax, spelling, and punctuation to pre-Neanderthal Man.

The newspaper even mentioned a teacher by name: "Consider this review of Florinda Fricke of Shite College in the United States: 'She is an old sourpuss with a bald spot, and she is so boring I can barely keep my eyes open in her class. I wish she would turn into mush and blow away. You would avoid her in person if you saw her coming at you on the sidewalk. So avoid her in the classroom. I truely believe she will steal your soul.'"

I'll have to find that on the website and print it out and have the Committee on Truth send it to Florinda Fricke. True or false, Florinda, you steal your students' souls? And here it was being quoted in the Holy Land as if it were Gospel!

Shall I join in the discussion? Nathaniel pondered. I'm entitled to free speech, or so I've heard.

> Hello,
>
> This is a message from Dr. Nathaniel Tack of the English Department. I just want to say that the review process on this site is seriously flawed.
>
> The reviews can be written by anyone about anyone. I have tried to point this out to the webmaster, in hopes that he will rectify the problem, but he apparently has not gotten the message. I wanted to add a Teacher's Statement in place of mine that was removed (by someone in charge, I assume.) However, I have decided that this website deserves no respect — just look at it — and so I refuse to participate in it in any way.

Except to send in a few fake Cro-Magnon/ Shite-like reviews of course, sweethearts. He wondered if he should add some misspellings to make his message feel at home on the site, but it was gone into the ether before he could think twice about it.

It was a mistake, as he was soon to learn.

The next day, after a particularly good 101 class in which they discussed fallacies, Nathaniel went to the website again, this time from home. Something told him he should stay away, but it was like some horrible accident that he couldn't take his eyes off, especially since he seemed to be riding in one of the vehicles.

His comments on SPEAK OUT LOUD had caused a furor. Here is a sampling:

> i was all for dr. tack until he put up that self-righteous message on this bulletin board. now i hope he gets what's coming to him

> PICK my nose, Dr. Tack. Pick my nose. Pick, pick, Tack, Tack!

> Now we know who is writing all these Messages criticizing the site, don't we? It's Nathaniel Tack of the English Department. Soon, I hope, to be l-a-t-e of the English Department. Tenure sucks!
>
> — Fly-on-the-Wall

Nathaniel noticed that indeed there were a number of messages finding fault with the reviews of certain teachers, but *he* hadn't written them. He'd only sent in those few silly ones of himself (now gone) and a few others (three or four). He decided to set the record straight:

> Hello, this is Dr. Tack again. Do not assume that everyone who criticizes this ridiculous website is me. Others may feel the same way. Thank you.

It was almost as if the man was lying in wait, the response came in so quickly. Didn't Fly on the Wall have a life?

> Squawk all you like, Nathannyboy. Some of us KNOW you have *f-l-o-o-d-e-d* this site with negative comments because you are such a <u>bad</u> teacher and don't want to admit it or change.
>
> — Fly-on-the-Wall

Nathannyboy? Who *was* this Fly on the Wall? Was this a real student of his who hated his guts, or just some cyberfly pouncing on the cybershit?

Nathaniel wrote back:

> Who are you? You don't know that I'm a bad teacher. How dare you! I am an excellent teacher, as any number of my colleagues will be happy to inform you!
>
> — Dr. Nathaniel Tack

This was posted:

Oh, my, Nathannyboy is mad now!! Yea, all you faculty stick together to cover your manifest incompetence. This is a student revolt that will change the world. If not quite off with your pretentious h-e-a-d-s, then at the very least out of the classroom with you. The only real education is self-education.

Well, at least Fly on the Wall could spell and punctuate, making him a bit harder to dismiss.

Nathaniel had never gone into a chat room before and found it sort of exhilarating, but annoying too, because you didn't know who was on the other end. It could be Tadd Dryer, for all he knew. Or even an ex-trick! Or Dean Visigoth and Heidi Ho!

The point I am trying to make, Fly on the Wall, is that this website is utterly unreliable and cannot be taken as a source of genuine information about anybody reviewed on it. People LIE!

Nathaniel hurt his fingertip he pushed the Send key so hard. Fly on the Wall was still online:

LIE? Why would anyone LIE on this site when they can be anonymous? No, Mr. Tack, it is the best means ever devised for students to have a valid method by which to control their own destinies. Maybe you are lying on it, Mr. Tack, but the rest of us are not

— F-l-y-on-the-Wall

It was liking arguing with a Jehovah's Witness in your hallway. What had ever possessed you to let that person in in the first place!? Maybe one more message and then Nathaniel would sign off:

I just want to point out to the many who might be reading the reviews of instructors on this site without a great deal of true skepticism as to the real motives of the people bothering to write in that this is the antithesis of everything a college education is supposed to stand for and a shameful illustration of the position that educators in this culture are put in. I am singing off now!

Damn! He sent it in with the typo "singing" for "signing" still there. Double damn! That's what was wrong with the Internet in a nutshell. You could act before you thought.

Fly on the Wall here!

Leaving so soon, Mr. Tack? just when I was beginning to enjoy your "singing." By the way, what position do you prefer — for teachers, I mean. (What else could I possibly mean? Pace: webmaster!) Alas, you have revealed your hand on Speak Out Loud, Professor, and now the g-a-m-e is up!

Why, you little shit! You big shit? The nerve! My *position*? Is that supposed to mean because I'm gay? We all take it up the butt, is that what you think? Bend over and I'll show you the position I prefer, Fly on the Wall!

It was so tempting to write back. No wonder FLAMING others was forbidden. Wasn't it? Of course on Teachersonparade you were free to flame teachers and they couldn't say boo back. American teachers were supposed to be suckers who took it up the ass from Fly on the Wall and his ilk and say: "Oh, my, what else can I give you, what more can I possibly do for you to get your through this insti-tution of higher learning? I'm so sorry that all the late papers and the missed classes and the missed assignments that I put up with, to say nothing of the absent grammar and the idiomatic nightmares, weren't enough for you! Please, please, what *else* can I do? Vent all your failures on your teachers. *We* alone have failed you so miserably! Of course never in a million years have you failed yourselves! We're the problem. *NEVER, NEVER YOU."*

He didn't send in another message. But the next time he looked, an hour later, somebody had sent this in:

> Hello, just a follow-up from Dr. Nathaniel Tack of the English
> Department. I wish Fly on the Wall (or should it be
> Niggerboy?) would cease his mewlings and pukings on this
> discussion site. Let's hear from STUDENTS!

Now it was really getting nasty. Nathaniel would never have used that word, not because blacks didn't have serious problems as students (unless they were gay) — this was well documented — but because that word itself was too inflammatory. Diction 101. Blacks could yell "faggot" at him in their blatantly homophobic way, with little consequence, but he or any other white couldn't say "nigger" anything under any circumstances, and he knew it. All might be racists in fact, but some were "more racist" than others. So Fly on the Wall (or whoever had sent this message in) wasn't afraid to forge Nathaniel's signature, in effect, and stink up the whole mess with this red herring.

SPEAK OUT LOUD had another flurry of messages on this new development, including:

> I had Tack he never said anything bad about blacks in class. So
> I am sorry to see him using "Niggerboy" on this discussion
> place. He as a teacher should know better. He taught us to be
> very careful about our language.

> Hey, Where does thisDr. Tack get off on calling somebody
> "Niggerboy" when he's nothing but a f"ing homo hisself!

> He should be ashamed! I'll never take no class from him!

Where do you go with this kind of madness? Were these even real responses, or had Fly on the Wall written them all to stir up controversy? Who was this mysterious Fly on the Wall character anyway? Was he part of the First Amendment Club? Was he even a student at Shite? Maybe he was just a passing hacker who saw this site as an opportunity to partake of the forbidden pleasures of the Internet.

He went back to the SPEAK OUT LOUD section and wrote:

> This is Dr. Nathaniel Tack. I did not write anything using the word "Niggerboy." Somebody else has pretended to be me in an effort to discredit me on this terrible website.

In no time at all this appeared:

> Don't believe Nathaniel Tack when he denies using the word Niggerboy. He is just feeling guilty after the fact and is trying to save himself from the punishment he so richly deserves. I had him in class, and I remember one vivid conference in his office when he called me "Niggerboy" under his breath. I never reported it, but now it can come out.

WHAT?! This had never happened! It had not even come close to happening! My God, what were they all dealing with here? Welcome to a new Paradise of Viciousness!

A copy of the "Niggerboy" comment in hand, he went to see Hanukkah Kaneesha Washington-Goldfarb, who taught in the African American Success Program, another sub-section of the English Department. Hanukkah Kaneesha was a rare phenomenon around the college, a mixed-race Republican, with roots firmly in both the black and Orthodox Jewish communities. He'd had only sporadic interactions with her over the years, but she always seemed fair and impartial, unlike some he could name. She had even voted with him on not granting tenure to a young male bleeding heart who called his students "Hey, man" and went out drinking with them during class hours — on what he called "field trips."

Luckily she was not busy even though it was her office hour.

"I wonder if I could talk to you about something very important," Nathaniel said.

She gave him a big smile and invited him to sit where her students usually did. He remembered being a student. He ought to; he'd done it for enough years! He didn't like being in this supplicating position either, but it's what you did when you were in school, and then you moved on and did something with your education. Yeah, look where *I* am, class — at Shite College!

"You look distressed, Nathaniel."

"Do I?"

"There's a big crease between your eyebrows."

"Really?" He put his index finger there and rubbed it a few times. "How's that?"

"What seems to be the trouble?"

Now he didn't know if he should show her the "Niggerboy" posting or not. What if she thought he'd sent it and was just trying to cover his ass? He sat quiet, unable to bring himself to speak.

Hanukkah tilted her head inquisitively. She had piled braids for days and several combs and strings of beads in the layers of her coarse black hair. Was it all right to think her hair was coarse? What did you call it if not coarse? Luxuriant? What was the name for this hair style? Afros were out of fashion, right? Or were they coming back? She had obviously taken a lot of time and trouble to arrange her hair in this elaborate manner. Was it all right to think it elaborate? She had light brown skin and dignified, pretty features, and she seemed slightly amused that he wasn't speaking yet. He noticed that her clothes were very Businesswoman Proper and her desk and bookshelves immaculate.

"Nathaniel?"

"I'm sorry. I guess I'm going through a bad time. Have you seen the review website for teachers?"

"I've heard of it."

"Have you looked at it?"

"Not yet. Should I?"

He had forgotten to look up her reviews. Maybe she had some nasty ones too, probably did because of her politics. He should have brought those. "I haven't seen your reviews. But students are reading lies about teachers and using those lies as the basis on which to pick their classes. At the very least it predisposes people to view a teacher in a certain light. It's sort of like Teacher Profiling."

He looked to see how that was playing with her. Racial Profiling of blacks was a big hubbub in the headlines. He hated catering like this, but he felt on the defensive and he wasn't that sure about this woman's exact racial agenda. Better to be safe than sorry and make a new enemy.

"Isn't it possible that students can see through the lies to the truth?" she said.

"Well, maybe," he conceded, not really meaning it. "But how can someone tell what's true and what's not true about a teacher if the person has never met the teacher and never seen the teacher teach. If you accuse someone of being an unfair grader, for instance, you have to know what the student actually wrote in order to judge the facts. You might be sifting through nothing but lies upon lies from disgruntled or failing students and stay away from targeted teachers when they might in fact be the best teachers around this place."

"Are there no positive reviews on the site? I read something that said they were sixty-eight percent positive ones."

"But the negative one carry more impact, whatever the actual percentage."

"That's true," she said. "I still remember the one negative examiner on my Master's orals more than anyone else. It was a black man, by the way. He thought I was too conservative. He actually called me Miss Oreo, although he denied it later."

"I made the mistake of going on the Speak Out Loud discussion part of the website and protesting the way the site is set up. Anyone can review anyone, without even being a student. Are you aware of that?"

"Really? I thought some sort of identification was required first."

"Most people assume that, but it's utterly not the case."

"Interesting."

Was he gaining an ally at last? He put the "Niggerboy" printout on her desk.

"Someone wrote this and attached my name to it."

He held his breath while she read through it.

When she looked back at him, she didn't seem unduly upset. "I've seen worse," she said.

"No doubt." (Suck up, suck up!) "My main point, my thesis sentence, if you will," (What the hell was all this essay writing for if you couldn't use it when you really needed it!) "is that I didn't write that, and yet any number of people think I did. And there's apparently nothing I can do to rectify that impression."

"Can't you go back to the site and leave another message?"

"I did. And somebody — somebody named Fly on the Wall, I suspect — merely came back and claimed that he had been in my class and that I'd said this word to him in a student conference!"

"And you didn't?" she asked.

No, I didn't! he shouted in his head. And you've never, as an Orthodox Jew and Republican black woman, ever used any words like "fag," "fucking queer," "fairy," fruit," "pervert," or "cocksucker," have you, my dear? Nor have you ever voted against gay rights now that you've got yours, have you, Ms. Bi-Cultural Hyphenated Last Name, my dear friend in the fight against oppression, have you!?

"Are you all right, Nathaniel?" he heard her ask.

"What?"

"There's a nervous tic in your cheek." She showed him where it was, on her own cheek.

He put a finger up to his face and, sure enough, he felt the convulsive twitch in the muscle just below his eye. "Oh, great," he said, "just what I need."

"You must be under a great deal of strain."

"I must be," he said amiably. "It's my first tic!"

"You always remember your first," she said.

He laughed. "Does that mean there will be more?" He could see himself after a few more months of this tension with a face twitching like Medusa's hair. "What a can of worms this is," he said to Hanukkah. "I'm almost at my wit's end."

"Surely no, Nathaniel. You'll find a solution. You're a clever man. And very amusing."

We homos always are.

"I enjoyed working with you on that tenure review we had. You facilitated that very well."

"Thank you." What a nice woman!

God, I'm a sucker for a compliment, he thought. But who isn't. If only I could find it in my heart to compliment people more! Yes, maybe that was the answer. "Miss Blutwurst, I just loved the semi-colons in your last essay." "Mr. Morales, never in all my born days have I seen finer penmanship than yours!" Even though the essay was supposed to be typed and double spaced!

"Take Dr. Nathaniel Tack!" the website would say. "He loves his students more than life itself and always finds something nice to say about them, unlike Mr. Tadd Dryer, who makes you use the subdunctive mood even when you're not in the mood to use it."

No, that way madness lay. Besides, I do compliment them sometimes. *I do!* What had he written on that student's essay last year? "It's been a pleasure reading your work." And the fucker hadn't even said goodbye at the final exam!

"So what are you asking from me, Nathaniel?" Hanukkah was saying.

"I'm sorry. My mind' been wandering quite a bit these days."

"What are *you* doing here, Nathaniel!" was the next thing he heard. It was Elita Braine, the other black woman in the department.

"Oh, *I* can't be here?" he said, somewhat prickly. What did she think, that she owned Hanukkah because they were both black and he wasn't?

"I'm just surprised, that's all. I've never seen you here before," Elita said. "I wanted to talk to you, remember?" she said to Hanukkah.

"I can come back some other time," Nathaniel offered, irritated but hiding it. He stood up.

"No, no," Hanukkah protested. "Stay." She got up and got another chair for Elita. "Let's talk about this website together."

"Oh, *that!*" Elita said, sitting down.

Elita Braine was a large woman with muddy skin (rich chocolate?) and very short hair. You might even call it "nappy," except that "nappy" was out, he was pretty sure of that. Not that it might not be back "in" the next semester. Elita was one of those P.C. people who were always a step ahead of you when it came to the Correct word of the moment. Just when you'd mastered Afro-American, it became African American, and then it might be turning into Sub-Saharan-American. Or Mid-American Saharan! She believed with all her heart and Soul in Reparations for slavery. She often wore African-style fashions — though not today— and she wore a large size, shall we say. And he swore he'd heard her brag that she bought all her clothes at some place called the Dress Barn. Look! I got *my* dashiki at the Dress Barn! — with a little twirl of her tent. She also always wore sandals, revealing her incredibly large, horny, ugly feet. For the cause I'll stay! he whispered and turned his eyes toward the ceiling.

"I haven't looked at that site," Elita said. "Somebody I know told me not to."

"Why not?" Nathaniel was trying to turn his body so that he couldn't see most of Elita.

"They said my reviews were racist."

"Really?" Hanukkah said. "That's just what Nathaniel and I were discussing."

"What did your reviews say?" Nathaniel asked.

"Whoever saw them wouldn't tell me."

He could guess. He had observed Elita teach a couple of times. She had a certain stage presence in the classroom, but she was monumentally disorganized, jumping from topic to topic like a scatterbrained parakeet. And every other word, literally, was how she had been the Victim of Racism. She supposedly had a Ph.D. from someplace. With the climate of Affirmative Action the way it had been for years, Elita, as a black female with a Ph.D., no less, should have been gobbled up by Harvard and Princeton *both*, or *someplace* good, but here she was at Shite, and Nathaniel knew why. If the website had any legitimacy, it was to get teachers like Elita Braine.

"Long ago I learned not to let racism get me down," Elita was saying with a sigh.

Yeah, Elita, two roads diverged in a yellow wood, and you took the one less traveled!

"I have printed out some reviews from the site and sent them to people," Nathaniel continued, "to see how they'll react."

"And what do you hope to accomplish by that?" Elita said.

"To be frank, I hope people get so pissed off they join me in getting this site shut down." Shall I send yours Special Delivery —as part of the Reparations program?

"Can you really shut it down, though?" Hanukkah said. "Isn't it free speech?"

"How can it be free speech to review somebody you've never had!" Why were people such knee-jerks!?

"Is that happening?"

"Yes." And I *helped* it to happen, he thought, but it didn't need much help, that's for sure.

"Maybe the school will shut it down," Elita offered.

Nathaniel tried not to roll his eyes. "At least we can fix it so that only real students are sending in reviews — thoughtful reviews," he said. "And only one review per student for any given teacher."

"Whoever told me about my reviews said they looked like they were from the same person," Elita said.

"It seems to me you know more about these reviews than you're letting on, Elita," he said coyly.

"It's just one person. One damn racist."

"Cough it up. What did it say? Otherwise, I'll look it up when I get home."

Elita was trying to decide whether to tell them or not. "You have a couple of good reviews," she suddenly said to Hanukkah. "They make you sound like you walk on water!"

"I do walk on water," Hanukkah chuckled.

"Aren't you going to tell us?" Nathaniel coaxed Elita again.

"I don't think I will." She picked at something down below — again! Where had this woman been born, in a Dress Barn? "Look at my toe," she said, holding up her foot. "See, it's all discolored and crusty. Do you think that's a fungus? And there's something under this toenail too," She pointed to her other foot.

Jesus, Mary, and Martin Luther King! Was there no end to her body parts!

"Have you put anything on it?" Hanukkah said solicitously.

"I've been too busy," Elita said.

Yeah, organizing your class lectures! Nathaniel cursed to himself.

"What this person wrote is that once she took my class she understood why racism exists. Can you imagine anyone saying that!"

Never! You're a poster girl for racial harmony, Elita!

"She also said that I was disorganized! *Disorganized*, her white ass! I run my class like Socrates. Topic leads to topic. The ancient Greeks were related to the Africans, you know." Elita nodded several times, reassuring herself. "A long tradition there."

Eek!

Yeah, you and Socrates, Elita! You team-taught that class. He'd heard her refer to Cleopatra as black on more than one occasion. Once he had actually tried to correct her, but she didn't seem to hear him or understand what he meant when he said: "And don't forget Alexander the Great and Genghis Khan on that list."

"I feel better talking about it already," Elita said, putting her foot down, thank god. "It was bothering me, I must say. But now I can see that it's just more of the same old systemic racism, year end and year out."

Am *I* like this woman? Nathaniel wondered. Am I as blind to my own faults as she is? I can't be, can I? Please no! Oh, *stop* me if I am!

"You know what else was on there?" Elita went on. Now that she had opened her heart to them, she couldn't seem to stop. "It says I'm clueless! Me — *clueless!* I've published seven articles, and *I'm* clueless? Not on your life, honky bitch! You're the one that's clueless, you white bitch!" Elita almost seemed to see the offending spirit of the reviewer standing in the corner of the office by the telephone table.

And whatever in the world were your articles about, Elita? He had read several of them. Surprise! Racism in academia. Racism in the line in the Duplicating Office. Racism in the Physics Department. There were *no* blacks in that department, you see! (None had applied.) Racism everywhere! And yet the plain fact of the matter was that this woman wouldn't have held down the job she had for even half a semester if she weren't black! Nathaniel thought, the tic in his cheek starting up again. He slapped his hand against it, like trying to stop a tiny mouse under his skin. Elita! Elita! he longed to say. Somebody can dislike you, even hate you — in your case — and still not be a racist. And they can dislike me too and not be a homophobe. Please, please don't let me ride that BORING hobbyhorse to oblivion! God knows all gays aren't wonder-ful. Hadn't he had enough gay loser students to realize that by now. The answer to genuine racism and homophobia was not this blanket bleeding heart blindness to some people's genuine shortcomings!

It's not true of me, these shortcomings, is it? Nathaniel panicked, fighting off another threatening epiphany.

Hanukkah Kaneesha Washington-Goldfarb turned out to have been a good choice as an ally. Soon after the meeting in her office she looked up her reviews and was upset with what she found. She even took it upon herself to send the Committee on Truth a copy of one, with annotations:

> Ms. Washington-Goldberg treets us like she is our=mammy.*
> She ain't my mammy. I would prefer a more professional attitute on her part. Otherwise she not to bad.

> *Dear Nathaniel:

>> I believe you are on to something here. We can't have students treating us like this. My comment on this review is as follows: Bullshit. I also looked for some place to counter the student's review, but I couldn't find any. Do you know where this section is? —HKWG

He sent her a note back at once:

> Hi, HKWG:

> As these reviews go, that one of yours is pretty mild, but I am glad that you see the danger here. Nobody else seems to, or they are keeping very quiet about it. As for countering the review, the only thing you can do is to put something in your Teacher's Statement about it. Of course that section is not near the actual review itself and thus loses impact and may not even be read — to say nothing of answering the review and thus putting yourself on the defensive, the very "suspicious" defensive, at that.

> I intend to gather teachers' comments like yours and then perhaps get some action going on this, and I don't mean just a petition. — Best, Nathaniel

> Dear Nathaniel,

> Keep me informed. —HKWG

Well, it wasn't quite "I am dropping my day job and getting the NAACP, B'nai B'rith, Jesse Jackson, the Jewish Defense League, *and* the Reverend Al Sharpton and the ghost of Nelson Mandela after their asses." But it was something.

The very next day he got some other responses to his mailings:

> To Nathaniel Tack:

> I urge you to leave this alone. You will get a reputation as a crank or, worse, as someone opposed to Free Speech.

>> Sincerely,

>> Dean Calvin Visigoth

Nathaniel didn't remember sending him a review. There must be someone telling the good dean that bad reviews were being disseminated. Who might do that — student activists, teachers sympathetic to the website? How could anyone be sympathetic to this website when it was so full of loopholes, never mind the EMBARRASSING illiteracy being displayed? Go to Shite College and learn to be a fool who can't even be bothered to proofread a "review" before killing a teacher's reputation. But actually maybe the fact that everyone could see the illiteracy before their eyes would help. Naw, illiterates probably couldn't spot illiteracy if it puked on them.

There was also a note from Florinda Fricke about her review reprinted in the newspaper in Jerusalem:

> Nathaniel: I'd rather not be sent these items. Thank you.
>
> FF

Why not? She was supposed to teach the Honors Remedial Reading section the next semester and might not get all the "Best and the Brightest" if her reputation was being sullied, in the Promised Land no less.

He also got back a response from Tadd Dryer:

> Nathaniel,
>
> I make it a habit never to read anonymous comments about myself. Were I to do so, I might, God forbid, be put in the untenable position of trying to figure out who wrote them, and that might lead to less than collegial rapport among the staff here. — Tadd

What did that mean — Tadd suspected Nathaniel had written it? He hadn't, just sent it:

> Mr. Dryair must drink his own peepee before every class, he sounds like a sissy i only stayed ten minutes before i had to get out of that christian classroom don't take him unless you want to hear his pee pee voice

Even Tadd Dryer (was *Dryair* some kind of clever pun? . . . Naw!) deserved more than a lousy ten minutes before having his head cut off. Nathaniel wondered if there was any truth here. Did Tadd in fact drink his own peepee before every class? Or only certain classes?

The one from Guy Mountain was interesting:

> Nathaniel,
>
> I must confess I was disturbed to read that nasty review of myself. Someone else had sent me a copy as well. I think I know who wrote it, some troublemaker in my 102. The class has told me privately before that they find him a nuisance and

wish he would leave the class. He has not attended since the review about "growths" on my hands appeared, so I suspect the problem has been solved. I still believe in the inherent right of students to evaluate thier instructors, so I hope you won't go too far with this Committee on Truth thing. — Guy

P.S. Thanks so much for your sympathy that day we discussed my mother's bowel operation. I'm happy to say it went very well and she is now functioning as well as she ever did.

Thank you for sharing. *Thier* students? Guy! Guy! You're an English teacher! Must I fight the fall of Western Civilization alone!? And, no, it wasn't all better now merely because one student creep had decamped from a class.

Nathaniel went to the library and checked the website again to be sure. Yes, Guy's reviews were untouched. Where was the webmaster and his so-called "standards" policy? Nathaniel was still in THE PITS, but the last review was sort of nice. Wasn't it?

— Hey, I had Dr. Tack twice, and I learned a great deal from him, sometimes painfully so. He is not interested in telling you what you want to hear, only what he thinks you ought to hear. He could be more Tack-ful at times, yes, and his hair color seems to fluctuate from time to time, but you could do much worse. I am now attending UC — Tienanmen Square Branch, and am doing well.

It was probably Madison Fuchs, to whom he had given two A's. A nice kid, smart, good writer. Fuck you on my hair color. I can't *find* Medium Brown, asshole! And he had had Mr. Fuchs as a student — what? — four, five years earlier? Wasn't there some kind of statute of limitations on reviews? "Yup, I had that Dr. Tack when I was a mere lad, and now I am eighty-seven years young. He was, if I remember rightly, a so-so teacher. I have the Alzheimer's, so I'm a little gaga about how so-so he was, but I saw this website here at the Home (I think) and I thought as how I should up my computer skills." Yeah, up yours, Grandpa.

When he looked at Elita Braine's reviews he winced a bit, even for her:

Miss Braine has none. She is a self-righteous, unpleasant individual. I know one isn't supposed to judge a person by her color, but her constant harping on the subject forces one to do no less. I hope she reads this and will mend her ways.

But she won't read it, dear girl, and she wouldn't mend them if she could (people only change in novels!). She's too set in her ways, has been coddled and encouraged to whine for too many years. But it might be nice to hear her scream if the Committee on Truth sent this to her. Hmm. Oh, stop me, God!

Or the next one:

I haven't bothered to review any of my other instructors, whom I find vary from very fine to adequate, but with Ms. Elita Braine I feel compelled to vent somewhat. She lost my first paper and blamed me. She couldn't tell me what my grade was for the mid-term because she had "misplaced" her records. I can speculate where they might be shoved up, but I refuse to take my cue from some of the other unfortunate writings on this website. Suffice it to say, that you'd be better off in anybody's classroom, even a dead teacher's, than in the one run by Elita Braine.

So maybe this site wasn't all bad? Maybe Elita *should* see these! But, no, this was no way to review anybody. Hey, but how about setting up a second site, to review Shite *students*?! Yummy!

I had Miss Kristin Blutwurst in my class. While she is not the very wurst student I've ever had, her offer to write me a good review on this site in exchange for a B instead of the C she deserved (?) insulted my integrity as a teacher and shows how total corruption of the grading system lies just a few more computer clicks away. . . . Professor Somebody

Or this:

Keith Early was enrolled in a creative class, i've heard. he was not my student, but I feel confident in reviewing him on the basis of what i overheard in the cafeteria. he goes around to all his teachers and THREATENS them with bad reviews on this website unless he gets the grade of his choosing. if he tries to enroll in your class, don't let him in (find any excuse) unless you want an EARLY grave.

The Professor from Heaven

P.S. Be glad I am sending in only ONE review of Mr. Early. He is not so moral about his teachers.

Delightful! The screams from the ALLIANCE OF STUDENTS would reach the outer reaches of cyberspace. "Someone reviewed a *STUDENT* on a website and gave their name! Why, that might mean a *STUDENT* might not get into a class they wanted and achieve the SUCCESS we are entitled to by God, the Declaration of Independence, and the Geneva Convention, because the teachers are ganging up on us! This is so UNFAIR!" (or more likely: "acheive," "SUCESS," and "Unfare!!!!")

And about time too. Maybe there should be a PLAGIARISTS LIST as well, a SLIGHTLY CRACKED LIST, a DOWNRIGHT DANGEROUS LIST, CANDIDATES FOR APPEARANCES ON THE "COPS" TV SHOW LIST, even a

Every liberal dewy-eyed dork should be thrown into an American classroom! Nathaniel raged. Especially one of the high schools from whence the people with these "skills" and "attitudes" emerged. Hi, I congratulated from Primordial Slime High. Give me an A — or I'll kill you!

No! Nathaniel told himself. Calm down. Meditate. (I don't want to.) Pray. (*Pu-leeze!*) At least think some good thoughts. (What are those?)

Okay, okay, I'm going to make a list of things I like. He took a piece of blank paper out of his briefcase. You must think only good thoughts for at least five minutes, he shamed himself. He looked at the pen in his hand. How many words have you written in your lifetime? How many of your books are out of print? How long had it been since you've had an agent? "Don't go there, Nathaniel!" he said aloud, under his breath.

The brown spot on the back of his left hand was bigger. Age creeping in, converting me into a . . . creep? Until I turn into one huge brown spot screaming in the grave. Or is that brown spot a crab? My, I haven't had crabs in years. Well, at least it isn't a KS lesion. *Is* it? Call me old-fashioned, but I long for the good old days when a man's brown spots just meant a crab in his pubes!

I will make a list of things I like in this old world. I will. Of course every religion in the world from Buddhism to Islam to Hinduism to Christianity thinks the same thing I do — that this world is a place of sorrow and misery and that there *has* to be something better Out There. So we agree on half of that, except there's no Out There. That's just Comfort Food for thought. But at least that means I'm not the only one who feels this life with burned skin.

I am here, therefore I must find solace in this vale of tears. (Didn't Descartes have a comma splice there?) Never mind, Nathaniel! Never mind.

All right, things I like:

Books. My garage is full of books that I'll never read again.

My books. The world will little note nor long remember what we did here?

Penises. Some more than others.

Christmas carols. And you an atheist! Especially "O, Holy Night." The dirty version. "Fall on your knees!" That got you so hot when you were an adolescent, and you thought it was religion.

Microwavable food. The one great invention of modern times.

Fan letters. One every six months without fail.

Orgasms. Why do I keep coming back to sex? Because you like sex. It's about the only thing that really does make life worth living. Why can't we have one life-long orgasm and then go to Heaven?

Hot fudge sundaes. That's why you're so fat. I am not fat! I am a Bear! Fuck you. As long as they want to suck my dick, I'm not fat!

Your dear friends. What friends? You've fought with every one of them. Well, I was right and they were wrong. And, besides, I still see Irene and Morgan every month or so for dinner. So they're almost eighty and both deaf, they're friends! They count. And Ludie Fauxville, when I see her! How many people can say they have transsexual friends? (or want to). See how P.C. I am!

Marty. Yes, you like Marty. But do you love Marty? What does love mean? What men call out when they're coming? Oh, oh! *oh! I love you!* Would you give up your life for Marty? C'mon, does it have to go *that* far? Marty is a drug addict and our sex life is on the wane. So? Everybody is an addict of some kind: religion (the worst), fame, food. Marty, you are a kind man, a good man, a sometimes weak man, and, when I don't hate you, I love you very much and am so grateful you are in my life. . . . Now am I just saying that to sound *nice*?

What else do you like?

The Carpenters. Admit it, you love Karen Carpenter's voice, no matter how corny that pair is supposed to be now. And it's a goddamned *shame* that she wouldn't eat so she could still be around as a lounge act in Vegas!

Homeward Bound: The Incredible Journey. The greatest movie ever made. An old dog, a young dog, and a sassy cat trying to find their way back to the family that loves them — how can you do better than that? You've shed more tears over that movie than anything else in your entire life. . . . And they say you're *hard*!

What else?

I'm thinking.

That's all you like in this world?

I'm thinking! Ty Hardin.

Who?

Never mind. My first "self-abuse." At twenty-one.

Nothing else?

I'm thinking!

Penises.

You said that.

I did?

Nathaniel looked down at his crotch. If my penis ever goes, I suppose all I've have left is Karen Carpenter, won't I?

And it is going, isn't it?

Yes.

"**W**ake up, Nathaniel! It's me!"

The voice was recording on the answering machine. Nathaniel hadn't bothered to answer because it was only five in the morning. He was an early riser, but not this early. And Marty was a night owl. So something had to be amiss.

"What's wrong?" he said, fumbling at the telephone next to his bed.

"Can you bail me out?" Marty sounded angry.

"Wait a second. I can't turn this damn thing off." The answering machine was still recording. "Okay, there." The red light was blinking.

"I've been here for three hours already. They just now let me use a phone." Now Marty's voice sounded depressed.

"What happened?"

"Those fuckers! I could kill them."

"Are you in jail?"

"Yes."

"Are they listening?"

"I don't care if they are. The fuckers!"

"Marty, be cool."

"Yeah, you're the one to talk!" He was referring to Nathaniel's penchant for losing his temper with meter maids.

"How many times does this make? It's becoming a life style, honey." The other arrest was because of some stupid neighbor dispute over parking. Only the two cops didn't know what was going on and had arrested Marty for "burglary." It had cost an un-pretty penny to get that all sorted out.

"Just cut the jokes and get me out of here!"

"Actually you could use a sense of humor, Marty." Sometimes Marty was even more depressed than he was!

"I don't have enough room on my credit cards for bail, or I'd do it myself," he said.

"Well, I'm not exactly flush either."

"So you can't do it?"

"I didn't say that. How much is it?"

"$7500."

"I don't have that much."

"Call that bail bondsman we used last time. What's his name? Uhh . . ."

"Something like Languish. With a slogan. 'Don't Anguish in Jail.'"

"'Call Languish for Bail.'"

"That's it!"

"Please, Nathaniel. I'm cold. I was just wearing my pajama bottoms and a light coat when they arrested me. And there are a lot of creeps in here who keep giving me the eye."

"Christ! Okay, I'll see what I can do. We never seem to have enough money, do we? Last time Languish accepted my condo as collateral for the loan."

"He did?"

"What's the charge?"

"I'll tell you everything when you get down here. Please, can you do it for your honey?" Now Marty sounded like he was going to cry. "The fucking fuckers!" Crying as he slit their throats!

It took another four hours to get the bail bondsman out of bed, down to his office to sign the papers, and to walk over to the jail. Languish was a man in his sixties, very short, who said very little. He'd seen it all. "Your friend should be down in under an hour, Mr. Tack," he said as he left to return to his office.

"It's Dr. Tack," Nathaniel said, knowing how pathetic the attempt sounded.

He sat on a rickety old green bench and watched the cops and the culprits come and go, talking of Michelangelo. Yeah, right. He hated being in places like this — everything he had run like mad from his whole lower-class life, the star-crossed, the crummy, and the lame brained. You could tell from looking at these people that they were born to be arrested. No, I must keep Christmas in my heart every day, he told himself. . . . Why? It just encourages them! And here I am, one of them.

It took Marty another hour to emerge from the scuffed elevator at the end of the corridor. His face looked drawn, his beard rumpled, the red pajama bottoms very noticeable. They met halfway. Marty would have hugged, but Nathaniel felt uneasy among the Forces of Fascism. He and Marty shared a deep dislike of police officers, except when you really needed one, of course, or for the occasional mutual masturbation fantasy.

"Those fuckers kept me an extra hour!" Marty was buttoning up his coat.

"What for?"

"Because I told them off. How dare they arrest me in my own car!"

Two porky pigs passed near them but didn't even glance at them.

"Maybe we should get out of here," Nathaniel said.

Marty had to tie his shoelaces, which were flopping as he walked. "This has been a complete nightmare," he said. "Let me catch my breath. I ran when they told me I could leave." He sat down on the rickety green bench and held the center of his chest.

Across the lobby some demented old man in a dirty raincoat was arguing with the policeman who was bringing him through the revolving door. "Shut, up, shut up!" the policeman was saying.

"I got friends in high places!" the demented old man was clarifying.

"Can we get out of here?" Nathaniel said. "Have you eaten? I think there's a diner down the block."

"I'm not hungry." Marty's eyes seemed bleak. There was a big red blotch on his forehead.

"What happened to your head?"

"I bumped into my car door when they pulled me out."

"Are you free now?"

"I have to appear in court in a few days."

"*For?*" God, Marty could be so tight-lipped sometimes!

"I was sitting in my own car just a few doors from my own apartment, minding my own business, listening to the new Neil Young CD, and the next thing I know two police cars are blocking my car and shining their fucking lights in my eyes."

"And you had some drugs?"

"A little bit."

"How little?"

"Some speed." Marty turned his head toward Nathaniel. "Not much! Don't look so annoyed."

"Was I?"

"You don't seem to realize that everything you think shows on your face. No wonder people don't like you."

"Some people like me!"

"Yeah, right. That's why you have all those bad reviews from your students!"

"Something tells me that is not the thing to say to the person who has just bailed you out of jail! And they're not necessarily *my* students! Why can't people seem to get this point?"

"Maybe most of them *are* your students! What then, Nathaniel?"

They both sat and stared at the dirty cement floor, not speaking.

"Sorry. It's just that these pigs infuriate me."

"Why would they surround your car?"

"It's that same jerk who had my car towed before. Remember that? My neighbor?"

"I do indeed. Thou shalt not have thy neighbor towed."

"He doesn't want anybody else parking anywhere near his house, and so he goes and reports 'suspicious activity in a black car.' A drug deal. That's what those fuckers said to me when they banged on my car. 'Caught you! We caught you!' Why don't they go arrest someone driving a hundred and fifty miles per hours around a racetrack! He's doing a lot more damage to himself and others than I am sitting in my own goddamned car having a goddamned joint!"

"I thought you said it was speed."

"So I had a little of each. So fucking what!"

"I agree. It's none of their business. Why is it that the Republicans always say government off our backs except when it comes to the things that really matter, like drugs, sex, and sitting in your own car at two A.M. in the morning?"

"So I like to sit in my car and you don't. Big fucking deal!"

"I'm agreeing with you!"

"I know you are. Sorry, I feel sick to my stomach." He was also rubbing the red splotch on his forehead, which up close looked like a bump.

"Maybe you should have that looked at."

"When? I've got to go to work."

"When?"

"In a couple of hours. Unlike you, I don't have my mornings off!"

Nathaniel decided not to answer back. "And they confiscated what you had?"

"They did." Marty was feeling the bump on his forehead. "This thing hurts. The fuckers! Luckily I had just used up most of the speed just before they got there."

"That's good."

"I said they could have it if they wanted to pry up my nose."

"That must have gone over well."

"Oh, fuck you!" Marty said.

"Marty, Marty, I know you're angry but . . ."

"I'm sorry. I'm sorry." Marty's eyes were full of tears now. "You didn't even hug me when I came out of the elevator! Would it kill you to hug me sometimes?"

"There, there." Nathaniel managed a couple of surreptitious pats on Marty's wrist.

The tears were spilling out now, Marty hunched on the bench. One of his shoelaces had come undone again, and the pajama bottoms were absurd.

"We'll get out of here and go to my place. You can take the day off."

"I can't afford to. I've already been warned. Officially."

"I see."

"Life is shit!"

"Pretty much."

"Don't agree with me," Marty said.

"Okay. Want me to take you to your place? Get a little sleep at least? Get cleaned up?"

"I didn't tell you, but there's no heat in my apartment and the shower doesn't work."

"Well, tell the landlord. He'll fix it."

"I'm too ashamed."

"What?"

"How long has it been since you've been over to my place?"

"I don't know. A month?"

"Try three. It's a mess."

"Oh, it's not that bad."

"You haven't seen it. It's a complete mess."

Nathaniel was no neatnik, but he had thought it was a complete mess the last time he had seen it, with at least a hundred and fifty library books piled up on the sofa, computer magazines spread everywhere, porn tapes all over the waterbed, thick dust on the lamps, every shelf. What must it be like now? So bad that Marty would rather live without a shower and a heater than have his landlord see it.

"Shall we go?"

"I guess," Marty said, making himself get up.

When they got in the car, Nathaniel put his arms around Marty and hugged him as if their lives, or at least their lives together, depended on it.

Later Marty snorted some crystal and went to work.

The one oversized letter that wasn't campus mail in his mailbox was addressed to NATHANIEL TACK, Ph.D. in large bold-faced type, with no return address. From the Una-bomber? They'd caught that guy, right? Of course there could always be a new Unabomber too. He felt it with his hand to see how heavy it was.

It did contain a bomb of sorts.

It was a printout of messages from the SPEAK OUT LOUD section of the review website. Nathaniel scanned it quickly, looking for a note with it, but there was none. Who could have sent him this?

He had not looked at the website for a week, busy grading papers and taking Slacker to the vet several times because she's developed some kind of digestive problem and wasn't eating. He'd even gone to court with Marty about the "possession" charge, down from the "dealing" charge the cops had dropped. But it was taking longer to clear up than they'd thought.

So he was somewhat surprised that the website had apparently gone on without him. Nathaniel at times thought the world ceased to exist when he wasn't thinking about it. He knew this wasn't factually true, but it was emotionally very comforting. He also at times thought that because he had clearly articulated a problem in his own mind it had ceased to exist in reality, or it certainly *should* have. Surely the many faults of the website were evident to anyone observing its workings by this time, were they not? . . . Of course he knew in his heart this wasn't true.

The printout showed some thirty messages back and forth between different discussants, with Nathaniel's name very prominent among them:

> Tack the Imperious, *Homo Supercilious.*

> His comments make me delirious!

"*Homo Supercilious*? Was that yet another gay slur? Or just a regular slur? And the rhyme was forced. Hah!

> Dr. Tack is a fine teacher. He, I thought, was even an easy grader. He gave me a B and I copies my my term paper! Thank you, Dr. Tack!

Thanks for the vote of confidence, you darling plagiarist, you!

this man's attacks on this revbiew site are distasteful and do nothing to rmedy the repitation that hes earning him with his continual canards!

Well, at least *canards* was spelled right.

Tick, Tock, Dr. Tack! We've cleaned your clock.

And your time is running out.

All right, this was getting a bit scary. My time for *what* is running out? Teaching? Living?

Then he noticed that there were any number of messages from a "nathan lack." One of them in particular caught his eye:

this site is spooky. it's clear to me that people who have never been in shite's classrooms are leaving reviews here. why does the webmaster not do something about this travesty of 'providing information' for students? — nathan lack

Followed by:

Almost clever, *Nathannyboy*, to use an anagram of your real name. But we have caught you r-e-d-handed. Squeal all you like. I like the sound.

— Fly-on-the-Wall

It went back and forth like this for pages, Fly on the Wall pouncing on every message sent in by this "nathan lack" and impugning his reputation ("belligerent," "elitist," "tenured asshole," with counter messages by either a "nathan" or a "lack" ("I don't know this teacher but respect his legitimate complaints about this site," "a friend of a friend told me Tack was damn good"). Lots of others had jumped in as well, some defending Nathaniel, others attacking him for sending in so many messages to the site. Very few of them seemed to be from actual students who had had him as a teacher, or who had even *seen* him. Yet he was the center of this maelstrom.

He hadn't sent in *any* messages as "nathan lack"! Not one! All he'd sent into the SPEAK OUT LOUD section were those few that he'd put his own name to. He'd decided that using this "chat" room was a blunder he should never have made. He'd only hoped to point out the fatal flaw in the basic way it was set up. So much for *his* Free Speech! He'd become a whipping boy, and he wasn't even into S&M!

Why had somebody mailed this letter to Nathaniel? Was it some teacher angry with him for sending a copy of a bad review? He hadn't heard back from most of the people the Committee on Truth had contacted. (A knock in the night! Oh, my God, no! It's the Committee on Truth!) Was it someone who wanted to make sure that Nathaniel knew this Internet wrangling was taking place because he knew that Nathaniel wasn't in fact sending these messages?

There was a separate printout, seemingly from the Reviews section of the website, that looked like it might be the answer to these questions:

> I know for a fact that Dr. Nathaniel Tack has sent in ALL the positive reviews of him that appear here. He is the "travesty," not this site. His belligerent arrogance knows no limits.

> One time in class he told us that none of us would pass. He has insane leaps in t-h-o-u-g-h-t and I can still remember the gleam in his eye as he tried to embarrass the quiet female Asian students as he called on them again and again, until there were tears in their eyes.

Fly on the Wall, again? Only now he was saying, "Look, Doctor, I can review you as a teacher with the same words I have used here on SPEAK OUT LOUD — but in a much, much better way. People will think I'm your student. Was Fly on the Wall his student or just taking stabs at random? No, he couldn't be a real student. Oh, Mr. Darcy, you have been most vilely maligned! I did not send in ALL the positive reviews of myself. The one from Marty is still there, but the other compliments are genuine. As genuine as anything on this cyberfarce is genuine. And I have never in my entire teaching career said that not a single one of you would pass a class. How preposterous! Yet we all know what they say about a Big Lie, don't we, Fly on the Wall?! I stopped dragging replies out of shy students years ago. In fact, I rarely *call on* anyone. If they want to speak, they can speak. Just raise their hands first is all I ask. Hell, I believe in Free Fucking Speech!

Nathaniel ripped the printout in two and threw the pages on the floor of the mail room. But then he saw Charlotte Wiggley coming toward him, still in her jaw brace, and he bent down and scooped up the pieces and tossed them into the trash barrel and hurried out before she got there.

It was a momentary consolation, however. He knew the Ur Reviews and messages he had just read, the Platonic Ideal ones, one might say, were still up on the website wreaking their manifold mischief.

"Dr. Tack? Can I talk to you?" A big, husky Latino young man in a hairnet, chinos, and a faded work shirt (Oh no, *no* stereotypes here at Shite!) was standing outside Nathaniel's office. Nathaniel shrank back, his stomach in knots. He even caught his breath. He didn't recognize the student. Who was this — somebody who had read on the website what Nathaniel had supposedly Said and Done and was about to settle the score on behalf of The People everywhere!? (Who among you would not but choose the wit and wisdom of Josef Stalin over that class-riddled bitch Jane Austen!)

"Yes?" Nathaniel said abruptly. "What do you *want*?" He found himself making his hands into fists, although he managed to keep them at his side.

The student blinked, somewhat taken aback. "Uh . . . I was thinking of taking your 102 next semester."

"Yes? *And?*" Nathaniel was trying to un-stiffen his face, but he couldn't.

"I was wondering about the reading assignments. Do you know them yet?"

Nathaniel was trying to regain himself, the easy congeniality he fancied — but with the distinct tone of "It's my class and I'm the boss of it" — that he preferred. Old World Charm — couldn't they tell Old World Charm when they smelled it in the sweat on his brow? They consider it arrogant? Arrogant? I haven't got an arrogant bone in my half-Irish, half-white-trash body!

"Are you okay, Dr. Tack?"

"Yes, I'm fine. I'm *wonderful!*"

"Maybe I'll come by another day for the syllabus," the student said, backing away.

"So you just want a syllabus, do you, huh?" Nathaniel said, following the student part way down the hall. "That's all you want, a *syllabus!* Is that it, you say?!"

The student looked positively scared. Great, now the word would go out that Nathaniel was chasing his students down corridors, a crazed look in his eye, bragging that he was wonderful!

I need help with this monstrous website, Nathaniel thought. It's driving me over the edge. He also realized that he was beginning to self-censor every word that came out of his mouth —the very quality that makes me lively as a teacher, for God's sake! Or am I just indulging myself, taking advantage of the Academic Freedom I enjoy as a professor? He knew that he didn't say one tenth of one percent of what he actually thought. (Did anybody?) But he hadn't been afraid to say controversial things before, knowing that tenure protected him, just as he had always graded hard (fairly!!), even when he'd been a lowly part-timer all those years, because that was his Duty. You can take the Catholic boy out of the clutches of the Church, but you couldn't take the Church out of the boy. Fuck their butts, or at least their minds, before the age of seven and you have them for life! That's what the Jesuits said. Well, I'm fucked, Nathaniel thought, because I can't shake this sense of duty. No, maybe I *could,* just give everybody an A, the way they do at Harvard, and I bet overnight I'd turn from the Gay Ogre from Hell into some lovable old eccentric. Yeah, take Tack. He goes on about weird stuff, but he'll give you an A.

No! No! Never!

"Is there not one among you who will rid me of this website!?" he all but screamed into the Void.

And then God answered Nathaniel's prayer, even though there was no God.

He saw Louise Beeze, the Cat Lady from the English Department, feeding the ferals under the ancient bungalows, which were corrugated Quonset huts left over from the Civil War. Or something. He waved to her, preparing to get into his car. Again he'd had to park far away from his office to find a parking place. Maybe I should kneecap myself, he mused, and get me one of those Handicapped Stickers. Hmm. Or should he simply wait until the student vigilantes got wind of "his" SPEAK OUT LOUD objections to the website and they would kneecap him on their own!

Louise Beeze was signaling to him to wait. She put down the sack of dry cat food she'd been carrying to fill the plastic bowls under the Quonset huts — some fifteen bowls all in a row. "Nathaniel! Nathaniel!" she called.

She came up to his car, her sixty-year-old hair a trifle askew from the wind, wearing some kind of outsized overalls and rubber boots, and kept looking back toward the ferals, who were nowhere in sight. "Some of them are not feeding! I'm afraid one of them, Suzy Q, is back under there very sick, even dead, and they may be cannibalizing her!"

"How are you, Louise?" he said. He liked her and he liked animals, but she really was becoming one of *those* people.

"I may have to have Ambrose Bierce put down," she said, shaking her head sadly.

"Ambrose Bierce?" he said, keeping a straight face.

"The big, fierce male with the gash in his hip. He killed some stray pit bull around here the other day. That'll teach 'em to keep their dogs from roaming on this campus!" Louise looked around for Ambrose Bierce. "He's right there under that second bungalow. If you get down on your hands and knees, you can just make him out." She tugged a little on Nathaniel's sport coat sleeve to lead him to the area.

"That's okay," he said. "I believe you. A cat really killed a pit bull?"

"Just a small one, probably still a pup. I had to bury it under the Equal Opportunity Office. The grounds crew doesn't like that, but I outsmarted them." Louise looked very pleased with herself. "Hey, what's this I hear about you trying to drum up opposition to that review thing. True?"

"Don't get me started. Have you looked at it?"

"Not really. I've been too busy with the ferals. Cinderella has developed a cyst under her left nostril."

"Has she?"

"And I haven't had her spayed yet." At least Louise believed in spaying and neutering to reduce the overpopulation of her world, which was more than could be said for a certain *other* species which would remain nameless.

"How much time to do you spend with these cats, Louise? Per week, I mean."

"Too much, too much." She seemed weary of it but apparently couldn't stop.

"Didn't you use to be active in the union?"

"I had to give that up when Tommy Twoshoes got diabetes. I've never looked back."

She did look back at the ferals, two of them now actually feeding at the bowls, very skittishly.

"They want to have these poor cats rounded up and euthanized, the grounds crew. Can you imagine. They call them vermin! No, they get *rid* of the vermin. I found two dead rats under Nimbus Hall — I mean Sitting Bull Hall. I keep forgetting the name change. And do you know who was responsible for those two rats?"

"Ambrose Bierce?"

"No, Lolita! That's her, right there! Louise pointed at a gray and white cat with bunches of fur in the wrong places who was feeding. "She's part Maine Coon! We've have tons of rats around this place if it weren't for Lolita."

Nathaniel waved. "Thank you, Lolita!"

"Anyway, I may have a lead for you," Louise continued.

"On?"

Louise looked conspiratorial. "Do you know Haywood Wire in the Statistics Department?"

"Can't say that I do, no."

"I saw him in the gym the other day. I work out once a week, without fail, and he told me he's very disturbed by that website but can't seem to find anybody else who wants to fight it. I've heard you're very upset by it as well, so I gave him your name. I hope you don't mind."

"Not at all. Sounds promising. I don't think I've even heard Haywood's name before."

"This campus is too big. We're all in our separate, separate . . ."

"Cages?" Nathaniel offered.

"No communication."

"Exactly! And that has left us vulnerable to this website. We can't even organize to protect ourselves." Louise fumbled through the pockets in her overalls and found a tattered piece of paper. "I got Haywood's phone number for you."

"Why, thank you, Louise!" What a jewel this woman was.

"It's his home phone number."

"Terrific!"

"Well, I've got to get back to the ferals, Nathaniel. Do you want me to name one of them after you? There's a new litter coming in a few weeks. I didn't get Catherine the Great spayed in time."

"That's okay," Nathaniel said, easing into his car. That's all he needed — a feral Nathaniel lurking under the buildings on campus, Louise calling out among the passing throngs: "Here, Nathaniel! Here, boy! Come and eat your rat!"

It took several left messages, but he finally managed to make an appointment to meet with Haywood Wire of the Statistics Department. A real ally at last! And somebody obviously adept in numbers. Nathaniel was not adept at numbers beyond the multiplication tables and was glad to have that strength about to be joined with his talents. (He'd noticed that he hadn't really needed algebra even *once* since the ninth grade. What had all *that* been about? Nevertheless, maybe Statistics would come in handy in this looming death struggle.

He'd agreed to meet Haywood Wire in the gym two days after their initial phone conversation. Nathaniel hated gyms in general because certain disgusting body parts tended to be on display in such places, despite some more agreeable upper male nudity, and Shite College's gym in particular because it stank of generations of perspiration and urine. Whoo-ee! Who sweated and peed here? Betsy Ross?!

(Out of respect, he didn't think Betsy Fucking Ross.) Hence Nathaniel had been to the Mike Tyson Memorial Gym just once in all his years at the school — he'd forgotten why — and thus he got a bit lost among its tangle of aromatic stairwells and bleak subterranean niches until he heard the sound of tap dancing in the distance.

Hark! That must be it! he thought.

Haywood had asked him if it would be all right to meet after the tap dancing class that he was taking twice a week in the gym. Anywhere, anything! Nathaniel told himself. Now it wasn't for himself alone. He'd looked up Louise Beeze's reviews:

> "Miss Beeze teaches good, but she is one freeky lady, and I bet
> she does it with her cats under them there bungalows!"

So now the fight was for Louise Beeze, Suzy Q, Ambrose Bierce, Cinderella, Tommy Twoshoes, Lolita, Catherine the Great, and the Rest of the Oppressed, Under-Represented Ferals of Shite College under them there Quonset huts!

The tap class wasn't quite over yet, so Nathaniel set on a chair next to the dance floor. Although as far as he could tell he had never seen Haywood Wire before, despite being at the same school, he thought he could pick him out — with only one man in the whole class of fifteen. There — in the middle of young women of varied hues, wearing varied snug leg warmers and leotards, not an un-toned one in the bunch. Hmm. What might Haywood Wire be doing here, methinks?

At the moment he was tap dancing like mad. And he wasn't bad for a fifty-something-year-old man completely out of shape. He had "enthusiasm," if limited motor skills, like some over-achieving, over-the-hill Mousketeer. He saw Nathaniel and saluted him, evidently guessing whom he might be as well.

The young Filipino woman instructor was pointing out something on the yellowed floorboards, perhaps splinters to be careful of, and then the whole troupe went into some kind of furious gyration and shuffle, arms reaching for the ceiling, with Haywood leading them in animation. The man had a full, white beard — well, almost white. Could those be tobacco stains in the middle there? The head was almost free of hair and rather long and gaunt instead of chubby. He had small, merry eyes, thick, white eyebrows and a round belly that shook, when he danced, like a bowl full of . . . jelly? He *did* sort of look like Santa Claus, only dead.

"Nice to meet you!" Nathaniel said when the class was dismissed, taking hold of Haywood's rather bony hand.

"You too!" Haywood said. "Maybe with the two of us working on this something can be done, you think?" His voice seemed deeper in person than on the telephone.

"Let's talk. Do you have to change your clothes?"

"Oh, I think I'm good," he answered. Actually he was a little ripe from the tap dancing, but Nathaniel said nothing. Smelling the sweat was better than having to watch Haywood change out of his tap shoes in the locker room.

He and Haywood eventually sat on a stone fence between the gym and the soccer field. It was a bit chilly out, but nothing they couldn't handle. "So you're taking up tap dance," Nathaniel commented. "For credit?"

"I audit. It's great exercise. This is actually the third class I've taken."

"Interesting."

"And did you see all the pretty girls in the class?" Haywood winked like a dirty old Santa.

Well, that answered a couple of questions. Haywood was straight and he was getting some kind of erotic delight from his surroundings.

"I bring candies to the class. They like them but feel sort of guilty about them. I also bring candies to my classroom. I throw them to the students."

"Aren't you afraid of hurting somebody when you throw the candy? Aren't they hard?"

"Oh, they've got thick hides," Haywood explained. "Besides, I toss overhand."

Hmm.

"I really haven't had any bad reviews myself. They like me because I joke with them."

"And throw them candy. I must say that I've never tried this as an educational tool."

"You do what you gotta do. Maybe I'm just protecting myself."

"Sounds very pragmatic."

"I am that. Most of my students are just fulfilling a requirement and will never use this stuff in their entire lives." Haywood threw up his shoulders.

"But they will always have that skill in catching candy, won't they?"

"You don't approve, I can tell." The deep voice was suddenly soft. "You ever tap dance?" he went on, pointing to his tap shoes.

"A couple of lessons when I was ten. But there was no noticeable skill in evidence, so I faded from the scene early," he said. "So what kind of reviews have you gotten, dare I ask?" Nathaniel said, the excruciating small talk done.

"Not too bad."

"So your objection to the site isn't personal."

"It could become personal. I feel as if any student can run to a computer now and trash my butt on the slightest pretext."

"Exactly!"

"But now they sit up for the candy instead! I see," Nathaniel said, tapping his fingers on the stone wall.

"They love it!" Haywood was picking up the knees of his pants, apparently sticky from the dance workout. "Sometimes they do get out of hand, but it's better than them just sitting there sleeping. It's an eight o'clock class."

"Is this a regular Statistics class or remedial?"

"Oh, regular."

Yet what if Haywood put out an eye? And if their insatiable craving for sweets ever became satiated before class was over? What then — bits of meat? Live mice?

"I must visit one of your classes one day," Nathaniel said to be polite. No way, Jose!

Still, Haywood Wire was the only fellow knight to come forth to slay the dragon, and he seemed intelligent despite all the off-putting trappings. "So we're in league then?" he was asking, extending his hand.

"To the death!" Haywood smiled.

They shook on it.

"Not too literally now," Nathaniel cautioned.

Haywood pulled a folded sheet of paper out of his shirt pocket. "Guess what I found out today. I printed it out to show you. A couple of reviews of Dean Visigoth. Know him?"

"I've had the pleasure, yes, if that's the word."

"I don't care for him either. And something fishy's going on with the dean's reviews."

"Oh?"

Haywood now seemed troubled by the state of the seat of his pants and kept flap-ping it, no doubt to aerate it. He was a strange bedfellow indeed, but whatcha gonna do? "These reviews of him appeared on the site last week." His pants at last attended to, Haywood finally handed Nathaniel the paper. It was bit soggy, but Nathaniel took the paper:

> Dean Visigoth should stick to being a dean. he thihks he's a teacher, but he's quite incompetent. His mind seems elsewhere and you get the feeling he's only teaching because its' a requirement. He also smells of cigarette smoke and I'm allergic to it! Avoid! ive never had a dean before, nor ever again. easy grader, no content. thinks the People created history, not Big Guys. boring speaker. big-smoker. hot wife and he knows it. we learn more about her than the People. needs hair transplant, or maybe brain transplant.

Nathaniel looked up. "I haven't seen these. Want me to send them to the dean for a reaction?"

"They're not there anymore."

"What do you mean?"

"Those two reviews have been removed from the site. Within minutes of being posted."

"By whom?"

"It must be the webmaster. Nobody else can remove them. I was lucky to capture them before they went."

"Great! And why were they removed?"

"By the way, I've read some of yours. I think they're homophobic. But yours are still there."

Nathaniel was beginning to see Haywood's point. "But these two have been taken *down*, right?"

"The faculty sponsor of the review site gets a couple of bad reviews, taking him *off* Tip of the Top, and then a few days later they magically disappear!"

"Putting him back on Tip of the Top?"

"He went back on this morning."

"And these two reviews of Visigoth aren't anywhere mean enough to be close to violating the so-called 'standards' that Dude Lather says he's following now . . .

". . . while downright mean and sick ones of those opposed to the site are left . . ."

". . . on, to prosper and grow. What a prick he is!"

Haywood seemed pleased that Nathaniel, in spite of his generally reserved demeanor, would swear.

"My Old World Charm!" Nathaniel said.

"What?"

"Just a private joke. One has to keep a sense of humor though this."

"I don't think it's funny one bit," Haywood said. "The webmaster protects his friends but gets his enemies." Then he grinned and did a little tap with his tap shoes on the ground below the wall.

"Nothing is either funny or not, except that thinking makes it so, I guess."

"Who said that?"

"Idi Amin."

"Really?"

"I'm joking."

"Do you mind if I say something, Nathaniel?"

"Go right ahead."

"You really shouldn't have sent in those messages to Speak Out Loud. Now they *know* what you think. Let's play it much closer to the vest from now on. When the website first appeared, I made a similar mistake and wrote in using my real name and expressed my objections to the site. Somebody named Fly on the Wall jumped all over me, and I decided never again to use my real name there."

"I wish I had known. Those who refuse to learn history are doomed to repeat it. So you know about Fly on the Wall! Do you know *who* he is?"

"I think we could figure it out if we parse his messages. I've been asking around the Computer Learning Department and Tang Pong Ping, the head of it, thinks it's this sociopath named Mike Something. Fly was dropped from a class and disciplined for misusing the school's computers about a year ago."

"I didn't think such a crime as misusing anything could exist around this place."

"For flaming his fellow students. Said to be about thirty, white, a member of the Komputer Klub, with a history of flaming and other cyberbullying mayhem. Real hate mail."

"Would we have a case if he's been using campus computers to write fake reviews?" (And what about against me, for sending fake reviews using campus computers?)

Nathaniel decided to keep mum about his early flurry of indignation.

"Maybe — if he's still a student. But even if he was expelled, he could still send in whatever he wants from any computer in the world."

"Well, I've decided never to write in to the site ever again."

"A little late. If I may say so, you really shouldn't have sent in those thirty some messages you did send to the discussion part."

Nathaniel had to keep his jaw from dropping. He turned more toward Haywood on the stone fence. "But *I* didn't send in thirty messages!

"You didn't?"

"I sent in two, maybe three, all with my name attached. Then Fly on the Wall or whoever started sending in the rest after I had stopped. To create controversy, like the snake he is."

The cadaverous Santa was all but shaking his head. And that *was* tobacco juice on his beard. Did he chew? "I remember asking a mental note to tell you if we ever met that that was a strategic error, sending in all those signed messages. You really didn't send them?"

"No, I didn't send them!" Nathaniel insisted. Jesus! If his one ally, someone who knew the capacity for lying on this website, was suspicious even when he denied sending in messages with his name "forged" on them, what were they up against? This was undeniably something important and not just for himself. "I don't want to be melodramatic," Nathaniel said, "but I believe this website can do more damage than the Inquisition. Vicious, anonymous charges. Accusations running rampart."

"Followed by burning at the stake?"

"Hopefully, it won't go that far."

"Don't be too sure," Haywood said. "I like to think I'm something of a student of history. Do you know what they did to the professors during Mao's so-called Cultural Revolution? It was worse than burning at the stake, because it lasted longer and was more humiliating. Any of this could return back in our time. Civilization is only this deep." Dead Santa Claus held up his thumb and forefinger a millimeter apart. "About like this."

"I hope you're very wrong," Nathaniel said.

"I'm never wrong!" Haywood laughed.

"I didn't write the majority of those messages. Fly on the Wall probably did. Or the First Amendment Club. Or both. Or somebody else entirely. It's a mess, but we have to track them down."

"Let me see what I can find out. It gets better and better, doesn't it?" Haywood said, doing another little tap dance in the dirt.

Yeah. Ho, ho, ho.

Guy Mountain was standing at the door of Nathaniel's office. "I just want to say a few words. I've got student conferences coming up."

As if I didn't know, Nathaniel thought. *Loud* ones! Guy had taken to holding his conferences not in his office but in the testing area nearby. He had a metallic voice and every out-of-place student paragraph had to be shared with the whole room. Didn't he realize that unorganized student essays could be cured by the teacher giving an organizational pattern in the *first* place! As if these students would ever again write an actual *essay* in their entire lives. They'd probably use algebra more!

"I just wanted to say that the review website is not going to work, Nathaniel, if it's abused."

"That's precisely what I've been trying to point out. Come in, sit down."

But Guy wouldn't. "I don't mean the student reviews, however thoughtless some of them might be. I mean reviews and comments sent in by instructors."

Nathaniel looked up at the Mountain. "You mean *me* in particular?"

"It's come to my attention that you have been sending in complaints to the discussion parts of the site, and that's your right, of course. But when you start sending in reviews of deans, you throw the whole thing off." Guy's body was moving around awkwardly. It was clear he was uncomfortable with confrontation, his size notwithstanding.

"The website has been off from the get-go!" Nathaniel shot back. "There isn't one review on there that anyone can vouch for as legitimate!"

"You're not helping by reviewing Dean Visigoth and saying his wife is 'hot' and that he needs a brain transplant!"

"Who says I sent in such a review?"

"It sounds just like you. The webmaster removed it, I'm happy to say."

Nathaniel was torn. Yes, he'd sent in a review of Visigoth, just not this one. Where was this all going? To a Sargasso Sea of endless denials, the flotsam and jetsam of I Think You Wrote This and You Think I Wrote That?! It was a journey he didn't want to take. The website had set its course long before he got on board. And he was not going to account to Guy Mountain for what he had written and what he hadn't. "It seems to me the pertinent issue here is not who wrote what but rather that we can even be having this conversation at all."

"You don't want to discuss it?"

"I wish I had the nobility to refuse to scream or cower or defend my reputation —"

"Nobody's impugning your reputation, Nathaniel!"

"Do you even look at the site, Guy, or just defend it on some kind of crazed principle?"

'I read the review of myself and how ugly I am that you sent me. It wasn't pleasant, but I still would defend the site's right to exist."

"I guess my point is — in the vernacular— that no one should have to deny writing something that wouldn't even *be* if this marvel of technology hadn't been set up by a horse's ass and defended by other horses' . . . stable boys and grooms." Nathaniel had backed off at the last moment.

"This site could be a really nifty way for students to have input and make constructive comments about their teachers, if it's left alone and not interfered with." Guy's face was all blurry and red now.

"I happen to disagree with you, Guy. If students have complaints against teachers — and I would be the last one to say that some teachers around here can't use improvement — then they can write them up and submit them to the chair of the department or the Grades Committee or any number of other legitimate places. They can even drop a note to the teacher, typed or even hand printed, and stay anonymous. But not this cyberbullying monstrosity, where every petty gripe is broadcast to the universe, true or untrue. What in the name of God will it take to convince you?"

"The school won't give the webmaster the ID numbers of students, so there's no way to verify who's a real student and who isn't. He's at a great handicap because of it."

"Then he shouldn't be operating the fucking thing!"

Guy was becoming very passionate too. "The greatness of the Internet is just the kind of untrammeled freedom that we're talking about! For the first time in human history people have this tremendous tool to effect change in their worlds!"

So maybe I'll drop a quick review of you, big boy, and say how much you disturb others with your very loud conferences. Maybe I can effect change in *my* world!

Nathaniel thought about standing up, literally, but he thought it might get even more heated, and, besides, he'd had garlic salami for lunch and hadn't brushed his teeth. No, he'd stand up for what he believed in by sitting down.

"The Internet must not be interfered with! It's a fundamental principle of the new technology!"

"You know something, Guy, I hate fundamentalists. Of all kinds. And the Internet is hardly something not to be tampered with, as though it's holy!"

"There are a few kinks to be worked out, but the Internet is going to change the world!"

"Just like the theory of the Divine Right had a few kinks in it."

Guy's face was doing all sorts of tricks. And Nathaniel thought his own come-and-go tic was bad! "You don't believe in the importance of the Internet, Nathaniel?"

"You sound like I doubt the existence of Betty Crocker or something. The Internet is just one more in the endless cycle of supposed panaceas for life's problems."

"Well, just because you're so *negative*, Nathaniel, it doesn't mean the rest of us have to be!" What a great red pumpkin Guy's head made.

This was getting way out of hand.

"I don't want to argue with you anymore, Guy, but I don't see it as *negative* merely because I don't accept the Second Coming of the Internet."

"You're always so snide!"

"I'm sorry. I was trying to be amusing."

"Well, you're not! Most students don't even know what you're talking about half the time! And I wish you would leave the workings of this website alone. In time it will prove to be extremely beneficial to this college."

"How can you believe that?"

"Because it will make teachers more accountable!"

"For every teacher it will make more accountable, it will make two others cowards! Above all, it will make *students* even less accountable than they are now."

"Do you have a kind word for anyone?"

"No, I let you handle that."

"Don't you realize that there are plenty of bad teachers around this place?"

"Not as many as there are bad students. I've observed plenty of teachers, and more of the *students* are bad. *Bad!*"

Guy looked positively shocked. Nathaniel had said the unsayable, the Masses had no clothes on!

"We have very hard-working students here!"

"No, we don't. We have just a few of those."

"And they want quality teachers!"

"They want easy grades and minimalist assignments." It crossed Nathaniel's mind that perhaps Guy, who was still probably under thirty though he looked older, didn't even know what real academic hard work meant.

"They put in a lot of effort in my classes. I can't speak for yours."

"And with what result, Guy? Do we reward effort or *results?*"

"Maybe it depends on the teacher. Students will exert more effort when they know they will be rewarded."

"Absolutely not true. They slough off and often turn in shit, and not just shit but runny shit."

"It could be you don't know how to *love* your students, and that's why you get the results you do!"

"Could be that you don't look closely enough at what's actually turned in to you because you're so busy loving them!"

"Perhaps you are in the wrong profession, Nathaniel. My students care for me!"

"It's a bit late in the day to change professions. And do they care for you or for the generous A's and B's you lavish upon them?" Nathaniel's heart was drained, but he still continued to sit there. He'd be damned if he would say "But many, many of the good students love me too!" However, he would say this: "I've had quite a few students after you've had them, Guy, and frequently they are — what's the polite expression? — ill-prepared, shall we say."

"First I've heard of this. Funny you should bring it up now!"

"I bit my tongue before. You've given B's to people who can barely read! Then I become the Bad Guy. Ah, wordplay! You're the Good *Guy* and I'm the Bad Guy."

"At least my students don't go crying to the counselors, saying 'Dr. Tack says I will never be able to write.'"

"I don't believe I've ever said such a thing to a student in my life."

"But they do go crying to the counselors!"

"Perhaps they do, because they've been told lies about themselves before they got to me. By people like you! They have plenty of self-esteem — and so little to warrant it!"

"Well, aren't you God's gift to education!"

"I did not say that. I know my flaws as a teacher. And it's not *loving* my students enough! What they need is some *tough* love!"

"Possibly you don't know your flaws as well as you think you do, Nathaniel."

Nathaniel considered that. "Possibly."

"I've heard that you don't treat your students as equals!"

"If you mean that I don't treat them as fellow human beings in this great pisspot before Nirvana, you're quite wrong. If you mean I don't consider the pre-literate in a holding cell like Shite College my equal in their writing skills, or even in thinking coherently, you couldn't be more right! Yes, and I *beat* them too."

"I don't think this is getting us anywhere," Guy said, wiping a piece of lint off his chin and starting to leave.

"Does language ever succeed in getting us anywhere, do you think?"

Guy turned back for one last thrust. "Just leave the website be, Nathaniel! Leave it *be*!"

Was that a threat?

It was too late to ask because Guy had disappeared into his own office. It was just next door, but it was miles away.

"Guess what I've found!" Marty said, opening the door to his apartment, sounding chipper, and yet speed-free. They were going to watch some television together, a program on some rock group Marty loved.

Nathaniel had a key, but he still usually knocked. It was more polite. "What's that?"

"You sound depressed."

"I'm all right. Had a rough time today with a colleague, that's all."

"Well, don't let the bastards grind you down. Look, I cleaned up the apartment!"

Nathaniel looked around. Cleaned up? Where? There were still library books everywhere, only now stacked — on the floor, on the sofa, next to Marty's computer, even under his desk. Marty was going to get arrested for overdue books next! Nathaniel got a glass from the bathroom for a drink of water. Marty was always on his back about how Nathaniel's dishwater left food bits on some of the utensils, but Marty's bathroom was moldy-looking with grout on the shower wall, a broken shower head, and three daddy long legs in one corner of the ceiling.

Say nothing! Nathaniel told himself. We won't have a fight. Maybe we'll even have sex. We're going to forget how. He called from the bathroom: "You sound very up, Marty! What did you find? A twenty dollar bill on the sidewalk?"

"No, this way cool website."

At the word *website* Nathaniel's tic began to pulse a little. "Another one about teachers?"

"Honey, not everybody is looking at your website. Trust me, okay?" Marty came into the bathroom and put his arms around Nathaniel from behind. "You're a worrywart, do you know that?" He pointed at the two of them in the mirror. "See it! He tapped on Nathaniel's tic "There's the worry wart. Right there." He kissed Nathaniel on the side of the neck, then tugged on his earlobe.

"Sorry. I'm becoming a bit obsessive about it, I know."

"*My* website is much better! Let me show it to you."

Nathaniel pressed on Marty's arms around him to make him stay a little longer. The tic was quiet now. He thought they made a nice couple in the mirror, virile. An Army of Lovers. Well, at least two. After a few moments he said, "Okay, I give up. What's your website?"

Marty headed for his computer. "Chad Manley has set up his own site!"

Nathaniel followed him. "Wow! . . . Who's Chad Manley?"

"This really sexy stud, with a cock out to here. Very hairy chest. Nice pecs. And it's *interactive*!" Marty held up a color printout of Chad Manley.

"The wily Internet wins again!" Nathaniel glanced at the printout and put it back if on the desk. He didn't care for pornography. It was like masturbation — it made him feel lonely, as if he couldn't get the real stuff. But Marty loved it. Sometimes he wondered if they were in a boat about to be capsized and stranded on a desert island and Marty had to choose between him and porn which he would choose. There are some questions couples should *never* ask.

"What have you heard from Haywood Wire — is that his name? Your new ally in the fight?"

"Nothing since that first meeting. I'll have to give him a call. He's a little strange, to tell the truth."

"Look at this!" Marty said, leaning in toward the computer screen. "Chad Manley is going to have a live sex show in fifteen minutes."

"Must be nice to be so ready, so efficient. Does he shoot on cue too?"

"Practically. Why don't you watch it with me?"

Nathaniel moved away from the computer. He'd watched porn videos a few times with Marty. It was Marty's way of re-igniting their sex life, he realized, but for some reason that he couldn't quite identify he found these situations uncomfortable and usually backed off.

"Why don't you like anything *I* do!" Marty suddenly snapped.

"I'm over here to watch a rock group I don't even care for! What are you talking about?" No, no, they mustn't fight! Who had said that a long-term marriage consisted of a year and half of rabid sex and the rest fighting? La Rochefoucault? Nostradamus? Judge Judy?

"All right, let's not fight," Marty said, spreading both hands.

"We're agreed on that."

"But don't you think Chad Manley is *sexy*?" He pointed to the printout. "Just look at that man!"

Nathaniel made an effort to appreciate the aesthetics of the porn star. Yes, nice pecs, slim waist, with something in front of him. "What's that garden implement he's holding?"

"His dick!" Marty laughed.

"Looks lethal. Don't you find it somewhat intimidating to see someone with a cock that large?"

"I thought you said mine was fine."

"I didn't mean that yours is small. But *that* one's unnatural! I don't even really find it attractive."

"Really?" Marty squinched up his eyes.

"Maybe in some kind of pagan, ancient, Greek-let's-celebrate-the-corn sort of way, but *practically* . . . And to tell the truth I'd rather be the Big Man on Campus when it comes to . . ."

"Showing off?"

"Exactly."

I wonder if we'd have more sex with each other if we had no other choice, Nathaniel wondered. Wasn't that true for most married couples? Nathaniel didn't even *want* to be married. Day in, day out, year out. Have we done it on the basement shelving yet, darling? Some anti-porn version of the Myth of Sisyphus! *Eeek!* No wonder there were so many horrible crimes of passion among straights — and even lesbians. Thank God for the bushes for me and Chad Manley for Marty!

He looked at the waterbed. How many times had he and Marty made love there? Countless. They'd even sprung a leak once, they were so fervid in their activity. Ah, youth.

"Chad Manley and his boyfriend have sex together," Marty went on, "and if you're a subscriber you get to watch and even discuss it with him later. He's a bottom."

"What does one say? To a porn star, I mean?"

"It's what I've always wanted to do, be able to ask questions."

"Most little boys want to be firemen."

"Yeah, I like firemen too," Marty joked. He pointed to another pile of porn printouts. "Firemen, cops, businessmen."

"Businessmen?"

"Doing it in suits. Don't get the different piles mixed up."

Nathaniel leafed through the pecs and the pricks, not even getting a hard-on this time. Usually he at least got a generic hard-on looking at such things, even if not very deeply interested. What's happening to me? he wondered, worrywart-like. This is not good. My dick, my dick, my kingdom for my dick!

They watched the TV show together and nuzzled a little bit and held hands on the sofa, but they didn't have sex, with or without Chad Manley's manly assistance.

How long had it been now? Who was counting?

Hmm. Or was it Eek?

Rather conspiratorial, Haywood Wire stopped by Nathaniel's office the next day, looking around to make sure no other teachers were within earshot. "I may have some thing," he said, but not before he'd walked the length of the big outside room to double check. "Should we go outside?" he asked, keeping his big voice down. There was only one other person around, in the most distant cubicle.

"I don't think they can hear us," Nathaniel said, keeping his voice down as well. "I'm supposed to be having an office hour and should stay here."

"Okay. I'll try to be *sotto voce*." It appeared that Haywood had recently indulged in a tobacco "chaw," like one of Nathaniel's grandpappies on his mother's side, because the otherwise white beard was very discolored. What color was that? Polluted-mill-stream? "Hey, look at these beauties," he said, slapping two more reviews from Teachersonparade down on Nathaniel's desk.

"You're on top of this," Nathaniel complimented.

"I have a copy of every review that's appeared since it began."

"We'll need them."

"We'll get their balls yet. What do you make of these?" Two of Haywood's bony fingers traced some lines in the reviews:

> Dean Calvin Visigoth is an outstanding instructor in the History Department.

> He's a kind human being who takes time to clarify topics any student has questions about. I urge you to engage with this man. You will not regret it— esp. his History 12.

"Suspicious, don't you think?" Haywood said.

"Because it doesn't have any errors in it and thus couldn't have been written by a student?"

Haywood looked sideways at Nathaniel. "Not that. I'm not all that perfect myself when it comes to grammar and all that crap."

Nathaniel winced. Great, just the kind of ally I need!

"I meant the two of these together. Here."

The second review said:

> Calvin N. Visigoth takes time to clarify any topic for his assignments for any student needing his assistance. He knows the People's history as it ought to be taught and is extremely competent and never boring. I urge you to engage with his classes. They are real.

"Notice how certain odd words are repeated — 'engage with,' for example."

"And they both promote his People's History course."

Haywood's eyes were bright with the hunt. "It's almost as if they've taken his negative reviews, the ones that were removed, and reversed the wording to make them into positive ones."

"And yet the webmaster hasn't pounced all over them, as he did when someone sent in multiple good reviews of me."

"Was that *you* who sent those in?"

"Time will reveal all," Nathaniel said quickly. He wasn't making any admissions to Haywood just yet. He barely knew the man.

"They not only counter the bad reviews that Visigoth got, but they push him further up the ladder on Tip of the Top. He's number two now."

"Could the dean have sent them in himself?"

"More likely one of his student cronies."

"Somebody from the First Amendment Club?"

"Possibly. Do you know that club?"

"I think it's a campus front for the website."

"I did a little investigation into what they're up to — by trying to get a membership application. It's supposed to be open to all. At least that's what their bylaws say."

"And?"

"They didn't respond to me. *Nada.*"

"Do you think they got your application?"

"I dropped a typed note in their campus box, identifying myself as An Interested Student — with caps."

"How long ago was this?"

"Probably a month."

"No reply of any kind?"

"None."

"Of course it *is* a Shite College campus organization . . ."

"I don't think there really is a First Amendment Club. I doubt they have the ten members you're required to get to be an official club. I looked up their so-called minutes, and they've had exactly one meeting since September. I don't believe they actually have any meetings!"

"And you think Dean Visigoth is in on this?"

There was a step outside Nathaniel's office. He and Haywood both stopped talking and held their breath.

They couldn't see though the small crack between the door and the jamb. "*Yes*, who's there?" Nathaniel finally called.

"It's just me," Guy Mountain replied, softly.

Was he trying to eavesdrop?

"I'm having trouble with my key ring," Guy said. There came an appropriate rattle of keys.

Nathaniel got up to check outside. He and Guy had been avoiding each other since their contretemps. Their eyes met.

"I hope I'm not disturbing you," Guy said, with a patina of sarcasm.

"No student conferences today?" Nathaniel parried.

"No, but I guess you do," Guy said, nodding his head at Nathaniel's office. He must have heard Haywood's voice.

Should he lie: "Just one of my students here." He said nothing and went back inside his office.

Haywood looked inquisitive about who this other teacher might be, and Nathaniel put a finger to his mouth to encourage silence and sat back down. They both waited to see what Guy would do next, for they certainly couldn't continue to talk if he stayed there. He belonged to the Enemy, and he had the growths on his hands to prove it.

"Will he leave?" Haywood mouthed.

"I think so," Nathaniel mouthed back.

Various sounds drifted over: papers being moved around, a dictionary or some other heavy book being opened. Then silence. Had Guy sat down? Usually he made more noise than this because he was so large.

I don't know what's going on either, Nathaniel shrugged. Was Guy standing on the other side of the flimsy wall listening to their conversation? It was sure taking him a long time to settle in or get out.

Suddenly Nathaniel heard himself saying "As I was saying, Mr. Smith, you need to move this paragraph from the top of your essay down to the middle. See?"

Haywood started to reply full voice until Nathaniel signaled quickly that he should only say 'huh uh' if anything at all. Who knew — maybe Guy would recognize the voice or at least guess it to be that of a faculty member.

Haywood muttered something.

Guy was still there, strangely quiet. Was he in cahoots with Dean Visigoth and the First Amendment Club? Their spy in the field?

"But you have *excellent* margins, Mr. Smith!" Nathaniel went on. "The best I've ever seen." He'd show Guy Mountain a thing or two! See, he complimented his students!

Guy didn't seem to be leaving.

"So you work on that aspect of it, okay?" Nathaniel continued. "And maybe you can come to see me another day and we'll get this baby tap dancing!"

Haywood gave him a slightly annoyed look but didn't say anything.

"Leave a message on my answering machine here when you want another appointment, all right?"

Haywood grunted something and slipped out the door, then stuck his arm back in and gave Nathaniel the V for Victory sign.

"Nice conferring with you, Mr. Smith! You're one of my very best students, do you know that?" he called as Haywood made his escape.

Irony will do me in one of these days, Nathaniel thought.

"I may have something else we can use," Haywood said on the phone. "Can you come to my office?"

They met in Haywood's office in the Dolores Huerta Statistics Building. It was one of the newer buildings and still smelled of fresh paint. But should you still be smelling fresh paint after a year? You're too sensitive to your environment, Nathaniel told himself. Yeah, and that's how gays have survived, one of his other selves answered back.

"Who was that creep who was hanging around yesterday?" Haywood asked.

"Name is Mountain. He's a big believer in Teachersonparade. Thanks again for picking up my cues about not letting him overhear us."

"No problem. Do you think he heard anything?"

Haywood looked like he had washed his beard — thank god. It wasn't as soiled in the middle. Nathaniel cast his eyes around Haywood's office to see if he could spot any chewing tobacco on the bookshelves. There wasn't any, but there were models of atoms, or molecular structures, made out of wooden sticks, sitting in a box just below eye level on the other side of the office. There were also small vinyl blow-up figures of cartoon characters on the bookshelves, five of them, some of which Nathaniel didn't recognize.

Did Haywood have blow-up dolls at home too? The *other* kind! Nathaniel, don't go there. Okay, but what was Haywood's sex life like? Was there a cadaverous Mrs. Klaus? The man was clearly heterosexual, but he had not mentioned a wife. Mentioning the wife was what straight men did all the time, usually by the second sentence of any conversation.

"Since our aborted meeting," Haywood was explaining, "I've been busy." He patted the computer on his desk.

"So you have your own computer here," Nathaniel said. "We don't have them in the English Department yet."

Haywood didn't seem overly concerned about this lack. "I use it a lot." He switched on the computer from the back. It wasn't the most up-to-date computer actually and the screen looked dusty, with a glare. There was a folded-up green blanket used as a cushion on the chair. "It's right here, available for our purposes." He patted his trusty computer.

"Lead the way! By the way, have you ever sent in false reviews of anybody?" Nathaniel asked.

"Never," Haywood replied immediately. "I vowed not to get into all that deception after my initial bad experience with those complains I sent in to Speak Out Loud."

"I'm sorry I missed all that."

"They're still there, only buried at the bottom. Many others have come in since then, thank goodness."

"But nothing every dies in cyberspace, right?"

"Virtually not."

"That would be a good ad campaign for a movie. Be Very Afraid. Nothing Ever Dies in Cyberspace!"

"Speaking of being afraid, Fly on the Wall is *still* after your butt."

"Well, he *can't* have it."

Haywood laughed. Actually laughed. What did straight men think when they met Nathaniel, the most openly gay teacher on campus? What images did he summon up for them? His legs in the air? In a dress? Fuck me! I'm Myrna Loy! Well, it ain't so, Mister! Did Santa Baby here think Nathaniel wanted him? That's what all those ugly, slop-bellied generals in the military seemed to think. The gays would be pestering them for their penises! *Pu-leeze!* Nathaniel could do with mature men, rather liked a good many of them in fact, but not the generals, and not the Dead Santa Klaus sitting here.

Did other people's minds race like this? Nathaniel wondered. Well, hyper-vigilance is the price of freedom! Didn't George Washington say that? "Do you know who Fly on the Wall is?" he asked.

"I've done some checking around, discreetly. He's a sociopath. And that's his own description! It was in one of the early exchanges."

"What's his real name?

"I haven't been able to find that out yet. I do know *you* didn't write most of those messages they're accusing you of."

"Didn't I mention that already?" Nathaniel said.

"You did, but now I know who did write them. A former student of mine, an adult man in his late thirties in law school."

What did this mean — that Haywood didn't trust what Nathaniel said? Well, okay, Nathaniel didn't completely trust Haywood either.

"And his name is Nathan Lack?"

"No, that's his *nom de Internet*."

"I wish he had chosen something else."

"Fly on the Wall and the others, however, still believe it's *you* writing in. He calls you

Nathannyboy, did you know?" Haywood grinned. There is something in the misfortunes of our friends that does not displease us. Besides, now they were going after Nathaniel instead of Haywood.

"I'm afraid all this has made me somewhat gun-shy," Nathaniel said. "I haven't looked up my reviews in a while."

"You're still near the bottom."

"Thanks."

"If it's any comfort to you, they're probably not from your real students. I'm still checking on reviews every day."

"I'm glad somebody is."

Nathaniel's cat was still sick and Marty was bleeding at the nose at work and the criminal charges from the arrest still hadn't been dropped completely, but he decided not to mention these things to Haywood.

"It's a conspiracy, pure and simple."

Nathaniel didn't believe much in conspiracies, too tabloid for his taste, but this time it seemed quite likely. "Fly on the Wall, the webmaster, and the dean?"

"It's as if the webmaster is lurking waiting for any bad reviews so that he can remove them. Fortunately the way he set up the site *all* the new reviews show up first, so I manage to transfer them to a diskette before they disappear."

"Good for you!" Positive reinforcement for Santa! "Do you think we should *tell* Visigoth that we know this is happening? Or is that tipping our hand?"

"He'd probably deny it. No doubt he wants to remain number one on Tip of the Top — for the enrollment for his History 12 class."

"Is he any good — as a teacher?"

"I've asked around, but nobody seems to know. I've counted at least six reviews that were there one day and gone the next. There wasn't anything in them that would make them objectionable, except that those didn't praise the dean to the skies."

"And no one else can't tell this, right, because they're not following the site as closely as we are."

"Most people have no way of knowing what was on the site first and what's there now. It's completely under the control of the webmaster."

"The cocksucker!" Nathaniel spat out. "Sorry."

"It's okay. He *is* a cocksucker."

Should he bother to explain that he didn't really think *cocksucker* should be a term of contempt? That indeed it was one of the higher compliments a man could pay another man, at least if the cocksucking was well done (no teeth). Nathaniel had only been using the term in a spontaneous outburst in the tongue of the peasantry. Come to think of it, wasn't it about time for some tongue from some peasantry, or any class for that matter. As a wise old woman (Gertrude Stein) once pointed out: From time to time men have to empty themselves. Not pretty. But, oh, Gerty, so very true.

Haywood had summoned up the site and was checking for new reviews. "Oh, my God!" he suddenly exclaimed.

That shook Nathaniel out of his semi-erotic reverie. "What?"

"My God."

"What?"

But he wouldn't tell him.

Nathaniel got up to look over Haywood's shoulder at the computer screen.

"The goddamn lying piece of shit!"

"Fly on the Wall?"

It was hard to read because of the glare, so Nathaniel tried shielding his eyes. He inadvertently bumped into Haywood's back and moved away a half-step as if scalded. Men don't touch!

Haywood tapped on the computer screen. "Look at this goddamned shit."

Nathaniel moved closer, careful not to brush against the other man. I can barely read this. I ought to get Lasik surgery on my eyes, he thought. This is ridiculous. But finally he could make out the source of Haywood's annoyance:

> Attention: Women
>
> Mr. Haywood Wire should not be teaching at this colledge, or at any colledge. He sexually harasses his female students and is a disguzting pervert who should have his candy shoved up his penis! When he goes after you, run to the dean. Report any and all instances of Wire's harassment.

"I think I know who wrote it," Haywood said.

Somebody you harassed? Nathaniel kept himself from saying.

"Some wacko I had last year."

"What happened?" (Are you truly a "disguzting" pervert, or merely a regular pervert?)

"I drew a picture of a double helix on the blackboard and said that its curves resembled the female body."

"And *that's* it?"

"I knew as I was saying it that it hadn't been a good idea. But it was that eight o'clock class of mine."

"And you're sure that's all?" Nathaniel didn't want to ask Haywood any more directly than this, but there were the tap dance classes and the nubile young ladies. They might create a Reasonable Doubt, mightn't they?

"You doubt me?" Haywood said, turning and looking up at Nathaniel, who stepped back even further.

"Just trying to get the situation clear in my mind." (You doubt *me*, for god's sake!)

"That's what so terrible about this website. You can just plunk down any old accusation and it plants seeds in people's minds."

Nathaniel moved back and tapped at the screen. "So you're telling me that because you drew a double helix and said it looks like a woman, somebody has accused you of sexually *harassing* women? We have come to this sorry state?"

"She came to see me about it here in this office, furious. I apologized and apologized and I thought she was satisfied. But apparently not. I even said I was sorry in the next class."

"Oh, I can believe it happened. Around here. In this country. There are women around the world who can't even uncover their faces, and here we have fanatics all bent out of shape because you compare a double helix to a woman." Of course *I'd* never say such a thing in class, Nathaniel knew. You have to pick and choose the taboos you thwart, and women's bodies were untouchable. You couldn't compliment them — that was horribly sexist. You certainly could not *denigrate* them. Basically you were not to notice them or possibly, just possibly, to speak of them in hushed and reverend tones. Her mantle laps over my lady's wrist too much . . . No, not even that. My wrist? You're looking at my *wrist*?!

I am so *lucky* to be gay! Nathaniel thought. It's bad enough watching every word in class, but to have to go out and court these Black Widows! Yikes!

"That student sure got me," Haywood said. He seemed a little stunned, his arms hanging down.

"If you really didn't do anything, isn't this libel?" Nathaniel asked.

"You think maybe? Liable?"

"The word is *libel*," Nathaniel corrected, as gently as he could. Funny, you weren't supposed to correct people in America even when they misused a word. But he had a feeling that this word was going to become a major part of their vocabulary from here on in and it was best to get it correct, right off the bat.

"Just two syllables?" Haywood said. "I never knew that." He didn't seem particularly pleased to be corrected, but at least he didn't attack back. "But I do think I know what *libel* is."

"Which is?" Nathaniel had a general knowledge. After all, he was a writer and sometimes used people he knew as models for characters — always thoroughly altered and completely unrecognizable from the originals!!!

"Sometimes it's hard to tell what's libel and what's permissible," Haywood said.

"Making it sound as if you're making unwanted sexual overtures to your female students crosses way over the line. Way over." (Unless of course you really did it.)

"You think so?"

"I *do* think so!"

"I've been sort of intimidated because I thought perhaps what I said wasn't the wisest thing I ever said."

"Wasn't it a joke?"

"I do think the double helix looks like a woman's body. I thought it might wake up some of the males in the class."

"You know something, Haywood, this would be hilarious if it weren't so serious. Not incidentally, have you checked your enrollment for next semester?"

"Think I should?"

"I think we both should."

Haywood was very adept at using the computer and had that information on the screen in no time. "Mine seem okay," he said. "But they're all required classes."

"And that one about harassing *just* came in."

"You think they might dis-enroll after they read it?"

"If I were a woman, I might think twice about taking an instructor who might harass me." Especially if he looked like you, Nathaniel continued the thought. Come here, Miss, and see what Dead Santa has in his candy sack for you!

"Here are your enrollments coming up," Haywood said.

Nathaniel leaned closer to the screen again.

"Jesus!"

Haywood counted for him. "Ten in one. Eleven in that one. Nine in Plays and Novels."

"And only seven in my Saturday 102."

"The word is getting out on you!" Haywood teased.

"You're a bundle of laughs," Nathaniel said.

"You only teach four classes? We have to teach five!"

"You want to switch?"

"Do you know statistics?"

"No, but I can throw candy at students."

Haywood almost laughed. "I guess I shouldn't have told you that."

"And what are we going to do with all the information we're gathering?" Nathaniel pressed on. "In the Information Age. I mean the Mis-Information Age!"

"We could always get the school to sue the webmaster."

"Do you think it would? I've encountered nothing but stonewalling so far."

"A friend and I made a videotape of the way the college's website is set up, with all those links to Teachersonparade all over the place."

"They're more than links. They're endorsements."

Haywood patted a videotape on one of his bookshelves. "I think it shows how the school has actively promoted the website, even allowed libel to be promoted on its very own webpage. Come and read about teachers who sexually harass their female students! Actually we should sue this goddamn *college* too!"

"Sue the college? This royal throne of kings, this scepter'd isle, this earth of majesty, this seat of Mars, this other Eden, demi-paradise, this happy breed of men, this little world, this precious stone set in the silver sea, this blessed plot, this earth, this realm, this Shite!"

"Hey, that's good!"

"I left some out."

"Why don't we sue their butts off?"

"I don't think I can afford a libel lawyer. Can you?"

"Let's see about our options," Haywood said, not answering his question, it seemed to Nathaniel.

"I've got to be going, Haywood. My cat's been at the vet's for a week and I have to see if they're ready to release her or keep her longer."

"Let me walk out with you."

"Sure. But should we be seen together," Nathaniel joked. "The word will go out that two wicked professors are plotting against the greatest boon to students since the downloaded term paper."

"I think my name has pretty much disappeared from the discussions, thank god."

"I wish I had talked with you sooner. I might have avoided some of the same pitfalls. But I think we're making progress, don't you?"

"I think we've just begun," Haywood said. "Suing the school will be far from easy."

"Hello, Mr. Wire!" a female student called out happily as he and Haywood walked down the steps from the seventh floor.

"Way to go, Mr. Wire!" another student, a light-skinned black male, said, with a big, warm smile.

Haywood certainly seemed to be a popular teacher. He obviously had something going for him beyond his off-putting appearance. Maybe that candy wasn't such a bad idea after all.

When they got down to the lobby, three other students also acknowledged Haywood. It seemed by this time a little *too* friendly. "How's it hanging, Mr. Wire!" "Hey, there's the Wire Man!" Where was academic decorum, for god's sake?

"Saw you, man!" a Latino male in his teens suddenly said, almost with a sneer, as he approached the two teachers.

"What you talkin' 'bout, Eduardo!" Haywood replied, in some kind of ghetto voice, high-fiving the male student.

"I saw you over there, like, looking through that window, man!" This was accompanied by a *mano-a-mano* grin that filled up his face.

"I don't know what you're talkin' about!" Haywood said, reaching into his coat pocket and pulling out a couple of hard candies, which he proceeded to lob, underhand, toward the student, before moving on. "Get your homework in this week, you hear me!"

"Mr. Wire he lookin' in the back window of the girls' gym! *Yes, sir!*" the student said, loping off, proud to have such a teacher.

Nathaniel looked toward Haywood for a possible clarification. Was this true?

"Oh, he's a moron!" was all Haywood offered, greeting yet another student.

Onward! Nathaniel thought. What else was there?

"Not too bad. Yourself?"

"Can't complain. Cold up there?"

"Not too bad. There?" Jimmy said.

"Okay, enough of this generic conversation. What's wrong?"

"Nothing's wrong." Jimmy's voice didn't sound *wrong* exactly, but it sounded like it had a touch of teenage Angst.

"How are your mom and Lana?" You do have to get the formalities out of the way.

"Mom got promoted. Now she's a master electrician. With her own truck."

Allah be praised! was the first thought. The second thought — did Allah approve of somewhat butch lesbians with their own trucks? Not any Allah that Nathaniel knew of.

"How's Marty?"

Been arrested, still sticking speed up his nose every chance he gets, mildly depressed, letting his apartment go to hell, and our sex life has all but dried up "He's fine. We're fine." And everybody seems to think I blurt out everything! "How's school?" he asked. You have to father.

"I got a D."

"Great. In what?"

"Intro to Theater."

"Nobody gets a D in theater. And your father is a playwright!"

"He is?"

"Don't make me trot out my many prestigious awards."

"Like what? The Pulitzer?"

"The Pulitzer is overrated."

"Like what then?"

"The Great Platte River Festival Contest – that's the one to win."

"Who?"

"Don't scoff. There were over four hundred entries."

"And you won?"

"Tied for third place. So there. So don't get a D in theater. You are betraying your genes."

"I didn't turn in the assignment. I did it, I just didn't turn it in."

"Please, I don't want to hear this. The computer ate your homework?"

"No, I just didn't get around to turning it in."

Hmm. Nathaniel wanted his child to be what any American father wanted: normal but not ordinary, bright and successful in school but not creepy, talented in something, the arts perhaps, with just a bit of his mother electrician's practical skills thrown in, adventurous yet well-behaved. Not quite yes-honored-father-what-is-your will. Still thankfully not—fuck-you-mom-I-hate-you-and-this-stupid-trip-to-all-the-world-capitals-you-gave-me-and-I'm-leaving attitude, like too many American kids. Certainly somebody who at least turned in his assignments.

"Your mother should get a birch rod."

"What's that?"

"So what's wrong?"

"Why do you always think something's wrong?"

"Just asking."

"How's that website you don't like?"

"Did I tell you about that?"

"You wanted me to send a virus."

"Oh, right. Well, don't bother." Nathaniel decidedly did not want Jimmy going to the site and reading those nasty things about him. Not that there was a thing he could do to stop it. "I'm working on it."

"Do you think you can really stop it?" Jimmy said.

"We're thinking of suing."

"I thought it was free speech."

"The Constitution of the United States does not protect lies. That's why we have libel laws. People are so knee-jerk, brain-dead 'liberal' about this. Yimmy, I don't want you to become a leftist fundamentalist any more than a right-wing one. Promise?"

"I just wouldn't try to stop people from saying what they want to."

"Suppose somebody said that you harassed the females at your school and put that comment up on a website that made it seem like it was something official from your high school, how would you like that?"

"And I hadn't done anything?"

"Maybe just looked through a window at some girls tap dancing or something."

"Does that count as harassing girls?"

"Let's not go there. The point is you wouldn't want everything about your sex life up on a public website."

"I don't have a sex life."

"If you had a sex life — and you will, trust me."

"When?"

"I was twenty-five before I —"

"No way!"

"In God's own good time, my son."

"You don't even believe in God!"

"But God believes in *you*, Yimmy."

"Whatever. What's on that website that you hate so much?"

"Never you mind. Suffice it to say, most people get run over by history. But I'm not going to let that happen to me."

"Wow."

Hmm. "Was that ironic?" Nathaniel asked.

"No," Jimmy said.

"The apple never falls too far from the tree."

"I don't know what you mean. Jimmy sounded slightly irritated.

"All I really mean is that my father was very, very passive. If there was a mistake on a bill in a restaurant, he simply couldn't bring himself to complain about it. It drove me wild as a boy. I am not like my father, as God is my witness!"

"I'm not like that either," Jimmy said.

"Good. If you mean you're not like *my* father. Turn in your assignments, and on time. And don't look through windows at tap dancing girls."

"Okay."

"Or you will be run over by history."

"Whatever."

There was a lull. Oh, no! Nathaniel thought. Not the father-and-son-we-really-don't-have-anything-to-talk-about syndrome.

"Actually I've been sort of seeing two girls!"

"Thank god."

"Really?"

"I wouldn't want my boy to be a goddamned queer!"

"Dad!"

"Sorry. Couldn't resist."

"But I can't decide which one I like best."

"Better."

"What?"

"Of the two. *Better*, not best."

"Yeah, whatever."

"Are these the same two you mentioned before?

"No. I don't like them anymore. I like Lindsey. She's very beautiful. She wants to be an actress. She's in my theater class."

"But?"

"She's a bit stuck up."

"Drop her."

"I haven't quite got her yet, so I can't drop her!"

"What about the other one?"

"Darla. She's sort of short, but she really seems to like me."

"How short?"

"What do you mean?"

"I mean, is she like a dwarf?"

"No that bad. She's sort of plain-looking."

"She looks like a plane?"

"Not an airplane! She's a lot shorter than me."

"But you're a giant."

"No, I'm not! There are seventeen boys in my class who are taller than I am. Plus Twyla Provoliak."

"Who?"

"This girl on the soccer team. She's six-nine."

"Don't date Twyla."

"We call her Twilight Zone."

"You kids."

"It's between Lindsey and Darla. By the way, my mom thinks Twyla is hot. . . . I don't need to know who my mom thinks is hot, do I?"

Lecture time! "Your parents are not just your parents, Yimmy, remember. They're human beings with needs and wants of their own."

"But my mom is with Lana."

"Even lesbians' eyes wander, my child."

"Whatever. Yuck."

Okay, I won't tell you about my dalliances in the fog-shrouded night. "Let me see if I can get this picture clear in my head. You really like Lindsey, is that it?"

"I do! The way she moves."

"But she's not sure about you, right?"

"Sort of."

"But Darla is after you."

"I guess. She's always smiling at me in the corridors at school. And giggling."

"Have you talked to both of them?"

"Sure, Lindsey at least. I wait for her after school sometimes."

"But you don't expose yourself to her, right?"

"Dad!"

"Just checking. No son of mine is going to be accused of harassing anybody!"

"Sometimes I think she really likes me, and then other times she's sort of cold."

"You don't want a bi-polar girlfriend."

"She's very popular."

"They always are, but remember, son, those types tend to fade immediately after high school. You see them at the tenth year reunion and they're as big as army wives, even when they're not army wives. They shop at the Dress Barn — and they wear the whole store."

Not a chuckle.

"Darla's always talking to me. She even let me kiss her once."

"Where?"

"On the steps."

"Darla has steps?"

"She let me kiss her on her mouth while we were on the steps at the back of school. Dad, I don't think you're taking this seriously."

"I'm sorry. You're just not the first, or the last, human being to go through this, Jimmy. You should know that. Go on."

"You sure you want to hear?" Jimmy was pissed.

"Of course." Nathaniel did want to hear. He also felt just a faint twinge of resentment. He recalled his own high school days — no way in hell could he ever, ever have told anybody, let alone his father, that he couldn't decide between Mikey Reynolds and Melvin Macintosh and needed help deciding! Hell for all eternity or Purgatory for seven billion years, yeah, we'll help you decide, you fucking homo!

"So, really," Jimmy said with some urgency, "how do I get Lindsey? Though maybe you're not the one to ask — you know, about girls!"

"Hey! I dated girls."

"You did?"

"Of course."

"How many?"

"Ten or so."

"Really?"

"Is that so hard to believe?"

"No, you don't seem gay. You've a big guy and everything."

"You think all gay men are little?"

"I didn't mean that."

"Not only *lesbians* like Twyla are big, son. I'm joking, I'm joking! Your mom and Lana aren't big, I know that."

"So, anyway, what did you say to get them to go out with you?"

"Well . . . to tell the truth they asked me."

"To go out?"

"Yes!"

"All of them?"

"Yes. Maybe I asked out one."

"Were they dogs?"

"*No*! Jesus. I was tall. I was six-one at fifteen."

"Did you ever sleep with them?"

"Jimmy!"

"Never?"

"No."

"I like the beautiful ones," Jimmy admitted.

"How odd of you."

"I can't tell if Lindsey wants to go to the Mating Ball or not."

Nathaniel paused. "Back up. Did you say Mating Ball?"

"A dance. Our class council came up with it. It's named after the way some snakes get all bunched up in a tree. It doesn't really mean we're going to mate."

"Still, you're going to try, right? The names of dances have sure changed since my day, sonny! We had the Spring Hop and maybe Cupid's Caprice and —"

"Cupid's what?"

"It meant a girl could ask a boy." Nathaniel started to say that it certainly didn't mean a boy could ask another boy, but he decided not to.

"I'm just not sure Lindsey wants to go with me."

"Then ask Darla."

"But Darla's a dog!"

"Jimmy!"

"Well, she is!"

"Maybe she has inner beauty."

"I don't think so. Besides, she giggles too much."

Fatherly lecture #2: "You might like her a bunch once you get to know her."

"You think so?"

"You never know."

Of course it doesn't mean you'll want to fuck her. My son, my son, I understand the male body — better than most, I do believe. All that bullshit about what men are supposed to be attracted to, but aren't, is just that — Grade A Bullshit. Men are deeply carnal beings, always will be. You cannot lie to your penis! Nor should you.

"If I go to the dance with Darla, maybe she'll . . . you know. She has her own car."

"And *you* don't — good. Wait until you're twenty-one."

"To get a car?!" Jimmy was scandalized.

"To lose your virginity. To say nothing of your first car wreck."

"You want me to be a virgin until I'm twenty-one years old?! I'm weird enough already because I'm still one at seventeen!"

"Not *that* weird! There are venereal diseases. Do they teach you that in school?"

"Yeah, in Pre-Marital."

"You have a class called Pre-Marital?"

"It's not exactly a class."

"I'm proud of you, Yimmy, that you aren't afraid to admit you're a virgin. Maybe you should get them to change it to the Virgin Ball instead of the Mating Ball."

Jimmy gave an insincere laugh. "Yeah, sure. I don't tell *everybody*. It's very frustrating."

"Sex is. Believe me, I know." He couldn't bring himself to ask if Jimmy masturbated. It might be *misinterpreted.*

"There will come a time, my boy, when you will look back on all this and wonder where the teen years have fled."

"You talk funny sometimes."

"Well, like, uh, you know, like, I'm weird. You *know?*"

"It's okay, Dad, the way you talk. I sort of like it."

There was a warm buzz in Nathaniel's heart. "Don't worry, Yimmy, a boy like you — you'll get laid."

Nathaniel was not getting as many responses back from the Committee on Truth poll as he had expected. What's wrong with these teachers?! he cursed. How could they stand to be demeaned on a public website, their integrity not simply questioned but trashed? Didn't they realize that insults and chaos in the classroom itself lay just a few heartbeats away? He'd heard more than a few teachers, especially females, say that they had noticed increasing rudeness among their students, more "misbehavior." "Misbehavior" in a college classroom, for God's sake. Wake up, you fools!

Or were they *not* lies?

Even Haywood Wire hadn't been in touch since he'd found that review accusing him of sexual harassment. Was it *true*, or was Haywood just ashamed now that he had shown it to Nathaniel, or because Haywood might seem to be at least a voyeur? Oh, great, my one ally isn't communicating with me, and he's a Fucking Peeping Tom Santa Claus!

So Nathaniel took one of the more unsavory reviews of Tadd Dryer from the growing Committee on Truth folder and slipped through the opening between their two offices and placed it on Tadd's desk. It said:

> i hate mr dryer. i hate him. i hate him. he is so BOREING he
> makes me want to puke in order to have something happend
> in that class. i am a christain myself. but he makes everything
> seem like the lord's will and how we must apreciate it and love
> it and i hate his guts and hope he retires and i hate shakespeere
> too!

It didn't take long for a reaction. Nathaniel was just about to leave and go home and give Slacker her new medication and then take a nap before his night class when he heard Tadd Dryer enter his own office, put his briefcase down on the floor as he always did, and then seat himself at his desk. There was an intake of breath, almost a snort, an angry snort, and then Tadd got up and threw open the door of his office and came over to Nathaniel's office and knocked hard on the already-open door.

"Nathaniel, are you there?"

Nathaniel's heart raced. Had he gone too far? "Yes."

Tadd came in, all five-foot-two of him. He had taken off his suit coat and his suspenders showed. His face was changing color before Nathaniel's very eyes. It had been a warm pink, but now it had become just short of purple. "Did you put this review on my desk?"

"Yes."

"Why?"

"I want teachers to see what is being said about them on the website." Nathaniel could feel his own face coloring.

"I thought I told you I don't read anonymous things. I thought I told you I don't want to see my reviews. Not even the good ones."

"There aren't any good ones." It had slipped out before Nathaniel could stop it. "Or not very many."

"I don't care how many there are!" Tadd roared. "I don't want to see them! I don't care what they say!"

"It's not whether you see them, Tadd. It's whether *students* are seeing them."

"What good does it do to show me these insults? I can't help it if some student jerk thinks I'm boring! *He's* boring! I know who it is!"

"But that's just the point. You don't know who it, Tadd. You could assume it's somebody and yet be completely wrong and that could even affect the grade you give a person. That's just one of the things wrong with this website."

"I'm quite capable of figuring it out."

"No, you're not. None of us are."

"I don't want to read them! Have you *got* that?" Tadd's eyes were two big pustules of anger about to explode all over Nathaniel. It didn't seem likely that he was going to turn the other cheek.

"I know it hurts to read those."

"I don't give a shit what they say!"

"But you do give a shit. That's why you're over here." In your suspenders.

"I wouldn't be over here if you hadn't put this goddamned thing on my desk!"

"There's another one here that's actually worse." Nathaniel began to look through the Committee on Truth folder. "And something must be done about them."

"I told you I don't want to see these! What's wrong with you?" Tadd's face was now beyond purple into something close to Jove on Mt. Olympus having a stroke.

"But they're accusing you not just of being boring but of being incompetent! Look what it says." Nathaniel had it in his hand.

"Not another word!" Tadd shouted. "Not another word about that website! *Ever!*"

"But it says you've been seen farting on the students' papers before you return them!"

Tadd was shaking his tiny fist in the air and shouting even louder. Nathaniel really thought that he might attack him. He threw down the "farting" review on the Committee on Truth folder. "Fine! Be a victim, Tadd! I won't give you any more of your reviews!"

"Don't you ever put anything on my desk again as long as you live!" Tadd slammed out of Nathaniel's office, got his coat, locked his own office, and stomped away.

"Fine!" Nathaniel muttered to himself. "Kill the messenger!"

There was an e-mail from Haywood Wire:

Sorry I haven't been in touch. Had dental work done. Wisdom teeth pulled.

Your wisdom pulled along with the teeth? Please, no! I need your help. And of course you had a beard de-staining too, I hope, all the better to tap dance with the ladies.

Nathaniel was home reading the message on his own computer. He looked at his own face reflected, poorly, in the computer screen. I have the face of a Minotaur, sort of bull-like. Half-man, half-bull. It shows a certain virility, waning virility perhaps, but there's life in the old prick yet! I will find someone's heartfelt fellatio soon! he swore, reading the rest of Haywood's e-mail:

> I have discovered a review on the site that may be the one that will open this thing up once and for all. That review about me harassing my women students is one of these to cite if we sue for libel, but it makes me uncomfortable to use my own reviews. It's seem self-serving. So I'd rather use other ones. Like this one below for Nona Dwibble. Do you know her. I don't know her personally myself, but someone informs me that she is a former nun who uses a wheelchair. Is this correct? Perhaps this awful review will get her on board with us.

The 'review' followed:

> I had had many teachers, but the one I had enjoyed the most is Miss Dwibble. When I went to see her in her office she made the eyes at me. At first I was suprised. But soon she had undid my fly and I was on top of her. Her wheelchair made it dificult to have the full position I prefer, but when I entered her her bosoms rose up to 'greet' me. She sighed so softly as I rammed my way into her sweet nunnery, or "love place" as she called it,

125

and she had to caution me not to cry out cuz her office is next to the Duplicating Office and we might be overheard. But all was well between us, and I liked her best when she was kittenish, but, no, maybe she was even better when she was a she-devil of desire. I recommend Miss Dwibble highly, and let it be known that she's got no GAG reflex! Even if she is in her sixties, she's one hot nun bitch!

Perfect! Nathaniel thought. *Now* we'll get the bastards! Clearly an out-and-out libel — her office wasn't anywhere *near* the Duplicating Office! Better than that, this was pornography!

He pondered the review for a moment. Sister Nona did it in her wheelchair? In her office? With students? She didn't seem to have any breasts at all, let alone breasts that would rise to 'greet' you. Nona kittenish? Well, maybe. Nona she-devilish? Even Nathaniel's ex-Catholic animosity toward the Church couldn't summon up images of Nona Dwibble being a she-devil in her wheelchair, although he *had* seen her clip a corner or two on the handicapped ramp at Arts.

He decided that the Committee on Truth should send Nona a copy of her review, in case she had missed it. She wasn't exactly up to speed in the New Technology, Nathaniel was pretty sure. As he was making the copy, it crossed his mind that Nona might take umbrage the same way Tadd Dryer had. Would she roll, in her wheelchair, from the other side of the English Department, both arms raised against Nathaniel. "How dare you send me this filthy review! Of course it's not true that I have intercourse! I've never had intercourse. Nor will I ever have intercourse! Intercourse comes from the Devil!" Or perhaps something quite different, though just as angry: "What I do in my office with my students is my own business, you bastard! How would you like to be an ex-nun in a wheelchair, you goddamned promiscuous pervert out getting your dick sucked night and day!" And there would be Nathaniel's body sprawled in the hallway, Nona doing "wheelies" across his forehead, the life gushing out of him.

He would send her the review anyway. Somebody had to call attention to the crimes being committed here, for god's sake! Either Shite College is a students' nightmare of abuse beyond bearing or irresponsible, evil cyberfuckers are having a field day at the faculty's expense. And I'm pretty certain the culprits are not the teachers. Oh, sure, some of them are boring and some of them are lazy and some of them come late and some have bad speaking habits, with a few as nutty as the students, but nobody deserves this kind of treatment!

He carried the review over to Nona's office and put his ear next to the door. No one was stirring inside, not even a mouse, so he double checked the name plate: Wynona Y. Dwibble, then folded the pornographic review and slid it under the door.

He felt quite anxious. Why kind of response *would* he get? Would she even answer? Nathaniel answered all correspondence immediately and didn't understand why everybody else didn't do the same. He didn't think that he was *that* much smarter than the others on the staff, but they were so *slowwww* in doing things. Maybe there's an underground resistance movement to Teachersonparade building right this minute without his knowledge? They'd find Dude Lather's hard drive and smash it with axes!

Yeah, sure.

As he was leaving, he noticed that there seemed to be more flyers for the review website posted outside the English Department. Maybe he should post Nona's review there as well! The nerve of these people. He stopped and read one of the flyers.

HAVE YOU REVEIWED YOUR TEACHERS YET???!

NEVER TOO LATE!

SEE WHAT OTHER'S THINK.

GET SATISAFACTION.

TRY ACTION!

Now the fuckers were even using rhyme! If you could call it that. The influence of Rap no doubt. I like that John Keats 'cause he got beats! Greeting card verse with Attitude. Nasty Attitude. Now there were separated tabs at the bottom of the flyer so that people could tear off the web address and take it with them.

Nathaniel reached up to tear down the flyer from the wall. Nothing was supposed to be posted on the walls. He would have torn it down anyway. This way he didn't have to care if anybody saw him and "reported" him. Dr. Tack is tearing down the only means STUDENTS have to get a better educashun!!!

Try studying. Most education is self-induced anyway.

Just as took the flyer down, he noticed a young man at the far end of the hallway who was stapling more flyers to a bulletin board. He was tall, thin-bodied, and horse-faced with blonde/blue hair, using a gigantic staple gun, holding a stack of flyers in his other hand. You could tell by just looking at him that he was a bad speller. My God, it's Dude Lather himself! Nathaniel all but cried out. Here in the English Department posting those goddamned flyers right in our faces!

Nathaniel hesitated. Were other people permitted to post flyers on the faculty's bulletin boards? Was there *nothing* the faculty could have for itself? He didn't know the actual rule, but at least this had not happened before. These bulletin boards were for class schedules and the occasional manila envelope with returned assignments and tests.

He made himself walk over to see if those were really the Teachersonparade flyers that the skinny young man was stapling with such gusto. Nathaniel's eyesight wasn't as good as it used to be; still, he could see that the flyers seemed identical to the one he had just taken down.

His throat raspy with rage, Nathaniel said, "What are you doing?"

The skinny dude glanced over his shoulder at him but didn't say anything, lifting his huge stapler to shoot two or three quick ones into the flyer he was holding against the bulletin board.

"Stop that!" Nathaniel said.

The younger man hunched his back as if warding off Nathaniel's presence, almost crouching.

"Did you hear me?

The young man turned around, his horse face showing all the deep intelligence of a . . . horse. He wore granny glasses besides and had the tiniest mouth hole Nathaniel had ever seen on a human being. "What's it to you? Who are you?" The stun gun looked downright menacing from this angle. The fluorescent lighting didn't help either.

Oh, great, now I'm going to be attacked with a staple gun! Nathaniel winced. He decided the better part of valor was lying. "I'm a dean here at the school. Those flyers shouldn't be posted here."

"A dean approved them!" Dude flashed the APPROVED FOR POSTING stamp. Ah, the Pope had spoken!

The student turned back and continued stapling, determined. But he did glance back to see if Nathaniel was going to attack him.

"Do you know the kinds of stupid, lying reviews that are on that website?"

"Most of the reviews are positive. 67.8 percent!"

"How do you know that?"

"I counted them."

"I'll bet! You're just making up the statistics."

"Who are you? Why do I have to answer to you? Dean Deane approved them!" Dude waved the approved flyers in the air.

"Did you tell the dean that you don't even have to be a student to use this ridiculous website?"

"It's for students! It's all for students!"

"Then why didn't you set it up so that only *real* students can use it then! And only one review per teacher!"

"Because the school wouldn't give me the students' ID numbers."

"But you went ahead anyway, is that what you're saying?"

"Yes, I went ahead. Students are entitled to this information!"

Nathaniel was somewhat surprised at the ideology glimmering in the not-very-bright eyes. But then why should he be surprised. Ideology often burned brightest in the dimmest eyes.

"Do you not realize that people are being accused of having sex with their students! Is this the kind of information students are entitled to know?! I just delivered an obscene review of Ms. Dwibble, under her door."

"Why did you write an obscene review of Ms. Dwibble?"

"I didn't *write* the review! I just delivered it to her office. It says she had sex in her wheelchair!"

"Well, maybe she does! Are you in her office all the time?"

Nathaniel's breath was temporarily suspended. "No, I'm not!"

"Then how do you know it's not true?"

"Because she's a nun and she's in a wheelchair!"

"If the review is not accurate, then the faculty member can send me an e-mail, and I will examine it to see if their complaint is legitimate or not."

"Why, you little shit!" Nathaniel said. "Who appointed you God? You'll *see* if the complaint is legitimate or not. *You'll* see?! You don't have enough decency to *see* if the website works properly or not, but you'll *see* if the faculty member's complaint is legitimate or not!" Nathaniel's neck was burning up. He felt like grabbing the staple gun and stapling Dude Lather's butt-ugly face hole to the bulletin board. But he could see the headline: STUDENT ASSAULTED BY HOMOSEXUAL TEACHER.

"Don't you think it's wrong to destroy people's reputations without any proof, and the people with the destroyed reputations have all the burden to disprove the charges?"

"Students have rights!"

"But accused people have none? Several thousand years of legal tinkering to guard against vicious rumors and mere accusations as "evidence," and this is what we have to show for it? The Internet is going to wipe all that out with a few clicks of somebody's computer keys?!"

"Students can tell what's legitimate and what's not!"

"You think students have some kind of clairvoyant powers unknown to the rest of the population? You can't even read and write!"

"They can sift through what's there and make the right choice! The Internet is at last the way to achieve true democracy!"

"Most people don't vote, and many don't even know what they're voting about. Democracy isn't perfection on earth, you jerk!"

"Students will bring justice to this school! To all schools!"

It was like arguing with a religious fanatic. Light the Auto de Fe! The STUDENTS have spoken!

Only Nathaniel felt just as fanatical. And he knew he was right and Dude Lather was wrong!

"Besides I think the review you're referring to was removed."

"You think? You're not sure?"

"I'm pretty sure it was removed."

"And why so?"

"That is the webmaster's decision." Dude Lather's eyes ignited. "Hey, I think I know who you are! You're not a dean!"

"How do you know whether I'm a dean or not?"

"Where's *your* ID?"

So Dude Lather was turning legalistic on him! "For you information deans don't have to carry no stinking badges!"

"Yeah, but they want to make the students have to carry identification cards to use the computers around here!"

"Good."

"Why is it the students have to prove themselves, but you deans don't?!" The staple gun was at the ready.

Nathaniel took a step back. "We are getting off the point. The point is you cannot put up flyers advertising that website where you're putting them!"

"And just where am I supposed to put them then? Huh?" Dude Lather shot back.

"Don't tempt me to tell you where to put your flyers, Mr. Lather." Again the potential headline screamed in Nathaniel's head:

GAY TEACHER TELLS STUDENT TO SHOVE IT

Sexual Harassment Charges Likely

"I'm afraid this website of yours is dragging me down to its level," Nathaniel managed. "I expect some TV scandal show to show up with a microphone in this hallway any moment!"

"Now I know! You're *Dr. Tack*, aren't you!"

Should he deny it?

"I've seen pictures of you, on your books."

Oh, a fan?

"When you were younger."

Fuck you.

"The point I am trying to make, Mr. Lather, or one of them, is that you as the webmaster enjoy far too much power over the lives of . . . of your betters." (Should he simply have said *faculty*?)

"That's exactly why my site exists!" Dude said, fully lathered. "You think teachers are *better* than students! Don't you! Don't you?!"

It was some latter-day Proletarian Inquisition crapola like: You say the People are not holy? Not holy — the *People!!!* We will show you who is holy and who is not!!!! Down with you elitist swine!!!! (Oxymoron be damned.) We will not rest until the world is free of punctuation!!!! And spelling.

"It's people like you," Nathaniel retaliated, "who give the People a bad name!"

"You *are* Dr. Tack, I'm sure now."

Dude Lather gave Nathaniel a good glancing-over, as if to memorize his features.

"You seem to believe that teachers were never students, Mr. Lather. We were, and for a long time."

"You have no sympathy for the problems of the students here!"

"In your case you're absolutely right. I have no sympathy for you or students like you.

You shouldn't even be in any college worthy of the name. All the signs of your 'educashun' call for a complete and utter condemnation of any system that passed you through it."

"I never had no easy time in school! I'm not gifted! But, by god, I got through, and I'm going to graduate this college at the end of this semester, and then I'll have my degree. So screw you!"

"Another turd passed at Shite College. I can hear the Chancellor crowing at the graduation ceremony already."

"You're mean! You're just mean!"

"And you and your ilk *made* me what I am today! You're a spoiled, brainless nincompoop who disgraces not only American education but the entire Great Chain of Being!"

"The what?"

"I rest my case!"

The young man turned back and began furiously stapling more flyers. "We'll see who wins this battle!" he spat back at Nathaniel.

"I guess we will. And it won't be staple guns at thirty paces. It'll have to be a lawsuit, I can see that now."

Dude Lather gave a scary smile. "Then you'll lose, because the law is on my side, asshole!"

His stomach was not doing well from its combination of white wine, pork fried rice, and Maalox. That's what I get for eating Babe, Nathaniel told himself, vomiting into the toilet. God, who invented vomit! Especially the part where the saliva trickles into your mouth but the real stuff won't quite come, and you're not sure if it ever will and you might have to stare down into the Toilet Void forever.

He wiped his mouth clean and got off his knees and went back to his office. He had a night office hour that he'd better stay for it, even though he felt terrible. Was it the aftermath of the run-in with Dude Lather? It had been three days. Post-stress syndrome? Nathaniel had of course gone back and ripped down all the vigorously stapled flyers he could find. Another person, presumably a faculty member, saw him and said, "They just come back the next day" and skulked off. He'd always had a cast-iron stomach. Was that about to go now because of this cyber sickness in their midst?

He hadn't heard anything from Nona Dwibble about the obscene review. Should he go see her in person?

The news was full of stories about students shooting their teachers: for any reason they damned well felt like: Failing grades. Bad Home Lives. Upset Stomachs. Maybe Teachersonparade wasn't all that bad compared to bullets in your chest. No, that way lay cowardice.

And where the hell was Haywood Wire? He hadn't been in touch for a week or more. Was he an ally or wasn't he?

The only person who came to the office hour was somebody who had simply disappeared from class a couple of years before and now wanted a Retroactive Withdrawal instead of the F he had earned. Nathaniel signed the paper. What the hell.

Then he went to his mailbox a couple of floors down. He hadn't been there for a whole day, tired of the same old spam from the offices on campus, losing hope that the Committee on Truth would get any help from pissed-off teachers. What did it take to get these people angry? Did they have no self-respect?

There was an envelope with a message inside — from Dean Calvin Visigoth, all nice and formal looking, letterhead and everything. Only two typos. So the staff was getting better! One sentence jumped out at Nathaniel: "Perhaps you would like to meet with me in my office next week, at your convenience, to discuss the teacher review website."

Aha! Was the Administration at last seeing the error of its ways? Why shouldn't the Administration be an ally of the faculty instead of an obstacle? Why had it taken them this long to see the problem? Or was it a trap?

Nathaniel set up an appointment for the first available day the dean had free. He spoke to a secretary with bad English skills, as usual, and was almost sure that he was supposed to go on Tuesday at ten in the morning.

At least he showed up at that time. Dean Visigoth's office was in the former Student Union Building, recently renamed the Chairman Mao Anti-Discrimination Building through the vigorous lobbying and picketing efforts of the Alliance of Students

The dean was dealing with a student discipline problem, and a little bit of the interaction seeped out of the inner office as Nathaniel waited on a rather ordinary hardwood chair in the outer one – a lawsuit waiting to happen, the dean sued by the Alliance of Students: "Confidential matters involving a Student were carelessly and even criminally allowed to leak out and be overheard by others, thus irreparably injuring the self-esteem of said Student . . ."

"So I will reinstate you in Mr. Crevasse's class, as long as you promise not to copy answers from any more tests. Is that clear?"

"I guess."

"Is it clear or not?"

"Yes."

Wow, the dean was coming down really hard on this student! He made him make an actual promise not to cheat again. Of course the student had already cheated and was being put back in the class after the teacher had probably asked for his removal. Welcome to Shite College! On your Left you will find the remnants of what was once called college education.

The student emerged a minute later, a ring in his nose and his pants seat down below the backs of his knees, and waddled off. In the Old Days this would have meant that the student had been — heavens! — punished, even paddled, in order for his nose, gait, and trousers to be in such a pitiful state. Now it just meant that he was wearing what was considered "cool." The ass of your pants so low you wobbled like someone with a brain disorder was now "cool." *Double Eeek!* Nathaniel had seen student fashions come and go over the years, but he simply could not abide these. Am I just an old fart about this, or is this not truly a fashion that will bring howls of laughter when eons to come look back at our time?

The dean would see him now.

Dean Visigoth was as ugly as ever, the fat, somewhat threatening leprechaun in the tight blue blazer. But he'd had work on his smoker's teeth, hadn't he? He had a handsome office, with lots of space and tidy file cabinets in off-cream. There was even a picture of the dean's wife and his two teenage children, turned just enough so that a visitor could see the lovely Heidi Ho and the two Eurasian sons, who resembled their mother.

"I know you've been upset by some of the reviews on the website," the dean began.

"I don't see why more people aren't upset."

"Perhaps you take them too personally. The students are just venting."

"Let them vent somewhere else. In the cafeteria, the way we vented when we were students."

There was a soft lift of a shoulder that told Nathaniel the dean was rejecting the proffered camaraderie.

"And there are always toilet walls," Nathaniel added.

The dean looked up from the paperwork left over from the cheating student who had just left. "As I believe I told you, I am the faculty sponsor of the site."

"I'm aware of that."

"I took on that responsibility because no one else seemed to want to. The students checked around and came to me when they had exhausted their options."

Nathaniel moved uneasily in his chair. "You should have said no too."

"But I chose to support the site. And do you want me to tell you why I did?"

Nathaniel was pretty certain the dean was going to tell him.

"I took it on because I believe in free speech. I believe that it is a very special right and one that needs to be nurtured."

"I'm a gay writer, Dean Visigoth. I also believe in free speech. I have some idea how difficult that has been for some people to get. I'll spare you the saga of my hardship days. ("How dare you send your fucking homo stuff to our magazine!" Plus the publisher of the *New York Times* admitting years later that his paper never reviewed gay books, or only reviewed them negatively, during the years when Nathaniel's works, virtually alone, were trying to humanize the despised image of homosexuals. And now again, after a generation, it was getting almost impossible to find an agent or a publisher for his work.)

"Yes, I hear you're a very good writer. I'm sorry to say I haven't read any of your books."

"Shall I drop some off?" Nathaniel said, smiling.

"Perhaps that'll have to wait until I enroll in one of your classes."

Ouch! A slap at the fact that Nathaniel used one of his own books in two classes? "I believe even gays count as part of the Beauty of Diversity Program here on campus. Do they not?"

"Of course they do," the dean said.

Yeah, sure, Nathaniel thought. Gays were finally included on the list with every indigenous cannibal tribe in the Amazon and every whining bellyaching, self-promoting Darwinian ethnic struggler in the Diverse universe, but there was always the sense that they weren't legitimate, not really. In fact, he was the *only* one in the entire English Department, no doubt in the whole school, who used a gay text.

Or am I just imagining the resistance?

I don't think so. Louise Beeze, the Cat Lady, had tried to use a gay history book once in her Reading for Our Times class and had had serious opposition, she'd told Nathaniel. It had surprised her. What a sweetheart Louise was. Too bad she was such a . . . such a . . . "Yeah, I gotta read this fucking homo book from this fucking Cat Lady!"

"I'm hoping that you have changed your mind about sponsoring the review website," Nathaniel continued.

The dean looked a bit aggrieved. "That's not my intention in asking you to see me."

"Hard to believe." Nathaniel feigned a smile.

"I think the site serves a very useful purpose, if used properly."

"But it's not being used properly! That's my main point." Nathaniel could feel his voice rising and tried to stop it.

"We cannot let its basic good qualities be driven out by its bad."

"I see very few good qualities in the website," Nathaniel said. How about sissy tears — would those work?

"Some teachers could benefit from a bracing review or two."

And what about a dean, if only *his* bad reviews weren't removed?

"I am no blind defender of teachers, including myself," Nathaniel said. "That's why we have faculty peer observations. A student can even write a letter to you, a letter of complaint, is that not so?"

"The students feel that the Administration ignores the genuine complaints of the students."

"That's funny, I feel that the Administration ignores the genuine complaints of the faculty."

The dean was quite calm. No sweat apparently had flowed over that forehead in many a year. "It's very difficult to get teachers to change their ways."

"And do you think they will change because lies are told about them online?"

"It's all rather complicated, isn't it?"

This time it was Nathaniel who rejected the proffered we're-all-in-this-problem-together move by the dean. "Have you seen this review of Nona Dwibble of the English Department? I've taken the liberty of bringing it today in case you haven't." Nathaniel drew it out from the inside pocket of his sports jacket. "You know who she is, correct?"

"Yes, I know Nona quite well."

Nathaniel handed over the obscene review. The dean even stood to take it.

Nathaniel waited anxiously as it was read.

The dean's eyes met his. "Is this still up on the site?"

"I really couldn't say."

"I doubt that's it's still there."

"I don't think how long it's there is the issue. If this were written on a hallway wall, would we call it free speech and leave it there?"

"I don't think the situations are the same."

"You're right. No one defends the filth on the hallway wall, but if it's on some review site of teachers then it's all right. Maybe it's even Scripture!"

The dean seemed to feel the heat coming off Nathaniel's words, but he didn't react with more than a slight flicker of the eyes. "I won't defend the content. Nevertheless, I don't think the entire site is to blame for an occasional aberration like this." The dean got up again and handed the paper back to Nathaniel.

"Perhaps you should keep it for your records, Dean Visigoth."

"That isn't necessary. That review is obviously inappropriate. I still nevertheless defend the principle of students reviewing their teachers. Even anonymously."

"What if they're *not* the students of the people they're reviewing? Do you still defend it?"

"I don't think that happens, Dr. Tack. I think you are trying to divert the issue from reviews about yourself that you may not like, to a more agreeable issue."

"Are you saying that I find this obscene review of Nona Dwibble agreeable?"

The dean's brow was furrowing somewhat. Obviously he was not happy with the way the discussion was going. "Perhaps my phrasing was not the most felicitous," he admitted. "I didn't mean to imply that you enjoyed that obscene review of Ms. Dwibble."

Oh, who are we kidding! Nathaniel thought. It's the funniest thing that's happened around the dopey campus in years.

"Well, I hope not," Nathaniel said, halfway up on his high horse.

"I just hope, Dr. Tack, that you will be able to live with the website, despite its shortcomings. Maybe it will even fade away if it is left alone."

"I don't think so. It's getting worse."

"Could that be from the attention you have brought to it?"

"Possibly. However, I don't think the answer to a vicious reality is to do nothing and merely hope it all goes way."

"I have seen such reviews in the past. Printed ones. They tend to fade with time."

"This time it's on the Internet. It's in cyberspace. It won't fade away. It just stays there, accessible by anybody in the whole world. The printed reviews in the past were supervised. I saw them too. And there was never anything about having sex in them."

"I fear you are getting a bit too exercised over this, Dr. Tack."

"It's the only exercise I get!" Nathaniel shot back.

Only the dean did not laugh, did not smile. The joke went over like an ex-nun in a wheelchair over Niagara Falls. "Why don't you just try to ignore the website?"

"There have only been a few causes I have fought for in my life, Dean Visigoth, and this is one of them. I will not ignore these reviews."

"I'm afraid we don't see eye to eye on this issue, do we?" Coldly, the dean stood up as though the interview were over.

Nathaniel held his ground. He was not leaving with the website still functioning the way it was. Never! "Dean, how do you think you'd feel if that were a review of *you* having sex? With your secretary." Nathaniel nodded in the direction of the unseen secretary with the bad English skills. "Would you say that it should be ignored, that it doesn't matter?"

"Is there any such review?"

"Not that I'm aware of."

"I guess I'll wait until it appears then, won't I?"

Was this a dare from the dean to write it? Don't tempt me! Nathaniel thought. Who was that gentleman seen riding his Heidi Ho "comfort woman" in the Anti-Discrimination Building, huh?

"The site should not be set up so that such things *can* happen! I'm sorry, that is not free speech! It's some horrible corruption of a wonderful principle. Just like this stupid college is a horrible corruption of the wonderful principle of education!"

Now he'd gone too far! He could see it in the dean's glaring eyes.

"I guess some of our faculty simply don't believe in the Constitution of the United States, it appears."

"What?"

"I perhaps should point out, Dr. Tack, that you've been *seen*."

"I've been *seen*? What does that mean?"

The fat "Leper-chaun" now looked more like a python. He struck: "You were seen ripping down flyers that had been approved by Dean Deane's office!"

Nathaniel's stomach went queasy. Should he deny it? Was there video of him doing it? Who had seen him? Of course it had to be Dude Lather! Well, it's my word against his!

"Those flyers should never have been approved in the first place. Dean Deane didn't even check to see if the site protected the basic rights of the faculty!"

"They were approved nonetheless."

"I don't care if they were approved or not. Who says they're right just because some activist crazies intimidated a weak dean into giving them the power to destroy reputations with no proof whatsoever!"

"The reviews that are on the site will not be used in school tenure or for promotions or for —"

136

"Pardon me, Dean Visigoth, but that's bull." Nathaniel held the "-shit" at the last second. "Of course they will be used. Because if a teacher stops getting twenty bodies in his classes, dead or alive, he won't have a job here."

"You seem rather sour about the school where you work. Are you sure you want to work here?"

"I am sour, but I haven't given up yet, the way quite a few around here have. They've simply thrown in the towel. I'm trying to make this place an institution of higher learning. *Higher*, not lower!"

"Did you or did you not rip down flyers in one of the buildings on campus? Perhaps even more than that?"

It seemed to be turning into charges against Nathaniel once again! Where did these people get their training as Administrators — with Milosevic in some Baltic nightmare?

"I'm not saying I did so, but what would my criminal violation be exactly?"

"Let's not be legalistic, Dr. Tack. Please! Although the Alliance of Students *is* drawing up a list of possible charges. I think they range from denying students their Constitutional rights to threatening a student with bodily harm while the student was acting on approved school business."

"What, no charges of interfering with a student's inherent right to staple gun the teacher of his choice?"

"Are you taking this all very lightly, Dr. Tack?"

"Don't mistake the tone for the depth of my feelings, Dean Visigoth. I'm in it for the long haul as well."

"I do have a meeting I must attend. Is there anything else you wish to say?"

"In my defense? Is that what you mean? When did *I* go on the defense in this ridiculous matter?"

"When you tore down those flyers, I would imagine," the dean said, sliding in the fangs.

"I never said I tore them down!" Nathaniel said, suddenly panicking.

"I'm sure we'll all be hearing a great more about this, Dr. Tack. We can sort it out at that time." He stood in such a way that there was no question that the meeting was at its end.

But Nathaniel wouldn't stand. Moist though his rear end was, he stayed where he was. "You do you know that you've been *seen* too, Dean Visigoth?"

"I beg you pardon?"

"Your reviews on the website are manipulated."

"I don't know what you're talking about." Maybe not, but the dean's eyes sure looked shifty.

"When *you* get bad reviews, they are removed. Furthermore, good ones are sent in to replace them — all no doubt to ensure that *you* stay on the so-called Tip of the Top, thus guaranteeing you enrollment for your History 12 class."

"This is the first I've heard of this."

Haywood's collection of reviews had better be right!

"Do you deny it?" I can play this game, Nathaniel thought.

"I don't believe I have to deny it," the dean said icily.

"The website is complete fraud from top to bottom, and some people are benefiting from it, and some are being screwed."

"Hope you aren't accusing me of anything, Dr. Tack. Are you?"

"I don't know you well enough to do that," Nathaniel said.

"The college has a set of lawyers that is quite formidable, I do believe." The dean was at the door.

"Perhaps we'll see, won't we?" Nathaniel rose from the hot seat.

"I suspect that you are biting off more than you can chew, Dr. Tack. You really don't want to fight a battle you can't possibly win."

Nathaniel started to protest more – to say that if these were reviews about students instead of faculty they'd not only be torn down but the culprits prosecuted and probably put to death! But he wouldn't give the goddamned dean the satisfaction. He'd rather fry in Hell first. (Be careful what you wish for.)

While he waited for one ax or another to fall, he got several interesting e-mails, one from Haywood saying that he'd joined the Bill Gates Technology Discussion Group on campus, an online group started by a visiting Palestinian instructor, who was based in the Yasser Arafat Wing of the Engineering Building.

The rest of Haywood's e-mail said:

> The college has just gotten a $7 million dollar grant to upgrade
> computer services on our campus. Although I have joined, so
> far I am just "lurking" till I get the lay of the land.

Nathaniel signed on for the discussion group and read through some of the threads, all about how wonderful the grant from Bill Gates was, how generous, and how the students were going to benefit enormously from having computers up the gazoo. A lot of the talk was about whether to wire every single classroom and office or to leave some "Pre-Computer Literate." The Pre-Literates seemed to be losing the word war.

Nathaniel sent a message:

> Hello, this is Nathaniel Tack of the English Department. Am I
> wrong or has there been little or no discussion of the harmful
> effects of computers on our campus?

Almost immediately there was a reply, pre-programmed:

WELCOME TO THE BILL GATES DISCUSSION GROUP

TECHNOLOGY ANSWERING TODAY'S NEEDS!

Dr. Hamid Huumid (of Engineering)

Nathaniel decided it was a bit too Nerd Idolatrous and sent in a response:

> Forgive me if this has come up before and been discussed and solved, but computers on our campus have been and can be used to send obscene, vicious, and fraudulent so-called "reviews" of faculty and administrators. Don't we need to work this out? I'm no Luddite. Mad things are going on.

Haywood must have been lurking online and sent Nathaniel a rapid reply, privately:

> Congrats! This topic has NOT been discussed to my knowledge on this discussion group. Thanks for bringing it to the fore. Let's see what kind of response you get. Dean Visigoth's and others' collusion in all this will be revealed!

The response was this:

> Mr. Tack,
>
> This is not an appropriate discussion topic.
>
> Dr. Hamid Huumid (of Engineering)

Haywood saw the reply and e-mailed Nathaniel at once:

> What kind of reply is that? What could be more relevant than a discussion of the misuse of this technology? I guess $7 million carries a big stick!

Nathaniel wrote back to the discussion group:

> If libel is being perpetrated via the computers on our very own campus, it seems to me there is every reason to discuss this topic. — Dr. Nathaniel Tack

Again privately Haywood wrote:

> Way to go, Nathaniel! You've got grit!
>
> Keep giving it to them! The college must pay!

This was followed by a message to the entire membership, some 48 staff and faculty members:

> Professor Tack,
>
> I must ask you to refrain from discussing this

topic on this discussion group!

> Dr. Hamid Huumid (of Engineering)

Nathaniel wrote back:

> We cannot discuss the most relevant aspects of the underbelly of the Internet here? Then where? Why is there so much discussion of Free Speech everywhere except where it clearly matters?

> GREAT! Keep it going!

This from Haywood, standing by, still lurking. It emboldened Nathaniel, as he thought it was meant to do.

> Are we just cheerleaders for Bill Gates? He can buy our hearts and souls for a mere seven million dollars?

Nathaniel almost put "buy our asses" but decided to keep to the high road since he was now becoming so visible on the Information Highway.

> BETTER AND BETTER!

> Go get 'em, killer! Money doesn't just talk.

> It shouts! Bring the bastards to their knees! — Haywood

Followed by another message from the discussion moderator:

> Professor Tack,

> I respectfully request that you NOT say anymore on this topic,

> which is secondary to the best employment of our recent grant,

> a munificent gesture granted to our humble campus.

> God is great!

> Dr. Hamid Huumid (of Engineering)

Well, yes, the campus was humble, even lowly and unworthy, and maybe even God was great, and Bill Gates was Great too, but that didn't mean you couldn't *discuss* the horror that was descending on them all. Nathaniel shot back:

> What does it profit a man if he gains the whole computer world but suffers the loss of his soul?

With a snappy rejoinder from Dr. Huumid:

> Professor Tack, I am going to have to remove you from our discussion group if you persist in beating this topic horse to death.

They didn't even want to hear about this problem? He had hardly mentioned it, let alone beaten it to death! He didn't know exactly what to say back. Then this came:

Allowe me to offer an option for the esteemed Dr. Tack.

He is welcome to come to a meeting of the ALLIANCE FOR STUDENTS any Wensday between 3-5 in the STUDENT UNION Arena 3B to ducuss the matter of seeming importance to some "disturbed" faculty who can meet and openly duscuss matters pertinent to ALL.

I[ersonally invite Dr. Tack to come this next time. Please advise.

Nathaniel was mulling the scatter-brained, unsigned offer over when this came in from Haywood:

DON'T GO THERE!

IT WOULD BE A KANGEROO COURT.

THEY'D LIKE NOTHING BETTER THAN TO HAVE YOU ON THE ROPES. I KNOW SOMEONE WHO WAS FOOLISH ENOUGH TO TRUST THE ALLIANCE OF STUDENTS.

STAY AWAY!

Then this:

Hello, Dr. Tack. This is Suze DiMentia of the Poly Sci Department.

We've never met. But I work closely with the ALLIANCE OF STUDENTS and I just want to echo Jake's words about your being welcome to attend a meeting next week. We can hash out the topic, which as the moderator says, is not appropriate here.

Nathaniel wrote to Haywood:

Do you know this Suze DiMentia? What about her?

Haywood replied:

I don't know her, but she's a protégé of Visigoth's and associated with the Alliance of Students. Watch out! I think she may be the one who teaches a course in 'guerrilla political warfare.' Jake is probably Jake Trosky, the president of the Alliance. A complete Weirdo! Had him in class. He has Afro hair even though he's white. Late thirties. Bad skin. Avoid like the plague!

Nathaniel responded:

> This Jake Trosky sounds like the one who sent in fake reviews of me — the same physical description. Maybe these people need someone to confront them? What if we went to the Alliance meeting together?

Haywood:

> You'd have to drag me there by my beard. I'm telling you AVOID these people. They think Josef Stalin was a wimp!

Nathaniel:

> Okay, I won't meet with them. But why don't you write into the discussion group and back me about the need to discuss Teachersonparade?

Haywood:

> Keep on doing it. You're persuasive. I've mentioned the website to a few in the Statistics Department and they are as pissed off as we are. By the way, they continue to trash *you* as "Nathan Lack" on Speak Out Loud, even though I know who Nathan Lack really is.

Nathaniel:

> Is that review about you harassing your female students still up on the site?

Haywood:

> Yes! Only it's not as noticeable now since other reviews have come in. Good ones. And, no, I didn't write them myself. I have NEVER submitted a review of myself or anyone else. I wrote only to the Speak Out Loud section.

Nathaniel:

> So you think I should keep pressuring Hamid Huumid to let us talk about the problem?

Haywood:

> He's in bed with Bill Gates and Silicon interests, as are a lot of the "teckies" around here and elsewhere. They have everything to gain from the Internet, or so they think. But it's likely to come back and haunt them.

So Nathaniel sent the following privately to the moderator:

> Hello, I don't mean to be obstreperous, but it makes no sense not to try to stop the abuses that we know for a fact are

142

occurring on the Teachersonparade site. Haywood Wire and I have been trying to expose the situation for what it is. Please re-consider your ban on talking about this issue. Our school doesn't need more places where lies and obscenity and FRAUD can be posted under the guise of reviewing instructors and administrators!!

He felt the two exclamations fully justified. What he was not prepared for was the response from Haywood:

Nathaniel,

How dare you use my name in an e-mail! I did not give you permission to use it. What if Huumid sends your message to the entire group? I want an apology and a promise that you will never again do such a STUPID THING! And you even put my name first! — Haywood

Nathaniel needed to rest his eyes, which were smarting from his "ally's" words. He looked down at the rug in his bedroom/office. He really ought to run the vacuum sweeper, to get the cat hairs and the food bits, or whatever those were. He felt sick to his stomach, partly from the pungent odor coming from Slacker's litter box — he had put off cleaning it because of this damned website crap — but mostly from "STUPID THING" — in caps, no less.

How should he respond to this smack across the face? Nathaniel had deep resentment about anybody (much of the world) thinking gays were little pansies to be knocked down and insulted whenever macho fuckers wanted to restore their draining testosterone. And he was not going to let Haywood get away with anything approaching that either. At the same time Haywood was the only faculty member who'd gone even this far to stop the website problem. But who the hell needed an ally in the cyber closet?! He wrote cautiously:

Haywood:

I don't really know you all that well. I took your en-couragement about discussing the problem in our midst with Hamid Huumid as tacit agreement, I guess, especially since you said you had mentioned your opposition to colleagues. I don't feel that I owe you an "apology" because I happened to mention your name to one person in an e-mail. — Sincerely, Nathaniel

Nathaniel:

I do NOT want my name out there. Already several students have hinted in class that they think I am on some committee to shut the website down. They can, I remind you, run to any computer on campus or anywhere else and write me up. I don't want to work with you if you're going to be so stupid about it.

Well, at least "stupid" wasn't in caps this time. Nathaniel was tempted, sorely, to flame Mr. Haywood Wire right back in his ugly Santa Claus kisser, but something told him he needed this man's support, however feeble, because at the very least he had copies of all the reviews that had been sent in, including ones that had now disappeared from view, and Nathaniel didn't.

He leaned down and stroked Slacker on the floor next to him — she was trying to Meow-Meow him into giving her extra food even though the vet said she was too fat — and wrote again, stiffening his back:

> Okay, Haywood, if you demand an apology, you have mine.
> — Nathaniel

It took several minutes, but this finally came:

> It's not much of an apology. — Haywood

Nathaniel fought the impulse to send back a nasty reply. God, how he wanted to! Yet this was partly what he was fighting here, people being vicious and too quick on the trigger to slice someone's head off. He knew that was a mixed metaphor, but he didn't give a shit. His mind was in too much of a jumble about what to do. He took a deep breath. He had to be careful what he said now. What is education for if not for moments just like this? he told himself.

> Dear Haywood,
>
> You're probably right. I shouldn't have used your name. I hadn't realized how strongly you felt about this. I won't use your name without your full approval in the future. — Nathaniel

This came back:

> I'm not "probably" right. I am right. — Haywood

Don't push it, man, Nathaniel seethed. This was as far as he was willing to "apologize." What a creep Haywood was! Why the hell didn't any of the other faculty seem to want to help? But I'm not dropping this, Haywood or no Haywood. If he had to argue it alone before the Supreme Court in his underwear and barefoot, he was not dropping this cause!

Hamid Huumid didn't send Nathaniel's mention of Haywood's name to the entire discussion group, and no more e-mails were exchanged that day.

The next day this message did come in:

> I can see why Dr. Tack doesn't like the website. I checked out his reviews and his students seem not to like him, with a few exceptions. Well, I also teach hard courses, in chemistry, and yet I manage to be well liked by *my* students. I have a 4 point rating on Tip of the Top, unlike Mr. Tack. — Dr. H.R. Gunther

Who the hell was H.R. Gunther? There were so many variables here, Nathaniel didn't know where to begin. How many of Nathaniel's "reviews" were even from his students? What kind of grades did this H.R. Gunther actually give? Maybe he just thought he was "hard." Maybe he'd sent in his own reviews to bolster his enrollment. Chemistry classes were notoriously under-enrolled at Shite. Maybe this was just an ad! Maybe he'd cajoled the students into writing in!

Fortunately, Hamid Huumid came to the rescue before Nathaniel could even reply:

> This is Dr. Huumid. Eventhough I do not wish this topic appropriate for this technology discussion group, I do beg to point out to Dr. H.R. Gunther of the Chemistry Department that it is unfair in him to blame Dr. Nathaniel Tack for his bad "reviews" when the review site has no real supervision and anything on there must be taken with a grain of pepper. Dr. Hamid Huumid (of Engineering)

So maybe the grammar was a little off-kilter, the man had the problem nailed! See, bad English doesn't *always* irritate me! Maybe Nathaniel should try to hook up with Dr. Huumid instead of Haywood? Terrific. What a choice — someone who didn't want to discuss the dark side of the Internet or someone who wanted Nathaniel to take all the flak! It was getting harder to find anything funny in this whole business. Yet god help you if you stop laughing, Nathaniel warned himself.

He must have been "forgiven" because this arrived the next afternoon:

> Did you reply to Suze DiMentia? Or Jake? Just curious. What did Dean Visigoth say to you? — Haywood

Nathaniel sent a cryptic:

> You told me it wouldn't be wise for me to deal with Suze and Jake. I wouldn't want to do anything "stupid."

Haywood came back with:

> Have you seen this review that Marcus Blatty got in Statistics? It's a humdinger. It could turn around people's thinking.

Attached was:

> marcus blatty is the bomb as a teacher, man. he teaches just so-so, and he looks like a 50-year-old cockroach, but he let me go early for an appointment once, and dudes he also gave me a great *blowjob*.

Nathaniel could indeed see the usefulness of this review.

> Who is Marcus Blatty? Is he gay? Is there any truth to this at all? — Nathaniel

Blatty is a black man in the office two doors from me. He's married, not gay as far as I know, and this is just pure libel. — Haywood

I'm going to make a copy of it from what you sent me, okay? — Nathaniel

Okay, but be sure my name and e-mail address don't show anywhere! — Haywood

Of course. — Nathaniel

So he and Haywood were partners again, he guessed. Not friends, just in this cyber mess together. See, blowjobs had their multi-purposes!

He went back to the discussion group and sent a copy of the "blowjob" review to all the members with this note, making sure, by checking fifteen times, that Haywood's ID was nowhere in evidence:

To the Bill Gates Discussion Group:

Is this "blowjob" the kind of thing the celebration of campus technology is meant to inspire? Why do administrators ignore libel of their faculty? Or why not have them arrested if the charges are true!

If it wasn't quite the "blowjob heard 'round the world," at least there were ten responses, ranging from annoyance with Nathaniel for having forwarded something "obscene" (two) to indifference ("I've been called worse to my face") (one) to dismay that such a review could have made it to the website (seven). There was even an apology, from Hamid Huumid (of Engineering):

Accept my deepest regrets, kind sir, that I forbade a engagement on this abuse of the computer. You are correct that something has to be done. A "blowjob" is a serious accusation. Dr. Hamid Huumid (of Engineering)

Nathaniel wasn't completely happy with the latter response, though it did include an apology. It seemed quite possible that Dr. Huumid wasn't just objecting to the false accusation but to any and all blowjobs. No, kind sir, the blowjob can be a fine and beautiful thing, and I think most men would be much nicer if they got a few more of them. Yet it was no time to split hairs, pubic or otherwise.

Another ploy:

Dr. Tack,

We haven't heard back from you about our offer to have you speak to the Alliance of Students. Can we count on you appearing Wednesday between 3-5 in Arena 3B? It need not last the entire time. — Suze DiMentia, full-time faculty member

Nathaniel Tack,

This is Jake Trosky, full time student, and am mostinterested in haveing you're appearence at counsel metting. Do you know were Arena 3B is located?

Have you even ever been there? Please do come and get off of your chest what you want to say in person. — JT

Come to us, we won't hurt you; we just want to talk to you, to embrace you . . . *sucker!* Plus: You fucker, you haven't even made a pilgrimage to Mecca, the office of the Alliance of Students?!

Nathaniel didn't like the smell of it. He decided not to respond. He did do a little research on the organization, seeking out the unfortunately hyphenated Mabel Wang-Chew in the Speech Department. She had worked with the Alliance of Students in the past and had not enjoyed the experience, he'd heard.

He asked Gladys in the English Department for Mabel's office hours, very aware of the fact that anyone in the world could find out his office hours as well — and his classrooms — and show up with a gun "to get rid of this fuck-ass homo who doesn't want students to have free speech." Please, don't shoot! I almost *never* fuck an ass!"

For once somebody actually seemed glad to see him, was even waiting for him when he arrived. Mabel Wang-Chew was fifty-something and tended to heaviness, especially her face, and was forever talking about diets, spas and exercise, but she always seemed to be just about twenty pounds over what she wanted. She wore her black hair upswept, no hairpins ever in view, and had a British (via Hong Kong) accent. Today she was wearing a dark velvet academic power business suit (if that wasn't an oxymoron). There was a perky white rose in a vase on the window ledge. She was also sporting a black eye patch.

"I would be extremely careful with those particular students," she said, jumping right in, offering him a seat on a couch. Mabel had the whole office to herself, somehow. "See what they did to my eye."

"Seriously?"

Mabel smiled. "Only psychologically. I had a little accident at home with my grandson and a fork."

"Ouch!"

She sat opposite him in an armchair. She was one of those who tried to make their offices as livable a possible. "The eye doctor tells me I will be all right. No, don't deal with those students because they are quite crazy. They think that the students around here should control things more, even the hiring of teachers."

"I hadn't heard that part."

"They want two student representatives on every hiring committee, with full votes."

"So they can hire student-friendly instructors, I presume."

"They are very, very adamant about it."

"It'll make us hire King Lear's bad daughters," Nathaniel said.

"Will it?" she asked, crinkling her forehead.

"My allusion is a bit forced perhaps. I meant that the teachers being hired will have to profess their love for students in the most sycophantic ways."

"Precisely!"

Mabel Wang-Chew turned and picked up some materials she had prepared for Nathaniel. "I worked with the Alliance on the Child Care Center last semester."

"You mean the Betty Freidan-Gloria Steinem-Susan B. Anthony Child Care Center, don't you?"

"Yes, the students pushed that name through."

"I didn't follow all that, but I can believe it."

"They even lied in their campaign literature."

"Really?"

She handed him a flyer he didn't remember seeing before. "They say here that the school was going to cut the funding for the Center."

"Not the Betty Freidan-Gloria Steinem-Susan B. Anthony Child Care Center!"

Mabel smiled again. "They've trained you well."

"Not quite yet," Nathaniel said.

"When in fact the school was increasing the funding. I forget all the mumbo-jumbo language they used. They're not very articulate, but they are certainly dedicated. What it boiled down to is that they wanted quite a bit of the money to pay themselves salaries."

"No!"

"They pay themselves for attending meetings — and they have many meetings — and also for getting ready to attend meetings. Jake Trosky, as president, makes the most, about twenty thousand a year. The rest of the board, some ten or twelve, depending, make about three-quarters of that."

"I've never heard of student officers being paid salaries."

"They claim there are others elsewhere, but mostly they're setting a precedent, they feel. I sat through many a harangue about how the work that students do is every bit as valuable and important as anything some old teacher might do."

"And their salaries are approved?"

"The Alliance of Students has its own budget, approved annually by the Board of Trustees."

"How much is the budget?"

"About $750,000 per school year."

"That's amazing. I had no idea."

"They don't think it's enough. They are lobbying the Board to double it next year. And when I say lobby, I mean phone calls to the Board's homes and mass attendance at the Board's meetings. Nobody else comes usually, so the twenty-five or so they can muster up seem very evident in the room, and they have a definite effect on the Board. Several members have told me that they're afraid of these students. So they never contradict them. They let the students bully them."

"You're making my blood boil. This is what comes of having a publicly elected Board, no doubt. Especially in this city."

"It gets worse. The Alliance wants to take their extra funding out of the budget of the Speech and Music Departments. They object to those departments inviting outside speakers, artists, and such."

"Because?"

"They say we are being 'elitist' by bringing in professionals. They believe the money should be used only for student artists and speakers, with possibly some, a little, going to campus faculty. But they throw a fit when we invite and pay distinguished artists."

"I have no idea how much such distinguished artists receive."

"It's really not even logical on the students' part, because the monies are in separate funds, and they get theirs no matter what. It really just some anarchist or 'progressive' principle or whatever. They never like to characterize what their political persuasion is, not precisely."

"I thought it was a little to the left of Mao. Let a thousand salaries bloom!"

"Let's just say they have less breadth of thought than your typical Muslim boys' school. And they have pretty much taken control of the budget, with very little oversight."

"Paying themselves handsome salaries to carry out their agenda with school funds."

Mabel sighed and sat back in her chair. "Yes."

"Does no one try to stop this?"

"Believe me, I tried discussing it with them at more than one meeting. They are very savvy in some ways, like making any visitor sit in the center of Arena 3B in the Student Union Building. To intimidate the visitor. Have you been there?"

"I've heard of it."

It has seats on three sides — raised seats. I think it was intended to be a stage or something, but now it's a classroom, except that nobody liked to teach in it. Because of the way it's arranged it makes you feel like you're on trial."

"The Joan of Arc Memorial Arena?"

"When I stood there — sat actually — I found that I could barely express myself in the face of the twenty-five or so who always showed up — and I'm a speech teacher! They may show a higher membership than that, but in actuality there are only about twenty to thirty on the entire campus with their —"

"Plan to take over the world? At least our world."

"They wore me out. Now they have no faculty supervision. Except for Suze DiMentia."

"So I've heard."

"What a piece of work she is!" Mabel adjusted her eye patch, which seemed to be irritating her.

"And she's in cahoots with Dean Visigoth, is she not?

"They share an ideology, so they're like this." Mabel crossed her fingers.

"They must be stopped! And stopped now," Nathaniel said, "before they fertilize the pods of the others!"

She didn't smile, just adjusted her eye patch again. "If you are planning to meet with them, don't."

"You're the second faculty member to tell me that."

"Oh?"

Nathaniel hesitated. Could he mention that Haywood had told him? Would that result in another burst of outrage? "Someone who doesn't want his or her name out there told me," he finally said.

"I can understand that. Ever since I withdrew as whatever I was in those dealings with the Student Alliance, they have been bad-mouthing me to the Chancellor, to various deans, saying that I'm anti-student, and all the rest of it. Actually, I've always been very pro-student. I was the one who originally asked the Board to increase the Alliance's budget and to give them more control over their own money."

Nathaniel shook his head. "Some parents, I've heard, eat their offspring. Here at Shite it's the other way around."

Mabel shook her head too. "Whatever you do, I'd advise you not to go to Arena 3B."

"Alone, you mean?"

"Not even with other faculty members. Unless you can perhaps get twenty-five or so of them to counter the students."

"Fat chance. I've had very little luck getting people riled up or riled up enough to the point where they'll do something! The teachers around here are such . . ." He wanted to say "pussies." But he said "passive-aggressives — without the aggressive part, at least in protecting themselves. They're living in some fool's paradise, like dopey, indulgent parents with a son in his bedroom with an arsenal of atomic bombs. 'Oh, our dear students wouldn't use the Internet against us, their dear teachers! My students love me!' Well, quite a few are not as loved as they want to believe."

"I've had some nasty reviews about me on that site," Mabel said.

"Care to share?"

"Some of them are decidedly ridiculous. I got a review for a speech course I don't even teach, and have never taught. I think they had me confused with Mabel Hu Chu, who used to teach here. I won't even go into the racism involved in confusing names as different as Mabel Wang-Chew and Mabel Hu Chu."

Nathaniel went into anti-P.C. rigor mortis. Oh, no, don't spoil my opinion of you, Mabel, with this kind of 'poor-me-industry' crap. Nobody should review the wrong teacher, but the names are very similar. Students often get the name Tack wrong and I don't start bleating about their anti-gayism. Please!

Happily she didn't go on with this boring "racist" point for long. "The reviews that bother me the most are the ones that accuse me of being a Hitler."

"You don't seem like a Hitler."

"I had a male student whom I had to kick out of class. I gave him three or four warnings, but he would not stop doing what he was doing!"

"Which was?"

Mabel seemed conflicted about revealing something private about a student. "I don't know that I can really . . ."

"What? I don't know his name."

"He used to rub his crotch when the female students were giving speeches."

"And you could see him?"

"Well, I wasn't looking, but it became obvious to me after the second set of speeches."

"And you kicked him out for masturbating in class. You Hitler, you!"

Mabel enjoyed the laugh with him. "Of course I never used the word 'masturbation' when I talked to him about it."

"Of course not. You might ruin his self-esteem. You said, 'Mr. So and So, I must ask you to leave the class because you have an itch that obviously needs medical attention. It's for your own improved health that I must request that you not attend the class until you feel better.'"

"More or less."

"Heavens, we wouldn't want to be sued for claiming that a student was actually masturbating in class, even though he was! What has happened to our world, Mabel?"

"I'm afraid you're right. Soon that student — although I can't prove this — started sending in bad reviews of me, saying I'm cruel and a Hitler and all the rest of it." Mabel suddenly looked tired, a general sag to her whole body, even her upswept hair, though she was still trying to look energetic and well-coiffed.

"More than one?"

"There have been five or six reviews using the word 'Hitler.' One of my other students, a good one, told me about these reviews. She was more upset than I was. But it is disconcerting to think that someone like that . . . that . . ."

"Masturbator?"

"Could get back at me so easily — and make it seem like lots of students feel the same way."

"Just the message I've been trying to get out!" Nathaniel said. "And what exactly is the ideological connection between Dean Visigoth, the Alliance of Students and this Suze DiMentia? I think I know, but spell it out for me, would you?"

"I've overheard her when I passed her classroom telling her students to use Teachers-onparade.com."

"Oh?"

"Suze teaches a course called Modern Guerrilla Political Warfare. How to use dirty tricks to get what you want."

"Only at Shite College! Where have I been?" Nathaniel cursed. I was so busy writing novels and plays I paid no attention to any of this scary nonsense. I feel guilty for having kept myself above it all. I should have acted much sooner."

"But what can we actually do?" Mabel asked, a definite note of defeat in her voice. Even her white rose in its vase looked a little deader than Nathaniel had first thought.

"It will be revealed to us in the fullness of time," Nathaniel said. "Or my name isn't Nathan Lack!"

☙

Despite the warnings, he still wanted to confront Suze DiMentia and the Alliance of Students. Something told him that it was some of them who were sending in the most fake reviews of him. Holding his breath, he took another peek at his reviews on the website. He had more than anyone in the school, forty-five, and was second from the bottom on THE PITS. The last one said:

> Nathannyboy Tack is losing the war with his silly words on
> Speak Out Loud. How many more inane complaints against
> this site can he make? B-l-o-w it out your gay spot, why don't
> you? You just don't know when to hush up, do you? — And
> get back to tearing down student flyers the way you like.

The 'review' gave him an F. It couldn't have been more obvious that this wasn't even his student. It looked like the work of Fly on the Wall, or maybe Jake the Cyber Anarchist. The Cyber Anti-Christ? There wasn't a word about his class or his teaching, only about comments he was making on the forum — comments he wasn't even making! Maybe he should ask Haywood to have his buddy cease and desist or at least use some other name than Nathan Lack. The "review" also was homophobic, was it not? It had been left up on the site for a week. How maddening!

When he checked on Dean Visigoth, there were absolutely no negative reviews of the man, just praise. He was at the very Tip of the Top. The webmaster is simply removing any bad stuff about the beloved sponsor of the site! If only we could prove it!

He looked up Suze DiMentia for the first time:

> Ms. DiMentia gives a killer course in how to employ modern
> methods to the oldest problem in the world, i. e., overcoming
> corporate America and it's tentacles. I recommend her hi-ly!
> She knows what shes talking about!! Does Suze.

Who was this from — Jake Trosky? Something was a little "off" about the syntax, to say nothing of the ahistorical worldview about "corporate America" being the oldest problem in the world. Bad spelling alone was not enough of a giveaway, naturally, since misspelling abounded in this crowd. (Was it contagious?) Nathaniel was no cheerleader for corporate anything; in fact, he felt the corporations and their conglomerate greed were destroying competition and ultimately themselves, but he wouldn't give Jake Trosky the satisfaction of knowing that he agreed with him about even this one thing!

Suze DiMentia wasn't as high up on the Tip of the Top as Dean Visigoth, but she was on it. There was also a new wrinkle. RECOMMENDED TEACHERS!!! HERE!! Teachersonparade itself was now recommending certain teachers? Just what is a Teachersonparade recommendation worth to you, Professor, hmm? And guess who was on it: Dean Calvin Visigoth and Suze DiMentia and nobody else. The bastards!

Nathaniel shut off his computer and rubbed his eyes. I'm going to go off the deep end if I don't get a break from this. A three-day weekend was coming up because of Veterans Day. What if he and Marty went somewhere, had a massage, made a little love?

He hadn't heard from Marty for two whole days. That was the longest they hadn't spoken in all their years together.

He tried Marty at the library, but his boss said that Marty had called in sick that morning. Oh, no. Nathaniel tried Marty's number, but there was no answer. He tried again. Sometimes Marty was in the bathroom, where he liked to read, sometimes for over an hour. He couldn't answer because his extension phone was broken and he hadn't had it fixed. It had been broken for over a year now.

When he got no reply, Nathaniel decided to drive over to Marty's place. Usually he made plans in advance before showing up, even though he had a key, but the two days and the lack of response were not a good sign. Even the answering machine didn't seem to be capturing messages properly.

The upstairs landlord of Marty's building had a nasty yellow mongrel dog named Gretel that sometimes got out from upstairs and chased intruders. That was all fine and good, but she also chased Marty sometimes. She'd even bared her no-nonsense fangs at Nathaniel a couple of times. The landlord, a little shrimpy millionaire in some business in Silicon Valley, usually came down and begged Gretel to come away, but one of these days the landlord wasn't going to get there in time. This time Nathaniel managed to get inside before the dog got down the steps to him.

Inside his apartment Marty was sitting on his couch upright, asleep. All around him were the library books he had not returned and stacks upon stacks of computer magazines. There was barely a pathway into the bathroom now. There was a plate of unfinished microwave something-or-other on the cushion next to him. Marty did at least look alive, his head resting on the knuckles of one hand, but the whole situation did not look good. What did it mean when even speed wouldn't keep you awake?

"Marty?" Nathaniel said, touching his knee.

Nothing.

"Marty! It's Nathaniel."

The eyes flickered and the head came up. "What?"

"It's me. Don't jump."

Marty came to and began rubbing his neck muscles. "I guess I fell asleep." He yawned.

"You didn't go to work today?"

Marty didn't reply. But he pulled his fingers over his mouth and beard, removing the bit of drool there.

"I called you at work."

"Yeah, I didn't feel good. I have some sick pay coming." Marty went into the bathroom with the drool on his hand.

Nathaniel sat on the couch, or tried to. He had to move books and magazines and even three porn tapes: Chad Manley in Kansas Fucking Company, Chad Manley Goes Down in a Mine, and Chad Manley Porn Outtakes. The last one didn't sound half bad. What were porn outtakes?

"Marty!"

"Yeah?" He was brushing his teeth.

"Why don't we go away this coming weekend? You have off, don't you?"

"Yes, but I didn't tell the clinic."

"Even a day or two. How long can you go without methadone?"

Marty came to the door of the bathroom and looked at Nathaniel, the toothbrush still in his mouth.

"We could leave Friday after you dose and get back early Monday. Could you do without methadone for two days?"

"I don't know. I start to have withdrawals after about a day."

"We could go to Calistoga to the Monks Spa." This was a spa run by an order of Dominicans.

"I can't afford it." Marty went back into the bathroom and turned on a faucet.

"I'll pay for it, if you buy your own meals."

"Really?" Marty was back, a towel to his mouth.

"I feel the need for a little rest and relaxation. I've mulling over going to see the Alliance of Students and Gorilla Woman."

"Who's that?"

"I just made up that name for this teacher in Political Science at school. Her real name is Suze DiMentia. She apparently teaches our students to screw other people to get what they want. A class in Political Guerrilla Warfare. Hence she's now Gorilla Woman."

"You and your names for people!"

"It's my way of disarming them, I fully realize. Gorilla Woman can have no power over me. Calling her that is better than envisioning her on the toilet seat."

"Maybe she doesn't go to the toilet."

"Like the angels. Anything's possible. Do you want to go with me to see the monks?"

"For the whole spa treatment?"

"Mud bath, herbal wrap, half hour massage, the occasional naked customer or naked monk to look at. And we don't have to peep through the gym window, either."

"What?"

"That's a reference to Haywood, my cyber 'buddy' in all this."

"I can't keep them all straight. How about an hour massage?"

"Beggars can't be choosers now."

"I might go if it's an hour massage," Marty teased.

"You're a whore, you know that?"

Marty came back looking better. He'd combed his beard and hair. "If you've got it, sell it."

"Now I don't want to go."

"I'll pay for own meals and put in an extra fifty for the massage!" Marty leaned down and kissed Nathaniel on the top of the head, then stoked his cheek. "Deal, Daddy?"

"I can't afford all this. Those monks aren't cheap."

"You're backing out?"

"I didn't say that. It's been a while since we've gone anywhere."

And a while since they had had "relations." Maybe a trip to a new environment — beds close together, the soothing waters of Monks Spa. What would Ann Landers recommend to spark the old flame? A three-way with the head monk? Not exactly. Brother Vassily was no Chad Manley. He was perfectly nice, but he was a shriveled-up little old man in his eighties with a large carbuncular nose that looked like a pomegranate, a friar/chiropractor who'd been in the business for almost fifty years and still believed in separate male and female facilities. God love him and his cloistered spa! It was all on the up and up, of course —none of *that* — but his monks would massage anything else you wanted.

"I could use some relaxation myself," Marty said, sitting next to Nathaniel on the couch. "I've got to clean up this place one of these days. Really!"

Marty said it with such conviction Nathaniel didn't have the heart to say "I'll believe it when I see it." They didn't need another fight right now. They needed to "bond" again, before their sex life dried up completely.

"Of course there is also the little matter of my growing flaccidity. Excuse the oxymoron."

"We'll play it as it lays, won't we?" Marty said, tapping Nathaniel's crotch. "I've been having trouble getting a hard-on myself lately."

"Even with Chad Manley's help." Nathaniel gestured at the porn tapes.

"Oh, he's a rip-off!"

"Chad Manley a rip-off? What's the world coming too when you can trust porn stars?"

Marty ignored the irony, as he usually did. "I signed up for his chat room, and he performed live twice. Just twice! I paid for a whole damn month's worth."

"What does he do exactly?" Nathaniel was curious despite his disdain.

"Has sex with his boyfriend."

"And you have to pay?"

"I don't mind paying — if I get what I pay for! He's supposed to do whatever the subscribers tell him to do."

"What am I hearing?"

"He has the computer in his playroom, and he and his lover do whatever the majority of the subscribers ask for."

"Democracy lives!"

"It's hot. When they do it!" Marty looked disgusted, a customer about to write the Better Business Bureau.

"It sounds like Teachersonparade, sort of. We do whatever the majority of our reviewers tell us to. Stand on one leg while explaining the comma splice! Dangle your participle out the window, professor!"

Even Marty laughed. "You haven't lost your sense of humor. That's good." He went back to put the toothbrush away.

"But I am losing it! I think I'm far less funny in my classes these days. That's why I need the spa and a massage."

And a couple of orgasms with my honey. Both he and Marty didn't like to plan their sex together. It could be in the offing, but they almost never spelled it out ahead of time. Even at the cottage at the Monks Spa, if sex happened, it happened. If it didn't, that would be what . . . yet more of life? Enough with the lessons, Life!

"Maybe I'll stop whining in the Wine Country."

"I doubt it." Marty came out of the bathroom.

"Thanks. And when I return, refreshed and purified, I will know which way to continue this quest against evil deans and evil students, like the brave knights of old!"

Marty snuffled a little bit. "You really think you're somethin', don't you?"

"I'm joking! I'm joking. It's called satire. I'm satirizing myself. Believe it or not, Marty, but I'm capable of satirizing myself."

"Not as much as you are of satirizing other people."

"Touché."

"I didn't mean it to be mean," Marty said.

"I know you didn't. That's why it hurts."

"You big old bear, you!" Marty suddenly nuzzled his bearded, prickly face into Nathaniel's chin, and they almost did it there on the couch among the apartment's litter. But they both pulled back at the last moment. It would spoil the trip to Spa Land. And anticipation sometimes could be better than . . . sex among all that litter in Marty's place.

"Think we should get Viagra?" Marty asked as Nathaniel was leaving.

"Never! I don't do chemicals!"

"Give me a break," Marty said, setting up his methamphetamine powder on the coffee table and beginning to chop it up with a razor blade. Yet one more time.

Nathaniel wanted to scoop it up and throw it into the toilet and flush it away with all the other troubles in his life. But of course he didn't.

When he got home, there was a message from his son on the answering machine: "Guess who called you!"

Nathaniel called back at once and got Jimmy's mother. "How are things going up there?" he asked as cheerily as he could.

"Not bad," Diana said tautly. "Do you want to talk to Jimmy?"

Good girl! Oops, woman! She knew that she and the father of her child had nothing in common except their child. Christ, she was hard to talk to, and Nathaniel might have taken it personally if he hadn't noticed that she was the same way with most people.

Jimmy came on the phone. "Yo!"

"Is this Yo?"

"Yo!"

"You need a new word."

"Yo!"

"Enough. Is anything wrong, Jimmy?"

"No. I just called."

"Yeah, sure."

"I did!" Jimmy's voice seemed to be getting deeper by the day.

"You're a seventeen-year-old American boy child. You don't just call your father for no reason."

"Let me go into my room."

Nathaniel waited, Slacker on his lap, two stacks of papers he hadn't graded yet on the end table next to him.

"Okay, I'm in my room."

"You never used to go to you room when we talked. Is it something you don't want your mom and Lana to overhear?"

"Sort of."

"I'm all ears. Did you go that Winter Dance — with the snakes — that you were talking about?"

"No." Jimmy sounded a bit disgusted.

"I thought you had two dates lined up."

"I did. But they both backed out."

"The bitches!"

Jimmy laughed. "That's what I thought."

"Don't tell your mother I said that."

"I won't."

"What happened?"

"I don't know whether you can solve it."

What would the Beaver's dad say? "Let me put on my heterosexual sport jacket and necktie and get right to that teenage problem of yours. I can't promise to solve it, but we won't know if you don't tell me, will we?"

"I'm still a . . . virgin."

"Technically I'm still a virgin."

"You are?"

"It depends on how you define the term. Didn't we discuss this before?"

"I don't think so."

"Sure we did. Wouldn't you remember discussing your father's virginity?"

"I don't know."

"A father's virginity — akin to one of the miracles of Mary, the Mother of God."

"Whatever."

Nathaniel felt strange. Not only didn't they have a Catholic upbringing to mock together, they were quite different in temperament. Nathaniel always remembered everything anybody said that was the least little bit negative about him, particularly if it was about sex. No doubt it was a Gay Thing, self-protective.

"Do you think I'm weird because I'm still a virgin?" Jimmy asked.

"Yes."

"Dad!"

"But nice weird. It's actually rather charming."

"I don't feel charming."

"I don't mean to make light of your situation. I know the male body's urges, and I sympathize."

Nathaniel's view was that most male sex consisted of animal appetite, the heavy biological duty to spew seed often and anywhere, Mother Nature having created such an urgency that she was not very fastidious about where it went, as long as some of it got into places where it could continue Mother's Reign of Terror. Women seemed to demand Love with it, for their own reasons, but men didn't and telling them they should only Do It when they were in Love was just Silly.

"I'm horny all the time."

"You'll outgrow it."

"I will?"

"When you're fifty-nine."

"God, can I wait that long?" Even Jimmy could joke.

"Time flies after forty."

"Forty!? That's ancient!"

"By the way, it really is true that time seems to go faster and faster, the longer you live."

"Fine, but what do I do now?"

"Excellent question, class. The immediate problem before us is . . . let's see now."

"Should I go to a prostitute?"

"I'll see if Chad Manley has a sister."

"Who?"

"Never mind. What happened to those two you were seeing?"

"Lindsey and Darla?"

"Yeah, the pretty one and the dog who giggles too much. Your words, not mine."

"Well, Darla let me finger her a little bit."

"I beg your pardon?"

"She let me stick my finger in her."

"Hmm. And that wasn't enough for you, my son?"

"It just got me all excited, and then she wouldn't do anything else."

"The slut! Worse — the non-slut!"

"It was sort of hot, but I wanted to . . . you know . . ."

"Oh, I know, Jimmy. I haven't been there, exactly, but I know. You don't have to actually go to Mongolia to realize that some people might want to visit there even though you yourself have no desire to set foot in such a place."

"Mongolia?"

"Forget my metaphor. I don't know what to advise you."

"I sort of asked mom and Lana, and they said I should wait until I'm in love."

"That's not such bad advice." Nathaniel slapped his own tongue. Sorry, ladies, this was a Guy Thing, how to cope when you aren't getting it regular and you're going crazy. Cum, like murder, will out! And yet Nathaniel steered away from discussing Jimmy's masturbation. As did Jimmy. They weren't *that* close or *that* modern! "I don't know what to tell you, Yimmy."

"My friend Timothy says I'm too shy around girls."

"Is he any better?"

"Well, he's got a girlfriend. But I think he just uses her."

"The cad!"

"And she's not even that pretty, really. Timothy is even younger than I am, and he's not a virgin."

"Your story is an old story, Jimmy. What can I say?"

"I know it's happened to other guys, but what do I do about myself?" You could hear the ache in the voice.

"And nothing will satisfy you except that one particular deed? The Deed of Darkness. The beast with two backs."

"What?"

"The man-woman thing, the yeasty pretzel . . ."

"Are you taking this seriously?" Jimmy sounded somewhat offended.

"I'm sorry, I'm sorry! Where are you exactly now with Lindsey and Darla?"

"I'm not seeing either one. I'm avoiding them. I guess they're avoiding me too."

"I read somewhere that people who are late bloomers in sex actually do better in school. So it may not seem so terrific right now, but in the long run you'll be happy about it." . . . God, that sounded so lame!

"Well, thanks anyway," Jimmy said.

"You're going to hang up?"

"Yeah, I gotta do homework. I have a science project to do."

"What is it?"

"I've really got to go. Thanks anyway. I'll be talking at you."

"Sure." Nathaniel felt bad that he couldn't help more, that the conversation was ending so awkwardly. "Let's talk soon, Jimmy, okay?"

"I'm going by Jim now."

"Oh."

"Bye."

They hung up, and Nathaniel punched the receiver with his fist. Jesus, why is it so hard? I'm just trying to get everybody I love, including me, laid!

Nathaniel was waiting for Marty in Marty's driveway, steaming. He'd come twenty minutes late on purpose, and Marty still wasn't ready. For the umpteenth time he checked on his small leather overnight bag on the rear seat, made more room for Marty's things, and even got out and emptied the trash receptacle into the city's trash container down the block. Then he flipped on the radio and listened to an awful song by some vocalist named Fiona Orange. Slacker sings better than that, he thought, and has a nicer personality. He knew that if he cell phoned Marty again, they'd have a fight, so he just sat and tried to control his temper. I must be patient. I used to be more patient, didn't I? When I was a teenager, a young man. I don't think I lost my temper much, or am I misremembering? Probably not — when you're young you don't realize how little time you actually have.

And, by god, I don't want to spend my remaining days in Marty's driveway!

Just as he picked up the cell phone to call again, there was Marty coming out of his four-unit apartment building. "I'll be right back," he said, putting two bags on the rear seat of the car.

What could he possibly want another bag for — yet more meth?

Part of the reason for Nathaniel's hatred of this perpetual lateness, aside from the obvious, was that it seemed "fem" to him, and he didn't want Marty to be fem.

"So get your butch butt out here," he grumbled under his breath.

Ten minutes later Marty emerged with the third bag and a knapsack. He still had a comb in his hand and was putting the finishing touches on his beard even as he loaded up the car. Well, one thing was for sure — Marty looked nice. He always looked nice — clean, pressed shirt and pants, his hair dark and a little wet. His apartment might be one of the lower circles of Hell, but he always managed to look nice himself. Wasn't there some psychological profile for that? Enough! I will not complain today. I will not lose my temper. I will not!

Marty got into the car. "I got a call from my mother at the last minute. It's her birthday." His eyes looked a little red.

"Yeah, sure."

"It is!"

"How is the old . . . darling?"

Marty buckled up. "She asked about you."

"If I was dead yet?"

"I think she respects you."

"Then why am I banned from her house?"

"You're not banned. Exactly."

Nathaniel backed out of the driveway and almost got hit by a speeding truck that hadn't stopped at the stop sign. "Jesus! These drivers!"

"It's clear now," Marty said, helping out.

"Not that I want to go to your mother's house."

"You shouldn't have killed her fish."

"I did not kill her fish! How many times must I say this?!"

"Well, she thinks you did."

"I was just standing at the fish tank and looking — looking — at her dumb old goldfish."

"Siamese fighting fish."

"And one of them up and died. I swear I never laid a hand on it!"

"She'd had that fish for a long time."

"You know what I think the real problem is?"

"She just doesn't like you?"

"Ha, ha. Mostly she doesn't like the idea of us. Because we're gay and because I'm fourteen years older than you."

"You could be nicer to her."

"I'm nice to her! Even though she wouldn't let me attend your family's Christmas celebrations."

"You're right about that."

"Ten years. But who's counting."

"You didn't want to go anyway. You don't celebrate Christmas."

"I don't exchange gifts. I have no objection whatsoever to the mindless giddiness of people celebrating the birth of their personal scapegoat savior."

Marty said nothing and looked through the stack of CDs he'd brought along. Marty was much more religious than Nathaniel. He even had a guru. To keep the peace, they didn't discuss the subject very much. "I brought the new Fiona Orange album!"

Nathaniel bit his lip. "Oh, good."

"Want to hear it?"

"Sure. Not too loud, though."

Marty slipped the CD into the slot on the dashboard. "I'm looking forward to this trip, withdrawals or not!"

"They should keep that clinic open more hours for its customers."

"Tell them that. They think they're doing us a favor as it is. I got a whiff of what they really think of all of us today when I dosed."

"What was that?"

"Oh, this new guy who hands out the dosing cards — I think it was his first day on the job. Anyway, he gives me a hard time because my counselor had put in a request that I see him before I dose. Well, I had already seen my counselor the last time I was there, and the request was an old one. When I tried to explain all this to the new guy so I could get my card and dose, he says 'You dregs can't even get your act together to get your goddamned drugs!' The nerve! And it really hurt my feelings besides."

"You dregs should have him fired."

"They won't fire him. The staff turns over there every three minutes. Nobody wants to work there."

Nathaniel wouldn't want to work there either. The clinic was down in the Tenderloin part of the city, surrounded by dirty, blowing papers and other stinky junk. The smell of urine filled the vicinity like a bouquet from Bosnia. The people there were trying to recover, but most of them looked like relatives you'd like to forget you had — creepy, strung out, wild of eye.

"Review him on ClinicStaffonParade.com."

"I might start it!"

Nathaniel hated the fact that Marty had to go there and pay lots of money every month. It meant they were hemmed in — by limited clinic hours, by addiction, by serious money limitations.

I will not get depressed! Nathaniel cajoled himself. "We're going to have a marvelous time in Calistoga with the monks!" he said. "We are!"

"I hope so, because that website of yours has really put you on edge lately," Marty said, lowering the back of the passenger seat.

"Oh?"

"You're on my back most of the time."

I am so not on your back, Nathaniel thought, tightening his hands on the steering wheel and heading toward a big bridge that led out of the city of Santa Francesca. "I guess we have different perceptions of the facts," he said, biting yet another section of his tongue.

"I guess we do," Marty said.

"Write me up on Teachersonparade."

"If you don't behave on this trip, I just might."

Nathaniel presented his teeth in a big, phony grin.

Marty leaned over and gave Nathaniel a kiss on the neck. "I love you anyway, you prick!"

It felt nice to be kissed on the neck. Nathaniel was grateful that Marty was so much more demonstrative than he himself was.

But the scary, un-relaxing part was that Marty could indeed, if they had a fight, or if he just felt like it, write Nathaniel up on Teachersonparade.com and say any damn thing about him he wanted to, and there wasn't a thing Nathaniel could do about it.

When they got to the spa, their reservation had been lost, but then it was located (O Lord, I was Lost but now I'm Found), and they were allowed to check in. "Is that for two men?" said the small-town teenage girl who worked for the monks, not exactly approvingly.

"Afraid so," Nathaniel replied. Is anything easy? he wondered.

They'd asked for two double beds, not out of any old-fashioned closetry, but because their bodies tended to get overheated when they shared a bed for a whole night. Still, Nathaniel was hoping — an hour or two of "spoons" might be nice.

The room was a "Victorian cottage" out behind the other structures. It probably had been a Twenties' horse stable or a Fifties' wash room. Or a penance room for wicked monks? Now it was a trendy "Victorian cottage" with about as much glamour as a Victorian Motel 6: plain beds, a rug sus-pect in its cleanliness, a "complimentary" coffee maker from Pyrex. But what the hell, they were on vacation, short though it might be. Damn the credit cards. Full speed ahead. Especially since a great stab of tension had descended between Nathaniel's shoulders, and his facial tic also seemed to be acting up.

Marty commandeered the bed he preferred and set up his paraphernalia. It looked like a pharmacy. He had more medications than any other person Nathaniel had ever known in his life: two for blood pressure, two for depression, another for triglycerides (whatever those were), three types of eye drops, a box for the methadone (before he got "dirties" and had to dose every day), some speed — you name it, Marty had it. He was chopping away already with his little old razor blade.

"Can't that wait until we have the mud bath at least?"

Marty chose not to answer, and Nathaniel dropped the subject.

"I'm happy!" Nathaniel said, throwing himself on one of the king-size beds. "I will be happy!"

"So am I," Marty said, leaning down to sniff some of the white stuff into a nostril. Then he did the other one, blinked, and hurried over and lay next to Nathaniel, his head back so that the crystals would work their magic. Nathaniel reached into the drawer of the night stand and took out the Bible the monks had been so thoughtful to put there.

"Aren't we a pair?" Nathaniel said, opening the Bible. "'Let not cripples come unto your altars,'" he read aloud. "That doesn't sound very wheelchair friendly, does it? Could you massage my neck muscles, just below the neck? It feels like a yoke there. Right here."

Marty held up a finger to signal that his nostrils were not yet quite in order. But after a few seconds he knelt on the bed and began squeezing Nathaniel's afflicted part (or at least one of them).

"Oh, that's great!"

"I expect a tip."

"Oh, yes, keep that up! A tip, a trip, anything, just don't stop!" Nathaniel let the Bible fall from his hand onto the bed.

"You're really tight all through here." Marty rubbed his fingers across Nathaniel's upper back.

Nathaniel lay with his face in a pillow that had seen fresher days. With a struggle, he managed to remove the outside pillow cover — ah, now the linen smelled fresh. "You haven't written any bad reviews of me, have you?" he said, not looking up at Marty.

"Just that one. It was positive."

"Nothing else?"

"What are you thinking — that'd I'd write something unkind about you?"

Nathaniel shrugged under the kneading fingers.

"I leave that to your students!"

"Ouch!"

"Can't take it, huh?"

Nathaniel turned over. "Maybe that's why it does feel so tight in here. Maybe more of them are from my real students than I want to admit."

"Is it bothering you that much?"

"It is."

"But you don't care what people think about you."

"Of course I do. I wish I didn't."

"I've seen you teach. You're fun." Marty turned Nathaniel onto his stomach again.

"Oh, you're just saying that."

"No, I'm not." Marty used his knuckles to beat on the tension.

"I won't need the massage if you keep that up."

"Is it too much?"

"No, never. I just don't want to feel that there's any legitimacy to any of the reviews."

"What do they say?"

"Oh, different things. I can dismiss most of them, even the homophobic ones, just glance through them sometimes. But there was one that said I want my students to fail."

"Do you?"

"No!"

"Don't bite my head off. You brought it up." Marty pressed hard with his thumbs on Nathaniel's spinal column.

"You're great, Marty. You could be a masseur."

"I'm being a masseur!"

"I don't want my students to fail. I want them to be better than they are. It would be a whole lot easier, believe me, if they were."

"You do complain about them a lot."

"Most teachers I've know, at least English teachers, complain about their students' work."

"Just pass 'em all. What's the difference, in the overall big picture?"

"It'd be a whole lot easier. Just let go. Standards? What standards?"

"Of course you shouldn't, silly. Give them what's fair."

"That's what I think I'm doing, but they're so spoiled, so easily satisfied with —"

"Believe me, I believe you. Some of the student workers we get at the library! They come late. They do very little actual work. They talk about their 'workers rights' all the time, and never their duties. And some of them even steal."

"Steal what?"

"Money has been missing from our fines box ever since our two Youth Workers, so-called, arrived. The problem is we can't figure out which one is doing it."

"Could it be both of them?"

Marty stopped massaging and wiped his nose or something. "Maybe it is both of them. Thank you for your suggestion. What a mind."

"Actually I wish I could be more like you sometimes."

"Me?"

"More trusting of people, less cynical. People like you better than they like me. I've seen it at the library. Your boss and the others actually seem to like you."

"Not all the time. Nor do I like them all the time. I just hide it better than you do."

"I thought I hid it."

"Nathaniel, are you serious? Every thought you ever think shows right there on your face! How can you be so blind to yourself?"

"Another review said I'm arrogant. Is that true?" Nathaniel turned over so that he could look right into Marty's eyes.

"Yes."

"No, I'm not!"

"Yes, you are."

"I was such a mouse as a kid. I had to get tough to survive."

"No doubt."

"Should I be less arrogant?"

"Could you be?"

"Yow! That hurt."

Marty held up both hands. "I'm not even touching you."

"I don't think I'm arrogant."

"Okay, you're not arrogant."

"But arrogant is good! Teachers are supposed to be arrogant."

Marty didn't reply, just twisted his lips in an unconvinced way.

"Well, teachers are supposed to exude confidence. I saw this tenure report at school, from Dylan Tante about some new teacher. He said — and this was praise — Miss Sloble treats her students as her complete equals.' Well, I'm sorry, students aren't the complete equals of teachers! They are learning from their arrogant teachers! In Europe, in Asia, in most of the world, the professor comes in, delivers a lecture, and walks out. There is none of this 'Hi-class-have-we-bonded-yet' crap! 'What do you think of Aristotle, Mr. Reading at the Sixth Grade Level?' 'What a wonderful insight, if I could figure it out, Miss Idiom-Impaired Spawn of Religious and Ethnic Overbreeders!'"

"You need to get down and wash your students' feet."

"Don't be disgusting!" Nathaniel rolled off the bed and stood up. He threw the Bible back into the drawer.

"I knew that would get you going."

"Let's not even talking about this anymore."

Marty came over and put his arms around Nathaniel. "I like you best when you're vulnerable like this. Do you know that?"

"Not for long, you wouldn't."

"What do you mean?"

"The pack descends on the weak wolf and rips its throat out. And the same goes for lovers!"

"You really believe that?"

"I do."

"I'll be here to protect you," Marty said, rocking Nathaniel back and forth. "I'll be here, come what may."

"Be sure to put the ripped throat patch back real nice and neat, would you?"

"Rest your weary body right here . . . right here . . ."

"I think we've reached the stage called Lesbian Bed Death, and we're not even lesbians!"

"There, there now . . ."

They rocked back and forth, and it was good. They didn't have sex, and that was good too. Well, almost good. There is no greater good than Sex *mit* Orgasm. But Nathaniel was beginning to see that he and Marty had reached that level he'd heard about, when just a massage, a few rockings or "spoons" and some "complimentary," soothing comments from someone who cared about you would suffice.

Those warm and fuzzies would have to suffice because Nathaniel's penis was definitely on strike, laid off, AWOL, or on a religious retreat. Because functioning properly it wasn't. He hadn't even gotten an erection in the herbal wrap, usually one of the highlights of a visit to Monks Spa.

The mud was luscious, though, as e.e. cummings noted. No, you didn't want to check too closely what had been sitting there in the mud before you, but the "mud boys," both monks in their Latino fifties, did a fine job of smoothing out the wrinkles in the muck (*mirabile dictu* — made from volcanic ash!) (Let's see you beat that, Vesuvius!) with long wooden rakes and even put cucumber slices over your eyes. (Eat your heart out, Caligula!) The mud even seemed to de-shrivel Nathaniel's penis, once he removed the sticky clumps from his pubic hair. As he showered, it hung down in a most becoming, if temporary, way. A very chubby man even seemed to be looking at the penis in a more than casual manner — at least until he caught Nathaniel's eye catching his eye. Not too shabby — fifty-nine, a bit long in the tooth and thick in the love handles, and yet Eye Candy for the even chubbier! Could life offer more?

The masseur, Brother Kyle, a long-fingered, thin, "spiritual" type who wrote poetry and whom Nathaniel had had before, although he never seemed to remember Nathaniel, began working him over pretty good. He had rolled up the sleeves of his Dominican robe, all the better to rolf. "Tell me if the pressure is not to your liking," Brother Kyle said, keeping his voice low. All through the massage area one could hear these hushed tones. There were even signs up saying QUIET PLEASE. RELIGIOUS MASSAGE IN PROGRESS.

Nathaniel mumbled something, not really wanting to chat.

But Brother Kyle wanted to. "Have you ever had a religious massage before, sir?"

"Oh, yes."

"Where you from?"

"Santa Francesca."

"I've been there. I'd like to live there. But it's too expensive. We had to shut down our monastery there."

Yes, yes, I'll give you a tip, Nathaniel thought.

"You're very tense in your shoulders," Brother Kyle noted.

"And I just had another massage before this one too."

"Oh? Where was that?"

"Not a professional one." I won't mention it was from my lover.

"Two massages and your back still feels like a brick."

"I know," Nathaniel said. "I'm under a lot of pressure."

"Do you work in Silicon Valley? A lot of our customers are from down there."

"No, I'm a victim of Silicon Valley."

"Beg pardon?"

"Silicon Valley is pushing the Internet without caring a damn what's on it."

"I'm afraid I'm not online yet." He tackled Nathaniel's torso.

"Do you ever get dissatisfied customers?" Nathaniel asked.

"Am I pressing too hard?"

"No, no, it's fine. I'm just wondering how you'd feel if Brother Vassily set up a website and let his customers send in reviews of the staff here."

"I can do less or more pressure, whichever!" Brother Kyle was beginning to sound worried.

"You're just fine. I'm just saying what if people could post anonymous reviews of you on this spa's webpage and everybody in the universe who might think of coming here could read them, would you like that?"

"Do you think that's going to happen? Are you building a website for Brother Vassily?"

It was too hard to go into all the subtleties with your face in a padded hole. "Yeah, I might build a website for the boss here," Nathaniel said.

"Most people like the massages I give, but if there's anything you want or don't want, just tell me!" Desperation seemed to be filtering into Brother Kyle's voice.

"And the reviews could be written by anybody — the other friar masseurs, even the mud boys. Maybe even rival spas!"

"The mud boys?"

"Because they want to be masseurs and take your jobs."

"Oh, my God!"

"Or suppose you see somebody with an obvious hideous deformity that you could fix by applying the right pressure to the right body parts. Only the customer won't listen to your suggestion, won't let you apply the right amount of pressure. Actually the customer prefers his deformed state!"

"Oh, my Lord!"

"And suppose, further, that you have a very cranky customer, one who just can't be satisfied, and you squeeze his . . . some body part a little too hard, just to teach him a spiritual lesson, and the customer brings accusations on the website."

"No!"

"He has it coming, of course, more than coming, but the way the customer words the complaint it seems like you're at fault, that you have done something very wrong. Actually you should have ripped his . . . whatevers off, but instead you've shown restraint!"

"My God in Heaven, does this happen on websites?" Brother Kyle's hands had almost stopped the massage.

Nathaniel was on a roll now with his analogy. "And then this customer says that you want your deformed customers to stay deformed, when in fact all you want is for them to walk tall and straight — straight backed, that is. Actually nothing gives you greater happiness than to see them walk from the spa of life into the sunshine with the scales fallen from their scabby eyes!"

"Are these deformed ones the same as those you almost ripped their whatevers off?" Brother Kyle forced his voice back to the expected hush. "I mean, I'm getting confused about which is which."

"Hey, nobody is going to review you on a website, Brother Kyle, and I'm going to leave you a nice tip in the envelopes provided."

"You are?"

"You've answered all my questions without even knowing it."

"I have? I don't seem to be having much luck getting rid of this tension in your back." Brother Kyle applied himself anew.

"I'll get rid of the tension, don't worry," Nathaniel said. "If it kills me. Or somebody."

He and Marty enjoyed the trip to the spa, but in fact Nathaniel barely slept the entire time they were there, staring at the ceiling, both his brain and facial tic racing with many grievances. And many plans.

Even though he had been warned, he went to Arena 3B, tucked away in the Student Union Building, a tacky old auditorium with flaking peach-colored paint and desks, some broken, arranged in tiers. They were already waiting for him when he arrived, about twenty-five students, again almost all "minority." And – god if ever single one of them wasn't as homely as sin. Why weren't they out protesting that? He thought he spotted what must have been Jake Trosky — he of the Caucasian dreadlocks and the Student Jihad — sitting in the top row, wearing just a thin, white tee-shirt although it was chilly in the room. Nathaniel had seen this kind of I'm-a-man-so-cold-weather-don't-bother-me nonsense before. He liked men sexually, but they could be such stubborn, dumb fucks sometimes.

"Where are the lions?" he joked as he took his seat on a backless stool in the center of the "stage" area. No one acknowledged the allusion.

I should not have come here, he admitted to himself even before the "meeting" got underway.

"So glad to see so many of you from my political techniques class here! I want to take this opportunity to thank Dr. Tack for agreeing to come today." Thus Gorilla Woman introduced him to the crowd. He had actually seen her around the campus before but had never attached a name to her. How could he not have noticed her. She was built along the lines of the Kelvinator they'd had in his kitchen when he was a boy. Hadn't that been diesel run? Well, Suze DiMentia was clearly Diesel run. When God invented stereo-typed dykes he used Suze for His mold: broad, squat, militantly unmade-up, even the hair drab (brown was too colorful a word to use), just a touch longer than a drill instructor's. A faded blue unisex "smock" completed her ensemble. The head had also obviously been transplanted onto the shoulders, along with all the predictable one-sided P.C. rhetoric from some previous owner.

"The good doctor has agreed to answer some questions for us today. Isn't that great?"

Nathaniel was leaking by now, at the temples, at the armpits. All that was missing was Dean Visigoth and his army of lawyers.

"Shall we begin with a short statement from Dr. Tack first?" Suze seated herself in the first row, with some difficulty.

Nathaniel looked up at the unsmiling faces above him. He was apparently Enemy Number One. Why hadn't he asked other teachers to come with him!? They wouldn't have come — and who could blame them — but he could at least have asked.

"I came here today," he began, "because I believe certain members of your organization, the Alliance, have been using the teacher review website to post reviews of me — and possibly of others, such as deans — even though these people have never been in my classes."

Nathaniel looked to see Jake Trosky's reaction. Far from screaming with guilt and running from the auditorium, thus revealing his foul crimes, Jake just sat staring hard at him.

"I don't know whether you know it or not, but there are absolutely no controls over who posts things on that website. It was made to be abused, apparently."

"So you want to be able to control what students say?" Jake cast the first . . . lion?

But Suze took control, looking back at Jake. "Now let's let him speak his piece first, all right?"

"All right," Jake agreed. (Not really, though)

The crowd was restless, with all sorts of bad body postures on display. One girl on the side was even clipping her fingernails. Snip. Snip. God, she had a lot of fingers! Snip, snip, snip, snip! Miss "Diverse" LaFarge awaits the decision of the Tribunal of the Equals.

"I don't know the exact connection between the review site and this organization, but it seems to me that because you have recommended that people use the site, when it's a downright fraud, that you need to re-examine your endorsement and —"

"The Alliance never gave money to the website!" Jake Trosky was quick to call out. "We never approved money for it. Never!"

"Well, somebody did!" Nathaniel said.

"The site is privately financed. No school money, no Alliance money has ever gone into it."

"I doubt that," Nathaniel said. He couldn't prove it, though.

"The webmaster asked us for money, but it was never given! I was the president and so I know what happened!"

So they were trying to cover their legal asses!

"Are you aware that the flyers for the website — which should never have been approved in the first place without knowing how it would allow the phony reviews it does — are being put up in all sorts of places they shouldn't be?"

This didn't impress the crowd. There was a general grumbling.

"Maybe there should be more places to post flyers then!" somebody snapped.

"Please!" Suze warned. "First let Dr. Tack have his say."

And then we decapitate him!

Nathaniel could tell his approach was not working. His mind kicked up — or down — a notch, and he said, "Are you aware that there are reviews on the website that claim that certain teachers have had sex with their students?"

"Maybe they did!" a voice said. "Teachers do a lot of shitty things to students."

"In a wheelchair?"

"That review was the only one like that," Jake called down.

"No, it's not!" Nathaniel retaliated. "There's also one that says a male teacher gave a student a blowjob." Nathaniel patted his pockets. He had intended to bring those reviews in printed form, but he'd forgotten to in his nervousness about going to Arena 3B.

There was a bit of interaction among the Alliance members. It appeared that some of them didn't know about the blowjob review.

"Maybe the teacher did it!" another Voice of Reason proclaimed.

"Why do you always assume the teachers are the culprits, that they're guilty without any evidence?"

"Because they deserve it!" another student, a big-faced male, said.

"No, they don't deserve it!" Nathaniel said. "How do you think you'd like to see Studentsonparade set up? How'd you like to see reviews of you posted there?"

"You already get to grade us!" Jake said.

"We give you a grade — and not even with a plus or minus anymore. And that grade is confidential. It's not put up on a website for all the world to see."

"Students need to see about the bad teachers so they don't take them!"

"What I'm saying is that you can't judge from fake reviews whether to take a teacher or not."

"Students can tell what's the truth and what's not. They can read! The average age at this college is twenty-seven. We're not stupid! Are you saying we're too stupid to be able to figure out the truth?"

Nathaniel didn't think it politic to say: In fact a lot of you are stupid and that's why you're here at Shite College, but he thought it was true and wanted to say it. Only you couldn't, not right now. "What I'm saying is that nobody can figure out the truth when they don't know the facts. If the reviews says the teacher gave a blowjob, how are you going to know what the facts are? That teacher is being accused of a crime, I hope you will note!"

"So noted!" Jake Trosky barked.

That brought a laugh from the crowd.

"And there are even worse reviews than that — worse because they may not be as gross, but they still spread vicious rumors without a shred of proof. You say the students can tell what's what, but they can't tell whether a teacher is an unfair grader or not! And being labeled unfair is devastating to a teacher's reputation."

"Are you fair to your students?" Jake tossed his second lion.

Nathaniel hesitated, momentarily tongue-tied. Should he start lobbing some lions of his own? What about the strong likelihood that Jake had sent in phony reviews of Nathaniel? Or they were working with the site's webmaster to doctor Dean Visigoth's reviews. If the accusations were made directly here and now, instead of online, what would be the result? Headline: Teacher Falsely Accuses Jake Trosky of Sending in False Reviews. Teacher Fired.

"Are you Jake Trosky?" he asked.

"What's it to you?"

Their eyes locked.

"Have you ever been in a class of mine?"

"No."

"Have you ever sent in a review of me?"

There was a hesitancy on Jake's part. " . . . No."

"Are you sure?" Trosky actually looked guilty, or was that just wishful thinking?

"What about you, Dr. Tack? Have you ever sent in fake reviews?"

"Me?"

"I think we're getting off the point," Suze interrupted.

"Right," several of the Alliance agreed.

Whew! That was close.

Nathaniel jumped in again. "My main point is that the website should not be set up so that people are actually able to send in fake reviews!"

"The webmaster is working on that," Jake said.

"No, he's not! And he should have worked on it before he opened the site!"

"A dean approved of what that site is doing," Gorilla Woman said.

"And that dean should not have."

"Are you an Administrator, Dr. Tack?"

"No, I'm not."

"And yet you seem to think that your decisions should override a dean's?"

What bullshit! As if Gorilla Woman cared two cents' worth about what some higher-up declared unless it was to her own advantage.

He could feel the "meeting" getting away from him — if he'd ever even "had" it. "What if a teacher set up a website and let teachers say whatever they want to about their students, or anybody's students? How would you feel about that? Student A — with the real named actually given — gave me a blowjob. I recommend him highly."

Several of the students were startled that Nathaniel was talking this way.

When in a stadium, do as the Romans do!

"Or Student B — you fill in the name — gave me an assjob, but, my, it was a terrible assjob. Don't ever let him give you one! Of course I'm sure you could all differentiate between the various blowjobs and assjobs, real and imagined, couldn't you? Whatever your limited experience might be!"

Nathaniel's back was soaked. Bring on the lions! Bring on the tumbrel!

"And you teach your own books about homosexuality, don't you?" suddenly came out of some mouth or other.

"Is that supposed to be a charge of some sort?"

"Well, do you? With sex scenes."

Nathaniel couldn't quite see who was asking the question; it was somebody short and brown in the second last tier. "The last time I checked I believe gays are included in the school's Beauty of Diversity Program, sex scenes and all."

"But not to teach that it's okay."

Great, we don't have enough home-grown homophobes. We have to import more! Nathaniel thought.

"I don't teach that's it's 'okay,' just that it exists. He sat forward on his stool. He thought the whole concept of promoting "the Beauty" of anything, including gayness, was ludicrous, especially when Diversity and everything else in life had more than a few drawbacks. Still, the Zeitgeist said plug this crap like paid hacks. Don't examine it like educators.

"Would you say some teacher couldn't teach about Filipinos?" Nathaniel shot back.

"That's different. You can't help being a Filipino." That brought several hisses. "I mean . . . you know what I mean."

"Again we're getting off the topic," Gorilla Woman said. "Now that's all right when you're trying to disrupt an enemy's meeting, but you shouldn't do it at your own meeting! I believe Dr. Tack is correct about gays and lesbians being included."

Thank God, gay rights had gotten at least this far. It couldn't trump in very many places, but it could at least in this room, at this moment.

"I don't think the issue is whether Dr. Tack is gay or not," Jake Trosky said from on high. "It's his opposition to a legitimate Constitutional right afforded even to students by the Founding Fathers."

"Yeah, Thomas Jefferson and Benjamin Franklin lived and died so that students could accuse their teachers of giving blowjobs!" Nathaniel said.

An hour or more of this kind of back and forth continued, but Nathaniel left not knowing if he had won the debate or not. Gorilla Woman and Jake Trosky went out of their way to thank him for coming, but something in their body language said they were furious with him, underneath the smiles. He thought it meant that they had expected him to be stodgier than he was — the "C" word — a Conservative! And in Santa Francesca!

Nathaniel knew he wasn't a Conservative. It was precisely this kind of glib, simplistic labeling that he fought against in his writing. He thought he did so in his classes as well, but evidently Dame Rumor and Dame Cliché had preceded him and shaped the way the others could more easily perceive and dismiss him. To his mind, both the Left and the Right took turns being arbitrary and preposterous; it was only that at Santa Francesca he happened to be bombarded more by the sins of the Left than the other. But I do think maybe I turned a few heads around in Arena 3B, if I must say so myself.

So it was with some chagrin that afternoon that he noticed an article in the school paper about an "English teacher" (unnamed) and his nefarious ways:

I have been told not to write this article, I might get in trouble. But I am not going to be afraid to speak of my mind! Like the Declaration of Indepenance. So let me point out some of the things this male English teacher has done to his students.

First, he makes them call him "Sir" and "Doctor." He makes it clear on the first day of class that he has no respect for students and they must grovle before him.

Second, he is a raceist because he says that you can tell the race of people from their names! In supposably teaching about conotation, this man puts names on the blackboard. I have not attended his actual classes (thank God) but a reliable source has, and this person says the teacher gave examples. My source could not remember any of these. However, it was something like "Kaneesha" and "Darnell" are African-American names!

When they're not. Lots of white people have names like that! We cannot allow this kind of stereotyping of the People!

Third, this man once said this to an actual class at Shite: "There is literature. And then there is feminist literature." Can you imagine anything so sexist?

He, also, was heard to say, "People who can't pucutate should be put to death." Is this the kind of person who should be teachung in a colledge!

I hope that a petition or action from a Dean will be started to have him removed. We need more teachers of our own color anyhow!

174

Oh? Why wasn't it "raracist" to demand certain teachers for their race alone? Only Whites could be racists, of course. More doublespeak bullshit. The article had a byline by a Jennifer Bouganoonigny, whatever example of the Beauty of Diversity that name was. I didn't even say that line about feminist literature! Nathaniel thought. But I wish I had! How dare this moron distort what he'd actually said and put quotation marks around made-up statements. What kind of journalism were they teaching the students at this school? Don't let facts get in your way! You are such a brave fighter in the land of Free Speech, defending America against those dreadful enemies: Competence, Accuracy, and White People! She hadn't even bothered to contact him to get his side of things! The school paper had just won an award for Excellence in Journalism, besides, from some national organization, all the members of which must have been blind (sorry, visually impaired) not to see all the spelling errors, typos, mis-matched paragraphs, and inane commentaries like this one. Poor Literate America, was there any saving of you?

The article elicited a number of responses, the first an e-mail from Haywood Wire:

Saw the piece on you in the school rag.

> See, I warned you that this ought to be a stealth operation on
> our part. At least they didn't use your name. What's our next
> step? Maybe you could sue the school? — Haywood

The next was a note under his office door from a student who had been at the "meeting" with the Alliance of Students:

Hello and Greetings, Dr. Tack

> I attended the gathering in Arena 3B and I thought you
> handled the situation very well. To be honest I went there
> prepared to hate you, as do most of the members, but I
> thought you brought up some good points.

> Like the reviews not being genuine. I must say no one had
> mentioned that possibility before.

> That article in the paper was not fair to you.

> I hope you won't mind if I don't put my name here.
> Somebody in the Alliance of the school paper might see it and
> give me grief. A Fan

How nice. There were some decent souls around after all. And a person in the college who could actually spell! But he or she was as afraid as Haywood to come out of the cyber closet. Yeah, Free Speech existed — for the Worst, who were full of Passionate Intensity, the others muffled by their fears or their apathy.

Even Gorilla Woman dropped him a note. Yay! It didn't come in a neat package like a Ted Kosinski Surprise. But what was to stop somebody from sending a bomb and precisely that way, in his mailbox or under the door?

Dr. N. Tack,

> On behalf of the Alliance and myself, I just wanted to thank you once again for your appearance at the meeting. There was a discussion after you left. I thought it only fair to mention that the Alliance has voted 13 to 12 not to proceed at this time with the lawsuit against you that originally had been anticipated. Yours truly, Suze D.

What lawsuit? For what? Removing their fucking, lying flyers? They were going to sue him? We'll see about that. Maybe *they* needed to be sued! Lucky old me, one vote saved me. See, class, verbal skills are extremely important in the real world. Not that Shite College had much reality about it!

He whipped off an e-mail to Haywood:

> Suze D. tells me the Alliance may try to sue me.

Haywood wrote back:

> Be on the alert. Let's sue them before they sue us. —
> Haywood

On the alert for what — a subpoena? You are hereby served for desecration of Sacred Student Flyers. Well, at least Haywood said "us," for what that was worth. Was he serious about suing the school?

Nathaniel sent off a note to the faculty moderator of the school newspaper, criticizing the unprofessionalism of the article and mincing no words about it.

He got back a terse little reply:

> Mr. Tack, the students run the newspaper.
>
> I act only as an advisor with no veto power. I would point out that I got the reporter to omit you name at the last minute. —
> Juan Cabo San Lucas

What a pussy!

By God, somebody had to do something. So Nathaniel took his office hour to create a flyer of his own, scotch-taping together words that he cut out of magazines and hand-printing the rest. He hurried over to Dean Deane's office in the Student Union Building, or whatever the hell it was called this week, to see if she would approve it. If she did, she was dead meat!

He couldn't help noticing that Dean Deane's office was just a few doors down from the Alliance of Students office. He could even see some students lounging in their office. No wonder they had her in their grip.

The dean was in, her secretary said, and went in to get her in the inner office. A weathered woman of fifty or so emerged, very Plain Jane. Daphne Deane — rumored to be part of the Lesbian Mafia on campus. She reeked of ordinariness more than anything else. She had pale skin, light eyebrows, and perhaps lips, of a color below pink yet to be named. He doubt that he could have picked her out of a lineup even if she was the only one in it.

"May I help you?" the dean asked.

"Yes, I'm Dr. Tack of the English Department."

There was no reply to that, but was that a tightening of the non-lips?

"I have brought a flyer that I would like approved for display."

"Oh?" She looked at her secretary, who was perkier, with good posture for days. In her fifties too, but osteoporosis was not going to get her, by god!

"Can I get it approved?" Nathaniel pressed. "I'm a big supporter of Teacherson-parade."

"Really?" She didn't seem to be that sharp. A person who'd approve flyers for a website that could spread libel about the school's faculty without asking some questions and putting some safeguards in place wasn't likely to be on top of other things.

"You do approve flyers, don't you?" he asked. "Like the ones that are already up?"

"The *office* approves them." Ah, so she was a little defensive. So maybe word about Trouble had leaked out despite the Administrative gag rule on the matter that obviously was in place.

"We approve most flyers that come our way."

He wanted to say "Would you approve ones for porn sites?" But he thought it best not to rile the dean too much until he got the flyer approved. Then he'd whack her with it, maybe even in court.

"We want our students to have access to lots of information."

Oh, *pu-leeze* ! Half of them hadn't even been to the library!

Nathaniel just smiled at her.

"I did approve the other flyers. Someone has got to look out for the interests of our students here."

"That's why I think this new flyer should be put up." He handed it to her and watched as she read it:

> REVEIW YOUR TEACHERS TODAY!!!!
>
> ANGARY ABOUT YOUR GRADE?
>
> GET SATSFACTION!! NOW!!!
>
> SEND IN REVEIWS. GET THE GRADE YOU
>
> DESERVE!!! NO ONE WILL KNOW WHO YOU ARE IF
> YOU USE
>
> TEACHERSONPARADE.COM!!!
>
> HAVE YOUR FRIENDS SEND IN REVEIWS TOO!!

He was nervous waiting for her reaction. He thought the exclamation points and misspellings especially nice touches, to say nothing of the tear-off slips at the bottom and the promised extortion of grades. She read it through twice.

"But I couldn't approve this."

Nathaniel's heart sank a bit. "Oh?"

"It has no contact number!"

"Well, put my phone number on it then."

"Are you willing to? With your name?"

He hadn't counted on this wrinkle, but, hell, he was "out" about this. "Yes, let me write my name and telephone number." He put down N. TACK and the number. "Is that enough?" It felt hot in the tiny office.

She read it again, apparently unfazed by the militant tone of the flyer or the not- so-hidden message of "student power." She seemed to be checking it for violations of form alone. Finally she said, "I guess it's acceptable."

"I just want students to get all their rights," Nathaniel couldn't resist saying as he grabbed his approved flyer and ran out.

Surely people would begin to see that this couldn't be right, no matter what any school rigmarole regulations said — advertising a way to browbeat teachers into submission on grades! It was like those Internet ads that came in the spam: GET YOUR DEGREE FOR YOUR LIFE EXPERIENCES. Have Your M.A. or M.S. in Three Weeks! Enroll now! With some "university's" name attached — the University of Total Fraud. Dean Daphne looked like she might have gotten her degrees online. "Well, someone's got to stand up for these alternative methods of education, Dr. Tack," she would insist.

"I want a bird so bad I can taste it!" Slacker was saying. She was sitting in the window just behind Nathaniel's computer. Nevertheless, she didn't move, merely sat there flicking her tail back and forth.

"You're just like the faculty — inert!" he scolded her.

She didn't care, just looked at him and blinked, then went back to wishing. Maybe the tail flicked a bit faster, that's all. "Well, you hate it when I actually catch something," she said.

"So I'm inconsistent! Sue me! Besides, nobody eats hummingbirds! Have you no sense of decorum?"

"Decorum-Schmorum, I'd like to have one of those tiny necks between my teeth right this minute, with feathers flapping and flying all over the place. What joy!"

"I could understand that if it was Jake Trosky or Dean Visigoth flapping his feathers under my teeth," Nathaniel said.

What was the reason for this "conversation" in Nathaniel's bedroom/study? Another review on Teachersonparade he had come across:

> What a pathetic sight Tack was trying to persuade the students
> to listen to his feeble, aging justifications for takeing up the

cause offaculty oppression over worker/students! (most of whom have to commute to campus). Tack's (or Lack's) days however are numbered! Votes can change. So can tenure!

The fucker had given Nathaniel another "F" as a teacher! Now he was at the very bottom of THE PITS. And Trosky had probably paid himself with school funds to write the review besides.

This will not stand! Nathaniel vowed. And yet he felt helpless. What can I really do about it? I feel pinned and wriggling on a wall. A chill ran through his spine, and the tension across his back had returned, not that it had ever really left, despite the massages at the spa.

So much for THE PITS. The PENDULUM came when he got a call from the chair of his department on his answering machine at school:

Hello, this is Spike Burns.

We're getting close to winding up enrollment for next semester, and your classes are still practically empty. I've checked registration to see if there's a glitch there, but there doesn't seem to be. Please advise A.S.A.P.

Advise what? — that I'm giving in and exposing my balls to the wolves at last?

Nathaniel was under no illusions about the fact that others could be found to fill his job. Part-timers would jump on those classes in a New York minute. Just the way the Administration liked it — part-timers paid a fraction of the salary and oh, so grateful for the leavings. Even Spike, under pressure, would probably cave in: "Well, they're signing up for our part-timers, Nathaniel! What option do I have?"

The Academic Senate? Toothless.

His mommy? No, his mommy was dead, and she could barely read anyway.

The teachers union?

The union was all but dead. It was made up of sleepy old Leftists more interested in freeing what they considered "wrongly convicted prisoners of color" than defending wrongly convicted teachers, especially if they were of "whiteness." They were supposed to represent the entire school, but eight of the eleven officers were from one department, ESL. It had over three hundred teachers compared to about sixty in the English Department, the tremendous influx of foreigner students having converted one department into a powerhouse, and — "Darwin be praised –what a guy! — quite naturally it ministered to its own needs and wants and could and did outvote any opposition.

He went out and bought a bottle of vodka at the liquor store down the block from his condo and had several stiff drinks before his microwaved dinner. Then he had several more, even though the vodka burned his throat. Even he knew this wasn't good. He was a very light drinker, giddy from two glasses of wine usually. But even these four glasses of vodka didn't put him out, the way he had hoped. He sat in front of some CNN program about tanks, stroking Slacker, and waiting for brain cells to die.

He was hung over when he awoke on the couch. The telephone was ringing, but he could barely move to get it. Slacker had taken over his lap in the meantime and didn't want to move. She dug her claws into his thigh as he staggered upward toward the phone in the kitchen. "Damn you!" he yelled at her.

It was Haywood. "I thought I should call you about it."

"About what?"

"Apparently you haven't seen it then."

"Seen what?"

"It's pretty bad. You sure you want to know?"

The hangover was dissipating, making room for worry and annoyance. "What is it?" And now the cat scratches were really smarting.

"Which one do you want me to read first?"

"There's more than one?"

"A couple of doozies." Haywood sounded downright gleeful. These had evidently made his day. He cleared his throat and began to read:

> Dr. Nathaniel Tack is a man who makes this campus unsafe for both women and men as he lurks outside the campus restrooms waiting for his victims.

"My victims?"

> Then he follows them in and attacks them. But not before he sits in the booths rubbing himself. Several women and one man have told me of their experiences of being traumatized by Dr. Tack. He is one sick mother and yet the Administration does nothing to end his spree of crime! Be alert if you see him on the prowl. You could be next!

"A pretty serious charge, Nathaniel."

"I'd say so. Is that it?"

"Of the first one. I didn't know you were bisexual."

"What?! I'm not bisexual!"

"Now you know how it feels to be accused of something you didn't do, like me."

"Haywood, I knew that before you even read me that review. That's why I'm fighting this whole thing!"

"Do you want to hear the other one? It's worse."

"Do I have any option?"

"These are still up there on the site. I captured them before they could be removed."

"Okay, I'm ready, Haywood." (And, yes, you're a good boy!)

I have read all what I needed to know about this Nathaniel Tack Tack guy. I can tell you right now that hatred is filled up in my eyes. I'm prepared to do whatever means possible to end his teaching career.

I know where he is at pretty much much most of the time. I have timed and recorded all his movements and his actions. The date has been set and my plan is underway. All I need now is a consensus of all the students who want me to go along and eliminate Mr. Tack from the face of the earth. So...if you are with me, give me a 666 sign.... I will check back to see what the results are. Time's a wastin'!!! Tick....Tock...Tack!. — XXX The EXECUTIONER

When Nathaniel didn't say anything, Haywood said, "Pretty scary, right?"

"It's terrible."

"These two might get removed eventually. The blowjob review is finally gone."

"Will it be removed before or after I'm killed?"

"Do you know who might have posted these?"

"I haven't a clue. My only real suspect is . . . the whole fucking world!"

"Don't lose your cool now, Nathaniel. Keep a steady head."

Haywood's words just called attention to the hangover. Nathaniel could barely think straight. He unbuckled his belt and pulled down his pants to examine Slacker's scratches. Two big gouges were already turning dark red.

"You should report this to the police, you suppose?"

"Oh, it's merely a death threat. I wouldn't want to interfere with anyone's free speech!"

"I don't believe death threats are protected."

"Maybe we need an Amendment to the Constitution protecting death threats then. I have a few of my own I'd like to make!"

"You really don't know who this might be from?"

"It doesn't sound like Jake Trosky or Fly on the Wall, but how do I know? Maybe Dean Visigoth sent it, but I don't really know his style yet!"

"I've poured over what I take to be messages from those two, and this last one at least seems to be a different person, a different style. The spelling is better."

"Always wanted to be shot by a good speller."

"He doesn't mention the weapon he'd use, does he? Did I miss that?"

"Sorry, not a gun after all. Probably a machete!"

"It could be a woman too."

"Or a whole death squad! All with lawyers!"

"You're positive you don't know who wrote this? I had another couple of bad reviews myself, but I think I know who it was."

"Who?"

"This joker I used to trade quips with in my 85 class. He turned into a heckler and I told him to shut up."

"And he went to the last refuge of the witty, the website."

"Except he's not witty."

"Hard to believe."

"What are you doing right now, Nathaniel? Maybe you ought to contact the webmaster and tell him to remove the reviews."

"I will not contact him!" Nathaniel decided not to tell Haywood that he was standing there with his pants around his ankles poking at his own scratched thigh.

"He'll probably remove these two if you call them to his attention."

"I'm supposed to call them to his attention? Why isn't he watching his own fucked-up website to prevent such things in the first place?"

"I think there's some Internet law that says the webmaster is less liable the less he actually edits his website."

"What?!" Nathaniel managed to pull up his pants, but the buckle was giving him trouble.

"I know, I know. We'll have to check that law out. In the meantime, you'd better do something about this."

"What do you suggest? Write in and say I don't give the 666 sign? Maybe you could write in too?"

"Is that the sign of the Devil?"

"I'd be willing to bet."

"There really is a Satanist Club on campus."

"Why does that not surprise me?"

"Of course this guy could just pretending to be a Satanist."

"Will the real Satanist please stand up."

"I've heard that Barney Rock is pretty upset about the website. Maybe you should contact him."

"Who's Barney Rock?" Nathaniel had actually heard of the man but wanted to hear Haywood's description of him. He also wanted time to get his belt re-buckled.

"A member of the Board of Trustees. I've met him a couple of times. Said to be a millionaire, and he takes things like this seriously, I'd think. He was a student here years ago and has an attachment to the place. I'm pretty confident that he would react to this death threat."

"I don't want to go online and retrieve it myself. Can you send me a copy?"

"Shall I fax it to you?"

Nathaniel gave his fax number. "Ain't all this communication peachy!"

"Let me know if you don't get it."

"I will. And thanks."

"I hesitated to let you know about this. But we can't just ignore it. Shall I send both reviews to you?"

"Why not? My cup runneth over."

"Are you afraid because of this?"

"Just because somebody might be waiting for me outside my condo right this minute?" Nathaniel moved to the window in the front room and moved the drape aside. The street outside was deserted. "But not to worry. I'll put Slacker on watch."

"You have a dog?"

"My cat."

"You'll put her on watch?"

"A joke."

"It's good, Nathaniel, that you manage to keep you sense of humor through all this."

"I hear machete wounds heal faster if you have a sense of humor."

Haywood laughed.

"Maybe I really should call the police." Nathaniel suddenly felt cold.

"Wouldn't hurt."

"Hello, this is the Bisexual Crotch Rubber calling. Can you help me?"

Haywood laughed some more, quite heartily. "Are you this funny in class? I'd think the students would love it."

"People tend to dismiss you if you're too funny. Better to be as serious as a . . . as a Satanist."

"I'm cutting back on the jokes and the candy myself," Haywood said. "I'm thinking about retiring."

"Really?"

"I have some money put away. And a pension. I've been here for twenty-seven years. And I can get another job doing statistics for people. Maybe you should consider retiring too."

"I don't have enough years in. I don't have enough credit for the years I do have in. But don't get me started!"

"Okay, don't get started."

Funny how people didn't want to hear about things like that.

"Where do you suppose these reviewers came up with the idea that you rub yourself in both bathrooms?"

Was Haywood fishing? "I haven't a clue." Damn this belt buckle!

"You haven't ever gone into the women's restroom by mistake or anything, have you?"

No, Haywood, that's your scene. He pinched a cat scratch so that he wouldn't say it. "Ouch!"

"What's the matter? Is someone there?" Haywood sounded quite worried.

"It's nothing. My cat scratched me."

"Oh."

"Or should I say my Familiar scratched me. Actually all this is very similar to being accused of witchcraft, have you noticed? Somebody says something about you, however preposterous, and suddenly you're on everybody's favorite witch list."

"Like what happened to me. That review accusing me of harassment is still there."

"That's why we've got to fight this, Haywood. It took centuries to establish proof and evidence and all those legal trappings, and they are being wiped out by the Internet in a few minutes!"

"I'm with you on this!"

"I'm glad to hear it."

"I'll be more than happy to help in any way I can, Nathaniel. Just don't use my name."

"I appreciate that, Haywood." It was as close to "bonding" as they had come, flawed though it was. "I'm not a perfect human being by a long shot, and I no doubt have a lot of opinions that are not popular, but I swear I won't be dragged to the fire without a protest and a major fight!"

"Right!"

"At the very least I want to be roasted for what I've actually done and said and not for fabrications made up by people who happen to have access to a computer and no clue that they're doing evil things. It's a sad day for the world when the Satanists start believing they're the forces of moral justice! The Bisexual Rubber indeed!"

"Amen!"

Nathaniel finally got his belt buckle back into place. "I think I will call the police. Can you contact Barney Rock of the Board?"

"I'll send him the reviews, but I don't want him to know where they came from."

"Okay. Let's do this, Haywood! Otherwise, I have a strong feeling that the combined forces of Dean Visigoth and the Alliance of Students, Academic Freedom or not, will have our scalp."

When Nathaniel succeeded, after numerous dead-ends on the voice mail, in getting through to an actual police officer, he encountered the following:

"Officer Grout speaking."

"Oh, good. I'm Dr. Nathaniel Tack of Shite College."

"Yeah?" She seemed in a hurry.

"I left a message about threatening messages about me."

"Yeah?"

"Is this the Special Hate Division?"

"Yeah."

"Well, I think I've been the object of 'special hate.' I'm openly gay."

"Yeah?"

"I mailed a copy of the threat to your office."

"Didn't get it."

"Do you want me to read the threat over the phone?"

"Just tell me what it says."

"It says someone knows where I park and teach and has promised to end my teaching career."

"Well, that could mean any number of things."

Nathaniel was surprised at her indifferent tone. "It also says that I'm to be removed from the face of the earth. Do you find that ambiguous?"

"Do you know who made this threat?"

"No, it's online."

"On your telephone?"

"No, online. On a website."

"I'm not up on all that yet."

"It's posted somewhere where anyone can read it — and act on it."

"Have you actually ever been threatened?"

"I'm talking about an actual threat." He could feel his facial tic kicking in again.

"I mean a real one. In person. Anyone waiting for you outside a classroom or somethin' like that?"

"Not so far."

"Oh, are *you* the Bisexual Crotch Rubber? I did get that message."

"I'm not actually bisexual — or a rubber, for god's sake!"

"Don't get mad at me."

"I'm not mad at you. I just don't like being referred to that way. How would you like it if the police department put up a website where any criminal could post things about you?"

"We get complaints all the time."

"But they don't go up on the police department's website, I bet." Make it personal, and they will come!

"What's your point?"

"No doubt you have a long list of 'special hate' crimes on your desk, but this one is not to be dismissed just because —."

"I'm not dismissing it."

Jesus! Nathaniel knew he was losing her, and he hadn't even had her yet! "Look, I'm trying to keep calm and rational about this, but your tone tells me that you don't seem to care very much about this threat."

"When did it happen, sir?" Uh oh — into "professional" mode.

"Three days ago."

"Has anything more serious happened since then? Assault? Any battery?"

"No! I'm trying to prevent assault and battery!"

"Hold on, hold on."

"The threat is still up on the website as far as I know!"

"You don't know for sure?"

"I don't want to look at it. Would you?"

"Maybe it was just temporary."

"Maybe it wasn't. Maybe the threatener is waiting outside my office right this minute to get me!"

"Don't you have campus police there?"

"Yes."

"Can't they protect you?"

"I doubt it. They don't carry guns. And they spend most of their time giving parking tickets — parking tickets to the faculty, I might add, instead of barricading the parking lots in the first place so that non-faculty can't get in and take the parking spots, thus preventing the faculty from parking in the faculty parking spots and thus causing the faculty to get tickets!"

" . . . Is this a separate complaint, sir?"

"It's all one big complaint. A cosmic one!"

"I don't like your tone, sir."

"Well, I don't like yours."

When he went in to see said Officer Ilse Grout, winding his way through a labyrinth of offices in the Rudolph Giuliani Police Headquarters Building until he finally found the Special Hate Crimes Division (two tiny rooms), it was with full determination to handle the situation better this time. She greeted him with:

"Oh, the Bisexual Crotch Rubber."

"I would point out that is merely an accusation. Without a shred of truth to it."

"I know that." Nathaniel could tell already that she didn't like him. Probably the "uppity" way he talked. Well, he wasn't going to say "he don't" to please her!

She was a tall white woman about thirty-five in full cop drag, a uniform of dark blue in some coarse cotton material, very form-fitting, with her plain brown hair pulled back into a pony-tail. She had a fussy, straight-arrow nose and all the charm of a meter maid with a hernia. She offered him a seat at her cluttered desk in the tiny, unimpressive office.

"I brought along the threatening review to show you, plus a few others." He laid them out on her desk.

Officer Grout pulled a pair of glasses on a cord from the top drawer and began to read. Not much showed in her face.

"I've included some others about other teachers as well."

She didn't seem to care overmuch.

"So that you can see there's an atmosphere at our college."

"Hmm."

"Note the one about the blowjob."

She turned a page.

"And the one about having sex in a wheelchair with a woman teacher."

"Quite a collection you have here." She looked up at Nathaniel as though he were some kind of pervert who relished this special pornography.

"I don't collect it! It's been forced on me — on all of us." Nathaniel felt utterly ridiculous.

Officer Grout stopped reading — he doubted that it was one of her favorite activities anyway — and looked him in the eye. "What do you want me to do about this?" She picked up a blank form and a pen.

"I want it to stop."

"Who's doing it? Do you have a name? A suspect maybe?"

"I believe I mentioned to you already that it's online — it's anonymous."

"How does that work now?"

It took all his effort for Nathaniel not to sigh out loud. "Let's just say that I think that one review in particular shows that a hate crime is being planned."

"But has it taken place yet?"

"No!" He realized he was being too aggressive, and yet he couldn't stop himself.

"Do you think it's likely to occur again? Is it someone in your personal life, a domestic partner maybe?"

Oh, she was one of those Neanderthals (Neandertalls, to be precise!) who might enforce the law, but she sure as hell wasn't going to go out of her way for them people. "No, I don't believe it's my partner, if that's what you mean. But it could be!"

"I beg your pardon?"

"What I mean is that the website is set up so that anybody can review a teacher even if you have never met the teacher!"

"And why would this occur?"

He felt like he was explaining algebra to Slacker.

"Why do people deface buildings? Because people are mean!" She nodded.

Oh, good, why hadn't he thought of this sooner. Of course she thought people were mean. She was a cop. They needed to be watched and punished and wiped clean of Original Sin with a good arrest and pistol whipping every now and again.

"Let's fill out this form," she said. She took his name and telephone number again and turned the form toward him to fill in the actual complaint. "I took a course at Shite once," she suddenly confessed.

"Really?" He looked up but then continued writing.

"English."

"You didn't have me, did you?"

"No."

"Good thing. Otherwise we'd know where the threat came from, wouldn't we?" She gave him a pinched smile. "I did all right there."

"Well, good. Who did you have?"

"I forget."

"Hmm."

"I think it was a man."

Was this a reflection of her poor memory or the sexual ambiguity of the instructor? After all, there were Seven Types of Ambiguity, weren't there? He found the pen hurting his fingers because he had to press hard, the form in triplicate.

"I read some of the other students' papers. We did peer . . . peer . . ."

"Evaluation?"

"That's it."

"And?"

"A lot of them were pretty terrible, I thought."

Yay, an ally! "Terrible in what way exactly?" (Let me count the ways!)

"Full of mistakes."

"Shocking, isn't it?"

"And the teacher was passin' 'em. I saw one with a B on it which I couldn't even understand."

Nathaniel wanted to hug her. "People have no idea what's going on in American colleges," I'm afraid. He read through the written complaint and caught a handwriting error he'd made. He couldn't remember the last time he'd actually written this much by hand. "Let me fix that," he said. "I'm always on my students' backs about their English."

"I'm glad somebody is. I'm sendin' my daughter to Shite next year."

"Is she in high school now?"

"She wants to be an English teacher."

"Is she a masochist?"

Officer Grout allowed a smile. "She's very good in writing and stuff like that."

"I'm pleased to hear that. But it also helps to be a masochist."

"I've never thought I was any good at that kind of stuff, but I was better than a lot of 'em in that class."

"What was it?"

"English 101."

"I teach that." Talk her up, Nathaniel. Maybe you'll get a police escort!

"America is in a sorry state."

"Indeed it is," he said. Now to keep her focused on illiteracy instead of the Moral Depravity that he, as a Practicing Homosexual, probably represented to at least a section of her mind. "Some of us are trying to rectify the problem, but it isn't easy. There's resistance, and now those with a hacker mentality have discovered a new way to undermine standards."

"I've heard of hackers," she volunteered. "They break into . . ."

"They do! And that's precisely what this threat is all about. Somebody can read vicious lies about a teacher on this website I mentioned and then decide to seek vengeance, maybe even kill someone, someone who has done nothing more than to try to maintain academic standards and not be a push-over for every whiner around this city."

She liked that, he could tell.

"How awful."

"As you no doubt know, there are a lot of weird and crazy people wandering around this city."

"You don't have to tell me."

"Now they can be weird and crazy on the computer."

"Progress!" she scoffed.

"Exactly!"

They were buddies now, in the foxhole together, fighting off the whining barbarians!

"It's been very nice talking with you," Nathaniel said, handing her his complaint form all neatly filled in.

"And you," she agreed.

"I hope my handwriting is legible," he said, tapping the form.

She gave it a glimpse. "It's fine."

They even shook hands.

A nd that was the last he heard from Officer Ilse Grout.

However, Nathaniel hadn't been born yesterday and didn't wait for her Special Hate Office to get off its donut-filled, hate-free butt and act. The form he'd filled out would get processed in time perhaps, but he suspected that the dangers he was fighting were probably too new to sink in very far to the typical police mind — or, worse, that they wouldn't know what to do about it *if* they did see the problem!

Haywood had been true to his word, and there was a message on Nathaniel's answering machine at school:

Hello there, Dr. Tack! This is Trustee Barney Rock!

I saw that threat on the site and think it's disgusting. Let's talk about this and maybe get some action going here.

He even gave his home phone number, which was very decent of him. The voice was gruff, a bit down-in-the-well, but warm too.

When Nathaniel called, he got Barney Rock's answering machine. Maybe he was at his business, whatever that was, making his millions. Nathaniel left another message. Something tells me this man might actually do little good here. I can't lose hope, I just can't!

It was an e-mail from Haywood that startled him out of the bout of depression he could feel forming at the base of his brain.

Glad to see you respond to that threat!

Both are still up on the site! See this new one!

Haywood included the following 'review':

This Dr. Nathaniel Tack writing in.

Whoever wrote that message about me and my bathroom "victims" should understand that their information is incorrect. I am sure that we can work this all out and resolve our differences. If I have offended anyone, I am deeply, deeply sorry. Yet there is no need to take any action against me.

I am sure that if you go to the Chancellor or to some other Administrator or to a Dean your complaints will be addressed. Please, please, whatever you do, don't do something you'll regret for the rest of your life! I beg you!

N. T., Ph.D.

"I didn't write this!" Nathaniel said aloud. He wrote back to Haywood immediately:

I DID NOT WRITE THIS!

Then who did write it?

I don't know. Did you?

Nathaniel, I think you sent it.

I did NOT send it! Why would I send it? To save my life maybe? BUT I DID NOT SEND IT!

When he got together with Marty that night for dinner — in the parking lot of a drive-in burger joint called Beep's — which should have been called Burps — he couldn't wait to tell Marty about the developments. Nathaniel didn't like being out of the streets like this, vulnerable to Santa Francesca's growing crime rate, but Marty wanted drive-in food because he was short on money again. He looked tired but smelled good. He seemed relatively free of speed, his beard newly trimmed. Probably getting too thin.

"What's that smell on you?"

"Aftershave. Walgreens. Menthol."

"Nice."

They put in their orders at the drive-in's walk-up counter. Just burgers and fries and Cokes. There were some "ghetto" youths (who probably made more than Nathaniel did) in Bad Ass clothes milling about, making drug deals on their cell phones. "You don't buy drugs from them, do you?" he asked Marty.

Marty just rolled his eyes. "Any more threats about you on that site?"

Nathaniel looked out at the street from the complete insecurity of his Rav4. The machine gun bullets no doubt would penetrate the doors, the upholstery, and him in a flash. Probably even a Saturday Night Special from Walt-Mart would do the trick. "Somebody posing as me sent in a begging, ass-kissing plea!"

"No!"

"It makes me sound like I'm peeing my pants." Nathaniel reached into his shirt pocket and got the piece of paper.

"Are you peeing in your pants?"

"I think I'm handling this very well, if I must say so myself."

"Why would someone else answer the threat?"

"I guess this is the only way to reply to any review. You send in a review of yourself. Only I didn't do it!"

"You sure?"

"I haven't touched the site since the very beginning!"

"I know," Marty smirked, refusing the review and patting Nathaniel on the crotch.

"What?"

Marty looked quite smug. "I did it."

"Are you serious?"

"I was checking the site, saw the threat, and raced to the defense of my honey."

"No!"

"Is that so hard to believe?"

"I guess not. I'm just surprised, that's all. I thought it was Haywood."

"I swear on my mother's kidney dialysis."

"Is she doing that now?"

"She sent me a picture of her favorite machine."

"Send her my gay love."

Their burgers were ready. Marty liked his rare, but Nathaniel had seen a TV expose about uncooked beef and always ordered his just short of burnt to a crisp. This time both burgers were rare. What the hell, when the machine gun let rip, he'd be pretty rare himself. He piled on relish and mustard and hurried back to the car.

Marty stopped for a cigarette. God, he was smoking again! He even asked one of the Bad Asses for a light. He stood there, the smoke swirling around him, under the severe light from the spotlights on top of Beep's, and he still managed to look good. Nathaniel wished he could lose some weight himself. Would it take speed?

Someone moved too fast at the corner of Nathaniel's vision, and he jumped and spilled his Coke all over his lap and his cat scratches. "Christ Almighty!" He began mopping it up with the two napkins he'd taken, but they were mostly soaked too. "What next?!" he sighed.

When Marty got back into the car, he didn't say anything snide about the spill. "Let me get that," he said. He seemed to feel that Nathaniel was about to crack under all the strain. Marty always took more napkins than he "should have," Nathaniel thought, but here he was mopping under his lap and the car seat and not complaining about it.

"Thank you," Nathaniel said, fighting off tears.

"It's the least I could do." Marty stuffed the soggy napkins into the trash container on the floor of the back seat.

"Can you give me a little arm-lovin', as my old hillbilly mother used to say?" He felt big and thick and crammed under the steering wheel. Even the scar on his chin seemed to be throbbing. At least the tic wasn't . . . ticking.

"Of course," Marty said, starting to put his arm around Nathaniel.

"Not here!" Nathaniel practically screamed. "Not with those homophobic Bad Asses around. We'll be shot!"

"Okay, okay!" Marty held up his hands as if in a holdup. "Jesus!"

"I'm sorry. Let's drive up to the top of Double Peaks and see the view." Nathaniel started to turn the key in the ignition.

"Okay, but the last time I was up there it was all Latino gangs, gunning their motors and acting tough, yelling and screaming 'maricones' and 'fuckin' fags' and . . ."

"The Beauty of Diversity strikes again. . . . And we're big-time 'racists' because we notice it isn't all beauty, not even close," Nathaniel said, shaking his head. "I'm afraid the city of Santa Francesca has seen its best days and is now descending into its twilight." He tried to smile. "Like me!"

"You've got lots of good years left," Marty said. "Miles to go before you sleep."

"I don't think so." Nathaniel was shaking. "I really don't think so. There comes a time in your life when you can see its end. And I'm there — and I don't mean just because of the death threat. But because of my age and . . ."

"Why don't you try writing something? A play?"

Nathaniel half-shrugged. "I can't write. Not now."

"Hey, I'll give you my Coke," Marty said, "since you spilled yours." He took the lid off. "Will that help?"

"Thank you, Florence Nightingale."

"I love you, bastard that you are," Marty said, touching Nathaniel's knee. "That's why I sent in that reply."

"I know. Thank you. Thank you."

They sat in the crummy parking lot and finished their unhealthy burgers and fries, and eventually Marty snorted some speed, and Nathaniel did not say "Oh, God, I don't think I really love you anymore, Marty."

After they kissed good night and Nathaniel felt yet another wave of guilt about what he was feeling toward Marty, he went home, prepared to drown himself in the evening news and maybe some vodka.

There was a message blinking red:

Hi! This is Jim. If you get in before ten call me.

Nathaniel called immediately and his son answered.

"What's wrong?"

"Let me go into my room."

"Sure."

He heard him say good night to his mother and her lover, distant female voices in the background. There was even some laughter or horseplay. So that didn't seem to be the problem.

"I'm back."

"No 'Yo'?"

"I don't say that anymore."

"Just when I was getting used to it. So how are you . . . Jim? You are going by Jim now, right?"

"Except around this place, where they insist on Jimmy! They're dorks."

Hmm. "Oh, they'll get used to it. What's the problem?"

"Yes, I'm still a virgin. But that's not the problem."

"It's not?"

"Something else."

"Sounds like your voice is getting deeper."

"Whatever." Jim/Jimmy hesitated. "Am I illegitimate?" He sounded almost plaintive.

Nathaniel hesitated as well. "What?"

"Am I?"

"Does it matter?"

"Yeah. I was talking to this girl at school."

"A new girl, this is?"

"Bethany. She's really beautiful. Really hot. Except that she's a Christian."

"They seem to grow Christians like weeds up in your neck of the woods. Pretty weeds, of course."

"She knows my parents are gay. She saw my mom and Lana at a play we did."

"You were in a play?"

"Yeah, sort of."

"Why didn't you tell me. I would've come up to see it."

"Oh, it was just a one-act. It wasn't in the real theater. This Christian group put it on and I was in it. It's a long story."

"You were in a Christian play? And it wasn't Christmas?" Now this indeed was a serious problem!

"I was only in it to get to know Bethany!" Jim/Jimmy sounded impatient.

"Go on."

"What happened is that she saw them at the play and figured it out. When I asked her out, she said she couldn't go out with me because I'm illegitimate."

The Christian cunt! he thought but dared not say. "Find somebody less narrow. Aren't there any non-Christians up there? A nice Islamic girl? Just kidding!"

"I like Bethany!"

"You know how to pick 'em, kid."

"So I told her I wasn't illegitimate, but she said I was because my parents aren't married."

"I don't know where this is going, but I'm not marrying your mother. Or Lana."

"I'm not asking you to!"

There was a bit too much of that American teenage parents-will-never-understand tone to suit Nathaniel. "What are you asking me to do. Life is not a Walt Disney movie, I hope you realize."

"I know that!"

"Ah, Jim, I'm going to ask you to cool the tone, okay?"

"Tone?"

"Your tone. I don't like it."

"Why?"

"Because it's too . . . too demanding."

"I'm just asking if I'm illegitimate or not."

"And what if you are?"

"Because Bethany won't go out with me. She won't introduce me to her parents."

"Those Bible seminars will just have to go on without you."

"I'm serious."

"You're seventeen! Everything is serious. Oh, my god, did I forget your birthday?"

"Yes."

"Sorry."

"Doesn't matter."

"I've been under a lot of strain."

"It's all right. My mom made me a cake."

They waited.

"What about this Bethany now?"

"She is just so beautiful. Everybody says so."

"I fear you lusteth in your heart, my boy. Mix not your carnal ways with the Good Book."

"What? Talk English."

"I am talking English!" Nathaniel was also getting irritated. He looked at the vodka bottle on the kitchen counter. "If you're illegitimate, no one cares about that technicality anymore."

"Bethany cares."

"If she's such a good Christian, she can forgive you — and go out on a date and give you head. Christian fundamentalist head!"

"Dad."

"Sorry, I'm feeling stressed these days. Besides, fundamentalist head is an oxymoron."

"So I'm a bastard then?"

"No, just becoming one."

"What?"

"It was a joke, a feeble one. I'm afraid my humor faileth me in my hour of need."

"You're not much help."

"Sorry!"

"Well, I can't talk to them about it."

"By them I presume you mean the people who support you, your mother and Lana."

"I can't really talk to anybody about it. Why'd you even have me if I had to be illegitimate?"

"Whoa now, Mister. Do not think you'd have no problems and instead would be enjoying the Biblical delights of Bethany Born Again if only this one little imperfection in your make-up didn't exist. It ain't so. It will never be so."

"It's my only problem right now."

"Others will develop. Trust me."

"You're so negative!"

Nathaniel bit his lip. "It's called the human condition, Jimmy."

"Jim."

"Whatever. Life is like a Woody Allen movie. Always a little bit disappointing."

"I've never seen a Woody Allen movie."

"Listen, you tell Bethany Born Again —"

"That's not her name! Can't you even get that straight?"

"I know that's not her name!"

"It's Limbaugh."

"What?! Is she related to the Right Wing radio host?"

"Yes. He has a lot of money and we don't."

"It seems to me, son, that you're hanging around with a bad crowd. Stay away from that girl."

"She doesn't drink or smoke or do drugs or swear or dance." Jim/Jimmy seemed to be consulting a list in his mind. "Or even —"

"She performs in the theater!"

"Only in Christian plays. They might do another one in the spring, too."

"Once is a lark. Twice is a lifestyle. Don't do another one with them, okay?"

"They said I was excellent in the one-act!"

"I'm sure you were. But they might have said that just to entice you into their world. Remember, those people recruit! They accuse us of it, but they actually *do* it!"

"I'd do just about anything to get to know Bethany better."

"I want you to go out right now and drink, smoke, and swear!"

"What?!"

"But don't do hard drugs. No son of mine is going to become born again! Your first birth was hard enough. Ask your mother."

"You're weird."

"Do you know that the Bible is based on incest?"

"It is not!"

"Bethany and her gang won't tell you this. They probably haven't even figured it out yet. But how did human life begin, according to them?"

"From Adam and Eve."

"Exactly. From two original parents."

"So what's your point?"

"How do you get more human beings from two parents? We know that Adam and Eve had at least two sons, right? Cain —"

"And Abel."

"Plus their handicapped child, whom we don't hear much about — Dis-Abel, the one they no doubt kept locked in a closet."

"I've got to do my homework. I've been putting it off and my mom's all over me about it."

"Wait! This is important. Perhaps Adam and Eve also had some girl children. Let's just say they did, though they aren't mentioned by name. How do heterosexuals reproduce? It's well documented. Either Adam had sex with his girl children or Eve had sex with her boy children — Cain and Abel — but probably not with Dis-Abel — unless that's where Tiny Tim came from — or at the very least the children of Adam and Eve had sex with each other. Anyway you slice it, dice it, or price it, it's incest."

"So?"

"So wouldn't Bethany and her family frown on incest even more than illegitimacy?"

"I guess."

"See, they believe in a so-called Holy Book that promotes and endorses the nakedest kind of incest you can imagine."

"They're not promoting it."

"If they believe that Almighty God, in all His Almightiness, couldn't come up with something better than a man's rib and incest to reproduce the human race, then they're worshiping up the wrong tree! I don't want those people telling me, or my son, how to live."

"But that was back then. Not now."

"Surely morality doesn't change! Heavens! If incest was good enough for God Almighty in the first place, then why in God's name isn't it good enough for Him now?"

Jim/Jimmy paused. "So you want me to commit incest?"

"Yeah, that's what I want, Jimmy."

"It's Jim. I'm just joking! Like you."

"The apple never falls far from the tree. The forbidden apple included."

"So am I illegitimate or not?"

"You just tell Bethany Holier Than Thou that she's not only descended from a long line of apes, but she's a product of God's holy incest. . . . Then she'll go out on date with you."

"I kind of doubt it."

They laughed together.

"Honestly I don't know what to tell you, Jim. It's true your mother and father didn't have a marriage license when you were conceived, but, believe me, Bethany and her ilk aren't superior because her parents bought a piece of paper that made their offspring 'legitimate' and everybody without that piece of legalism is supposed to be 'illegitimate.' It's what the person actually is that matters! That's where real legitimacy comes from."

"Yeah."

"I'm sorry it sounds so lame. But it's the truth. And being a bit different from other people can make you creative besides."

"I've got to go. Homework."

"Does that help? Even a little?"

"Got to go. Mom's on my case. Later!"

And then Jim/Jimmy was gone.

Nathaniel the father sighed.

He took the bottle of vodka from the kitchen counter and a large glass, then fished a set of student essays out of his briefcase on the couch, sat down and began to drink and grade. Grade and drink. It was the very first time in his life that he'd ever graded papers drunk. (The students did much better.)

Nathaniel finally arranged to meet up with Barney Rock, the Trustee on the Board of Shite — for some action at last. The Trustees, being elected politicians and having to cater to the special P.C. pieties of the city of Santa Francesca, were not entirely to be trusted of course. Still, Nathaniel felt stymied and didn't know where else to turn. At least he had finally gotten his back paychecks. The bastards.

They had agreed to meet in the Non-Faculty Dining Room, and naturally Barney Rock was late. The usual suspects were there, some librarians from the Jesse Jackson Memorial Library, a large tableful of math and physics people, the odd retired faculty member dining alone, shaky of limb and desiccated of face, ignored and forgotten. Yes, I gave my life to this institution . . . and now nobody gives a crap.

Nathaniel ordered the special drink of the day, a Vanilla Manila, named in honor of the college's Filipino Activism Week, and tried to look busy. He'd brought along a book, but he kept looking up for Barney Rock Somebody had painted a new mural of what looked like caricatures of the staff and faculty, really quite grotesque, the whole bunch of them. Then it dawned on him that they were pictures of "Our Friends the Mentally Ill." At least that's what the plaque underneath said. Well, at least the food was usually good here. He adjusted his chair slightly so that he wouldn't have to dine with "Our Friends the Mentally Ill."

Barney Rock, it turned out, was a handsome man of some sixty-five winters, all piled right on top of his hair, which looked like it had never been anything but white. The face was Italianate, not quite marble, but firm, noble-looking, well-nosed. He was wearing a knockout, very expensive suit of black silk. He'd better watch himself, Nathaniel thought, or the Masses will tear him to pieces. "Did you see that elitist suit he had the audacity to wear while the poor Homeless couldn't even find a seat in the Lowe-Rankin Dining Experience!" the Student Alliance would charge.

"Nice to meet you," Barney said, sitting at the small table after Nathaniel waved to him.

"And you."

"Did you happen to bring along that threatening review?" Barney asked. "I forgot my copy."

"I did indeed," Nathaniel said, having anticipated as much, taking it out of his shirt pocket, where it had become a bit moist in his anxiety over whether Barney was going to show up or not.

When Nathaniel presented the review and even opened it, Barney just skimmed it. He had the politician's air about him — not given to close readings of things, shall we say, sharp, but not a micro-manager.

"I think that is the worst thing I have ever seen," he said, indicating the somewhat wrinkled and wet review on the white tablecloth between them.

"There are lots more, old ones and new ones both," Nathaniel said.

"More threats?"

"Not threats exactly. Just vicious lies."

"Like what?"

"I brought some." Nathaniel opened his book and removed the envelope of "choice" reviews from the website. "I want to emphasize that it's not only the ones about me that are the problem."

"I fully understand. Are there any about the Chancellor?"

The question surprised Nathaniel. "The Chancellor?"

"I've never looked at the actual site," Barney said.

"I believe there is one about the Chancellor, yes."

"Is it awful?"

My, what had we here! "Awful?"

"I heard there was one saying the Chancellor takes bribes or something like that."

"I haven't found that one."

"Do you think you could?"

Obviously Barney Rock didn't like their beloved Chancellor. "I could look."

"Maybe you could send it to me?"

"I'll see what I can do." (You scratch mine, I'll scratch yours.)

"By the way, is the threat against you still up there?"

"I believe it came down yesterday. The Mole told me."

"Who?"

"Somebody who doesn't want his identify exposed. So I call him the Mole now."

"Did you call the police about it?"

"I went to see the police about it. They didn't seem overly frightened for me."

"Yeah, the police are problematic around this city." Barney took a bread stick and broke it in two and began nibbling on it. "Where's that waiter? I can't stay very long, I'm afraid. I have a meeting with some of the other Trustees."

This too didn't amaze Nathaniel. He knew he'd better get in his sound bite between the other bites. "Are the other Trustees aware of how the site is being used?"

"They're aware of it, but we haven't discussed it. It's one of the items I mean to bring up at today's meeting. The whole website thing is a pretty hot potato."

"Which they probably don't even want to touch."

Barney nodded. "Do you mind if I take this?" He meant the threatening review.

"Take the whole envelope if you wish. There are plenty more were those came from."

"I'll just lose them." Well, at least that was honest. Barney stuck the lone review into his wallet.

Finally one of the student "servers" came over to take their orders. Nathaniel was surprised that "server" hadn't been 86ed along with other offensive terms like "waitress." Surely "server" more than smacked of "servant."

"Hello, I will be your servant today," a young woman said — really. She proceeded to read the specials to them, not particularly well. You weren't supposed to notice.

He and Barney both ordered the Salade Nicoise, or at least that's what they thought it might be. Barney even went out of his way to thank the "servant" for her kindness to them. He also noticed that Barney was working the room with his eyes and giving big, warm Italianate hand waves to several other tables.

"Must be exhausting," Nathaniel said.

"What's that?"

"Politicking."

Barney smiled a little bit. "I have a ranch to get away to."

"Lucky you." (Maybe I'll join the Masses and take over your ranch.)

"Have you met our Chancellor?"

"I've seen him around. He's very short, isn't he? With a Boston accent."

"An interesting man."

Nathaniel took that to mean, The Chancellor's a full-fledged dick and I hate his guts. "Do you think he might help us?"

"No way. He's already given money to the Student Alliance for its proposed lawsuit."

"I beg your pardon?"

"He gave at least fifty thousand dollars to the Student Alliance in the lawsuit they were — or are — planning against you. You didn't know?"

Nathaniel choked on his bread roll. "I had no idea, although I've heard about the possible lawsuit of course."

"They got to him first. He's a real sucker for student activism. His Ph.D., so called, is on the rights of students."

Nathaniel's stomach sank to the floor. "Oh, great."

"I didn't vote for him when he was being interviewed, but he seemed to impress the other Board members. Now I think they're having second thoughts." Barney's eyes came up to Nathaniel's, a bit jumpy, as if maybe he had revealed too much. He bit off some more bread stick.

"I'll get you that awful review of the Chancellor," Nathaniel said. It's Pimp Time.

"I'm just curious," Barney said self-protectively.

"Of course you could always write one yourself."

"What's that?" Barney was working the room again — charm, eyes aglitter. He spotted some gargantuan woman who was leaving and waved. Maybe she was a whole 'minority' by herself?

"Should you choose to. You do know that anyone can send in reviews to the website."

"Anyone?"

"This information is taking longer to sink in than I thought it would. Yet, despite my reputation, I'm actually an optimist. People will eventually see what I'm bitching about. Yes, you can send in a review, or several, if you just damn well please."

"You can't send in reviews of the Board members, though."

"Oh?"

"I checked. Only faculty and Administrators."

Of course you'd make sure the Board covers its ass and can't get pilloried like the rest of us. "Call me a crybaby, but I don't think the faculty should have to put up with this . . . this . . ."

"Fucking crap?"

Nathaniel smiled. "A man after my own heart."

"Have you thought about suing the school?" Barney asked.

"What?!"

"Suing the Chancellor maybe, or the whole school. Of course you didn't hear this from me. As a Board member, it is my sworn duty to protect and promote the college under all circumstances." Barney Rock smiled the smile of Machiavelli. "Just between you me, and the Vanilla Manila, I don't think you'll get any satisfaction about that website unless you sue."

"Really?"

"Think about it."

"I don't think I have the money for a lawsuit."

"I can probably suggest some lawyers. They might do it pro bono — since it's about Internet law. Could be precedent-setting."

How about you being precedent-setting and giving me the money for the lawyer, Nathaniel thought.

"You interested?"

"It has come up from time to time — from the Mole especially."

"Your anonymous friend."

"Friend would be going too far. My strange bedfellow, I guess you could say."

"I've whored around enough to know about strange bedfellows," Barney said. "Call me and I'll see what I can do about getting you a lawyer." He took a business card, very nicely engraved, out of his wallet and slid it toward Nathaniel. "Do you have a card?"

Nathaniel found an old tattered one tucked away in his wallet. "Can't wait to hear from you," he said.

Their Greek salads didn't come, but two Nicaraguan Du Jours did. Barney had time for just a few quick bites before he had to leave. However, he stopped at three other tables before he finally got out of the dining room. But I like him, Nathaniel thought. Under the guile there's something else.

I just hope it's not more guile!

He found the awful review of the Chancellor when he got home to his computer:

> Chancellor Gavin P. McTooney should be fired.
>
> He is a known crook. Back in Boston they still refer to him as "Hands Out" McTooney. He left there in virtual disgrace after accusations of him accepting "donations" for certain administrative decisions he made, like contracts for certain buildings, surfaced. He'll do the same here at our college. We don't need this.

Nathaniel didn't even bother reading the "information" provided. It was obviously not by a student — it had no spelling, punctuation, or grammatical errors. For a moment Nathaniel wondered if perhaps Barney Rock had actually sent it in and just made up the story about not having seen it, knowing that Nathaniel was likely to spread it around through his Committee on Truth and thus get it wider exposure. Hmm. It was sort of like a spy game, and Nathaniel knew that he was not good at spy games. Whatever his faults, he was not duplicitous. But he was aware that there were some people in the world who planned — even plotted — much more elaborate schemes than he was capable of. Maybe Barney Rock wanted to get McTooney out so that he could be Chancellor himself?

He sent a copy of the damning review to Barney Rock's office. I just don't want to be somebody's "mule" or whatever it is they call the sucker who gets caught in the middle.

He decided to send a copy of the review to the Chancellor as well, with a note attached. How could that hurt? Yeah, right.

> Dear Chancellor McTooney,
>
> We haven't met. Perhaps you've heard of me. My reputation seems to be spreading on campus. Alas, it is all more devious than it appears to the naked eye. I thought you might appreciate a copy of the enclosed review about you. It shows how easy it is for a person to sully someone's name. I'm sure there is no truth to any of this.
>
> Wishing you well, — Nathaniel Tack, Ph.D. (English)

He decided it best not to ask, quite yet, if the Chancellor had indeed given at least $50,000 of the school's money to the goddamned Remedial Reign of Terror Alliance of Students in order to take him to court.

This Chancellor was the first non-minority one in a decade, and there had been a rather public squabble over that fact that he'd been hired. He didn't belong to any of the approved Diversity or Affirmative Action groups. Perhaps he got in under the Americans with Disabilities Act because he was so short? Did a Boston accent count? Naw, it was most likely because the Chancellor immediately before him, a Korean had done absolutely nothing for his entire four years in office and then had retired with a handsome pension. By contrast, this Chancellor had been touted as "pro-active," and he had indeed seemed feisty when he'd given his inaugural address the year before. But Nathaniel had always tried his best to avoid the politics — and the political players — at Shite and even gone out of his way never to sit at the Big Table in Lowe-Rankin, where the Chancellor sometimes held court.

Now the situation called for some politicking of his own, if he was going to save his job, to say nothing of the universe.

He got a call almost immediately from the Chancellor's secretary (again English-impaired). He thought he understood her to say that the Chancellor would like to meet with him the next day. My, my, maybe the snotty reviews about the higher-ups were finally about to result in some changes.

Nathaniel put on his best sport coat, a blue tweed one that didn't make him look too large, and even donned a tie, something he hadn't worn in ages. The tie was too narrow for the fashion, with ugly yellow circles on it besides. He rolled himself all over with the Pet Hair Picker-Upper from the shelf in his closet, freeing himself of Slacker's exfoliates and several other forms of detritus, including little bits of clinging notepaper from his students' essay pages. To meet the faces that you meet.

There was no waiting this time. The Chancellor was out in a flash once Nathaniel's name was delivered by the secretary (apparently a different one, because this one could be understood). Chancellor McTooney was under five-foot-two despite the elevator shoes he was wearing, and seemed to convey a certain Puckishness in his fifty-two-year-old face. He still had all his sandy hair, fringed over the ears with strands of gray. Despite his dark blue suit and big red tie, he looked like a choirboy getting on in years, one possibly violated by some priest or other in his past, and determined, by god, to get even.

They met tie to tie.

"I want to thank you for calling that review to my attention," said the Chancellor in his opening gambit. The Boston accent was not in evidence.

My pleasure? No, that wouldn't be the wisest response. "I'm only sending people their reviews because it seems so many have buried their heads in the sand about the problem," Nathaniel said.

"Some may not like receiving them, though, I suspect."

"You wouldn't believe."

There was a certain twinkle in the Chancellor's eye. Either he was slightly amused by all this or else a practiced liar of considerable skill. I don't suppose you get to be a Chancellor of a school with over sixty thousand students on six campuses without a certain amount of acting ability.

"I know who submitted this review of me," the Chancellor said, lifting a folded slip of paper from his large, magisterial desk.

"Oh?"

"There are certain people around here who don't see eye to eye with me on a number of issues. They're not hard to identify." Ah, there was the Boston accent on the *hard*. So McTooney thought it was Barney Rock.

Nathaniel considered it strategic that he not mention Trustee Rock just yet, maybe not at all. Let the Chancellor reveal his hand first. "I don't suppose any Chancellor escapes censure, does he?"

"You wouldn't believe," McTooney smiled. Was that a smile?

"What about the Board members? What do they think about all this?"

"They're examining all options."

To cover their legal asses, no doubt.

"At the moment Trustee Rock is the one most exercised about the reviews on the website. Or at least that's his public posture."

There was something about the way in which the Chancellor bit down on the "p's" in "public" and "posture" that indicated he hated Barney Rock's guts. Good to know, Nathaniel thought. They hate each other. Now to keep from getting crushed between the two of them. No doubt either one of them, if incensed enough, could find some loophole to get him fired. "One does like to feel that one's reputation is not being made only by one's enemies, wouldn't you say, Chancellor?" I can make this man like me, Nathaniel said to himself. At the very least he won't think I'm the ogre that the "reviews" are creating. "It's fortunate that your tenure as Chancellor doesn't depend on what's up on the site about you, is it not?"

"Are there other reviews? I've never looked at the site myself."

"I believe the one you're holding is your only review — at present."

"Perhaps it comes with the territory," the Chancellor said, shaking the still-folded piece of paper.

"I know it's shamelessly un-modern, but I don't think it comes with the territory of being a teacher to have lies and threats distributed online about you," Nathaniel said.

"Believe me, the topic has been discussed at great length, Dr. Tack."

It was Nathaniel's turn for the deft smile. "Has it? You'd hardly guess."

"We didn't want to call attention to the website."

"No? A dean approved it. Several deans did — its creation and its promotion on campus. Flyers have been approved." And I've got one I'll put up all over this campus if this nightmare isn't ended, choirboy!

"That sounds a big legalistic of you, Dr. Tack."

Was that a warning? "Does it?"

"But, yes, we are looking into that. I believe you were the object of a threat of some kind. Is that true?"

"You haven't seen it?"

"No. A member of the Board mentioned it in passing at our last meeting."

"I guess a casual mention of a death threat is a start." Cool your sarcasm, Nathaniel, he warned himself.

"Trustee Rock brought it up, but he didn't have a copy of the actual threat with him."

And I gave him an extra one! Nathaniel cursed silently. "I can get you one," he offered.

"I got the gist. Trustee Rock was quite upset about it. As was I. It's my understanding that you reported it to the police."

"I did. It didn't seem to go very far. The city's District Attorney hasn't called on me, shall we say."

"Why didn't you bring it to my attention?"

"Perhaps because my earlier messages to the Administration about the site went unanswered."

"They did? I don't recall getting any from you."

"No doubt a breakdown in communication," Nathaniel said crisply.

"It seems to me that this whole matter is best handled out of the courts."

"Does the Alliance of Students feel the same way, Chancellor?"

"I can't speak for the Alliance, I'm afraid."

"Did you give them money?"

"Money?"

God, I can't hold my tongue! Nathaniel railed to himself. "Money to take me to court."

"They feel very strongly that their right to a better education is being threatened by the website's being interfered with."

"I hardly know where to begin with some clarifications here. First of all, the last thing most of them want is a better education. They want an easier education! They want even more grade inflation than there is, and it's already obscene. And not just here."

"Now, Dr. Tack —"

"Let me finish, please."

The Chancellor pretended to defer. "Of course."

"I have become their *bete noir* because I was foolish enough to publicly criticize the inane and cruel way the website is set up and operates. They can't seem to get it out of their craw that I am not the only person who thinks the review site is disgusting, if not downright criminal. Libel was a crime, I believe, the last time I checked." (I'll give you legal if you want legal! Nathaniel thought.) "Don't you consider that review about you libelous?"

"I think the law on libel is somewhat fluid," the Chancellor answered.

"You said you think you know who wrote it, but it's quite possible you think it's one person when it's actually someone else. Don't you see how this leads to suspicions and recriminations, when the whole thing is just a tissue of lies? Maybe it even came from Boston. And why should someone be able to gratuitously accuse you of crimes on a website? 'Hands Out McTooney' — that may be the only thing most people ever see about you. It does not come with the territory, like Greek fate! Why just us? Why just sucker academics?"

The Chancellor let the moment cool with no comment. Then he said, "I've spoken to Mr. Lather, the webmaster/owner of the site."

"You have?"

"I called him in for a little chat a few days ago."

"And?"

"He was quite nice."

"Was he? I guess I missed that part."

"He said he had 'encountered' you one time — in a hallway, I believe. He was stapling flyers."

"Funny, I can hardly remember that."

"I think he is quite sincere in wanting to provide a place to express opinions."

"So was Joseph McCarthy. Dude Lather is a total jerk, and I'm surprised that you condone what he is doing in any way, shape, or form. And if you gave the Alliance $50,000 you should be ashamed of yourself!" (God, am I blowing this!)

"I can understand your being upset, Dr. Tack, in that your students have often found fault with your teaching and . . ."

Nathaniel was dumbfounded. "I feel like I have been screaming for months and nobody hears what I'm saying. Sure, some of my students don't like me, and I don't like some of them. But the bulk of the nastiest reviews about me come from people who are *not* my students. Why is this message not getting through?"

"And who would those be?"

"I can't prove who's doing it, but I know it's being done. And not just to me!"

"If you can't prove it, it's best to be cautious, wouldn't you say, in making any allegations against specific persons, especially students? They are very legalistically minded, I might point out."

"And so you gave them even more money than they already have to do it with?"

"I'm merely trying to facilitate the educational experience for them."

"Do I hear what I'm hearing? What gives these students or whoever the hell they are the right to spew hateful, incautious to — to put it mildly — lying vitriol about their teachers, but the teachers are supposed to be cautious and careful and . . . and . . ." Nathaniel was so enraged he ran out of words.

"We are supposed to set a good example for our students, are we not?" The choirboy looked like he was about to sing some Gregorian chant.

"Chancellor, that is the biggest bunch of horsepucky I've heard in years! Who in the name of God or anyone else says that teachers are supposed to be namby-pamby floor mats and whipping boys? That's precisely what's wrong with American education. These students come from a tradition of thwarting, insulting, abusing, and even shooting their teachers! Enough! It's not going to come to the colleges now, as God is my witness!"

You go, Scarlet! And you don't even believe in God.

"Thank you for coming in today, Dr. Tack. I believe we've cleared up some things."

"We have? What?" Nathaniel was quaking inside.

"Mr. Lather has promised to pay more attention to what's on his website from now on."

"Is he going to remove the fake reviews of me?"

"I couldn't say."

"He won't because he can't tell the fake reviews from the real ones! What power that must give him! He's calling the shots now, the academic failure from Hell!"

Nathaniel knew that his face had turned completely crimson and he could do nothing about it, and his tie was choking him. His tic was galloping.

"Mr. Lather managed to remain quite calm during our discussion," the Chancellor noted.

"Did he?" Nathaniel said. "Maybe that's because he's not being libeled on a website. The little shit! Or maybe it's because he's dead in the head. Or should be!"

"I really don't believe you should make threats against our students, Dr. Tack." The choirboy was pissed now.

"It's okay for them to make threats, but I can't defend myself? What is wrong with you, Chancellor McTooney! I can't believe this. You're on the wrong side of this issue."

"I guess we'll see, won't we?" the Chancellor said, his choirboy eyes not pleased, not pleased at all.

Well, that went well, you politician you.

When he e-mailed Haywood about the confrontation, he got this back:

My name didn't come up, I hope!

No, it didn't.

Good. There's another threat (sort of) against you on the website today. See attached.

The attached said:

Nathaniel Tack is floundering in his own ineptness, going

around shouting at the top of his lungs that he wants to kill students. This man is mentally ill as the Administration has duly noted. All good t-h-i-n-g-s come to those as wait. He will get what's coming to him when the Savages display his h-e-a-d on a pole.

It sounded like Fly on the Wall. He had to have some eyes and ears at the school to be picking up these "facts," half-assed though they were. The secretaries? The Chancellor was Fly on the Wall? Anything was possible in all this manifest insanity. And *I'm* mentally ill!

Good old Haywood wrote:

Nathaniel, did you or did you not threaten to kill somebody?

Rumors are flying.

Haywood,

I got a bit carried away because the Chancellor seems to

be on the other side and took the threat against me much too lightly.

Nathaniel, I can't work with you if you are going to make mistakes like this!

I'll have to terminate all connections with you.

Haywood, please, don't! I need your assistance.

It took several hours before this came back:

NEVER again threaten anybody. It will just backfire on you. Do you promise?

Hey, I was just exercising my Free Speech!

Nathaniel, this is not funny.

DO YOU PROMISE?

It took Nathaniel several more hours, and most of his pride, to write back:

Okay, I promise not to threaten anybody. It doesn't seem, however, that the webmaster is keeping his promise to watch the site more carefully. Why would he when he doesn't have to? — Nathaniel

Frankly, I worry about you going off the Deep End. —
Haywood

Nathaniel was also worrying a bit about himself. Just how much more of all this could he take? But Haywood had all the reviews as evidence, along with the dates of added and deleted material. Now that this seemed to be going toward the courts, he simply had to eat the shit for now:

Haywood, I need your help. I promise no more threats. —
Nathaniel

P.S. It was an idle one anyway.

Nathaniel, even idle threats are not permitted. Or I am out of here and you're on your own! — H

Okay, Haywood, I agree.

Out near the ocean he trudged up and down in the sand as the sun set. I'm getting physical exercise, he told himself, so that my mind will hold up during the coming battles. The sky lay before him like a patient . . . autopsied upon a table — all violet reds and pinks and blue streaks. Quite stunning. If only Nature were enough to soothe the savage cock.

He crossed over to the cruising area, trying to be grateful for his blessings. Not only the ocean, the sky, the upcoming sex but he could even pick up some groceries at a Safeway just a short drive away!

The weather was warm for November. Almost humid. The twilight slowly crossed the sand dunes ear the ocean and then spread to the cypresses where he was beginning his moves. There were cars parked along the surrounding streets with men coming and going from them. Nathaniel had parked farther away since there was a sticker from Shite College on his windshield, and the last thing he needed right now was his name and picture in the newspapers:

TEACHER WHO THREATENED

STUDENT WEBMASTER

ARRESTED ON HIS KNEES IN BUSHES.

With a sub-headline: Long-Term Lover Heartbroken at Sexual Betrayal.
EEEK! I need some sex! Right now! Or I'll die!

I just hope I can get it up.

He had put on his other Sex Clothes: Levi's and a bomber jacket. It was rather retro, but it's amazing how potent cheap retro can be. He had touched up his mustache with some hopefully non-poisonous "gel" he'd found in the back of his medicine cabinet. He caught a glimpse of himself in his rear view mirror. I don't look too bad tonight. See, what stress can do for you!

As the evening fell, some fog trickled through the area, swirling slowly, like incense in a cathedral. How wonderful! Nathaniel thought. How many of the Bored Monogamous had a church like this to go to!

But there was something in front of him, and it wasn't a fellow celebrant like himself. It was small, furry and . . . maybe black? What was that? It had stopped on the path directly in front of Nathaniel. Was it Gorilla Woman's Familiar, sent to rip his heart out? A video camera on wheels, sent to rid his world of joy? He didn't move, nor did It.

As his eyes adjusted to the darkness, Nathaniel realized that it was a skunk. An adolescent skunk, to judge from the size of it. And it didn't seem to be moving on either. Where is my trusty sword? He didn't know if skunks bit or not. Yes, they sprayed, but bite? All Nathaniel had on him was a ballpoint pen. He'd emptied his pockets of wallet, coins and everything else, hidden away under the front seat of his car in his so-called Sex Box.

After a few more moments, the skunk decided that Nathaniel was not going to attack and scurried off to do whatever skunks do.

As Nathaniel continued further on his mission, there seemed to be some activity down a small incline near a meadow, which had some construction vehicles parked in it. Leave it to the queens to find the heavy machinery! But when he got closer, he saw that it was two raccoons humping. Really now! Get a room! Their eyes gleamed fiercely in the rapidly failing light when they heard him, and they were obviously staring him down. He deemed it wise not to venture any closer to the beasts. We gays should do the same instead of running like cowards when the police patrols come by. Nature likes a good fuck, officer! Gay Power now!

Onward he quested, his lance at the ready!

Of course I'll probably shoot in two seconds, he reminded himself. Seize the night, but take your time.

Suddenly a phantom appeared out of the construction machinery and the wisps of swirling fog. He was tall, but not too tall. Nathaniel didn't like to do it with men who towered over him. Fortunately he was tall himself, and that problem didn't occur very often. This person was wearing a trench coat, it seemed, and a cap — a sea captain's cap? Nathaniel's eyes still hadn't adjusted totally to the weak light. Hmm, maybe Captain Ahab was out trolling? It was amazing how some office dork could become downright sexy with just the right application of body language and fetching sea costume.

But, no, it wasn't a sea captain after all. More like a homeless person. Was that a new trend. Homeless Chic? Naw, this guy looked like an actual homeless person, a term Nathaniel had grown quite weary off. Why not vagrants? Beggars? Druggies? Alkies? Anything but another euphemism to continue hiding the problem.

The man was probably trying to find a spot for the night, in a cardboard box, or he might even put up a tent. Nathaniel felt sorry for the man, but he didn't especially want him there in the cruising area. Just one more reason for the cops to try to butt in. Besides, it tended to crimp one's style to trip over sleeping bodies. He'd even had a few of these gentlemen yell homophobic epithets at him in years past. The homophobic homeless — go figure!

However, this one seemed to be cruising — and cruising Nathaniel. No way! Nathaniel moved off. But the man followed.

Well, it won't hurt to look, will it? He hated it when cruisers got haughty and slapped away hands, hated it even when he was younger and more marketable too, and never did it. Miss Manners was right when she said a gentleman never slaps the hands of those probing one's delights, just politely moves away. Nathaniel kept to the trees and let the man go by. He seemed to be in his early forties, of modest built. The trench coat was really a raincoat that had seen better days. The man's face had seen better days as well, but it wasn't too bad, a bit puffy from drink, possibly even battered a touch from the streets, but there was no mistaking the enormous lance protruding from his pants front. My, was he ever glad to see Nathaniel! Or probably anybody, for that matter.

They fenced, they parried. They paired. They wound up in a part of the park where the grasses hadn't been mowed for years. The weedy aroma of the dew-dropped grasses mingled with a breeze coming off the ocean. Even the moon was showing now, emerging from some low clouds. The moonlight did not exactly enhance Mr. Homeless's facial charms, in particular the missing front tooth, but the moon didn't lie about his imposing weapon of choice, which he held in one hand and waved with a most beseeching mutter: "Do me! Do me!"

How could Nathaniel ignore the plight of the homeless as one of them called out in his hour of need? Here was a beggar's begging that he could appreciate. Here was someone who could in fact be saved. Thus Nathaniel the fag knelt and became both Sir Lancelot and the Catcher in the Rye for several enthralling minutes. Ain't literature grand!

Thank you's exchanged (but no telephone numbers), the two parted, and Nathaniel continued his quest for the Holy Grail. He was hungry, but raw sex was better than food. And, yay, he hadn't come right away this time! His erection had even been noticeable, if not remarkable. Fuck Fly on the Wall! Fuck the Chancellor and his $50,000 for those student goons! He thought. Fuck Haywood Wire and his insatiable demand for apologies! No matter what anybody says, there is no greater happiness than sex on this sad planet!

To prove it, he watched and waited and walked. Yes, officer, I often take my exercise here. Why don't you go bother some criminals? Happily, there were no police and no screaming homophobes about that night. Just loads of men with Gay Agendas on their minds. Yummy, yummy! Maybe I could actually be happy, the Human Condition notwithstanding, Nathaniel thought, if I could merely have sex (and don't forget get published) all the time.

But talk to me after I come.

Someone was walking his dogs, talking softly to them. The dogs seemed to be sniffing something they shouldn't. "No, Princess! No, Laddie!" The speaker was a young man about twenty-five, with short, fair hair. A veritable fair-haired lad. As best Nathaniel could make out, this fellow was a hunk, and, boy, did that make Nathaniel want to make out. He moved closer. A pullover sweater and chino slacks, no costume. Or was that a costume? The lad smiled at him. Oh, danger! Who smiled in these situations? Smile? Sex was much too serious for that! Maybe Nathaniel should not approach.

But he did anyway, not foolishly by any means, just a survey of the potential of the scene. Damn, his eyes weren't as good as they used to be! Maybe he should have that surgery. What was that? No, not the one to remove the testicles! On the flaps of the eyes. Makes you see like a baby again. Was that the ad? There were so many ads.

Oh, my god, the man with the pet dogs was unzipping his pants. "Sit, Laddie! Sit, Princess!" Well, who did this guy think he was! Did he really believe Nathaniel was going to go over there and suck him, just like that? What nerve!

Actually the lad was just taking a leak. Sorry.

A peek wouldn't be amiss, would it? What is it they always said? Don't regret the things you did, only the things you didn't do. Was this one of the Things He Was Meant To Do? I'm easy, Nathaniel thought. Naturally, if he wants to do me, I can live with that too. You know, I bet there are some men who have never had a blowjob in their entire lives! The mass of men lead lives of quiet desperation. You tell 'em, Henry David, out their cruising your own woods!

The peek at the leak led to a kiss on the cheek. And more. Up close and personal, the lad seemed a bit wild-eyed, possibly from retardation or mild schizophrenia. Well, these people have their needs too! Nathaniel said, in a liberal mood. In fact, the night was becoming fuller and fuller of people of Diverse backgrounds. Well, good, you didn't have to speak good English or have perfect mental health to give good head. "Suck me," Nathaniel told the lad. And he did. But he seemed more interested in the welfare of his dogs, two elderly Collies with arthritis, than he was in Nathaniel's somewhat under-performing tool.

"Here, let me," Nathaniel said, trading places. He stepped on a dog tail, causing a whimper. "I'm sorry, I'm sorry!" He felt down and patted the dog's head.

"She's old. They belong to my grandparents," the lad said. Yeah, he was a little goofy.

"It comes to the best of us," Nathaniel said, getting on his knees.

It was swift and the dogs didn't bite him, and he spat it out too. You couldn't catch schizophrenia from sperm, could you? Those doctors, always coming up with something new!

"That's two!" Nathaniel triumphed, a fist in the air, like the Count of Monte Cristo.

It took another hour for the circumstances to be efficacious, and by that time he was cold and hungry, but his body felt alive. Even his brain raced with puns and jokes and plans for things to write. The moon was overhead now, as big as sin. Sometimes it was good to be mooned. Nathaniel found himself wanted by quite a few. "Hey, big guy, what you want!" was said by more than one interested sex therapist. He likewise watched others enjoying themselves. He had a whiff of poppers. It was all good.

But the best was the last. There would be worst ways to leave the world, by far. To die, perchance to dream. He saw some activity off the beaten path, and he soon became part of a three-way in a by-way — and, thank the Lord, they don't mind doing it My Way! Nathaniel crowed. Both of them were blowing him, first taking turns, then both at once, and his cock was rampant and full of gay pride. One of the pleasure-givers was a leather man complete with cap and chaps, his lovely butt exposed to the elements. No, I won't go there! Let's not be greedy now. And the other succulent was about thirty-five with a swimmer's defined body, a face like a movie star's, and a Big Thick Thing sticking out of his swimming trunks. He was actually wearing swimming trunks, despite the creeping cold. Plus heavy balls as a bonus. And everybody was groping everybody else in this tight little unit, but mostly they just couldn't seem to get enough of Nathaniel's cock. It was porn, and it was real, and he was starring in it! He was trying to hold back — trying and trying. But the warlock in his loins was shouting to be let out, and he didn't see how he could hold off even one more second, but he thought of Jake Trosky and Fly on the Wall and Gorilla Woman and Dean Visigoth and all the rest of the tangled mess he was in, and thus he didn't come until he was good and ready. And both of his New Best Friends were ready, and, my, were they ever good!

It was the greatest sex he'd ever had in his life. "Thank you, thank you. You absolutely saved my life!" he sobbed in their arms when he finally reached his zenith. He'd always been sure the Holy Grail would turn out to be a dribble glass. Who would've thought it would be so full of cum?

It was his office hour — back to the dull puke of everyday reality, as a poet had said, an obnoxiously self-aggrandizing poet that Nathaniel had met once, to be sure; nevertheless, the line was great.

He could hear Tadd Dryer and Guy Mountain next door discussing a paper that Tadd had just received from a student. Nathaniel had given up trying to talk to either one of them, timing his exits and entrances to a different drummer.

"Unbelievable!" Tadd was fuming. "Unbelievable!"

"What class is it?"

"The last time I checked I thought this was supposed to be sophomore college English!"

"Now, Tadd, they work hard on those papers. Don't be so grumpy."

"They had two hours to write this. They could use their notes! Two hours! Let me read this to you."

"I've really got a class to prepare, Tadd."

"Just this part."

You could feel Guy's resistance, but Tadd was not to be denied.

"It's about *The Importance of Earnest*. Have you ever taught it?"

"No, but I've read it."

"Listen to this! 'This play emphasize the important of being Christian.'"

"Well?"

"The English, and the play isn't a Christian play. I'm a Christian and that isn't a Christian play!"

"Why are you so excited?"

"Because this isn't college English. Listen! 'One side is based on doing innocent deeds, while the other side is always thinking of something dirty like sex.'"

"Well, you think sex is dirty, Tadd."

"No, I don't! I tried to explain double entendre to them, and this is what I get back! It's hopeless!"

"Anything else?" Guy said, all but groaning. "It doesn't sound that bad to me. At least your student read the play. Lighten up, Tadd."

Tadd threw the essay on his desk and perhaps even kicked his desk. "There's no use talking to you, Guy. You're as bad as they are."

"Well, don't teach imperialist literary works then! I certainly don't."

Ah, my colleagues, Nathaniel thought, caught in amber, for future archaeologists to marvel over. He agreed wholeheartedly with Tadd that it was not college work. Too bad he and Tadd weren't talking to each other.

To hell with the both of them. And Guy's big, fat mother too!

He hadn't gotten back to the chair of his department about the poor enrollment for the upcoming semester. Now here on his desk was a note from Spike that he hadn't opened yet, out of fear of what it might say. He picked it up:

> Dear Nathaniel, did you get my voice message? We need to talk
> about your classes for spring. Please come by the office. They are
> better but still only about half full. Urgent! – Spike Burns

Well, he'd just have to bump a part-timer, that's all! He'd taught pre-101 classes before. It was a swamp, but he could do it again. "Hello, I am your teacher despite what the schedule says — Nathannyboy!" Would they run screaming from the classroom? "I am here to whip your remedial asses into shape." Hell, what was the use. The Chancellor had just issued his Proclamation of the Expedited Success Program, meaning that you could get through Shite in two and half years with a full college degree. Soon you'd probably be able to graduate with a major in Success. "Me so thank Shite for give to me education!" (Where was Jonathan Swift, that dead white male, when you needed him?)

Yet I've simply got to get some students, living or dead, for the first four weeks, Nathaniel advised himself. So when an emaciated Arab-looking male carrying a class schedule came to his office just at that moment, he was downright hospitable.

"Professor Tack?"

"That's me! Please won't you take a seat, Mr. —?"

"Fazwa Umar Shaikh."

214

"How can I help you?" Nathaniel asked, polite to the spine.

The student seemed to be in his mid-twenties, with lots of black eyebrow, one, almost joined in the middle of his forehead. The eye sockets were hollow and the eyes lacking in merriment, one might say, but the eyelashes were long and lovely. He was also wearing sandals in November and had the ugliest long, bony toes ever made in God's image. Best to look on the bright side. He had no tattoos, nose rings, or weapons.

"I am thinking to take your English creative next semester," he said.

"My creative writing class?"

"Yes. I am most proficient in the writing of the creative."

"Well . . . good." Nathaniel maintained his smile. (Let me sign you up! Perhaps your whole family, all in the same sandals of course, might fly over for a course in the creative?) "I'm sure Mr. Burns in the main English Department will be happy to sign you up. Do you know where he is located?" Nathaniel got up to lead him there.

Mr. Shaikh remained seated. "However, there remains to be one problem."

"Oh, and what might that be?" Nathaniel sat at his desk again.

"There is one favor I must be to asking before I can take the creative from you."

A crash course in English idiom by any chance? Okay, that can be arranged. Or I can blink a lot when I read your papers. "And what is that, may I ask?" he said.

The student was very nicely dressed, perhaps even in designer clothes — with sharp creases in his trouser legs.

"It is most delicate what I must request, Professor."

"Ask away!"

"I would like to enroll, but I am unable to attend the first classes in the semester that is forthcoming."

"I see. How many classes would you be missing?"

"Perhaps only of first two weeks."

Nathaniel let out his breath. "Well, we can handle that. God willing! That's not a problem. As long as you pre-enroll. You do plan to enroll early, correct?"

"That is my dilemma — on the horns," Mr. Shaikh said with a sudden smile, because of what he evidently thought was a nice turn of phrase.

"Dilemma in that . . . ?"

"I hope to return to America, which I soon hope to make my home, but I may be delayed for as much as three to four weeks."

"You can always probably make up the assignments. I'm sure we can work it out." Nathaniel got up again. Better get this guy to Spike before he got away.

Mr. Shaikh raised a very manicured and royal finger. "You see, I must participate in the honor killing of my sister."

Nathaniel blinked a couple of times. "I beg your pardon?"

"I hope you will treat of this information with appropriate silence," Mr. Shaikh went on, again with a very busy forefinger. "For some reason, you Americans do not seem to appreciate customs that are different than your own, despite your very loud advertisement of your so-called interest. My economics professor, by example, would not give me this permission — and I must point out that I do not pay the resident tuition. Instead, I am forced to pay the out-of-state!"

The Royal Bank of Bahrain must really be hurting.

"Did you say the honor killing of your sister?"

"She has shamed my family." Mr. Shaikh looked decidedly displeased.

I should let this man fold his tent and depart, Nathaniel was sure. Yet, never mind the enrollment, it was fascinating in an Arabic Edgar Allan Poe kind of way. Were they planning to bury her alive? "What, may I ask, has your sister done to merit such an honor?" he said.

"She had sex!"

The incredible slut!

"With a man not her husband!"

Death is too good for her!

"Are you of interest in this matter?"

Yeah, I wonder what your lovely culture would do to me if it caught me having sex. As if I didn't know! But, hey, come on in and give us that old-time Sharia law!

"Professor?" Mr. Shaikh had noticed that Nathaniel was not saying anything. "You do not approve, it would seem. No wonder the United States has moral bankruptcy! With your rapes and your out-of-wedlocks!" Mr. Shaikh was having a low-key hissy fit.

How far should you go to get a student to enroll?

"I'm afraid they're not my rapes and only one out-of-wedlock," Nathaniel said. "And as for what is honor, I think the point can be argued."

"There are some points that cannot be argued as well!" The student rose from the chair. "I was hoping that you would find room for me — I am the first cousin of a prince, in case it is not evident to you! — because I have been reliably informed through a search on the Internet that your classes are available, is that not so?"

Nathaniel stood up too. It was the last straw. "Your Internet sources are quite wrong, Your Highness. My classes are overflowing with students. They may not be able to spell, write, or make the subject agree with the verb, but they don't participate in the honor killings of their sisters! Good day to you."

And they said he didn't love his students!

No doubt this refusal wasn't going to save the poor girl's life, but it sure as hell felt good to tell off the bony-toed bastard.

Despite the "urgent" message to call him, Nathaniel kept avoiding the chair of the English Department.

Barney Rock called the next day with a suggestion for a lawyer. "I don't want this coming back on me, via our Mick pygmy Chancellor or anyone else, so I can't write this down for you."

"Okay, no paper trail," Nathaniel agreed. Had Rock really said "Mick pygmy Chancellor"? How deliciously incorrect.

"But try Suzanna Oznick. I've told her that you would be calling."

"Thank you."

"Something has to be done about these reviews. I did a quick check on the site this morning. The threatening one about you is gone, but there was a new one this morning."

"I can hardly wait to hear," Nathaniel said.

"It said that you are racist against Muslims."

"I can guess where that might have come from. I had a student in here who —"

"You aren't, are you?"

"Trustee Rock —"

"Call me Barney."

"It seems to me that the word *racist* has been so widely and cavalierly applied that it has lost all currency and should be banned from the language."

"I know what you mean. Like the little boy who cried wolf."

"Exactly!" Nathaniel was liking Barney Rock more and more.

"Only you still can't say anything out loud, you must realize. They can get you with it."

"How can you put up with it?"

"I'm in public life. I have to put up with it. But maybe not for long."

"You aren't quitting, are you?"

"I may serve out my term, and that's it."

"How long is that?"

"Another year. Eleven months and a few days."

"Do you think we can get rid of this problem in that amount of time?"

"I haven't a clue, Mr. Tack."

"Nathaniel. You're the only member of the Board or the Administration even to attempt to help out in this situation. And I want you to know I'm grateful."

"You're welcome. Now, to be honest, I don't know how much the Board can really do about it. But I'm going to bring some of these awful reviews to the meeting next month. Most of the activist students will be gone by then, because it's at the end of the semester. They're still hot for this website, but I think I can perhaps win over a few of the Board to our side by quoting from them. They're pretty rank, a lot of them."

"The Board or the reviews?"

"Both."

"I've stopped looking at the site."

"Who's this Nona Dwibble?"

"Is that one still up on the site?"

"The sex one?"

"I thought that had been removed."

"It says that she takes all comers, especially priests, in her wheelchair."

"That must be a new one. What does it say exactly?"

"I don't have a copy of it with me, but it says something like Nona Dwibble spreads her flying nun's wings for all-comers during her office hours. With a discount for priests. Really filthy. Do you know this woman?"

"Yes, I know her. Want me to get you a discount? A special appointment during her office hours?"

Barney Rock guffawed into the telephone. "You're shameless!" It was said almost with affection. "I think when I show this to some Board members — I don't know how many, now, so I can't promise anything — there might be an outcry, and that could be the beginning of some action on all this abuse and filth." He gave the name, address, and telephone number of the lawyer, which Nathaniel wrote on Barney Rock's business card.

"I thank you. Nona Dwibble thanks you — I guess. I still haven't heard from her and haven't seen her around. Do you think I should send her a copy of this latest review?"

"Up to you. Got to go!"

Okay, no time for small talk.

As soon as he could, Nathaniel called the lawyer's office, but he was careful to use his cell phone because he didn't want anyone at school to overhear the call. After all, now it looked like he might be about to sue the school itself. The fuckers. A child answered. She said that, yes, Ms. Oznick and her partner could meet with him the very next day at three. Great! He'd be there! (But why were they letting a little girl take their messages?)

He hurried to see Haywood in his office in the Statistics Department. He was just leaving for the day, but he invited Nathaniel in. The room looked cluttered, and Haywood himself looked spooky. He'd trimmed his Santa Claus beard somewhat, but he'd probably done it with a butcher knife. It looked ragged, and of course stained.

"What's up?" The Mole seemed a bit put out with Nathaniel.

"I'm sorry if I've been making you nervous during all this, but I have good news finally."

"Which is?"

Nathaniel hadn't been offered a seat, but he took one any way. "Someone has recommended a lawyer for us."

"This is for a libel suit?"

"Yes. It was your idea. . . . Wasn't it?"

"I guess so."

"Do you want to go with me to see the lawyer? I have the information here." Nathaniel had copied everything onto a note card especially for Haywood so that he wouldn't see Barney Rock's business card.

"When are you going?"

"Tomorrow at three. I'm off all day."

"So am I."

Nathaniel's heart leapt up. "You're willing to go?"

"Now I'm not signing anything, Nathaniel."

"You won't have to sign anything. We're just going to meet and discuss the possibilities."

"Do you have any money for a lawyer?"

"No."

"Did the lawyer say they'd do it on contingency?"

"No. But maybe we can persuade them to do that. The two of us!"

The Mole mulled it over. "I guess I can come. My tap dancing class has been canceled."

Because of a Peeping Tom? Nathaniel wondered. Oh, give the Mole a break. The poor guy's probably not getting any, and this is the best he can do.

"Wonderful! Here's the address." He laid the note card on the desk and watched while Haywood fingered it. "Shall we meet at the lawyers' office?"

The Mole stroked his beard. What was that he was wearing? Under the sport coat it looked like a black shirt made of netting. Was it a see-through shirt? Believe me, nobody wanted to see through Haywood's shirt! Nathaniel withdrew his eyes.

"At the lawyer's then, just before three?"

"Okay," the Mole said. "I've been studying up on the libel laws. I think we just may have a case. I read something that even calling someone 'incompetent' in their job could be libelous."

"Terrific!" Nathaniel said, getting up to leave. "See you tomorrow then. And thanks, Haywood. Thanks a lot."

The next day Nathaniel sat in his car, waiting. It was time for the appointment. In fact, it was two minutes after three, and still no Mole. In panic Nathaniel fished his cell phone from the side pocket in his car and called.

"Haywood? Are you on your way?"

"No."

"I thought we had an appointment with the lawyer at three."

"I'm not coming."

"May I ask why not?"

"Well, to be frank, Nathaniel, I think you've handled this without really consulting me."

"What do you mean?"

"I wanted more say in the selection of a lawyer."

"Have you contacted any lawyers?"

"Not yet. But I know someone who knows a very good lawyer."

"Well, we don't have to take the very first lawyer we meet with! If you get a lawyer, we can talk to that one too. I just thought since this possibility presented itself, I should go for it."

"I'd really prefer that you didn't act so impulsively. That's one of your lesser personality traits, if I may say so."

"I'm sorry you feel that way, Haywood. But it's time we took some action here. I thought you agreed."

"I do agree. I just don't want to be rushed into things. You should have cleared the appointment time with me before you set it for sure."

"But I didn't even know if you wanted to go or not!"

"Well, let me know how the meeting comes out," the Mole said. "I've got to grade some tests I've put off."

"Okay, Haywood, I'll keep you informed," Nathaniel said, biting his tongue in two big chunks. Almost.

Now late, he went in to meet with Suzanna Oznick and her partner, Jordan Kurd. Their office, grandly called The Offices of Oznick and Kurd, was in a run-down storefront near the new Chinatown in the north part of the city. There was a visible hole in the ceiling near the back with a bucket underneath catching the drip. "Sorry about our leak," Ms. Oznick said, gesturing at it. So it was her voice on the phone. Not a child after all. Whew, thank god. She looked to be in her late twenties or early thirties, drab, with an un-handsome gap between her front teeth, and possessed of a very "fem" — that childlike — voice. Hmm, did she get it on when she went to court perhaps, like some actors who had to have an actual performance to show any energy?

But of course the first part was getting this child-woman to agree to take the case at all, since her very next words were:

"My partner and I unfortunately have more cases than we can handle already. We're swamped. But when Barney described it, I thought it sounded somewhat interesting. I'm afraid my partner can't be here today."

"Mine either."

"Do you want to tell me about it?"

Christ, now he had to lobby a lawyer!

His throat was dry and he asked for a glass of water. She got him one — and not from the bucket under the leak, as far he could tell. You've got to watch these lawyers every minute!

"Do you ever get disgruntled clients?" he suddenly asked Ms. Oznick. It had worked on Brother Kyle.

The eyes narrowed. "Disgruntled? My clients?"

"I'm sure you have many satisfied customers. But hasn't there been one, somewhere along the way, who was less pleased than you had hoped?"

"I don't know about that," she said. She was taking notes on a notepad. Was that a good sign?

"Just hypothetically then. Of course I'm not a lawyer . . ."

"Go ahead."

"Let's say there's a client or even possibly another lawyer — yes, a rival lawyer — who takes it into his mind to find fault with your work — more than that, to lambaste your practice, to get your clients to come over to him. That person then sets up a website — no, a bullhorn outside your office — yes, a bullhorn right across the street from this office!" Nathaniel pointed through the covered windows. "And then this angry person, whoever it is, begins to make accusations and call you names at the top of his lungs."

"Mere name-calling doesn't get very far in most libel cases. What kinds of accusations?"

Good, Ms Oznick was actively engaged.

"That you're incompetent at your job, for instance. That you're dishonest as a lawyer."

"Now whoever would believe that?" Miss Oznick said slyly.

Terrific! She even had a sense of humor.

"And then other people come along and borrow this bullhorn and begin to say even worse things about you — that you're mentally ill, that you're unfair to your clients when they're from . . . Poland, let's say."

"From Poland?"

"But of course you're perfectly fair to all of your clients, no matter where they come from. Only some of them shouldn't have come from Poland to file that lawsuit they filed!"

"What?"

Okay, okay, the analogy was breaking down. Nathaniel always told his 101 students in the Critical Thinking section of the course that all analogies break down eventually.

"I do think I get the essence of what you're saying, Dr. Tack."

"Oh, good. I'm a little flustered." (This was more gut-wrenching than the Inquisition in Arena 3B!)

"You're saying that people are using the website in question to spread malicious slander. Yet what if they think it's true? You realize that the First Amendment protects opinion. It was meant to protect political opinion originally, but it has been more widely interpreted over time."

"I'm a gay writer, Ms. Oznick, with a lot of less-than-popular opinions besides. I know what it feels like, and how hard it is, to try to get free speech."

She looked impressed.

So you'll pull out a P.C. stop or two yourself when you need one, is that it, Nathaniel?

Oh, shut up, I never said I was perfect.

"Furthermore, the people using the bullhorn sometimes haven't even been your clients!"

"Why would they do it then?"

"Because . . . their friends have been your clients and they're just trying to destroy your reputation to help out their friends, who have slanted everything in their favor and against you."

"Do you think someone would really do this?"

"I know for a fact this is happening. I just can't prove it. Yet."

She seemed to be evaluating his performance. Perhaps to see how he'd hold up on the witness stand? He looked at his hand to make sure he wasn't twisting any ball bearings. He knew he was perspiring, but he didn't think it showed.

"There is a dark side to people, Ms Oznick, and some of them will do things if they can get away with them, for the sheer hell of it. I believe this observation about humanity, if I'm not mistaken, lies at the base of the law itself."

She nodded and said, "There are studies showing that people will do even extremely cruel things if they think no one will ever find out what they did."

"The Internet is made for just such cruelty, Ms. Oznick."

Did that sound a little too "Twilight Zone"?

Well, fuck it! He was living a "Twilight Zone." And it was a hell of lot longer than a half-hour episode, too!

"The Zeran ruling has been the standard legal decision for some time now."

"Zeran?"

"He sued America On Line because someone online accused him, falsely, of selling memorabilia about the Oklahoma City bombing. He got vicious hate mail and death threats, and AOL didn't remove the accusations even after the man informed them about the problem."

"And?"

"America On Line and the other Internet Service Providers have a lot of money and are, as a major corporation, more than willing to spend it to keep things the way they are. They don't want to be held responsible for what people post. They claim they can't keep track of all of it, for one thing, and it goes against the free spirit of the Internet, for another. Zeran lost."

"I don't want to hold AOL responsible either. But if somebody gets libeled or threatened, that somebody ought to be able to do something about it."

"So you believe that a webmaster should be held accountable for what's on his website?"

"Absolutely."

"So you would make the case that the webmaster is similar to an editor of a newspaper or magazine?"

"I guess. Is that the right argument to make?" Was this a trick question?

"It may or may not fly in court. The Internet was given special privileges by Congress, unlike newspapers and magazines."

"Why would Congress do that?"

"To encourage the Internet's growth."

"I think it's grown — like Topsy. The last time I looked. It's everywhere, in fact."

"No doubt the same kind of big money greasing a few palms. A lot of big money, a lot of palms."

"Of course there are those who would ride to the rescue of what they might consider a poor student with his lonely website just trying his best to stop teachers from oppressing their students."

"Not if they understood what's actually going on, they wouldn't."

"People often have a limited amount of information, about most things in fact; nevertheless, they act on whatever they know. Don't forget I deal with juries, Dr. Tack."

"You're scaring me, Ms. Oznick."

"I've printed out some of the reviews on the site. There are quite a few glowing ones about teachers — especially of a Dean Visigoth. He comes highly recommended."

"What I question is who actually wrote them, or why, especially the dean's. There are absolutely no safeguards on who writes the reviews, or how many get written, or on which ones stay there and which ones come off. I suppose most people can't conceive of a website being set up in such a stupid manner to begin with. But I find it a perfect miniature of what is sick about American education these days."

Ms. Oznick's eyebrows went up, and Nathaniel stopped.

"But don't get me started," he demurred. The true nature of his contradictory opinions couldn't be presented in the few sentences he was being allowed. "Maybe some day I'll write a whole book about it," he said.

The lawyer went to a file cabinet in the rear and brought back a folder. "These are the reviews I have printed out."

"And I brought some too," Nathaniel said. holding up his own Committee on Truth folder.

"You first," she said.

Nathaniel extended his hand. "After you."

She opened the folder. The leak in the back was making a pip-pip-pip noise into the bucket now. Maybe it was some kind of lawyers' water torture device?

"I skimmed the site, reading at random, for half an hour or so."

"Did you leave a review?"

"Of?"

"Of anybody you felt like."

"No, I didn't."

"Why don't we go online right now, and you can write a review of me, or anyone else, and it will be posted."

"Are you sure about that?"

"Try it! A picture is worth a thousand words, no?"

"I don't think I'll do it just now, Dr. Tack. However, I did notice some reviews that possibly could be called libelous."

"Oh, good! I mean . . . Not that I want anybody libeled."

"Of course you don't."

Of course I do! Nathaniel thought. The more the better! Obviously it's the only way we're going to overcome AOL, the free speech nuts, and the hackers — unholy alliance that it is.

"This one, for example," Ms. Oznick was pointing out. "It's about a professor named Wire."

"Oh, yes, Haywood."

"So you know him?"

Could he admit he knew him? Are you now, or have you ever been, a friend of Haywood Wire? And it would be Haywood himself asking the incriminating question! "Yes, he teaches in Statistics, I believe."

"Have you talked to him about this review, Dr. Tack?"

"Ah . . . what does it say?"

"It accuses him of harassing his female students."

"And that he's a pervert? That one?"

"Exactly."

"Yes, I've read it."

"Do you know enough about the man to know if this might be accurate?"

Sure, Haywood's a pervert. A tap-dancing one. But aren't we all? Who's to throw the first stone? "I know enough about Mr. Wire to believe that he is not guilty of actually harassing his female students."

"Has he discussed using this review for legal redress?"

"It's come up." (Fuck the Mole for not being there and making it twice as difficult!)

"I think that particular review might be very useful in a lawsuit — and that threatening one of you. Not that my partner and I really have the time to take it on." (Drip, drip, drip.)

It crossed Nathaniel's mind that he might be charged for this get-together after he was pushed out the door.

She picked up another review. "And this one. Have you seen it?"

Nathaniel leaned forward.

"It says that Dr. Titus Ashe in Astrology — you have an Astrology Department?"

"What can I say, Ms. Oznick. It's Shite College."

She didn't flinch. Despite the little voice, she seemed pretty tough. "It says that this Titus Ashe, and I'm quoting, is a 'monster' who 'berates his students in class,' teaches 'drunk,' and 'plays with himself' — through his pants pocket.'"

"I haven't seen that one," Nathaniel said, taking it from Ms. Oznick. "To be honest, I hate to look at the website anymore."

"Do you know this Dr. Ashe?"

"Not at all. It's a big place."

"I've been on the campus. It's really quite attractive — the views there. Wouldn't you say?"

Was this to see if he was a "totally negative" and un-American 'monster' too? "The campus has its delights, Ms. Oznick." He put two fingers to his mouth to stop the words "Education just doesn't happen to be one of them."

"If these charges against Dr. Ashe are untrue, he might have a case. Have you tried to get other teachers to join a lawsuit?"

"I have contacted any number of teachers. Most have not responded. I do know one other person who's expressed some interest. And there has all along been some discussion, apparently, of suing me!"

"You?"

"Some of the student activists. A surly bunch."

"That would complicate things."

Oh, God! I shouldn't have told her that! "It's not definite, however. In fact, I don't think it's going to take place."

"What about this other person, the teacher you mentioned?"

"I can't use the person's name until he or she agrees to let me. But there is a chance that he — or she — might agree to meet with you and come on board." (That's Haywood's nasty review right there!)

"A chance?"

"A good chance." (If I have to drag Haywood there by his ugly old beard!)

"I'd think some sort of class action suit might work here. We'd need at least five or so teachers to agree, though."

"Really?"

"There's another bad one here about you that might work. Let me find it."

"There have been so many!" he said lightly. (See what a charming person I am!)

She found it. "It accuses you of mental illness. She says she was in a class where you yelled at a student who was doing nothing."

"I told the student to stop reading a newspaper during class. Twice. Call me narrow in my teaching methods, but we were discussing a textbook at the time."

"She says that you didn't grade her fairly. She got a B when she — I'm quoting — 'clearly deserved an A.'"

"If that's the person I think it is — and you can never be sure, I do point out — then it's probably Shirley Knott, whom I had in a Saturday 102 class — probably four years ago. I remember her well. She wrote decently, but she didn't even deserve the B she got. It was a three-hour class every Saturday morning, and Ms. Knott came late to at least fourteen out of the seventeen classes. And not just a little late — anywhere from twenty minutes to forty-five minutes late, every single time, interrupting the class with her umbrella or her cell phone or her whatever. It was something different every time! Then she had the gall to miss the two classes right before the final exam because she had already planned a vacation! No wonder she didn't know half the information for the final exam. And now she writes me up! The incredible bitch!"

Ms. Oznick stared at him.

Time for damage control!

"Excuse me for saying 'bitch,' but that woman's comments are so lopsided and distorted it makes me furious."

"I can see that."

In fact "bitch" is actually a euphemism! . . . *Grrrr!*

"Nobody knows the teachers' side of this. That fool, that self-serving anti-student has the nerve to find fault with her goddamned B! I even spoke with the teacher who had her for 101, and that teacher said the same thing happened there — and that Miss Knott even yelled at her for not getting an A. She didn't have to yell at me. She went to Teachersonparade! This is not right. This is not just. And her fucking lies are on the website and can be read and absorbed by the entire world!"

Shit! He'd sworn again.

"Are you sure that people are even reading the reviews?"

"My classes have half the enrollment they usually do."

Ms. Oznick made a note of that. "If you do lose any classes, that could be very good," she said.

"Very good?"

She smiled her lawyerly (cobra?) smile. "Because it would show a financial loss. That's even better than hurt feelings."

"How about starvation? Would that help too?"

"Will it go that far, Dr. Tack?"

"It's also more than hurt feelings, Ms. Oznick. These are festering, compounding lies! Isn't that what libel is? Does the Constitution protect pathological liars?"

"You seem passionate about it, Dr. Tack. Is it that you don't want your students to review you at all?"

"My students, the real ones, can review me — and anonymously too — in the regular evaluation process."

"Do students have access to these evaluations?"

"No."

"Do you think they should?"

"No."

"And why not?"

"Because they make teachers into pussies." (Oh, god, another wrong term to use here!) "By that I mean there is an overwhelming temptation to cater to people who have that much power over you." (Just like I'm sucking up to you now!) "A professor cannot make objective judgments if his job depends on merely being 'popular.' I believe there's a direct correlation between a teacher having to get high marks and that teacher having to give high marks. Or to dumb down the content and make everything lowbrow. The intellectual life, the college environment, is not supposed to be like some product on TV — some hit of the minute. I feel that my integrity is being undermined by this website, as is the integrity of the entire teaching profession."

"I see."

Had he been convincing enough? Be careful of the words you use, class!

"Why don't you see who else you can round up to join you. We need at least five teachers. And then we could talk again perhaps?" She handed him the folder of the reviews she had collected.

"And if you took the case, the cost would be . . . ?"

"If we take it, it will be on contingency."

"No cost?"

"Not until there's a settlement in our favor."

"Great!"

"But let's not get ahead of ourselves, shall we? No promises."

"Of course."

Yet Nathaniel couldn't help getting his hopes up. What else did he have?

The death threat from the Satanist was evidently going unacknowledged — he heard nothing from anyone with power at Shite. Maybe the "666" threat was a hoax. Maybe it wasn't. It was certainly making him nervous and irritable, with not only an upsurge in his facial tic and a renewed bout of vomiting, but his joints seemed to be turning arthritic as well. This thing was making him an old man before his time.

And it wasn't just the one death threat. Haywood had sent him another one the night before, from Speak Out Loud:

> There is a rumor going around that N, Tack of the English

Dept., is threatening a lawsuit against this website. If he does follow threw, he may see not only his class enrollments deflating, but, his tires as well. And then Re-inflating. Be Warned.

Who wrote that one — the Oracle of Delphi? What did the "Re-inflating" part mean? His tires blown up again? God, this was horrible. He was in a war zone.

He kept his office door closed now, not even a crack. Visitors had to knock. He probably looked like some old geezer checking them out to see if They've Come For Me, he realized, but he still had a great deal of pure animal desire to live.

He looked under his own car for bombs and booby-trap. He didn't see anything suspicious, but did he really know what to look for? It probably wouldn't be marked BOMB, right? Or maybe it would be, as some kind of sick joke. Teacher blown to pieces in killer Dot-Comedy.

Two days later, near the lot where he parked, he saw Nona Dwibble in her wheelchair and raised his hand in greeting, but either she didn't see him or else cut him dead. He watched her getting into her car with great difficulty, but you had to give it to the skinny old biddy. She still managed to drive, to say nothing of entertaining all those troops in her office. Maybe Nona wouldn't acknowledge him because she thought her wheelchair would get bombed too?

Okay, if the college wouldn't protect him, then he would protect himself. He drove down to Pier 39 on the waterfront of the city and found the store he had looked up in the yellow pages: PERSONAL (This Means You) PROTECTION DEVICES.

How cute. . . . Sort of.

May I have a personal protection device, please?

It sounded like something you'd wear as a diaper. Well, Nathaniel hadn't quite crapped in his pants yet, but he could feel the temptation. Somehow Depends jokes weren't quite as amusing as they had been.

He looked at revolvers, shotguns, pepper spray, Mace, stun guns, and tazers.

"Can I show the gentleman something in designer shotgun, yes?" the clerk asked. The clerk was a Bosnian refugee, or had the look, feel, and accent at least. A lean and hungry look. The Bosnian teeth were a bit rotten and jagged.

"I'm just browsing," he said.

Did he really want to shoot somebody? Better than being shot yourself. But a shotgun was so . . . permanent. Did he want a handgun then? Wouldn't he have to get a police permit — a designer police permit? Officer Ilse Grout hadn't suggested a gun to him. The police wanted all the guns for themselves.

"Nice pepper spray can make them weep like crazy man and fall down!" the clerk said. Business seemed to be pretty slow. He got out a can and held it out like somebody on the Shopping Channel. "Sir, you like?"

Maybe I should have gone online and bought an arsenal, Nathaniel thought. I'm too conventional.

"Our new tazer can hit your personal enemy from up to four meters away," the clerk advertised. "Want I should demonstrate?" He held up the tazer, playfully. Maybe this was all part of the plot? The Satanist had known that Nathaniel would race to the most obvious place for a weapon, and here was this paid assassin waiting for him! An empty store, a taste of tazer, the body in the dumpster:

PROFESSOR MISSING. PRESUMED SUICIDE.

Feeling despondent over his bad reviews, Professor Nathaniel Tack, police fear, has taken his own life and left no trace . . .

"What would you like then?" the clerk persisted, spreading his arms to indicate the cornucopia around them. Well, if he wasn't an assassin, he sure as hell was working on commission.

"I don't know yet," Nathaniel said. "I'll let you know."

The clerk looked offended. "Am sorry." He skulked over behind a display case and pretended to rearrange the merchandise.

Clerk zaps surly customer.

Nathaniel thought about it and thought about it and finally asked for a demonstration of a stun gun. The clerk put in a fresh battery and showed Nathaniel the various switches. "You like try it, sir?"

Nathaniel fumbled a bit with the apparatus but finally held it out, examining the two prongs between which the voltage would flow — like viper's fangs. "You talking to me?" Nathaniel said. "You talking to me?"

The clerk looked a little nervous, Bosnia or no Bosnia behind him. "Sir, like?"

Nathaniel flipped the side switch down with his thumb, and the volts sizzled and crackled like current in a miniature Frankenstein laboratory. "It's alive! It's alive!" he said.

The clerk didn't seem to be getting the allusions and might even be re-thinking his offer to sell it.

"I'll take it," Nathaniel said.

The clerk grinned, glad to be rid of him.

He put it into the glove compartment of his car. "Bring on the goddamned Satanists!" he said, with more bravado than he felt.

He wrote Haywood Wire as strong an ultimatum as he dared:

Hi, Haywood,

Have you found a good lawyer yet?

I think I have, in the one I met with two days ago. She noticed that the review accusing you of harassment might very well work in a libel suit. No, I didn't point it out to her. She discovered it on her own. She seems willing to represent us if we can get five souls with the willingness to sign on. Are you game? — Nathaniel

He also dropped a note to Titus Ashe in the Astrology Department. He made it handwritten to personalize it:

Hello, Mr. Ashe,

We have not met, I do believe, on our spacious and lovely campus. I am gathering aggrieved parties for a class action lawsuit against Teachersonparade. com. Are you aware there is libel about you there?

Sincerely,

Nathaniel Tack, English

It might be best not to show Ashe the precise review just yet — about the man playing with himself while he taught his classes.

He noticed in the folder that Suzanna Oznick had given him was a review of another teacher he didn't know, Lillian St. Jude in the Business School:

Mrs. St. Jewd she a racist. she fail me because she hate Black people. I did as much work as the White Ones. But, n, not good enough for this bitch, who is so crabby because she aint' gettin none. . . .

It went on for several paragraphs, tedious in the details of its particular gripe. But maybe Lillian St. Jude would see the light (anti-Semitism if they were lucky?!) and jump aboard. Choo choo! Hear that whistle blowing, Lillian? It blows for thee.

He thought he'd also try Krista Prandemonia, because of the review in the folder:

Mrs. Prandemonia has no ability to teach. She just stands there, incmpetent, with a book in her hand. She gave everybody a C for the mid-term and an A for the final. No talent, something of a Greek activist, but I'd like to be a little beep up her bonnet one time.

Krista was in his department, but fairly new. He'd been at a party with her somewhere one New Year's, and she had asked him the strangest questions, putting him off a bit. "Are your novels user friendly?" and "If I were to get an agent for my non-fiction novel, would I have to leave my teaching position?" She was pretty but more than a little spacey. And what exactly was a Greek activist? Did it have something to do with her sex life? Hell, whatever, she was worth a try.

Now who else? Nathaniel could play the race card if he had to. Who did he know that would fit the criteria. Not Marcus Blatty — he of the blowjob review. Nathaniel had heard indirectly through someone or other that Blatty had just laughed when he heard of the review. But what about . . . Vernon Daniels in the Music Department? Hadn't he seen a bad review of him one day? Was it still there?

Sure enough, it was:

> Vernon teaches his Bongo class with a decided elitist emphasis. He doesn't respect his students and tries to make them fit into his Afrocentric view of world music. I'd avoid this man, if I was you, and just make your own mistakes instead of makeing his. I expected more, just didn't get it.

But was it libelous? Hmm.

Nathaniel got all these into the campus mail and went to teach his afternoon class, carrying his new stun gun in the upper pocket of his favorite sport coat. About half the students were no longer attending — the half that shouldn't haven't been attending in the first place. There was much talk among the Administrators of "retention" of students, but he thought the emphasis was totally misplaced. Decorum in the classroom might be retained, yes, but why retain remedial life forms in so-called university courses? He'd been able to grade as he knew he should grade despite the dropout rate and the parade of easy graders before him, but now he feared that the review site was going to make him give in. He patted his trusty stun gun and Walked Tall.

Mr. Bhatangsombatuisit had departed, along with a bunch of others, and so the grading chores at this stage of the semester weren't as onerous. The remaining students by and large were competent, but both they and Nathaniel were counting the days until the end of the term.

When he began his 101, he was startled to see a stranger sitting in the back. Who was that? He waited for the person to identify himself, or, more likely, for a regular student to come up and ask if it was all right for a guest to attend the class. When none of this happened by the time he'd taken the roll, Nathaniel was a bit irritated. Still, I mustn't stun gun just *anybody* he told himself, patting his coat pocket again. Amazing how good it felt to have some protection. "Yes?" Nathaniel asked of the stranger, who was an androgynous male in his twenties. This long-limbed stranger was covered with more chains than Marley's ghost, with one even in his nose, and sporting a blue Mohawk hairdo. When Boy Bands go Bad? Was it the Satanist, his hour come round at last? What were Satanists wearing this season?

"I'm with him," the stranger said, indicating Mr. Badermann, the pudgy lad who sat in the center back.

"Is it all right," Mr. Badermann asked belatedly, "to have a guest?"

"Sorry," Nathaniel said, "you're supposed to ask in advance." Where did these people learn their manners?

"I have to leave?" the stranger said, making a face.

"Afraid so," Nathaniel said.

"Really?"

"Only enrolled Satanists are permitted."

The stranger conferred with his friend and then got up, jarringly so, and adjusted his tangle of chains and headed toward the front of the classroom.

Nathaniel held his place at the lectern. Do you worst, dread Satanist! Nathaniel thought, setting his face. He would, upon the slightest move, go for his stun gun and have the Evil One on the floor in no time, begging for mercy, chains abuzz with electricity.

The weapon of choice of Satanists was?

The stranger hesitated at the door and gave a high sign to his friend in the back, then gave Nathaniel half a dirty look.

Don't make me hurt you, Nathaniel thought, arranging his lecture notes.

But the stranger left, and Nathaniel sauntered over and closed the door. "Really!" he said, glaring at Mr. Badermann. Of course there was nothing to stop the stranger or anyone else who was determined from barreling through the door of the classroom, which had no lock, and doing the Devil's work. "What were you thinking?" he asked Mr. Badermann?

"He was considering enrolling in your class next term," Mr. Badermann explained.

"Just my luck! Another Phi Beta Kappa down the drain!"

The first teacher he heard back from was Titus Ashe, who came to his office, a very beefy-faced, heavy-set man in his late fifties. His ears stuck out more than they should have. Nathaniel thought: Don't you know they have cosmetic surgery for that now? But he was glad to see somebody taking an interest — he guessed.

"I'm the man who plays with himself in class!" Titus Ashe announced.

"Is this a confession?" Nathaniel asked.

"I jiggle my keys while I talk." He demonstrated with his hand in his pants pocket. "It may be annoying, but it's not masturbation." What a loud voice the man had. And what a bossy demeanor.

"Do you want to join the lawsuit?" Nathaniel was tired of preliminaries. Jump on or get off.

"I might."

"Sign here."

"Already?"

"I just meant metaphorically."

"Are there any others joining the suit besides you?"

Nathaniel decided, against his nature, to attempt a bit of prevarication. "As a matter of fact, a good number of people have expressed interest." Was that alluring, yet vague, enough?

"And their names?"

"They have not authorized me to release those yet."

"Our names would have to appear on the lawsuit, wouldn't they?"

"I don't really know."

"Although I think it can be one name and then a class of people. Would you be willing to be that one name?"

". . . Sure," Nathaniel answered. What was he getting himself into?

"How much is this going to cost me?"

"The lawyer has mentioned working on contingency."

Ashe grimaced. "You get the legal help you pay for — or don't pay for."

"I can't sue if I have to pay," Nathaniel said honestly.

"Okay, I'm in," Ashe said. "Put me down."

"Would you mind signing your name and a telephone number?" It was all happening so fast now Nathaniel hadn't even been prepared. He grabbed a blank sheet of paper and scribbled Possible Litigants across the top. Ashe signed it and made as to leave. "We'll be in touch," he said. "And the fairy shitass who wrote that about me is going to suck my cock!"

"Okay . . ." Nathaniel opined, unable to follow up because Titus Ashe was out of there in a hurry.

The next day he heard from Krista Prandemonia, who also stopped by his office.

"It's my day off, but I wanted to speak with you," she said, catching him in the corridor on his way out. "Sorry I'm late." She looked a bit disheveled and overheated, as though she'd been running. She was wearing high heels that were mud-spattered, and her flame-rinsed big hair and low-cut dress made her look like a thirty-something old-timey country singer. "I heard of those rotten reviews about me from somebody, but I ignored them. However, now I want to do something."

"Welcome."

"They're making me see upside down!" Krista's eyes did look a little odd, not upside exactly but pupil-enlarged and bloodshot.

"Who is?"

"These damn girls in my class!"

"And that's because . . . ?"

"Because they've got me scared witless!"

Indeed, Krista Prandemonia seemed a bit witless at the moment, hopefully a transitory state. And, no, she didn't seem to be the perfect candidate for the libel lawsuit. But Nathaniel was committed to the principle that the position of the teacher has to be safeguarded. If everyone who teaches has to go into the classroom and earn the territory every single moment, the world will soon be an American high school. EEK! Maybe Krista could be excused from the lawsuit if somebody more presentable came along.

In the meantime . . .

He could see that tears were welling up in her eyes. She was actually quite a sexy woman with all that big hair and those curves and all that predictable stuff. He held open his arms to her, and she fell on his breast, as they used to say. In fact, she began to sob on his collarbone.

"There, there," he soothed.

"Where do I sign?" Krista sobbed.

He let them back into his office and he hugged her some more — careful to keep the door wide open — by god, there would be no sexual harassment suits if he could help it! — and had her put her John Hancock on the list of possible litigants.

"Thank you. You've been very nice to me today," Krista said as she prepared to leave.

"I could do no less," Nathaniel said, standing at his office and waving goodbye.

Aha! Two names and counting!

Later that day he was having dinner at a Chinese restaurant near school, before his evening Creative Writing class, when he was approached by a big woman with large hoop earrings. "Dr. Tack?"

Nathaniel caught his breath.

Was this the Satanist?

"I'm Lillian St. Jude — of the Business School."

He sighed in relief. "Oh, you scared me."

"I'm so sorry! I didn't think."

"Sit down. Please." He gestured toward the other side of the booth.

She slid in, but just barely. My, she was a hefty gal. Full-figured. Watch it, Nathaniel, he told himself. Some might say the same about you.

"How did you know I'd be in this restaurant?"

"I called the English Department and asked for your schedule."

"They know where I dine?"

"Some woman there said she thought you usually ate at Jenny's Hot Wok on Tuesday nights."

"That must have been Gladys, our secretary."

"I didn't ask her name."

"I must have mentioned dining here to her sometime in the past. She has a memory like an elephant, and she's nearing eighty, would you believe?" He'd have to have a word with Gladys, that was clear. Oh, you want to shoot Dr. Tack. Go to Jenny's Hot Wok at Salinas Street and Juniper between six and seven and he'll be waiting for you.

"I sought you out because that review you sent me upset me so much."

"I'm sorry if it caused you pain," Nathaniel said. "But it seems to me some of us have to act now if the pain isn't going to get worse."

"I agree with you."

"No kidding?" Nathaniel became all smiles. "Do you want some of my food?" He pointed to an egg roll he hadn't touched yet.

"I am eating later with my husband, but I might have a glass of wine."

Nathaniel stood up and signaled to the staff. Fortunately the place was not busy, one of the reasons he went there.

"A glass of house white," Lillian St. Jude ordered, and the male staff relative hurried off for it.

In addition to the big body and the big hoop earrings, Lillian brought a firm, possibly face-lifted countenance to the table. She looked Jewish. Could you say that? You had to be so careful! And we say the Victorians had their taboos! You could say she looked Irish or Scandinavian — but Jewish? There were certain facial patterns, for God's sake. It didn't mean you were prejudiced because you saw them!

If anything, Nathaniel was prejudiced in favor of Jews. He found the men sexy and their culture intelligent — just cool that hard-nosed Orthodoxy about gays, all right? Anyway, Mrs. St. Jude was possessed of personable brown eyes and a high color to her cheeks, the hair very dark. She was probably forty-five. (Could you say that?)

"How did you find that review?"

"My lawyer showed it to me." It felt good to say "my lawyer." He hoped it was true.

"I think I know who wrote it."

Nathaniel raised a quizzical eyebrow, continuing with his meal. He also cast an eye on the big round clock near the entrance to the kitchen. He would have to leave in a few minutes to make his class.

"It was Rasheeda Tompkins, this black student I had last year. She was not passing the course by any stretch of the imagination. I had other black students who were."

"Of course," Nathaniel nodded. I hear what you're saying, lady.

The white wine arrived, and Lillian was gracious to the waiter. "I am certainly not prejudiced against African Americans. In fact I worked for civil rights when I was a young woman. I even participated in many demonstrations."

I'm sure you'd drink black wine if they made it. But be careful of what you work for, lady, Nathaniel wanted to say. It comes back to bite you in the butt. Every social or political movement, it seemed to him, went from a grade A (maybe) to a low C-minus in about twenty-five years and then into various lower stages of self-serving poo-poo. It had happened to the civil rights movement, the feminist movement. Was it going to happen to the gay movement too? There were signs. Poor chunky Lillian St. Jude, another foolish liberal half-eaten by her "children." Would these people never learn? Of course he didn't tell her this. He needed her.

"This case went all the way up to the Chancellor's office," Lillian was clarifying. "At every step I was vindicated. My grade book was examined. The exams were double checked. Triple checked. I even offered to have Miss Tompkins examined by another instructor."

"But?"

"She would not be satisfied."

"Of course not. She's riding the Zeitgeist." Nathaniel was way past worrying about whether he was mixing his metaphors or not. "If you're faulted, it can't be because it's her. It's got to be racism."

"She finally found Teachersonparade.com and left that review of me. As a matter of fact she's left it on at least three different occasions."

"Meaning?"

"I contacted the webmaster, as we're supposed to, and informed him. He removed it the first two times. But this last one has been up there for some time now."

"It must be so difficult for the webmaster to raise that finger to delete it." Nathaniel let the irony waft across the booth along with the aroma of his lemon chicken.

"I can see that you're not a fan."

"To say the least, Mrs. St. Jude."

"Lillian, please."

"Nor do I consider it the obligation of the maligned to beg for the webmaster's kind mercy."

"I didn't know how else to get the review off there."

"Believe me, I'm not blaming you. What I'm saying is that he has usurped enormous power for himself via the Internet, and we must not and cannot let him control our lives this way. Nor any of his hooligan compatriots, however computer literate."

She took a sip of her wine. "I have come to see that something must be done. "That's why I have come to you."

Come to me, all ye who are heavily laden and I will . . . Stop! One Jesus was enough. Talk about a good idea gone bad!

God, her wine looked good. "The lawyers have said they'll do it for a part of any settlement we might obtain. Not that I'm doing it for the money."

"They'll want a third. They usually do when it's on contingency. I had an uncle who was a lawyer, and I touch on business law and lawsuits a little bit in one of my courses."

"Better and better."

"This student was very belligerent towards me from the start, and it made me wonder if she had picked up some of that anti-Semitism you find sometimes in certain portions — limited portions — of the African- American community."

Yes, Lillian, your liberal credentials are impeccable, and safe with me. Would these Mayflowers never get over their guilt? Nathaniel was emphatically over his. Indeed, if you wanted a new cause, why not Reparations for Homosexuals! Let the other ethnic "minorities" start lining up to donate — for their long history of sins against My People!

Guess that would have to wait for another day.

"I'm somewhat reluctant to go into a lawsuit," she said.

"You would be our second woman," he sprang on her, feeling nervous that she might be about to back out. He suspected that she might go for women's causes.

"Oh? Who else?"

He guessed it was all right to use their names, now that they'd signed the list. "Krista Prandemonia in my department. Do you know her?"

"I'm afraid not."

"She's very nice." And almost normal when she isn't seeing upside down. "She too has had obnoxious students giving her a very hard time."

"How awful."

God, he hated being a politician like this. But war was war.

"She may have to take a medical leave."

"Really!"

"She was sobbing in my arms just recently, I'm sorry to report."

"Well, Ms. Tompkins did not make me weep, but she made my life hell for several semesters. She even threw a copy of that review on the floor of my office. Tossed it from the doorway."

"Like you were trash."

"That was her message. Maybe I should have passed her or tried harder or —"

"I think we may have an African-American man joining the lawsuit," he said, totally without foundation.

"How wonderful! That would really show what this site has turned into."

"I'm working on it right now," Nathaniel lied through his lemon chicken. Vernon Daniels, I need you!

"And what has brought you to this willingness to sue?" she asked.

"You haven't looked up my reviews?"

"No, but your name seems to be bruited about quite a bit on the site."

"I always wanted to be a household name," Nathaniel said. "Maybe one day I'll write a play about it. A Greek tragedy."

"Oh, I hope not!"

"A comic Greek tragedy then. The Greeks, I am beginning to appreciate more and more, truly had a grasp on the fundamentals of life."

"But surely we're not fated," Lillian said.

"Maybe it just applies to other people, not us," Nathaniel said. "For we are not going to let the Internet permit the disgruntled and the slack-jawed in the cyber posse to have their way with us."

"I'll drink to that!" Lillian said, toasting Nathaniel's glass of water with her white wine.

She signed her name on a separate sheet of paper with her home address and phone number and even accompanied him as far as the edge of campus. He had walked to school, to throw any potential tracker off his scent. Lillian didn't turn out to be a hit man (hitperson?) for the Satanist, thank god, and he didn't have to stun gun her.

That meant he now had four people willing to sue for libel. For some reason he kept forgetting to count himself. So he needed just one more person. Just one more! He hadn't heard back from Haywood or Vernon Daniels and wondered if he should go to see them in person.

Maybe he wouldn't even need Haywood Wire. What a godsend that would be — although Haywood's libel was definitely better than Vernon's libel, and you had to figure that in to the equation. My libel can beat up your libel, especially in a court of law. And my death threat trumps your harassment charge and her sexual put down. Except that nobody seemed to give a rat's ass about his death threat. Maybe the college was hoping it would come true, and they'd be rid of his annoying gay butt. Naw, they weren't that bad. Were they? He'd better hurry and write a note to Marty and Jim/Jimmy telling them to sue for wrongful death if the Satanist got him.

He was writing the note in his office when Haywood showed up looking like a million bucks. Well, a buck ninety five. He had on a new white vinyl jacket and new boots. Tap boots? He'd combed his beard and what was left of his hair and smelled of lilac cologne. He must be on his way to see the ladies. Er . . . to learn the beauty and grace of Beginning Tap. Or maybe Haywood was up to Intermediate by now.

"I want to join the lawsuit," Haywood said.

Damn. He'd rather have Vernon, even though he'd never met Vernon.

"What made you decide?"

"I of course have to be extremely careful where I sign my name."

Haywood would make five, but still . . .

"Maybe you won't even have to sign," Nathaniel dared, feeling just this side of cocky. Maybe the lawyer would even go ahead with just four?

"You don't want me to sign?" Haywood snapped.

"I don't want you to do what you don't want to do, Haywood."

"Who are these lawyers? Are they any good?"

"I don't really know, but they're the only lawyers we have."

"If you'd left it to me, maybe we'd have better ones."

"It's still not too late for you to bring in these wonderful lawyers."

Haywood seemed to sense Nathaniel's irritation, although Nathaniel was forcing himself to curb his voice. "I just might. I have some money saved."

"Are you willing to use it for the lawsuit?"

"I didn't say that."

"And who did you have in mind for counsel? Perhaps Ruth Bader Ginsburg can take a couple of months off from the Supreme Court to help out an old friend?"

Haywood's mouth looked a little pulled. "What's gotten into you?"

"Nothing. I'm the same lovable old coot I've been all along."

"It's because Titus Ashe has signed on, isn't it? You're feeling flush."

"How do you know he signed on?" Nathaniel was positive he hadn't mentioned it yet.

"Titus and I know each other."

"If he told you, it must be true."

"Titus is a handful."

"I sensed that. Do you think he really plays with himself while he teaches?"

"What an idea!"

"Some of the students play with themselves. Maybe we have a class in it? Guerrilla Masturbation 101?"

"Titus is prickly. He gets on my case sometimes."

Hmm. "Will he stay the course? He did sign this piece of paper in my office." Nathaniel flashed it.

"But did he sign with the actual lawyers?"

"Not yet."

"He can surprise you, that Titus."

No doubt you're the stable one of this duo, Haywood. "And two women have agreed as well."

"No kidding? You've really been working this, haven't you?"

"There is no stone I have left unturned. And nothing that has crawled out from under that stone have I ignored."

"You still want me to join the suit, don't you?" Was this almost a plea?

"I thought you weren't sure about it, and that's why you didn't come to the first meeting."

"I was also feeling a little under the weather that day."

"No doubt."

"You probably need my assistance."

"Could you give me copies of all of Dean Visigoth's reviews?"

"You don't want me to sign? I thought you needed people."

"I'm not saying I don't want you to sign, Haywood. The lawyer said five people. I have four. I'm planning to go to see Vernon Daniels on a hope and a prayer. I have no idea what he thinks of the website or of his reviews on it. I am just trying to gather as much information and support as I can get. If you'd give copies of anything relevant that you have, including missing reviews and that videotape you made of the way the school's webpage looked when this first started, I would be extremely obliged to you, and then you might not even have to sign anything. Because if there is a lawsuit, and you're in it, you probably will have to sign your name, somewhere — although I am a complete novice at the law and could be wrong. Possibly there is some way to sue and keep you as a John Doe, but, frankly, I doubt it."

"Sounds to me like you're backing off of me."

Not completely, you incredible jerk, although nothing would make me happier than not having you on board — except possibly viewing the Satanist laid out in Arena 3B, his death threat pinned with a stake to his devil-loving heart.

"Why don't we go see Vernon Daniels together?" Haywood said.

"Together?"

"I've met him. He teaches Classic Bongo."

"So I've heard." What the hell was Classic Bongo?

"He's a very dignified older gentleman. He's been around here for thirty-five years or more. I've talked to him from time to time."

"And what's your take on him?"

"I think he'd be very upset with any kind of review that didn't speak kindly of him."

"Have you seen his reviews?"

"I've seen everybody's reviews."

And they're driving you even crazier than you already are! Nathaniel shrieked (a quiet shriek that never left his throat).

"And are his reviews libelous?"

"I've been reading up on what constitutes libel. The law is all over the place. And when it comes to the Internet, we're the cutting edge, Nathaniel, the cutting edge."

Pardon me, while I bleed. "And as for Vernon's reviews?"

"Unkind — a touch race insensitive maybe, but not exactly hard-core libel."

Oh, Jesus, does that mean I'm stuck with you? Nathaniel thought. Mother of God, what have I gotten myself into!? Can I get out of it, short of suicide or murder?

Yes, maybe that was easier. He'd go and murder Dude Lather and take his hard drive and that would be the end of the website. Of course! Why hadn't he thought of this before?

What was wrong with that plan? Absolutely nothing. It was a brilliant plan! Was he overlooking something? What was it?

"Nathaniel?"

He came to. "What?"

"Did you conk out there?"

"Sorry. Just a reverie. What were we saying?"

"Let's see if we can find Vernon Daniels."

"I was just about to look up his hours."

"I'm way ahead of you," Haywood smirked. "If we hurry, maybe we can catch him right now at the end of a class."

Maybe Haywood was worth something after all.

They raced across the campus, and again umpteen students greeted Haywood Wire as he were Aristotle. Had Aristotle tossed candies to Alexander the Great? What if Aristotle had had students like the ones at Shire? He'd be known as Alexander the Remedial.

"Are you still getting reviewed on the site?" Nathaniel asked as they trudged along a path between buildings.

"My number has gone way down, I'm happy to report. Soon I'll be just a bleep and no one will know I'm even there."

"But they seem to like you." Nathaniel nodded at the grinning students in clusters standing along a ramp that ran down to Visual Arts (the Helen Keller Building).

"I wish I could retire," Haywood said. "They are so bad!"

"Hi, Mr. Wire!" a girl with a club foot said.

"Hi, Elizabeta!" Haywood called. "She's taking me for the third time. I'll have to pass her this time, just to be rid of her."

Haywood didn't seem to think any more highly of the student body than Nathaniel did, but, boy, he was much better at disguising it.

They caught Vernon Daniels talking with a bongo-carrying student in the Music Department in Arts, one of the funkier areas of the school. Evidently they all worked up quite a sweat playing their various instruments, from kettle drums to marimbas. There seemed to be even more than the usual assortment of scraggly bearded, tam-wearing or long-haired would-be musicians in that section, coming and going from the rehearsal rooms with their bad sound leaks. Many a day Nathaniel had to contend with rising, seeping, and conflicting melodies interfering with his afternoon class.

He and Haywood waited for Vernon to finish with a student in a funky hat with ear flaps, but he seemed to go on and on, a jovial old "character" who favored his right leg and had a brier-patch beard and bifocals, burly and black as the Ace of Spades. Yeah, maybe he was about to be their Ace!

"Vernon!" Haywood said, at last gaining his attention.

He seemed to recognize Haywood. That was a plus.

Introductions were made, and Nathaniel got right to the point. "Are you aware of the review site about teachers?"

Vernon's face went cold, the eyes suddenly very un-jovial. "Yeah? What about it?"

"Have you seen your own reviews?"

"Yeah, I know the prick who wrote that!"

Nathaniel wasn't sure which review they were talking about it, but it didn't matter. Vernon Daniels was pissed, and that was good.

"I teach my students the fundamentals. I give 'em some history. But they don't want — some of 'em — to learn anything. They want to come in here and start banging their nuts off, and that's exactly what it sounds like — nuts banging!"

"Some of us are gathering supporters for a lawsuit."

Vernon's eyes looked somewhat suspicious. "Suing who?"

"Probably the webmaster and his site."

"Maybe even the college," Haywood tossed in.

"The college?"

"It has supported the website from the start and isn't doing a damn thing to stop it now. It's been almost a whole semester."

"But the college — don't they have a lot of money to fight a lawsuit? Some friend of mine tried to sue a few years ago. He got run over by a delivery truck, one of the school's, and he couldn't win shit."

"Maybe he shouldn't have tried for shit," Nathaniel said.

Vernon laughed.

"Would you be interested?" Haywood pressed.

"Is this for big bucks?"

"I was reading about some man who got libeled in a business publication and won a million dollars in the settlement," Haywood said.

"I don't think money is the real reason for this," Nathaniel was quick to add.

"Still, you won't turn it down?" Vernon said. "Right?"

"No, I won't turn it down." Vernon sounded like Nathaniel's mother, who had been raised dirt poor and whose every other thought was about money. "It's possible that your reviews aren't actually libelous, it should be pointed out."

"They certainly are!"

Nathaniel looked at Haywood. "The one I read wasn't that bad."

"Then why are you asking me to join?"

Nathaniel hesitated. How did you say, We're loading our Race Deck?

"As I understand it," Haywood jumped in, "it's to be a class action lawsuit. That way any particular review wouldn't have to be that bad, as long as there's a pattern. Isn't that correct?"

"The lawyer and I didn't get into it that far. But it sounds like Haywood has been doing his homework."

"Well, I'll definitely consider it," Vernon said. "I've got to be going now. I've got a gig tonight. But they're not getting away with saying I'm elitist!"

They all shook hands, in the non-elitist way possible, and he and Haywood walked back toward the Statistics Building.

"What do you think?" Nathaniel asked. "Is he in?"

"Sounded like it."

Yeah, and you sounded like you were coming to meet with the lawyer and you didn't even show up or call!

"But how reliable is he?"

"To tell the truth, I don't know Vernon that well."

I'd better cover my ass, Nathaniel calculated. "So do you want to sign on, Haywood?" he said. "Right this minute?" Nathaniel was not much for conventional wisdom, yet a bird in the hand was worth two in the bush, was it not?

Through an elaborate series of telephone calls and visits to their offices, Nathaniel managed to get the possible litigants to commit to a meeting with Suzanna Oznick and her law partner. It was deep into the semester with finals approaching, but he prodded and cajoled and flattered and made promises which he only hoped he could keep just to get them all there. He said he would get a date they could all agree on.

Then he had to call the lawyer four times before he got her again. "Yes?"

"Ms. Oznick?"

"Yes?"

"It's Nathaniel Tack."

"Who?"

"The college professor you spoke to."

"Oh, yes."

"You're still interested in the case, right?"

"I thought you had dropped it."

"What?"

"I haven't heard from you."

Nathaniel's heart sank. "I haven't dropped it. I've been gathering the five people you said we'd need."

"You have?"

"I thought that's where we left it."

"Well, people say they're going to do things, but they quite often don't."

Not me! Nathaniel thought. "I have the five! In fact, I may have six!" Vernon Daniels had proved elusive after the initial enthusiasm.

"Well, my partner and I just got in thirty boxes of materials we have to go through for the case we're currently handling."

"Oh?"

"I doubt that we can find time to meet with your people."

"What if they just came in one at a time and signed?"

"Did we agree to sign? I don't quite remember agreeing to that," Ms. Oznick said. This was, as they say, not a good sign.

"You mentioned getting five people who were willing. I've got them!"

Nathaniel hated too much pushiness in people, and it did not come naturally to him. He worked at his. But he could tell this was a crucial moment, and he'd knocked himself out arranging all this. "Please, Ms. Oznick. I can help you with anything you need. I can write up whatever you want, if you haven't got the time. You just tell me what and I'll do it!"

"Well . . ."

"Please!"

"Let me look at my calendar."

She was gone for what seemed two eternities, and then she was back. "How about the fourth?"

"At what time?" he asked.

"In the afternoon."

"Three?"

"Three on the fourth is fine," she said.

"We'll be there, or else I'll have the teachers stop by your office individually to sign."

"God, that sounds complicated. Can't you just all come at three?"

"I'm afraid they have different teaching schedules."

"I don't want to have to explain it five or six times."

"Just tell me, and I'll explain it to them."

She seemed to grow reluctant again, and he thought she was going to say it was just too difficult.

"I could drop by and pick up the form, if there's a form to sign, and bring it to each person. How would that be?"

"That's a possibility."

"I'll be happy to do it. These are lies about these teachers, Ms. Oznick! Vicious lies."

"I'm sure they are, Mr. Tack."

Well, there are at least more lies than truth, Nathaniel thought. You've got to deal with life's mixed bag as you find it. After all, this was real, not a goddamned Perry Mason!

Somehow, magically, he got all five to agree to meet at the Offices of Oznick and Kurd at the appointed time. Vernon Daniels said he would try his best, and even Haywood got there early.

This is too easy, Nathaniel worried, when he saw them all sitting there in the office. There weren't enough chairs and more had to be brought from the back. These were old and rickety and the leak in the ceiling was still not fixed. The heat didn't seem adequate either.

Yet even Oznick's partner was present, a small, dapper brown man with a chipped front tooth and big whites in his mercurial brown eyes. He looked to be about thirty, seemed feisty, and was wearing an expensive-looking sweater made of light blue angora, perhaps hand knitted by slave labor in the land of his birth, which he had said was northern Iraq. "Hi, I'm Jordan Kurd," he said in a very American accent to each possible litigant as he or she arrived. He even handed out business cards to everybody.

"I'm so glad that you're taking the case," Nathaniel breathed, trying to make it irrevocable on their part. But nothing had been signed yet.

The last to arrive was Titus Ashe, who seemed a little the worse for wear. He looked bloated and closer to seventy than his late fifties. He probably did drink too much, and time had not been good to his earlobes or his eyebrows, sending them forth in all directions. Maybe Nathaniel should have sneaked into the back of one of the man's classes to see if he did indeed play with himself. Titus could be "excused" from the case perhaps.

"I see that all of you are white," Jordan Kurd said, half-sitting on the back of Ms. Oznick's chair.

"You got a problem with that?" Titus barked.

"I didn't say that."

"Then why did you mention it?"

"Just as a factor in the look of the case."

"White people don't have rights?"

Jesus, not right this minute, Titus! Nathaniel cringed. Let's sign first and bitch later!

"Didn't you say you had an African-American litigant?" Jordan asked Nathaniel.

"He said he would come."

"I wouldn't count on him," Haywood said, slumped in a chair that made his legs jut up like ship's timbers.

"What?"

"I think he has a gig this afternoon."

"I am glad to see two women involved," Ms. Oznick said, acknowledging Lillian St. Jude and Krista Prandemonia, who both looked very nice. They had tarted up, the two of them, and Nathaniel was grateful — although when he looked at the drab, un-made-up face of Ms. Oznick he wondered if perhaps she considered make-up "male oppressive" or some other P.C. thing. You also couldn't help noticing that the woman was so shy she was scary.

"Shall we begin?" Nathaniel urged. "If Vernon comes, that's a plus. But we have five!" He felt giddy and a bit queasy. He'd had some of that vodka before he'd left home, and he wondered if anybody could tell. I'll probably die in a gutter from all this, he thought.

Haywood had taken a seat as far from Nathaniel as it was possible in the cramped front area of the Offices of Oznick, Kurd, and Drip and seemed displeased about something.

I won't look at him, Nathaniel promised himself. We don't leave this room without a lawyer!

Ms. Oznick finally took the initiative, despite her tiny voice, and laid out the legal plan. "I think you might have some very legitimate legal grounds for a lawsuit."

The litigants lit up and nodded at each other.

"However, libel is never easy to prove."

Nathaniel looked around at his catch. I think it's going to happen — finally! Then he caught a glimpse of Haywood out of the corner of his eye. He had his chin down and was stroking his ugly old beard and shooting nasty eye-darts Nathaniel's way. What have I done now? Nathaniel wondered.

Titus was interrupting Ms. Oznick already. "I must say your office is not very impressive," he was telling her.

Ms. Oznick looked at Jordan Kurd.

"It sort of looks like one of the classrooms at Shite College," Jordan shot back.

"Were you a student?" Titus asked. He had a pot belly that made Haywood's look petite by comparison.

"No, I never had the pleasure of being a student there."

"You look like somebody I had," Titus said.

"One of your stellar ones, no doubt," Jordan joked.

"No, one of the morons."

Yikes! For God's sake, Titus, shut up!

"You were about to tell us the law?" Nathaniel prompted.

"To continue," Ms. Oznick said, "there is a possibility that some free speech group might come in on the other side, to defend the webmaster."

"Why?" Nathaniel asked, his mouth dry.

"As a poor, defenseless student."

"He's got more power than we do."

"I'm just throwing it out there as a possibility."

"So what are you saying?" Titus said, not a whit less gruff.

"That we most likely should not sue the webmaster."

"Not sue the him?" Nathaniel asked.

"You mean we came here for nothing?" Haywood griped. Now he was turning his body away from Nathaniel. What was wrong with this man?

"You could still sue the school."

"But the school will claim it doesn't run the website," Titus said. "And it doesn't."

"Somebody's running it," Haywood said grumpily. "I hear it's privately financed."

"Maybe by a dean of our school," Nathaniel threw out. "There's a real possibility he's supporting the site and using it to ensure good reviews to maintain enough enrollment in a class he teaches."

"Can you prove that?" Ms. Oznick asked.

"No. I mean, not yet."

"Who is this dean?"

"Dean Visigoth. But he's not alone. Any number of the reviews are frauds. And look — one of the other deans approved these different flyers for the website." Nathaniel pulled them out of another folder he had brought. "I even managed to get Dean Deane to approve this flyer I made up." He passed around copies. "It practically invites students to extort grades from their teachers."

Everyone examined the fake flyer.

"You posted this? "Ms. Oznick wondered.

"No, I just wanted to see what would get approved. And this did. It should never have been approved."

"You're sure you didn't post it?" Ms. Oznick asked again. What legal horrors was she suggesting?

"Not even one. But there are hundreds and hundreds from the dean."

"Very interesting. Now it seems to me that the following is the best legal case —"

They were all ears as Ms. Oznick looked at her notes and they passed back the flyers to Nathaniel.

"Accusations have been made, some quite serious." She looked Titus Ashe's way. "May I ask you all something?"

"Fire away," he said.

"Are any of these accusations true? Any of them at all?"

"I don't masturbate when I'm teaching!" Titus replied in a huff.

"I don't harass my female students," Haywood said, his body turned away.

"I am not incompetent," Krista Prandemonia protested. Her eyes looked almost normal.

"I am not racist and I grade fairly," said Lillian St. Jude. Thank god for Lillian. She was looking better and better.

"I'm not any of the things I'm accused of, especially lurking outside the men's and women's bathrooms" Nathaniel said. "Well, maybe I am a little arrogant," he tried to joke, but nobody laughed. And I'm being cured of that pretty damn fast, he thought.

"So," Ms. Oznick concluded, "if none of these charges are true, then why isn't Shite College trying to shut down the website that permits these blatant lies to be broadcast about its own staff? If, on the other hand, the charges are factual, then why isn't the school taking steps to prosecute the guilty faculty members?"

"Good point!" Nathaniel said, trying to cheerlead. He'd thought of this argument himself. All these accusations couldn't be true. Sure, I see flawed humanity here before me today. But Jesus Christ in Heaven — not *that* flawed!

"I've studied a little law," Titus jumped in. "I'm not sure this should even be a class action suit."

"What do you think it should be?" Jordan Kurd asked airily.

"Do you know the principle of false light?"

"Yes, I'm a lawyer," Jordan said.

"Then why didn't you think of false light to build the case on?"

"How do you know that we didn't?" Ms. Oznick said, showing a little steel.

"Maybe you'd rather represent yourselves?" Jordan asked, standing up.

"No! We want you!" Nathaniel all but cried out. He hadn't worked this hard to get this far to have some Titus Ashehole ruin it all!

"You sure?" Ms. Oznick said. "Perhaps you can find someone with a more impressive office." She too stood up.

Oh, my God! We're going to lose the lawyers! Nathaniel panicked.

Just then, Vernon Daniels showed up, like a deus ex machina. "I made it!" he said, banging on the window. Jordan had to unlock the door to let him in. But you could tell the lawyers were glad to see him. "I canceled my gig to be here today." They found him an ottoman to sit on, bad leg and all.

"So we have more than enough people to sign on, don't we?" Nathaniel said, trying to salvage the day.

"I'm not sure how committed all of you are," Ms. Oznick said, looking around at the group.

"I'm willing to sign right now," Lillian St. Jude said.

"Me too," Krista said.

"And me — I'll sign it," Vernon Daniels said. "Nobody calls my Bongo class elitist!"

"With me, that's enough!" Nathaniel said. "Where do we sign?"

"I'd have to read the agreement through," Titus Ashe declared. "I don't want any funny business in the small print."

Jordan rolled his eyes.

Haywood wasn't saying anything — didn't he want to sign now? Even Haywood was better than Titus Ashe.

"And you, Mr. Wire?" Ms. Oznick was canvassing.

"I haven't made up my mind yet." His body was turned away, his arms folded, in case the others didn't notice that he was angry about something.

"What is it, Haywood?" Nathaniel said, trying to ask gently.

"You know!" Haywood looked like he wasn't going to bring any presents to Nathaniel's house that Christmas.

Here he was about to sign legal papers, and he was still fretting abut his name getting out? If not that, what in the hell was it?

"Four names should be enough, don't you think?" Nathaniel appealed to Oznick and Kurd. "We can let Haywood and Titus off the hook that way."

"I'd really like five," she said.

Maybe it was her way of getting off the hook?

The meeting ended an hour later, with various legal strategies and responsibilities having been presented for consideration and discussed to death — but with just four signatures on the attorney/client agreement (Nathaniel's, Lillian St. Jude's, Krista Prandemonia's, and Vernon Daniels'). Both Haywood and Titus refused to sign until they took it home and had sex with it, or whatever it was they wanted to do before they'd join the lawsuit.

"I must get somebody besides those two!" Nathaniel was telling Marty, who was taking a shower in Nathaniel's bathroom. "Especially that Titus Ashe. What a pill. And The Mole has become totally unbearable. I still don't know why he's mad at me. He stormed off after the meeting."

"Who else do you have?" The bathroom was full of too much steam, sending the little spider who lived over the mirror scurrying for cover. Nathaniel could see the silhouette of Marty's body through the shower curtain. He liked to foam up and then let the water cascade through his hair and beard for what seemed to Nathaniel eons. He himself was always in and out in a couple of minutes, but he didn't complain even though there was a drought and water was supposed to be rationed. He wanted Marty's company, one way or the other.

"Want to jump in here with me?" Marty said, poking at the plastic shower curtain.

Maybe it was a chance to Renew Their Love, but then Nathaniel thought about it and wasn't sure he wanted to. "No, thanks," he said, poking back at the shower curtain.

"You really should get Viagra," Marty said, soaping away.

"I believe Viagra is forbidden. Leviticus."

"You've never let that stop you before," Marty said, sticking his fingers through the shower curtain.

Nathaniel couldn't tell if Marty really wanted to have sex or was just teasing. At least he didn't seem to be on speed, or maybe he was just getting slyer at hiding it. It was pretty clear that he didn't want any more lectures from Nathaniel about it.

"So what about your arrest?" Nathaniel asked, cracking the bathroom door more, to let the steam out.

"Hey, it's cold now!" Marty said.

"No, it's too hot with the steam."

"I like the steam."

"Well, I like the cold." There they were Jack Spratt and his Domestic Partner (though not legally) chewing the fat about steam and the law's delay. "What have you heard?"

"The cops are being nasty. They haven't dropped the charges completely yet," Marty said.

"What is it this time?"

"Some crap about my car not being properly registered to park in my neighborhood. I got a notice today."

"I thought you had a permit."

"I do — only I was a little late sending in the check."

"Did you spend the money on speed instead?" Nathaniel said, before he could stop himself.

"What?" There was an edge to the question.

"Never mind!"

"Did you say something about speed?"

"Yeah, I said those cops need to get up to speed on your case."

Marty may or may not have believed him, but he didn't say anything else.

I've got enough on my plate — all fat, and I hate fat, — right now, Nathaniel told himself. So let's not have a fight about drugs! "You want some pizza? I can put one in the oven?"

"All right," Marty agreed. "Are you still swilling that vodka?"

Nathaniel thought he had hidden the vodka glass pretty well behind the electric toothbrush, but Marty must have spotted it before he got into the shower. "What are you talking about?"

"You're coming down on me all the time for speed, but you seem to be developing a drinking problem of your own."

"A little alcohol is good for you. Prevents heart attacks."

"That's wine, not vodka!"

"It's any alcohol."

"Not when it's done to excess!"

"I'm not doing it to excess!"

"Says you. And I'm not doing speed to excess either!"

Nathaniel got the glass for vodka from behind the electric toothbrush. "I'm throwing it out!" he said.

Marty stuck his head out of the shower to check. Nathaniel wiggled the empty glass at him and turned to rinse it out. "Good!" He closed the shower curtain again. "But I'm not stopping the speed."

"Why not?"

"Because it's the only way I can get through my job — or my life."

"Is everything really that bad?"

"Yes, it's really that bad. I've tried 'normal' and it sucks."

Unfortunately Nathaniel had to agree. Life was a pain. Or if it wasn't a pain, it certainly was more to be endured than enjoyed. And then you died.

"Slacker?" Nathaniel called, going to see how she was. She was watching a cat-sitting video he'd bought her a few years earlier: *Rodent Adventures*. All it was was some healthy-looking lab rats chittering and clambering on each other. Okay, where were the "adventures"? But Slacker had loved it the first couple of times, but she turned out to have the attention span of most Americans and barely opened her eyes to look at it now. "You want some Cheetos, glamour puss?" he asked her, and she turned on her back and stuck her paws into the air. She liked a good rub now and then, and Nathaniel would serve. "You slag!" he said, rubbing her belly. She wasn't averse to her lower areas being stroked as well, but Nathaniel didn't indulge her. DR. TACK MASTURBATES CAT would be up on Teachersonparade as sure as shootin'.

He put the frozen pizza into the oven and looked to see what was on television. Not much except "Frasier" re-runs. He loved them, but he'd seen them too many times now.

Maybe I should take some speed myself. Whatever gets you through the night. Even Slacker's Rodent Adventures looked more promising.

"How much longer before you're finished?" he called to Marty, hinting the shower was taking far too long.

"Fix the pizza!"

"Yes, master!" He put it in the oven even though he hadn't pre-heated.

He went to the window in the living room and started to draw the drapes. Marty's old car was below in the driveway, and he could see some of the other condo owners across the narrow street: the busybody on the condo board and the hairy, old man who walked around in his underwear. Ah, home!

Off to one side he saw somebody lurking in a doorway where the light had been turned off. Who was that? It was a male in dark clothing, and he was carrying a . . . was that a flashlight? A pen light? Was he trying to read the numbers of the various units?

Nathaniel drew the drapes but kept his eye on the figure across the way. After a minute, the person (the Satanist?) walked over below Nathaniel's second-floor condo and pointed the pen light upward, then moved it back and forth slowly, very deliberately, as if he knew that Nathaniel was standing there watching.

By the time Marty got out of the shower, the visitor was gone. "What are you staring at?" Marty asked, toweling off.

"Nothing," Nathaniel said. "At least I hope it's nothing."

He got a call the next day from Susannah Oznick. "I can't deal with that man!" she said, crying. Little girl tears.

"Which man?"

"Titus Ashe."

"What happened?"

"He called and said he was willing to sign the lawsuit, but he wants to see our law degrees. He said our law school passes too many people! He said he thought Jordan and I were doing a lousy job. I've never seen anyone so mean before!"

"I'm sorry he's been such trouble. I really didn't know the man or I wouldn't have asked him to join us, believe me."

Her tears went on. "I didn't even want to take on the case, but you make me feel sympathetic when you laid out the problem. I haven't even had time to work on it, and here's this Ashe person finding fault with everything and telling me how to argue the law! He even said he thought our leak was a sign of our inability to handle our landlord and therefore what kind of lawyers were we anyway!"

"I'm very sorry." She wasn't going to back out, was she? Nathaniel didn't even want to mention the possibility. "We can do this without Titus Ashe. We don't need him. How about Haywood Wire? Has he agreed to sign?"

"I thought he was acting very strangely when he was here. Is that man all right?"

"He was just a little bit upset with me. We've worked it out."

"Upset about what?"

I haven't a clue, Ms. Oznick. I am dealing with mad people, from the administration to the students to the goddamned faculty! "He's a bit leery about his name getting out. Actually he shows the validity of our case, don't you think? Haywood's been terrorized into fearing that his students will write him up on the website and destroy him."

"Maybe they've already destroyed him."

"He can be very nice. He's not always that bad." But Haywood actually did seem to be getting worse.

"I'm not sure I want to defend these people. Any jury would side with the students."

"But you haven't seen the students!" Nathaniel protested. Surely a jury can separate the chaff from the . . . chaff? Off with their heads, the whole lot of them!

"I'm really not sure this is going to work out, Dr. Tack."

"Oh, please, don't drop out! Please! I can do the leg work for you." Out of shape and overweight though I be!

"We really only have the two of us, Jordan and myself. Titus Ashe said we couldn't seem to afford a clerk. And he's right!" More tears flowed.

"I can be your clerk!" Nathaniel pleaded. "I can research the law. Just set me at the right computer or send me to the proper library. I don't mind. Please, Ms. Oznick, I think you're doing a fine job so far."

"You do?"

You're the only lawyer I have! A poor thing but mine own. He didn't know how good she and Jordan might be, but they were willing to do it on contingency. They'd had a meeting! "What if I get a replacement for Titus Ashe? Would that work?"

"Who have you got?"

"I'll look through the reviews and find somebody. Have you looked at any more yourself?"

"I haven't had time. Those thirty boxes that came in."

"Can I help you with those? I can read quite well and can make notes for you? Would that help?"

"I really think we're going to have to withdraw."

"Please don't! My classes are going to be canceled next semester because of lies about me. And last night I think I saw somebody lurking outside my condo."

"Who was that?"

"Titus Ashe probably," he said.

Ms. Oznick sniffled through a laugh. Which was better here, tears or laughter? "You ought to call the police and get some protection."

"That was a joke — my way of dealing with the stress, I guess, but in fact last night there was some man outside with a pen light. He very well could be the person who sent that death threat to the site. I actually met with the Special Hate Division, did I mention that? And so far nothing. And I don't expect any help from them. So the site has to be stopped from providing a place where stuff like this can fester and turn into what it's turned into. Please help us. We're not perfect. We're just human beings. But nobody deserves what's happening to us!"

"Do you think you can find a replacement for Titus?"

"I'll do my damnedest."

"And Haywood Wire hasn't signed yet."

"I'm on both of these things. Now when would you like me to come by your office and help with the leg work?"

There was a long pause while she wiped away the tears. "How about next Monday, between one and three?"

That was his nap time, but — "I'll be there. And thank you so much for not withdrawing. Thank you! I'm sorry that Titus made you cry."

He hung up and took a deep breath. What should he do now? Dare he risk calling Haywood and getting an earful? Maybe an e-mail?

He checked his own e-mail. Teen Sluts of Bangladesh a wanted to perform acts with large animals for him. He'd just have to wait on that! He sent Haywood an e-mail:

Hi! Are you still in? — Nathaniel

He waited in dread and had some more vodka, right from the bottle, which was getting empty. Either he'd have to get some more or Just Say No. God, and he had essays to grade. These stuck out of his briefcase like the Teen Sluts of Bangladesh. Eeek! He watched the daily horror show called the news and wondered if he could get Nona Dwibble or Marcus Blatty to rise in outrage about the sexual accusations about them on the website. But maybe he had this all wrong. He should give up teaching and set up a website of his own: Nun Sluts of Shite!!!! Obvious that's where the money was — and the true heart of the Internet.

Then a call came — from Haywood. He sounded stuffed up. "I can't stand that man another minute," he said.

"Who are we talking about?"

"He said I had my head up my ass when it comes to the lawyers." So Titus Ashe had made Haywood cry too.

"We're dropping Titus."

"We are?"

"He's nothing but a liability."

"He said he had a lawyer friend we could use."

"We have a lawyer. Two of them. They may not be everything we want, but they have agreed to stay on despite the behavior of Mr. Titus Ashe."

"Did you tell him we're dropping him?"

"You're closer to him than I am."

"I'm not telling him!"

"We'll tell him he waited too long to sign." Nathaniel would dread doing it, but if he had to, he would.

"He said I didn't show much judgment in dragging him there the other day."

"All he does is complain. Well, Titus can just drag his key-rattling, alcohol-saturated, old bloated body anywhere he wants to. We don't want his signature!"

"You sure? I'd rather have him with me than against me."

"As long as we have your signature, Haywood, we have the necessary five." Would they be known throughout legal history as the Necessary Five?

"I'm still not sure about all this."

"Exactly why now?"

"I wasn't speaking to you the other day in the lawyers' office. Didn't you notice?"

"Oh?" Nathaniel pretended.

"You made me furious."

"I did? And why was that?"

"You don't know?"

Nathaniel realized that Haywood would browbeat you to death with his litany of slights and that he should tell him to join Titus Ashe in Hell. But he didn't have that fifth signature yet. "Why don't you tell me?"

"How could you not know what you did?"

"I guess I'm just not sensitive enough."

"Well, I'm not going to tell you!"

"I'll try not to do it again."

"How can you do that if you don't know what it is?"

"Maybe in the fullness of time you'll tell me."

"Are you being smart with me?"

"Haywood, I don't know what I'm being with you, smart, dumb, or in-between. All I know is that we have two lawyers willing to represent us if we can get our act together. There may be finer lawyers in the universe, and no doubt even finer lawyers are up Titus's ass, but I'm going with the lawyers I see."

"You didn't offer me a ride."

"I beg your pardon?"

"I thought you should have offered me a ride to the lawyers'."

Nathaniel's mouth gaped open. "That's why you were mad at me?"

"I don't like to drive in heavy traffic, and the meeting was in the afternoon. Don't you remember I told you that?"

"No, I can't say that I remember that, Haywood."

"So I had a terrible time getting there, and the parking was horrendous. I scraped my tires and they're old!"

"I'll be sure to drive you next time. How's that?" Eeek!

"You promise."

"Of course. Would you like me to drive you to the lawyers' office today?"

"They want thirty-five percent, do you know that? Not the usual thirty-three."

"As far as I'm concerned, they can have it all — as long as they win."

"I'm not giving up whatever I win. There's another review on there today saying I put out somebody's eye with a piece of candy."

Should he ask?

"It was just a little scratch on his cheek. He's the one who begged for seconds!"

"You can get revenge in court, Haywood. I mean, complete vindication."

"Come and get me."

"Now?"

"Do you want me to sign or not, Nathaniel?"

"Where are you?"

"In my office."

"Let me check to see if the lawyer is there."

"All right, and I'll finish the small print."

Nathaniel called, Jordan Kurd answered, said he was there and would accept the fifth signature.

He called Haywood back. "I'll pick you up in fifteen minutes, outside Statistics, okay?"

"You don't want to come inside?"

Who the fuck did Haywood think he was — Scarlet O'Hara with her beaus? "It would just be faster if you'd come down and meet me."

"All right."

Nathaniel threw on a coat and raced down to his car in the garage. Maybe he could get there before Haywood changed his mind again — or found something to quibble about in the small print.

Louise Beeze was down on all fours feeding the ferals under Fellon Hall and waved to him as he drove by. And, by god, there was Haywood coming out of Statistics. Nathaniel sucked in his breath and drove very carefully to the lawyers' office, breaking no laws along the way, including hitting Haywood Wire, who was still not sure if he should sign or not.

They reached the office, found a parking spot, amazingly, and went in. The leak had been fixed, Jordan Kurd was efficient instead of snotty, and Haywood Wire actually put his name down, saying once and for all that he was willing to sue Shite College for libel, spreading false light, and providing a hostile working environment.

It sounded good to Nathaniel.

He should have known better.

The next day the chair of his department seemed to be waiting for him as he arrived for his office hour. Was Spike the Satanist?

"You seem not to have gotten my messages," Spike said, just this side of surly.

"I'm sorry. I've been meaning to come by."

Spike looked shorter and less imposing standing than he did behind the desk in the English Department. Still, he had what looked like enrollment figures in his rickety old hand. "Unless you come up with some more students, I'm going to have to cancel two of your classes."

"Really?" They went into Nathaniel's office.

"You have seven in your 101 and eight in your Plays and Novels."

"People always show up on the first day wanting to add."

"Have you done any outreach this term?"

'No." Where? Cemeteries? Chain gangs? The school does that!

"Why not? Electives always have trouble."

"I've taught Plays and Novels for years and years and it's always made it."

"Some other classes are down too. It's that damned website, I suppose."

"Do you want to join the lawsuit?"

"What lawsuit?"

"Five of us have signed on with a lawyer."

"To sue?"

"Yes, the college."

"Why don't you sue the guy who runs the website?"

"I'd love to. But the lawyers think it's not a good idea."

"The Chancellor is not going to think it's a good idea."

"The Chancellor has any number of bad ideas. He's all for the faculty except when he's not. Our Chancellor speak with forked tongue."

"And he's likely to stick that forked tongue right up your twee-twa!"

"Surely not there!" Nathaniel said. "My twee-twa?"

Spike allowed a smile to surface. "I've seen that man when he's mad. It's not pretty. He's very stubborn besides."

"So are some of us. The school has done nothing to stop this verbal assault on its own faculty. Who wants to work here in this hostile environment?" You want legal, I'll give you legal! "If classes are canceled, the school has nobody to blame but itself."

"Trust me, it will find somebody else to blame, Nathaniel." Spike put the enrollment

256

page on Nathaniel's desk. "I've got a Curriculum Committee meeting to go to."

"Thanks for stopping by."

"See if you can't wrestle up at least fifteen in each of those classes, okay?"

"I'll do what I can."

Nathaniel the teacher sat down at his desk, suddenly very weary. But at least now it was in the hands of the lawyers. He opened his mail and noticed a note from Marla Grab in the Horticulture Department. He didn't know her, but he read her note with interest:

> To the Committee on Truth,
>
> I would be interested in joining any lawsuit that may be pending about Teachersonparade.com. I have been libeled on the site several times. The enclosed review is but the latest.— Marla Grab

The review was attached with a paper clip:

> Mrs Grab has crabs, of which she imparts on her male customers, though she is a little bit of a bi, I think. I found a Grab Crab on the Christmas wreath I made in Ornamentals 90, and theres only one place it could of come from, Mrs. Grab's crab patch. Avoid this b**** unless you want crabs on your Christmas wreath too. My Amendment rights I hear whereby do declare.

How tasteful the "b****" was. And they say our students don't know nothin' about decorum.

All right, so where had this b**** been when he needed her?! He could have gotten around Haywood Wire and used her instead. Surely this was libel. What did it take in this country to say: Enough of This? In England Liberace had collected because a tabloid had said he had fruit juice in his veins. Here you could say your teacher had rubbed crabs on your no-doubt remedial Christmas wreath and think you were a Fucking Founding Father.

Nathaniel sent her a nice reply, saying that maybe she could perhaps join the rest of them in the lawsuit and giving her the lawyers' telephone number.

A couple of students came by. One wanted to know what double spacing an essay meant. (It was near the end of the semester) The other was upset because Nathaniel had objected to seeing the very same errors repeated in the mandatory re-write. "But your instructions say to re-write it. So naturally I just re-wrote it!" he explained. (He had gotten a B too.)

Nathaniel of course was the epitome of patience and understanding, as a teacher of college-level English should always be. (One of them could have been the Satanist besides — only held in check by the lovely demeanor of this gentlemanly professor.)

Nevertheless, the Satanist, or a reasonable facsimile, caught up with him just as he was about to begin his afternoon 101 class, now down to thirteen souls, two of them first-rate students, the rest bedraggled people who said very little in class and waited for the light.

Nathaniel was arranging his notes for an onslaught on *ad hominem* arguments, wondering if he dared use some of the personal attacks from the website as living, breathing examples, when suddenly a young man not in the class was standing in the doorway. "Your time has come, dude!" he said right at Nathaniel.

Nathaniel's breath stuck in his throat.

"You do remember me, don't you?"

Nathaniel wasn't sure if he did or not. The young man was somewhat familiar, about twenty, clean-cut, with short, blackish brown hair, in baggy-ass pants and an ordinary white shirt. The only odd thing about him was the pen light in his hand, whose strong green beam he proceeded to aim at Nathaniel's eyes.

"None so blind as those who will not see," said the baggy-ass specter at the door. And then he was gone.

Nathaniel was unable to move, his fingers fumbling at his notes. He hadn't even gone for his stun gun, even though it was in his inner coat pocket.

"Who was that?" Miss Ricco asked.

"I don't know," Nathaniel mumbled, at last managing to move to the doorway. He looked down the hall to see where the young man had gone, but he couldn't see him now.

"Was that a joke?" Mr. Badermann asked.

"I don't know yet," Nathaniel said, feeling his body, looking for bullet holes. He ran his hand over his face. "Is my hair falling out yet? Are my eyes in their sockets? I can see you. Can you still see me?"

"Maybe you should report that," Miss Ricco said.

He was particularly funny that day, as several students complimented at the end. "I'm always at my best when the Grim Reaper knocks on my door," he replied. Miss Ricco, a sweet young woman who could think and punctuate at the same time, seemed especially disturbed by the visitor. "You mustn't let this go!" she warned.

He went to report it to the campus police as soon as the class was finished, walking over to the office in Sitting Bull Hall. He tapped on the closed dutch door.

"Yes?" The officer on duty was Mr. Early, the tattooed student who had dropped out and most likely written five or more bad reviews about Nathaniel on the website. The tattoos were now hidden by the campus police uniform.

"Mr. Early, you work here?"

"Yeah, I took a part-time job on campus. It's just temporary."

It seemed fairly useless to be reporting this crime to somebody who didn't like Nathaniel and who was probably committing a few cybercrimes of his own in his off-hours. "Is there anyone else I can talk to here?"

"Something wrong with me?"

"Never mind."

"You want to fill out a report, Dr. Tack?"

"Never mind."

"What happened? You look upset."

"Thanks anyway."

Nathaniel walked away, a bit dazed. Was his karma that bad?

He went to his office and called his son. "How you doing?" Nathaniel wanted some kind of confirmation that something in his life was going well.

"Can't talk now. I have rugby practice. I was just on my way out."

"Are you okay? How's school?"

"School's fine. I got a date with Heather Hodges."

"Is she a Christian?"

"No."

"Well, that's a start."

"How are you, Dad?"

"Fine."

"I have a separated shoulder."

"From rugby?"

"I guess. I'm going to see about it tomorrow."

"That's good."

"You sound down. Are you?"

"I'm fine," Nathaniel said.

"I also have a tumor in my throat," Jim/Jimmy said.

"What?"

"I'll find out about that too when I go to the doctor tomorrow."

"A tumor?"

"Got to go! Keep in touch!"

"Don't separate anything else at rugby! Call me!"

What was going on here, his personal version of the Ten Biblical Plagues?

He didn't know what to do next. Should he call the regular police again? Oh, it's that whining Bisexual Crotch Rubber again! Yeah, what do you want this time, Prof? Maybe he should tell the lawyers? We're counting those thirty boxes and trying to get your case going to. Could you call back?

Should he get off campus at the very least? The young man with the pen light knew where he lived, didn't he? Was it the same person, or more than one? Was it the Satanist, the First Amendment Club, Fly on the Wall or Jake Trosky and the Alliance of Disturbed Students? Was that their name? Disturbed Students? Was he making that up, or had he seen it on a flyer on the way to the campus police?

He re-traced his route and stopped before the flyer, which was taped to a food vending machine that had been vandalized, of course, but just a little bit.

JOIN THE ALLIANCE OF DISTURBED STUDENTS!!

Yes, that's what it said.

And the rest of the flyer was about him:

> Faculty Member <u>Nathan Lack</u> has brought a lawsuit against Teachersonparade.com (Use it!!!) to stop students from finding out the truth about their abismal teachers. He will not be happy until he has silenced the Voice of the People. But he must be stopped!!!

> Come join the ALLIANCE OF DISTURBED STUDENTS and help create some disturbance on this sleeping campus!!! Drpe the scales from you're eyes!!!! Revelution lives!!!!

Disturbed all right.

And how did they find out about the lawsuit? They could get that part right, if not his name and any other word in the English language.

Nathaniel wandered through the halls of several buildings. All of them had the same flyers, dozens and dozens of them. He even saw some students reading them. He waited and then tore them down and stuffed them into waste baskets. How dare they put his name (sort of) out there like this? He was out of breath when he finished with the flyers and headed back to his office. It was late afternoon by now, the campus almost deserted.

When he played his office messages back, he heard this:

> You fucking homo pig! Do you squeal when you shit? I guess one day soon the world will find out. Homo shit!

"That is very terrible" said a voice outside Nathaniel's office.

Who was that?

Nathaniel peeked out and saw Abdullah Rooshdie, from the ESL Department. He'd had lunch with him a few times but couldn't say that he knew him at all well.

"You heard it?"

"I did. It is indeed terrible!" Abdullah Rooshdie was from Bangladesh and a devout Muslim as far as Nathaniel knew. He was a slight, dark-hued man in his late forties, the skin sagging around his eyes, mild of speech, but he had studied at Cambridge and could get excited about William Wordsworth. "I think you are very brave," he was telling Nathaniel. "I have heard of your lawsuit."

"You have?"

"I was going to join with you, until my brother in Bangladesh was killed in a riot and I had to attend to his business and his family."

"How terrible," Nathaniel said back.

"I have a review myself," Abdullah confided, taking it out of his wallet. "I have been losing sleep over this, I must say."

"What does it say?"

"I will paraphrase it for you." Abdullah wagged the review. "It maintains that I will not let the older students talk in class."

"Why would you do that?"

"I encourage all my students to speak up. This review was written by a man who wants to dominate every class. He believes, quite wrongly, that he is all-wise and the others are not as knowledgeable as he."

"So he said —"

"That I am a terrorist!"

"Really?"

"It is right here!" Abdullah shook his review. "It is terrible to say this. I am not a terrorist."

Nathaniel was sure the man wasn't even close to being one.

"Who has called you a homo pig on the machine there?"

"I have no idea."

"You suspect no one?"

"As a matter of fact, I suspect many."

"It is terrible, a terrible thing!"

"Perhaps it will sound better recollected in tranquility."

Abdullah crinkled his eyes. "You are being clever, aren't you?"

"I wish."

"Are you a fan of the great Mr. Wordsworth?"

"One of the few poems I know by heart is 'She Dwelt Among the Trodden Ways.'"

"How splendid! That too is my favorite!"

They quoted Wordsworthian lines back and forth to each other, and Nathaniel thought his new best friend was going to orgasm right then and there. Poor man, it was probably the only time since he'd left Cambridge that anybody, particularly at Shite, had known who Wordsworth was, let alone consent to recite him aloud.

"You must not discontinue the fight," Abdullah said. "You must end this website."

"We're not even suing the webmaster."

"I will give you some money — for your fight." Abdullah got his wallet out again and pulled out three twenties. "This is all I have right now. For my brother's death has depleted my resources for the moment. However, I want you to have this money for your legal battle." He pressed the bills into Nathaniel's hand.

"Why, thank you." Nathaniel was touched. He wasn't sure where Abdullah stood on gay rights, but the man seemed to be acting out of simple human decency.

"You must erase that terrible message from the machine." Abdullah gestured toward Nathaniel's office.

"Alas, no, I had better save it — as evidence."

"Ah, yes! Evidence."

"Give me that review you got," Nathaniel said. "I'll show it to the lawyers."

Abdullah found it in his wallet and handed it over.

"It has been most pleasant talking with you today."

"And you," Nathaniel agreed.

Abdullah Rooshdie wandered off and Nathaniel thought: Where were these people last week?

He was tempted to cancel his classes and lie low, but there was a need for some review of the course material before finals. The world had to go on — as no doubt it would if the Satanist, or whoever, got him.

He thought he might give Dean Visigoth one more try. He didn't bother making an appointment since he might be dead before the dear dean got around to it. Instead, he went directly to the office.

"Dean Visigoth, may I speak with you, please?" he said, bypassing the "bilingual" (give me a break) secretary.

The dean was filling out a report, no doubt about the Success !!! the school was having, something to impress the legislators who dispensed the funds to run the cogs of this educational unfunny joke machine. It was odd, but the dean seemed to be getting better-looking every time Nathaniel saw him. His snaggle teeth were less noticeable, and he even had a new tan sport coat that fit him. The Machiavellian, reptilian eyes, however, still held sway. "Yes? What is it?" he asked brusquely.

"Are you aware that there have been several serious threats on the website? I have heard nothing back."

"We've been looking into those — just one, I believe."

"Nobody mentioned that to me."

"We didn't want to alarm you."

"It wouldn't have alarmed me to think something is being done to make the faculty feel safe on this campus."

The report would have to wait, the dean's impatient body language said. "Perhaps you should take some time off, Dr. Tack."

Time off? Was this a way of easing him out of their hair — and probably out of the school altogether?

"I don't want time off — just some action would be nice."

"I looked at that so-called threat about you. Legally it won't stand up."

"Oh?" So the dean had heard about the lawsuit. "And why is that?"

"It's obviously a joke. Poor taste of course, but clearly a joke. That's what our lawyers believe."

"Funny, the joke is not that clear to me. Nor the humor in the young man standing outside my home or outside my classroom and saying my time is up."

"These things happened?"

"Would I make such things up?"

"Did you report it?"

"I went to the campus police, but . . ."

"But what?"

"There was a student I'd had a problem with taking the report, so I didn't bother."

The dean smirked. "You seem to have more than your fair share of problem students, don't you, Dr. Tack?"

"Perhaps I wouldn't have if the school didn't try so hard to attract the students it does attract."

"You don't seem to be aware of our mission here at Shite."

"Oh, but I do. To convert the heathens. I'm afraid the baptisms aren't working."

"To provide a quality education at a very reasonable price."

"Well, at least you got the price part right."

The dean was not pleased. He squeezed his temples. "I believe Shite College has one of the highest transfer rates in this entire area and our students stand out from other similar schools."

It was probably true. Eeek!

"When was the last time you read some student essays, Dean Visigoth?"

"Yesterday."

"And they didn't bother you?"

"I grade them on their ideas."

"And you just blink at the rest?"

"Perhaps your standards are unrealistic, Dr. Tack. Has that ever crossed your mind?"

"Call me old fashioned, but when did a college education mean you can't read and write?"

"They get by."

"What are you telling me — that I should just give in and accept the inevitable?"

"I don't know, Dr. Tack. We have any number of strange events on this campus. A student came in not long ago to say that she was mentally slow, and so she's entitled to pass all her classes because she qualifies under the Americans with Disabilities Act."

"And you told her what?"

"It's still pending."

"I would think, Dean Visigoth, that with anecdotes like the one you just told me you and the Administration in general would see the serial craziness of this place and try to do something about it."

"I seriously doubt that one can do much about craziness, Dr. Tack. And yet one must deal with what is before one's face, it seems to me."

Ah, we had a philosophical impasse here.

"You are more accepting of the status quo than I am."

"I may not agree with what people say or write on the website, but I will defend its right to exist. Have I not made this clear?"

"As long as you yourself don't have to get unpleasant reviews, of course."

"I'm afraid you haven't convinced me that that is happening, Dr. Tack."

"You say that after having conducted a thorough investigation of what is put on the site and what is removed — and the motives of the people doing so. Is that correct?"

"I'm afraid I have been too busy to conduct any such search. Not that I would wish. Pure democracy doesn't trouble me."

You pompous ass! Nathaniel thought. And I'm the one who's supposed to be the pompous ass. There isn't room in this office, pardner, for two pompous asses. Get out! Let me be the dean. There'd sure be some changes around here.

"Students at times are guilty of hyperbole. I've seen it many times in my role here — and when I was at a previous college. It's all part of the package. The law firm we keep on a retainer assures me that a threat like the one you say you have experienced is not serious and not actionable. If a student came to your classroom, it was probably what is called 'opportunity,' not out of any concerted effort to track you down."

"How nicely parsed, Dean Visigoth. What about the person outside my condo? What legal phrase dispenses with him?"

"The same person? Is that what you're claiming?"

"Both times the person had a pen light. A coincidence?"

"I couldn't say. Pen lights, it seems to me, are fairly common."

"Have you ever had one trained on your eyes?"

"Can't say that I have."

"You should try it. I'll ask my Satanist if he has a friend for you."

"You seem to enjoy a laugh, Dr. Tack. Why can't you just laugh all this off? I'm sure it will die down and blow away. Most things do."

"I guess I don't want to do that because I'm afraid I might be one of the things that dies and blows away."

"Do you mind if I ask you a blunt question, Dr. Tack?"

"Be my guest."

"Have you, or have you not, filed a lawsuit against the college?"

"Do I look capable of such a thing?"

"Perhaps you should take a sabbatical and think it over."

"Is that an offer?"

"I've looked at your records. You're eligible for a sabbatical."

"For next semester?"

"Yes."

"It's past the deadline."

"Perhaps not."

"I don't believe a sabbatical is going to solve the problem. A lawsuit may."

"And it may not. It may make matters worse."

"I believe matters can certainly get worse, and may very well do so, but it won't be from the lawsuit. It will be from letting things continue as they are."

"Do you know Boris Leifsogger in the Theology Department?"

"No."

"He brought a lawsuit against the school a few years ago. He didn't win, and it cost him a fortune."

"Sorry to hear that. Perhaps this time around it will be different."

"I wouldn't count on it. The Internet — I have discovered — does not have to abide by the same restrictions that print and other media do."

"Maybe we can change that."

"You're in for the battle of your life, Dr. Tack."

"I'm aware of that. And it is my life — and that of every other teacher — that I'm fighting for."

The dean smiled as only a reptile could. "Save the rhetoric for the courtroom, Dr. Tack. You're going to need every ounce you can get. We are going to fight you on this, I hope you fully realize."

"I must say it's becoming clearer by the moment."

The dean slammed his fist on his desk. "If you're so opposed to this site, why did you go to Dean Deane's office and get a flyer approved?"

"I —"

The fist came down again. "Why didn't you try a little harder to settle this with the school before you jumped into a lawsuit?"

Nathaniel was a bit taken aback. How could people have such different views of the same situation? He knew that they did; it was just always startling to hear it. "I think I waited quite long enough, almost an entire semester. I haven't had the courtesy of a reply. Now that the lawsuit is about to commence suddenly I'm hearing about magical sabbaticals and legally bested theologians and many other wondrous things. I don't know if I can stand the shock of so much attention."

The dean looked him square in the eyes. "You haven't even begun to feel the shock yet, Dr. Tack. Trust me on this one. In the meantime, would you like a campus police officer to escort you to and from finals?"

Nathaniel accepted the police escort, but when nobody showed up at his office to go with him to his first final, he just shook his head and packed his stun gun. Blow, winds and crack your cheeks!

They say a teacher should always learn from his students, to say nothing of his dean. Here is what Nathaniel learned when he read the final exams from his 102 on *King Lear*:

> "When the day a king needs to announce the succor of his
> kingdom, a new era would begin."

What a fresh insight on a classic play, Ms. Hubgub! Could you be a touch clearer? See Dean Visigoth for suggestions. He'll grade you on your 'ideas,' whatever those may be." Every sentence in the exam was equally strange. Obviously she'd had "help" on her out-of-class papers.

Another exam said:

> "While the heavy storm is a-monstering, King Lear chooses to
> go into the storm rather than with her daughters."

Her daughters? Indeed the storm on the heath is severe, but it causes a sex change? Did that make Lear march in the Lesbian/Gay/Bisexual/Transgender Parade the next year?

While the storm is a-monstering? Now that was almost poetry. It wasn't meant to be poetry, but you must find beauty when it sits on your face.

He had left several messages and even gone to a law library downtown and done research on libel laws. It was tedious and the language arcane and almost as mysterious as Ms. Hubgub's. But he managed to glean a few pointers. Some of the books even spoke of libel that was evident "on the face of it." Surely some of these accusations against the faculty could not be defended as opinion or hyperbole or anything else except what they were: vicious, illiterate lies told to destroy reputations.

Nathaniel wondered if you could sue for aggravated illiteracy. There was gross indecency. Why not gross illiteracy? His side would win in a heartbeat. Whoa — what if the jury was illiterate too? A very real possibility. Maybe he should take the dean's offer of the sabbatical. No, it was an offer he could — and had — refused.

Now what other bridges could he burn?

Marty?

His son?

He called his son, to see about the tumor. But he kept getting the answering machine. Maybe he should drive up there. It had been almost a year since he'd seen his own flesh and blood. Finals were almost over and there would be a Christmas break. Hey, teaching wasn't all bad! Nathaniel wept and gnashed his teeth and threw some of the exams on the floor of his condo and somehow came up with grades and turned them in ahead of time.

He called the lawyers and left several messages. They must be busy with those thirty boxes. Couldn't they call back at least?

He asked Marty if he would feed Slacker while he was gone, and he agreed. "I wish I could go too," Marty said.

"Do you want to try to get away?"

"I didn't tell the clinic, so I can't get my methadone in time. Why didn't you tell me sooner?"

"I just decided to go."

"I can't get off anyway. I've missed too many days. So never mind."

"I appreciate you looking after Slacker."

"Tell Jimmy hello."

"I will."

Nathaniel sometimes felt that Marty resented Jim/Jimmy, although it was difficult to pin down the resentment precisely. Marty was never snide, but he'd let drop a hint or two about the boy being "a lot of trouble" and "young for his age." Marty's relationship with his own mother and father had been very troubled.

"I love you," Marty said.

"Me too."

He left another message on his son's answering machine. Maybe they weren't even there?

Whatever. He needed to get out of town for a few days.

He got in his old Rav4 and zoomed up the middle of the state, stopping at the play festival in Ashland, where he saw an Affirmative Action *Coriolanus*. Once again politics triumphed over art. The audience of mostly Mayflowers applauded like mad, congratulating themselves on how liberal they were.

At least his son was home when he got there. He came out when he saw the car. "Dad? What are you doing here?"

"I couldn't get hold of you."

"I left a message last night."

"I didn't get it. I stopped in Ashland."

"You want to come in? Are you going to stay here?"

"I can stay at a motel. That would be fine."

"My mom and Lana are at work. Come on in. You can stay here."

It all seemed rather awkward, including the perfunctory hug and the help with Nathaniel's suitcase.

"Really, I don't have to stay here."

"We can make up the back bedroom. It's got some drape crap on the beds that Lana's making, but I can move it."

They went inside the house, which sat pretty much out in the country surrounded by large trees. There were even some cows in the distance, plus two potbellied pigs in the barn out back. A couple of dogs were barking in the garage and the place didn't look all that clean. It was quite modest, with a wood-burning stove and a burnt-orange shag rug that had seen better days. But it smelled of cooking, good smells.

"You look great," Nathaniel said. And Jim/Jimmy did. He was filling in, not so teenage-looking anymore, the face fuller, the arms and legs muscular — all that rugby, no doubt. He was three or four inches taller than Nathaniel now, but they avoided the back-to-back measurements that had characterized so many of their earlier visits.

His son was on vacation too, and the TV was still on, tuned to some sci-fi movie. Jim/Jimmy's room was small for him now, a single bed that he had to be too long for, the metal shelves loaded with broken action figures and baseball hats and deflated balls and other brick-a-brac of youth.

"So what's new?" Jim/Jimmy said when they had everything settled and were sitting on two separate couches next to the wood stove.

"Getting by. You?"

"Fine."

"The last thing I heard from you was about a tumor in your throat."

"I told you that?"

"Did you have it checked?"

"Not yet."

"Do you want me to look at it?"

"Naw." Jim/Jimmy shrugged his big body and rubbed at his throat. He was wearing short pants, mid-calf, the legs hairy. Funny, when Nathaniel had been a teenager, no boy would have been caught dead in short pants. But he'd never seen his son wear anything else.

"You should have that tumor looked at."

"My mom looked at it. So did Lana."

"And?"

"They think it's a polyp or something. I think that's what they said." He shrugged again.

Oh, God, apparently machismo would never die.

"I did not have a son so that he would die of a throat polyp. Have it checked by a doctor."

"Lana thinks I should have holistic acupuncture."

"Really?" Nathaniel looked around. Well, to look at the place, at least they didn't seem to practice feng shui.

"How's that website you were worried about?"

"Still functioning. I might not have classes this coming semester."

"Really?"

"It's possible."

"What do you do in class that makes you so unpopular?"

"I tell the truth. It's supposed to make me free."

"I wonder if I'd like you as a teacher."

"Probably not."

"I wonder if you'd like me as a student." Jim/Jimmy jumped right in: "Probably not!"

They laughed together, and that broke the ice a little bit.

"So what's happening in your life?" Nathaniel the father said. He'd noticed that when you had a kid, everything was about the kid. "Had any good dates lately?"

"I'm still a virgin, if that's what you're wondering."

Nathaniel shrugged, the same way his son had. "There's still time."

"I don't know," Jim/Jimmy said. "I'm not doing too well on that score. And don't laugh at me!" He was serious.

"What about Bethany and Lindsey and all those girls in their Christian dresses?"

"I've been sort of interested in somebody else."

"Who's that?"

"Oh, just somebody."

So mysterious! "It's not a teacher, I hope."

"No!"

"Nobody under twelve?"

"Dad!"

"Just checking."

"You don't know who it is."

"I didn't know who the other ones were either."

"Just somebody."

"Maybe you should date a nurse. She could look at your polyp."

His son paused, as if wondering whether to say something or not.

"What is it?" Nathaniel prided himself on his intuition about people's unspoken feelings.

"Oh, it's nothing."

"What?" Nathaniel was thirsty and hadn't been offered a welcoming beverage, but it could wait.

"You sure you want to hear?" Again that barely muted angry tone.

"Of course."

"Sometimes I wonder about myself."

"Introspection is good for you."

"I used to cry a lot when I was little. Did you know that?"

"Yes."

"I was a crybaby."

"I'm glad I have a son who's sensitive."

Jim/Jimmy rolled his eyes. "Yeah."

"I believe you even cried when your mother first showed you my picture. Your mother and Lana both told me that."

Jim/Jimmy seemed to blush a bit. "I've forgotten, but I guess I really carried on, for a long time."

"I had a beard then. Maybe it scared you."

"I guess I didn't know what you were exactly to me, not for sure."

"Maybe it was Oedipal."

"Edible?"

"Let's not go there. You haven't heard about the Oedipus complex?"

"I guess not."

"Freud was wrong a lot, but he probably had that one right."

"What does it mean?"

"How do you feel about Lana?"

"She's all right."

"Did you always feel that way?"

"I didn't used to like it when she kissed my mom. They did it in there." He pointed toward the kitchen on the other side of the wall.

"I think we're getting close."

"I wanted my mom to pay attention to me."

"She paid attention to you."

"I wanted all her attention."

"Your mother has a right to a life of her own, you know."

"I know." Jim/Jimmy folded his arms.

"I guess you've resolved your Oedipal complex then."

"Whatever."

"What about my edible complex?" Nathaniel said.

"Your what?"

"I'm hungry and thirsty."

"Oh, sorry."

"Where we you raised? In a barn?" Nathaniel nodded toward the barn out back.

Jim/Jimmy got up and brought him a Pepsi and a coconut cookie. "You want to see the pigs?"

"Sure."

They went through the glass doors in the kitchen, across the big lawn. In the barn the two potbellied pigs heard them coming and began snuffling. "Quiet, Elmer! Quiet down, Sally!" Jim/Jimmy grabbed a handful of corn from a wooden barrel and tossed it into the pen. The barn was open on both ends with long, exposed overhead beams and bits of straw and feed on the floor. The pigs looked fat but sort of scruffy, their eyes almost closed from dirt or mucus or God knew what. "Are they all right?" Nathaniel said.

"They're fine. You want to feed 'em?" He handed Nathaniel another handful of corn. It was dry and hard. "Don't give 'em any of your cookie."

Nathaniel threw the corn on the floor, and both pigs squealed and snorted around for it. There was an opening in the wall of their pen so that they could go out into the yard behind the barn if they wanted to. There was pig shit out there. Big clumps. Little clumps.

"They stay in here most of the time," Jim/Jimmy said. He had the offhanded weariness of somebody who deals with animals on a daily basis and isn't the least bit sentimental about them.

Something seemed to be troubling his son, the talk about the pigs and everything else just barely masking it.

"So you're growing up, it seems,." Nathaniel said. "Where did the time go?"

Jim/Jimmy shrugged.

"Is there something on your mind?"

They were leaning on the inner wall of the pen, not looking at each other, watching the pigs, who were noisy, competing for the corn.

"Maybe."

"What?"

Jim/Jimmy blew out a puff of air. "Oh, sometimes I just wonder . . ."

"Yes?"

"Sometimes I wonder if I might be gay, Dad."

Nathaniel snorted.

"You think it's funny?" His son seemed a bit put out.

"Sorry. Just be glad we've gotten to the point where being gay can be considered amusing. Believe me, it didn't used to be. I've been there."

"It doesn't seem funny to me."

They moved out of the barn, not making much eye contact, and watched the cows in the neighbor's field beyond the fence. His son was tall, strong, the Irish ancestral genes showing, right down to the pug nose and red highlights in his hair.

"What makes you think you're gay?"

"Oh, I don't know."

"What does that mean?"

"I used to think I might be gay."

"When?"

"Before."

"You mean attracted to men?"

The topic was making Jim/Jimmy uncomfortable. "I don't know!"

"What do you know? You brought it up."

"Let's forget it." Jim/Jimmy started back for the house. "My mom will be home soon."

"Have you discussed this with her?"

"No."

"Why not?"

"I don't want to!"

"Do you want to discuss it with me or not? Believe me, you're never going to find a more accepting audience than your gay father."

"It's hard to talk about."

Jim/Jimmy was shaking the wire fence at the rear of the property with one hand, out of nervousness, although he tried to make it seem like he was straightening it. "This thing keeps coming loose!" he said, giving it another good shake and fiddling with a metal pole. "I think the cows hit it. When did you know you were gay?" he asked.

"As soon as my daddy's sperm hit the egg."

"No, seriously."

"Early on. But it was a different time, and I denied it, fought it. The past is a foreign country, somebody wise once said. But I lived to tell the tale."

"Did you cry a lot?"

"About being gay?"

"Because you were gay."

"Is that what this is about? You think gays cry more? And you used to cry? So you're gay?" What homophobic nonsense was going on here?

"I don't know!" The pole got another rigorous adjustment. "My friends aren't virgins, but I am!"

"You think men are gay because they can't get laid by girls? It's a matter of what you're attracted to that makes the difference. It's attraction to your own sex sexually. By the way, it's part of the normal distribution in human beings. Somebody in the world has to have talent!"

"What talent — your novels and stuff like that? Didn't you ever play sports?"

"Why are you asking?"

"I'm just wondering."

"You think gays don't play sports? Some don't, some do."

"You don't seem interested in sports."

"I think people spend far too much of their time obsessed with balls of various sizes. It's hardly the height of human accomplishment."

"That sounds like somebody who didn't do well in sports."

"Not true. I was very well coordinated. I just thought it was much ado about nothing. 'Look, I hit a round thing with a stick!' Look, I slammed this round thing through a hoop.'"

"It takes skill."

"Maybe they'll find a cure for it someday," Nathaniel snapped, growing more irritated. His son had gay parents and he still had all this fear and contempt just beneath the surface. Wasn't that what was going on here? "This person you said you're seeing — is it somebody male?"

"I'm not seeing him! I just like my friend Damian a lot, that's all."

"Who's he?"

"He's a sophomore. I play rugby with him."

"Have you had sex?"

"Dad!"

"Why all this pussyfooting around? Real men get to the heart of the matter, don't they? Except they don't! They run from the heart of the matter any chance they get!"

"I just like being around him."

"And you think that makes you gay?" Nathaniel threw the remainder of his cookie in the direction of the cows.

"I don't know. I feel more comfortable with him than with girls." Jim/Jimmy was blushing to the roots of his manhood.

"Then there's no question about it."

"What do you mean?" His son's eyes went big.

"You're not gay."

"I'm not?"

"Most men like their men friends better than they like their women. They just don't want to poke them with a body part — or at least not that body part. In my experience, gay men like women far more than straight men do — they just don't want to poke them at all."

"Jeez, I'm sorry I brought it up."

"I'm sorry I haven't handled this as well as I should have."

The stood there near the cow field and didn't touch.

"I thought I'd ask you since you're gay and everything."

"Yeah, I'm the expert."

What was he supposed to say now?

"I don't think you're the least bit gay," Nathaniel said.

"You think so?" Jim/Jimmy looked so grateful Nathaniel the father wanted to cry.

"Of course if you turn out to be, I'll love you anyway," Nathaniel said, grabbing the top of the fence.

"And what if I turn out not to be gay?"

"It'll be more difficult, but I guess I'll still have to love you."

Nathaniel didn't know if his son smiled or not, because they weren't looking at each other.

He stayed the night and somehow managed to be on his best behavior through dinner and breakfast and made small talk with his son's mother and Lana. Both had aged, Lana a little more tight-mouthed and prim than before, Jim/Jimmy's mother tall and quiet. Her eyes, at least in the morning, looked a little poached. He complimented their food and their house and their cows, even though they weren't theirs — until he ran out of compliments.

Nathaniel made sure that he and Jim/Jimmy played tennis before he left — and he made damn sure he *whipped* his straight ass.

When he got home, Slacker was fine and allowed a few hugs before going out to torment something smaller than herself. There were telephone messages from the other litigants wanting to know what was happening with the lawsuit. Even Titus Ashe had called, but Nathaniel didn't return the call. There was an e-mail from Haywood Wire as well:

> What's up with those lawyers you got?
>
> They're taking forever to file, aren't they?
>
> You got some more bad reviews. Want to see them?—
> Haywood

No, he didn't want to see them. They could have been by Dean Visigoth — the Administration loading the site as an excuse to get rid of him.

He called the Offices of Oznick and Kurd and got Jordan. "No, we haven't filed. We've just been so exhausted with our other cases."

"Do you want me to write up whatever you need? Just tell me the legal terms."

"We really can't find the time at present."

"How long is this thing expected to be — what's it called again?"

"A Complaint. Probably about seven pages."

"You're too exhausted to write seven pages?"

"I've got to go now."

"The other teachers who signed on are wondering what the delay is."

"Got to go. Sorry."

Nathaniel had been too afraid to ask if this meant they were backing out. It wasn't like there were other lawyers calling night and day to take over the case.

He e-mailed Haywood:

> They say they're exhausted. But they haven't dropped us. I remain hopeful. — Nathaniel
>
> P.S. I don't need to see any more "reviews."

> Nathaniel,
>
> You've got to be firm with lawyers. Are you being aggressive enough? — Haywood

No, I'm the fucking "sissy" who has pushed and pushed and pushed, and that's why they haven't written up the legal Complaint yet! So what does that make you, Haywood, a fucking straight sissy who doesn't do anything except carp and hide!

He called the other litigants and assured and soothed them, but he was really beginning to think Oznick and Kurd had changed their minds.

On the first day of the new semester, when Ms. Ricco, who had taken him in 101, came to see him, he was still a little gun shy. After all, anyone could just walk up to his office and remove him from the face of the earth. Maybe that would be easier when all was said and done. He was looking at the census sheets from his four scheduled classes, and the numbers were not encouraging: 9, 7, 13, and 12. You were required to have twenty in each section.

Over the semester break Ms. Ricco had frosted her black hair. She was small boned and small breasted, with tiny wrists. She was a good writer, one of his better students. She looked to be about twenty-five or so. He suspected that she might be from Italy, but most of her accent was gone.

"Did you report that incident that happened?" she asked. "That guy who came to the door of the classroom with the pen light."

"So it wasn't my imagination."

"It was scary. I almost didn't want to come back to class."

"I don't blame you."

"Did you get it taken care of, Professor Tack?"

"Not exactly. I'm working on it."

"Do you know who he is?"

"Afraid not."

"What if you looked back through your grade book?"

"I did."

She winced. "That's scary. Thank you for the A in 101, by the way."

"You deserved it."

"I was thinking of enrolling in your 102. Is there still room?"

"On Saturday mornings."

"I'm not a morning person, but I did enjoy your class."

Nathaniel tried to fight the relief he felt. He must not be beholden to students. He must not be! That way destruction lay. And yet there were only seven students enrolled in that class.

"I think we can find room for you, Ms. Ricco," he said. "Would you like an Add sticker?" He fumbled through the mail he'd just picked up, looking for the manila envelope.

"My one reservation is this . . ."

He looked at her tiny wrists. "Yes?"

"Do you think that scary student might come by the classroom again?"

"I can't say."

"I really don't want to get caught in any crossfire."

"Few do." His own wrists looked small. He turned one over and could see his pulse throbbing through the skin.

"The nerve of that person!"

"Tell me about it."

"You're a very good teacher, and I learned a lot. You said things I've thought but haven't heard said aloud very much. You're controversial, and I like that."

Don't tell me! Run to Teachersonparade and tell the world!

"Thank goodness for good students like you, Ms. Ricco."

She looked pleased. Maybe he should turn on the old compliment machine more often. No! He wouldn't cheapen himself and his compliments. He wouldn't!

"I know you've had some troubles this past semester."

"When troubles come, they come not single spies but in . . . Italians?"

"Italians?"

"Battalions. Excuse my feeble attempt at humor. I think I'm running out of gas." Jesus, had he insulted his one fan?

"I hope not. You made that afternoon class lively."

What a jewel this woman was!

Okay, what did she want — besides another A of course?

"I've looked at that website, and I think it's been completely unfair to you."

God, could he go back and give her an A+? Did she have any more at home like her who might enroll? Just look at the intelligence beaming from her eyes!

"Did you leave a review?"

"No."

"Don't bother."

"I didn't think to leave a review."

"Don't worry. It's meant only for people who don't like me or who haven't taken my classes."

"Isn't the school doing something about it?"

"Aiding and abetting, with both benign and malign neglect."

"I think students should be able to review their teachers, but the things I've read on there! And not just about you."

He wanted to tell her to review Dean Visigoth and give him umpteen what-fors. You want Free Speech? I'll give you free speech, asshole! But he kept control of his emotions. When the funeral service was held and the world trooped in to leave the lilies on his casket, everyone would say, What a saint he was through all the Bad Times. Too bad he had to die from that awful anarchist flame-thrower in the Lowe-Rankin Dining Experience.

Ms. Ricco took the Add sticker and went on her way. "You're one of the best teachers I've ever had," she said as she left.

Nathaniel felt all buzzy and fuzzy for about ten seconds, and then he had to go to his first class. There were eight students there, not nine. And nobody else showed up except Spike Burns, the chair. "I thought I'd drop by to see how your enrollment is," he explained, peeking into the classroom. "Not too good, Nathaniel."

"Maybe they're waiting for Thursday before they show up."

"Enrollment's a little weak throughout the department this semester, but I can't possibly get the dean to sign off on eight students for this one."

"Did you count the one hiding under the teacher's desk?"

"Let's give it till this Thursday, just in case."

"I will go out into the highways and byways and make them come in."

"I hope you won't want to bump any other teachers. It's very tight for everybody this term."

"We'll just have to stop putting our crabs on students' wreaths," Nathaniel said.

"What?"

"And just when I'd mastered my technique."

"What are you talking about?"

"It was a review written about somebody."

"It's all a mess, I know. I heard you were suing. True?"

"I'd love to. The lawyers are playing hard to get."

"If you do sue, the school will try to get back at you."

"I have so much to look forward to!"

"Already I've heard that they're floating the idea of offering an alternative to your Plays and Novels course — in the theater department, this would be."

"Really?"

"The dean has signed off on it."

"What does that mean?"

"The chair agreed, plus the dean. Now it's up to the Curriculum Committee."

"We get about twenty-two students each semester — in a good year — who want to take that kind of course. If the theater department offers it, it will split the enrollment and neither section will go."

"I told the dean that."

"Is this Dean Visigoth?"

"Yes."

"The self-serving prick!"

"He says it will broaden the appeal of the course."

"I introduced that course to this college!"

"They don't care."

"I'm trying to keep this school from falling into total shit! I get the best students in that class."

"They think you made the review site worse by attacking it. Now it's grown and they blame you."

Nathaniel wondered if that were true. Had he made it worse?

"There's always a different perspective on things between the Administration and the faculty," Spike said. "You just don't want to get ground up in the maw of the beast." Spike's was the voice of wise and weathered old academician.

"What if I really don't get the necessary enrollment?"

Spike hemmed and hawed before he said, "You can always make them up next term."

"What if my classes don't fill up then?"

"That's never happened before."

"These are new and parlous times. But the Internet shall make us free!"

278

"I wouldn't worry about it overmuch."

"I can always teach the lower courses, you mean."

"You did it before, right?"

"I was young! I was foolish! I needed the money!"

"Some people actually prefer the remedial courses."

"I'd prefer to have burning coals on my eyelids."

"By the way, is it true that some student came by your class and threatened you?"

"Yes."

"Why didn't you tell me?"

"I've been avoiding you, because of the poor enrollment."

"Nathaniel, you really shouldn't let things like that go. Malachi Moorcock was killed by a student here, did you know that?"

"I've heard about it. I was hoping it was urban legend."

"I think it was in your very office."

"Oh, great."

"That was twenty-one years ago, and things are getting worse. I see it every day."

"I'm counting the moments."

"Until you retire?"

"I can never retire, unless the school buys me out."

"Won't happen."

"I know. I'll get me a tin cup and hang out on the ramp to Arts, crying "Alms for an old professor! Alms for sweet charity's sake. Poor Tom's a-cold!'"

Spike tried various schemes to get the enrollment up, but the long and short of it was this: two of Nathaniel's classes, his afternoon and evening101's were canceled.

I'll have more time to think good thoughts about students, he told himself, not having so many. I'll finish that play set in Ireland. I'll play with Slacker more. I'll be nicer to Marty. Best of all, there will be fewer "opportunities" for the Satanist to show up at his classrooms and send him to his (the Satanist's) Maker.

To say nothing of having more time to help the lawyers write up the Complaint.

Except that they didn't call.

Haywood did call:

"What's taking those lawyers so long?" Jesus, he had a big voice.

"They say they're busy. Do you know any other lawyers?"

"I thought we were going with these two lawyers."

"I hope we are, but maybe they won't come through. We could use a backup."

"Now you want a backup?"

"Haywood, all along I've been open to any number of possible lawyers. If you have one, let's talk to him."

"Oh, now you want my lawyer."

Nathaniel's teeth were grinding. "If you have one."

"I thought we had Oznick and what's his name."

"I don't know if I have them or not. That's as plain as I can make it."

"Titus was asking why you didn't get back to him."

"What did you tell him?"

"I didn't know what to tell him."

"We don't need Titus — unless he's got a lawyer? Do you think he has one?"

"Not really. Titus talks a lot, but it's mostly talk."

"That's why I acted and went for Oznick and Kurd."

"Yeah, but you don't always make the best choices."

Grind, teeth, grind! "I'm doing the best I can, Haywood."

"We should have interviewed at least a dozen lawyers and then selected one."

"In an ideal world that could have happened. Everybody seems to mention a lawyer, but nobody actually comes up with one."

"Well, you came up with two and now they aren't even doing what they promised."

"Maybe we should sue them," Nathaniel said. "You know a lawyer we can get?"

"I'll tell you what I think we should do."

"Okay, what's that?"

"Somebody should contact the server that carries the website."

"Meaning?"

"Tell the server that there is libel and filth on there and that they are helping convey it."

"Do you think that will do any good, Haywood?"

"It might."

"You mean they might drop Dude Lather and his evil baby?"

"It's worth a try."

"And the down side of this would be?"

"The server can refuse to drop the website, I suppose."

"Can I legally threaten a server?"

"With legal action! Don't get violent now!"

"Maybe I should ask Oznick and Kurd to do it?"

"They don't seem to be doing very much of anything."

"True. Is this really a good idea, Haywood?"

"Even if this works, the webmaster could take the site to another server. But it would be trouble for him and most likely interrupt service."

"One small step for mankind. Do you know who the server is?"

"I looked it up. It's called TeleTruth." Haywood spelled it.

"Really?"

"I think it's based in Seattle. You want the address?"

"Sure."

Haywood gave it.

"I'll write them tomorrow."

"Somebody's got to stop this. Did you see that review of Arlene Buboe-Pitsky in your department?"

"No."

"It's a pip."

"Don't tell me! Don't tell me!"

"You don't want to know?"

"I was doing an impersonation of Arlene Buboe-Pitsky when I told her about the site's existence. She was one of the first I mentioned it to. Total denial. Quick — what does it say?"

Haywood had to find the review. "It's here somewhere. I have about twenty-five disks full now. I should probably put them all on one CD — for the jury to look at. Wait. It's here somewhere!"

"It better be good, after all this."

Haywood finally found it, cleared his throat, and read it to Nathaniel. "'Mrs. Buboe-Pitsky should change her name to Mrs. Twitsky. Or something else that rhymes with Clitsky. Because that's what she is, besides full of Shitsky.' The words that rhyme are in capitals."

"How classy."

"There's a little more. 'Arlene, why are you so mean! I'd like to get you on the ground and stick something in-between. I wonder if your hair — down there — is as red and hard as what's on your big old head.'"

"I love the internal rhyme."

"Do you know this poor woman?"

"She's hardly a poor woman, yet I must resist this chance to gloat. Could you re-read me that part about her hard hair?"

"I'll send you a copy."

"Send Arlene a copy. Maybe she has a lawyer! It's even possible her husband's a lawyer."

"I don't know them."

"Thanks, Haywood. That made my day. Is the webmaster removing these things?"

"When he feels like it. A lot of the insulting ones are still up. Of course anything bad about Visigoth comes down immediately. Are you going to contact that server or not?"

"I'm on it — like a hawk on a . . . on a submarine!"

Here is the letter that Nathaniel sent:

Dear TeleTruth,

It has come to my attention that your company provides the server for a so-called review website called Teachersonparade.com. If for any reason I am mistaken about this, please excuse this letter.

The reason I am writing to you is to alert you that your acting as the server for this website permits degrading, libelous, and even pornographic "reviews" of teachers at Shite College to be posted — by anyone. I can't emphasize the *anyone* enough. Absolutely no controls exist to prevent fraudulent "reviews" from being posted and providing the basis of a so-called grade point average for the teachers. Many —if not most — of the "reviews," both positive and negative, are utter misrepresentations of the facts, and yet they are taken to be reliable because they seem to have the endorsement of the Administration of Shite College and various campus organizations, such as the Alliance of Students. Classes have been canceled on the basis of lies and distortions on the website, whose webmaster controls it like the despot he is, rewarding his supporters and injuring his opponents. His name, according to public records, is Drew A. Lather.

Five faculty members, including myself, have obtained the Law Offices of Oznick and Kurd to represent us in a lawsuit against the responsible parties. We expect to file a complaint momentarily. We hope that we won't also have to file a suit against TeleTruth. This letter is an attempt to call these offenses to your attention — and to persuade you to drop Teachersonparade.

I'm sure you would not wish to have it as a client if you examined it carefully and saw the kind of material that is there. Please stop letting your company be a conduit of libel and obscenity.

I enclose copies of some of the reviews that have appeared.

Sincerely,

Nathaniel Tack, Ph.D.

He enclosed the Arlene Buboe-Pitsky "poem," the nasty sex allegations about Nona Dwibble, and Marcus Blatty's blowjob review. He thought about including some of the homophobic ones about himself, then decided not to ride that hobbyhorse. For he would indeed rise above his personal objections to the website!

Alas, before he heard anything from TeleTruth, four days later he got a letter from Oznick and Kurd in the afternoon mail at home:

Dear Nathaniel Tack,

We have been informed by TeleTruth Corporation that you have told them that we are repre-senting you in a legal action against them for carrying Teachersonparade. We have never agreed to such an action. Nor would we.

We must, therefore, withdraw as your attorneys for any and all proposed lawsuits. We did not authorize you to use our name, as you well know.

Note: Please inform the other faculty members of our withdrawal. We wish you the best in any future endeavors.

Your truly,

Susannah Oznick + Jordan Kurd

Whack! Take that!

Nathaniel called Marty, whom he felt he'd been neglecting, at the library. "Can I cry on your shoulder tonight?"

"Sure. I was going to call you about doing some laundry over at your place anyway. What's wrong?"

"The lawyers have dropped us."

"What?"

"They used a letter I wrote to the website's server to get rid of us."

"I'm on the desk. Let's get together. About eight?"

"Fine." Nathaniel knew that meant after nine. Marty was never on time.

Should he tell Haywood and the others? He looked at the agreement he had signed with Oznick and Kurd. Of course it had an out clause for them, near the end.

He was just about to call Lillian St. Jude, whom he thought would be easier to talk to than any of the others, when he got a Special Delivery letter. It was from Krista Prandemonia, she of the upside-down eyes.

> To Nathaniel Tack,
>
> This is to inform you that I am withdrawing from the lawsuit we discussed. Please do not use me or any of the reviews about me from the Teachers Website to solicit other possible litigants. Is this clear? I no longer wish to be associated with your lawsuit. I'm out! I have signed with Oznick and Kurd to represent me individually in another matter. — Very truly yours, Krista Prandemonia, M.A.

What the hell was going on here?

He showed the letter to Marty when he showed up at ten o'clock with his five bags of dirty laundry. They kissed, a chaste little cheek kiss. Marty looked a bit hollow-eyed and undernourished, his beard showing more gray hairs. "Let me get started on my laundry, okay?" he said, opening the doors to the recessed washer and dryer. "Hi, there, Slacker!"

he called to the cat, who was sitting on the window ledge in the living room.

"She's on guard for the Satanist," Nathaniel said.

"Then God help you!"

"You're so reassuring."

"Have you heard any more about all that?"

"I just pray and fast and await my fate."

"You don't look like you're fasting that much." Marty threw some jeans and shirts into the washer. "Look! I brought my own detergent!" he called, holding up a plastic jug.

"Thank you. Have I put on more weight? I've stopped the vodka."

"You're fine."

"You're sure? What about your police report?"

"I think they've forgotten about it."

"You're not positive?"

Marty shrugged and threw some more clothes into the washer. "So what about these lawyers now? I thought they had signed."

"I see now why lawyers are hated. They've been trying to back out for a long time now."

"Can they do that?"

"Even if they can't, do I want people representing me when they don't want to? Why kind of representation would that be?"

Marty flipped the lid on the washer and started sorting through the remaining laundry bags. "What are you going to do about it?"

Nathaniel felt grateful that Marty was there, that he had someone to talk to about this mess. "I got this too." He showed him the Special Delivery letter.

Marty read it through. "Is she the goofy one you mentioned?"

"She is."

"Why is she doing this?"

"I have my suspicions. I think she was looking for a lawyer for herself, and she stole mine."

"But why?"

"I think Spike Burns is trying to get her out of the department. There have been rumors that she didn't hold classes for six weeks and instead sent her students to the library to study."

"Really?"

"She's a total flake. I knew she was a total flake, and yet she was better than Titus Ashe. I bet you she gave Oznick and Kurd some money to take her on."

"Because they'd rather represent somebody who's paying them?"

"That — and maybe they figured they can't win. I don't know!" Nathaniel went over and stroked Slacker. At least there was nobody outside with a pen light.

Marty read through the letter from the lawyers. "What A-holes."

"Do you think I was wrong to write the server?"

"What did you say?"

Nathaniel found a copy of that letter too and showed it to him. He was apprehensive that Marty would say it had been a bad move, and then they would have a big fight. "What do you think?"

"You just hint that you might sue. You don't say for sure."

"Yes! I was trying to be oblique. I guess TeleTruth must have phoned Oznick and Kurd as soon as they got my letter. I thought they'd write me, not the lawyers. I guess I'm not as clever as I'd like to think."

"I don't think you did anything wrong."

"You don't?" He came over and gave Marty a hug from behind. "Thank you. I need to hear that." He moved back to the living room and closed the drapes. "I'm afraid to tell the others what's happened, especially Haywood. He'll be all over my case, even though writing the server was his idea. He'll say I should never have hinted at suing them or something."

"You should drop him too. What a baby. Don't you have anybody else?"

"I referred a couple of people who belatedly expressed interest to Oznick and Kurd, and I suppose they turned them away. Now we have no lawyers and just a handful of teachers willing to pursue this."

"Can't you get another lawyer?"

"I have no idea."

"At least try." He was taking out the lint filter in the dryer. "Look at this! You really should clean it more." He scraped the lint away with his fingers and put it back.

Who are you to talk? Nathaniel thought. "I should quit now. Accept my fate, I suppose."

Marty looked up from the dirty laundry, now in piles on the floor, on the machines. "That doesn't seem like the Nathaniel Tack I know."

"You bet your bippy it isn't!" Nathaniel said, with more conviction than he felt. After all, maybe there really was no way out of this.

The next person he heard from was The Mole by e-mail:

> What's this all about? Have you seen this posting on Speak Out Loud from Fly on the Wall? See attached. — Haywood

> Who's laughing now, Dr. Tack? Can't keep your lawyer, boobie?

> What's wrong? Maybe you don't have a case? Maybe the gods

are telling you something. Vengeance is mine, saith the Lord. And you are by no means the Lord. Gain some t-a-c-k and stop your at-Tacks!

They're tacky.

—Fly-on-the-Wall

It's tact, not tack, asshole — was the best Nathaniel could come up with. He e-mailed The Mole back:

It's true. Oznick and Kurd have withdrawn. They say they didn't like the letter I wrote to the server, but I think they just wanted an excuse to get out. How does Fly on the Wall know about these things so quickly? — Nathaniel

Before I know them, apparently. What did you write?

What did you say? Huh? — Haywood

I don't want to go into it. I tried to speed things along. It didn't work. I don't know what to try next. — Nathaniel

He'd be damned if he'd apologize to Haywood again!

Nathaniel,

Maybe we lost the lawyers, but something seems to be wrong with the website. Good news? There's a message there saying: TEACHERSONPARADE WILL BE UNDERGOEING A RE-LOCATION TOMMOROW. WE HOPE TO RETURN SHORTLY.

Nathaniel summoned up the website himself, and sure enough the message was still there. Had TeleTruth blinked? He even steeled himself and checked THE PITS and TIP OF THE TOP. He wasn't at the very bottom, merely third from last, but he had the most reviews. He decided not to read any of them. He wasn't going to change any more than he already had, come hell or high water, canceled classes or the Devil at his door.

What was surprising is that Greg Pewiston in Math was at the very bottom. Wasn't he the one that had a direct link from his personal web page to Teachersonparade? Nathaniel checked — yes, it was true. USE THIS SITE. REVIEW ME. As big as life. And sure enough, somebody — one, two, any number — had creamed Greg Pewiston. The last one said:

Pewiston is crazy. Cann't teach. Big bullshitter. Attend and you'll get youre A. Then get out of this madhouse! One more semester and Im free!

Pewiston. You sucker. You moron. He didn't know anything about Pewiston's teaching, but this reviewer had one thing right — Shite was a melodramatic madhouse, from top to bottom. And Nathaniel wanted to be free of it forever too!

Retiring — wasn't there some way? Could he live on the thirteen years he had in at Shite? Fat chance. Not in the city of Santa Francesca. Maybe he could sell his condo and move to some cheaper place. Afghanistan? I mean, how many land mines and warlords could there be? They say Sudan isn't that bad except in the summer. And the winter. And the spring and the fall! Eeek!

Maybe the website really was re-locating. Was there a shred of hope there?

He wrote back to The Mole:

> There is obviously a network of interested parties keeping each
> other informed. I'm starting to think they have better technical
> skills than I can ever hope to achieve. Maybe the Day of the
> Word is over. Long live our new god — the Holy Internet! —
> Nathaniel

He didn't hear back, and he actually felt relieved. He wasn't up to some harangue from Haywood (Nobody Knows My Name) Wire. He called the remaining litigants (Vernon and Lillian) and told them about Oznick and Kurd and Krista Prandemonia all dropping out. They were upset.

"Know any other lawyers who might take on the case?" Nathaniel asked.

Both said they didn't, but they would ask around. Lillian St. Jude seemed the most upset of the group. "A student told me that she didn't enroll in my Business 70 because she'd heard I was a racist! She was extremely cold and wouldn't listen to my explanation."

"Racist is probably the most common word on the site — and in the air we breathe. It's bull, thrown out these days like skunk stink. It's supposed to make you stop dead in your tracks, unable to argue back. Don't take it personally and don't let it stop you from being honest. 'Racism' is an idea that's gone from being truthful and needed to a vicious, lying cliché! And it won't stop being used as a hammer for other people's self-aggrandizement until we speak up. How are your enrollments this term?"

"Down."

"I had two classes canceled."

"No!"

"Afraid so."

"You're not going to let this go on, are you, Nathaniel?"

"I don't know enough to be my own lawyer. What do you suggest?"

"I feel so frustrated!"

"Have you ever called any of the Administrators and told them how you feel?"

"No. Should I?"

"Tell Dean Visigoth. He's the faculty sponsor of the site, and its main beneficiary. Call him up and tell him what you think. Try Barney Rock, the Trustee as well. He seemed sympathetic, although I don't think the Board has done anything to solve the problem."

"What about asking the webmaster to require a name from anybody who sends in a review?"

"That's precisely what they don't want. They don't even want to be able to trace general sources of e-mails. But I bet the webmaster has those. Or some of them."

"Those could be traced back somehow. The people writing this stuff could be sued individually. What about in Small Claims Court?"

"It's worth a try, I suppose. But I really think the integrity of the teaching profession is bigger than Small Claims Court. Don't you?"

"We can't let this continue! We can't!"

"Teachersonparade says it's re-locating. Let's see how that works out. Maybe Mr. Lather won't find another server. It would serve him right. Maybe the site will die for lack of a home."

He left Lillian St. Jude — and himself — with that small hope.

About three A.M. Nathaniel's telephone rang. He reached up from his bed to lift the receiver. "Hello."

". . ."

"Hello?"

". . ."

"Who is this?"

"Is this queer teacher?"

"What?" Nathaniel sat up in bed, disturbing Slacker.

"I had you class. You bigot!"

"Fuck you, Bigfoot!"

"You unfair, just because we not know English! Why should we English? Why no they offer degrees in other language? You ruin my life! I hate you! You sick!"

"Your life was no doubt a ruin before you got to me. How dare you call me at my home!"

"America land of the free! You be sorry one day! Very sorry!"

The caller hung up.

He knew he mustn't take it personally, and yet the call left him with an ache in his chest. After a bit, he did a *69 to see where the call had originated.

"Hello," a voice answered.

"Is this Jimmy?"

". . . Dad?"

"Did you just call me?"

". . ."

"Did you?"

"No."

"I did Star 69 and you answered."

"And you got me?"

"Were you playing some kind of trick on me?"

"Of course not."

"What's going on here?"

"I don't know. What did the caller say?"

"Another threat. I might have to change my land line number."

"You're getting threats? Isn't there something you can do about it?"

"Sure, pass all my students. Sing their praises to the skies."

"You're not serious."

"As serious as a Muslim fundamentalist. Now those are students! I'm sorry I woke you up."

"I fell asleep on the couch. Luckily mom and Lana are gone for the weekend."

"I hope I didn't scare you."

"Naw."

". . . Well, good night."

"Good night."

"How's your tumor?"

"It's just part of me, the doctor says."

"My son is part tumor?"

"It's okay, for now."

"Did the doctor look at it?"

"He felt it."

"He didn't actually look at it?"

"How are you doing, Dad?"

"Surviving."

"Good."

". . . Well, good night."

"Goodnight, Jim."

They hung up. Something wasn't right. Was his son lying about the prank? In his grogginess had Nathaniel hit the Favorite Numbers Re-Dial Pad? Had the person who had called fixed his phone to make sure that he couldn't be traced? Nathaniel shivered even under the covers, counting the tics in his cheek.

❧

When your life is falling apart, call it old-fashioned, but you might as well have a blowjob.

The next night Nathaniel went out to his favorite trysting area near the ocean. He didn't look his best, his hair still in need of a touch-up and a haircut, and the air was nippy, but he found a man who seemed to want to administer just what the sex doctor had ordered. The man was old, ugly and thin with a frumpy warlock beard, but he didn't make any special demands and removed his teeth and began the treatment. The fact that he somewhat resembled Haywood Wire only added to his allure. "Take that hot dick!" Nathaniel said. "You take it now, goddamn it!"

It was took, and it was good, and both parties were entirely satisfied with the arrangement, and thus Nathaniel went home and had a good night's rest, living to fight another day.

It doesn't necessarily take love — dirty, old, raw sex can save a life.

❧

Of his two classes that hadn't been canceled, the 102 people seemed a little subdued and Nathaniel couldn't tell yet if there was much talent to reckon with, but they listened attentively. He didn't mention The Problem.

The class had seventeen people in it now, a couple of transfers from the dead afternoon section and the inevitable late-adds. It looked like the dean and the chair were going to let it continue. Spike had said, in the hallway, that even one more student would make the dean happier. "I live to make Dean Visigoth happy," Nathaniel had said.

He arrived early so that he could go through both Johnnie Cochran Arts and Helen Keller (one building over) to see if there were any flyers for Teachersonparade. And there were. He went down the corridors, methodically taking them down and stuffing them into trash containers when he could find any, trying to be discreet. A few he saved and dated as "evidence," just in case another savior miraculously appeared on the legal horizon. The flyers had many of the tear-off tags at the bottom removed, so students were still using the website apparently. Nathaniel stopped and wrote ABUSE THE TEACHER OF YOUR CHOICE HERE!!! on top of one of the flyers near the women's restroom. He knew he was taking a chance: DR. TACK SEEN DEFACING STUDENT FLYERS WHILE WAITING FOR HIS VICTIMS. SATANIC ACTION DEMANDED IMMEDIATELY!!!

He was sweating and out of sorts when he got to his classroom. A young black man was waiting at the door, but he didn't seem to be bent on destruction, just on adding the class. He was as tall as Nathaniel and sturdily built, nothing outlandish about his wearing apparel — a light shirt and dark pants, just one ear stud — except that he had a wristwatch on each wrist. What did that mean? A personal quirk or a sign of trouble? I'm getting completely paranoid! Nathaniel told himself. But he knew the old saying — that doesn't mean they *aren't* out to get you!

"May I help you?" Nathaniel said.

"Are you the instructor for this class?"

"Yes."

"I was wondering if I could add."

"Can you show your eligibility?"

"I took Subject A and got a B."

"Who did you have?"

"Ms. Washington-Goldfarb."

"Can you show me the proof?" Nathaniel should simply have signed him in to shut the goddamned dean up, but his experience had led him to be cautious about students from the remedial classes (the lower classes?!) — even when they had passed. But Hanukkah Kaneesha was pretty good about maintaining standards, wasn't she? He didn't really know.

"I don't have it with me. But I can bring it next week."

"I'm not supposed to give you an Add sticker without the proof."

"Oh, I can get the proof!" The student gave Nathaniel a big smile. "I was president of the Alliance of Students last year."

An icy hand gripped Nathaniel's heart. "You don't say?"

"I believe that we've been on opposite sides of an issue," the student said. He seemed to notice the flyers that Nathaniel had placed on the lectern.

"And what issue would that be?"

"Teachersonparade."

"I can't think of a single thing that would make me less want to add you to the class than what you've just told me, Mr. . . . ?" Nathaniel had kept his voice down, but a couple of the other students overheard.

"Antwan."

"Mr. Antwan."

"Antwan is my first name."

How non-stereotypical of you, Nathaniel thought. I must make a note of it to send to that Politically Correct basket case who wrote the article about me in the school rag. "Didn't you think you would need to show proof in order to add, Mr. . . . ?"

"Timmons. I forgot it."

"Let me make something perfectly clear, Mr. Timmons," Nathaniel said, tapping the small bundle of flyers. "I think Teachersonparade is an abomination and the people running it and a good many of them using it are criminals and should be prosecuted."

"I know it's not perfect yet."

"If you were to judge from that website, why would you want to take me for a class anyway? I'm in the Pits, to say the least."

"I really need this class this semester."

How many times had Nathaniel heard that over the years? "I don't think you'll be happy with me, Mr. Timmons."

The dean be damned!

But the student didn't go away. "I thought maybe you've changed."

"To what?" Your personal pussy?

"I did get a B in Subject A and that entitles me to take 101."

"And I'm a little short on enrollment in this class, I'll tell you frankly, Mr. Timmons. But I don't think we'd be a good match. I see problems ahead."

And this is the first of them!

"You can't really keep me out of the class."

"Oh, I can't?"

"Not if I qualify."

More heads looked toward the front of the room. What was this all about?

"I believe the teacher is still in control of his individual classroom — the last time I looked anyway. I don't have to accept discipline problems."

Mr. Timmons was looking a bit grim around the gills. "I haven't been a discipline problem!"

"Not yet perhaps."

All the signs are there, however.

"I don't want to argue with you, Mr. Tack, but it is the student's choice as to which class he or she wishes to take."

Nathaniel was actually a little unclear about the precise rule here, but he knew for sure now that he didn't want this person in the class.

It was getting close to ten after nine and time to begin. "I don't want to argue with you either, Mr. Timmons. That's my decision."

"So I can stay then?" Mr. Timmons said.

What?

"Why don't you come back next week with your proof of eligibility?" Get this guy out of the room now!

"Won't it be too late to add then?"

"We can always do a late add."

"I need this class. I'm transferring to State next term."

Our loss, I'm sure.

"I need to start the class, Mr. Timmons."

"Okay, I'll sit in then," he replied. He went to the back of the room and took a seat.

Was it deliberate defiance? He was taking out a notebook and didn't look particularly defiant. Had he misunderstood what Nathaniel had just said? Plenty of students couldn't seem to follow the simplest directions. Or was it — possibly — part of a plan by the Alliance of Students to write down remarks Nathaniel might make and use them against him somewhere, somehow? There! Mr. Tack said students have too much self-esteem! See! Mr. Tack denied with his own mouth that students' shit don't stink!

Nathaniel was not going to make a stink in front of the other students and began the class. He noticed that Timmons was watching him carefully. And the same went double for him watching Timmons.

"Let us begin our review of the major punctuation errors — those true evils in contemporary society — the comma splice, the fragment, and the fused sentence. We must act now, before these corrupt our souls further and send us all screaming to perdition. Shall we begin?"

There were four smiles on the shining morning faces.

Right after that class Nathaniel made a beeline for Hanukkah Kaneesha Washington-Goldfarb when he saw her in a passageway between buildings. She was talking to a student, and so he waited. She looked nicely dressed — in a skirt, no less, every hair in place, a tidy brown briefcase in hand.

"Can I ask you about a student?" he said, wasting no time.

"So how are you?" she smiled. "I hear you're behind a lawsuit. True?"

"I'm trying. It isn't easy."

They walked along together.

"I've gotten several unflattering reviews myself."

"Do you want to sue?"

"I can't afford it."

"We had two lawyers, but they backed out."

"Sorry to hear that."

"Do you know any?"

"Not really."

"Lawyers seem to be like cops. Never one around when you need one." Nathaniel opened the door for her, students whizzing by. There was a buzz saw noise coming from behind another building. Such noises were commonplace on campus. The repair-"persons" didn't seem to know or care that there might be classes going on.

"Which student do you mean?"

"I have somebody trying to enroll in my 102. He's one of the student rabble-rousers, I think. He said he took you for Subject A. His name is Antwan Timmons"

Hanukkah Kaneesha frowned. "Oh, him."

"Trouble?"

"You can't trust him."

"Really?"

"I caught him in several lies about papers that were due and even who wrote them. He had me call his grandmother, and she lied for him as well."

"Did he pass?"

"He managed to get a C or B, I believe."

"How disappointing. Does that mean I have to accept him in my class?"

"Technically yes, I suppose."

"Was this a regular Subject A or —"

"It was the African-American Pride section."

"And he cheated there? Am I missing some irony here? Has my irony meter simply conked out?"

"My advice to you about Antwan is to keep him out of your class any way you can."

"Wow." Coming from her, this was important information.

"And you're correct. He's involved with the Alliance of Students. He may even have helped set up Teachersonparade. That was part of the reason he didn't do his essays, or something like that. He told me so many stories I finally just quit listening to him."

Nathaniel felt like telling her that she shouldn't have passed this student on to the rest of the faculty, but he held his tongue.

"He's very student-oriented, shall we say? Anything else I can tell you?"

"I guess that's enough."

"Just watch yourself with that young man," she said as they parted.

Nathaniel called the teachers' union and asked for legal help on his potential lawsuit. Yes, there had been complaints from some other instructors and the matter had been looked into, but the lawyers that the union kept on a retainer thought the law Congress had passed — ostensibly to reduce pornography on the Internet — was now being used to *protect* websites like Teachersonparade. How could this be? Well, the law had been badly worded and had been turned on its head. There really was nothing they could do. Goodbye.

That afternoon Haywood Wire dropped by Nathaniel's office with a handful of new reviews. "These are getting completely out of hand," he said. "What about a new lawyer? We've got to stop this."

"Do you have one — a new lawyer?" Nathaniel said.

"I thought you were working on it."

"You're not working on it?"

Haywood looked tired. "I haven't been feeling well." His face did look sallow and his eyes itchy red.

"What's wrong?"

"Indigestion. I probably don't eat right. And I think I have an allergy to trees I didn't have before."

"I was just on my way out," Nathaniel said, getting up from his desk.

"Don't you want to see these reviews? There's one of Suze DiMentia calling her a Leftist fascist."

"She is a Leftist fascist. This city attracts more than its share."

Haywood fished one out of the little bundle he was carrying. "Well, look at this from Fly on the Wall."

"Read it to me."

"'Good news for Shite College! The intolerable Dr. Tack of the English Department has lost his lawyers and can't seem to get anyone else to take on his pathetic lawsuit. Why would anyone when this is clearly a free speech issue, pure and simple.'"

"The truth is rarely pure, and never simple."

"Hey, that's good!" Haywood said.

"Yes, it is. I wish I had made it up." He zipped up his briefcase. He didn't really feel up to Haywood at the moment.

"Fly on the Wall goes on. 'Maybe one of these days the good Dr. Tack will retire to his gay retirement home and scare the horses there.' What does that mean?"

Did Fly know about Nathaniel's sex life too? "Your guess is as good as mine."

"And here's the part that really grinds my ass. 'The professor in a 'calculating' department who has been assisting the passionate but fruitless plans of Dr. Tack may have to give up his shenanigans and calculate his own pension as well.'" Haywood looked up from the page. "That's me, right?"

"I told you that if you signed with Oznick and Kurd —"

"I know, I know. I'm just checking that you didn't bandy my name about some other places."

"No, Haywood, I didn't." Nathaniel could feel his own cheeks drawing in, his teeth about to gnaw on something.

"I've been off THE PITS for some time now, and I don't want to get back on there!"

"How are your enrollments this term?"

"About normal."

"Mine are so low I may have to let in a student who helped create Teachersonparade."

"Really?"

"He somewhat flaunted the review site in my face while trying to add."

"The nerve of these people!"

"Perhaps they've won and we should admit it."

"No! Nathaniel! They can't make us swallow this. They can't!"

"Oh, but they can. They can make me eat shit. And they can make me say it's delicious too."

"Well, at least you haven't lost your sense of humor."

"Yes, I have."

"Don't say that."

"It's true. They are making us eat shit."

"Not me!"

"What's that little brown speck near your mouth?"

Haywood rubbed the back of his hand at it, couldn't stop himself. He even looked to see if anything had come away.

"Try it. You might like it," Nathaniel said, without expression. His briefcase seemed heavy.

"There must be something we can do!" Haywood said, his voice almost begging.

"We are mere teachers, my friend, in a culture that despises genuine education. Powerless ninnies. The pen may be mightier than the sword, but the Internet is mightier than the pen. The slow erosion of civility, grading standards, and classroom control has now, at last, reached the world of the colleges. We thought all our fine advanced degrees would protect us from the hordes. At least I did, but I was wrong. And all the king's horses and all the king's men — to say nothing of all your bribe candy — can't put them back together again."

And with that, Nathaniel walked out, leaving Haywood at a loss for words. "Will the last sane person please close the door when you leave," he added.

Despite what his mind told him, he let Antwan Timmons enroll in his 101 class. It didn't of course take long for Mr. Timmons to play his hand. As soon as he had his Add sticker, he passed out flyers for Teachersonparade, to each and every student, while Nathaniel was erasing the blackboard, which was covered by a previous teacher's scribbles. Even the desks had been moved for another class and not returned to their usual positions. When Nathaniel grumbled about the desks, Mr. Timmons said, to no one in particular, "The way desks are arranged in a classroom of course are not preordained by God, and they do usually make it seem like the teacher has more authority than the students — some sage on the stage."

Nathaniel gave him an eyeful but didn't know what to say. You can't pass out those flyers in here? Why not? They're clearly marked APPROVED by a dean's office. .

"What do you think of this thing?" one of the students asked Nathaniel, holding up the flyer Mr. Timmons had just passed out. "I didn't know about this."

Mr. Timmons was back in his seat, notebook at the ready, very attentive to what Nathaniel might say, perhaps to report it to Them. The other students seemed excited by the flyer too, were turning and twisting and showing it to one another.

"Oh, I haven't seen those," Nathaniel lied. "I'd just be careful what I get as 'information' on the Internet, that's all."

"You haven't seen these?" Mr. Timmons asked. He had more to distribute. "Maybe that's because they keep disappearing from walls."

"Perhaps they spontaneously combust," Nathaniel said, getting out his class roll. "From all the lies on them."

"Perhaps they are torn down by somebody," Mr. Timmons said.

"Perhaps they're in places they shouldn't be."

"Perhaps they upset some people."

"Why would people be upset?" Nathaniel said. "Merely because those flyers distort the truth and spread vicious lies and congratulate themselves on being a fountain of truth."

"Perhaps they are the truth," Mr. Timmons ventured.

"And perhaps they aren't," Nathaniel said.

"They are the truth because they're brought by the truth fairy."

What did that mean? Was that an allusion to Nathaniel? Was Mr. Timmons saying he himself was gay? The atmosphere in the classroom was all "fun," except that it was actually un-fun.

"You mean we can review you, Professor Tack?" one of the students asked, eyes newly bright with anticipation.

I'd better change the subject before this gets ugly, Nathaniel thought, wiping the chalk from his hands. Already he was bespattered with chalk dust, and he hadn't even begun the class. How much chalk had he inhaled over the years? he wondered.

It was Trustee Barney Rock calling. "I'm planning to present some of the reviews before the Board at our next public meeting. Can you come?"

"Present them for what purpose?"

"I plan to speak from the speakers' podium we set up each time, not from the long table."

"And this is for what now?" Nathaniel hadn't attended very many Board meetings, maybe one, and wasn't clear on what he was being told. He wondered if he had lost a few brain cells from all the stress, or maybe it was just that Barney Rock had called during his nap.

"It might get the Board of Trustees to take some action."

"I'll come," Nathaniel said. "Just tell me when and where."

"Maybe you can speak to the Board too?"

"If I have to."

When he got to the meeting, he noticed that Gorilla Woman and the student activists were present. Even his student Antwan Timmons was there. They didn't acknowledge each other. It was being held in the James Madison Center, one of the other campuses of Shite. How in the world had the name James Madison been allowed to stay?

The Board, composed of seven members elected by the city at large, consisted of two black women, one black man, two Asian women, one white woman and one white man (Barney Rock). All Nathaniel knew about them is that most of them were political hacks for sale to the highest trumper of Political Correctness. They sat at a long table with water pitchers, glasses, and various budget memos in front of them. The Chancellor, the molested choirboy, sat in the middle, his glasses pushed up to the front top of his head.

"Trustee Bolus is clearly right about that," one of the black women was saying, unctuous to an extreme.

"Indeed," several others said, nodding agreeably.

"Madame President, faculty member Suze DiMentia wishes to bring a proposal before the Board," some man on the end, not one of the actual Board, was saying, again in a very Parliamentarian-phony way. He may have been the college's counsel: another Asian male.

Gorilla Woman got up from her chair and advanced to the speakers' podium to make her presentation to the Board, applauded heartily by the activists. "Honorable Trustees, Students, Faculty, Guests," she began, "I would like to pass out this list of demands from the Beauty of Diversity Committee." She held up a sheaf of papers. Gorilla Woman looked very heavy-set and lesbian standing at the podium, her hair cut short, her body cut short by Nature. Lots of people are indeed stereotypes, Nathaniel thought, and nobody's going to tell me not to see what I see, just because it's not flattering. "I am here tonight to demand that the Board take steps to increase the success and retention rate of students by race and ethnicity!"

Cheers went up.

Suze DiMentia went on with some gobbledygook formula that was supposed to create a Math Bridge and an English Bridge — no doubt to Heaven — for – yep — "underrepresented minorities." Underrepresented as determined by her, apparently, and her cohorts. Albinos weren't on the list. Nor were ability, work ethic, and actual personal performance skills.

Nathaniel looked at Barney Rock. I came for this?

Barney wagged a finger as if to say, "In time, in time. Hang on."

"Our second demand," Gorilla Woman was demanding, "is that there be an immediate implementation of The Return of Students Program, by which we mean that there need to be greater incentives for Shite College students to return to Shite as instructors. We simply have not done enough to insure that this happens. We must take steps to insure a more diverse faculty!"

It was curious to Nathaniel how nobody questioned the basic assumptions in Gorilla Woman's words — all those nodding heads up there on the dais. What if Shite's students weren't any good, and why should they, more than students from elsewhere, be entitled to have faculty positions? What next — guaranteed faculty positions? You want to find "racism"? Here was your "racism." As big as life. And the only thing "under-represented" around here was Truth.

"Further," she was saying, "we want teachers to integrate the experiences of three or more ethnic groups into the basic subjects in all areas of the college. For Diversity equals quality!"

No, it didn't. Nathaniel encountered it every day, and it caused more problems than it brought benefits. The mantra simply did not hold up under scrutiny.

His eyes met Barney Rock's. There was a flicker of a smile there. Barney looked elegant in yet another expensive dark suit, his hair as white as snow on Vesuvius. (Did it snow on Vesuvius? Would Barney/Vesuvius explode and wipe out this nonsense from Gorilla Woman?) Barney poured himself a big glass of water from a pitcher and took a sip.

Okay, Gorilla Woman, I'll integrate the experiences of three or more ethnic groups into the curriculum, Nathaniel thought. We'll start with "insidious institutionalized" homophobia among blacks, Latinos, and Asians. We don't have another home-grown homophobia in the U.S. We've had to import more! And how about ethnic crime rates while we're at it? How about looking at those, honey? Gorilla Woman seemed to assume that this kind of ethnic educational quota system would only show the groups to advantage. Maybe not, dear one, if it is real education and not the cheerleading propaganda you undoubtedly "demand."

"Moreover, there will be a committee to monitor and insure that teachers are really doing this in their classes and to assist them in doing so."

What?!

Gorilla Woman was going to send her Thought Police into the classrooms. "Professor, you're under arrest! You have not complimented an underrepresented ethnic group although we have been watching you for fifteen minutes!"

Nathaniel wouldn't have believed anyone could be saying such things, let alone demanding them, if he hadn't been sitting there listening with "all his ears," as a student had written once.

The Board members seemed to think this might be a good idea too. They at least were looking receptive instead of howling with laughter at the incredible racism and preposterous silliness of what this woman was "demanding."

Suze thanked the Board and returned to her seat, to handshakes and pats on the back from her student satellites. Antwan Timmons seemed especially appreciative.

"Thank you, Ms. DiMentia," Madame President was saying. "I'm sure everyone here agrees with you and wants a more diverse faculty."

We already have a more diverse faculty than any other school in the universe! Nathaniel raged. All it did was make them fight and scrabble for living space and jobs even more than human beings ordinarily did, all the while speaking in tongues like the Tower of Babel — that shining beacon of the Beauty of Diversity. There was budgetary business that took up another hour. It was so boring that Gorilla Woman and her band of warriors left. Finally Barney Rock said, "I'd like to say a few words to the Board, but not from up here. From down there." He pointed at the speakers' podium.

"The President recognizes Mr. Rock."

Barney stood at the podium holding what looked like the folder Nathaniel had given him. He was tall and his suit was handsome, but there was a small piece of string on the back of his jacket and there were wrinkles on his butt from the way he had been sitting.

"I have brought some reviews from the website to show to you tonight," he said. He looked at his watch. "I know we don't have much time left, but I would like to call these to your attention, have you look them over, and maybe have us do something about them."

"And what website is this?" Trustee Bolus asked. He was an elderly man and evidently didn't keep up.

"The one the students use to review their teachers," the Chancellor explained, fiddling with his glasses.

Well, not exactly, Nathaniel thought. But he didn't have a podium in front of him.

"Now you may find some of these offensive, but it seems to me that that is the problem. They are offensive, and they are directed at our dedicated staff of instructors."

Barney actually looked behind him to see if any of the student activists were still around. Nathaniel wondered if Barney had arranged the boring budgetary items to be inserted into the meeting where they had been to guarantee that the troublemakers would leave before he got around to the website. Very few people of any kind were left, actually.

"Do you think this is an appropriate review to post on a website about anybody, let alone a teacher?" Barney said. "'Alice Mae Fast likes to take it up the ass.'"

There were several gasps from the Board.

Even Nathaniel's ears pricked up. Who was Alice Mae Fast and where had this review come from? Had Haywood missed it?

"Let me read the entire review," Barney Rock continued. "I know it's upsetting. 'She keeps a dildo in her desk in Room 307 in Arts and she scoots down and uses it on her hind quarters while we are forced to write on current social issues. Alice Mae thinks that we can't see her, but we can, as her dildo is quite large and makes a distinct buzzing noise. I am unable to concentrate on my answers and have received failing grades when this is not my fault. I think this teacher should be fired.'"

"That review is not typical!" a voice from the back of the room said. It was Dean Visigoth, just arrived. He had on his Tweedledum overly tight blue jacket this time and his lovely wife, Heidi Ho, somewhat stout, was with him.

"Does it matter if it's typical or the only one?" Barney Rock was quick to respond. "Is this any way to treat a member of the faculty of this school?"

"One review doesn't make a summer!" the dean retorted, not quite apropos but maintained with gusto.

The meeting went on from there, and somehow the subject got shifted by the invading dean and his equally militant wife to the fact that Barney Rock had "violated" some statute or other about "revealing a faculty member's name without permission at a public college function."

Huh?

It was typical Shite behavior.

Nathaniel wished he had brought a machine gun to mow down the bastards. He closed his eyes and envisioned the scene. But all he had on him was his stun gun. He was pretty sure Gorilla Woman would be all over him before he could stun more than a few.

He stayed around, despite his great desire to flee, and told Barney Rock that he appreciated his efforts. "Do you think any of this will do any good?"

"I can't tell," Barney said. "I'll have to poll them individually later. I'm sure there's some reluctance. They'd rather do nothing — it's safer."

Dean Visigoth and Heidi Ho seemed to be lobbying the Board members toward their side of the issue. The former Beauty Queen had thickened over the years, from hips to face. She was wearing a red women's suit that was too tight for her. Luckily she'd left her crown behind. What was with this couple and their ill-fitting clothing? Yet they seemed pleased with themselves that they had managed to re-direct the focus of the meeting from the pornographic trashing of a teacher to some "violation" by a Board member.

"Of course there's really nothing we can do to stop that website," Nathaniel overheard the Chancellor saying.

The little punk. The little choirboy punk!

"I may not agree with the content, but I will defend its right to exist to the death," Dean Visigoth added. He even glanced around at Nathaniel and Barney Rock.

"Maybe we should try to lobby the Board too?" Nathaniel asked.

"I don't think it's the right time."

"When is the right time?"

"I'll have to feel them out."

"Can they really get you in trouble because you mentioned Alice Mae Fast by name?"

"I'll apologize. I probably shouldn't have done it, but I couldn't resist the rhyme of Fast and ass. I got their attention, didn't I?"

"You sure did. At least you got around the student activists."

"For tonight anyway. We'd actually be better off holding off on this until the end of the term. Most of them are gone by then."

"Can we wait that long?"

"Grind them down, slowly but surely."

"But are you going to be back in the fall?"

"No." Barney gave him a wink.

I'll have to do this on my own?

"I'll try to do what I can before I'm out of office." Barney Rock obviously was looking forward to his departure. "I can't believe I lasted this long at this place," he sighed.

Can I believe a word this man says? Nathaniel wondered. Was this all he could manage — the hubbub over the dirty review? Maybe Barney Rock would simply drag it on and on until he was safely out of office. Christ!

※

"Did you enjoy that meeting?" Antwan Timmons asked Nathaniel before the next class, as the students were trickling in.

"Which part?"

"The presentation by Ms. DiMentia. I thought she spoke very well."

"Did she?" Nathaniel was not going to get into this right now. He wanted to discuss some of the mistakes he had found — *quelle surprise!* — in the first set of papers. "Actually I enjoyed the part most where Trustee Rock read that review of Alice Mae Fast," he found himself saying.

"Actually most of the reviews are positive," Mr. Timmons said.

"That must be comforting for Alice Mae Fast."

"I believe the students around here are adult enough to see through all that."

"You think so?" Nathaniel asked, feeling hot under the collar. His sport coat was too heavy for the warm spell they were having.

"Nobody believes that she uses a dildo in class." Mr. Timmons looked as cool as a cucumber.

"I believe it," Nathaniel said. "Why would somebody say it if it wasn't true?"

"It's just one person mouthing off."

"I, for one, am glad somebody at last has exposed Ms. Fast. Maybe she'll turn down the buzzer on her dildo. It was interfering with my classes. Now if the students will just turn down their cell phones as well."

Antwan frowned. "Getting back to Ms. DiMentia, I am happy to see that she has the courage to present the new Diversity Demands to the Board of Trustees. She's not afraid of anybody."

"It seems to me it takes more courage around this place to object to such racist demands," Nathaniel said. He could feel his face coloring. (Would that count as being a person of color?)

"Maybe I can give you some articles that you could pass out in class," Mr. Timmons offered.

"Glad to see them," Nathaniel said, trying to pull the folder with his class notes out of his briefcase. It stuck. And he even cut the back of a knuckle on the zipper. You can pass them out over my dead body.

Better not say that aloud — might be taken as an invitation. Nathaniel looked at the doorway. My, he hadn't had a death threat in weeks!

Mr. Timmons wouldn't leave it alone. "I'm going to be on the Oversight Committee," he said.

"Be sure not to overlook anything," Nathaniel quipped. He looked up to see where his pun had gone.

Evidently nowhere. Mr. Timmons was looking at Nathaniel as if he would stare a hole through his heart. This was a new attitude for college students, so naked. Say something I don't like and I'll be on Teachersonparade so fast your head will spin!

Nathaniel plunked his notes down on the lectern. "No one is going to force me to teach something I don't want to teach," he said, glaring back at Mr. Timmons.

"The world moves on," the student said.

"Not all movement is progress."

"There will be changes, you watch," Mr. Timmons said, licking his tongue into the corner of his mouth. He looked away to say something to another student who was sitting down, but then his eyes darted back toward Nathaniel's. If the eyes are the windows of the soul, Nathaniel was in big trouble.

Am I really the extinct species to be in this Darwinian struggle? Nathaniel thought. Is this what Triceratops felt looking up at that asteroid? Not me! Not me! I'm Under-Represented!

"Well, how did it go?" Marty said on the telephone.

"So-so." Nathaniel was taking a nap, except that he couldn't sleep. Slacker lay up against his side. Holding the phone was uncomfortable, but he twisted until he got it to his ear.

"I'm sorry I couldn't go with you."

"That's all right. Barney Rock brought up a review I've never seen before — a really crude one."

"Yeah?"

"Why is it people always want to know the crude ones? If I'd said I found this marvelous rave about some teacher, nobody would give a damn."

"C'mon. What did it say? I've got to get back to work. I'm on the desk."

"It accused some woman teacher of using a dildo."

"That's all?"

"During class and up her butt."

". . . That's all?"

Nathaniel laughed. "Thanks. I needed that."

"Are you getting depressed?"

"Only when I'm not depressed."

"You can't give up now!"

"I've also got this troublesome student, who used to be president of the Alliance."

"Boo, hiss."

"I feel like I'm in a death struggle with him."

"Ignore him. Smoke some pot."

"You know I don't like pot." Nathaniel looked at the new bottle of vodka he had purchased that morning. He was keeping it on the floor beside his bed. He hadn't opened it . . . yet.

"Can't the Board of Trustees do you any good?"

"I don't think they want to. They're more afraid of the students and Gorilla Woman. I saw them with my own eyes."

"Maybe we should do something to make them afraid of you."

"Like what?"

"Get some dirt on them."

"It would take too long. I'm beginning to realize just how powerless I am. I always thought — swore — that I wouldn't be like my parents, who let history push them around, and here I am being pushed around by history."

"I looked up the site again."

Nathaniel felt his stomach clench. "I don't think I want to know."

"There was some review saying that a teacher in one department by the name of Haywood Wire is telling his students not to take classes from you because you're a terrible, incompetent teacher."

"You're joking."

"I wish I were. It mentions both of you by name."

Nathaniel sat up on the side of the bed, making Slacker cranky. "My god, is Haywood really saying such things just because I left him stranded in my office? He's never seen me teach."

"Maybe he's just vindictive."

"He has many faults, but I didn't' think he'd do something like this."

"Well, that's what it says. He gave you an F as well."

"You sure you don't have to get back to work?"

"Did you get another lawyer?"

"Not so far."

"What about a gay lawyer? A lot of those reviews have been homophobic, right? I've got to go. Patrons are lining up. Mandy is supposed to work the desk, and she's always disappearing!"

"Which gay lawyers?"

"What about Modos & O'Harromog? They have an ad in the gay papers."

"You really think it's worth a try?"

"I've never known you to be so down before. Get up from that nap. Call Modos & O'Harromog!"

"I don't think I have the energy." The bottle of vodka looked mighty appetizing.

"Call them!"

Nathaniel looked again at the bottle of vodka on the floor. He could hear the screeching theme music from *The Lost Weekend*. He looked at the walls to see if he could see any bats. Maybe Slacker could jump on them when they came.

"Talk to you later," he said to Marty as he rolled off the bed and forced himself to get up. He opened the bottle of vodka and found a paper cup in the bathroom.

It was the alcohol that gave him the nerve to call Haywood at home a few hours later. "I just want to say that you are a complete slimeball." Nathaniel took particular care not to slur his words.

"Nathaniel?"

"You bet it's Nathaniel! You are an utter son of a bitch!"

"Hey!"

"How dare you! You tap-dancing pervert!"

"Nathaniel, I'm not going to listen to this."

"Yes, you are!"

"I'm going to hang up."

"Hang up? Well, why not! Lord knows you've got enough hang-ups to fill up Teachersonparade for twenty years!"

"Are you drunk?"

"Are you stupid? What a fucking pill you are. Making me apologize to you because you're so goddamned cowardly you're scared shitless somebody might see your name on something that shows you have the balls to fight having your goddamned balls cut off!"

"Nathaniel!"

"I'm not finished yet. And now you go and tell people not to take my classes because you think I'm a bad teacher. Well, I'm not a bad teacher. You're the bad teacher. And I just may go on the website and tell the whole world not to take your classes unless they want fucking candy thrown at them!"

There was a pause. And then Haywood said, "I do know what you're talking about. I would've called you, except that you seemed to want to have nothing else to do with me that day in your office."

"Don't try to make excuses."

"Nathaniel, let me say something."

"I don't want to hear what you have to say. You fucker!"

"Nathaniel," Haywood sounded surprisingly calm.

"You've never seen me teach, you disgusting creep. You know what — I think maybe you really do harass your female students!"

"I didn't write that review, Nathaniel."

The vodka was beginning to turn into a headache already. "What?"

"I think Fly on the Wall wrote it."

"What are you saying?"

"Let me get the review. It's right here." Haywood moved away from the phone.

Nathaniel slapped his own face and couple of times. He could barely feel anything.

"Here it is. Fly on the Wall or somebody wrote it using my name. Here's what it says: 'He's usually a kindly gentleman, but Professor Haywood Wire is telling all his classes about his former good buddy, Nathaniel Tack, informing them they should avoid him like the plague because they never know what they might get from Tack — including communicable diseases and low grades. Besides, he is a bad, downright incompetent presenter of information to any student unfortunate enough to cross his path. I heard Professor Wire say these things myself since I'm in one of his classes.'"

"Oh, my God."

"I repeat, Nathaniel, I did not say this. I would never say this."

"They're now turning us against each other. Oh, God."

"And it's working. I'm a bit hurt that you would believe such a thing of me."

"I'm sorry, Haywood." My God, here he was apologizing to this man again!

"It doesn't matter. I'll overlook what you just said. It's all getting very sinister now."

"I don't really think you harass your female students." Actually, he didn't. Maybe the man sniffed a few panties.

"Never mind." Haywood was all forgiveness, sort of. "Fly on the Wall is a true sociopath. He's got to be stopped."

"It could be anybody. We might wind up murdering Fly on the Wall and it could be someone else entirely doing it — the Christian in the next-door office, Tadd Dyer, or Guy Mountain or his large mother. It could even be the Chancellor trying to drive me out. I already have two canceled classes."

"With this review, you could have none. I'm sorry you think I'm cowardly about this, Nathaniel, but it seems to me the better part of valor is discretion."

"At least we cleared this up. Thank god for the vodka. I wouldn't have called you without it."

"You'd better watch how much you're drinking, Nathaniel."

"I know."

"This shows, once and for all, the true evil of what this website can do. Don't you?"

"No doubt."

"We've got to fight it."

"Absolutely."

Actually Nathaniel didn't think the full evil of the website had been tapped yet at all. So there he was — allies with Haywood Wire again, wherever the hell that would take him.

Immediately he called gay attorneys Modos & O'Harromog, and even got through.

"Yes, I've heard a little bit about this case," Modos said. "I had some dealings out on your campus not long ago and was told a few details."

"Might you be interested?" Nathaniel was too afraid to hope. "Perhaps you've read one of my books? I believe I have some reputation as a gay writer."

See, see, we're gay brothers!

"Afraid not. But I do think I've heard of you. Didn't you write a book about S&M."

"Not that I remember."

Ah, fame!

"No?"

"I'll write one if you want."

There was no chuckle on the other end. "I'm wrapping up something in the next day or two."

"I have lots of time off. Two of my classes were canceled."

"Sounds like monetary loss. Is Thursday good for you? About three-thirty?"

"I'll be there."

"Just to explore."

"Of course."

He even got Haywood to go with him, almost without an argument. Nathaniel offered to drive and met him in the parking lot at school. Haywood looked presentable, a stain or two on his pants notwithstanding. Both he and Nathaniel had brought folders with relevant materials in them. They were a bit estranged at first and made only small talk.

Then, as he drove, Nathaniel turned and asked, "Do you know if Vernon Daniels is still interested?"

"I haven't been in touch. Titus might be."

"Let's see if we can get by without Mr. Ashe. Just as we'll get by without Ms. Krista Prandemonia. She took our lawyer to save her job. I hope the school fires her ass."

"What about that other woman?"

"Lillian? The last I heard from her, she was very interested. I've also heard from some other people who say they're interested. And no doubt we should check out Alice Mae Fast."

"I did. She's not interested."

"Why? Is the dildo story true?"

"She wouldn't give me a reason. I got the impression she was extremely offended by the whole business."

"All the more reason to do something about it. Is her review still there?"

"It came down yesterday. I didn't want to tell you, but . . ."

"But what?"

"Don't you look at the site anymore?"

"No."

"You have to, in order to keep up."

"I know I tell other people to look at it, but I can't bear to. What did it say now?"

"There is an annotation where the nasty review of Alice Mae Fast used to be — it says the webmaster thinks it was posted by a faculty member to discredit the site."

"Oh?"

"It says that the guilty party's initials are probably N.T."

Nathaniel gripped the steering wheel hard.

"Is it true?"

"Haywood, we've just been through this false accusation business!"

"I'm just asking."

"I'm just denying. I have not visited that website in ages, almost from its very beginning. And yet my monsterhood seems to grow daily."

"You wouldn't mind discrediting the site, I'll bet."

"I hope everyone will send in fake reviews — to prove what's going on here. But I don't want it to be only me discrediting it. On my mother's grave, I have not reviewed Alice Mae Fast. Have you sent any yourself?"

"Not one!"

"You have my permission."

Haywood puffed through his lips at that. "I'd like to beat them legally." He looked almost vulnerable, his hands in his lap, big, ugly hands with age spots on the back.

"Maybe we're hopeless throwbacks, Haywood. The Internet is going to have its way with us. But let's give it a good fight, okay?"

"I'm game!" Haywood agreed.

The Offices of Modos & O'Harromog were palatial, a huge green-yellow-and-blue Victorian mansion high on a hill looking down on the business center of Santa Francesca, with street parking in front and a white stone pathway slinking its way up to broad doors with gold-plated handles. In the driveway were parked a Mercedes, a Bentley, and a new Volkswagen, in no particular order. "I want a driveway like that one day," Nathaniel said, nodding at the cars.

"When we win this lousy lawsuit!" Haywood said. He seemed more committed than Nathaniel had ever seen him before. Had he gotten more charges leveled against him on the website? A backbone transplant?

Inside the Victorian there was even a secretary, a stunning, young, dimpled man with very good diction and a gay accent. At least I can understand this one, Nathaniel thought.

They had to wait a few minutes, but then Mr. Wolfgang Modos, LL.B., began to descend from his upstairs empire, using the long spiral staircase that made a mere Hollywood set look anemic by comparison. He appeared to be a man in his early sixties with short legs, professionally dyed dark black hair, and a bulkiness to his upper body that clearly was the result of working out at a gym — too much so, since the top half didn't seem to go with the lower half. As he got closer, on the bottom step, despite the suit and tie, he looked more and more like a grim grandma with various bumps on his face. There may have been a smile or some acknowledgment, but mostly the eyes seemed to be fed by some reservoir of ice — electric ice. Nathaniel had thought it cold in the Victorian and had ascribed it to the architecture. Now he could see the true source of the coldness in the place.

"Glad you're on time, Dr. Tack," Modos said, offering his hand to Haywood.

"He's Dr. Tack."

"And you are?"

"Haywood Wire."

"Oh, I didn't know you were coming too." Modos gestured at Nathaniel with his ice cube eyes in a mild reprimand; then to the male secretary he said, "Twenty minutes." He extended his arms and began to usher them into the conference room. "My partner — legal partner — may join us later. Shall we?"

The conference room itself had multiple windows, all double glazed and immaculately clean. In the center of the room was a long oval table made of mahogany, not a speck of dust on its dull gleam.

"Your place is quite something," Haywood said, looking around, then going to a window to take in the view of downtown.

"We like it," Modos said, in pretended deprecation. He seemed to take the proffered compliments as his due. "Would you like coffee?"

"Sure," Haywood said.

Modos went to the large sliding doors that separated the two rooms and said to the male secretary, "Would you bring coffee for three, Conor?"

"Yes, sir."

Using his considerable upper-body strength Modos pulled the sliding doors shut and indicated which chairs Nathaniel and Haywood were to sit in. Nathaniel noticed framed newspaper articles on the walls, every single one of them showing Modos under some headline about winning some judgment for his gay client. $5 MILLION IN SETTLEMENT, one of them read. I think I can withstand the chill in here for five million, Nathaniel thought.

"So what have we got?" Modos said, intertwining his fingers as he sat at the end of the wonderful table. "How much can you afford?"

Oh, no, I knew it was going too well, Nathaniel thought. "Not too much, I'm afraid," he said.

"I might have a little," Haywood said.

"We're not cheap," Modos said.

Maybe they should just leave?

"We've been vilified," Haywood said.

"All sorts of lies are being told on a website," Nathaniel added.

"All very interesting, but libel is very hard to win, you realize."

"We've heard that," Nathaniel said.

"Are you the only two?"

"There are many more."

"Are they willing to sue?"

"We can get you some," Nathaniel said.

"Besides defamation, have you thought of common law harassment and infliction of emotional distress?"

Nathaniel and Haywood looked at each other. "Sounds good to us," Nathaniel said. "We're not lawyers."

"Though I've been studying up of late," Haywood said.

Modos's eyebrows lifted above the ice cube eyes, just enough to register mild contempt.

"I'm sure you know much more about the law than we do," Nathaniel said, rushing in.

"I'm sure I do," Modos said.

Just then the male secretary pushed open the sliding doors from the other side and came in with the coffee. As long as he didn't speak, he really was quite a handsome fellow, the best that money could buy, no doubt, and he served the coffee from a silver tray with great aplomb, pouring it into the white china cups, with real milk and sugar, even a dish of chocolate-tipped profiteroles on the side. Nathaniel sat there in the little cocoon of aromatic, coffeed air and felt surely somebody this wealthy had to know what he was doing. But could they afford him?

"Will that do it?" the male secretary asked.

"Thank you, Conor."

He slid the doors closed again. "Have you filed the Notice of Claim yet?" Modos took his coffee black.

"What's that?"

"If you're going to sue a public institution like a college, you've got to notify them first."

"This is the first I've heard of this," Nathaniel said.

"I thought the previous lawyer did that," Haywood said.

"What other lawyer?" Modos asked, not thrilled.

"We had Oznick and Kurd, but they were swamped with work and never got around to actually filing anything."

"They were terrible!" Haywood snapped. He seemed to burn his mouth on his coffee.

"They wanted to do it, just couldn't get out from under their load." Nathaniel was sure it was better to be complimentary to the other lawyers, pretty sure that lawyers would stick together if came to choosing sides.

"I don't know Oznick and Kurd," Modos said. "Are they gay?"

"We weren't pushing the gay angle," Nathaniel said. He noticed that the milk curdled when he poured some into his cup. He didn't say anything and just stirred the coffee as though nothing was wrong.

"I'm not gay," Haywood said. "Though I have nothing against such people."

Shut up, Haywood.

"Big of you," Modos replied. "I specialize in gay cases." He raised his arm toward the gallery of photographed legal triumphs on the walls.

"Very impressive," Nathaniel said.

"A lot of the reviews of Nathaniel are inspired by homophobia," Haywood said. "My friend here seems reluctant to go that route, but that's what I think."

"I am somewhat reluctant," Nathaniel said, wondering how honest he should be. "I'm just fed up with the way 'minorities' whine and carry on as though they are the only ones who have problems, or that all their problems are caused because they're 'minorities.'" And who said we were friends, Haywood?

"Oh, really?" Modos said. "Believe me, gays have special problems, lots of them." He had finished his coffee already. The ice in his mouth must have cooled it.

Christ, now I'm going to lose my gay lawyer because I'm not gay enough! Nathaniel thought. "But aren't problems mostly the result of the 'human condition?' he added lamely.

"What's that?" Modos said.

Nathaniel smiled. "I guess it's not something you can sue for."

"You don't like your coffee?" Modos asked, noting that Nathaniel wasn't drinking his.

"I'm waiting for it to cool."

Just then the doors slid open again and another man stood there. "Oh, Seamus, come in," Modos said. "Meet Mr. Tack and Mr. Wire. My legal partner, Seamus O'Harromog."

The partner was younger, perhaps thirty-five, tall, slim. He was not wearing a suit and tie and looked pallid and Irish – clawed-his-way-up-from-the-bogs Irish. His hair seemed somewhere between setter red and day-old beef stew. Even though he shook hands with Nathaniel and Haywood, he seemed, if anything, even colder than Modos, the small eyes far back in the head, watching everything. The Ice Brothers. I'd have sex with him, but I sure don't like this man, Nathaniel thought.

O'Harromog was carrying a top-of-the-line portable computer. "I thought we should look at the website itself," he said, setting the laptop on the table, although he continued to stand.

"Good idea," Modos said.

It didn't take long for Teachersonparade to come into view, and all four of them stood around the laptop to see what they could see.

"Why don't we try accessing it from the Shite College website?" O'Harromog suggested.

"Yes," Modos said, "let's see if there's enough of a connection to make a case here." It took a while, but eventually the website came up.

BE A WINNER! GO TO SHITE!

That was the fetching new banner.

"I don't see any links to Teachersonparade," Modos said.

"Try Information," Haywood said. "Then the Alliance of Students."

There apparently had been some adjustments to the website, perhaps because of the rumors about a lawsuit, but there were still the endorsements, like the one from the Alliance of Students:

CHECK OUT THE GOOD, THE BAD, THE UGGILY.

CONTROL YOUR EDUCATION

"You can also access it from other campus organizations," Haywood said.

"But you can't sue for links," O'Harromog said.

"It seems to be part of legitimate information being offered by the college," Haywood said. "And there's still a review on there that claims I harass female students!" O'Harromog scrolled through Haywood's reviews and found that one. "It's been on there for months," Haywood said, not seeming to mind the curdled milked in his coffee and almost through his profiteroles.

They also found endorsements from two other campus organizations.

"What about yours, Mr. Tack?"

"I haven't looked lately."

They looked him up. The very last review was surprising:

> Dr. Tack is an excellent teacher, clever and fair. He may not please the Masses, but he is more than a notch or two above most of the teachers I've had. He has, I believe, been under a lot of stress because of threats and insults directed at him, but he has always conducted his classes with complete professionalism. I recommend him.

"So what are you complaining about?" Modos said.

"The ones who can spell tend to like me."

"Did you write that, Nathaniel?" Haywood asked.

"No — but I could have. I don't know if it's clear to the lawyers that there are absolutely no controls over who writes reviews."

"Really?" O'Harromog said. "There must be some filtering system to be sure they're actual students."

Nathaniel resisted sighing. "There's no filtering system whatsoever. Anyone can send in a review. The webmaster alone decides what stays there and what gets deleted."

"Surely not," O'Harromog said.

"Go ahead, send one in," Nathaniel said. He was getting excited. Once they saw how it worked they would have to be outraged.

"I don't think we should risk that," Modos said.

"Go ahead. You can review me or Haywood."

"Should we?" O'Harromog said.

"Don't review me!" Haywood said.

"Give him an A."

They dickered about whether to send a review or not, but ultimately they decided not to.

"But you see now that you could send a review, don't you?" Nathaniel was not going to leave this alone.

"It does seem very easy," Modos agreed.

They scrolled through some of Nathaniel's other reviews. There were several other nice ones. Apparently some people were coming to his rescue.

"And still you're upset?" Modos asked, reading another glowing review.

"I object to the principle of this site, even when I get good reviews. The whole reason behind any review appearing at all is flawed and corrupt. It doesn't matter whether the actual reviews are good or bad."

"Here's one!" Modos said, delighting like everybody else in the nasty stuff.

> Nathaniel Tack is a butthead from another planet.
>
> He should take his socialy impared crap to Outer Space and get a life. He is aslo a raving homo-maniac! Avoid his classes. Find anybody else. Youve been warned.

"I'm a homo-maniac?" Nathaniel said.

"Vague," said Modos.

"I don't think it's a compliment," Haywood the Gay Liberator said.

"What I don't see is absolute proof that the college is involved," Modos said.

"There isn't even a disclaimer, or you can hardly find it," Haywood said. "Not that anyone reads disclaimers."

"What about the fact that campus organizations recommend it, and those campus organizations are funded by the college?" O'Harromog asked Modos.

"And the website calls itself a "resource" for students at Shite College," Nathaniel chimed in.

"If it's not a resource, then the college should not endorse, or appear to endorse, something that is defaming their own faculty, right?" O'Harromog asked again, running the argument by Modos more than by Nathaniel and Haywood.

"We could go for the school district itself," Modos said. "It controls the money."

"What about the webmaster? Does he have any money?" Modos asked Nathaniel.

"I doubt it."

"It's his money that supports the website — and maybe a dean or two of the college as well," Haywood said.

"That would be good," O'Harromog said. "High administrator involved."

"A dean of the school approved flyers advertising the site all over the campus — hundreds of them. And they're still up, lots of them."

"Do a search," Modos instructed O'Harromog.

Sure enough, Teachersonparade came up six different places, including Information and Student Benefits.

"It does look like the college is behind it," Modos said.

"Harming its own staff," O'Harromog agreed.

Were they on a roll?

"And have you seen this," Haywood said, taking a flyer out of his folder.

He hadn't even shown it to Nathaniel. "What's that?"

"This is a flyer that the Alliance of Students just put out." Haywood laid it on the table.

THE ALLIANCE OF STUDENTS

RECOMMENDS

TEACHERSONPARADE.COM

READ ABOUT AND REVIEW

YOUR TEACHERS, INCLUDING THOSE

ARE TRYING TO SHUT THIS

WONDERFULL INFORMATION SITE DOWN

There must be a proofreader working for the Alliance now — only one spelling error and the missing *who*.

"Maybe we should go after the Alliance of Students too?" Modos asked O'Harromog.

"They do seem very much involved."

"They're part and parcel of the whole damn problem!" Haywood said, finishing off the profiteroles.

Modos looked at Nathaniel. "Does the Alliance have any money?"

Nathaniel blinked a bit at the nakedness of the inquiry. "It does."

"Much?"

"I believe they have an annual budget of over $750,000. They use it for their agenda — and to pay themselves salaries."

"Really?" O'Harromog said.

"They're a nest of vipers," Haywood said, looking hungry.

"Shall we sue them too?" Modos said, looking quizzically at his partner.

By god if the new lawyers didn't agree to take on the case! They even said they'd do it on contingency. Nathaniel was overjoyed — well, *joyed* at least. These two men clearly knew what they were doing, and they were gay hard-noses to boot. Although it smelled a bit too much of the pursuit of money, they had to have come to their decision on likely legal grounds. So when they offered him and Haywood a contract with a thirty-three-and-a-third deal for themselves for any monetary settlement, plus legal costs deducted from the litigants' share if they won, he didn't hesitate for long. He didn't see any alternative.

It was Haywood who hesitated. He even had the pen in his hand and was about to sign when he backed off and said he wanted to take the contract home and look it over. Modos seemed to take a little umbrage at that but said he understood.

"I have something of a lingering resentment against your college," Modos confessed, standing in the hallway, O'Harromog gone, it was now understood that any aggrieved teachers, including Haywood, would get in touch to sign on as soon as possible.

"Oh?" Nathaniel said.

"I ran for the Board of Trustees out there. It was not a pleasant experience."

The male secretary was taking away the remnants of the coffee even as Haywood stopped him, wetted his finger, and picked up the last crumbs from the profiteroles. "Would you like more, sir?" he wryly asked Haywood.

"No, oh, no!"

I'd like some more of the male secretary. Yum, yum, Nathaniel thought. But business was business. "What happened?" he asked Modos.

"I sought the endorsement of various individuals on your campus and was asked a lot of grueling questions — many of them none of their business, frankly — and despite all

315

that, I did not get much support. And I did not win a seat of the Board."

Just a glimmer of this came back to Nathaniel's memory. "I'm sure you would've been a far better Trustee than some of those we actually have," Nathaniel said, hoping that was polite enough.

"You seem to have a lot of horses' asses out there," Modos said. The sting was evidently still being felt.

"I can't disagree with you."

"Now perhaps they will taste the whip of the law," Modos said, ushering Nathaniel and Haywood out the front door.

"Can we hope?" Nathaniel said, shaking the man's hand yet one more time.

Almost immediately the Notice of Claim went out to the School District that controlled Shite College, and Nathaniel could barely contain his excitement. His lawyers returned his calls and several other teachers wanted to join the lawsuit now — except Haywood, of course. He kept worrying about some clause in the contract with Modos & O'Harromog that said they didn't necessarily have to represent them if there was an Appeal.

"Let's worry about that when we get that far," Nathaniel argued.

But — again — there was no convincing Haywood. He wouldn't sign, and yet he wouldn't go away. He had suggestion after suggestion for Nathaniel.

While they waited for the District's response, which no doubt would be a denial of responsibility, the Complaint for Damages was prepared by the Offices of Modos & O'Harromog:

WOLFGANG MODOS, SBN 888661

SEAMUS O'HARROMOG, SBN 097666

33 Transvaal Ave.

Santa Francesca CA 94116

415-233-6700

Attorneys for the Claimants

CLERK OF THE CITY OF COUNCIL OF THE CITY OF SANTA FRANCESCA, SUPERIOR COURT OF THE STATE OF CALIFORNIA, COUNTY OF SANTA FRANCESCA

NATHANIEL TACK	) CASE NO: _____
VERNON DANIELS	) COMPLAINT FOR DAMAGES
LILLIAN ST. JUDE	) (Libel) (Gov. C. 900, et. seq,)

KARMA SUDRA)
)
Plaintiffs)
)
v.)
)
TRUSTEES/ SHITE COLLEGE,)
SHITE COLLEGE,)
SANTA FRANCESCA COLLEGE)
DISTRICT,)
TEACHERSONPARADE.com,)
ALLIANCE OF STUDENTS,)
of SHITE COLLEGE,)
JOHN/JANE DOES 1-100)

How lovely to see such Diversity, and so randomly selected too! A white gay male, a black straight male, a straight Jewish female, and a straight female of color. The individual names hardly mattered. Thank you, Gorilla Woman.

Next was a paragraph containing all the plaintiff's addresses and a request that all notices be sent to the lawyers. Then the Complaint continued:

Plaintiffs complain and for causes of action allege as follows:

1. DEFAMATION (LIBEL)

2. COMMON LAW HARASSMENT

3. VERBAL AND SEXUAL HARASSMENT

4. INFLICTION OF EMOTIONAL DISTRESS

5. INTERFERENCE WITH CONTRACT

6. Having duly filed a prior NOTICE OF CLAIM, we claim that Defendants are public (or private) entities and now, and all times mentioned in this Complaint, were residents in Santa Francesca, California, and that the Plaintiffs have worked as college instructors for many years, and have resided in the Santa Francesca area for many years. The Plaintiffs have during all this time enjoyed a good reputation, both generally and in his or her occupation. Defendants are now, and all times mentioned in this Complaint, were educational entities organized and existing under the laws of the State of California, or official adjuncts of such educational entities, or Internet website(s) purporting to provide reliable and accurate Educational Information about Plaintiffs.

7. Commencing on or about September of last year, and continuing to the present day, Defendants have allowed to be published on TEACHERSONPARADE.com,

which appears to be, and is, an integral part of the architecture of Shite College's website (not merely a link to a distant entity) comments that any reasonable viewer would assume to be an official source of information about Shite College instructors, and these comments constitute gross insults, libel, outright lies, accusations of crimes, and other indignities, without having insured that these so-called anonymous "reviews" are by actual students or that multiple "reviews" are not being posted to target teachers recklessly and viciously and without accountability, and thus constitute egregious ongoing verbal and in some cases physical threats and sexual harassment.

There followed samples of the reviews of Nathaniel, Vernon Daniels, Lillian St. Jude, and Karma Sudra.

A few words about the latter.

Karma Sudra was a teacher in the Nursing Department who had sought out Nathaniel when the news began to leak, once and for all, about a real lawsuit. She was a tiny woman from India, who, to judge from her name, hadn't been given much chance for a very good start in life. Time had also not been good to her face, like a Red Skelton comedy sketch, almost funny, somewhat embarrassing, with assorted puckers and discolorations, and the red jewel in her forehead somewhat tarnished. She likewise seemed to have one leg shorter than the other, with perhaps a slight hump on her right shoulder. She was somewhat difficult to understand because she spoke too fast. But, hell, she was committed to defending her name and willing to sign on the dotted line.

"I am taking no more insults from life!" she had told Nathaniel when they had met. The review of her that was included in the Complaint was this:

> Karma Sudra is a demented, miserable woman with a victim complex. She bullie's students, run's off on tangents, she's cofused and confusing, carrie's a big chop on her shoulder and resents the chair of her department. Not only is she strange, she is a horrific teacher. She treat's her students like their in first Grade, then is suprised if they act like it, she'd disrepectful, and really incapable of rising our levels of undrstanding. I felt oppressed by Ms. Karma Sudra, who's class was a hugh aste of time.

Perhaps both this student and Ms. Sudra would do better in another life?

The Complaint went on:

13. See Appendix for numerous other such remarks about these Shite College instructors and dozens of others.

14. The Defendants neglected to foresee this defamation in permitting Teachersonparade to function despite the existence of official methods of teacher evaluation that are already in place, or to end the continuous vilification despite the repeated pleas of the Plaintiffs and others, and have in point of fact given active support to Teachersonparade through college funding, approval of flyers by the office of Dean

Daphne Deane as well as other Administrative support of Teachersonparade, by others both known and unknown to the Plaintiffs at this time.

15. Teachersonparade clearly exposes the Plaintiffs to hatred, contempt, ridicule, and obloquy, as well as loss of authority, death threats, threats of physical violence, sexual harassment, damage to reputation, emotional distress, and prospective loss of future earnings, and prospective medical and hospital care.

I can feel that obloquy all the way to the bank, Nathaniel thought, relishing each paragraph. There was a little bit more:

16. Because Teachersonparade is on the Internet, it continues to be seen and read by any and all who wish to view it or use it online from anywhere in the world, and it can be reached easily through the official webpage of Shite College of Santa Francesca, including its search engine and several related official campus organizations.

17. As a direct and as a proximate result of the above-described online publication, Plaintiffs have suffered gross loss of his or her reputation, shame, mortification, and injury to his or her feelings, all to his or her damage in the total amount of $50 million or, if the action is brought in Superior Court, a total amount to be established by proof at trial.

We'll take a check for the $50 million, Nathaniel smiled. I'll take a check for fifty cents! Just as long as we win!

18. The above-described publication was not privileged. It was published through the negligence and/or intention of the Defendants, and has permitted malice and ill-will toward the Plaintiffs without proof of facts and dissemination of innuendo, rumors, and lies and thus injury, in some cases merely to "get back at" teachers for grades. The Plaintiffs seek additional punitive damages in total amount of $25 million, or, if the action is brought in Superior Court, a total amount to be established by proof at trial.

I guess seventy-five million dollars might just begin to soothe the ache, Nathaniel told himself, shaking with anticipation as he read through the last part of the Complaint:

WHEREFORE, Plaintiffs demand judgment against defendants, and each of them, for:

1. Compensatory damages according to proof;

2. Punitive damages;

3. Interest as allowed by law;

4. Costs of suit; and

5. Such other and further relief as this court may deem just and proper.

It had been dated and signed by both Modos and O'Harromog.

Besides the expected pro forma denial of wrongdoing by the college, what more could one possibly want?

"Do you think I'm weird?"

"This must be my son."

"Do you?"

"It's considered normal to introduce yourself before launching into intimate questions."

"Sorry."

"What's wrong now?"

"Are you busy?"

"Never too busy for you, my child!"

"Yeah, right. How's your lawsuit?"

"We're just waiting for the school to deny our claim and then the actual legal Complaint can go in. It's written and ready. I think it's finally going to happen."

"I wish we had something like that website at my school. There's a teacher I'd like to tell a thing or two, Mr. Shaver."

"Maybe the teachers would like a site for their students too. Have you thought about that?"

"I got another D."

"No son of mine gets a D! Who is this evil Mr. Shaver?"

"I didn't study."

"What was it in?"

"Theater Arts."

"Again?"

"I don't think I want you for a teacher, Dad. But that's not why I'm calling," Jim went on. His voice was getting very mature, the manly tones falling into place.

"You lost your virginity?"

"That's not it either!"

"You haven't become a Christian? Or a Satanist?"

"Satanist?"

"A little problem at school. Possible stalker."

"Not me."

"That's my boy. What is it then?"

"Did you really have to have a child?"

"I beg your pardon?"

"You and my mom didn't even know each other, did you?"

"Only Biblically. As in The New Testament, the really new Testament."

"I don't think it's funny." There was more than a little wasp in the words.

"Well, excuse me."

"I'm a freak!"

Oh, God.

"No, you're not!"

"People ask where my father is, and I don't know what to tell them."

"Tell them he's an illustrious author in California."

"I don't want to lie to them!"

"Ha! Well, as a matter of fact I just won another play contest. I just got the notification today."

"Which one?"

"It's a theater in Hollywood. I won first prize in a one-act contest. For a non-gay play, by the way."

"Do you get any money for it?"

"You sound like my mother — your grandmother. Too bad you never got to meet her."

"I have a grandmother. Oma. I don't think you'd like her."

"Why's that?"

"She's really down on gays."

"She's down on her own daughter?"

"Pretty much. She still thinks my mom might outgrow it. And my mom's almost forty."

"Jesus H. Christ, when will these people grow up!? She's got a grandchild. What more does she want?"

"She says I'm going to turn out weird."

"Is this where all this is coming from — your grandmother?"

"She says she can see certain traits in me."

"Like what? You haven't killed or tortured any small animals, have you?"

"No!"

"Of course you'd tell me if you had, wouldn't you?"

"You're weird!"

"I'm not half as weird as your grandmother. She has a fine daughter who has given her a fine grandson."

"She's German."

"Maybe she'll outgrow it. And if she doesn't, I forgive her."

"She says I twitch my face too much."

"Do you?"

"I can't help it! I just do it."

"It's probably temporary. You'll outgrow it. I mean really."

"That's what my mom says."

"Sensible woman."

"But Oma says it's because I have gay parents."

"Oh, please! Does she actually say that?"

"She was here this week to visit. She slipped me a couple of twenties and shook her head and said she felt sorry for me and the burden I have to carry."

"Give me a break. You poor thing, you. It must really be a burden carrying those twenties around."

"I put them in the bank."

"You're a total freak; that's pretty obvious. Using a bank at your age!"

"I had an accident."

"What?"

"I rolled the car over."

"Oh, my God."

"I didn't hit anybody. In the rain. It rains here a lot."

"Were you hurt?"

"Not too bad."

"What exactly?"

"Oh, I have a scar on my forearm."

"A scar!?"

"It's starting to heal. It's only about eight inches long."

"Does it hurt?"

"Naw, it's still a little red. In fact, I had two accidents, a week apart."

"Didn't you learn anything from the first one?"

"It was in the same spot. The second time was worse than the first." There seemed to be some pride about all this in his son's voice.

"Some people have to learn the hard way, I guess."

"So I've been home the past few days, resting up."

"You poor thing, you."

"Is that sarcastic?"

"Not at all. Are you going to be scarred for life?"

"Naw, it'll disappear."

"Well, I sure hope so. You've got enough to cope with as it is — being the twitchy, scarred son of gay parents. Make that gay and lesbian parents. Gay/lesbian/bisexual/transgender/and questioning parents!"

"What are you talking about?"

"Never mind. I live in a crazy city. How's your tumor?"

"It's just something on my uvula."

"Don't talk dirty."

"I've got to. It's dull here."

"But then Oma comes to town and livens things up. Bless her old ooompah pah German heart."

"She's all right. She doesn't like Lana either."

"Did she say that?"

"She criticizes her cooking."

"Sounds like any old mother-in-law to me. It's not gay-specific, I hope you realize."

"I overheard her tell my mom that she could do better than Lana."

"The meddlesome old biddy. I'm glad I haven't met her."

"My mom knows how to handle her. She doesn't snap back at her."

"Good."

"My mom's pretty cool."

"For a lesbian?"

"For anybody."

"I'm teasing. I hope she doesn't turn into your grandmother down the line."

"She won't."

"Kids turn into the parents quite often, you know."

"I won't."

"Hmm, I don't know if I should resent that or not."

"I don't think I'm like either one of you."

"Yes, you are."

"I don't think so."

"Yes, you are."

"In what way? I'm not gay. I'm sorry I brought that up before. Now I know that I'm not the least bit gay."

"Perhaps you're a lesbian," Nathaniel said, a bit miffed at the homophobic relief in his son's voice.

"Or a transgender? Would you like that?"

"Don't put me on the spot."

"You're not all that liberal, are you?"

"I outgrew it. Go ahead, be straight, see if I care."

"My mom is having some problems with Lana."

"You're just full of news for such a dull place, aren't you?"

"They go out in the back yard by the barn, but I can still hear them. They try to keep their voices down, but . . ."

"What are they fighting about?"

"I'm not sure. I know that Lana doesn't like Oma coming here."

"Who would? Hitler?"

"She's not that bad!"

"I'll give you a couple of twenties not to like her. What do you say?"

"It's possible they may break up."

"Seriously?"

"My mom asked me how I would feel if she and Lana didn't live together anymore."

"No! . . . How *would* you feel?"

"I don't know!"

"'Divorce — the words hit Caitlin between the eyes like a ton of bricks.'"

"What?"

"Oh, sorry. It's something some student wrote in my Plays and Novel class. I don't mean to make light of this. I certainly hope they can work it out."

"My mom is very good at working things out. She doesn't always say a lot, but she's smart."

"See, you are like your parents. They're smart. You're smart."

"Yeah, right."

"You don't think your old dad is smart?"

"A smart ass maybe."

"You got it, kid!" Nathaniel laughed. "Watch your language!"

"So you don't think I'm going to turn out weird?"

"Actually, it's too early to tell."

"Hey!"

"I do see quite a bit of you in me."

"I think I'm more like my mom."

"Since when?"

"Since always."

"You ask questions about things. You worry. Just like me."

"But I don't always say what I think — right out of my mouth."

"You mean like me?"

"My mom is more cautious."

"It takes all kinds. Maybe you got some of each of us."

"I can fix things like my mom. Can you fix things?"

"No, but you got those two D's in theater from me! You're set for life."

"Why don't you ever talk to my mom?"

"We don't have very much in common."

"I think most parents talk to each other."

"Put her on."

"She's not home now."

"Tell her I said hello."

"I guess that'll have to do, won't it?"

"Jim, parents talk, sure. They also scream and fight a great deal. Your mother and I have never had a quarrel in our lives."

"Grateful for small favors, huh?"

"I don't think you're doing so badly."

"I have a twitch, two car accidents, and my parents don't even know one another. Am I cool or what?"

"Please, whatever you do, don't inherit my streak of self-pity."

"I won't!"

"It's not becoming."

"I said I won't!"

"Good!"

"I think I've got to go now. Lana and mom are coming home soon."

"I hope they stay together. Keep me up to date, okay?"

"If anyone can handle it, my mom can."

"Superwoman, huh?"

"I really appreciate what she's done for me. Always being here and everything."

Nathaniel could hear the missing words. "I appreciate it too. And what Lana has done in taking care of you. They're both great."

"If anyone ever hurt my mom, I'd hurt him!"

Whoa!

"Is that aimed at me?"

"Whoever."

"I have no intention of harming your mother, and I'm sure Lana doesn't either."

"Good. Because I'd really hurt them if they did."

Yow, work out that Oedipus complex, boy! Work it out! Nathaniel thought, before they said their good-byes and hung up. Kids, yikes — even at a distance!

Amid growing rumors that the college was indeed going to be sued, the Chancellor (the diddled-with choirboy from Boston) called a special Legal Hearing of the Board of Trustees.

It's not necessary to describe all its self-serving posturings, merely to mention that every single lawyer invited to give an opinion gave the same one: the college could not be held responsible for the online libel of its faculty. Nathaniel attended with Haywood

Wire and Karma Sudra and expected Modos and O'Harromog to show up to argue the other side. He had informed them of the hearing, but they were no shows. Boyd DeLucca, the president of the Academic Senate, was present, and tried to address the Board on two separate occasions, only to be told that since he was not a lawyer it was inappropriate for him to be speaking that night.

"This is total bullshit," Boyd said during a fifteen-minute break. Nathaniel didn't know the man very well, but he liked his attitude. He'd been around the campus for years; they just hadn't connected before. Boyd tended to wear rumpled suits made of light blue seersucker and red bow ties. His eyeglasses were as thick as safety glass. Overall, he gave the impression of being unfocused and wouldn't look you in the eye, even came off as somewhat of a stumble bunny. But tonight he was focused and he was pissed. "This hearing is so stacked I can't believe it!" he said.

Barney Rock came over and joined them, looking regal and yet flustered. "This is a waste of time," he said. "They don't want to hear anything that might make them liable."

"I'm going to give McTooney a piece of my mind," Boyd said, darting unhappy, bubble-eyed glances at the Chancellor, who was fraternizing with some of the student activists, including Antwan Timmons from Nathaniel's 102 class.

It sounded like the noises of two men realizing they held no power around the place whatsoever.

"Do you know Karma Sudra?" Nathaniel asked, to both men. He would have introduced Haywood as well, except that he was hiding on the other side of the room, pretending not to know Nathaniel.

The small Indian woman barely came up above their belt buckles. Nathaniel hadn't realized that she was quite that tiny since he had only seen her sitting down until now. Her hump seemed less noticeable than before. She was wearing a heavy wool sweater over her sari.

"Karma and I worked on the Honors Program," Boyd said.

"We have an Honors program?" Nathaniel said.

"The Remedial Honors Program, don't you know it?" Karma said. It was evidently her baby and she was proud of it. She spoke in that formal manner of well-educated Westernized Indians.

"I'll have to look into it," Nathaniel said. Already he could feel the pressure on him to watch his tongue about the educational nonsense surrounding him.

"How can these lawyers say the school is not accountable for the website?" Karma went on. "My students tell me they are convinced the college has installed it, and that is indeed why they use it!"

"The Chancellor told me he was going to have a variety of legal opinions tonight," Boyd said. "The little liar."

"I will try to say something," Barney Rock said. "But I'm afraid it's all going the other way right now."

"Surely the lawyers haven't seen the lies being spread, have they? How could they defend those?" Nathaniel said, exasperated.

"I just want to help my students learn traditional, drug-free birthing techniques!" Karma said. "And that one insane student I had in summer school is preventing me!"

"I'll try to get you some satisfaction," Barney Rock promised. But he didn't sound convincing.

"I don't hold out much hope," Karma said. "I don't know if you are aware, but I tried legal action against this school before."

"You did?" Barney Rock said.

"I was knocked down by a shipment of school catalogs during my second term here. They had placed them outside my classroom in Sitting Bull Hall, stacked twice as high as me!" She held up her hand. It wasn't that high.

"And what happened?" Nathaniel tried to keep a serious face.

"I had broken my spectacles the day before, and was thus unable to see very well. I nevertheless did my duty and met my class. Upon my departure, I inadvertently stumbled upon the stacked school catalogs, which proceeded to topple from on high and pinned me beneath them. That's why I limp to this day." She raised a tiny finger. "I was born with the hump but not the limp."

"I remember this now," Boyd said. "How terrible it must have been for you."

"It was even worse than that," Karma went on. "Because it was late on a Friday, I was not noticed as I lay under the catalogs, and so my cries went unanswered."

"No!" Nathaniel said.

"Needless to say, in addition to the limp, I received numerous paper cuts from my ordeal as I struggled to free myself. I eventually fainted from the loss of blood."

"Oh, my God. How long were you there?" Barney Rock asked.

"It wasn't until the following morning that a janitorial employee discovered and extricated me."

"I've never heard of this. When did it happen?"

"Five years ago this month."

"Before my time on the Board."

"And you sued?" Nathaniel asked.

"I attempted to, but the college disclaimed all responsibility — even though I sustained a small fracture of my tibia in addition to two hundred and twelve different paper cuts." She pointed to her tibia.

"The college wouldn't even pay her medical expenses," Boyd said.

"The heartless corporate educational entity at its worst!" Nathaniel said. "But this time we'll get satisfaction, don't you think?" He looked to the other three.

Not one of them looked sanguine. Karma Sudra in fact said, "My instincts about this are not good. Not good."

Nathaniel didn't want to hear it.

"I also tried to sue the school another time," she continued to regale. "I did not win that one either — even though I was trapped under a bungalow for several hours,

327

surrounded by at least six feral cats. And none of it was my fault!"

Nathaniel naturally was eager to hear about the episode, but the Legal Hearing started up again and they all had to listen to the lawyers explain how Not Guilty the college was.

Even though the college had disclaimed responsibility, hence allowing a lawsuit to proceed, and whereas a legal Complaint was drawn up and ready to be filed, and should have been, and whereas and so forth and so on, it wasn't.

Nathaniel offered to carry it down to the appropriate office of Superior Court. But Modos & O'Harromog said they weren't ready to file. Yet no reason was given. Shades of Oznick and Kurd began to raise their ugly visages in Nathaniel's mind.

Haywood Wire kept sending e-mails and even phoning, trying to find out why the lawsuit was stalled. "Do you want to sign on at last?" Nathaniel said.

"I don't trust them," he replied.

"I don't either," Nathaniel said, "but who else do we have?"

Other potential litigants on the faculty began sending notes to Nathaniel, saying that they had taken his advice and called Modos & O'Harromog, and yet their calls hadn't been returned. There were ten other people angry enough now to sign on. Surely this was all to the good in terms of a legal victory, was it not? It wasn't just one or two bad apples trying to defend their rotten cores by silencing their critics. And yet the lawyers were getting harder and harder to reach.

Finally the attorneys called and asked Nathaniel to come to their offices. There was something they wanted to "discuss" with him. Hmm. He did so the very next day.

It was the younger one, Seamus O'Harromog, the tall, bog-Irish-looking one, who was present this time. (Even the male secretary was nowhere in sight.) He held the Complaint in his hand and didn't even invite Nathaniel into the Room of the Oval Table with the Client-O'erwhelming Views. He looked a little peaked, the eyes allergy-irritated, some stubble on his considerable jaw. He was no warmer than before.

"We now think it would be best to have just one litigant," he said, flashing the legal Complaint.

"Why so?" Nathaniel asked, panicked.

"We'll have a better, more focused case with just the one."

"I thought you told me to send as many people as possible to sign on."

"Originally. Now we believe that just one strong litigant will work much better."

"And who is that?"

"We think Haywood Wire's harassment review is one of the strongest ones for libel. Can you get him to be the main litigant?"

"Haywood?"

"He isn't the most . . . court-presentable one perhaps. But he is being accused of a crime. The review remains on the website as of this morning."

"But Haywood won't sign."

"Well, why not?"

He couldn't tell O'Harromog that Haywood had said he didn't trust them. "He doesn't want to sign, that's all."

"Why not? I thought he just wanted to check some clauses. Isn't that what you said?"

This is what he got for protecting Haywood. "I think he's simply changed his mind about signing on. He's very reluctant to have his name mentioned in any of this. I'm sure that was clear about him, wasn't it? You met him."

O'Harromog moved his mouth into a disgruntled position. "We thought he was more committed than that." He looked at the Complaint in his fist. "We haven't put a name on this yet."

"Do you want mine?"

The man didn't seem all that excited about the idea.

"You don't think my reviews are libelous?"

"It's not that. You've had the death threat and plenty of libelous reviews. It's just that Haywood's is stronger, less exaggerated. I am assuming that there is no truth to the charge against him. Correct?"

"So far as I know." Well, probably not! If it were true, why hadn't the "harassee" come forward and tried to cash in like so many others?

"Can't you persuade him to sign?"

"I don't think so."

"You're not even willing to try?"

You don't want a flake like Haywood Wire, closet litigant, to be your poster boy for this case! Nathaniel wanted to scream. "I have tried. He won't budge."

The Iceman didn't exactly cometh at the news. "We're re-examining the direction of the lawsuit," O'Harromog said.

"You're not backing out?" It was better to hear it now and hear it bluntly instead of the slow bleeding of Oznick and Kurd.

"We're not backing out," O'Harromog said. "Why — do you want us to back out?"

"No! No!" Nathaniel cried out. "I very much want you to continue with the case, in any way you believe we can win."

O'Harromog seemed to ponder the legal vagaries for a few long moments.

"It's for the integrity of the teaching profession!" Nathaniel begged. "No one can teach honestly under these conditions!" He wanted to add that it was also probably the end of several teachers' careers and the Fall of Western Civilization as well, but he held off while his counsel waffled.

"All right, we'll go with you as the single litigant," O'Harromog decided.

Oh, goody! . . . I think, Nathaniel thought.

Louise Beeze asked if he would help in the effort to move the feral cats from the Equal Opportunity Bungalow, where they had resided for many a year, since that building was soon to be demolished, and participate in moving them to another area of the campus. "You've got to help these poor babies!" she said. "I'll even contribute to your legal fund."

"What legal fund?" Nathaniel said.

"You should definitely have a legal fund," Louise said.

"You're probably right," he said.

And so he joined the Feral Rescue League, as it was known officially, or the Pussy Brigade, as it was called by the cat-haters on campus.

He liked animals, and it was a way to distract himself since the lawsuit still wasn't filed and Marty wasn't speaking to him, apparently — hadn't spoken to him for several days.

He asked Slacker if he should help save the ferals, and she said, "Fuck 'em. I've got mine."

He ignored her.

The plan was to entice the ferals to move from under the Equal Opportunity Bungalow to a somewhat protected section under the rear of the Lowe-Rankin Dining Experience. Louise supplied him with wet food, dry food, bottled water, and a rubber pad to kneel on so that he could get down and reach under the building and fill the various dishes. He wasn't getting any younger while the lawyers dawdled, so it wasn't easy.

Louise said that the SPCA could possibly come and get the cats out before the bungalow was demolished, but then that would be the End of Them, because nobody would adopt a feral. They'd be Put to Sleep — only it Wasn't Sleep. So, instead, the Pussy Brigade was summoned to move the food and water every other day, further and further toward the intended new living area, enticing the cats, slowly but surely, to take up residence in a safer place, where they would live happily ever after. Naturally, they wouldn't lift a paw to help themselves.

Nathaniel followed procedure after his night classes even though he didn't see a single cat. Even after a week he didn't see any cats. He wondered if possibly this was all some deluded hallucination on Louise's part — there were no ferals on campus and she was actually eating the food herself! At Shite College a feral-cat-food-eating fetish didn't seem stranger than anything else. But no. She was just good-hearted to a fault.

So there Nathaniel was at ten o'clock at night, down on all fours. "Here, kitty, kitty!" he said to alert the ferals to the replenished food supply. Some workers from Rent-To-Kill, who were there to fumigate the Restaurant Department for rats and roaches, looked at him oddly as they got out of their truck. They would just as soon have fumigated the ferals and been done with them.

"Just feeding the cats!" Nathaniel said, smiling, his knees creaking. He moved the dishes a few yards away from where they'd been the night before. Now they were sitting on the edge of the driveway. Could that be right? What if the kitties got run over? "You put the dishes where?" Louise would say. He decided to move the dishes to the other side of the driveway. The fumigators were still watching him, whispering to each other. Maybe they'd call the campus police and Nathaniel would be arrested. The school paper would read: DISGRACED PROFESSOR CAUGHT: CAT ABUSE SUSPECTED. "Some of us are feeding the ferals!" he explained. "There are quite a few of us. Really!" The fumigators went inside, convinced or not, snickering.

Yet there didn't really seem to be a sheltered area for the cats to move to. Was he even putting the dishes in the right place? Proud member of the Pussy Brigade, he felt like he was nine years old again and he had missed some adult mumbo-jumbo about why such and such had to be done in just such and such a way.

Suddenly he heard a noise over by the proposed new feeding area. Whatever it was, it sounded too big to be a cat, even a herd of cats. He crept over, being very quiet, and there he saw a raccoon that seemed to be lurking under a bush near the building. It was either injured or drunk. Its eyes were bright but unfocused, and as it moved away it seemed to be dragging a hind foot. Oh, Christ, the poor thing. It was scurrying now, terrified of Nathaniel and yet erratic in its movements. How do you rescue a raccoon, for god's sake? It would rip him to shreds.

"Fuck 'em. I've gone mine," he started to say. He re-thought it and realized he didn't have squat, and he was losing that, and by god if he'd let the goddamned ferals and the bedraggled raccoon be crushed by the Equal Opportunity Bungalow! He fed on. And left some extra for the raccoon.

"Marty, pick up!"

Marty didn't answer.

"Marty, pick up. Are you okay?"

Nathaniel was just about to hang up when the receiver on the other end was raised. "Yeah? What?"

"I'm worried about you."

"I was sleeping."

"Don't you think you're sleeping too much?"

"That's for me to decide."

"You don't sound too good."

"What do you want?"

"To see how you are. I haven't heard from you."

"My fucking neighbor got my car."

"What?"

"I think it's the same one who reported me pimping for shemales before. This time he punctured two of my tires."

"You're joking."

"I'm not joking! He used an ice pick or something."

"Why would he do that?"

"Because he can't stand me sitting in my car!"

"Why should he care? Are you sure he can't hear your music?"

"I have the windows up. It's because he can see me from his upper window."

"Why doesn't he just not look out? You weren't pimping, right?" Nathaniel asked, mystified.

"Of course not! I was smoking a joint and listening to a CD."

"What's his problem then?"

"I don't know!" Marty was mad and taking it out on Nathaniel.

"Maybe I should call back later."

"Wait. I'm sorry. It's not your fault."

"Isn't there something you can do about this man?"

"I already went to his house and confronted him."

"You did?"

"He denied everything. And he said he was going to report me to the police again, this time for threatening him."

"Did you threaten him?"

"I told him I was going to get his tires if he didn't stop."

"Maybe you should just have done it, but without telling him."

"I'll do it, I swear."

"Really?"

"I would now, except his car is in his garage. The son of a bitch!"

"Maybe you should try to videotape him."

"With what?"

"You can borrow my camera."

"Where am I going to hide?"

"You can borrow my car if you like. You could park opposite your car."

"And sit there all night waiting?"

"Do you have another suggestion?"

"I'm thinking about reporting him to the police."

"I think that's a good idea. That man has no right to tell you can't sit in your own car."

"I got to go." Very grouchy.

"Where?"

"Back to bed."

"You're sleeping too much."

"I don't want to talk about it anymore. Goodbye."

"Marty, I can help you catch him perhaps. I think there's a camera you can buy that fits under your car."

"For what?"

"It shows who's approaching the car."

"I can't afford it."

"You can't let this go on like this."

"I'm going to go to sleep. The fucking goddamn shithead! I ought to throw paint on his house!"

"I'll talk to you in the morning."

"Maybe I'll be dead by then."

"Marty —"

But Marty hung up.

It was April, and it was the cruelest month. The Alliance of Students had forced the Board of Trustees to hold another hearing, this time to "debate" Teachersonparade. Flyers were appearing all over campus. Hundreds of them.

WHO PUT THE PUS IN OUR CAMPUS?

FACULTY ARE TRYING TO SHUT DOWN

YOURE RIGHT TO SPEAK.

SAVE TEACHERSONPARADE!

ATTEND! FIGHT!

You could even hear old Gladys the secretary and other people in the English Department's meeting room talking excitedly about the upcoming confrontation. The day (evening, to be exact) was almost upon them, the location the Lowe-Rankin Dining Experience. Tables would be removed and chairs set up. No one knew how many people might attend; however, there seemed to be a general buzz that it was likely to be the largest turn-out for a Board meeting ever. Antwan Timmons, of Nathaniel's 102 class, said they were expecting five hundred students. If so, that would have been two hundred more than bothered to vote for student officers, out of the 60,000 who went there.

"Are you going to show up, Professor?" Antwan had asked.

"I don't know yet," Nathaniel had answered.

"We need at least a few to defend the other side."

Smug asshole.

Boyd DeLucca and Barney Rock said they'd come and maybe speak. Boyd had already written a testy letter to the Chancellor about the one-sidedness of the Legal Hearing that had been held, and Nathaniel was glad to see it distributed to a few individuals, but it really didn't have any teeth because the Academic Senate had no power. Boyd might not even follow through, not with so many on the other side. At heart he was a politician just like Barney Rock.

"The Chancellor has given us a total of $100,000 to fight your lawsuit," Antwan said, after class. "That is, if that lawsuit ever comes."

"Some rough beast is slouching toward Bethlehem even as we speak. Never fear," Nathaniel said. But he was fearing. The rough beast might very well be slouching toward him. Despite repeated calls, he heard nothing from Modos & O'Harromog.

"Is that rough beast a paper tiger?" Antwan asked. "That's a term I've never quite understood, Professor." He started to leave before he got Nathaniel's explanation.

"See you at the debate!" Nathaniel said under his breath. Debate, my ass. The Alliance and its cohorts would try to drown everybody else out if they could. For all their talk about the First Amendment, they considered it something for use by themselves and nobody else.

He managed to talk Marty into going with him, even though Marty was still depressed and out of sorts about his punctured tires, which by now had become a symbol of his life for him. So far his neighbor had punctured six tires, and yet Marty wouldn't park his car anywhere else. "It's very, very hard to find a parking space around my house. Besides, that prick is not going to make me move! He won't!"

Nathaniel admired his grit. At the same time backing off for a time wouldn't hurt. But then he wasn't backing off on the website. Not if Antwan Timmons and five hundred students ran after him at the debate and punctured him with five hundred ice picks. He didn't even take his stun gun with him. It wouldn't have been any use anyway against so many.

He did have four banners made at a print shop. He tried to get a fourth person to hold a banner, but he succeeded in getting only himself, Marty, and Karma Sudra to agree. He'd had quotations from some of the "reviews" transferred to strips of heavy paper attached to long wooden sticks. He anticipated that some of the students would be carrying placards themselves. Tit for tat. And they wouldn't be expecting a mere faculty member to actually fight back and do something!

Sure enough the room was packed when he, Marty, and Karma arrived. There were not five hundred students present, but it could easily have been three hundred, including some organized groups: UNITED NEO-ANARCHISTS and FRIENDS OF JUDY, a gay Internet Discussion Group. All the old standbys were present and licking their chops: Suze DiMentia (Gorilla Woman), using her cell phone to direct the troops, Jake Trosky (although he supposedly had transferred to State), looking pitted, bony, dreadlocked, and revolutionary. Antwan Timmons and some others that Nathaniel recognized were making a list of proposed speakers and getting all excited. Even Dean Visigoth and Heidi Ho were in attendance, sitting near the webmaster himself. Dude Lather had changed his hair color from blue to bright yellow; otherwise, he looked his same tall, bespectacled, skinny self. If you looked closely, you could just make out some new chin whiskers. The Alliance members were gathered around him and seemed to be very pleased that their Hero had been able to make it. The Board of Trustees looked nervous and vulnerable to see so many of the committed milling about. The noise in the room was zooish. Even Chancellor McTooney looked unsettled, although he must have thought he'd bought at least a little time with the money he'd given to the Alliance. Of course Haywood Wire was nowhere to be seen.

"Is anybody scheduled to speak against the site?" Nathaniel asked Boyd DeLucca, who looked bow-tied, rumpled and shifty-eyed.

"Do you want to?"

"Maybe I'll just inflame the situation if I do," Nathaniel said. He was pretty sure that he would get angry and thus lose the "debate" if he tried to speak in front of so many hostile forces. Nevertheless, he filled out a speaker's card and had Marty turn it in. He had the banners as his main ammunition. Would he get a chance to display them — and what would be the effect on the crowd?

Barney Rock came over and said, "What's happening to the lawsuit? Is it dead?"

"I don't think so," Nathaniel answered, more out of hope than anything else.

The president of the Board, a middle-aged black woman with small, nervous eyes, a little vague on the rules of parliamentary procedure, heavily prompted by the Chancellor on one side and another black Board member on the other, called the "debate" to order. The sides were to alternate — first Pro and then Con. When she was handed the speakers' slips, Madame President counted through them dutifully and announced the following:

"There are three speakers to speak against Teachersonparade, and one hundred and twenty-two to speak for it." She saw one of the activist students get up and hand yet another slip to her. "Make that one hundred and twenty-three Pro," she said.

More students arrived with yet more placards and signs, late as usual. Nathaniel turned around and tried to read them.

SAVE TEACHERSONPRDE

LET SUDENT VOICE'S BE HERD!

YOU WILL NOT LET YOURE FACTISM

RUIN MY EDUCATION!!!!

He even saw one that was spelled correctly. It was held by Dean Visigoth:

I MAY DISAGREE WITH WHAT YOU SAY,

BUT I WILL DEFEND TO THE DEATH

YOUR RIGHT TO SAY IT —Voltaire

I guess he really, really wants to teach that People's History course, Nathaniel concluded. Human beings were strange creatures when you stood back and looked at what they believed, what they did. The weirdest ideas could be taken up and forced on others: "I am going to have seventy-two virgins attend to my every need because I am blowing you up." "You didn't have water poured on your whole body, or at least your forehead, so you can't be admitted to Heaven." "A Great Raven dropped an egg — or maybe it was a turd — and that became the Earth, and the Great Spirit molded that turd and threw it at the sun, who baked it and patted it and crossed it with T." "Oh no, misguided ones, this world doesn't matter. Everything is illusion and pain isn't real."

Eeek! Whatever! Nathaniel thought. The world feels real enough tonight — but it's not going to get me! You can't let them eat your brain! he swore to himself. You must fight or die. And if you die, at least let it be for your own ideas.

First up were two members of the First Amendment Club. They seemed to be the same two "minority" members who had spoken up when Nathaniel had appeared before the kangaroo court in Arena 3B. Both spoke animatedly about how important Teachersonparade was and why it must not be shut down. "Because of this website I not take certain teacher's course, once I learn he make his students read homosexual book!" the second one pointed out in terrible English that (once again) you weren't supposed to notice.

Several people looked Nathaniel's way and cringed. This young "minority" speaker obviously had not yet gotten the message that it wasn't okay to be so blatantly homophobic at Shite College. Could it be the — ahem — lack of command of the language, to say nothing of the marvelous cultural heritage, that got in the way of a new idea in his Beautifully Diverse brain? And these were the "Progressives." Progressives, Conservatives — a plague on both their asses, as far as Nathaniel was concerned.

When those two were done with their two minutes' worth, a Con speaker was called for.

At first nobody got up, and Nathaniel was afraid that nobody would. Finally Boyd DeLucca's name was called, and he went to the podium in front of the Board and said that the website was "unregulated" and being abused and he "regretted" it. It was all a bit weak. He added that since he taught only non-credit classes he was not arguing against the website for himself. He had no reviews. But he was siding with the credit faculty. He spoke better as he went on and took some flak from some of the more boisterous activists present. "Calm down now!" the Madame President said. But they didn't calm down until they were good and ready. "I do not ask that the website be shut down," Boyd concluded, "but it must be run responsibly!"

The next Pro speaker was a butch, snub-nosed woman in boots and a denim top and denim bottom, her dark hair cut as short as any penis that might come her way. She strode to the podium and gripped it with both hands and leaned right into the microphone. "Hello. I'm Wanda What-a-Kunt — and that's with a capital K." She turned and acknowledged the cheers of her cronies. "That's my movement name," she explained. "And that's how change is made in this country! By Kunts!" She spoke better than most of the activists he'd heard, and Nathaniel had no doubt that her name was well chosen. Talk about co-opting offensive words for your side. Wanda What-a-Kunt was a whole dictionary!

Highlights of her speech included:

"Teachersonparade is but the beginning of a major change in educational power structures. Our day is coming!" she said, lifting her arm in a salute to the future. She was practically Biblical in her enthusiasm. No doubt if left to her, the Mighty would be brought low and the Remedial exalted. And then she added a P.S. that was just as revealing as her self-righteousness: "I want to state my displeasure that there are ten things I have to do — boring forms and such — to transfer from this place to UC. That should not be! Ten things!"

You poor little butch dear, how oppressed can one person be!

Now when I was your age — yeah, I don't want hear it either, Nathaniel changed the subject in his head.

Karma Sudra went to the podium next. Despite the high heels, her limp was hardly noticeable. She came up to the lip of the podium, but not to the microphone, and one of the technicians had to find her something to stand on after he couldn't get the neck of the microphone to reach down to her. All he could find was a milk crate from the kitchen area, and even that wasn't too helpful because of the high heels, which kept going through the holes in the milk crate.

"I was born to the lowest caste in my native country," Karma began. "In a country that supposedly has banned the caste system I nonetheless was labeled unfit and unworthy. However, I would not accept that fate. I decided early in life that I would not be an Untouchable. I left my homeland and came to America, land of opportunity. I struggled and struggled, and somehow I got my citizenship and a Master's degree, and yet that is how I am being treated now on Teachersonparade – as an Untouchable! I had a student last year who was psychotic. She wanted to be a nurse, and I knew I had to stop her. So I failed her, and what is her revenge? She goes on that website and calls me demented and unhappy! I am here to tell you that I am not demented and unhappy! I am perfectly normal and very happy! And it is the moral duty of this Board to shut down this venomous website, if it can possibly do so, and end this catastrophe of caste-ism!"

Nathaniel and a half dozen others applauded.

Karma went on, once she had removed a recalcitrant high heel from the milk crate:

"Let me tell you how pernicious this website has become. Two students of mine came into my office last month and threw that despicable review on my desk and then just left. These are two D students, I want you to know. They were saying that if I didn't give them at least C's they would write things just as bad — or worse." Karma hard looked at the Board. "I am afraid that I am now going to pass those two students when I should not! And it is all because of the pressure of Teachersonparade! Thank you."

As Karma stepped back on the floor at the end of her two minutes, Wanda What-a-Kunt, prompted by Gorilla Woman, hurried back to the podium. She'd already used her two minutes the first time, but she was not one for niceties. "I forgot to add during my time that any teacher who lets Teachersonparade affect their grades is a bad teacher and should be fired!"

"I'll fire you!" Karma yelled, tottering on her high heels. "You had your turn already!" She was a little spitfire — forty-five, limp, hump, or not.

The room erupted in various cat-calls, grumblings, and rattled placards, and the beleaguered president of the Board was having a difficult time maintaining order, parliamentary or otherwise.

"I have a right to speak," Wanda What-a-Kunt went on. "I didn't use up all my time before!"

Not only had she used all her time before, she had gone overtime. Her teacher in Guerrilla Politics, or whatever the fuck it was, had taught her well. "I will not be intimidated by the phallic atmosphere of this room!" she proceeded to add.

"Oh, sit down, you dreary P.C. dyke and give somebody else a chance to abuse the First Amendment!" Nathaniel heard himself shouting.

Wanda What-a-Kunt heard him and turned sideways, giving him a lethal look. "Certain faculty members will no longer be on the staff here, ruining the lives of poor, progressive, underrepresented groups once Teachersonparade and its truths spread throughout this city, this nation, and the world!"

The applause for her was thunderous.

Maybe he should just go home? The chair felt like electric needles in Nathaniel's butt. But Marty was patting his banner and whispering, "We'll kill 'em with these. We'll kill 'em with these!"

Just then Lillian St. Jude and Vernon Daniels walked into the room together. Yay! Some of Nathaniel's own people were finally showing up. He tried to signal them to come and sit with him and Marty, but they didn't see him in the throng. He got up and went over to them. Lillian looked like she had lost a little weight, or maybe it was just the black dress. She had omitted her usual hoop earrings, possibly because she feared the students would swing on them.

"So glad you could come," Nathaniel said. He inadvertently brushed against somebody with his rolled-up banner.

"Hey, watch it!" the person protested.

"Sorry," Nathaniel said, squeezing in between Lillian and Vernon. The long sticks made it hard to negotiate.

Vernon smelled of intense lime aftershave. He'd taken to shaving his cheeks above his brier-patch beard, giving him a smaller face. He also was using a cane for his bad right leg. Good! Nathaniel couldn't help thinking. One elderly black man with cane — you use what you have, yes sir.

"Do you want to speak tonight, Vernon?"

"Should I?"

"You have to put in a speaker's slip."

"Can you put one in for me?"

"Happy to. Would you hold my banner?" Nathaniel managed to wind his way through the crowd, got a speaker's slip from the box on one of the tables, wrote in

Vernon's name, and tried to hand it to Madame President. "It's too late," the Chancellor whispered, glaring at Nathaniel.

"What do you mean it's too late?"

"The speakers are all set. It's past the sign-in time."

"Shhh!" several people ordered. A student recently emigrated from the Pacific Islands, not white, not male, and not American, was defending Teachersonparade, and so everybody was supposed to be especially hushed and attentive. "Let her speak! Let her speak!"

"Sorry. Sorry," Nathaniel said. To Madame President he argued, "We only have three speakers! They have a hundred and twenty-three."

"A hundred and twenty-five," she replied, displaying several more speaker's slips that must have come in when Nathaniel wasn't looking.

"It's too late," the Chancellor said. The little Beantown Mick. Prick.

But then Madame President noticed that it was Vernon Daniels' name on the slip and showed it to the Chancellor. They both nodded.

"That's different. He may speak," Madame President said.

"Thank you," Nathaniel said hoarsely, getting up from his squatting position, his knee joints popping. "Christ, I'm too old for this!" he cursed into the noise of the applause for the Pacific Island speaker.

"For the other side, the Board now recognizes Vernon Daniels."

There was some clapping as Vernon got up and made his way to the podium. He was burly, bow-legged and slow-moving — but his cane sure was pretty! It took him quite a while to make it, and when he got there he had to find his bifocals and put them on. Nathaniel had made it back to the seat next to Lillian St. Jude. She was now holding his banner and took his hand and squeezed it with her free one as Vernon began to speak. Who knew what he'd say.

"Some of you know me. And I recognize some of you." Vernon looked around the room, his glasses on his nose. I have been around this college for many, many years now. I have come here this evening because people are telling lies. Not just little lies. Big lies! I don't really know what the Board can do about these lies, but if you want your teachers to stay here and teach your classes, you'd better get off your asses and do something!"

"Amen!" came from somebody. And it wasn't Nathaniel.

"You who know me and my music know I have devoted myself and my talent to upgrading the students around here. I try to share with 'em what I have learned as a black man in a white world — and just as a man in any world — and you know what I teach my students? I teach 'em to be honest. Play from their hearts. Learn some technique and then play from their hearts. And you know what else I tell 'em?"

"What's that, brother?" the voice called out again.

Thank you, God! Nathaniel said silently.

"I tell 'em the music business has a lot of cheats in it. A lot of cheats! But don't you be one of 'em. Don't sell your soul — even if you ain't got soul." Vernon smiled at his little joke, no doubt well polished from long use. "And do you know why I tell 'em this? Because I want my students, I want all the students at Shite College, which is my alma mater, by the way, to be standup folks who do what's right and say what they mean and mean what they say. But that website — that's from the damned devil himself."

There were a few hoots, but Vernon silenced them by looking first to one side of the room and then the other.

"I repeat — that Teachersonparade is trying to make me dance to their tune, to march in their parade. But Vernon Daniels ain't marching to anybody's tune but his own, and lies about Vernon Daniels are not going to be paraded before anybody. You hear me? If you want to know what Vernon Daniels is like, come to his classes and talk with him face to face, man to man, and then you tell me what you think to my face. Don't go sneaking around writing up stuff on the Internet like a little Ku Klux Klan member afraid to show his ugly face!"

"Right on, Brother Daniels!"

"That's all I've got to say to this Board," Vernon concluded. "You can do something about this if you want to. The question is: do you want to? I ask again: do you want to? . . . I thank you." The applause didn't match that for Wanda What-a-Kunt, but it wasn't bad. Several people even got up and shook Vernon's hand. My demagogue can beat up your demagogue, Nathaniel thought. But is this any way to run an educational institution? Logic? Fairness? Oh, grow up! Who said those had anything to do with contemporary life?!

The next speaker was Drew A. Lather, Hero of the Post-Literate. He was a long drink of water — polluted water. His face, chin whiskers or no chin whiskers, was so elongated it looked like it had been squeezed by something mechanical. Maybe his unfortunate mother had had an encounter with a forceps. Maybe she'd tried to abort her baby by slamming herself with a dictionary, had failed, and Dude had been frightened of them ever since. Such a cruel thought, Nathaniel reprimanded himself. No, let's see what he has to say — and then we'll have a some truly cruel thoughts.

"I am not real good at public speaking," the webmaster began. He hunched over the podium, the top half of his head colored like a cornstalk, the rest the dull brown he'd been born with. Even though he knew the two-tone hair was a fad, somehow it was a perfect symbol to Nathaniel. Dude couldn't even dye his hair right! Nathaniel reached up and touched his own hair. It felt dirty and in need of some dye itself. He must get that Medium Brown Loving Care if it killed him.

"I started Teachersonparade 'cause I took a class to learn how to play the piano. In summer school this was. I had always wanted to learn how to play the piano." The Dude's voice wasn't carrying very well.

"Speak up!" somebody encouraged.

Dude turned and grinned in a goofy way. Nathaniel almost felt sorry for him. Almost. When he turned back, he still didn't get any closer to the microphone. "I didn't learn to play the piano that summer, and it occurred to me that it was the teacher's fault. Did you know that most of our greatest people in history weren't successful students? Education stifles creativity. So I decided to start a website that would allow students to evaluate their teachers, anonymously, without fear of retribution, and —"

"Why not make sure only real students use it then!" Marty called out. Bless his heart. If it took punctured tires and speed to get him riled up and fighting, then so be it!

"Quiet, please!" Madame President scolded.

"Yeah, shut up!" some of the student activists yelled, shaking their placards.

"All I want is for students to prosper," Dude went on. "A country full of prosperous students is a prosperous country!"

The crowd was beside itself with this rallying cry. There was a march up and down the back of the room, orchestrated by Gorilla Woman, still on her cell phone, possibly summoning more troops from other parts of the campus.

"Did you know that a country of preposterous students is a preposterous country?" Nathaniel muttered to Lillian St. Jude.

"We'll win this yet," she replied, squeezing his hand again.

The march at the back eventually ended, and Dude Lather sat back down and was surrounded by supporters, who clapped him on the back and congratulated him on his speech, poor though it had been. Dean Visigoth and Heidi Ho leaned over and said something encouraging as well.

"Is there another speaker for the other side?" Madame President was inquiring, holding a speaker's slip in her hand. "I can't make out this name."

"It's mine," Nathaniel said, having made his way back to Marty and Karma. "Are you ready with your banners?" he whispered to the two of them.

"Is there another speaker for the Con side?" Madame President was pressing. "Or shall I turn to the Pro side again?"

"It's me!" Nathaniel called out this time. Marty was standing, holding his banner, ready to unfurl it when Nathaniel gave the signal. Karma was standing too, but because she was so small the banner was threatening to overwhelm her. Maybe she wouldn't be able to hold the sticks far enough apart so that the banner could be read. And she had the best one!

Nathaniel hurried to the podium. Somehow a baby had been placed near it in the last few minutes — by the student Trustee's wife. The baby was hiccuping, and Nathaniel wondered if it was intended to prevent him from speaking. He said nothing about the baby, realizing that if he did he'd be known thereafter as the Man Who Had Denounced a Baby.

He stepped up to the microphone, even though he could feel the animosity pressing around him. "I am that speaker," he said, pointing at the slip in Madame President's hand. "But let our banners speak for us!" He motioned for Marty and Karma to come forward, and they did, opening their banners on the move. Marty was tall and big enough to hold his two sticks over his head and far apart, but Karma was indeed having trouble. They were supposed to be "Teachers on Parade," but Karma was spoiling the configuration because her arms wouldn't reach very wide. Even Nathaniel's banner ripped on the lower edge when he spread it, and he was afraid the paper was going to come undone from the stick. Marty was waiting for the other two to get their act together, itching to be up and about — "on parade."

Finally somebody in the crowd jumped up from his chair and held one end of Karma's banner by the stick while she held the other. It was Biff Thorgoode of the Physics Department. He had a pot belly and seemed winded, yet Biff was more than doing his part to help.

"Unfurl your banners!" Nathaniel called.

I FEEL LIKE KILLING HER . . .

Nathaniel's banner read. He had left out the rest of one of Arlene Buboe-Pitsky's recent reviews: BECAUSE SHE'S SO BORING.

All eyes immediately went to the words the print shop had transferred to the long sheet of paper. The room even grew quiet, except for the Student Trustee's baby, who kept hiccuping. Nathaniel pointed at the baby, trying to make sure that Marty and Karma didn't knock it over as they paraded with their banners.

DUDES . . . HE GAVE ME A BLOWJOB!

read Marty's sign, and Marty turned this way and that to show it to all elements at the gathering. He even said the words aloud, in case anybody couldn't make them out.

"Is this how you put teachers on parade?" Nathaniel yelled, although his throat was dry and the words didn't carry as far as he wanted.

Karma stumbled once or twice in her high heels — the limp had returned, the limp worse, alas. Biff Thorgoode looked uncomfortable and out of shape, but they kept going around in a circle in front of the Board. Their banner read:

SHE LIKES IT DOGGY STYLE!!

Karma's banner had been the last to be unfurled and caused the most mouths to gape. Some of the women in particular didn't seem to care for the sentiment being displayed, just as Nathaniel had anticipated. He had cleared the review with Karma — it was one of hers — and even shown her the banner, but he wasn't sure that she really knew what "doggy style" meant. Maybe he should have told her?

"Woof! Woof!" Karma said, getting into it. "Doggy style! Doggy style!" She made the paper in her banner shake. "Woof! Woof!" she barked on, one leg up, one leg down as she limped around the Lowe-Rankin Dining Experience.

Just then Wolfgang Modos of Modos & O'Harromog came through the double doors carrying a thick sheaf of papers in his hands. He went right up to the Board and started passing out copies of something. Some of these members must have been the ones who'd given him a hard time when he'd campaigned to be a Trustee and had been denied an endorsement. They looked a bit surprised, yet they took the paper from him.

"Woof! Woof! Somebody wrote this about me!" Karma was shaking her banner. Marty and Biff Thorgoode joined her. No, she probably didn't know what "doggy style"

342

meant or she wouldn't have been quite so . . . canine specific in her chant, would she? (It must be said that Karma did give good woof.)

"The lawsuit has been filed. Expect media reaction." Modos said, handing Nathaniel a copy and then leaving without another word.

The contingent was taking more than its two minutes, but Karma cupped her free hand, trying to elicit more "Woof-woofs" from the audience. But nobody else would join in. Reactions varied, from irritated to amazed.

"You think your teachers are dogs, huh?" Karma cried out. "We are not your dogs! Oh, no, we are not your dogs!" She went on woof-woofing like a pro.

⊛⊱

G od, that was great!" Marty said. He was talking about the coup that had won them the night — even though another fifty speakers had labored on and on, on behalf of the website until time ran out. Unfortunately "great" wasn't applicable to their sex life, which they had tried to revive at Nathaniel's after their splendid rabble-rousing effort in guerrilla politics.

It wasn't just Nathaniel's growing impotence and Marty's drug abuse — oh, no, that was too simple an explanation (?????). It was the result of too many orgasms together over the years. You weren't supposed to say that, but it was clearly true. All the usual efforts were to no avail.

Nathaniel had an idea and did his best as they lay in bed, telling Marty raw — but artfully constructed — porn stories about the police who had arrested him. (Marty had a love-hate relationship when it came to cops, especially his erotic feelings.) Nathaniel even threw in a subplot about the neighbor who'd punctured eight of Marty's tires by this time — the cops fucked the neighbor with a truncheon, and then the neighbor fucked the cops with a tire pump. Nothing worked, and both Marty and Nathaniel felt frustrated. They held each other for an hour, and that wasn't all bad. Other people with the problem just lump it, or hump other members of their families, Nathaniel supposed. This was just part of most people's sex lives, and knowing that helped

. . . . Didn't it?

Still, Nathaniel couldn't sleep because of simple sexual discontent, and after Marty went home, he went out for sex. It was much later than he usually went, and it was good to see the full moon over his trysting place near the ocean. The cypress trees looked like lurking beasts in Gethsemane as he walked along the path, hoping somebody might still be out at two-thirty A.M. He'd changed into sex clothes (torn jeans and flight jacket and even sunglasses. It was hard to see, but, boy, did he feel sexy!) The cruising crowd of course was there and on the prowl — that's why you lived in Santa Francesca instead of, say, the Gobi Desert. He had his eye on a man in his mid-thirties who was wearing a military uniform of some undetermined nation (Switzerland?) and even had a butch shock of hair cut at a weird (but sexy) angle. The man in the uniform, however, was not interested in Nathaniel but rather in a Filipino with a skinny build and a flat nose, while the Filipino seemed to be interested in Nathaniel, who was not interested in the Filipino.

There's no arguing taste, of course. Still, it was annoying not to be able to celebrate and relax with a friendly orgasm with your companion of choice. *Pace* Marty.

Even though Nathaniel didn't like the fact that his chest kept barreling forth almost on a daily basis, there seemed to be some there who actually preferred his type. As he stood in the shadows, someone stopped and gave him the eye, and before he knew it he was engaged in a kiss with somebody he hadn't been Properly Introduced to. Somehow it didn't matter. Somebody else approached and began to massage Nathaniel's nipples — a touch too hard at first until gently reprimanded with a firm hand. Now there were three of them, and it had become, as the nuns might have said, an "My God an Orgy!" There were worse things if you and your lover couldn't get it on anymore than trading slurps and nipple rubs with a couple of fellows under the full moon. *Pace* Sister Mary Lucille.

Nathaniel was busy keeping his tongue occupied, his mind likewise occupied — worries about what the next step in the lawsuit might be now that it was finally filed, worries about Marty and his problems, worries about his son and his problems. He was so occupied in fact that he hardly paid attention to the fourth person who had joined the "My God an Orgy!" — somebody on his knees, stroking Nathaniel's pants and unzipping them. Nathaniel's penis was cooperating more than it had with Marty, not exactly at full staff, but the newcomer didn't seem to mind and soon enough had Nathaniel's member well in hand, and then well in mouth. My, this sure covered a multitude of sins, Nathaniel felt. Tongues, licked nipples, rather sweet kisses (mixed with a bit of tartness when the saliva got a little old) and your dick in somebody's happy mouth giving you tremendous head and not demanding any money or a marriage license for it — and the world thought this was a Bad Thing???? The world could go fuck itself. It didn't know how to have a good time. It was the most blessed experience Nathaniel could think of to soothe the pain and anxiety he was going through. And this was Safe Sex besides. And if oral sex killed you then, then so be it. It was worth death.

You can imagine his surprise when he looked down to see who was sucking him off, as the climax was about to occur. It was a young black man, it seemed, with a full face and his own sizable member in his right hand, having a good pull on himself. The young man's eyes were looking up at Nathaniel, and they looked familiar, but he couldn't quite place them, possibly because of the angle from below.

Mirabile dictu, Nathaniel's mature, but not yet dead, penis roared to its full dimensions — not pornographic maybe, but not too shabby, certainly nothing to be ashamed of, and he began to shoot into the willing, fully functioning mouth down below. The other two kissers/rubbers stopped to watch and listen to the rising tide of passion. "Give it to him!" "Take that load!" they said, quite sincerely. Happily and totally, the load was delivered.

When the blower rose to say thanks for the memories to the blowee and perhaps even share a creamy kiss, you can imagine Nathaniel's mix of feelings when he recognized Antwan Timmons, he of the two wristwatches, his 102 student and militant member of the Alliance of Students, staring him in the face.

"My God!" Nathaniel said.

"I've wanted to do that for a long time," Antwan said.

So it hadn't been an accident, a result of bad eyesight or the late hour. Antwan had seen him and sought the prize, such as it was.

Would they have to get married now? Would this mean an A for Antwan? He was barely earning a B-minus. Don't count on it, kid.

Antwan leaned close to Nathaniel and gave him a Gethseminal kiss on the cheek. "I still hate your guts," he whispered, wiping something off his upper lip. "It's just sex," he said, moving off.

"Hey! Understood," Nathaniel said, moving in the opposite direction. And he did indeed understand.

The next morning before eight he was awakened by a telephone call. The excitement, in all its forms, of the night before had kept him unsettled and unable to sleep except fitfully, and he almost didn't answer.

"Is this Mr. Tack?"

"Yes?"

"This is Nella Salmon of the *Gater*, at Santa Francesca State."

"Yes?"

"You sound guarded. Not happy with the way things went last night?"

"What are you talking about?" He was half asleep.

"I was there."

She was in the bushes watching sex acts?

"What's the purpose of your call?"

"I'm writing a story for our paper about your lawsuit, and I was wondering if I could get your answers to a few questions."

"What questions?"

"Why do you feel the need to file a lawsuit in the face of the obvious student sentiment in favor of the website?"

"Why wouldn't students be in favor of something that gives them a way to twist their teachers' arms."

"You don't think teachers can twist students' arms? I'm a student and I have exactly that experience."

"I thought journalists were supposed to be objective."

"I haven't asked you very many questions so far. How can you tell if I'm objective or not?"

"You sound hostile, with your mind made up."

"And so do you."

"Do you usually call before eight in the morning?"

"I apologize for that. I have a deadline today. Basically I've already written my piece and just thought I should get a comment from you. Why don't you believe in the First Amendment?"

How not to sound too condescending? "I don't think that reflects my attitude. Don't put words in my mouth."

"Well, I believe in the First Amendment!" she said, her voice glowing with pride.

"What about accountability? Do you believe in that too?"

"I thought the students made an excellent case last night. They can figure out what's true about teachers and what's not. Why are you trying to prevent them from having this information?"

"Miss Salmon, I can't believe that you think the crap on Teachersonparade is necessarily true in any way. Didn't the banners show that?"

"And do you really think you accomplished anything by having that poor little woman from India making a fool of herself with that obscene banner?"

"Ms. Sudra was exercising her First Amendment rights, I believe. It also shows the contemptible side of the website."

"I believe teachers should act with dignity."

"Oh, you do, do you? Teachers are treated with libelous contempt, but they're supposed to be saints and just take it. Perhaps we need some dignity lessons from the students."

"Many of the reviews are positive about the teachers. Only a few are like the ones on your banners."

"Let's hope so, Ms. Salmon. But one is too many."

"We're going to have a similar site at State."

"No doubt that will improve the level of journalism there."

"I certainly wouldn't want to take a class from you, Professor."

"And no doubt I wouldn't want to have you as a student if you think you're a journalist. I am not going to give you any quotations for your article. I can imagine how they would be used."

"That's quite all right, Professor. I have more than enough already."

And with that she hung up.

The article that followed in the *Gater* was principally an interview with Dude Lather, who was all set to transfer to State in the fall. It was a puff piece par excellence, dwelling on how many miles Dude had to bicycle to class and how he had overcome a bad background as a "Dutch-American." (What?) What seemed to be overlooked was the fact that he had not in any way, shape, or form overcome his background. He had simply brought it with him to college. There was a big picture of the webmaster addressing the Board of Trustees and a smaller picture of him riding his bicycle on his Journey to Success. (real caption). Nathaniel was quoted as saying "I refuse to give any quotations to your student newspaper" and "Teachers should learn some dignity from their students."

Still upset, the next day Nathaniel called Modos & O'Harromog and got through to O'Harromog. "I was surprised at how nakedly unfriendly she was," he said about the amateur journalist who had called. Sitting on the edge of his bed, he was still in his pajamas. So was Slacker.

"Just tell them you don't want to talk to them. Refer them to us."

"Are they all going to be like this?"

"They'll try to make you say things, some of them. They'll twist your words. We can handle it."

Nathaniel thought he knew more about the case, especially what was in the reviews, than the lawyers did. "I want to speak to the press. I guess I just wasn't prepared for Ms. Nella Salmon."

"Well, just be careful. We issued a press release to all the wire services and such. Didn't we tell you this?"

"Not exactly."

"It's our usual practice."

"What's the next step now?"

"To see if the school settles."

"You think the school is going to settle out of court?"

"That's what we hope."

"Really?" For how much?"

"Fifty thousand."

"That's all?"

"That's what we got for that library employee there."

So for all the talk of "millions," the lawyers actually thought this was an easy in-and-out snatch job? "You don't think the reputation and integrity of teachers are worth more than fifty thousand dollars?"

"I have another client coming."

"What if the school won't settle out of court?"

"Then we'll take them on in court."

"Do you think we can win?"

"The complication is this. If these things were printed in a newspaper or a magazine or said on the radio or TV, then we'd have firmer ground, legally, to stand on. Because they're on the Internet, they may be protected. I've been re-reading the Communications Decency Act, and the wording is murky, but it seems to rest on whether the webmaster is granted the same immunity for what appears on his website as a server like AOL is granted — the Zeran ruling."

"That's a completely crazy law. The webmaster isn't a server."

"It was written to reduce indecency online, and now it's being used to protect indecency."

"Why should the Internet have special rights like this?"

"Go ask Congress."

"And I hate using the term 'special rights,' because right-wingers use it to fight gay rights. But in this case, it really is a 'special right.' Correct?"

"Pretty much," O'Harromog replied.

"How long before we go to court, if the school doesn't settle first?"

"A couple of months."

"But you're committed to following through on this, right?"

"Of course. Got to see my client now. Talk to the press, if you must, but don't let them trap you. This is your lawyer talking."

And then O'Harromog was gone.

There was a call on his answering machine at school from Fox News wanting to talk to him. Somebody named Tex Wallobee had left two numbers, and so Nathaniel called back, but cautiously. This was supposed to be the network without the "liberal bias." That just meant it was the network with the "conservative bias." I am neither one nor the other! Nathaniel wanted to scream. Why must I be put into a box?

By ten o'clock Tex Wallobee and his camera crew were meeting with Nathaniel in his campus office, making both Tadd Dryer and Guy Mountain in the next office curious as hell, but still too mad at him to ask what was going on. Nathaniel had even gotten there early and re-arranged his own novels on the bookshelf — just in case the camera should come to rest there. Then he decided that he was not going to use any of this media coverage to promote his writing. He'd seen others blatantly getting in mentions of their products for sale. Cheesy. I'd like to sell some product myself, he realized, but not here, not now, not this way. He moved his books to a desk drawer.

He didn't have to worry. The camera concentrated on his face, and when he saw the story later that day he was struck by how jowly he looked despite the liposuction he'd once had. He got in a sentence or two amidst the comments elicited from students and others on campus. Most of the students thought, the review website was a "wonderful idea," whose time had come. And there was jowly old Professor White Face saying the website was a "tissue of lies." Later that day he caught several students in the hallways glancing at him as though they recognized him.

Antwan Timmons didn't seem to be attending his 102 anymore. The sex act had probably made him skittish after the fact. It made Nathaniel skittish too, and he feared the false accusations that might emerge around the episode. How would an indignant "Well, I hardly made him suck my cock!" sound on the follow-up story on Fox? Having Antwan in the classroom would have made teaching a bit awkward too, though Nathaniel knew the awkwardness would only last a minute or two. That's what being a "professional" meant!

"There he is!" one of the goofier students said when Nathaniel walked into the classroom. "The media star!"

"That's me," Nathaniel said. Yeah, I always wanted to be famous, and now I'm getting there – for being a bad teacher!

⟋

Haywood saw the TV news story as well and sent an e-mail:

> Nice job on Fox! Did you see what Fly on the Wall said about you on Speak Out Loud?

Here was the attached:

> Dr. Nathannyboy Tack has taken to the a-i-r-w-a-v-e-s now in a vain (very vain) attempt to sway the multitudes to his side. Too bad his teacher's Grade Point Average continues to decline. For all that he is now a media d-a-r-l-i-n-g, he can't seem to keep the bad reviews from coming in. I hear he had but two classes this term. Next term maybe none? I'll drink to that. He also really should have those j-o-w-l-s attended to. — Fly-on-the-Wall

I'd like to de-jowl you, you manipulating fucker! It sounded almost like an admission: I'm sending in bad reviews of you, and there's not a damn thing you can do about it! Maybe Nathaniel should finally ask the students he thought liked him — and there were more of those than the world seemed to believe — to send in some positive reviews? How craven. No, he would not do it!

He sent an e-mail back to Haywood:

> I'd be happy to share my media duties with you. Interested? — Nathaniel

> No way!

> Good luck with the lawsuit, though. — Haywood

⟋

Karma Sudra seemed a little peeved with Nathaniel when she came to his office the next day. "I have been informed what 'doggy style' means," she said. "I wish you had told me."

"I thought you knew," Nathaniel answered, not entirely honestly.

"I am told I made quite a sight saying 'Woof! Woof!' that night."

"You were magnificent."

"It does not matter. I would do it again," Karma said. "It is important that we fight back!"

You go, girl! Nathaniel thought. "What have you got there?"

She was holding a large sheet of yellow paper with what looked like several signatures on it. She was wearing four metal bracelets, two on each wrist, and a pale pink sari and seemed to have darkened her eyebrows. She'd given a good polish to her bejeweled forehead as well. All in all, Karma, if a little tacky, seemed flushed with vigor and purpose.

"I have here a petition to the Board of Trustees," she said. "Which I would like you to sign."

"For . . . ?"

"To protect their faculty. It is proving most difficult to get people to sign." She gestured at the office next door. She meant Tadd and Guy but didn't want to name names.

"They're not there now, I'm pretty sure," Nathaniel said.

"I hoped to catch you yesterday, but you weren't around. So I asked both of them. At first Mr. Dryer said he would sign, and yet by the end of the conversation he backed out."

"He's a wienie," Nathaniel said.

"Mr. Mountain said that he supports the website."

"He's a wienie too — and a masochist. Who have you got so far?" Nathaniel leaned down to see the names.

"Two people from Nursing."

He didn't recognize the names.

The petition said:

> We, the undersigned faculty of Shite College, condemn the practices of the online website called Teachersonparade and would speak out publicly against it, but we fear abuse, harassment and retaliation since our positive reviews could be removed and negative ones could be sent in by anyone who wants to target us, thus affecting our class enrollment and our general safety. In the light of these threats and others, we cannot appear before the Board, but we beg the Board to protect its faculty and not allow this situation to continue.
>
> Thank you

"You could get only two signatures?"

"Several more wished to sign, but they're afraid their names will get out. I assured them I will hold all signatures and report only the total number to the Board."

"What about the people who were willing to sign on, like you, until the lawyers said they'd use only my name? Have you tried them?"

"I'm not completely clear on who they may be. I thought perhaps you would go with me to find them."

"Let's go!" Nathaniel gathered some ungraded papers and stuffed them into his briefcase, combed down his hair with his fingers, locked the door, and then led Karma toward the main office of the English Department, not sure what good such a begging petition would do, but why not? They got Spike Burns to sign, but three others refused. "I'm up for tenure. I can't risk it," one adenoidal-voiced woman excused herself.

"Another wienie," Nathaniel said under his breath.

Tall, skinny Gilda LaMatresse saw them coming and deliberately turned around and hurried off.

"I don't want Gilda's signature anyway," Nathaniel said. The woman had sent to all the members of the department copies of a poetry chapbook she'd had printed, detailing her adulterous affair with a Honduran field worker during her sabbatical the year before. The title was *O! Hands of the Field*, if he remembered correctly. Not only was the plea for looser immigration rules misplaced and self-interested, the poetry was the kind that only a creative writing teacher would read.

They didn't see anybody else they knew, since it was in the late afternoon. "Let's try the Academic Senate," Nathaniel said. "Do you mind if I stop and feed the feral cats while we're at it?"

Karma didn't seem to be much of a cat person, but she didn't say no. So Nathaniel got some wet food, some dry food, a bottle of water, some plastic plates, and his knee pad out of his car, and they stopped by the Equal Opportunity Bungalow. "Here, kitty, kitty!" Nathaniel called. "It's picnic time!"

"Might you not be contributing to the vermin on campus?" Karma asked disdainfully.

"We are the campus of vermin, and it is all good!" Nathaniel said, trying to improve his own karma, throwing away the leftovers and the cans and other trash into a barrel.

They passed other wondrous sights on the campus: six open-air marts for CLOTHING FASHIONS OF THE THIRD WORLD, a sign that read: BE PREPARED FOR COLLEGE — DIRECTIONS TO FINANCIAL AID OFFICE, one R.O.T.C. recruitment table (which had once been picketed by GLOP, the Gay/Lesbian/and Other People campus group — except that the R.O.T.C. had outlasted them, at least for a while). There was a rag-tag reggae band playing loudly even though classes were still going on.

There appeared to be a large collection of souls at the rear of Shite Quad, near where the Academic Senate office was located. When Karma and Nathaniel got closer, they could see what had attracted the crowd: a pimply young, naked male student holding a small sign:

I WARE NO CLOTHES

IN SOLIDARITY WITH

"Maybe we should take off our clothes and get signatures that way," Karma said.

Nathaniel didn't answer.

"You don't like him?" Karma asked.

"No wonder the desks smell the way they do around here," he said.

All in all, they managed to get a total of five signatures.

On his computer at home Nathaniel got an e-mail that evening that was more than a little disturbing:

> Saw You! You And Your "little" Woman Out Trying to Gather Ammunition. Butt Your Campain Is Doomed. No Petition. A Ridiculous Lawsuit U Will Never Win. Give up and Die!

> GOT IT? GIVE UP AND DIE!

He would have tried to have the message traced, but no doubt it had come from one of those services that assured absolute anonymity. What if someone had left this on his answering machine? Wouldn't it be considered a crank call, actionable in some way? Had the writer carefully crafted the "Give Up and Die" instead of "Give Up Or Die"? And who had sent it? Was this just one person or several? Cut off one head and more would grow?

All he could do with this one was delete it — and hope it also didn't carry a virus. Technology will save us from human nature! Yeah, right.

Just to be sure, before he deleted it, he forwarded a copy to Haywood Wire. He would have preferred discussing it with Karma Sudra, who was, if not quite a friend yet, at least someone he could rely on. But she wasn't online yet, naturally.

Haywood wrote back:

> Nathaniel,

> They're watching your every move. Be careful!

> This is what comes of courting the media!

> Have you thought what might happen if you lost the lawsuit? You could wind up paying the legal expenses of the opposing side. Did the lawyers make this clear? I'm glad I didn't sign on after all. How awful to be humiliated in public if you lose! — Haywood

With friends like this, the Satanist was looking pretty good.

> Nathaniel,
>
> I have devised a method by which to flood Teachersonparade with multiple reviews. I have been working on this for some time now, and might be able to saturate the site in such a way that the fake reviews coming from our enemies can be counter-balanced by our fake reviews. I will only send positive reviews. — Haywood

> Haywood,
>
> Won't these fake reviews become obvious very soon? — Nathaniel

> Nathaniel,
>
> But removing them might keep Doo Doo Boy (the webmaster) so busy he'll want to pull the plug on the site.

> Haywood,
>
> How many reviews are we talking about?

> Nathaniel,
>
> Hundreds. I've devised a program to automatically go through the list of faculty names on the site and spit out reviews. I still need to make it more random, so that Doo Doo Boy won't be able to counter-program!

This just in, world! Tap Dancing Santa Claus in Face Off with Doo Doo Boy! Stay tuned!

> Haywood,
>
> I don't know if it will do any good or not, but I am glad to hear that you might participate in the cause. — Nathaniel

And get off your scared, tap-dancing ass at last!

Nathaniel,

By the way, there's a very glowing review of you on the site now. Have you seen it? It says you're an excellent instructor. Shall I send it to you?

Haywood,

Don't bother sending it. I will not live and die or teach — by whether someone has praised me or assailed me this minute or in the minute to come. I'm hopping to enough tunes already.
— Nathaniel

Nathaniel,

Suit yourself. I'll let you know when I'm ready to roll with the Cornucopia (spell?) of Reviews! — Haywood

I'll believe it when I see it, Nathaniel thought.

Nathaniel didn't believe that dreams foretell the future or even reveal psychological truths. They were probably no more than real events being chewed up and eliminated from the brain. He was dressed in his pajamas, full of holes — not just the pajamas — even his body was full of holes, and he was holding something like a big paper towel and kept squatting and trying to pick up this huge messy turd, but he kept dropping it.

Now what could that dream mean?

The dream had seemed to take up the entire night, and so when Nathaniel got to school he was un-rested and more than a little cranky. Who should be waiting for him at his office hour but Antwan Timmons. "Do I need an appointment?" he asked.

"Not at all," Nathaniel said, unlocking the door. He put his handful of mail on the desk and left the door ajar. Antwan took the chair near the desk. He didn't look particularly nervous, even though their last encounter had been in the bushes. Maybe the "diamond" stud in his left ear was new. Otherwise, he looked about the same, tending toward plumpness, round-faced, neatly dressed. He was still wearing two wristwatches, one on each wrist.

"You missed some classes," Nathaniel said, sitting down, his insides a bit tight.

"I'm afraid I'm going to have to drop the course, Professor."

"Really?" What a relief, but of course that sentiment wouldn't be expressed. "Do you want me to give you a 'W' on the final census sheet, or do you want to take care of it yourself?" Nathaniel never asked students why they were dropping. That was their business.

"You can do it for me?"

"Would you like that?"

"If it's not too much trouble."

"No trouble at all. Is there anything else?"

"I did enjoy the course."

"Did you? Well, thank you for being in the course."

Cum wouldn't melt in their mouths, it seemed.

"I disagree with almost everything you say, but you're still a good teacher."

"Thanks. I'm sure I'll remember you too."

"Of course I did get A's in my other courses. Not just a B-minus."

"Is that why you're dropping?" Oops!

"Not really. I have to devote more time to the lawsuit — your lawsuit. As the new president of the Alliance, it's my job to coordinate our efforts with the lawyer."

"This is the lawyer the Chancellor paid for?"

"He paid for two lawyers actually."

"Did he? I guess I'm out of the loop. I don't believe he got a lawyer for the faculty. I'm pretty certain about that." Nathaniel moved his mail forward on the desk, for something to do.

"There are in fact separate lawyers for each of the parties you've sued."

"No kidding. Must be scared, huh?"

"Our lawyer thinks we will prevail and that the other side — you — will have to pay us. The legal expenses could be . . . what's the word I want?"

"Considerable?"

"That's it! For the expenses of our lawyer, the college's two lawyers, and the lawyers that Dude Lather will probably get."

"And who might all these lawyers be?" Know your enemies.

"You'll see their names on our legal response to your Complaint."

"Can't wait."

"It looks like the American Civil Liberties Union is going to represent the webmaster."

"What?!"

"I believe they're negotiating even as we speak."

"Why would the American Civil Liberties Union defend lies about teachers, especially homophobic ones?"

"That's what I hear. We're very excited about it." Antwan's smile made him look a bit checkmatey.

"I doubt the ACLU will take on the case once it sees the kind of crap that's actually on the site!" Nathaniel was getting hot under the collar.

"Don't be too sure."

"How can you sit there and tell me you enjoyed my course and not be upset by the unfair and queer-baiting stuff that appears there?"

"Not all the teachers are as good as you, Dr. Tack."

Yeah, right. Was some kind of offer being made? We'll let up on you, Professor, if you withdraw your lawsuit?

"I'm sure some teachers are not everything they should be. Some may even be terrible. But this website is not the answer."

"You haven't seen them teach, have you?"

Nathaniel faltered. "Not all of them, no."

"The students are just trying to get the best instructors they can."

"That sounds pretty, Mr. Timmons, but I don't believe it. There are other ways than anonymous ranting online. It doesn't make the teachers change, and it certainly shows the students at their worst."

"The site might work if certain people didn't try to interfere with it." Antwan folded his arms across his chest.

"What is that supposed to mean?" Had they heard about Haywood's plan to flood the site already? Were they hacking in to his e-mails?

"Someone who shall remain nameless caught a teacher sending in fake reviews."

"Oh?" Nathaniel wondered if this meant him — the few early reviews of teachers he'd sent in. "It's not only teachers who are sending in fake reviews!"

"You don't trust students to be fair?" Now Antwan was getting hot under the collar.

"Are you kidding? Of course not!"

"Don't know how you got so cynical about students, Professor."

"Years of experience!" Nathaniel said. This was too easy! He swung around in his chair to look directly at the student.

"It seems to us to be a vicious campaign to undermine the credibility of the website."

"Its credibility is already undermined."

"This teacher who caught someone sending in fake reviews is on our side. He says that one of the reviews sent in is about you."

"I didn't ask any teacher to send in a good review of me. Just as I am not asking you to send in a good review of me. My point is, and always has been, that the website allows this kind of distortion to exist and to proliferate. It can't be allowed to go on without destroying the integrity of the entire teaching profession."

"Isn't that a little 'grand,' Professor?" Antwan went on. "This teacher was using a computer in the library and was spotted red-handed."

"I don't know who it is — if that's what you're asking."

"It was Mr. Thorgoode of the Physics Department — as if you didn't know." Antwan's lips were pursed.

"I don't know, as a matter of fact."

"He was helping you with your banners that night we were all in front of the Board. So he's your ally."

"I think he was helping Professor Karma Sudra because she was having trouble. I don't know the man very well at all. If he's an ally, it's news to me."

"And do you approve of what he's done — misleading students?"

"Everybody is misleading everybody! Don't you see that? The technology is allowing the worst traits of human beings to surface."

"Well, Thorgoode has made it worse. He was caught and he will be dealt with."

"Oh, will he? What does that mean, Mr. Timmons?"

"He was using campus facilities in an effort to distort the reviews."

"How many students have used campus facilities for the same purpose?"

"Not very many."

"You're wrong, Mr. Timmons. I don't know how many there are myself, but there is a group — a cabal, if I may. It could be just one or two people. I don't know how many it takes to create a cabal. The point is they are targeting the teachers of their choice, especially anyone who dares to stand up to this new form of the Inquisition — anonymous, unproven charges, destruction of reputation — wanton, flippant destruction at that! You can't tell me that you defend this?"

"It's all we have to defend ourselves! The teachers have all the power! This way we can level the playing field."

"So the playing field can be what it is in most American schools? Playing fields, my ass. Educational sink holes!"

"When was the last time you were in one of these schools, Professor? Recently?"

"No, not recently."

"Yet you're so sure they're bad."

"All I have to go by is what shows up in my college classrooms. I'll be happy to show you some proof." Nathaniel reached out a hand toward a pile of discarded student essays and exams never picked up for one reason or another.

"That's not necessary."

"Sure?"

They seemed to have come to an impasse.

"I guess I'd better be going," Antwan said, standing up.

"By the way, who was this teacher snitch who reported Biff Thorgoode?"

"I'd rather not say."

"Why not?"

"I'd just rather not, that's all."

"So he can live to snitch again? Which part of the library was this in?"

"I don't know. I don't consider him a snitch either."

"That's all right, Mr. Timmons. I'll find out on my own."

"I doubt that you will."

There was a pause. It was obvious as Antwan stood next to Nathaniel's desk that the student was "interested." There was a pause as Antwan stared down between Nathaniel's legs. "Want to fool around?" he mouthed very quietly.

Nathaniel grew aroused instantaneously. That old Viagra wouldn't work this well in a million years, he'd bet. But he didn't move.

"No, thank you, Antwan," he said just as quietly.

It didn't even seem to be a trap — just that Antwan liked risky sex.

"I'll take a rain check," Nathaniel said.

Antwan smiled. "See you in court, Professor." And with that, the young man disappeared.

CLONE THE POPE!

That's what the sticker on the office next door said. There had been a growing movement to continue the reign of the presiding Pontiff, who was ailing in a very noticeable manner, by taking some of His Holiness's DNA and reproducing a clone that could then continue the same conservative policies as his "predecessor." Nathaniel wondered if the sticker was Tadd Dryer's or Guy Mountain's. He knew Tadd was Christian, but wasn't it some Protestant denomination? And he didn't remember Guy being especially Catholic. He hadn't talked to either one in months, had barely seen them. It didn't get any better than that. But hadn't he heard that Guy sometimes worked in the library — in the Rodney King Study Lab?

He hung around his office, grading some papers and waiting for Guy to show up. It didn't take that long. Teachers were easy to find.

It took a lot longer to swallow his pride, but Nathaniel considered Machiavellianism the better part of valor, at least in fighting Machiavellianism, and so he stuck his head around the door of Guy's office. "Long time, no see," he said, almost choking on his own words.

Guy, if anything, had gained weight. He looked like one of the leads in *Beauty and the Beast*, and it wasn't Beauty. The pits in his nose may have been hereditary or from adolescent acne, and no question were not his fault. The page boy hairdo was. So was the bad posture. He gave a non-committal "Yes."

"I was wondering how your mother is." Nathaniel hadn't been invited in, so he stayed half in the hallway.

"I'm afraid my mother passed."

"No! I'm sorry to hear that."

Guy looked up, vulnerable. Aha, the way to this man was through his mother's bowels! "Yes. About a month ago."

"So the transplant didn't work, I guess." Nathaniel shook his head in sympathy.

"She had a second transplant, but to no avail."

Two anal transplants, and yet God took her. (There had to be a message there somewhere.) Nathaniel stopped short of asking if he'd saved any of his mother's DNA so that he might, possibly, have her cloned too.

"Did you want something?" Guy asked. He was obviously unforgiving of the argument they'd had about Teachersonparade.

"You still working in the library?"

"Two nights a week. Been trying to earn some extra money in the Study Lab. I won't need to next semester, since Mom is gone now."

Should Nathaniel just come right out and ask him if he was the one who'd snitched on Biff Thorgoode? Perhaps this pussyfooting around wasn't even necessary. "I'm sorry about our quarrel. What's your feeling about Teachersonparade these days?"

"Still a supporter. I understand you're suing a bunch of people over it." Guy was squatting down with his broad back to Nathaniel, getting something out of a file cabinet. At least he didn't show Plumber's Butt. "You may be biting off more than you can chew, I hope you realize. Personally I don't wish you any ill will."

"The generic ill will is bad enough."

Still squatting, hands in the file drawer, Guy looked around at him. "Are you trying to find out if I turned over some information I learned in the library?"

Yikes! I'm a terrible spy, Nathaniel thought. But he was adaptable. "Did you?"

"I saw Biff Thorgoode sending in what I took to be phony reviews of various instructors around here. I forwarded this information to the young man who runs the website."

"Are you as assiduous in turning in students who're sending in fake reviews?"

"I haven't noticed those, I must say."

"That could be because they do it from the comfort of their own homes or anywhere else they please."

"Biff Thorgoode chose to come into the Study Lab —"

"The Rodney King Study Lab."

Guy shrugged that off. "— and in my presence sent in any number of reviews that I could tell were not written by students."

"Did you sneak up behind him?"

"I didn't have to. It was obvious enough." Guy got up from his squat with a couple of file folders in hand. Nathaniel thought they might be intended for him, but they weren't.

"You're positive he sent in actual reviews, not just comments on Speak Out Loud?"

"I did walk over, to be sure. I saw your name on a review. Thorgoode has never been your student, I presume."

"Doesn't all this prove to you that all the website is a fraud? If Biff Thorgoode is doing this, why don't you suppose lots of other people are doing it too?"

"If they would stop doing it, the site could function as it was intended!" Guy snapped.

"Not true, Guy. That would just let the other side get to do all the manipulating of the reviews."

"It would work if people let it work!"

You hopeless liberal! Nathaniel thought. To think I used to be as sappy as you.

"People will act decently if given the chance."

"Guy, are we living in the same universe?"

"I'm busy with something I have to do. Do you mind if we stop discussing this?"

Nathaniel was startled by the abruptness. "Of course not."

Guy sat down at his desk with his back to him. "You're going to be very sorry you ever brought this lawsuit, Nathaniel."

"I doubt that," he answered.

But doubt it he did.

Not long after, his lawyer called with some bad news. It was Seamus O'Harromog. Modos seemed to have dropped off the face of the earth. "He's busy on another case" was the cold explanation he got when Nathaniel asked.

"The ACLU has come in to defend Teachersonparade and the webmaster. I just had it confirmed this morning."

"But why would it do that?"

"I doubt they have even looked at the website."

Nathaniel felt sick to his stomach. He had once belonged to the ACLU, back when he was young and it wasn't foolish.

"I spoke with Minna Thicke, one of the officers. She was one of the attorneys at that legal meeting at Shite called by your Chancellor," O'Harromog said.

"He's not my Chancellor!"

"I know Minna well. Wolfgang and I are on the Board of the ACLU."

"Don't you get priority or something from the ACLU? You were there first."

"I spoke with her half an hour ago and asked her how she'd feel if people reviewed lawyers like her on a website and said she had accepted drugs as bribes from her clients — or sex. She said she was sorry if any teacher's feelings have been hurt —"

"For Christ's sake, it's far more than hurt feelings! What's wrong with that woman!?"

"She said the principle of free speech overrides anything else."

"Doesn't she realize non-students are sending in reviews?"

"I don't think it matters to her."

"How can it not matter to her that people who aren't students are reviewing teachers while pretending to be students?! This is crazy!"

"The ACLU pretty much believes in an absolute interpretation of free speech guaranteed by the First Amendment."

"They're as bad as the right-wingers with the Second Amendment and guns. Words can kill just as much as guns."

"I argued with her, but she wasn't having it."

"And that means?"

"They are getting another firm — a large one — to handle the day to day. Tether and Shaft, I think. I'll let you know for sure."

"You're still handling the case, though, right?"

"We are." There wasn't a whole lot of enthusiasm in the man's words.

"Great. Thank you."

"There is something of a conflict of interest now, since we're on the Board of the ACLU."

"There is?"

"We can probably work around it."

"Great! I really appreciate it."

"This case is getting more complicated than we first thought."

"I really, really appreciate you taking it on and sticking with me. Would it help if more teachers signed on? I have a number who are willing to now."

"No, we'll go with you. How are the media treating you?"

"I've just had two reporters."

"Well, expect the ACLU to put something about you up on its webpage. And don't expect it to be flattering."

"Maybe I can sue them for libel!"

O'Harromog didn't laugh. Nathaniel doubted that he laughed at anything.

"Just be very cautious with any media that may get in touch with you. Remember, they aren't your friends."

"I'll be careful."

"God, I was hoping against hope that the ACLU wouldn't come in on the other side. It has hundreds and hundreds of lawyers at its disposal." This was the most emotion Nathaniel had ever heard out of O'Harromog's mouth, and it wasn't encouraging.

The ACLU did put something up on its website, saying that Dr. Nathaniel Tack of Shite College "is attempting to stop his students from saying what a bad teacher he is." It was an out-and-out libel, and the organization had hundreds and hundreds of lawyers to defend its libel, never mind the libel from Fly on the Wall and any number of crackpots and failed students who felt the urge to have at Nathaniel and anyone else they chose to.

A big radio station called and asked him to be on the morning call-in show with the host, Lon Owens, but he turned it down. He heard some of the program anyway, and most of the talk went against him. It was just assumed that he was a lousy teacher. The fact he had been invited to appear on the show and had refused also indicated — did it not? — his guilt? I'm not turning down any more offers, if they come, he vowed.

Like most of life, the rest of the time was waiting, waiting. When would the ACLU file its Special Motion to Strike and its fucking Demurrer?

The bastards even had the gall to offer Nathaniel an out before they had to spend any more of their precious time and money writing up their legal response. He could "get out now" if he would agree to the following items:

1) He would remove all legal Complaints now filed.

2) He would never again file a Complaint against any of Said Parties and their Assigned — or was it their Asinined? — until the end of time. Whatever.

3) He would agree to pay the ACLU's expenses, as to be determined by them.

4) He would write a Public Apology, which would be distributed to the press. A copy of an acceptable Apology was included in the packet sent by Modos & O'Harromog. It read:

1) I, Nathaniel Tack., Ph.D., instructor in English at Shite College of Santa Francesca, hereby abjure and disown any and all legal Complaints made against the website known as Teachersonparade, its webmaster, as well as against the Board of Trustees of Shite College and against its official affiliate, The Alliance of Students.

2) I, further, express my profound regret and confess shame at having tried to undermine the First Amendment of the Constitution of the United States of America and its Possessions in having brought this legal Complaint in the first place.

3) I, in addition, promise to work to better educate myself and others in the principles of protected Free Speech, as is only fitting for someone in a position such as I myself enjoy.

4) Lastly, I will promise to encourage my students to use Teachersonparade and to avail myself of the offered advice there presented.

That plus a scarlet T (for Teacher on Parade) and a "ye olde fucke up the arse" with a broomstick from Dude Lather, and how could Nathaniel refuse?

Unlike Galileo, he declined the order of recantation from the Holy Office. The ACLU had better not win this, Nathaniel realized, or they might indeed force me to acknowledge the Internet as the Center of the Universe.

"I was nearly arrested again," Marty said on the telephone. His voice was almost metallic in its bitterness.

"What happened?" Nathaniel was trying to check Slacker's butt. She seemed constipated and uncooperative about solving the problem.

"The cops pulled up in three separate cars and put their lights in my eyes. They made me stand with my hands on the roof of my car and then frisked me. Again!"

"When was this?"

"Last night. This morning."

"So you're still sitting in your car and playing music."

"You bet I am!"

"Did you have any drugs on you?"

"A little grass. Don't tell me I can't sit in my own car!"

"I didn't say a word." He started following Slacker around the condo. "Come here, you!"

"Who are you talking to?"

"Nobody." The cat was trying to squeeze behind the sofa.

"Then the cops said I was running a drug business out of my car."

"What?!"

"They're insane! They believe everything that asshole neighbor tells them."

"Why is that?"

"They're so stupid they assume it's true before they even get there, and nothing will change their minds."

"Did they see any drugs in your car?" He was kneeling on the sofa now, reaching down, only the cat's tail sticking out.

"Marijuana – which is not a 'drug.'" Marty's voice was up to whatever comes after metal.

"I'm just trying to get the picture. Hah — got you!" Slacker wasn't happy.

"What are you doing?"

"I'm checking Slacker." He was holding her tail up so that he could see if there was some impaction in her backside. He knew that if told Marty this, he'd be angry and accuse him of not caring about Marty's problems. You're more interested in your fucking cat's ass than in anything that happens to me!

"What's wrong with her?"

"She's a little under the weather."

"Take her to the vet's. Do you want to hear my story or not?"

Nathaniel forced his own voice into neutral. "Of course. They frisked you and then what?"

"They searched my car and took my pipe."

"Why?"

"Because they're drug-obsessed fuckheads."

"Stand still."

"What's Slacker doing now?"

"I'm examining her eyes."

"Has she got that yucky stuff she gets sometimes?"

Nathaniel was actually looking up the car's butthole, trying to pry without getting anything on his fingertip. "Then what happened?"

"They looked up my 'record.' It said I'd been questioned for being a pimp for goddamn she-male prostitutes."

"Now don't get mad, Marty. But were you doing that on the side?"

"I'm going to slam this phone down!"

"Don't do that. Ouch!"

"What?"

"Slacker scratched me. You bitch."

"Where did she scratch you?"

"On the back of my hand. But she didn't get away."

"What are you doing to her? Christ!"

"I'm checking her eyes!"

"Did you poke them?"

"Yeah, I poked them out, and that's why she scratched me."

"I don't think you know how to handle pets. You still let her out, don't you? No wonder she gets things wrong with her eyes."

"You like to get out of your house. She likes to get out of hers. But she doesn't have a car to sit in."

"You'll be sorry one day when she doesn't come back."

"She hardly leaves the house anymore. So what happened to the cops? Why do they believe him and not you?"

"Because they've got me down for a number of arrests now."

Am I really here? Nathaniel thought. Am I alive and in the known world and talking about my lover's non-existent she-male prostitutes while looking up a constipated cat's butthole?

Apparently so.

Yet things — Praise God! — have a way of working themselves out. Marty had convinced the cops that he didn't have any she-male prostitutes in his car and they'd let him go with a warning, and Slacker had a good crap on the side and rim of her litter box that wafted throughout the condo for only a day and half.

Come to think of it, these events weren't any more absurd than the ACLU defending the right of people who had never taken a class from a teacher to write a review, and a libelous review at that, or numerous libelous reviews if they felt like it, and claiming that the Founding Fathers of the United States of America had intended this nonsense when they wrote the Constitution, or even that Congress had intended this with Article 247, Paragraph 230 of the U.S. Legal Code. What was wrong with people anyway? They were always claiming some parchment or some tablets or some book had come out of the sky and was to be followed blindly, however preposterous it might it be.

The ACLU's legal response to Modos & O'Harromog contained some of these marvelous inanities:

1) The Teachersonparade website is a "welcome addition to the Shite College Community."

2) The website is open to post and read reviews of the "teaching performance of instructors." [liking it "doggy style" being no doubt a major component of any good teacher's performance]

3) Each review is just ONE student's opinion. [except when it's not, which is often]

4) That opinion may also have been submitted by a non-student or teacher, as is clear from the many Disclaimers and Content Guidelines on the site. [one, in print so tiny and so buried at the end of the prefatory material as to be equivalent to the head of a pin, or the head of the webmaster, whichever you prefer, to say nothing of the fact that these "Disclaimers" were added in the last few weeks before we wrote this and nobody reads Disclaimers anyway!]

5) As the webmaster of the Teachersonparade website, Drew A. ("Dude") Lather is a "provider" and a "user" of an "interactive computer service" within the meaning of the Federal Communications Decency Act, 47 U.S.C., Section 230. [Yeah, Dude was just like AOL, and Fly on the Wall was his Prophet!]

6) The third-party statements complained of by Plaintiff comprise opinion, invective, and hyperbole and parody that are not provably false, and therefore are protected by the United States and California Constitutions. [How does one prove the false Karma Sudra versus the true Karma Sudra? Will it please the Court to take her word that she doesn't like it "doggy style"?]

7) The Plaintiff has failed to show the probability that he will prevail as required by the anti-SLAPP suit statute, Code of Civil Procedure [Blah Blah Blah.]

The lawyer that the ACLU had sub-contracted for all this legal mumbo-jumbo was named Gus Strappado, of Tether & Strafe, and he and his staff had churned out thirty-one pages to Modos & O'Harromog's seven. It made you want to anti-slap his face. Online Nathaniel looked up Strappado's picture at his firm. He looked to be about forty-two with a bilious complexion and sour expression and a nostril-filled nose that arched up in a very unbecoming manner. The theory of humours wasn't in fashion any longer, of course, but this guy seemed to have more than his fair share of yellow bile combined with a legal writing style that leaned toward the smarmy. Smarm — wasn't that the lost fifth humour? Easy for him to say the case was "clearly meritless."

And what kind of law made you have to prove your case before you got a chance to prove your case? Not all these reviews were "reviews," either. They were vicious libels, most of them, not about actual teaching and not funny in the least, and thus not to be dismissed as humor or parody. Nathaniel was beginning to see that by laughing at the defamation and singling out the most outrageous ones he was actually making the case harder to prove. But the people accessing the site didn't think the accusations against the teachers were jokes. In fact most of the comments seemed to be offered and accepted as the outraged — and therefore legitimate — cries of oppressed students, who were the victims of endless "raceism," "sexeism," "youtism," "unfare grading," and every other sort of crime a teacher can commit against a student, up to and including "Mr. Wuckdurst want to have sex with me and when I said No and he gave me a F." With more coming in daily!

Maybe I'll have to stop making it seem like a big, nasty joke or I won't win this thing in any court, Nathaniel told himself. Modos & O'Harromog weren't humorless ice bags for nothing, and they had the headlines on their walls to prove it.

The court date was less than a month away. *The New York Times* had called the day before, having been referred by his lawyers, and asked Nathaniel a lot of questions. He thought he'd done a fairly good job of arguing his side. He was getting more practiced in getting his points made in quotable media bites. Like most, the reporter found it hard to believe that there were no restrictions on fake reviews by any and all who wanted to write them. Nathaniel knew he'd have to keep hammering this point to overcome the misconceptions, now made worse by the ACLU's blatant lies on its website. But the woman reporter wasn't hostile and after a while even sounded sympathetic.

When O'Harromog called him to "come and discuss the case," he was a bit apprehensive, but at last they were getting down to the nitty-gritty of how to argue before a jury. Thus Nathaniel was feeling upbeat when he went to the lawyers' mansion and was invited in by yet another handsome young male legal assistant with a warm demeanor. He continued to feel pretty good when O'Harromog came down from upstairs, holding some folders, and ushered him into the room with the long oval table and the impressive views. There was just the beginning of a hesitation of the heart when O'Harromog, tall and elegant in a black turtleneck sweater and expensive, retro "Farm Boy" trousers, closed the sliding doors in a way that somehow portended bad news. It almost seemed as if he was blocking anyone from overhearing what he was about to say.

As he sat to Nathaniel's right at the table, he placed the legal papers just so and looked up. A smile rose from somewhere deep in the ice pack and locked into place on the not-unpleasant face as if it had been arranged there by the interior decorator who had done the whole office. "So how did the interview with *The New York Times* go?"

"Fine. It should be out in a few days."

"I gave the reporter a quotation too."

"Wonderful."

The smile was replaced with a more serious expression. This too seemed manufactured, prepared in advance. "I'm afraid we're going to have to withdraw from the case, Nathaniel."

Something broke off Nathaniel's heart and fell to the pit of his stomach. "You what?"

"I'm afraid there's a conflict."

"What do you mean?"

"I believe I mentioned to you already that Wolfgang and I are both on the Board of the ACLU."

"Yes."

"Therefore, we feel we have to withdraw, now that the ACLU has definitely come in on the other side."

"But you were there first."

"That's true, but we can't handle a case with such an obvious conflict of interest."

"Why doesn't the ACLU drop out then?"

O'Harromog smiled indulgently. "I'm afraid it has a bit more leverage than we do. Besides, I am planning to take a six-month sabbatical and go to Australia. That won't leave much time to deal with the case."

"What about Wolfgang? Can't he handle it?"

"I'm afraid he's busy with other cases. We have quite a few cases, you realize."

"I'm sure you do."

"And then we just lost a staff lawyer, and we have to do a long search for a new one."

"Well, I can wait," Nathaniel said. "I've waited before. Can't we get a postponement of some kind?"

"A continuance? I'm afraid that's not possible in this situation."

"We can't wait six months?"

"We have discussed it and made up our minds. I'm afraid not."

Nathaniel felt like he had been whacked by a two-by-four. But he didn't know the half of it yet.

"We'll get you another lawyer."

"You will?"

"Of course you should try on your own. Do you have the number of the Bar Association?" He wrote it down on his card and handed it to Nathaniel.

"But I had a very hard time getting a lawyer in the first place."

"I think I know someone who will want to take it on. It's very cutting edge, legally-speaking. There's a lot of interest in the case."

"Who do you have in mind?"

"Karl Nino is a lawyer we've worked with quite a bit. I'll give him a call."

"Thank you." Nathaniel wanted to say a lot of things, such as: "But we've signed a contract and it's less than a month until the court date. How can you drop out? Conflict of interest? You knew the ACLU might come in on this. Why didn't you bring up the conflict of interest before, instead of now, after you've seen their hefty legal response?" However, he didn't know the law. Sure, lawyers had a bad reputation, shall we say, but Modos & O'Harromog had a legal obligation, didn't they, and they were his gay brothers, weren't they?

Snap out of it, Nathaniel!

"So there is a paper you'll have to sign." O'Harromog shuffled the papers before him.

"I will?"

"And then I'll get right on it — about getting a substitute lawyer for you."

"You definitely will get me a new lawyer, right?"

"Definitely. But you have to work at it with us."

"I'll do what I can. But you won't just abandon me, is that correct?"

"You'll have a new lawyer before you know it."

"And just as good as you?"

"Better."

He slid a paper toward Nathaniel. "I'd like you to sign this in two places, once on each line."

"What is it?" He read it through, but the print was tiny and his eyes weren't what they had been. There were also Latin phrases here and there that didn't help.

"It's just a standard form for transfer of legal representation."

"There's nothing specific here." There were some boxes that were unchecked.

"I'll fill them in later and make sure that you get a copy."

It was suspicious as hell, but if you couldn't trust your own lawyer, who could you trust? "I guess I have no choice then?" Nathaniel said. He was careful not to put a check mark in any of the boxes.

O'Harromog looked like ice wouldn't melt in his mouth. "You'll have a new lawyer in no time."

So Nathaniel signed the paper twice.

When his copy arrived the very next day in the mail, O'Harromog or a secretary had typed in Nathaniel's name and address and checked the boxes about the client requiring new legal representation. The new check marks seemed a little odd, but nothing jumped off the page. Nathaniel showed it to Marty and even Karma Sudra, his new best buddy. Neither noticed anything particularly untoward.

It wasn't until a few days later when Modos & O'Harromog weren't returning Nathaniel's calls about the new lawyer they were getting for him, and after his own unsuccessful attempts to get any interest from another lawyer, despite the rather favorable write-up in *The New York Times*, that Nathaniel picked up the paper he had signed and looked at it very carefully. It said "in pro per" about the new lawyer that he, as the plaintiff, wanted and would be getting. And then it finally dawned on him that it said that *he* was the new attorney that he wanted and would be getting!

He didn't want to represent himself! Never in a million years! He knew the old expression about having a fool for a client. He felt like ten fools for having trusted O'Harromog. He felt worse when his gay lawyer brother made copies of the agreement and mailed them to the court and all the lawyers for the other side, giving the impression that he had asked to represent himself, making him look ridiculous in the extreme, and giving the other side an unmistakable legal advantage. Since Nathaniel had no lawyer and couldn't seem to interest a new one, it looked like he might have to withdraw and agree to the humiliating terms of the Settlement proposed.

It was the lowest point so far in the whole low business, and Nathaniel felt stunned. He sent a letter to Modos & O'Harromog when they wouldn't return his calls:

Gentlemen:

I signed a form in your office the other day at your instigation so that you would substitute another comparable lawyer since you were withdrawing — and only because you were withdrawing —after all these months of representing me and all other defamed teachers, especially withdrawing so close to the date of the court hearing. I did NOT check the box saying I wished to represent myself, nor did I initial it. Nor did I agree to have it checked after I left! Nor would I have ever agreed to such a substitution of legal counsel under any circumstances, as you well know. That would leave me vulnerable to financial ruin. I cannot defend myself since I am not a lawyer. Giving me the telephone number of the Bar Association is not getting me a substitute attorney — and in fact is an insult. You should have obtained a comparable substitute attorney for me before you even informed me of this sudden extremely embarrassing and emotionally hurtful change (immediately following the response from the ACLU, no less) and certainly before you rushed off notices to all the other attorneys as well as to the court and who knows who else, leaving me stranded without the legal representation that you agreed to. I thought you were men of integrity and conscience. Was I wrong?

Please inform the courts, the relevant attorneys, the press and any other relevant parties that you are my attorneys until you and I agree that a comparable substitute attorney or attorneys have been obtained. At that time you can transfer my file to that new attorney or attorneys. Anything less is unethical and a violation of our agreement.

He sent a copy to the Clerk of Superior Court, Unlimited Jurisdiction, of the City of Santa Francesca.

A lot of good it did him.

Nathaniel kept trying to find something funny in what had just happened to him, his usual method of coping with the vicissitudes of life, but how could he? His lawyers — former lawyers — were filthy bastards, that was all. It was obvious now why they'd rejected the other possible teachers (at least ten) as litigants and kept him — much easier to get out of their obligation by hoodwinking just the *one* goose instead of a gaggle.

"I told you not to trust them," Haywood said when he was told.

That helped a lot.

"I'm about ready to send in those multiple reviews I told you about. I've got them ready."

"And that's supposed to do what now?" Nathaniel was still reeling from being stabbed in the back.

"To counter the nasty reviews. Do you want to write some reviews I can send in? Positive ones only. The ones I have are all very similar."

"I don't think I should get involved in that, but you do it if you think it will help." It seemed pretty obvious that the webmaster would catch on fairly soon — and probably Nathaniel would get the blame for writing them, whether he had or not.

"More and more of the reviews being sent in are suspicious, it seems to me. Yet the webmaster still lets the bad ones stay for people he doesn't like and removes the bad ones for his friends. There are two more glowing ones for Dean Visigoth just this morning that I suspect were written by Fly on the Wall."

Nathaniel could barely hear Haywood's words his mind was so clouded. There was a physical ache in his shoulders and the back of his neck, reaching all the way up to his skull. "I've got to go," he said.

"I'll let you know when the cascade of reviews starts flowing," Haywood said.

Nathaniel went to bed and stayed there for a whole night and a day. Even Stalker thought he was there for too long and meowed at him to get up. Marty didn't call, and he hadn't heard from his son in weeks. Even the vodka that remained in the last bottle he had bought didn't look tempting. His electric blanket wasn't working properly — with one side burned out. He felt sticky because he hadn't washed in over a week, and the hair on his face was grizzled and hurt when he moved on the pillow. He still had a few classes and final exams to get through. He felt like he didn't want to live anymore.

He heard nothing from Modos & O'Harromog about the letter he had sent them, and he knew that he wouldn't. They had written him off, and there wasn't a thing he could do about it. Sue a lawyer? With what?

Radio station KQED got his home number and called and asked if he would do an interview about his case. He felt terrible, but he made himself sit up in bed and answer the questions.

When he was asked about his lawyers, he told the interviewer the truth — O'Harromog had duped him into signing a paper that got the lawyers off the hook and made Nathaniel his own attorney, and they had made it seem as if this was his idea and his wish. He even used the words "deceived" and "abandoned their client."

He got calls from Irene and Morgan, old friens, who had heard him on the radio in their car. Even Marty had heard it. But Nathaniel just listened to their messages as he lay in bed, not picking up the telephone. "Are you there?" Marty asked. "Pick up, Nathaniel!"

But he didn't pick up.

He missed classes the next day. He knew he was sinking into despondency, and yet he couldn't stop himself. He managed to get up and eat a piece of toast and go down to his mailbox, still in his pajamas, which were rumpled and even starting to tear at the crotch. He always had his mail to look forward to, it seemed. Sometimes it even had an acceptance or a check in it. Today it had a letter from O'Harromog saying that he'd been told that Nathaniel had made "defamatory accusations" on KQED radio and they were considering pressing charges against him if he didn't stop.

He didn't stop, however. A local TV station called and wanted to know if he was proceeding with the lawsuit, that it had heard that Modos & O'Harromog might sue him, and what did he think of all this. "I'm trying to find another lawyer," he managed to say.

"Aren't you representing yourself now? That's what we heard."

"I have never asked to represent myself, nor would I ever do such a thing," Nathaniel answered. "Modos & O'Harromog are representing me until they get me a comparable lawyer, the way they promised to do."

He called the Lambda Defense Fund and was turned down. He made himself call the Bar Association and got several possibilities. He talked to four lawyers on the phone who had heard of the case, but they were unwilling to take it on contingency. He even dragged himself out of bed, shaved, and arranged with Haywood and Karma to meet with a famous lawyer who had represented the losing side in a *New Yorker* libel suit. The office was lavish; the lawyer was impressive — and he'd just won a million dollars for a bonds salesman who had been mildly defamed — nothing as bad as the "reviews" on Teachersonparade. But the comment had appeared in a business publication. Obviously the reputations of businessmen were of great consequence, while those of teachers were as important as shit. The famous lawyer said that Nathaniel's case was "interesting," "possibly ground-setting," "hard to win," and that he might consider taking it on — if $100,000 could be guaranteed upfront, with more to follow.

Karma offered to sell some jewelry she had. Even Haywood said he might be able to come up with $5000, but Nathaniel had nothing, not a penny, just credit cards and credit card debt. He could possibly borrow against his limited retirement savings, but he was almost sixty years old and they were all he had between him and "the State Home," as his mother used to call it. There was no way they could come up with that kind of money.

Sick to his stomach, he left the office of the famous lawyer ready to end his life — or the lives of the people who had allowed this situation to come into existence. He sat in his car and thought of going to a gun shop and buying an automatic weapon and then going to Dude Lather's house and blowing him away. Then to the Board of Trustees meeting to mow them down one by one. Maybe the Alliance of Students would be there screaming for something, and he could kill them at the same time. He was not just fantasizing, either. He parked in front of a gun shop downtown and sat there for hours, missing yet another day of classes. He then went inside and looked around at the guns. He could see the bullets entering the glasses on the furrowed forehead of Chancellor

McTooney, blood splattering everywhere. Then he'd seek out Dean Visigoth and his Heidi Ho and put them out of Nathaniel's misery, execution style — the back of their heads, but only after they'd begged for their lives.

Oh, he'd probably be caught, even shot and killed before he got off campus. But who wanted to be on this shitty campus any longer anyway? Besides, this was the American Way. Kill a bunch of people and blast your name onto the evening news. Your cause would get publicity, mangled and misrepresented, but by God they wouldn't think you were a wimp they could just screw over. You'd show them! You'd show them their brains spattered from one end of Shite College to the other. A man dedicated to education resorting to violence like this? Well, FUCK irony! When did irony ever get you anywhere?

❧

Nathaniel ultimately didn't buy the automatic weapon and even threw away his stun gun in a garbage dumpster he passed. He went into the garage of his condo and closed the door and rolled down the windows of his aging Rav4 and left the engine running. He put the seat back and closed his eyes. CONTROVERSIAL TEACHER KILLS SELF, said one small headline on page 18 of the *Santa Francesca Chronicle*.

And that is the end of the story.

❧

It very well could have been. But there were two things that saved Nathaniel from despair. Here is one of them:

(Incidentally, he did write a suicide note, never a good sign, and planned to get some pills from a doctor at his HMO. He tried to keep the self-pity to a minimum. However, that's hard when you're writing a suicide note, for Christ's sake. He named guilty names as best he could and told Marty and Jim/Jimmy that he loved them. If there was any money left after the debts were paid and his manuscripts were archived, these two were to split it. He hoped that Marty would take Slacker and treat her well. He hoped that she hadn't eaten parts of his body because he hadn't fed her for a few days.)

But the suicide note was useless because he couldn't finally get the barbiturates from his HMO and the suicide instruction tape from the Hemlock Society never did arrive. Damn those HMO's and the U.S. Postal Service! There was no alternative but to stay in bed and rot to death — or to go out and have sex.

He went to the usual place near the ocean with the cypress trees and the Holy Fog of Forgetfulness. He had received a free sample of Viagra in the mail that day, and he took it as a sign from God, as indeed it was, that he should continue to live and fight. He didn't know what the effects of the Viagra were supposed to be, not exactly, just in general, and his reluctance to over-medicate made him hesitate almost as long as at the gun shop. Eventually, though, he took a whole pill instead of a half, and now here he was an hour later — Pan, somewhat long in the tooth but roaming the spring fields with an anticipatory hard-on, fields that the Pope, the Ayatollah, the President of the US, and any other number of people would like to see shut down and boarded up. Unfortunately, even though it was spring and Pan was anticipatory, there was a mean wind blowing in off the ocean that said Not Tonight, Pal.

Nathaniel also thought he looked like hell: still had his pajama bottoms on underneath his pants, and they were just his everyday pants at that, nothing particularly "sexy." He hadn't bothered to scrape the hairs off his face, and they were very gray, as were the ones in his pubic area. He had lost maybe a pound by not eating the previous few days, but he was still bulky. There were red marks around his waist from his belt being too tight. But it was his birthday, his sixtieth birthday, and the Viagra seemed to be working at least a little magic.

Somebody's dog was wandering among the trees, a pit bull/Maltese mix. Sort of like me, Nathaniel thought. Don't underestimate a Maltese/pit pull mix! It looked like it was sniffing for wild cats, skunks, or raccoons and would have been happy and eager to tear anything it found to pieces. "Move along there!" Nathaniel commanded the dog, whose owner seemed to be nowhere in sight. The dog actually obeyed him.

It wasn't quite dark yet, and there weren't many men cruising because of the cold. Across the way he could hear the distant voices of soccer players, both male and female, caught up in the oh-so-important business of kicking an inflated, round object up and down a field. Nobody would be arresting them for tearing up the field and wasting great lengths of time. Hey, having sex was just as valuable for the participants — more so! Much was always made of how nasty old sex leads to Ruin, not nearly enough about how it really was — crucial at any time but now, at this time, to his very life.

"Hi, big guy," a man in his early thirties said *sotto voce*, standing next to Nathaniel beside a small wooden shed, long neglected. He was virile-looking and handsome of face, could have worked in a garage to judge from the oil spots on his jacket. He was showing an erection, not *sotto voce*, as he spoke. His welcoming words and the proof positive sticking out of his pants' front were more than enough to spark the Viagra to flame. Nathaniel hadn't had an arousal this impressive since . . . ever. Talk about flaunting it!

He took the friendly man's friendly member into his friendly mouth, and it sure beat toast, even hot chocolate and manna from Heaven, if only because sex was more reliable. He had to be careful not to spill over from the sheer joy of the experience. Eros — hot damn! — this was what the scribes surely had been describing all these centuries, impure, unadulterated Eros. Not grading papers. Not long walks along the beach with a barefoot Significant Other. Not fighting stupid and evil tormentors protected by a stupid law! This surging, spiraling cascade of hot, buttered cum — forget the forthcoming cascade of fake reviews by Haywood — this, this indeed was the Meaning of Life!

When the man bent over and took the Viagra-enchanted penis of one Nathaniel Tack (beleaguered faculty member at one benighted college of lower education) into his mouth and moved that mouth back and forth until that penis and adjacent parts welled up and flooded his body and brain with sensations beyond mere human words to convey, there was indeed no more to be said about how good life could be and why it was necessary to hang on to it and suck it dry.

Fifteen minutes later, when the same man did it to Nathaniel again, and this time it took a lot longer, he knew that he would live. "Take it. Take it! Please take it!" he cried. Now here — Sweet Mary Mother of God! — was Free Speech!

Sitting un-bathed and a touch post-orgasmically discontented at his computer, Nathaniel was deciding whether to get a substitute teacher to administer his final exams for him, his virus scanner checking for infected files in his Temporary Internet Files directory, surely one of the newer human experiences, though not that far removed from some poor soul in the past checking for signs of the Black Death in his groin.

His doorbell rang, and he thought it might be Marty come to see why he wasn't answering his telephone, but it was Biff Thorgoode. Biff had helped Karma Sudra with her "doggy style" banner that night before the Board of Trustees and might have sent fake reviews to Teachersonparade, but Nathaniel didn't really know the man. Yet here he was ringing his doorbell. Maybe the school had been burned to the ground. There had been growing rumors of a group of Student Suicide Bombers organizing under the aegis of Gorilla Woman, to protest something or other. Could they have acted already? No doubt, being who they were, they had blown up the whole place by mistake.

"Can I talk to you?" Biff said, through the window in the downstairs door of the condo. He was a big roly-poly man nearing retirement age, with thinning hair, a squint in one eye, a bit slump-shouldered. He was wearing work-out gym clothes — a complete sweat suit made of off-white material.

Nathaniel opened the door. "Yes?"

"Do you know who I am?"

"Yes."

"Can I come in?"

Nathaniel hesitated. "What's it about?"

"I thought I'd take you to lunch. I work out in the gym on the next block, so I was in the neighborhood." He patted his pot belly.

It seemed suspicious. "How did you get my address?"

"My wife teaches in the English Department. She has a home directory."

"Who's your wife?"

"Mary Ann Lubbock."

"May Ann Lubbock is your wife?" He didn't know her very well, either.

"She keeps her own name. Can I come in? It's about the website."

"I suppose." Nathaniel wasn't that sure where Biff stood in all this, but he led him up the steps to his condominium and offered him a cup of coffee.

"Looks like you've been ill," Biff said, sitting on the couch. Slacker didn't like the intruder and skulked off to the bedroom.

The remark made Nathaniel self-conscious, and he grabbed his own face, trying to cover the whiskers on his chin that he still hadn't shaved off. His mustache and hair were more gray than brown, he realized. At least I still care what people think of me, he thought. That has to be good, doesn't it?

"Have you eaten?"

"A little." He didn't clarify that there may have been a small exchange of leaking semen on both sides the night before.

"Let me take you to lunch. You look like — look like you need to get out." Biff had a slight stammer.

"I do. I just can't quite make myself do it."

"I've been in touch with Karma Sudra and Haywood Wire about joining forces with you. I don't know if you know — if you know that I have been experimenting with the review site."

"In what way?"

"I have sent in reviews of people, including you. My wife tells me you're an excellent writing instructor."

"She flatters me."

"I didn't believe you at first when you kept saying that non-students are sending in reviews. But then I tried it — tried it myself." The stammer was annoying, but the words themselves were beginning to sound delightful.

"And what did you discover?"

"I discovered that I could change the grade point average of any instructor I cared to. Haywood has also been sending in multiple reviews the past few days. Have you noticed?"

"I can't bear to look at the website anymore."

"Between the two of us, we've managed to make quite an impact on the site."

"And no one has noticed?"

"I spoke with Haywood on the e-mail this morning, and he said there's been a — been a shutdown of the site!"

"Really?"

"The webmaster put up some message about 'a temporary glitch that needs repair' or something like that. I think we've got him going."

Nathaniel smiled. "I'm glad, but is it going to do any permanent good?"

"Maybe not. The webmaster will no doubt find how to stop Haywood's flood of reviews, at least that."

"Can he trace them back to Haywood?"

"I don't know. I think Haywood most likely has protected himself."

"Most likely."

Biff and Nathaniel exchanged a look of understanding that was worth several thousands words. Thank God for Biff Thorgoode!

"Haywood's quite the character. You've been taking most of the flak in this, haven't you?" Biff was hardly touching his coffee.

"Ours but to do or die," Nathaniel said.

"Shakespeare?"

"'The Charge of the Light Brigade.'"

"I think we'll do better than those folks did."

"One can only hope."

"Why don't you get dressed and let's go to lunch? There are some other aspects of this I need — need to discuss with you. What do you say? I think you need to get out."

Thus Nathaniel got dressed and went to lunch with Biff Thorgoode. In fact, he went to lunch with him three days in a row, and that is the second reason — the kindness of another virtual stranger — that Nathaniel did not kill himself.

To the second lunch they invited Karma Sudra, who didn't eat much and had to leave early in order to get down the Peninsula for another part-time class she taught, this one at the Institute of Tantric Birthing. But, if anything, she seemed more committed than ever to fighting the lies about her on Teachersonparade. Apparently Karma's latest review claimed that she had peed in the Ganges. "They will not beat us into the ground! I have never peed in the Ganges!" she called, tiny fist in the air as she hurried off.

Biff Thorgoode did more than take Nathaniel and Sudra to lunch — he offered to join the lawsuit, in shambles though it was. He said he knew a lawyer who specialized in defamation cases, but he was pretty sure the lawyer would want to be paid something upfront. "I can probably contribute a couple of thousand. How about you?"

"I can use my credit cards." *Après moi, la Deluge.*

"What about Karma?" Biff asked.

"Bless her big soul in that tiny body. We really can't ask her for money, though."

"Does her name mean what I think it means?" Biff asked. "Isn't it an assumed name?"

"What do you think it means?"

"Isn't it a take-off on the *Kama Sutra*, the sex manual?

"I don't really know. I've never asked her."

"That's why I helped her with her banner when she was having trouble that night. I mean, there she is barking and holding up this embarrassing quote about taking it — taking it like a dog, and all I could think about was that sex manual and the different positions it describes, and I knew I had to help that poor woman. I really ought to know more about India."

"I think the *Sudras* are the lowest caste, the Untouchables, and it has something to do with *that*."

"God, the poor woman! She gets it from every side, doesn't she?"

"It would seem so," Nathaniel said. Both he and Biff did their best not to laugh, looking away from each other, because they knew it wasn't funny. Except that it was! There is something in the misfortune of our friends that does not displease us, as a wise man once said. And it wasn't Lord Krishna.

Biff promised to get the information about the defamation specialist to Nathaniel no later than the following week — yet another legal try. In the meantime Biff had some business with his daughter, an aspiring opera singer, to take care of. He was even driving down to Los Angeles to help her out with something to do with nodules on her larynx, if Nathaniel had heard correctly.

Before he left, Biff issued a statement that he e-mailed to all the people on Shite College's list and to Speak Out Loud on Teachersonparade:

To Whom It May Concern,

Hi! I'm Biff Thorgoode of Physics. I want to take this opportunity, as does my wife, Mary Ann Lubbock of the English Department, to speak up against the website known as Teachersonparade. We both, life-long liberals, feel that this is a new form of McCarthyism. Anonymous character assassination and false accusations without accountability occur constantly on this website, which seems to have the approval of Shite College and the Alliance of Students and others. I love Shite College and have devoted almost thirty years of my life to her. I hate seeing this scourge descend upon her. I am hereby announcing that I have, though my wife has not, sent in some forty reviews of teachers. Teachers that I have never had. I did this as an experiment, just as I would in the lab, to see if I could altar the reputtions of various teachers. I sent in only positive reviews and only about teachers I believed I had some legitimate information about, albeit some of it hearsay. What amazed me was that it was so easy to change the entire perception of any given instructor merely by choosing to send in one or more reviews of that instructor. I had been struck by the plight of a part-timer from India in the Nursing Department when she addressed the Board of Trustees and admitted that she had been intimidated into giving higher grades than she wished to do because of the threat by students to write her up on the website. I vowed to myself to help her as best I could. No teacher should have such a weapon held to their throats.

I consider this message I am sending to be something of an experiment itself. I think Teachersonparade may have started as a good idea, but it has become dangerous, even criminal and threatening, and if I can write fake reviews, then anybody can.

So let's see what happens to me because I am pointing out how easy it is to misuse Teachersonparade. I hope I dont regret doing this.

—Bifford G. Thorgoode

Good for you, even with the few errors! Nathaniel thought, as he went off to give his first final exam. But I fear for you. Oh, I fear for you, Biff Thorgoode.

Within a few days the website of course had "corrected the problem" of Haywood's cascade of phony glowing reviews, managing somehow to detect and stop them before they were posted. Why the webmaster couldn't do the same for reviews containing words like "doggy style" and assorted other obscenities of the more typical variety only he knew. In fact there was no reason he couldn't read them *all* before they got posted and then *remove* the ones that libeled somebody. But the incredible law of the Land of the Free and Home of the Stupid said that people like the webmaster were more liable to charges of defamation if they removed offensive material than if they did nothing at all. It made no sense whatsoever and it permitted the webmaster, Fly on the Wall, and their cronies to have the field day they were having writing and posting whatever they wanted to, fearless in their sanctioned, glorious People's right to manufacture whole cloth the sterling reputations of their allies and to destroy the reputations of their enemies.

There was even an editorial in the school's paper, *The Ram's Head* (*The Butthead?*), in which the student editor wrote: "What Mr. Thorfgoode did was wrong. But any student is free to review any teacher that student wants to, whether he or she has had the teacher or not. That's what the First Amendment means!! Get use to it!!"

Naturally, the school paper also crowed with the news that it had been awarded an AWARD FOR JOURNALISTIC EXCELLENCE from the College Journalism Association of Lilliput, or Somewhere. What must that say about the newspapers at other schools? EEEK!!!! did not begin to say the half.

It didn't take long for Them to "get" Biff Thorgoode. It was final exam time and so the campus was less crowded, but still flyers went up from the Alliance of Students:

SAVE OUR WEBSITE!!!

Bifford Thorgoode ADMITS sending bad reviews of teachers.

Physics prof joins Nathan Tack of English in effort

TO DEPRIVE STUDENTS of their rights!

THEY MUST BE STOP!!!

And, yes, some dean had stamped the flyer SHITE COLLEGE APPROVED FOR POSTING.

Because of the use of actual names, the flurry of flyers caused quite a buzz. Gladys, the old gal secretary in the English Department, had several on her desk, and even Spike Burns, the chair, asked Nathaniel what was going on when Nathaniel came in to make copies of an exam. "Only time will tell," he said. "But at least we have a lead on yet another lawyer. And please note that Biff did not 'admit' to sending in a single bad review, only good ones."

"I don't know how you keep at it," Spike said. For him that was a cheer, and Nathaniel took it as such.

"You stop these punks. They come in as rude as you please, ordering me around," Gladys said. She'd been there forever and seen the changes, few of them good.

Biff was out of town, so Haywood started e-mailing Nathaniel again:

> Have you seen what's happening on the website?
>
> Biff is getting bashed left and right. — Haywood

Several examples were attached:

> i say don't take Thorgoodes classes cuz he's an asshole who is trying to f*** with students. give him a taste of his own medicine take another teacher. any other teacher. i had him he stinks.

> Until I heard what Mr. Thorgoode did, I was not in favor of this website. Now I am. We must show this man and his faculty stooges that they cannot undermine the integrity of this review site.

> Notice to my fellow students:
>
> Prof. Thorfgoode of Physics can't teach and is a raving racist. If you care about your grade point average looks at his on Teachersonparade.

> It's as low as he is. B-o-y-c-o-t-t his classes. If you're a minority, you won't feel comfortable there.

> Nathaniel,
>
> Some of these sound like Fly on the Wall to me.
>
> What do you think? — Haywood

> Haywood,
>
> It looks like what Biff was afraid of this happening.
>
> He's getting bombarded with negative reviews because he condemned the site. He'd a brave man. I hope this doesn't

affect his class enrollment in the fall. — Nathaniel

Nathaniel,

These just in. Now Biff's wife is getting it.

I went back and checked. She had several good reviews — three out of a total of six.

Now she has just the three so-so ones. It looks like the webmaster is tamperingwith her reviews —removing the good ones. — Haywood

Haywood,

This doesn't surprise me in the least. They've been doing this kind of thing from the beginning. Maybe people will start to notice at last? — Nathaniel

Nathaniel,

Most people can't tell what was on the site before and what's on there at present. I can, though, since I have copies of every single review that has ever appeared there. It would entail lots of work, but it would be possible to compare the current reviews with the missing reviews to prove a pattern of deliberate manipulation and distortion on the part of Doo Doo. The latest with Biff and his wife is just the most flagrant. It would be harder to trace if it's somebody else besides the webmaster doing it, like Fly on the Wall and the First Amendment Club. Bu maybe you could subpoena the site's hard drive and find out just who wrote what to whom and about whom? — Haywood

Haywood,

Please hang on to your copies of the missing reviews. Could you make me a copy on a CD? These may yet be the evidence we need if and when we ever get to court. I'd really appreciate it. — Nathaniel

Will do! — Haywood

Biff got back from L.A. — his daughter's nodules attended to by special emergency surgery that Biff had paid for. When Nathaniel went over to Biff and Mary Ann's house for breakfast, they seemed welcoming, serving him up a huge mess of grits and scrambled eggs, but they were worried about their daughter. She might have to have more surgery or extended therapy, and they weren't sure they'd have the money to join the lawsuit now. Mary Ann Lubbock was in her early sixties, her face weathered, altogether big-boned but skinny, now on a complete fruit diet, she said, showing the mango and guava slices on her plate. She pinched an inch on one upper arm to show how much she'd lost. She seemed obsessed with her daughter in general. Her Texas twang combined with her liberal politics made her a little jarring. She was very active on all sorts of school committees. It was just that Nathaniel had avoided all such until the recent Troubles and so hadn't had much to do with the woman.

"Whatever Biff ultimately decides, I don't really want to sign on to the lawsuit myself if you get it going again, but I want you to know I support you," Mary Ann said.

"Are you aware that your reviews have been tampered with?"

"What?" They both looked surprised.

"Haywood informs me that both of you have been placed near the bottom."

"THE PITS?"

"That's it. You're in them."

"Really?"

"They're having their way with you."

"So soon?" Biff said.

"Mary Ann's good reviews just disappear, and your 'students' suddenly start bashing you as a teacher. To the general user of the website, nothing is amiss."

They went upstairs to Biff's study to check out the reviews. The study was very neat, not a speck of dust in sight. The three huddled around the computer screen.

The look on Biff's face told Nathaniel that Biff had probably written some of the now-deleted positive reviews of his wife, but he didn't ask. "The point about this website is that it's a tangle of deviltry, and yet it's still being pushed as a legitimate source of information with the backing of the school," he said. Of course if Biff was distorting his wife's reviews, even though it proved the point, it complicated the issue legally.

"My wife taught me how to write," Biff volunteered. "Now it wasn't in a formal classroom, but she used to sit with me and make me write — make me write paragraphs and then correct them, and over time I improved my writing skills a lot. So she was my teacher." He sounded defensive.

Biff re-read the review about his being a "raving racist." "That bothers me," he said. You could see on his face that it did.

"If there's anything he's not, it's a racist," Mary Ann said.

"Charges of racism are the last refuge of the scoundrel," Nathaniel said. "No, they've become the first refuge of the scoundrel. But don't get me started."

"How could they say such a thing about me?" Biff seemed genuinely hurt.

"I hate to say I predicted these people would stop at nothing once they had this power," Nathaniel answered. "All we can do is not back off now. You can't let the 'racism' industry that's developed in this country grind you down."

Biff and Mary Ann looked worried, their ultra-liberal leanings clearly under duress. Nathaniel practically gagged on the English muffin he'd brought upstairs with him.

He went on. "Unless you give nothing but flattery and compliments to so-called 'minorities,' you're accused of racism."

"We'd better get ready," Mary Ann said nervously. It was the land of Free Speech?

"You don't believe me?" Nathaniel pressed.

"We do have several appointments," Mary Ann said.

God, why were they so silly about this! He could tell he'd stepped on their bleeding hearts.

"We've got a bike ride to attend at noon," Biff explained.

"Bike ride?"

"In solidarity with Bikers Are People Too."

Naturally Nathaniel had heard of this organization — militant bicyclists who rode en masse once a month to protest automobiles. It had become more silly over the years, like everything else, and now motorists had to watch out for bikers out to "key" their cars on Teach Them a Lesson Day (every other month) or even being isolated as a driver by twenty or more biker riders and undergoing Recreational Vehicle Re-Think harangues. Several drivers had been beaten with bicycle chains.

"Aren't most of those people in their twenties?" Nathaniel asked.

"Yes, but we older citizens have got to do our part," Biff said, getting his a bike helmet out of his closet.

"Aren't you old enough for an exemption?"

"And then we're going to an Asian Infusion workshop," Mary Ann said.

"Dare I ask what that is?" Nathaniel said.

"Dean Visigoth set it up. Didn't you see the notice? It's a workshop on how faculty can incorporate more Asian influences into their classes and homes."

"You're joking, surely."

They weren't.

"What if you don't want to incorporate more Asian influences into your classes and home?"

"You're not xenophobic, I hope, Nathaniel!" Mary Ann was all but aghast.

"I look at things a little differently," he replied. "I see Asian influences as homophobic and cruel to animals, often superstitious, to say nothing of overpopulating the environment. Maybe some of its values shouldn't be encouraged."

"You don't mean they're the Yellow Peril?!" she said, flushed.

Christ, couldn't anybody have a sane discussion in this city? Because you thought one thing, it didn't mean you thought anything else!

"I'll see if I can get that lawyer for you," Biff said, getting his red-and-white spandex riding costume out of the closet. "Let me think about it some more before I reach my final — my final decision, okay?"

Mary Ann had gotten her helmet from the next room, a bright blue one. She also had a spandex biking costume in hand.

I probably said too much! Nathaniel cursed. Hope I haven't lost them. But damn their amorphous, good-must-surely-come-out-of-everything, bike-riding, bleeding hearts! They don't seem to realize that they'll be the first to go when their liberal culture gets kicked aside by one far less sentimental about such cherished soppy beliefs. 'Minority' collective virtue, my ass! Feng shui this! "Gosh, I was just too polite to say anything when they infused me," they'd say. Didn't these people know any history about how human beings acted?!

But if they weren't who they are, I suppose they wouldn't have done as much for me as they have, "our gay friend," Nathaniel consoled himself as he left. May God have mercy on their daughter's nodules!

Biff didn't produce the defamation lawyer he'd promised. Was it because Nathaniel had said some things that weren't P.C. enough? "He's tied up on another case," Biff said. Weak.

Luckily one of the lawyers Nathaniel had contacted through the Bar Association called back and said he was willing to have a meeting. Nathaniel wasted no time in going to the man's office. He could tell at once that the two of them had a good rapport. Jared Toste was a handsome young man in his late thirties, balding in front, immaculate in a dress shirt, tie, and loud, check suspenders. He listened to Nathaniel's spiel and said, "I'm in." Just like that.

"I don't have much money, but a couple of friends said they —"

"The law on the Internet is all being worked out right now, and I'd like to be in on it. I'll do it on contingency."

Nathaniel couldn't believe his good luck. Toste's even agreed to send in a false review to see how the website could be misused. They chose Dean Visigoth, who was still on the Tip of the Top.

"I'll give him a C," Toste said. And he did, and the new grade point average shifted the dean from #1 to #2.

"See how vulnerable a teacher is," Nathaniel said, trying to drive home the point even though he was pretty sure it had been made.

"Have Modos & O'Harromog send over their file on your case. I'll look at it over the weekend. All right?"

They shook hands, and Nathaniel felt exhilarated. Maybe everything would not die after all. He hated to, but he called Modos & O'Harromog's office and got one of the male secretaries and explained about the transfer and gave Toste's address. When he checked with Toste's secretary later in the afternoon, by God if Modos & O'Harromog hadn't sent the file over already. No doubt they thought now they were off the hook.

Toste's secretary's comment: "We got the file, but there was practically nothing in it."

"Meaning?"

"It looks like they didn't do very much work on your case."

"These gays — see how they love one another," Nathaniel said.

"Mr. Toste will do a good job for you. You can count on that."

"Would it be okay if I brought some other teachers to the meeting on Monday?" he asked.

"I don't see why not."

"Great!" Nathaniel got on the phone and tried to get Karma to accompany him to the meeting. Unfortunately she had come down with some pains in her earlobes and couldn't go. She'd had her ears pierced and an infection had set in in one of them.

He called Haywood and asked him, and he actually agreed — if Nathaniel would pick him up at school and drive him home. "Of course," Nathaniel said.

He wanted to ask Biff Thorgoode too, though worried that Biff was trying to get out of his commitment. I will not be my passive father! I will not! Nathaniel swore.

To his surprise, Biff agreed to go to the meeting.

Fantastic!

Nathaniel got the three of them into his car and to the lawyer's office with five minutes to spare. They sat in the lounge almost giddy with expectation. It was a modest office with fake plants, but who cared.

"I hate to sue my school," Biff said.

"They deserve a lot more than that, the way they've treated their faculty," Haywood said. He looked grumpy, his arms folded across his chest.

Nathaniel had to agree with Haywood.

When Toste finally came in and shook hands with all of them, there was something about his expression that did not bode well. He held up a white file folder. "This is what Modos & O'Harromog sent over. It contains your signed contract and a copy of the Complaint they filed. Nothing else. Oh, and your request to be your own lawyer."

"I told you not to sign with them," Haywood said.

"Maybe I shouldn't have," Nathaniel said. "But that's all behind us now." He made himself smile at Toste.

Toste shifted in his swivel chair, then said, "I'm afraid I can't take on the case after all." He was nervously intertwining his fingers.

"What!?" Haywood said.

"Why not?" Biff said.

Toste untwined his fingers. "Because I think you'll lose."

Nathaniel felt like he'd been punched in the side of the face. He could barely breathe.

"I'm sorry, but I looked over Title 47 and some other rulings this weekend. I think you'll lose if you got to court." You could see that he felt bad about it.

"But how can that be?" Nathaniel asked, aware of his own desperate voice.

"The law was written to accommodate Silicon financial interests — to spur development of the Internet. And you have a formidable opponent in the ACLU."

"To say nothing of the fledgling Hacker Community," Nathaniel added bitterly.

"But I read that even just calling somebody 'incompetent' is considered libel, never mind all these other terrible things on the site," Haywood argued.

"And my wife's reviews have been tampered with!" Biff said. "To say nothing of mine!"

Toste listened to what they had to say, and it went on for another fifteen minutes, but then he said, "I'm sorry. I think you should settle. I would. I could handle that for you, if you wish."

Nathaniel could taste the vile crud of eaten crow on his tongue.

"Do you want to settle?" Toste asked.

"Never," Nathaniel answered.

He'd thought it couldn't get any worse than when Modos & O'Harromog had tricked him into signing off on them, but this might be even worse. . . . *Wham!*

"I'll get us a lawyer," Biff said out in the parking lot as they stood there, stunned.

Even Haywood looked about to cry. "I thought we shouldn't have gone through the courts in the first place," he said. Oh, shut your Santa hole! You change with every wind.

"This can't be right!" Nathaniel fumed. "It simply can't be! I don't care what the law says. There have been plenty of evil laws that have been overturned, including ones against gays!"

"I won't let this drop," Biff said.

Yeah, right, Nathaniel thought. He drove them home, a funeral procession with just one car in it.

It took three more days, but Biff called Nathaniel and said, "Blake Lancet says he'll meet with you, if you — if you can come tomorrow." Hurray! Biff was following through.

"Where's his office?"

"In the East Bay."

"Did he make any promises?"

"No."

"Of course not. When will I learn."

"I'm afraid I can't go with you this time. My daughter is visiting, and I have to spend some quality time with her. She's recuperating."

"I'll go by myself," Nathaniel said.

What was this epidemic of bad nodules and infected earlobes? He didn't even ask Haywood this time. In this world the only person you could count on was yourself.

While he waited for the day of the meeting, he checked with the Bar Association to see if any other lawyers had expressed interest. Zilch. So it was down to one last try — this Blake Lancet in Prickeley across the bay, whoever he was.

He and Marty finally got together the night before the meeting. It had been the longest they hadn't spoken in all their years together. Marty didn't look especially good, a little skeletal in the face, the eyes stoned, his beard ragged and sprinkled with white hairs. Was it crystal, the usual? What happened to you if you kept using speed? Did you build up a tolerance? Did you shriek and clasp your hands in elemental ecstasy and then watch your brain collapse? Nathaniel didn't want to know. Marty wasn't going to stop, whatever the consequences. We're somewhat alike, Nathaniel realized. We won't give up what we find necessary in order to live.

"How's your neighbor? Still loving you as himself?" Nathaniel said. They were sitting in Marty's ancient car, on top of a city hill, a place they'd gone to a lot when they'd first met, had even had sex there. Now there was a roadblock at the end, and you couldn't get out to the section with the nicest views. At least nobody else was up there with them. The lights below looked like Christmas lights, but they weren't.

"I'm thinking about throwing garbage or paint on his garage," Marty said. "I've stopped turning the other cheek."

"Have you tried to videotape him? A little camera you can put under your car? Did you get one?"

"No."

Nathaniel knew that meant no more was to be said on the subject. God, Marty was stubborn. Oh, hell, maybe Marty's was the right approach after all. Do very little. Here I am running around with this lawsuit like a chicken trying to put its head back on, and what good am I doing? He and Marty, as different or same as they were, when you looked at it closely, were about in the same place.

"And how's your case going?" Marty asked.

"Not that well."

"You giving it up?"

"Maybe."

"You should report Modos & O'Harromog to the Bar Association. They should be disbarred," Marty urged.

"I haven't got the strength right now. I doubt that it will do any good, either."

"You're always telling me not to give up."

"I know."

They held hands on the seat. Marty's felt cold, physically. But not emotionally.

"I almost killed myself over this," Nathaniel said.

"I tried to get through to you."

"I know."

"I thought you didn't want to talk to me," Marty said.

"I know."

"It's not a very good time for either one of us right now, is it?"

Nathaniel squeezed Marty's hand. "But we can't give up."

"Who says? The next time around will be better. It has to be." Marty believed in reincarnation. Nathaniel wished he did.

"I appreciate you sticking by me through this," Nathaniel said. "I don't always say how much you mean to me . . . "Now he felt the words were too sentimental. "You do, though," he said, forcing himself.

"I don't wish I were you, but sometimes I wish I had your determination," Marty said.

"You have it. It's just quieter than mine."

"I think I'm losing the little bit I have," Marty said, lighting up a joint. The pungent cannabis aroma quickly filled the inside of the car. "No, you aren't," Nathaniel said, rolling down the window an inch.

"I can't go on much longer like I am."

There was something sinister in the casualness with which Marty had said the words.

"I think my time is about up."

"Don't be ridiculous."

Marty shrugged as he took another drag on his joint. He dropped it and it fell between his legs.

"Christ!" Nathaniel said before he could stop himself.

"It won't burn the seat!" Marty said. "It always goes out." He was patting around, unable to find the joint, which was made with dark brown paper.

"I'll probably get arrested one of these days for having marijuana in my car!"

"It's always about you, isn't it?"

Nathaniel said nothing. Couldn't they even have five minutes without a quarrel? Is this where "love" always led? To no sex and lots of fights. Funny, they never mentioned this in the romantic comedies.

Marty found the missing joint. "See! No damage." He brushed some ashes off the seat between his legs.

"I don't want to hear you talking like you just were," Nathaniel said. "Promise?"

"There comes a time when you have to let it go."

"That's nonsense." Nathaniel was aware of the irony that he was the one who had just tried to commit suicide and here he was attempting to cheer up Marty. Fuck irony.

"Life sucks," Marty said. The resignation in his voice was truly terrible.

"And that's on a good day." He patted Marty's hand. "No, life is not good," he said. "But at least it's hilarious."

"Yeah." So flat, so unconvinced.

"At least a little hilarious?" Nathaniel said.

There may have been a vague grunt from Marty, as he turned and looked out at the twinkling view on his side of the car and took another drag on his joint.

Nathaniel didn't want to leave Marty alone that night and invited him to stay over at the condo. As always, he refused. He liked his own bed. Nathaniel waited for an invitation to sleep over at Marty's, but it didn't come. "I still haven't cleaned it up," Marty said. "Just like everything else in my life."

"We'll have a spring cleaning party. And I'll help. Is that a deal?"

"Any century now. Good night," Marty said, getting out of the car. His eyes did not look good, bleak. He flicked the joint away into the night.

"I love you!" Nathaniel called.

Marty didn't look back.

Because he had a hard time finding it, Nathaniel got to Blake Lancet's office across the bay late. It was a converted gingerbread house set back off a side street, with three lawyers sharing the premises and the two secretaries. Lancet turned out to be a light-skinned black man on the short side of average. His hair was clipped close to his skull and his nose looked like it might once have been broken. He had thick, big hands with broad fingers. He looked a bit rumpled, but he splashed some kind of aftershave or cologne on his cheeks and neck to refresh himself. "Care for some?" he said, offering the bottle to Nathaniel.

"That's all right."

The office began to smell like mint. Lancet rubbed his hands together and sat behind his long desk. There were piles of documents, but they were neat piles. Everything seemed fairly new, as if perhaps he hadn't been a lawyer very long. He appeared to be about thirty. "So what's this all about?" he said. "Biff Thorgoode tells me you've got trouble." Lancet's voice was a little throaty, maybe raspy. "Excuse my voice," he said. "I've been arguing a case for about a month now."

"No problem," Nathaniel said.

"I have about three weeks left to go."

"I'm supposed to have a court date pretty soon myself."

"Then I won't be able to help you," Lancet said.

Nathaniel panicked. All the law books — volumes and volumes of them — around the room pulled at his eyes. He wished he knew the law. He couldn't stand being in other people's power like this.

"But why don't you tell me a little bit about what's been happening," Lancet said encouragingly, as if aware how abrupt he had sounded . "Biff's told me some of it. But I'd like to hear more. Please."

"Even though you can't represent us?" He was fed up with the whole business.

"Do you know what a continuance is?"

"Sort of."

"It's a continuation of a case, a postponement. Do you know how to get one?"

"No."

"If I told you how to, do you think you could get one?"

"Would it do any good?"

"It might." Lancet grinned, a nice, warm grin. Was a nice, warm grin enough to go on? Well, what else have you got? Nathaniel told himself.

Nathaniel held out the file folder of "reviews" which he had brought along. "Tell me if you think these are protected speech — or hate speech."

Lancet took the folder and opened it. His gaze fell onto the top page. Very soon he frowned. "These were posted on the website?"

"Just in the past few days."

"Pretty raw."

"Tell me about it."

Lancet held up one of the sheets of paper. "'Mr. Thorgoode likes to give demonstrations in his Physics classes. Too bad he likes to experiment on his male students.'" Lancet looked across the desk. "A student wrote this?"

"Probably not."

"I don't know Biff that well, but I don't think he's into male students. Last I heard, he wasn't gay."

"Not even those of us who are gay are necessarily into male students," Nathaniel replied, trying to be light. Not succeeding.

Lancet picked out another page and read it aloud. "'Bifford Thorfgoode — a typo — is a racist who calls his black student 'pickannies' and 'boy' — like his good buddy Nathaniel Tacky of the English Department." Lancet's eyebrows went up as a question.

"That's what free speech means, right? You can say whatever you like," Nathaniel answered, surprising himself.

"I know Biff Thorgoode, and he doesn't think like that. Or talk like that."

"But he could say those things if he wanted to. Isn't that correct? The ACLU apparently thinks so." God, he hated injecting race into this. But here it was.

"Biff might have the right to say them, but whether he said them if he didn't say them is a different matter, it would seem to me," Lancet said.

That sounded good to Nathaniel. "What's going on here is unscrupulous people putting nasty buzz words into other people's mouths in order to discredit them."

Lancet took out a third sheet. "'Nathaniel Tack of the English Department hates French students and bashes them in class. He goes on and on about how awful the French are. I will never again take a class from this monster.'" Lancet tossed the paper onto his desk. "What's that all about?"

"I said I had a bad time in a French restaurant in Paris — that is, I said it maybe five years ago. There is no time limit on when you can review a teacher. Wouldn't you like to have an open-ended Lawyersonparade connected to the Bar Association?" Nathaniel asked. "Of course all your clients — every single one of them — have been overjoyed with you as a lawyer. So if they told clients to avoid you, you probably wouldn't mind, right?"

Lancet smiled a smile that said "Hardly."

Nathaniel was weary of his own arguments. But the weary didn't inherit the earth. "Suppose anyone — disgruntled clients, competing lawyers, your ex-wife — could go onto Lawyersonparade, endorsed by the Bar Association, and say any damn lie they felt like putting there — and say it as many times as they like, and say it today or say it fifteen years from now? The lawyer for the ACLU said in his legal brief — and I quote — "this is the brave new world of Internet discourse.'"

"Hmm," was all Lancet would say.

"You could not write a letter to the editor like this, using people's names and trying to destroy their jobs. You could not say it on the radio, on TV, in a book or magazine, but you can say it online. It's taken a long time to work out these rules for the other media, but nobody can seem to fix this. Call me an old fascist, but I think this is wrong. Wrong!"

Lancet registered the anger. He rifled through the rest of the folder of reviews. "You're not alone in the reviews, I see."

"Biff has become the whipping boy of the moment. He had six or seven a few weeks ago. He spoke out, and now he has twenty-five, as of this morning, the last nineteen or so complete filth and lies. They claim to be from his real students, but they are not."

"I thought the ACLU said they were."

"They're not!"

"How do you know they're not?"

"That's the beauty of this website. You cannot tell who really wrote them. Still, people who don't understand what's going on think students — Biff's students in this case — wrote them. In all likelihood they certainly did not. If we could just prove it!" Nathaniel bit his lip because he bit on his words so hard.

"I was talking to him this morning. He's supposed to teach a summer lab. Says he's got only two students enrolled," Lancet said.

"It's even worse than I thought then."

Something caught Lancet's eye. He picked up the sheet. "This one goes on for several pages."

"Does it?" Nathaniel felt his bitten lip, pressing a finger down on it. Damn.

"'Nathaniel Tack tells the critics to slam my plays whenever I put one on. His critic friends in the theatre world do his bidding, and they call my work incoherent garbage. I don't write incoherent garbage. I write works of poetic genius, and if it weren't for Fucking Tack the world would notice!'" Lancet looked up. "What's that all about?"

"I didn't read the whole thing before. That one's probably really from a student of mine. Some cretinous loony I had in creative writing a couple of years ago. As if I have theater critics doing my bidding! I wish. I'd have them strangle that talentless asshole with his typewriter ribbon. We get more than our share of wackos. We do outreach, you see. 'We've done everything we can for you here at the Home. It's time for you to enroll at Shite College.'"

Lancet grinned. "You have to be careful that these reviews aren't so outlandish that the law won't take them seriously. They might be taken as jokes."

"We are a joke," Nathaniel said. "Hear me laughing? Ha! Ha!"

"You sound bitter."

"Why would I be bitter?"

"But I'm serious about these not being dismissed as too far over the top to be believable."

"Who can tell the jokers from the jokes?"

"Who do you think is writing these reviews about Biff?"

"Somebody named Fly on the Wall, possibly the webmaster. Anyone who wants to."

"Biff thinks some of them are from a retired teacher in the Physics Department — somebody who doesn't like him."

"How could anybody not like Biff?"

"He gave me the name, but I didn't write it down. Biff has been an expert witness for me in a few cases. Has he told you that?"

"No."

"He's a very fine man."

"He seems to be."

Lancet seemed to be mulling over whether to come aboard or not. "I do owe him several favors."

Nathaniel refused to let himself want this too much. And his lip was smarting besides.

Lancet read through a few more pages of reviews, shaking his head. "The ACLU is defending this crap?"

"It's often homophobic and it's always degrading, but apparently the ACLU thinks students have a God-given right to shit on their teachers."

Lancet's eyebrows went up again. "Some people might say it's the strength of the United States to have websites like this. Anything goes. Not controlled in any way. What do you say to that?"

Nathaniel didn't hesitate. "They can make me eat shit. They can probably make me eat a lot of shit. But they can't make me say it's delicious."

Lancet grinned and nodded. "I like that. Do you think you can give me $5000 now and then at least another $5000 sometime later?"

Nathaniel took out two credit cards, which were already nearly full. "Will these do?" he asked. laying them on the desk. He'd worry about the money later. (And he *would* worry about the money later.)

So, yes, Lancet would take the case — if Nathaniel could get a continuance from the court.

He finished reading final exams. On a long scene from a play that one of his creative writing students had turned in as a final project he wrote: "You have great talent. I expect great things from you." He was exaggerating, but he was just happy to find something he could compliment instead of always being disappointed. Most of his students were never heard of again.

And most people have never heard of me, either. Thirty years of writing and jumping up and down saying, "Hey, look at what I did!" and the reaction tended to be, "Nathaniel Who? I think I've almost heard of you. Didn't you write the *Scarlet Letter*?"

He turned in his final grades. And then he was bored. Wasn't that what life was — irritation and pain most of the time, followed by boredom, with an occasional orgasm to keep you going? And even those, with him, tended to be premature. Eeek! No, half an Eeek.

Nathaniel knew he had to get on that continuance Lancet had told him he must get from the court. But he was losing his resolve. He was supposed to prepare a form and go down in person to Superior Court and argue for the postponement. It might be turned down, too. It most definitely would be turned down if he didn't go and do it. Maybe I need some speed to get me going? Nathaniel thought. Should I ask Marty for some? Marty had been hard to reach, though. He seemed to be withdrawing, his line busy — online watching porn perhaps. That had to be better than some of the other alternatives, didn't it? He was still alive if he was watching porn or snorting speed. God, what you wound up taking as a minimum in life.

His son called from Oregon, and that helped. Your own flesh and blood sometimes actually helped! Not too often, though, to be honest.

"What's what?" Jim said, his voice noticeably lower now. Apparently he was late in developing, just as Nathaniel had been.

"Just so-so," Nathaniel said. "What about you?"

"I'll be a senior next year."

"How did you do? Better grades?"

"Okay."

"How good is okay?"

"B's and C's."

"No D's."

"One little D," Jim said, his voice trailing off.

"Why even one? Oh, I know — you forgot to turn in your homework."

"My electronics teacher said I can make it up."

"They always do. Don't get me started. Good to hear from you. Is this my son, the lesbian?"

"That's me!"

"Just teasing."

"It's true."

"What's true?"

"I've become a lesbian."

"How do you know?"

"I live with two. Believe me, I know."

"Do you want to tell me about it?"

"Let's just say I feel like a lesbian sometimes." A hint of impatience.

"What should a father say? It's all right for you to be a lesbian. But only if you want to be one. Don't let your mother or Lana influence you now."

"I might make a terrible lesbian."

"No way! You'll be Lesbian of the Year, or my name isn't Tack."

"You're weird."

"It's okay to call me that. Just don't put me in a box."

"Other than my lesbianism, it's pretty dull up here."

Nathaniel laughed. "You're pretty funny sometimes."

"A chop off the old block."

"Isn't it chip?"

"Do you know what an oxymoron is?" Jim asked.

"I think so. Why?" Don't change the subject.

"I just learned that word. Give me an example."

"You don't think I know what an oxymoron is? I'm an English teacher."

"Give me an example."

"Army intelligence."

"Is gay pride one?"

"Ouch. Nasty. But good. . . . you homophobe."

"I'm not really. But I couldn't resist."

"Whatever makes you happy, my child. Isn't that what the American parent is supposed to say?"

"You sound a little down."

"It's just a syndrome I'm going through. How are your mother and Lana?"

"They're good. They're playing softball right now."

"And you're not there to cheer them on?"

"I'm studying for the SAT."

"Really?"

"I am."

"I don't think you're a real lesbian then — if you're willing to give up softball for the SAT."

"If my mom could hear you!"

"She'd what? Send my child back to heaven?"

"I get a little tired of their Political Correctness sometimes. I really do."

"Yay!"

"I read about you."

Nathaniel didn't like the feel of that. "Where?"

"I looked up Teachersonparade."

"Oh, Jesus. What did you do that for?"

"I wanted to see what students are saying about you?"

"They're not necessarily students. Or my students."

"They're not?"

"I guess I can't say it too many times."

"They're pretty awful."

"Are they? The reviews or the students?"

"Some of the comments."

"I'm not the only one getting blasted."

"Do they bother you?"

"Of course they bother me. By the way, who are you dating now that you're a lesbian?"

"Tinsel. She just graduated."

"Did you say Tinsel?"

"That's what her parents named her. Tinsel Fawn Ackerley."

"The poor girl."

"But never mind that right now. I'd like to talk about those reviews. Do you mind?"

Nathaniel's stomach began to churn. "I mind, but what do you want to know?"

"You come off as sort of a . . ."

"What?"

"Why don't you put a teacher's statement or something on the site?"

"Because I don't really want to defend myself against what's being said there."

"Why not?"

"Because the site doesn't represent the whole me."

"Do I know the whole you?"

"Most people don't know the whole of anybody, most likely."

"Is there something about your hole that you want to tell me?"

"Jimmy!"

"Jim. Sorry. Couldn't resist."

"Would you tell the chip to get back on the block, please?"

"It hurt to read some of those reviews."

"I'm sorry you read them."

There was a pause. "I don't know you all that well, but from what I know you seem actually pretty nice."

"I'm not nice."

"You're not?"

"But I'm not the monster painted on that Devil's plaything, either."

"They accuse you of a lot of things."

"All I'll say is this — the website caters to and favors the angriest people. What they say isn't the whole truth and nothing but."

"A lot them can't write or spell. Jesus." He seemed to be testing the cuss word.

"Hurray! Somebody else has noticed! All is not lost yet!" He's no longer a boy. He swears. "Watch your words."

"Are you mean to your students?"

"It's complicated, Jim. I try to maintain a professional atmosphere in my classes. I try to apply what used to be known as college standards. For a whole host of reasons, something has happened to education — maybe not just in the United States, but at least there for sure. You're part of it. Sorry, but you are."

"I am?"

"Always turning papers in late. And do you study very much?"

"Of course."

"Do you?"

"No, no that much."

"Thank you. A lot of the flak I'm taking is from trying to stop grade inflation and incredible laziness and carelessness. Some is because I have opinions that aren't popular, especially here in Santa Francesca. I don't think it's necessary for a teacher to tell his students they're better than they are."

"They need encouragement."

"They get too much mindless encouragement. They need a reality check, and I don't want to say things are what others claim when, I see something entirely different."

"But do you make them cry?"

"Only when I beat them to death."

"No, really. Do you?"

"To be perfectly frank, I don't think a great many of them should be in college, if 'college' means anything. They shouldn't even have graduated from high school, if high has any meaning anymore. Education has become just some form of factory farming."

"What's that?"

"Herding the stock through the pens — only they come out with degrees instead of nails drilled into their foreheads."

"Is it that bad?" I'm losing him.

"Not everybody. Just too many. I used to be able to do what I could and save those worth saving and weed out the rest and laugh it all off somehow. Now, because of the website, I'm finding it harder and harder to maintain my integrity – or my sense of humor. At least that's how I see it. I suppose somebody else could see it some other way. But you know what — endless relativism is really not the answer. On some things you have to take a stand." Applause, please.

"That's what Tinsel's father says. He's a Pentecostal minister."

"Not that kind of stand!"

"How can you tell which stand to take?"

"God, Jimmy, how do I know! I'm just a grown-up sperm floundering in the morass like everybody else. But you — you stop dating those fundamentalists, you hear me?!"

"I don't believe them," his son said.

"The fundamentalists?"

"I don't believe those reviews. I actually think you're pretty cool."

"No way!"

"I think you are."

"No way I'm cool."

"You are, Dad. I think you are, and I bet you're a good teacher too. I'm glad you're my dad."

"Glad/dad — don't you go rhyming on me now, you hear me?" Nathaniel's voice broke and he felt tears trying to get out. Down, wantons, down!

They were both embarrassed and hung up soon thereafter. Nathaniel was ashamed of himself for wanting to hear those words so desperately from his boy. How sharper than a serpent's tooth it is to have a thankful child.

It was taking Nathaniel forever to draw up the petition for more time, not his usual style at all. Just two or three pages were needed, but he felt that he didn't have the legalese necessary to shape the continuance. Not only did he have to notify the court, he would have to send copies to the different lawyers for the college, the Alliance of Students, the ACLU, and the webmaster as well — so that they could show up and argue that he shouldn't have more time. He wrote up a preliminary draft, with the help of Slacker, who said, "Scratch their eyes out and then play with them until they're numb and then half-eat them." That certainly sounded like an excellent plan, but the final result was merely a plea to the court to excuse "his lack of knowledge of the law" and to let him have "an extra couple of months" so that his new lawyer could take over. He did manage to include: "At no time did I ever tell anyone, including my former lawyers, Modos & O'Harromog, that I wished to represent myself." Those bastards would be eaten — and not just half — all in good time, if there was a God in Heaven.

It took twenty-four tries to get the goddamned vertical parentheses to line up on the home-made legal stationery, and because of something known as "*ex parte*" he was required to go in person to the court downtown, and early in the morning besides. He asked Marty to accompany him if he possibly could, and Marty agreed, neither looking his best. Marty was more skeletal, sharp-nosed, his clothes a little stale-smelling. Nathaniel had fallen the night before — tripping over his cat in the half-light on his way to the bathroom — and had sprawled headlong on the floor and hit his mouth on a box of manuscripts he should have thrown away years before. For a moment he'd thought he might have lost a front tooth. He hadn't, but he did have a gash above his lip, and the upper lip itself looked swollen — somewhere between stung by angry bees and that of a very bad Brigitte Bardot impersonator.

The court would have been intimidating, even with both lips working properly, because it was a new one, large and granite and marble and full of innumerable hard-to-find offices and surly, bored clerks who told you to this way, no, that way, and didn't really care where you went as long as you got out of their hair.

Finally he and Marty found the right courtroom. You had to sign in and wait. Of course the judge (Judge Jesus Garza) had been delayed. Nathaniel had expected that. They sat in seats that resembled pews in a church, only ripe with the sanctimony of the law instead of religion. (Judge Jesus?) He looked around for representatives of the Defendants. He didn't really know what they might look like. Maybe some of the Alliance would be there. Dude Lather himself? He went back up to the sign-in sheet and checked to see if he could recognize any names. He didn't. So far, so good. He wondered if he'd freeze when he eventually got before His Honor and not make the judge believe how important it was to grant more time. Wasn't that the story of most lives? Just a little more time, please! Then I'll be good! Please, Your Honor Mr. Jesus! Please!

"Thank you for coming with me," he whispered to Marty. They even sneaked a hand clasp below the level of the seats.

"You'll be fine," Marty said. "I don't worry about you. You'll knock 'em dead."

Nathaniel had always been articulate. But you never knew, did you? You might suddenly develop a horrible stutter. Your swollen lip might refuse to move. "Next!" the judge would call out. And then there would be no continuance — in this life or the next.

Oh, no, a young woman in a severe business suit was signing in! There was something about her that said she worked for Tether & Strafe: the Plain Jane face, the hint of anorexia — what was it? The blonde hair pulled back and tied? The cruel lip and sneer of cold command? Look on this lawsuit, Ye Lowly, and despair!

Sure enough, when Nathaniel went up to check out what she had written, she had signed herself in as "Miranda Wright, of Tether & Strafe."

The cocksuckers. Oops! I mean, the cuntsuckers! They really were sending a lawyer to try to convince the judge not to allow more time.

Nathaniel kept stealing glances at her. She did indeed look cool and collected, sitting there ahead of them, with a small briefcase, from which she has extracted a portfolio that looked immaculate. She looked extremely competent, even formidable, and she didn't have a swollen lip, either.

He wondered if she'd even read any of the reviews or was just doing this because her firm had taken on the case. He wondered if she liked it doggy style and wanted the world to know. One day there would be Lawyersonparade.com right there along with Studentsonparade.com if he lost this case. Sauce for the goose! Except it wouldn't be the same. Only Teachersonparade seemed legitimate and on the up and up — after all, deans were endorsing it, Chancellors paying to defend it, and poor, downtrodden students dying on their barricades to defend it against their wicked, wicked teachers.

After an hour Judge Jesus was at last available — only Jesus still didn't show his face. He was somewhere in the back, and the parties were supposed to come up to the law clerk and make their argument standing right next to each other. Oh, my god, Nathaniel thought. I didn't have time to brush my teeth, and my mouth hurts. I should have taken some aspirin. Or some Viagra? Maybe he'd feel more confident with a stiffy.

The law clerk was a another female, young and "ethnic," Plain Jane #2. They'd stick together, these two! Women in Solidarity. Never in a million years would Nathaniel be granted the postponement.

He had to go first. Somehow he went into automatic. There was something to be said for thirty-five years of gas in the classroom. He made his pitch and handed over the formal petition he had finally put on legal stationery. Then Ms. Tether & Strafe made her counter-pitch. It seems that the webmaster "had already suffered enough" and "his valuable time wasted" because of the Plaintiff's "said such and such." Yeah, his valuable time spreading insults about teachers — his own and other people's, putting handcuffs on teachers with each passing day, or writing up fresh compliments for Dean Visigoth and anyone else who liked the "brave new world of Internet discourse" which the website provided. It was "time to move on" since Mr. Tack "obviously should not have asked to represent himself if he didn't have sufficient time to handle the matter."

You know, maybe it wasn't too late for Slacker's plan after all. Nathaniel looked at Miranda Wright and imagined her half-eaten body lying under the feet of a hundred thousand lawyers coming and going from the court. Oh, I mustn't have a thought of

Violence Against a Woman! Nathaniel panicked. That would be Wrong. . . . Fuck that. And fuck her! The hired executioner in her tidy tailored suit, ready to walk off with Nathaniel's head in her neat little briefcase.

The law clerk grabbed Ms. Wright's legal paper and disappeared. Both the Plain-tiff and the Defendant's counsel returned to their pews. "You were fine," Marty said.

"Could you hear?"

"Not really. But you sounded good."

Well, it was the sentiment that counted, Nathaniel guessed. They sat and waited. And then waited some more. Other lawyers and their ilk went up and did the same before various clerks. Meanwhile, backstage, His Honor was mulling and musing, apparently. His Great Legal Mind was parsing and dicing the niceties presented by both sides — Tether & Strafe in conjunction with the ACLU and its ideologues versus Tack & Who?

After thirty minutes, His Honor decided that Nathaniel could not have the two months he'd asked for — but he could have one.

So he would live to fight another day. He informed Blake Lancet's office of the legal "victory," such as it was, and his credit card was charged in no time at all. At least Lancet bothered to call back and leave a message: "Let's go for it. I'll do an Amended Complaint as soon as I can. I'll be in touch. I'll need more facts, though."

Now, as usual, there was nothing to do but wait for the courts to grind on and hopefully come to his case. Then at last somebody would legally grind somebody else's face into the dirt. His lawyer would beat up their lawyers. Or not. Both sides would present a distorted accumulation of "evidence," and out of that would come The Truth. Or not.

The case seemed to be getting more media attention almost daily. The other side must have been sending out press releases. Nathaniel wasn't. Not that he objected. This thing might very well be decided in the media as much as in the courts. God, he wanted his jowls worked on!

When he got a call from a woman producer at Tech TV asking if he wanted to appear on her show (*Cyber Crimes*) naturally he said yes. What bad could come out of that, right, jowls or no jowls?

It was amazing how fast the TV crew showed up, three of them — just one day later. They wanted to use a classroom, and they found one that looked photogenic, even though it wasn't one Nathaniel ever used. "Shouldn't we spill some coffee on the floor and wad up some Kleenex, possibly set a fire in a waste basket — to look authentic?" Nathaniel asked.

"We probably won't show the floor," the woman producer replied. She was tall, athletically lean, brown hair streaked with red highlights (a la mode), pretty, but pretty in that cable television second-tier kind of way. But she seemed sympathetic as she ran down some questions she was likely to ask him. She was just a young girl when you looked at her close.

It was a quiet time on campus, after finals and before summer school, so there were only a few people around to look suspiciously at the TV crew and what was going on. Nathaniel caught a glimpse of Guy Mountain and what could have been Gorilla Woman passing by in the hallway, not together, but both curious. Still, neither one ventured over to ask.

"Do you want some make-up?" asked the woman producer (Ashleigh Nashe) as Nathaniel was running over in his head what he was going to say.

"Just don't make me look like Dan Boatwright." Dan Boatwright was a local anchor who wore too much make-up and looked like a painted lady. "Could you hide the jowls maybe?"

"Of course," the producer said. She actually got out some pancake make-up from a kit and applied it herself to Nathaniel's face. How nice. Or was he just being set up?

"A star is born," he said, looking at himself in the small mirror she held up. "Frankenstein was a star, right?"

"The lights will wash it out. You'll look great!" she reassured him.

"When will this be broadcast?"

"On the weekend." That was just three days away. "Do you get cable?"

"Oh, yes."

"We have about twenty thousand viewers for every episode. Most 'teckies.' They'll be very interested in this case."

Two technicians were with her, both in their twenties, pulling cables and light shields around on the floor and trying to position a large camera, but they seemed to be disagreeing about something or other.

"It's okay. I'm not ready for my close-up, Mr. DeMille," Nathaniel said, getting more nervous. Was this really a good idea? What if the 'teckies' hated him?

"Any butterflies?" the producer asked.

"Nothing ventured, nothing gained," he answered.

"We'll need to get some establishing shots later."

"Meaning?"

"Shots of you walking, sitting."

So that's where those odd shots of TV news figures came from. No wonder they looked so posed. They *were* posed! Nathaniel was beginning to get the hang of this.

"We'll be rolling in just a minute," she informed him.

He cleared his throat and made it worse. What was his main point now? His mind felt a little fuzzy. Have a thesis sentence, class. A sound bite was the same thing. His lip had gone down somewhat, but it still had some puffiness to it. She hadn't touched it up, probably thinking he always looked that way.

"Let's do a volume check," one of the crew said, affixing a microphone to Nathaniel's lapel.

"What's your name?" the producer asked, coming up and straightening Nathaniel's collar. She flicked a piece of lint or dandruff off his sport coat.

"My name is Nathaniel Tack, and I am the resident ogre here at delightful Shite College," he said into the microphone.

"Don't look down at the mic," she cautioned. "It'll pick you up."

He repeated just his name.

"Fine," the crew member said.

Then they were rolling and Ashleigh Nashe identified herself to the viewing public and swung her hair fetchingly. Nathaniel would have to ask her what kind of fans she had. In fact, he asked her right then and there on camera: "Do people ever write reviews of you?" he said.

"Sometimes," she answered.

"And they're always positive?"

"Not always."

"Any filthy ones?"

She wanted to ask the questions, but she also knew that Nathaniel's questions might make a strong opening for the show. "There are some kooks out there, I'd have to say," she said.

"Do they write in and comment on your appearance?" And jack off on the TV screen looking at you — what he really meant.

"It happens," she said.

"Well, that's what's happening on Teachersonparade — filth and lies," Nathaniel said, launching his sound bite.

And they were off.

She asked him lots of questions, well over the required number for the eight-minute sequence planned for the program. Nathaniel thought he answered them reasonably well. One of the last questions was, "Do you as an openly gay teacher think any of this whole controversy has anything to do with homophobia?"

"I wouldn't want to make that the main issue," Nathaniel answered. "The main issue, as I see it, is that the Internet is permitted actions that give it special privileges, and those privileges are being used to abuse teachers and compromise their integrity in their professional duties."

Everyone seemed happy with the way it had gone.

It turned out none were happier than the 'teckies' who watched it that weekend. Here are some of the reactions:

I saw this asshole on TV. I know teachers of this type; they will all burn in hell. This teacher is so scared of his students that he sues them. What a wuss. Get a life Mr. Tack, and wash your face.

Or this:

YOUR'E JUST GONNA HAVE TO PUT UP WITH IT, FAG! you heard me, why tell everybody your'e gay, you know your'e gonna get pounded! COMMON SENSE, JERKOLA!, seems that nobody in America will understand this, because everybody is aggresive at everybody and they omit LOGIC in order to get as much from everybody else as they can. I suggest you change your attitude torwards everybody and start taking advice and using other teachers (top 15) as role models. Oh, and keep your emotional life out of class, If your'e a fag, I don't give a rat's ass, that just takes one more guy out off the planet, and gives me less competition to get a female. By the way you don't know what your'e missing... mmmm...girrrls.

Or:

What kind of a Fucking Asshole would sue their students -ON TECHTV!, this MotherF is nuts, he has he either has emotional problems, or needs to get a life. What kind of role model are you giving to your students? Besides he looked like a piece of crap on TV, like the kind of teacher that wants to flunk their students just because. If your reading this, "Nathaniel the faggy", I hope you understand that this displays exactly whats wrong with America. People suing other people for "emotional disturbance" you know you don't feel that way, you just want the money. "It's a cybercrime. It's cyberevil," Let me tell you something, People have the right to say whatever they want, and if they say You Suck, well then, you must, why else would they say it?

There were, in fact, some 327 messages sent in to the Feedback section of the program, many along the line of the above.

There were also some like this:

i disagree. i think the prof made some good points. you can't just say anything about anybody if it's a lie, just because you can get away with it on the Internet. the law on this is still not worked out. it's possible the law will be changed if asswipes like some of the guys on here don't show more responsibility.

Ashleigh Nashe and her bosses were thrilled with the response. Nathaniel, shall we say, was less so. It was frightening to think there was that much misdirected hate out there. When the "discussion" started turning into "reviews" on Teachersonparade, the nightmare became complete:

Hi, I'm Nathaniel Tack and hot for some dick riggt now, I'll even let you fuck my boyfriend, steve, he likes it when I shove big cilindrical objects all the way up his ass until he starts crying, the, i hope he does the same for me.

That's to teach you a lesson Nathaniel Tack, you fucking piece of shit fag ass hole, maricon, puto, miefdero, ass lick, donkey fucker, you really do pick up boys on broad st. you cuntfaced fairy, queer. Ohhh yesss, please harder harder, moooooo, quack quack, oink oink, bark bark. Farm animal fucker!!!!

Tack's #1 student was probably a hot-looking stud who refused to get rammed up the ass by Tack. His own ass is probably brown from all the black faggots that have shoved their big ass dicks up his asshole. I wish you kill yourself, there's no need for faggots in this world, they are an abomination.

YEAH, I took his butt-fucking class, and he raped me in front of the whole class, it was awful. And he also raped my friend's 3 yo brother and almost turneg his rectum inside out.

I do not understand what he thought he was doing when he killed that student last year for not handing in his assignment. He routinely keeps the pretty girls after class for 'extra credit' assignments, and they come out screaming a few minutes later.

Nathaniel Tack is a Fucking Faggot, he should get a life and be straight, faggots are a major threat to humanity and nature, they disgust everybody, especially if they're teachers.

Tack whipped out his cock and tried to shove it down my throat in the middle of class! I sit in the very front and he always was making passes at me, that faggot. Several times he invited me to the bathroom because he wanted to suck my dick but I told him toget the fuck away and he grabbed onto my balls so tight they almost exploded.

Then his grip gave out and I decked that boy-fuckig queer.

I got failed and he told me he was gonna kill me if I told anyone here tried] to rape me. He was always making fun of us girls and he was always trying to grope me!

Yep +++ I seen Tack tooling for anus on Polk Street.

Instead of questioning the student he should follow them—I know where Nathaniel (the Spaniel) Tack lives.

Why doen't you burn in hell now, you evil piece of garbage? Die now.

In fact, my teacher—a usually gentle and forgiving   person— warned our whole class against taking Tack's class. My teacher also p-o-i-n-t-e-d out that sometimes he sneakily changes his name a little so people won't know that they are signing up for his class, so be careful this Fall! My teacher also told us that he/she re-routes his/her walking about campus specifically to not have to run into Dr. Nathaniel Tack!

He ain't no man, he's a bitch!! Oh shit, man just let us put down this queer. We all know he's a Ass Hole.

Needless to say, these "reviews" put him at the very bottom of Teachersonparade, to say nothing of the very bottom of a severe depression. But he was "cheered up" by Haywood Wire:

Hi Nathaniel!

Sorry I haven't sent you those disks or the video of the school's webpage that I promised. They've altered it now —trying to cover themselves.

Well, you have been hit big time. You will have lots to show the Judge! The site is showing itself as the defamation center of the USA. After capturing the reviews, I could not get back on to capture your whole file. I recommend you check Teachersonparade regularly today and the next few days to document everything that appears. No one can claim that these are not libel and nothing but! You've hit the JACKPOT!

Whoo . . . pee, Nathaniel thought, still shaking from having read the "reviews" and the thought of having to read more.

"Your students really don't like you, do they?" This was from Gorilla Woman as Nathaniel was waiting for the elevator to take him up to his office. He was about to finish his grades and fill out the paperwork for the thirteen Incompletes.

"I beg your pardon?" he said.

"I read your latest reviews." Suze DiMentia had not gotten any lovelier in the last year. She was still broad and squat, and if Nathaniel wasn't pretty sure she was a vegan he'd have sworn that she'd just eaten a big bullfrog and it was still trying to get out of her mouth head first. Oh — that was her face? He knew she couldn't help her face, but it seemed to reflect her soul.

Should he even talk to her? She was the one who was had convinced her "babies" they weren't babies but were the reincarnation of the Weather Underground and the Black Panthers. When nostalgia goes bad . . . Whew. "I don't believe any of them are from my actual students." He couldn't resist.

"Yeah, sure."

Where was that elevator? One of them wasn't working of course, but one maybe? She headed around the corner toward the stairs. Gorilla Woman had just been passing by.

He needed the exercise and went right after her. "You can't possibly believe that filth came from my students!"

She didn't look back at him as they moved up the stairs. "What do you expect when you act like an old Nazi?!" Her big old rump was ahead of him

"You're a lesbian," he called out, "and you're defending this?!"

"It's making you hop, isn't it?" she snapped back. They were both getting a little winded.

He caught up to her two flights up. "I was on a TV show and that's why those reviews showed up on Teachersonparade. Don't you go around saying they're from my students!"

"I heard about it," she smiled. No, smirked. "It's one way to counter your commandeering of the media." The look on her face told volumes. She knew they weren't reviews from his students, but she didn't care. In fact, she liked it. All this was as a method to her guerrilla politics madness. "For the first time in history the little people have a chance to be heard!" She might just as well have pulled out a flag and draped herself in the Red and the Black. And she wasn't auditioning for *Les Miserables*. She really believed this. He knew more about the Little People than she did! He came from them!

"I think you're downright crazy."

"Because you hate women, that's why!"

"Oh, God!" Was there no exhausted, D-minus idea these people wouldn't pull out for ammunition?

"I don't hate women. I just hate you. You deserve to be hated."

"Well, you deserve to lose. Your lawsuit is absurd, and it's going to bankrupt you, and then you'll probably not have a job by spring, if all goes as expected." She flicked a little invisible booger at him.

"And then what? You'll be Chancellor and the Anarchist Pax DiMentia will reign in the land?"

"The students will run this place and get some real changes implemented."

"They already run this place. And look at it!" He pointed at some strips of paper that had been put up on the windows for some demonstration or other and then half-ripped down. "It's a pigsty!" He shook the forms in his hand. "And look at these Incompletes!"

"You ain't seen nothin' yet," she said with cool control. She thrust one of the sheaf of papers she was carrying into his hand and kept on going up the stairs. He was too winded to go any further. Besides, she probably would charge him with sexual harassment if he did.

His eyes were swimming, but he managed to look at the paper she evidently was about to distribute. It was marked APPROVED FOR SHITE COLLEGE POSTING and was yet another list of DEMANDS:

WE, THE COMMITTEE ON

THE BEAUTY OF DIVERSITY,

HEREBY DEMAND:

1) Increased Success/Retention Rates by race and ethnicity

2) Set-Asides for Shite College students to be Shite College Instructors

3) All Staff Hires to be Monitored by the Alliance of Students

4) End to the use of The Bullshead as the mascot of Shite (as demeaning to animals)

5) Removal of Bobble-Head Sports Figures from the college bookstore (as insensitive to sufferers of Parkinson's Disease)

Nathaniel would have screamed right there in the corridor, but he was all EEKED out about the world he lived in. "We are indeed the *Miserables*" was the most that he could mutter.

He got together with Biff Thorgoode and Mary Ann Lubbock at their house and showed them the latest filthy, homophobic reviews. They had already seen them because of Haywood and were properly appalled. Nathaniel realized that, for all the excesses of the Politically Correct in his hometown, he could count on sympathy about this, and that was not true in many places in the world. They especially found it appalling now that Biff was getting slammed as well, of course. He showed Nathaniel a "review" he had printed out that morning:

Bifford Thordgoode will ram your butt if you take his class, just the way he's getting rammed by his fag friend, N. Tack. The two of them goes at it and shit flies outa both their asses cuz they get so excited. It could happen to you!

They were sitting at the dining room table, with legal Complaints and possible new evidence spread out between them. The house was cold and it was raining outside, raining much too late in the season. Not a good omen. Mary Ann looked drawn, her hair askew, and Biff looked puffy-eyed and rattled and was shaking his head. "I'm supposed to teach summer school this summer, and the enrollment in my two labs is terrible."

"They might be canceled?"

"Some people might show up at the last minute, but I can't count on it."

"How can anyone believe these things?" Nathaniel waved his hand at the print-outs. "I shouldn't say that, because our lawyer wants to make the case that these are taken as factual. But honestly now!"

Mary Ann pointed toward the ceiling. "I'm afraid we'll have to be quiet or else move. Maria Callas's bedroom is right over us."

They had named their budding opera star daughter Maria Callas, and she had decided to use her mother's last name. Parents live through the kids, of course — but Maria Callas Lubbock?

"Sorry."

"I suppose students are being careful about taking my labs. They don't know for sure, but most likely they don't want to be hit by the shit flying out of our assholes."

"Maybe you could give them extra credit for ramming their butt?" Nathaniel said. They had to laugh, but it wasn't easy. Especially since they didn't want to wake Maria Callas Lubbock.

"I think I know who's writing these," Biff said.

"Fly on the Wall?"

"Not only him. I think it's Desmond DuSnood."

"Who?"

"He used to teach in the Physics Department. We quarreled over something years ago, and he never forgave me. I looked up his reviews, and he has all these puff pieces — and the man isn't even on the faculty — on the faculty anymore! I think he wrote the puff stuff for himself and the nasty stuff about me."

Biff went on elaborating the intricacies of the feud, and who knew what was true and what wasn't. The point was that no one should have access to this much power over another person's life.

"And all my positive reviews are gone now," Mary Ann added. "This is what I get for expressing my Free Speech rights." She was indignant, in a wishy-washy liberal kind of way.

See. You can't be goody-goody tolerant of everything! Nathaniel wanted to shout. People aren't nice just because you want them to be. Not everybody's ideas can co-exist.

They clash, and something or someone has to give. And it very well could be *us*. "Haywood wants me to keep track of the site, but I'm finding it very difficult to do," he said.

"Those reviews of you are still up there," Biff said. "I sent an e-mail to the webmaster about them."

"What did he say?"

"He said he'd remove them. But he added that he would be taking a real risk if he did."

"Because of the stupid Internet law, right? So he thinks he's doing us a big favor by removing what shouldn't even be there in the first place!"

"I guess. Maybe you'd better follow up and make sure they're removed. He told me he removed Mary Ann's because I had written them."

"I won't get down on my knees and beg that fuck for one thing!" Nathaniel almost yelled. He didn't ask if Biff had in fact written the removed reviews.

"Shhh!" Mary Ann cautioned, eyes uplifted to the bedroom above them.

Biff answered without the question. "Yes, I wrote some of her reviews, but I didn't write all the good ones. The webmaster removed every single one of them, however."

"Because he's a drooling, ignorant moron with all this technology on his side!" Nathaniel exploded.

"Don't get overly wrought up now," Biff cautioned. Both he and his wife looked concerned for Nathaniel.

Sure enough, he had awakened their daughter. There were thumps above.

"I'm sorry. . . . I feel so powerless." Nathaniel ran his fingers over his goddamned jowls, holding them up.

"It's time she got up anyway. She has to practice her belly dancing."

A belly dancing opera singer? Nathaniel didn't ask.

Biff looked at his wife. "I know a Godfather — a real one — I could call on."

"What?"

"I did a favor for some fellow when he was in jail."

Mary Ann held up a hand and tried to make Biff stop.

But he didn't. "That fella — that fella knows a Godfather, and that Godfather would do a favor for my friend."

Maybe they wouldn't need all these legal papers and a lawyer after all. "Tell me more."

"Now, Biff," his wife said.

"Why not?"

"Because we live by the rule of law," she answered.

"Desmond DuSnood doesn't live by the rule of law!"

"Honey!"

"I say let's go for it." Biff was on a roll now. Nathaniel's anger and the filthy review about him had fueled some rage that hadn't seemed apparent in the surface of the man before.

"I also have a buddy in Chicago. A big-time lawyer. I could contact him."

"No, tell me more about this Godfather," Nathaniel said. It was just a fantasy, to be entertained for a little while. No?

"He's had several people killed. A car salesman, for one. And the crime was never solved. He could probably take out Dude Lather. Why don't you start keeping a journal of your activities?"

"Why?"

"Just write down everywhere you go and what you do. It may prove useful. None of us can be anywhere near Lather when his time comes."

"Biff!" Mary Ann was getting annoyed, even a little scared at how this was growing.

"Why not? There's nothing I'd like to see more than the webmaster's and Desmond DuSnood's brains blown out and rotting in the sun."

"Why waste those brains?" Nathaniel said. "We could feed them to the feral cats on campus."

"You two are going to wind up in prison," Mary Ann said.

"I'll even put the brains in the dishes," Biff said.

"Of course, in the case of the webmaster there wouldn't be much for the ferals to eat."

"I bet the reviews would stop if there was no webmaster to run the site."

"And the dead body might prove a deterrent to anyone considering taking it over."

"And maybe I can have Desmond DuSnood's testicles made into a lava lamp, and I'll put it right there." Biff pointed at an end table. "Then whenever I'm playing the piano, I can watch those testicles — those testicles swirling around."

"Dibs on Dude Lather's testicles," Nathaniel said. "I'll give them to my cat, Slacker, as a chew toy."

Mary Ann got up from the table, impatient with the two of them and went upstairs to check on her singing, belly dancing daughter.

Biff and Nathaniel went on for a while longer with their revenge riff, and then they got back to work on the legal proof they would need to help their lawyer. Nathaniel could tell that they were both tingling with the vicious imagery pulsating through their brains.

The rule of law wasn't nearly as thrilling as this. By God, it had better work

Marty came out of his hibernation long enough for him and Nathaniel to go out and celebrate their anniversary. Eighteen years. Marty looked liked hell — the face elongated, no doubt from not eating very much, the beard invaded by those little white dead hairs, and apparently he had been missing a lot of work as well. He didn't want to talk about it. They sat in the same "early Mussolini" restaurant they had dined in for many years, happier years. They were bored with the menu, bored with each other. "Well, my neighbor did it again."

Nathaniel didn't want to hear about it. Why wouldn't Marty get that camera that went under the car and capture the villain on videotape? Why couldn't he do *something*!? Why did this same act keep happening week in, week out? The rule of law and endless patience weren't helping Marty, that was for sure. "This wouldn't keep happening to me," Nathaniel said, buttering his bread.

There were black bullets in Marty's eyes, and they were aimed at Nathaniel. "And what would you do? Tell me, O wise one."

"I've told you this. If you're not going to do something, then don't keep parking in the same spot."

"If you don't want your students to say bad things about you, then don't keep saying the same things in the classroom, especially about how bad they are!"

"They're not the same thing."

"Yes, they are."

They had a stand-off over the bread basket. Thank God the ante-pasta arrived. The elderly waiter could tell there was some tension in the air. "How are we tonight?" he asked.

"Fine," Nathaniel grumbled. Shut your fat face.

"All we do is fight anymore," Marty said, exasperated, once the waiter left.

Nathaniel looked at his own fingernails. They needed trimming. He was neglecting his own bodily upkeep. Even his knuckles looked loose-skinned and unhealthy. "We'll make it," he said. "Somehow."

"I wonder," Marty said. "I really do."

The words sent a jolt through Nathaniel's heart. Things weren't good, but he didn't want it to end. All that bread they'd broken together. All the kisses. There had been kisses in the past. I'll use it for the title of a book someday. *Where Are The Kisses of the Past?* — a romance novel by Nathaniel Whatshisname.

"I'm sorry," Marty said. It almost sounded sincere.

"So am I."

They took some bites. "Good, isn't it?" Nathaniel prompted.

"Too much salt." Marty spat out the bite of beef brochettes.

"You could take it out without spitting on your plate."

"Could I?" Marty poked at the salty chunk of flesh on the edge of his plate with the tines of his fork. It looked hideous.

"Do you want to go home? We don't have to finish this meal," Nathaniel said.

"I don't know what I want."

"Isn't that the story of your life?" Nathaniel regretted the words immediately, but he didn't say anything.

"Fuck you."

They both put down their forks and looked to the side of each other. Oh, damn, that it should come to this, and on their anniversary. Outside, in the courtyard of the restaurant, were small, shaped hedges that were shaking in the wind. "I think I'll order another glass of wine," Nathaniel finally said.

"You would."

"How's your speed?"

"Great. I can see how your wine is. It's making you fat and jowly. That's jowly, not jolly."

Nathaniel held his tongue. I must! This could be the end of us. Something in my bones tells me that. I must not say another word right now.

The silence began to corrode around its edges.

"I bought something," Marty suddenly said.

"What's that?" Nathaniel pretended indifference.

"This." Marty reached inside his coat, which was on the back of his chair. He brought out an ice pick, the point half-hidden by his thumb.

Oh, my God! Nathaniel thought. He's going to stab me with that! He flinched and pushed his chair back.

Marty laughed. "Afraid?"

"It's not funny." Nathaniel took the napkin off his lap and was prepared to throw it in Marty's face.

"It's not for you. It's for my neighbor."

Nathaniel wasn't so sure. He put his hands on the bottom of his chair so that he could jump up and get away.

"Is everything all right?" their waiter wanted to know.

"Perfect," Nathaniel responded.

The waiter wasn't convinced, because their food was mostly untouched, but he went away.

Nathaniel lowered his voice. "You're going to kill your neighbor?"

"Could be," Marty said, revealing the ice pick in all its lethal glory. It had a yellow wooden handle and a pick about seven inches long. "I always wanted a dick like this," Marty said.

"Jesus!"

"My neighbor is going to get a taste of his own medicine." This was getting out of hand. Marty was dead serious. "It's for his tires!" he went on. "What did you think I meant?"

Nathaniel felt creepy. His eyes kept jumping back to the ice pick. "I thought you couldn't get to his car. Isn't it in his garage?"

"Contrary to what you think, I've done some spying on the prick. I've noticed that on Sundays between two and four — at least sometimes — he leaves his car in his driveway. If I time it right, I could stick this in one of his tires, maybe several, and be gone in a flash."

Nathaniel chewed on that. "In the daylight, this is?"

"Yes."

"What if you're caught?"

"I won't get caught."

They didn't finish the meal, didn't even ask for doggy bags, didn't speak as Nathaniel drove Marty home, and didn't say good night.

Happy Anniversary!

They had hoped to include Karma Sudra in the Amended Complaint that Lancet was about to draw up (possibly as soon as the following week), so that there would be three Plaintiffs instead of just one. Unfortunately, something had come up — something about Karma's nursing degree. It seems that she might be an un-registered nurse instead of a registered one. So Lancet said that he'd have to go with just Biff and Nathaniel. Karma was heartbroken, and there was an investigation now into all her credentials — led by Dean Visigoth, naturally, who seemed to be the front man appointed by the Administration to oversee the school's side of the lawsuit. The dick!

The credit card bills were coming in, including Lancet's, and Nathaniel of course couldn't begin to pay them off. The interest was usurious, but what could he do? He had come this far, and now it was Them or Him. "You're getting me cheap, you realize," Lancet reminded him. No doubt it was true.

One of Biff's labs was in fact canceled for lack of enrollment, but he managed to eke out the other with ten students. The chair of the Physics Department wasn't happy, but he said he'd let it go — this one time. God bless Biff Thorgoode! Not only was he lending his name to the lawsuit, summer school or no summer school, he had agreed to share all the expenses with Nathaniel. He didn't even want any money if they won some. He was just happy that his daughter had recovered her singing voice and gotten a gig in Los Angeles and was already down there in rehearsal.

Biff didn't say any more about his "Godfather" friend who was going to take out the webmaster, so Nathaniel supposed they'd have to kill him with a lawyer instead.

Lancet said that the disgusting, homophobic reviews that had come in after Nathaniel's Tech TV appearance would be useful in the Amended Complaint. But there was a real concern that His Honor Judge Jesus Garza might not even accept an Amended Complaint. He might decide that Nathaniel's side was not likely to prevail, and that would be the end of that. Excerpts were lifted like the garbage they were and used in place of the libelous comments that Modos & O'Harromog had had access to. "How would His Honor feel if these things were posted about him on a website? Would he be able to dispense sentences impartially if he could be lied about so easily?" Nathaniel asked. But Lancet said they could not argue this in the Amended Complaint. Why not? They couldn't mention the judge, that's all. Shit!

Ashleigh Nashe of Tech TV called and asked if they could re-run the interview with Nathaniel because it had garnered such a reaction. He agreed, but he asked if she could at least remove the onscreen link to Teachersonparade that had been there before, making it virtually effortless for anyone in the viewing world to write up Nathaniel as a teacher instead of as a guest on a TV program. She agreed, and there were only two hundred twenty-one responses the second time around, and only four fake reviews on Teachersonparade. The first batch had finally been removed by the webmaster, after several weeks, but the new ones were just as bad:

> pick my creamy peehole pick my creamy peehole, fagg! eat my ass while your at it

> I can write hinm up any time I want to. SHUT UP.

> You teachers are all shit anyway! Freedom rules!

> don't take his classes.

The webmaster removed those too, but he left one bad one and one good one, probably because — Solomon that he was — he thought he was being "fair."

The good one said:

> I recommend Dr. Tack highly. He is an impressive and energetic instructor, from whom you can learn much if you apply yourself. I enjoyed his 101 very much. Do not be influenced by the other reviews here. —Tommy

> Hi Nathaniel,

> I see that most of the filth is gone and Doo Doo left the review I wrote about you. I signed it "Tommy" to make it sound more authentic. Did you see it?

> How's that lawsuit coming along? — Haywood

> Haywood,

> Do you still have the disks with all the reviews you've collected? We can use them now that Lancet is finally free and able to work on the Amended Complaint. I have some reviews, but we can probably use them all, or at least have them as backup ammunition to show both the defamation and the complete fraud that is Teachersonparade. — Nathaniel

> Nathaniel,

413

Can you meet me on campus tomorrow? I'll bring the items you mentioned. Noon?

It's better to use codes. You never know who might be reading our e-mails. — Haywood

Haywood,

I'll be there. And thanks!

Haywood dropped off just two of the disks at Nathaniel's office — in a brown paper bag, in his best espionage mode. "I couldn't find the rest," he said. He still seemed terrified of being identified with the Counter-Revolutionary Forces led by Nathaniel. "It's still not too late to sign on with Lancet," Nathaniel said, mostly to get a rise out of him. "Karma had to drop out."

"I wish you the best, but you've got an uphill battle." Haywood looked so silly and scared, his eyes darting around for other spies, that Nathaniel felt sorry for him more than anything else. He was hoping that maybe a check would be in the brown paper bag, but there wasn't.

He sent out a flyer for donations to his newly founded Teacher Integrity Fund. Because it was summer school, most people were gone and the donations were limited, but Trustee Barney Rock and Academic President, Boyd DeLucca, and a few others came through. Nathaniel ran, not walked, to the bank to be able to make a credit card payment. He ran into Louise Beeze, the Cat Lady, and she gave him some money too. He was still feeding the ferals for her twice a week but hoping that she would round them all up. She said she was moving and taking her own twenty-eight cats with her to Southern Utah. "I thought I had all the campus ones, but then I had to let Mommy Lamb go, because she was nursing. I had her in the trap and everything, and then I saw suckie marks on her titties, and so I had no choice."

If I put suckie marks on my titties, will His Honor Judge Jesus let us have our Amended Complaint? Nathaniel wondered.

Lancet got the Amended Complaint finished, and it seemed very good to Nathaniel and Biff. It was only nine pages long, but the obscenities certainly leapt off the pages. How could His Honor not agree that these were interfering with being a "judge" of students, even if they couldn't spell this out in the legal work? Some of the crimes against decency were clearly worse than some of the cases that came before him!

The ACLU sicked Tether & Strafe on the Amended Complaint as soon as it was received. Apparently its Gay/Lesbian Taskforce was taking it up the ass from the Free Speech Absolutists who were in charge of this lawsuit. Lancet reported on a meeting he'd had with Gus Strappado, the lead attorney: "He's a really big, slimy guy. Total smarm." So his picture hadn't lied. This from Lancet, who chose his words carefully and didn't seem to have a spiteful bone in his body. "He wants us to settle.

"We're not going to settle, are we?" Nathaniel asked.

"Not unless you want to pay their legal costs, which by now are over $100,000."

"What?! How could they possibly be that much?"

"They started the clock ticking as soon as the ACLU contacted them."

"I don't want to settle. You don't think we should, do you?" Nathaniel felt a bad taste in his mouth.

"Strappado was bragging and puffing about what an excellent case they had and how we had changed our whole argument, and so the judge was unlikely to give us the Amended Complaint."

"And what did you say?"

"I let him go on. He's a very forceful person. But I know Judge Garza, and he doesn't like lawyers that come on too strong."

"You know him?"

"I mean as a judge in the courtroom. He's arrogant, but he's usually fair."

"Usually?"

"We'll get the Amended Complaint. Don't fret."

Can my *lawyer* really beat up their lawyer? Nathaniel worried.

Nathaniel tried to write something "creative," but he couldn't concentrate. It was the first time in his life that he'd suffered from writer's block. He tried a poem and it came out like something on Teachersonparade. At least the grammar was better. He wanted a massage but couldn't afford one. He didn't want sex, so he knew he was in a bad way.

Marty was being remote. He always seemed to be half-asleep when Nathaniel managed to get through to him.

"Are you all right?"

"Yeah."

"You don't sound it."

" . . . "

"Did you use the ice pick on your neighbor's car yet?"

"No."

"How's your car?"

"I don't want to discuss it." That meant it had been attacked again.

"Do you want to go for a drive?"

"No."

"Do you think this car business is because of homophobia?"

"The guy is gay too."

"I'm worried about you, Marty."

" . . . "

There was nothing more to say.

As soon as the Defendants' legal response was submitted by the smarmy Gus Strappado, Nathaniel got three offers on his answering machine at school for interviews about the case. They already seemed to know about the nine-page Amended Complaint and the thirty-six-page response, with its numerous smarmy gems:

"Nearly two-thirds of the students' reviews on Teachersonparade rate their instructors 'Superior' or 'Good,' a fact that Plaintiffs Tack and Thorgoode cannot accept because they are such bad teachers themselves."

There was nothing about the fact that no one could validate that a single review on the website was written by the person it purported to be from and that many of the 'Good' and 'Superior' reviews could have been written by the teachers themselves. Fred Nouveau in French even admitted to Nathaniel in the note he sent with the check for the Teacher Integrity Fund that he had posted three reviews for himself and he knew two others who had done it too.

Strappado also pointed out that "many of the recent reviews of Nathaniel Tack are not student reviews at all, but that fact does not materially affect the usefulness of the website" and maintained that "the earlier sharply negative ones are all apparently authentic."

This was bullshit, however you worded it. And not a word referring to the raving homophobic slander crossed Strappado's slippery lips.

He chose to characterize Biff and Mary Ann's complaints that they had had their good reviews removed and negative ones inserted in their places as "the efforts of self-appointed guardians of 'correct' thinking to undermine the Bill of Rights in their attempts to destroy any online forum for the exchange of ideas on any topic interesting enough to be controversial."

As for any threats against any teachers, these were "hyperbole understandable by one and all in having been elicited from students under immense academic pressure."

On and on it went. It was clear Gus Strappado liked it doggy style, and his sense of social good extended about as far as a Mafia don's — to his own and nobody else.

Nathaniel talked to a local legal newspaper reporter and a radio station in Canada. He even was contacted by the "Larry Felders Show" in L.A. He had no idea who Larry Felders was, but the young-voiced setup man who arranged the call-in appearance said it was the most popular drive-time radio program in the nation.

It soon became obvious why.

It was a Geek Show. And Nathaniel was supposed to be the Geek of the Week.

But the competition was stiff.

Larry Felders had one of those impossibly deep radio voices that were supposed to make you roll over and fetch. He did a ton of commercials while Nathaniel waited. The setup man checked back from time to time. "Are you still there?'

"I'm still here."

"It won't be long now."

"Our guest today is Dr. Nathaniel Tack from up north in the city we love to hate, Santa Francesca! And he's gotten himself involved in a case of man bites dog. Up at Dr. Tack's school, Shite College, you see, it's the students who are grading the teachers! Are you there, doctor?"

"The doctor is in," Nathaniel said.

"Let me say upfront that I think you shouldn't be trying to stifle what your students want to say. Is this America or what?"

Nathaniel was more prepared now than he'd been when he'd started this. "I'd be happy to have my students say what they want to say — if I could be assured they are my students and nobody else."

"What are you saying?"

"It apparently has not yet penetrated that anyone in the world can, and does, send in reviews to that website. I have been a particular target because I have been outspoken in my opposition."

"But why do you object to people speaking their minds about you?"

"For the same reason that you don't want people speaking their minds about you — and affecting your ratings — when they've never listened to your radio show."

"And so you're claiming that these aren't your students — none of them?"

"Some of them might be. I didn't say that."

"Well, then."

Oops. Never apologize, never explain. Just keep hammering your points home. This is Talk Radio.

"Our first caller is on line two," Larry Felders' macho voice informed the radio audience. "You're on, caller."

"These damn professors think they can get away with anything. My daughter had a class where this damn sociology teacher swore all the time, and when she objected he told her to take another class. This damn guy here sounds like one of those."

"Are you one of those?" Larry Felders wanted to know.

It seemed a bit off the topic, shall we say, but Nathaniel didn't teach at damn Shite College for nothing. "The comments about teachers on this website are so filthy I can't even repeat them on the radio. I'd be bleeped out."

"He's right about that," Larry Felders said. "I've read some of them." Right on, Larry!

"Do you want me to read some of the obscenities that have been posted about me? I have them right here."

"Whoa, Professor. You'll get me thrown off the air."

"It seems like we have a double standard here. Doesn't it seem so to you, Larry?"

"At the same time you do identify yourself as openly gay, do you not?"

"Yes. So?"

"Then shouldn't you expect a certain amount of flak because of that?"

"What century are we living in? Would you say an African American man has to put up with a certain amount of flak these days just because he's African American? Or a woman? Or any other minority?"

"Of course gays aren't a real minority."

What?! Nathaniel recovered. "No, not when it comes to legal protections apparently. Just in the way they're kicked around." Gotcha!

The next caller quoted Leviticus — the "abomination" of a "man laying with a man" and said that Nathaniel was going to burn in Hell for all Eternity because he was a "perversion."

This was too easy, but Nathaniel didn't have to say anything because Larry Felders cut off the caller and said, "We're not going to have that on my show."

Yay! Nathaniel thought. "But, Larry," he said, "aren't you being inconsistent? You want me to take it online but not here on the radio. What's that? And aren't you suppressing this poor religious bigot's Free Speech while criticizing me for trying to do the same thing?"

But it was time for a commercial. Sixteen commercials. Nathaniel counted while he waited.

"Can you stay on for another segment?" the setup man wanted to know.

Why not?

They love me on Talk Radio! Nathaniel crowed.

"We're back!" Yet, before they were, Larry Felders managed to squeeze in a plug for some other show he had and three more products. Pretty soon every other media word would be followed by a commercial, just like baseball games: "That double play sponsored by Spearmint gum!" "This pitch brought to you by Pennzoil!"

"Go ahead, caller. You're on with Larry Elders and Dr. Nathaniel Tack, whose students just don't seem to like him. But why? He seems like a nice guy to me!"

Fuck you, Larry.

"If this guy's got all these bad reviews like you say, especially the same one over and over again, it's because there's something wrong with him. He should act nice to his students and listen to 'em, and then they'll like him. That's all I gotta say."

"What do you say to that, Professor?"

"Your listenership seems a little heavy on the retarded side, doesn't it?"

That lit up the phone lines.

It eventually came down to a screaming match. On one side was some thick-tongued old codger saying Nathaniel was "an effetist" and should be brought before a firing squad for "saying things against the First Amendment" and Nathaniel yelling back, "You don't seem to get it. They claim I murdered a student! They claim I raped a three-year-old boy!"

It was just awful, so awful they invited Nathaniel back for another show in two weeks.

The truly awful part was that, amidst a fallacy fest or not, Nathaniel loved it. He was not averse to having his fifteen minutes of fame, even for the wrong reasons. And anything was better than having to sit and wait for Judge Jesus to make up his mind. Garza's ruling on the Amended Complaint was slow in coming — in fact, about as slow as the Second Coming. Come on, Jesus, get the lead out and save poor teachers from Hell!

He even got some letters and e-mails about his media appearances, mostly sympathetic. See, class, you can use language to win a few for the Gipper. But he didn't much care for people sending e-mails to his personal computer, a little spooky. One of them said the sender wanted to "meet you and pick your brain." Hmm. Maybe he'd have to shut down his own website or remove his e-mail address. I am no technophobe, but still . . . His transsexual friend, Ludie Fauxville, actually heard Nathaniel mentioned on a South Bay TV station Nathaniel didn't even know about and was "thrilled" and "concerned" for him. They promised each other they get together "real soon." I haven't done a good job of keeping up my friendships, he realized, not since Marty and I became a couple. The same old mistake "real" couples make. And once the couple uncoupled, what did you have left?

But maybe he could save him and Marty yet?

Only Marty wouldn't answer his telephone.

Nathaniel drove over to the apartment and used his key to get in. He thought Marty might be sleeping, even though it was only nine o'clock, but he wasn't there. The place was an unbelievable mess. It looked like it hadn't been dusted or vacuumed for years. There were computer supplies and a scanner along with new shelving in boxes that hadn't even been opened yet. Hundreds of library books were still spread all over the sofa and stacked on the floor. The kitchen was sticky with grease, dishes in the sink, on the sideboard. The trash was spilling out of the plastic wastebasket. The refrigerator was an old model. Inside there were moldy pizza slices and desiccated oranges and little else, and the ice cube tray was frosted over so badly it wouldn't come out.

Nathaniel wrote a note and left it taped to Marty's computer:

> Dear Marty,
>
> I came by to see how you are. I hope you are okay.
>
> I care very much about you. Are you eating? Please call me.
> Your once and future lover. — Nathaniel

As he locked up the apartment, he occurred to him that Marty might be in his car. And sure enough there he was, down the block, sitting in the very spot that had given him so much grief, kitty-corner from the evil neighbor who didn't love Marty as himself. Asleep. The driver's seat was tilted back and Marty was face up, his mouth open, the breaths coming in loose waves. It did indeed look like he wasn't eating — he was so skinny it was frightening. His color wasn't good, either, but that could have been from the streetlamp.

Nathaniel tapped on the car's window, careful not to do it too hard lest he startle Marty. "Marty! It's me."

Marty stirred at once and his eyes came open, his head turning. "What do you want?"

"Let me in."

"I'm sleeping."

"I don't think you're supposed to sleep in your car."

"It's my car. I'm protecting it."

"What if the cops come by again? You don't want to get arrested again."

"I don't care."

"Of course you care. Let me in, okay?"

Marty reluctantly pulled up the car lock, and Nathaniel tried to slide inside. But there were tapes and CDs and magazines on the passenger seat. Marty grabbed them and tossed them onto the back seat.

"How are you?"

"I was fine until you woke me up."

"Why don't you sleep in your bed?"

"Because I want to sleep here. Is it any skin off your nose?"

". . . I suppose not."

"How are you? I hear you're on radio and TV. My boss heard you."

"Sometimes."

"I haven't seen it. I bet you enjoy it."

"At least I get to defend myself."

"How's your lawyer doing?"

"We're still waiting to hear from the judge — whether we can proceed to the actual trial or not."

"It's tedious, isn't it?"

"Exceedingly."

"Everything is tedious."

"Don't you get a vacation soon? Maybe we could go away for a few days. Wouldn't you like that?"

"I've used up all my vacation days."

"What do you mean?"

"I've used them up — by missing work."

"We could go up to Oregon, go white water rafting, or something."

"Yeah." It wasn't a real yes, just a flat acknowledgment.

"We both need some exercise."

"Yeah."

"Do you want to go out for something to eat?"

"I don't have any money."

"I don't either." He turned and looked at Marty's thin neck. "My treat."

"I don't really feel like it."

"You look like you're not eating."

"I'm eating." He gestured at some candy bar wrappers on the dashboard.

"Come on. Let's go eat." He gently tugged on Marty's arm.

Marty pulled the arm back. He didn't want to be touched.

"You're slowly killing yourself, Marty."

"Mind your own business."

Nathaniel didn't reply, and they sat in silence. Could you help someone who didn't want to be helped?

"Are you still going to the clinic for your methadone?"

"Yes."

"Have you had a checkup there lately?"

"I'm fine."

"Can I hold your hand?"

Marty looked at him sideways. "It's a little late, isn't it?"

"Do you want me to go kill your neighbor for you?"

Marty should have smiled, but he didn't. "He popped my tires again. Two of them."

"Have you punctured his?"

"He hasn't been parking in his driveway."

"How long have you been sitting in the car?"

"Two days."

"It's not worth it, Marty. You need to . . ."

"I need to do what I need to do. If he comes out here and touches my car again, he gets this in the face." He patted his coat pocket where the ice pick could just be made out.

"Be sure he doesn't have a weapon himself."

"Everything is so horrible, just so horrible."

"I know."

Marty was crying, the tears gleaming in the streetlights. "Why is everything so horrible?"

"I don't know."

"I don't want to live anymore."

"Yes, you do."

"I'm serious."

"I know you are. Sure you don't want something to eat? I think that little Arab grocery story up the street is still open."

"I don't want anything."

"Wait here. I'll get something."

"Some juice."

"I'll be right back. Okay?"

Nathaniel hurried to the grocery store, bought some food and hurried back. This time he saw that the two curbside tires were flat. He hadn't noticed the first time. Marty had fallen asleep again, but he woke him, gently, and they sat in the car and drank guava juice and ate baloney slices straight from the package, and didn't touch each other.

"Good, isn't it?" Nathaniel pushed.

Marty didn't answer, the tears rolling down his cheeks and onto his baloney slice.

Lancet called with the news. Judge Garza had accepted the Amended Complaint!

"Now let me get this straight," Nathaniel said. "This means we can go to trial?"

"That means we can proceed with our final legal argument."

"It doesn't mean we've actually won anything?"

"The judge didn't cut us off at the knees, and that's good."

"And Tether & Strafe and the ACLU can reply to us afterwards?"

"You can count on it."

"And *then* we can go to trial?"

"Hopefully."

"Before a jury or a judge?"

"Sorry you got into this?"

"I've fought passionately for only two causes in my life. One of them is gay rights — to be more exact, gay literature, which to me has never meant more than telling the truth about gays instead of the lies perpetrated over the centuries. If we're to be condemned, let it be for the truth, not somebody's wild surmise. The other cause is this one — for the teaching profession. Things are bad enough now, but if this website wins, then it's all over for any kind of standards or sane working environment. Teachers will be at the mercy of anyone — not just your everyday school shooters, the way it is now. As flies to wanton boys are we to the Internet. They kill us for their sport."

"Have you been practicing that speech?"

"A little. Does it sound that way?"

"Don't become too literary now."

"I won't if Strappado doesn't become too legalistic."

"That's not possible."

"Yuck."

"You've become a media darling, I understand."

"At least I'm changing the discussion. It's not always and only about Free Speech and how I'm taking it away from the poor students. I read the journalists a few quotations about Biff and me fucking each other while the shit flies out of our assholes and the like, and — guess what! — the whole tenor of their questions changes."

"Just be careful, Nathaniel."

He was not about to ask Lancet if he thought he shouldn't be doing the interviews. He was going on his own gut instinct. He'd trusted lawyers enough to last him a lifetime. Three lifetimes. Thank the Lord he'd gotten Lancet or he might have developed a Bad Attitude toward the entire legal profession. Couldn't have that!

Now it became a waiting game, as if hadn't been! Waiting, waiting, waiting. Lancet had another case he had to deal with, and that delayed him. And delayed him. And delayed him.

Oh, please, not again! He wasn't backing out, was he?

This time Nathaniel sent a fax asking him directly.

Lancet's fax came back with a handwritten note on it:

> No, I'm not backing out! We have until fall!
>
> I've noticed that Title 47 requires "good faith" on the part of a webmaster. Dude Lather has shown anything but "good faith."
>
> It could be the key to winning this!
>
> Blake
>
> P.S. Can you work on this?

Nathaniel and Biff got together and tried to hammer out a rough draft of the final legal Complaint, concentrating on the "good faith" clause. Biff had mentioned that he'd had a year of law school. That was good. However, he had flunked out. That was bad. He flew to Chicago to see his old buddy the Top Notch Lawyer to see if he might help out Lancet and them. He was glad to see Biff "as always" but far too busy to take on the case. But, yes, the "good faith" argument "sounded promising."

Several newspapers interviewed him. "The Lon Owens Show" on KGO, with a guest host, called and wondered if Nathaniel would reconsider and come on. But he didn't get the message for several days because it had been left at school and he was trying to stay away from there. Except when he wasn't. He'd go over and look for teachers teaching summer school and talk to them and send them begging notes for the Teacher Integrity Fund. Nona Dwibble, former chair of the department and former nun, donated fifteen dollars. Elita Braine was at the bank that she and Nathaniel both used and promised to put some money into his new Integrity Fund and even got the account number. And then she didn't do it. At least she didn't take any out.

He thought about going up to Oregon to see his son, who had gotten a job as a counselor in a Boy Scouts camp. But it didn't work out, and Nathaniel didn't go. It might have been awkward anyway, when Jim introduced him: "I'd like you all to meet my homosexual father, who just happens to be an atheist and who has several other unpopular opinions that have caused quite a stir down there. Let's hear it for my dad!"

He and Marty had two desultory telephone conversations and no other contact. Marty was still making it to work, at least most days. "I worry about you," Nathaniel said both times.

"No need to worry about me," Marty said, in a worrisome way.

News came that Nathaniel had won First Place in the American New Play Competition for a play he had submitted ages earlier. It was based on his relatives and in what he considered a realistic mode, but the award committee specifically complimented him on the "absurdist elements" in the script that "made such a powerful statement." Whatever. It was two hundred dollars and free trip in the winter to the convention of Theater South.

He had sex a few times. No matter how many times you have it, it doesn't take up as much time as the boring and painful parts of life. He had a mosquito bite that lasted longer.

A one-act of his was selected for a bill at the Edinburgh Fringe Festival, produced by an acquaintance of an acquaintance of Marty's. It was called "Alcoholic Nuns" and was about five medieval wine-making nuns and their struggle for salvation. It should have been done in campy drag, but apparently the group doing it took it seriously. He probably wouldn't be able to afford to go to Edinburgh to see it, though.

In June he wrote a couple of songs, managing to hum the words and melody into a tape recorder. One was country ("She's Got the Pretties"). Nathaniel hated country music and this was really about Slacker, but it actually sounded good. He hoped to get a demo made if he won the lawsuit.

In July he went to lunch at a nice restaurant located on one of the refashioned piers of the city, treating Karma Sudra, who was still fighting Dean Visigoth about her nursing credentials. Oh, leave her alone! Since she was from India she obviously knew a thing or two about birth!

She had called to ask Nathaniel his advice on something she was considering.

"And now what's this all about?" he said after they were seated. He looked out at the ocean washing up below them. There were long-unused piers on both sides, brown, dead weeds growing between the slats. A seal stuck its head out of the water a little further out. It was perfect. He needed something perfect.

"Perhaps you would rather not discuss this subject while we are eating," Karma said.

She really was considering doing it doggy style?

"It's about my being so short," she said.

She didn't look that short today. But maybe she was sitting up tall in her chair. She actually looked nice. Her infected earlobe had cleared up, and she was sporting new earrings with two Hindu gods he didn't recognize. They matched her "*bindi*," or whatever that red jewel in her forehead was called. She had big black eyes in her sweet, miniscule face. She didn't limp when she was sitting down.

Their "baby squash soup with piquant radish whirls" came. The seal was romping in the water.

"Anything but the lawsuit. I need a break from thinking and talking about it."

"I indeed admire you very much for persisting with this. That is why I seek your advice. I think that you will tell me the truth." She kept her back stiff, her spoon just so. "My husband does not approve of what I am considering, but then he is very old-fashioned."

"Fire away."

Karma spooned her soup away from her to cool it, very formal, very Old World. "I know, of course, that I am short."

"Not at all."

"I am. I have come to accept it. I am forty-six years old, and one must know one's place in the great scheme of things." She spooned away from her again and then took a taste of the soup. "Is yours piquant enough, Nathaniel? Mine is very."

He looked away from the seal and toward Karma.

"Yet I am leaning toward having an operation to improve my height," she said.

"Isn't there some medicine you can take now?" (Viagra for the legs?)

"I inquired. However, there is nothing suitable at my age. Perhaps with children who tend toward dwarfism. But I, of course, am not a dwarf."

"Of course not."

"My proportions are completely normal, just small."

"You look wonderful. I love those earrings."

"But I am not happy with my height."

"What operation would this be?" Nathaniel looked back out at the pier's old weeds and the murky ocean beyond. A freighter was passing by. Maybe he could swim out and float away on it. . . . Maybe the seal would let him ride on its back to . . . ? Probably not.

"I have read about an operation whereby the legs are lengthened, thus giving the individual as much as six more inches in height."

"Really!"

He didn't want to know.

"It involves stretching. Major stretching."

Now he really didn't want to know. "You don't say."

"You don't mind talking about this at lunch?"

"Me?"

"You're sure?"

"Of course not." The woman needed a break from her many troubles.

"First the vertebrae must be freed — I believe that involves a small incision or two. And then the vertebrae need to be manipulated."

Nathaniel wished he had ordered wine.

"Next the patient is placed onto a pallet, and the limbs are attached to rubberized rings and pulled and pulled, over a number of sessions, each lasting but half an hour, though the entire procedure could last as long as a year."

"I thought we agreed not to talk about Teachersonparade," Nathaniel said.

She smiled. "Oh, but this is gentle pulling. The pain is minimal, I have been assured by my chiropractor. Then medicinal herbs are applied."

"Really."

Have you tried our New Age Rack?

"Oh, I forgot to mention that plastic prostheses, sturdy but flexible, are inserted — to maintain the desired height permanently. In a year, they say, it is all but impossible to tell what was stretched and what was not, once the bruising and the swelling subside."

"And you can walk after this?"

"Evidently there could be some motor skill problems. Most are not that noticeable."

A limp on top of your limp? You'll be walking like Frankenstein in no time!

Their seafood entrees arrived, "petrale almandine with seasonal capers for the lady" and "crabcakes Antoinette for the gentleman." The seal and the freighter were no longer in view. The brown weeds were still there.

"I may be of normal height following this operation — perhaps even on the tall side. I have always wanted to be tall."

"Amazing."

"Of course one must return for some periodic stretchings. Unfortunately, my husband does not approve."

Couldn't you just walk around on stilts, as needed? Nathaniel thought.

"So . . . do you think I should do it?"

He choked a little on his crabcakes Antoinette.

"I don't think you approve either, Nathaniel." She was tucking in to her petrale almandine with seasonal capers.

"Couldn't something go wrong — terribly wrong?"

"Not with my luck!" Karma said, her black eyes and "*bindi*" twinkling — and without a speck of irony. "The doctors said I would not live two days when I was born, that I was too sickly, too tiny, and yet look at me today — about to change my size! They said I would not find a second husband, but I did. They said I would have to throw myself upon the funeral pyre of my first husband in compliance with suttee. Little did they know that a monsoon would drench the flames of that funeral pyre before my husband's relatives could throw me on it and I would escape to this great country! " She twirled her fish fork like Don Quixote.

Nathaniel ultimately didn't know how to advise Karma, but he went home and called a plastic surgeon for himself. Those jowls were coming off, goddamn it. Then he scheduled Lasik surgery. The scales were going to fall from his eyes as well, if it killed him.

Come on, media! Come on, you legal bastards! How can I lose?! Karma Sudra is my guru, and I cannot but take inspiration from such a brave, strong, and optimistic woman!

He and Biff managed to pull together a revised Final Legal Complaint that emphasized "lack of good faith" in the webmaster for not keeping lies off the website, tied in with "false light," "defamation," and "verbal and sexual harassment." Lancet of course would have to get it into final, final shape. He said he would be finished with his other case "pretty soon."

It was much easier to read small print now, because of the Lasik surgery on his left eye, and all it had taken was a scalpel lifting a flap on his cornea and a few zaps of a laser. He stung like hell for twelve hours. It was like having sand kicking in your eye, but once that was over, Nathaniel didn't have to use glasses anymore. The operation on his jowls, which included everything that sagged under his chin, was more problematic. It involved the doctor giving twelve injections with a needle in Nathaniel's lower face, an experience not soon forgotten, then cutting out the excess, and stitching it up.

But, hallelujah, both doctors took credit cards!

Then Lancet called. "I don't think we should sue the school."

"What?!"

"I believe the school is culpable, but I don't think we can prove it. We should also drop the part about the Alliance of Students."

"You're kidding."

"Instead, we should just concentrate on Teachersonparade and the webmaster."

"When did all this develop?"

"I've been talking with Gus Strappado. He says you're in over your head."

"Fuck him. . . . *Are* we?"

"Maybe. The school has four lawyers. And that's just for itself. It also got a law firm for the Alliance of Students. Why did you sue the Alliance, again?"

"It was Modos & O'Harromog's idea."

"Once they heard the Alliance had some dough?"

"Yes."

"I've heard they're ambulance chasers."

"That's the least thing they are."

"You should have come to me first."

"I wish I had, believe me."

"If you and Biff agree, we'll try to get out of suing the college and the Alliance."

"But we're not dropping the whole suit, right?"

"It will be simpler and more winnable this way."

"Just the ACLU against us."

"And Tether & Strafe."

"How big is that firm?"

"They have about a hundred lawyers."

"Oh, god."

"I've talked with a Trustee named Barney Rock. I forget where I got his name and number from."

"I gave them to you."

"You did? Good. He seemed amenable to working it so that the school and the Alliance are dropped, and they won't ask for any money."

"Money?"

"If you drop defendants without their agreement, they can demand legal expenses."

"Will this never end?"

"It's the way it is, Nathaniel."

"You really think this is the way to go?"

"I do. Can you talk to Barney Rock and see what can be done?"

"I guess."

"That will leave just one target. Got to go. Keep me up to date."

So the rest of the summer was spent negotiating with the school via Barney Rock and the Chancellor. It all had to be carefully crafted — not because the school wanted money but because the Alliance of Students didn't want to drop out. They even had a sit-in with placards in the Chancellor's office, led by Gorilla Woman on her cell phone outside in the parking lot:

OUR FREE SPEECH NOT UP

FOR NEGOTAITON

THE ALLIANCE NEEDS YOU'RE HELP

TO END COLLEGE'S OPPRESION!

The usual signs and the usual suspects, including Jake Trosky and Antwan Timmons, minus some because it was summer school, out in force.

The sit-in really pissed off the Chancellor, who seemed to be a very busy — too busy — man, but it was necessary for Nathaniel to talk to him about half a dozen times on the telephone. "I didn't realize how nasty they could be," the Chancellor confessed in a weak moment. "I've given them everything they asked for!" When Nathaniel asked why he hadn't supported the faculty in the lawsuit, he replied, "I was advised that the student activists would be an even bigger thorn in my side." The squeaky thorn got the grease, it would seem.

The candor was refreshing, in a kind of curdled, stinky way. At least now the Chancellor wasn't as friendly to the Alliance as he'd been. Or was he just schmoozing Nathaniel?

Barney Rock was terrific. So was Boyd DeLucca of the Academic Union. Nathaniel talked often with both the rest of that summer, and hence all the details of the settlement with the college and the Alliance were hammered out.

Except for one thing.

The Alliance of Students wanted $100,000 in order to be dropped from the lawsuit— even though it had used the lawyer which the *school* had provided for free. These Under-Represented Thieves wouldn't let go without some money crossing their palms.

Besides that, Slacker, who almost never went out, went missing for three days, and Nathaniel finally gave up on her. She wasn't at the Animal Shelter. She wasn't in the Dead Cats Folder. She wasn't lying dead on a street anywhere in the neighborhood. No neighbor had seen her.

Then suddenly, without so much as an explanation, she was back, apparently no worse for wear. She gave out that sad little plaintive (Plaintiff?) meow she pulled out when the food wasn't to her liking or she was bored and wanted "rubbies." Nathaniel found himself hugging her and trying not to cry into her fur. With Marty not calling thrown in, it was all just becoming too much.

"**M**arty, are you there?"
It had been two weeks now, and Marty still wouldn't answer the telephone.

"Marty, are you all right? Please call me."

Nathaniel knew that something was very wrong, and yet he was afraid to go to Marty's apartment.

"Marty, please pick up. If you're there, please pick up!"

Then Marty's answering machine stopped working. A mechanical male voice came through: "This machine is full. We are unable to accept your call. Please try later."

When Marty's mother and sister called saying they hadn't heard from Marty either, Nathaniel feared the worst. The mother didn't like him, so it had to be very serious for her to get in touch. The sister said it had been a couple of weeks, and that Marty had sounded despondent then, was still battling with his neighbor over the punctured tires. In fact, it had escalated into a confrontation on the sidewalk. Marty hadn't wanted to talk about it in detail, but apparently he and the other man had traded punches, and the neighbor had used pepper spray on Marty. The last thing Marty said to her was that he was going to press charges for assault.

It was a week before the fall semester was to begin and Nathaniel had some lectures he wanted to re-do, and Lancet was re-working the settlement with Shite and the Alliance and getting the final, final, final legal Complaint against the website in order and wanted Nathaniel and Biff's input, but he knew that he couldn't use any of those as an excuse. Nathaniel told the mother and the sister that he would go and check.

When he parked, he saw Marty's car, parked on the corner opposite the uptight neighbor's house. It had three punctured tires and two tickets under the windshield wipers. CDs and tapes of Marty's favorite music were scattered over the backseat. There were Kleenex and more CDs on the passenger seat and both floor mats. Not good. At least Marty wasn't in it.

The landlord's horrible dog came snarling down the stairs at Nathaniel as he inserted his key into the lock of Marty's door. She had fangs the size of icicles, her eyes bright with rage. Nathaniel kicked toward her and rushed into the apartment. He could hear the landlord's voice saying, "You bad girl!" She scratched at Marty's door with fierce nails first, and then she trotted upstairs.

The smell hit Nathaniel as he stood in the tiny entrance way that led into the studio apartment — an odor that was both fusty and uric.

Marty was lying on top of the bed, fully clothed. As Nathaniel drew closer, he could see a yellowish green color to the face and hands. The eyes were shut and the lips pulled back slightly into a rictus smile, only it wasn't a smile. The beard had not been trimmed for some time and probably had continued to grow, as many white hairs in it now as black. The ice pick's yellow handle stuck out of the chest, right above where the heart was. The hand that had jammed it there had let go of the ice pick and fallen back to his side. Blood that had seeped out of the wound down his shirt had long since dried. A hint of pepper spray lingered in the air.

Nathaniel sat on the side of the bed, sobbing, wanting to touch this man he had loved, but the body was in no condition to be touched, must not be touched because, if he did, that is what Nathaniel would remember for the rest of his life.

He considered getting into the bed and pulling out the ice pick and stabbing it into his own heart. Lying there next to Marty. How long would it take to die? Too long? Not long enough? "Sweet, sad prince," he sobbed, "why couldn't I help you?' His body heaved. "And goddamn you too! Goddamn you, Marty!"

Some of the library books and the other items that had filled the place before had been stacked neatly in cardboard boxes as if Marty had been cleaning up. Then on the screen of the computer Nathaniel saw a post-it note, sideways.

IT'S ALL SHITE! — You see, Nathaniel!

IT'S ALL OVER.

Don't have a memorial for me. Don't!

Nathaniel opened a window. There were several flower pots on the table nearby with orchids that Marty had let die. He touched one of them and the spindly leaves came away in his hand.

He went into the bathroom and washed his face with cold water, dabbing at his eyes until the tears stopped. He could see in the mirror that he had aged a great deal the past year. He no longer looked young, the forehead not so much furrowed as loosened, the area under the eyes crisscrossed with a thousand little . . . ugly punctuation marks. Life is right there, sitting on my face, he thought.

He had to notify the landlord, he supposed, and when the man walked in behind Nathaniel he looked surprised to see the shape the apartment was in. So this was the person Marty hadn't wanted to tell that the shower wasn't working, that the bathtub drain was clogged, that the heat didn't work, all because Marty was afraid that the landlord would think poorly of him. And here he was lying dead in his bed, an ice pick in his chest, and the landlord could see it all anyway, so what the fuck did it matter?

"I haven't been in here for several years," the landlord said. He was a dumpy little redheaded dot-comer whose wife had left him and moved into the apartment above Marty's and then had a series of "lovers" who had banged her silly, and noisily, until she had finally moved out and left him with just his building and his vicious dog.

"You can have it cleaned," Nathaniel said. "I'll pay for it."

"It can come out of Marty's deposit," the landlord said. He was trying to be nice. "I didn't realize he felt so bad. Is it . . . ?"

"It's a long story," Nathaniel said.

"I tapped on his door about a week ago and asked if he was all right, and he didn't open the door but said he was fine." The landlord was looking at the library books everywhere. "He did sound okay," he added guiltily.

"He's at peace now, as they say," Nathaniel said. Bullshit, of course, but what you gonna do!

"You don't suppose somehow our neighbor got in here and did this, do you? I know Marty was having some problems."

"He just managed to get inside Marty's head. I understand it completely. You have so much rage you can't direct against the people who deserve it, so you turn it against yourself."

"You've been involved in some case yourself, I believe. Isn't that right? Marty mentioned it, and I heard you on the radio."

"Thank you." Is that what you said? Thank you?

"I hope you win your lawsuit. That's not right, what they're doing. We have hackers where I work. They're vicious. It used to be just a lark, but no more."

"Maybe I'm winning after all," Nathaniel said, his heart aching as he took a blanket from the chest where Marty kept them and placed it over the body. It was a blanket Nathaniel had bought when he'd been in Ireland on a trip, bought for him especially because the green looked like the color of a marijuana plant that Marty was fond of.

"Shouldn't we'd call 911?" the landlord asked.

Nathaniel nodded, arranging the blanket. The ice pick underneath seemed more prominent this way, but he couldn't bear to look at the face, at the discolored skin a second longer.

The paramedics were the first to arrive, and Nathaniel and the landlord went out to meet with them. An ambulance had been sent, even though Marty was long past needing one. The driver sat in the ambulance while the two paramedics, a man and a woman, both young, came into the apartment. They examined the body while Nathaniel and the landlord stood near the entrance way. They seemed to register the smell in the room and were eager to get outside in the main hallway. The landlord's dog was inside upstairs but barking like she wanted to rip all their throats open.

"What was the name of the deceased?" the female paramedic asked.

"Martin Wheeler Dent."

"And you are — a friend?"

"Yeah, a friend."

"A close friend?"

"Yes, his lover."

She gave Nathaniel a look that said, Did you kill him? She glanced at the body again and seemed to determine that it was suicide. "Looks like nobody's been around here for a while."

"We were estranged."

She looked back. "And who are *you*?"

"His landlord."

She called the police and got Marty's name wrong, but they got it straightened out eventually. They all went out onto the street in front of the building. "Did you check for other weapons?" the male paramedic asked and then went back for a second look. It was apparent that the woman didn't want to stay in the dead man's room any longer. After a bit, the male paramedic came out and said, "I didn't see anything, but it's hard to see with all that stuff laying around. It looks like a suicide." He looked up at Nathaniel as if he might have offended him in some way. "We'll notify the medical examiner's office. You'll wait?" Nathaniel and the landlord nodded. The paramedic climbed back into the front of the ambulance and got on his cell phone. The woman joined him up in the cab.

Two male police officers, also young, straight, arrived about ten minutes later. They went into the apartment, and Nathaniel followed but didn't go all the way in. They asked him if he lived here and what his connection to the deceased was. The landlord came in and opened a second window to let in some fresh air. Nathaniel noticed one of the cops lift his eyebrows toward the other one at the state of decomposition of the body.

"He was a city employee," Nathaniel said, feeling silly as soon as he said it. He thought it might make them treat the body better somehow. See — Marty was like you. Here it was the very liberal city of Santa Francesca, and yet Nathaniel felt some of that old attitude coming from the cops — that after all he and Marty were just queers.

"Did he have any diseases that you knew about?"

"Not really," Nathaniel said.

"You're positive?"

"No, he didn't have AIDS." So you don't have to worry.

"Did he have jaundice?"

"I don't know. Maybe at the very end he did."

The cops had of course spotted the marijuana on the dresser and the rolling papers and the pipe that went with it, plus a small tin box of speed on the nightstand beside the bed. No doubt they would seize all these. "There may be some liquor and cigarettes in the kitchen too," Nathaniel said.

They didn't seem to understand the lecture he was giving them, but they let it drop. They weren't too bad, actually. They waited outside with Nathaniel and the landlord for the medical examiner to arrive, making small talk.

The medical examiner, a balding male in his early fifties, and his assistant, a sloppy, heavyset one in his twenties, arrived in a car that was clearly marked Santa Francesca Coroner's Office. But apparently "Medical Examiner" sounded more euphemistic. The older man introduced himself and his assistant to Nathaniel and the landlord. The cops already knew him.

"Does one of you want to accompany me?" he asked. "There should be a witness." He evidently knew the rules very well. He was already pulling on blue rubber gloves, as was his assistant, taken from his medical bag.

The landlord agreed to go, and Nathaniel waited in the outside hallway with the cops. Nathaniel turned to the wall, overcome by a new welling of grief. He didn't want the cops to see him weeping, but he couldn't stop himself.

Several people on the sidewalk outside looked in, curious because of the ambulance, the patrol car, and the coroner's car parked in front. "What happened?" a youthful, wide-eyed Asian woman asked, coming to the propped-open door.

"A tenant died," Nathaniel said.

"Oh, I'm sorry," she said.

God bless her, she didn't ask if there was going to be a vacancy soon.

The dog upstairs was still barking, not quite as much. Another resident of the apartment building, a crippled old man, came in and said, "Is Marty all right?"

"He died," Nathaniel said.

The old man looked sad but said nothing more and slowly went up the stairs to his own apartment. "For God's sakes, Gretel, shut up!" Nathaniel yelled as at the dog he slammed his door shut.

The coroner's assistant came out of the apartment and gave Nathaniel a look that seemed to say, It doesn't seem to be murder, so you're off the hook. "We'll be bringing him out in a minute, if you want to move."

Nathaniel moved out of the hallway onto the sidewalk as the coroner and his assistant came through with the white body bag. It looked heavy and "loose" and unbeautiful and terrible, and Nathaniel had to look away as they lifted it into the back of the ambulance, helped by the two paramedics, who then got in and drove away.

The coroner stayed and came back into the hallway. He seemed more physically fit than his assistant and spoke in a quiet, "sensitive" voice. "I'll have to go back in now and collect valuables. I'll need somebody to be a witness again, someone familiar with the place?"

"I've got to check on my dog," the landlord said.

"I'll go," Nathaniel volunteered.

"Thank you. And you are?"

Nathaniel gave him his name. "Marty and I were partners, but we didn't live together."

"I understand."

Inside, the coroner did a quick once-over of the kitchen, the bathroom, and the bedroom/living area, still wearing blue rubber gloves.

His first question was, "Was the deceased Caucasian?"

Oh, my god, what didn't that say. "Yes."

"What medications did he take?"

"A lot."

"Codeine, anti-depressants, Hydrocodone?" The coroner was looking at old bottles stacked in the closet, which was partially blocked with "things."

"Probably. Though some of that stuff is old."

"Methamphetamines?"

"Yes."

"Anything else?"

"I don't know. . . . He was also on methadone."

The coroner gathered up the speed, the weed, the pipe and some other bottles from the nightstand near the bed and put them inside a plastic bag. "Seen worse," he said.

Nathaniel had to excuse himself and went out into the hallway, where the cops were still waiting, just outside the front door. One of them was having a cigarette and being careful to blow the smoke away from the building.

In a few minutes the coroner came out with two plastic bags full of "valuables" and asked Nathaniel and the cops to join him. He knelt down in the hallway and took out a card that had blank lines printed on it. "I'm going to show you what I took and record it here," he explained. He began to itemize:

"Ten keys." He counted each one. Two of them were for Nathaniel's condo, the front door and the inside door.

"Seventeen dollars in cash." He counted out the ten, the five, and the two ones. "There was also a penny jar that I left inside," he added. "Various ID — a driver's license, a city ID. Right?"

"Yes."

The cops looked on impassively.

"Seven credit cards, assorted slips of paper." He held up a bunch of them. "Looks like receipts for *tire* repair. Quite a few of those. Yes?"

"Yes," Nathaniel replied. The bastard, Satanist neighbor.

"And a checkbook." He wrote VOID on the two remaining checks. "Do you know who the next of kin would be?"

"His mother, his sister."

"Do you have their numbers?"

"I do. At home."

"Do they live in the city?"

"The sister does. The mother lives about three hours away."

"It might be good if you got a note from one of them that authorizes you to handle his valuables, so that you can pick these up at the Medical Office later — if you want them, that is."

"I'll see what I can do. I'm not on the best terms with his mother."

"I can call them — the sister and the mother — if you'd rather."

"I'll do it."

"You sure?"

"I'll do it."

"You don't happen to have the mother's number on you?"

"It's in Marty's address book."

"I didn't find that."

"I'll call her, rest assured." Nathaniel thought: She'll probably say, "This is what Marty gets for being gay!" And he would have to restrain himself from saying, "No, this is what Marty gets for you telling him when he was fourteen that you'd rather see him dead than gay!"

"Anything else we should look at inside?"

Nathaniel shook his head.

The coroner put the plastic bags and itemized list into his medical bag, then pulled the door shut and took out a black-and-white sticker and placed it across the doorjamb. The landlord came back just then, and the coroner said, "When Mr. Tack here calls you and says that he's been authorized by the next of kin and has that piece of paper, then Mr. Tack can go in. Otherwise, if this seal is broken, notify the police."

The police officers nodded.

The landlord nodded.

And they all left.

"VOID" and "next of kin" and "Was the deceased Caucasian?" somehow said it all.

Nathaniel called Marty's mother, breaking her heart. She went on and on about how she "should have understood him better," how she "should have pushed him more," and "now it was too late." Nathaniel let her say what she had to say. Surely, she thought, there should be a memorial service — a Lutheran one, Missouri Synod — for her son. No, Marty had explicitly written in the note that he didn't want one. The sister was better, and somehow, though it took a few days, Nathaniel got the authorization to take care of Marty's property, such as it was. There were some stocks that were not worth much and a city pension fund. No beneficiary was listed. Marty had probably thought he'd outlive Nathaniel. It didn't matter. Nothing much mattered.

Getting the death certificate was hard, the signing for it. It said the death was "Self-Inflicted." Yeah, right. The "valuables" were returned, except for the dope and the pipe and the cash. They were even kind enough to include the ice pick. Nathaniel took them all and threw them off a pier into the ocean near where he had sex. Maybe he'd have sex again some day, no doubt he would. Only not that day. Not that day.

The hardest part of all was going back to Marty's apartment and trying to deal with the mess, to see if there might be a will or other papers. Some pictures of them together. Mementos. Whatever. He found two photographs. They had gone to Maui once, but the clinic had screwed up the methadone transfer and Marty had had withdrawals most of the time in beautiful Hawaii. At least in the photograph he was smiling and the beard was dark and young.

Nathaniel played back the messages on Marty's answering machine. Many of them were from him:

"I know you're there, Marty! Pick up!"

"Martin. Enough of this!"

"Marty, honey. It's your honey. . . . Are you dead?"

There was a message from Marty's mother as well, in a small, whiny voice:

"Why don't you ever call me? Please call. You're my only son. What's wrong with you? Just call me and I'll never ask you to call again. Okay? . . . This is your mother. Please!"

The sister had called a week before he died:

"Hey, Big Martin, it's your Big Sis here. Give us a tinkle sometime. Miss you."

There were also calls from creditors:

"Mr. Dent, it is very important that you call USA Credit immediately. Our toll-free number is . . . "

"Mr. Martin Dent, this is Maximum Credit. You need to reach us in the next day or so to deal with your late payments."

And from the branch where Marty had worked as a library tech:

"Marty, are you coming in today? We're understaffed. Is something wrong? Please, see if you can make it in at least for today."

"Marty, are you going to make it in today? It's Wednesday. Marty, this is not good!"

There was a call from Marty's speed dealer, or so it seemed. Somebody named Jack. It was the only name on the speed dialer. How amusing.

"Hey, Marty. You still want me to come over? You were supposed to confirm. What do you want me to do?"

There didn't seem to be any calls from friends. Marty had fewer friends than Nathaniel did. Would friends have saved his life? Nathaniel thought, Nothing can save your life if you don't want your life anymore.

There was no memorial service for Marty, but Nathaniel did visit with the sister and they told each other little anecdotes about him. At twelve Marty had been voted Best Picker-Up in the Lutheran Boys League, which was dedicated to picking up trash on the bad side of town, part of its spiritual outreach program. Marty had burned out on picking up trash, it seemed. Nathaniel told the sister that Marty had died of a heart problem that had gone undetected. He didn't think she believed him, but she wanted to and didn't ask to see the death certificate. She'd tell the mother the lie, he supposed.

Marty's car was towed by the city before Nathaniel could deal with it, and he decided to just let it go. Within a week, the landlord also had all of Marty's possessions removed from the apartment and placed in a dumpster in front. Nathaniel tried going through it, furious, cutting his hands, unable to reach most of it. The truly sad part was that most of it was junk and had no meaning except to Nathaniel. He threatened the landlord with a lawsuit, but he knew he wouldn't follow through. He'd had enough of lawsuits.

Now all he had to do was decide how to continue his own life in all its shitty, unfunny turmoil.

Lancet called Nathaniel and Biff to see if they could come to his office for two days of conferring on the last legal Complaint. The semester had started, and both had department meetings and first classes, and that made it difficult.

But they'd better! Both also had low enrollments. It looked like Biff would lose another lab, and Nathaniel might have only one class instead of four. Spike Burns had said he'd tried to put some students into Nathaniel's sections, and they had balked because they had heard that he "graded too hard" and "made controversial comments" and "had done something bad to a male student." Biff's chair said there was a rumor going around that Biff "performed dangerous magic tricks" using his students as guinea pigs. The bubble reputation was blowing up in their faces.

It was proving harder to show the tampering with Biff's and his wife's reviews than they had expected, because they needed to show that ones which Biff had not written — legitimate student ones — had also been removed. Of course what was "legitimate" and what wasn't lay in the ass of the beholder. They needed access to the webmaster's hard drive to see who in fact had written what. Biff was convinced his old arch enemy in Physics had orchestrated the series of bad reviews in the past few months, and the handiwork of Fly on the Wall seemed evident, but how could you prove he was the culprit unless you could subpoena him? Lancet said he didn't think Judge Garza would grant "Discovery" about very many people, but maybe he would allow it about Dude

Lather and Fly on the Wall. Was it possible that Haywood knew the real name of Fly on the Wall? Plus a note from Haywood verifying that he had read and captured reviews and seen them manipulated and deleted, especially the ones about Dean Visigoth and other supporters of Teachersonparade, would likewise be what they would need to nail this down.

"Haywood said he'd give me anything to help us win," Nathaniel said.

Late in the afternoon of the second day, after they had completed the almost final draft of the last legal Complaint, which ran to twenty-five pages, they felt pretty good about it. The filthy reviews about both Nathaniel and Biff leapt off the pages — including new ones daily. They accused them of having "scat sex" with each other, of "butt raping" their students, of having "unclear, unfair, racist, and impossible standards," and many other things that were hard to read, even though they knew they weren't true. How galling — that people were reading these things online and deciding at that very moment to take their classes or not, using this "Brave New World of Internet discourse." Nathaniel and Biff and Lancet sat there in the crowded office and tried to parse lie from lie. What discourse? When the teachers weren't even permitted to respond to these libels? Not that they would have! There is some s***, as the poet said, I will not eat.

When Nathaniel left a message on Haywood's answering machine about the help they needed to finalize everything, here is what he got in return on his:

> Hello, Nathaniel, it's Haywood. I thought I made it clear to you that I wanted nothing more to do with this case. I'm sure I told you that at the beginning of summer school. Didn't I? In any case, I am not willing to go on record with what I know about the site. I am burned out about this and into a project of my own right now. I also have classes to prepare. I'm teaching an extra one this term. I'm sorry, but I can't help you. I thought you knew that. I think you should just drop it.

What was there to be said about such a person? No, Nathaniel thought, this can't be about any one fucked-up person, any one teacher, good or bad. It's about the principle.

Later — he'd deal with Haywood Haywire later. He called Lancet and told him they couldn't count on any testimony from the Mole. He'd never delivered the rest of the disks, either. "We'll work around it," Lancet said. "I've got to get this Complaint in by tomorrow afternoon at the latest."

What Nathaniel couldn't understand was why these "reviews" weren't considered Hate Speech? There were posters and flyers all over campus condemning Hate Speech about any group you cared to name, except teachers, all self-righteous in the extreme about not using Free Speech in this way, though it was perfectly fine to use it online AGAINST TEACHERS in the most hateful of ways.

Yet Lancet didn't take up this tactic for some reason that was never clear to Nathaniel. Maybe he thought the First Amendment arguments from the other side would override any arguments about Hate Speech.

The issue of "bad faith" on the webmaster's part also seemed a promising route to take in winning this thing. It seemed to Nathaniel that the fact that Dude had set up a website where any review could be a fraud was ipso facto "bad faith." In fact, when this thought came to him, he thought he'd found the legal knockout punch: The webmaster knows the site is corrupt, that not a single review on it can be verified as coming from where it claims to come from, and yet he continues to run it. That's bad faith, right?

"We can't use it," Lancet said.

"Why not?

"The judge won't consider it."

"But why not?"

"It would be prior restraint."

"It's prior restraint of free speech to make sure that somebody doesn't pretend to be a student when he isn't?"

"It won't fly."

"It's not 'bad faith' to allow fraud?"

"But we can't argue it that way."

"I don't understand. He sets up a website that permits, even encourages, this kind of deception, and it's 'good faith' when he removes the reviews he feels like and leaves the ones he doesn't?!"

"I'm sorry, Nathaniel."

"This is something out of Kafka, right? I'm not really alive. I'm in a weird story, yes?"

"The way the law is written is certainly poor, and definitely wasn't the intention of at least some of the lawmakers who passed it. They meant to stop obscenity. But it's what it is, and we have to argue within its confines."

"I guess I'll never be a lawyer," Nathaniel said.

"Let's just hope we can continue to be teachers," Biff said.

And indeed their classes did not get enough enrollment. Biff lost his second lab in a row, and Nathaniel wound up with just one section, an English 102 on Saturday morning. The fact that he had three students he'd had before was mildly comforting — so he wasn't a total monster, at least to those who could read and write at the college level. But how was he going to live on one quarter of his regular income? He already owed the department units from the previous semester.

When he went to see Spike Burns about it, Spike said that he could either get him some tutoring in the Malcolm X Writing Lab or possibly he could carry Nathaniel for one more semester, but by Spring Semester Nathaniel would have to make up the missing classes "one way or another." And if there was no making them up? Well, we'll have to "deal with that then, won't we?" Nathaniel chose the spring showdown. Anything was better than the Malcolm X Writing Lab.

He missed Marty. He thought he hadn't loved him as much as he should have, and yet now that he was gone, there was an emptiness, a raw sadness that wouldn't go away. Life is empty most of the time, Nathaniel felt. That's what accounts for religion and marriage and sports and philosophy and almost every other thing you can name. People are just plain empty. And even when they have everything, they feel empty. Always somewhere in the back of the mind was that gnawing, scratchy feeling saying, "This isn't good enough. Is that all there is?" Singer Peggy Lee had said it all? Peggy Lee was the greatest philosopher of all time? And he didn't even like Peggy Lee.

Ah, Marty, I miss you. I miss having somebody in my life, but I also miss YOU, with all your annoyances and stubbornesses and insecurities and whatever else it was that made us work, however flawed and far from perfect, it made us work as a couple for what it was worth. And it was worth far more than I thought it was worth. And now that I don't have it anymore, all I can do is what most other poor suckers have done, trouble deaf Heaven with my bootless sighs.

Slacker didn't seem to miss Marty, unless lifting her leg high and licking her hind end counted. I should have been a pair of ragged claws, scratching at the furniture, Nathaniel thought.

The telephone rang often, both at his condo and at school. The media seemed even more intrigued with the case now that the final, final, final, final legal Complaint had been officially filed by Lancet and all that remained was the response from Tether & Strafe.

The BBC called, and Nathaniel was hooked up for a live interview at some inconvenient time, but since he had so much time off, he didn't mind. In fact, it kept him distracted. Wasn't that the secret of life — keep yourself distracted and you might not see what was really happening to you?

The show was for the BBC's World News Network, and the woman who did the interview wasn't nearly as nice as the setup woman, who had said she hoped Nathaniel won his lawsuit, that such slanderous things as she had read on Teachersonparade would never have been allowed in Great Britain. "That's what makes America such a great nation," Nathaniel said, not sure the irony carried across the telephone line. The actual interviewer was Mature and Veddy Brittle of voice and gave him no softball questions. "Why are you trying to curtail your students' opinions?" and "Why do you suppose you more than others have so many rude things written about you, Dr. Tack?"

But he'd had practice enough by now and was ready for her: "I'm only trying to curtail the opinions of people who are not my students but who have the gall to pretend to be my students," he replied. "I guess they're so rude because I butt rape my students," he said, catching the interviewer off guard at first. But she was sharp and caught on. "In fact, I probably should be arrested, don't you think?" he continued. "And did you hear that I also murder my students. To say nothing of being a hard grader. Why wouldn't students be rude?"

USA Today called and even sent a photographer to Nathaniel's condo. The pose the newspaper chose was a bit melodramatic perhaps, him leaning forward, head in his hands, brooding, but he certainly looked butch. He also looked tired. *How can I be tired?* he thought. *I'm practically laid off.*

The large picture and article in *USA Today* sparked an even greater amount of interest. Fame feeds upon itself, apparently. It was great to have some access. People sent him some supportive letters.

But Biff seemed a bit hurt that he hadn't been asked to do any interviews. "Is it because of — because of my slight stammer?" he asked.

"Not at all." Nathaniel started giving Biff's phone number to the journalists who called. Biff seemed happier once he got a taste of the camera. He appeared on CNN and made his points well, though he looked forlorn in the nearly empty classroom. The webmaster was interviewed on the same program, slouched in a chair with smarmy, archnostriled Gus Strappado by his side. When the interviewer said, "Mr. Lather, aren't you upset that you might be providing a place to destroy Professor Thorgoode's reputation?" the "Not really" reply and the smirk that accompanied it were priceless condemnations, it seemed to Nathaniel. But the CNN piece aired on a Saturday afternoon, not exactly prime time.

A writer for *People* magazine called. Nathaniel knew he was supposed to spurn this as "pop," even "tabloid" and surely beneath contempt. But he accepted. The middle-aged woman writer came to his house and he tried to seem as direct as possible. He knew that she could slant him any way she wanted to. The photographer from *People* was very curious about the case, though not up on the details, and spent five hours photographing him – some in classrooms, some in front of various campus buildings, including the Johnnie Cochran Arts Building, some with Slacker, some with him holding a large picture of Marty, and the magazine's fact checker called back three times and somehow got his real age although he wouldn't give it, so maybe *People* wasn't so bad after all. The story would be out just about the time that Tether & Strafe would be turning in their "terminal" legal response.

The Today Show called and asked if he would like to be on.

Okay. Why not?

How about going to the local Santa Francesca studio and being interviewed live at 4:15 A.M. his time — 7:15 A.M. New York time?

Sure.

Of course they would want Dude Lather to appear as well.

"I'm not appearing on a TV show with that dumb prick!"

"You'll be in two different studios."

"I won't have to sit next to him?"

"He'll be upstairs and you'll be downstairs."

"You're sure?" Nathaniel didn't want to be ambushed, the way it happened on atrocities like the *Jerry Springer Show*. Who knew — Antwan Timmons might rush onto the set and play video of Their Night Together, mutual — and fleeting — though it had been. Today's topic: TEACHERS WHO MAKE THEIR STUDENTS GIVE THEM

HEAD. He'd wind up having to throw a chair at Antwan.

"We will also pick you up in your own limousine," the setup person promised.

He even went out and found some Medium Brown Loving Care and dyed his hair.

Smell me!

The two limousines — both Lincolns – delivered Nathaniel and Dude at the studio within a minute of each other, at three-thirty A.M. It couldn't get much more glamorous than this, could it?

Nathaniel had hoped to avoid seeing the Dude anywhere except on the monitor, but there he was, stepping out of the limo, his narrow-shouldered, skinny twenty-six-year-old self, in a turtle-neck sweater, his hair now both blond and green, the spiky green on top. Horse-faced, or maybe he was just a centaur? Nathaniel had worn an old, trusty blue sport coat. I suppose I look square, he realized. That's all right. I want to look square! I'm queer and I'm square and I'm proud! Why couldn't I have been on TV when I was in my prime!

It was so early in the morning a cleaning person opened the door for Dude. Nathaniel sat in the limo and let him go in first. Then he got out and rang the bell, and the cleaning person let him in too. Soon a technician in chinos and everyday shirt came from somewhere in the back and escorted Nathaniel to his studio. "Where's the other guest?" Nathaniel asked.

"Upstairs." The technician, who seemed to be in his boozy thirties, pointed to the ceiling. "You two will be separated."

"Suits me."

It was a big building, quiet, almost spooky at that hour. They passed assorted sound stages set up for local newscasts and a children's show. Everywhere there were rows of lights hanging like bats. The technician placed Nathaniel on one of the sets in a cushy chair, though it did have a stain on one arm.

"Do you want some coffee?" he wanted to know.

"Sure."

He poured Nathaniel a Styrofoam cup full and heated it up in a microwave and handed it to him. "Sorry, haven't got any milk yet. Too early." He began to arrange the tiny microphone on Nathaniel's lapel.

"This'll do." He took a swallow. It tasted like Slacker's piss — not that he had tasted his cat's piss. It tasted like that smell — that morning, stale-coffee taste that fills the whole mouth and makes you worry for your breath. Thank god, the host was in New York. The bad breath wouldn't carry that far. Probably.

A few minutes before four, the monitor came on, and Nathaniel could see the mediagenic hosts, cutesy Katie Couric and strong-jawed Matt Lauer, getting ready. Last-minute make-up was being applied to their million-dollar faces, and Lauer seemed very concerned about his hair in front. Yes, it was thinning — but he was fighting it. Where's my make-up and toupee? Nathaniel thought. Let it go. It's just another class. With how many millions of viewers, did you say?

The technician was adjusting the TV camera and asked Nathaniel to do a voice check. Then New York came on and asked for another voice check. Maybe my tongue is as bitter as the cud of vile, incurable sores on innocent . . . No, the voice check was fine. They would be on in ten minutes.

Katie Couric did a piece on . . . something or other. Nathaniel couldn't quite tell. The volume was turned down, and besides he was getting nervous and self-conscious. What if he couldn't talk? What if Dude Lather had been coached by Gus Strappado into silver-tongued glibness?

And suddenly he was there on a screen in a silent three-way with handsome Matt Lauer and green-haired, equine-faced Dude Lather. On the air reporter George Lewis was doing a news story about him and Shite College and the review site. "Turmoil at West Coast college" and other snippets came through, and then the technician realized he hadn't turned up the volume loud enough for Nathaniel to hear. He apologized and then all the words came through, including carefully selected fragments of reviews: "An openly gay teacher is accused of . . . The young webmaster, however, claims that . . . ."

There was nothing about 'butt raping' or 'butt fucking' his students. You couldn't say that on the air. Maybe *I* should say it? Nathaniel thought. Yeah, maybe I should use those exact words (but which ones — 'raping' or 'fucking'? —) to prove my point about the double standard operating here. Do I dare? And do I dare? Dare I eat a peach? How my hair is growing thin! And how the color has turned from brown to half-dyed gray! And, moreover, I have measured out my life with coffee tongues!

He was hoping that Lauer, who apparently was going to do the interview, had been given the questions that Nathaniel had suggested to the setup person, a man who'd said he was teaching a course at a college in New York and had a problem student who had complained about him. "Imagine that student going on a website and blasting you to his heart's content and you unable to say boo about it," Nathaniel had said. He thought he had made a convert, but you never knew in this business. "Tell them to ask me why people who aren't students are allowed to write reviews," he had requested. "Let me read some of the reviews to your audience, what do you say?" Enough of this crap about freedom of speech and about how Nathaniel was taking it away. "You have a God-given right to review people you've never had as a teacher? This is freedom of speech? Give me a break! I am supposedly 'butt fucking' my male students, and it's costing me my classes!" Yeah, he had some sound bites at the ready. But would he get the right questions? Surely, Dr. Tack, you as a teacher, didn't expect to have the questions in advance?! What kind of message would this send to students everywhere? Duh, I don't know — don't be a blubber-mouthed 'fucking piece of shit fag ass hole, maricon, puto, miefdero, ass lick, donkey fucker' maybe?

And then they were on the air.

"We have both Professor Tack and Mr. Lather as our guests this morning. Gentlemen, how are you?"

Nathaniel lifted his Styrofoam coffee cup in a toast. "Great."

Dude Lather mumbled something.

The host's questions were pretty standard, and the webmaster gave his boilerplate response. "I wanted to apply modern technology so that students can have access to real and honest information about their teachers."

"What do you say to that, Professor?"

"The webmaster should have made sure his technology was giving real and honest information. It isn't. The entire thing is a fraud."

"How can you be sure it's a fraud, Dr. Tack?"

"I invite you and your entire audience out there to go online right this minute and send in a review of any teacher at my college you feel like writing a review of. Don't bother to be a real student. Just say you are. Your review will be posted immediately, and the teacher's grade point average will rise or fall accordingly." Nathaniel even lifted his arm and encouraged the audience physically.

Who knew what effect his Call to Fraud would produce?

"Shouldn't you have guaranteed that this kind of thing which the professor speaks of couldn't occur?" Lauer pressed Dude. Good man! Good question!

"The website has a few flaws," Dude answered. His glasses made him look scholarly — but it was just TV. "It still gives students valued information to use in selecting their classes. Besides, most of the reviews are positive." The webmaster was as terrible a speaker as he was a speller, mumbly, frozen-lipped, no intonation.

"Not true!" Nathaniel jumped in. "None of the information on the site is valuable. Even the favorable reviews are fake. Teachers review themselves. My colleagues have told me they have."

"Just you and Thorgoode review yourselves!" Dude shot back. He still didn't speak clearly, but at least he showed more life.

"Professor Thorgoode and I are hardly the only ones to review ourselves. You simply can't tell which reviews are genuine and which ones aren't. It's a pack of lies. The webmaster and his cronies are having a field day."

"You're just mad because your students don't like you," Dude said.

"What about that, Professor Tack?" Lauer said.

"When my real students review me, as they will this semester, I do well." Oh, god, now I sound like I'm tooting my own horn.

"However, don't you have a D-minus average on Teachersonparade?" Lauer asked.

"But they aren't my students! Every time I appear on TV or radio I get yet more reviews of me in my job from people who have only seen or heard me here. They've never been in my classes. No one can tell me this is right!" Nathaniel knew he mustn't blow it now, get so angry that he tangled his words.

"You're trying to discredit the website!" Dude said. "It would work fine if you left it alone."

"The website is a mockery of everything education is supposed to stand for, honesty, integrity, and literacy, and it deserves to be discredited. I hope to hell it is discredited!"

"Students just want to get the best teachers so that they can have success, wouldn't you say?" the host asked.

"That's right!" Dude said.

"No, they don't," Nathaniel replied. "They just want to intimidate their teachers into passing them. I'm sorry you were always such a failure as a student, but you just want to provide a means by which failures like yourself can get revenge on people who tell you the truth about your own incompetence. You love to have your teachers by the balls, don't you?"

He had said "balls" on national TV — and in the daytime too.

"I do not!" Dude protested.

"Gentlemen, please!" the host said.

Nathaniel could tell his face looked snarly and wrinkled, a bit puffy in the chin, despite the surgery on his jowls, though still ten years younger than he was. Thank you, Loving Care. He might even be winning this round. If he just didn't come off as too mean. His opponent was SO BAD he had to be cautious about seeming to take unfair advantage.

"I am going to graduate college this time!" Dude said, almost pleading.

"Surely, professor, you wouldn't deprive underachieving students of their right to a college education?" the host asked.

"I know people like to get all weepy about underachievers getting off drugs and off the streets and into their caps and gowns and marching proudly up to receive their diplomas, but, frankly, much of that is total B.S. None dare care call it what it is."

"And what you would call it?"

"I'm on the front lines of this, don't forget." I bet I know about what's going on in colleges than you do, Matt Lauer!

"Would you answer my question, Dr. Tack? What would you call it what exactly?"

Okay, pal.

"I'd say America is full of buttheads, and far too much of what we call education is just butt fucking our minds."

He could hear the words being bleeped out already. Lauer didn't blink, though, or not much. He seemed not to know whether to pick up on that or to leave it alone. Maybe it was too complicated for seven in the morning. Oh, dear, not just "balls" but "butt fucking our minds" too!

"I'm sorry if that's offensive," Nathaniel said. "But there are much worse things on Teachersonparade. Much worse. I just can't say them here in the mainstream media. Why should the Internet be permitted what the other media are not?"

"Let's get Mr. Lather in here," the host was saying. "Don't you think you should see about amending the way your teacher review site actually operates?" he asked. Great question!

The webmaster appeared incapable of saying anything that didn't sound like rote. "Our website is the brave New World of Internet discourse." If that was Dude's sound bite, it wasn't working. In fact, it was biting him.

There were a few more questions, which Nathaniel almost didn't hear. He was buzzing from having used Dirty Words on national TV.

"Well, thank you both for coming on."

"Yes," Dude said.

"Sorry I had to be here," Nathaniel said.

❧

He got a letter from a ninety-year-old grandmother in Iowa who said she was "appalled" at his language and that he looked young enough to "learn to be a nicer person." Fuck her.

It turned out that some eight hundred people took Nathaniel's challenge and sent in phony reviews of teachers at Shite College. Most of them were about Nathaniel, as he expected, but some were about other teachers. He captured them, flattering ones and insulting ones alike. He was almost inured to them, in particular because they weren't coming from actual students. A number of the "reviewers" commented on how odd it was that they could review a teacher never having had that teacher. Some thought it was "cool." The webmaster removed most of them, but he didn't catch them all. Sherlock Holmes he wasn't. Not even Inspector Clouseau. Many of the reviews mentioned that Dude Lather hadn't "defended his cause very well" and "seemed sort of pathetic." Yeah, right.

Nathaniel also got offers from *Court TV* and *Moral Court* to be on and debate the webmaster again. The producer from *Court TV* said, "Fax me the filthiest quotes you can from that website."

He did, but the shows didn't go on. Nathaniel was willing. More than willing. Lots of people saw *The Today Show*, friends and foes alike, and even Barbara Walters and the other women on *The View* discussed the case — without much knowledge of the facts, alas. Of course that hadn't stopped them before. Wow, suddenly he was indeed a media darling.

Maybe that would wipe the smirk off the webmaster's horse face. Maybe not. All Nathaniel knew for sure was that he was indeed winning the media war. Now if nobody knocked that gloat off his own face he'd be fine!

❧

You are one hell of gauy, tryeing to prevent your students from kicking your homo BEE-hind on that website as you desurve. When I run into you, I won't be so kind.

Jerry M.

Nathaniel should have been used to this kind of threat by now. Still, it was disconcerting to find it there on your computer in your bedroom. He didn't reply to it, but he did send a copy to the University of Utah at Provo, from whence it seemingly came, plus a copy to the server. He got no response. Maybe it was an idle spur-of-the-moment threat. No, maybe all the theateners of Nathaniel's recent past were getting together on the Internet and planning to finish the job together? Hackers and Satanists United?

There were also several nice e-mails from people who had seen him on *The Today Show* and were very concerned "that educators were being abused in this manner." He seemed "very nice" and "quite articulate" and if there was anything they could do.

Dear fans, yes, there is something you can do. Kick Jerry M's hetero-BEE-hind for me. And be sure to get his stinger while you're at it. If you can't find him, then kick Dude Lather's hetero BEE-hind instead.

The webmaster and Nathaniel did yet another early-morning program on FOX TV. This time there was an echo in Nathaniel's ear that made it harder to answer the questions quickly, but he knew he still whipped Dude Lather's dumb ass. Without his technology to protect him, it wasn't hard to do.

Soon thereafter, according to Lancet, Gus Strappado advised Dude Lather not to do any more TV appearances. He wasn't helping his cause.

He most definitely wasn't.

Without the webmaster as an opponent, the TV shows now of course didn't want to do the segment. So the TV programs began to dry up. To have to be bound to Dude Lather in this way — YUCK!

But there was still interest from radio and newspapers. *The San Jose Mercury News*, right in the heart of the Internet-loving Silicon Valley tech industry, called Nathaniel and asked if it could do a front-page story about the case. The reporter, by the name of Something Hernandez, wanted to know if she and her photographer, Something Jefferson, could come and watch Nathaniel teach a class.

Oh, my God, the pressure!

But if he said no, they'd think he had something to hide.

The only class he had was the Saturday morning 102, Introduction to Literature, with twenty-one students in it, some worthy college material and some writing like this: "The literature is most readable that make it seem notable." Huh? He'd have to keep even those students for a while to make it seem like a full class until the journalists had examined him and found him wanting or not wanting, properly P.C. or not P.C.

The students were excited by the robust, black photographer in the rear of the classroom, and Nathaniel wondered if perhaps it wasn't all too distracting somehow. Yet how often did this kind of thing happen? It would probably be the only time in their whole lives. So let the cameras role. The reporter also wanted to speak to the students at the end of class and get some quotations. Yikes. Pick Ms. Plucked Eyebrows there. I gave her an A on her first paper. She even deserved it. Or Mr. Steel Bar Through His Nose. I can't stand to look at what he'd done to his face, but this is the second time he's taken me and I gave him a B in 101.

Ms. Something Hernandez was still in her twenties, short and dark, though with more Spanish than Indian showing in her features. She had gone to Stanford, she mentioned, and Nathaniel hoped that the terrible Grade Inflation at places like that, which had once been pillars of sound learning, hadn't turned the so-called "Best Schools" into places hard to get into yet turning out puffed-up straw men as the actual student product.

So there was Nathaniel teaching his little heart out, trying to be his usual self, cordial but professionally distant, amusing, but not catering, open to comments from the class, but still the main provider of the information — the teacher of a college course, in other words. Duh.

Ms. Something Hernandez took notes, and after he got his roll of film of Nathaniel writing on the blackboard and talking to the class, the photographer sat in the back and listened. It could have been a bad class. There are those days. But that day seemed to be going pretty well, even with the nasty ravens outside on the lawn across from the classroom *caa*-ing and carrying on, even with a truck delivering and dumping sand on Halle Berry Drive — no doubt because it was a Saturday and the school traffic was less — even with Nathaniel's nerves on top of his skin and his insides working counter-clockwise and two students coming in late. It was about critics and the theater, and it caused a lively discussion, which wasn't just a bunch of Class Discussion Bullshit, but a class in which there was some factual information involved, some specific theatrical performances referred to and documented.

Ms. Hernandez came up to Nathaniel at the end and asked if she could stay after the break. "Of course," he said, hoping that was intended as a compliment. He suspected it was even more so that she could "get quotations" from the students about the class . Already he could hear her asking them out in the hall. He pretended he was above it all, but of course he was concerned. At least here they had to give their names to be quoted in a newspaper. What moved Nathaniel most was when the black photographer went out of his way to wait until after Nathaniel dealt with a couple of students who had questions during the break and then said, "I just wanted to tell you that was an excellent class. I never had a teacher as good as you when I was in college."

"Really?" Nathaniel said, feigning modesty. "How nice of you to say so."

Both stayed till the end of the two-and-half hour class and again came up and complimented him. He was pretty certain they were being sincere. Or was this a setup for a smear article?

"And I didn't murder or butt rape a single student today!" Nathaniel said. "I must be losing my touch."

"Maybe next time?" Ms. Hernandez asked.

He smiled and let her have the last joke. He was no dummy.

The article did appear on the front page. It was well-written, but it was so technical probably no one read beyond the fold, where the best parts were, at least from Nathaniel's perspective.

One of O.J. Simpson's lawyers — not Johnnie Cochran — saw it and called to say he had discussed the case with some "high-powered" lawyer friends of his. Oh? Did he want to come aboard and help Lancet? He was more than welcome. He thought the legal points were interesting, but he didn't think it would really get the attention it merited until "some judges get reviewed the way you teachers are. Then we'll see how much we hear about free speech," he said, cynical to the bone. He didn't come aboard.

Mavis Spielberg of the *Santa Francesca Chronicle* called and wondered if she and a photographer could come that next Saturday to observe a class and do a piece. He knew her articles on education and the way she always referred to "under-represented groups" and the like. She didn't read the essays he had to read. What about the literate – now there was an "under-represented" group! He wondered if he could stand the pressure of being watched two classes in a row. He was also scheduled to be evaluated by Peer Review in a few weeks, and this time his committee consisted of Guy Mountain, Tadd Dryer, and Arlene Buboe-Pitsky, none of them exactly favorably disposed toward him.

The *Chronicle* reporter was already eliciting student comments as he arrived. He hoped that she got some good ones before he gave back their papers at the end. "King Leer had a lewd gesture" and "Edgar was ethnically superior to his brother, Edmund"? No and no — and somebody had to tell the students this. Him. The Lasik surgery made him now see the errors without reading glasses. Progress was indeed a wondrous thing.

He overheard one girl in the back say, "He's just okay." The bad students always sat in the back, to the teacher's left. Miss Lousy Jean Pool was just "okay" herself. Somebody smarter would have lowered her voice when she saw her teacher come in. It was NOT the teachers. It was the students!

Mavis Spielberg was in her twenties. Was nobody but him sixty years old?! She had frosted, blandish blondish hair, toothpick-thin arms, big eyes, and a notebook as large as the Gutenberg Bible. She acknowledged him with a nod as he entered the classroom, as did her photographer, a white man in a baseball cap.

"We'd better begin," Nathaniel said, raising his eyebrows when she didn't stop whispering to the students she was getting quotations from. I will not scream at her, he thought. Nor will I kiss any of their asses today, or any day. That is my mantra. He opened his folder of notes, somewhat worn from his centuries in the classroom. I'll re-do some of these, he vowed, if I live to tell this tale. He wasn't married to the notes as it was. He used them as a jumping off point and made an effort to bring in fresh examples of the "general principles he was elucidating."

"How come Dr. Tack can't talk English like we do?" would be the sidebar student quotation in the newspaper.

He was a bit tired of *King Lear*. If he had a character abruptly change personality like Edmund does at the end of the play he'd be ridden out of theater on a rail and asked for his National New Play Contest Award back.

Onward!

He passed out some articles on Elizabethan times — portions of articles. They were for the mid-term in a few weeks. "I want you to consider some fragments of another time period, another civilization than our own, and see if you can pick out signs of the Great Chain of Being in operation," he explained.

Mr. Not Very Academic and That's Why I'm Here at Shite College had a last-minute question: "Doctor, when will you be passing out the fragments of that other civilization?"

He caught the eye of Mavis Spielberg. He knew it was a dumb question. She knew it was a dumb question. Obviously fragments of a civilization couldn't possibly include something you just *read*! Of course Nathaniel would never say it was "dumb," the press there or not.

But he had a sudden impulse to say, "What a splendid question, young man! It's so splendid, in fact, that next week I'll bring in some bears' teeth from a real bear baiting! And I think they have an exact copy of the corpse of Queen Elizabeth I. Let's find out for ourselves whether she was a virgin or not!" No — he wouldn't be sarcastic, just bubbly with enthusiasm, trying to get those poor under-represented groups represented, for God's sake.

Maybe he should raise the grades and write a comment on every paper during the break before he gave them all back at the end: "This essay made me understand why I went into teaching! Just splendid! Success!!! awaits you in all your endeavors!"

He restrained himself from both excesses.

The class went well enough, though he noticed he, more than the students, was distracted by the journalists present. He kept wanting to play to them, to be "ingratiating." He tried to be funny some of the time in any class, but now he felt like he was a comedian in a club trying to impress the critics, probably trying too hard to win over the "customers." I am a college professor, he repeated over and over in his mind. I am not a crowd pleaser! I am not!

Mavis Spielberg and the photographer said they weren't going to stay after the break, and that was worrisome. But could they take some pictures of the students who had volunteered comments? Of course. Nathaniel went to the men's faculty lounge to wait it out. "What's going on?" one of the other Saturday teachers asked.

"I am being judged in the media," he said.

"Who is it?"

"*The Chronicle.*"

"Oh, I wouldn't trust them."

But the deed was done.

When he came back for the second half of the class, Mavis said, "How about a few more pictures?" The photographer in the baseball cap was waiting.

"Is it true that your lover committed suicide?" she asked as the camera snapped away.

What did they want? A shot of him bawling his eyes out? He'd seen enough in the press to know that Journalism Lesson #1 was Weep and They Will Come.

"Yes," he said.

"With an ice pick?"

"Yes."

But he would not cry for them. He had a class to finish.

"And how did they make you feel?"

"How did my lover's death make me feel?"

That was a dumb question too. But he wouldn't say it was a dumb question. He wouldn't be that impolite.

No, no, no, he wouldn't cry for them. They couldn't *ever* make him cry for them!

He got a call before seven in the morning from Boyd DeLucca of the Academic Senate. "Have you seen it?"

"Seen what?"

"You're famous!"

"I am?"

"Your picture's on the front page of the *Chronicle*."

"My fifteen minutes of fame are now complete."

"It's a good picture."

Nathaniel wondered which one the newspaper had used. He had always known that the press can slant anything anyway it cares to, with the photo or the text, but now that it was him being slanted, it had taken on a — shall we say — more than academic interest.

He went down and got his own copy from the mat in front of his condo. His co-owner neighbor was getting hers too. She was an elderly, wild-eyed woman who had been hyper jittery the day Nathaniel had moved in and was hyper jittery now, all these years later. She must have thought he was a burglar or a murderer or something, the way she jumped when he came down the stairs. He knew she was likely to do this and usually avoided her. However, today he'd been distracted by the Fame at his doorstep. She held her palpitating chest and said, "Oh, you scared me to death!" and then hurried back up to her unit. Why should she be scared? Didn't she know that he only murdered his students!

When he opened to the front page there he was on the left side, as big as life. And smiling! Teaching and smiling, his arms up, a "fragment of civilization" in his hand. The headline read: TEACHER TRIES TO STOP ONLINE HATE. So they had decided to be on his side. Good. This is what it had come to: I AM MORE OPPRESSED THAN THOU. But that was the name of the game they were playing. And if you had to play it, damn it, it was better to win than to lose!

They were winning, weren't they?

So who was in that old, beat-up car below his condo? Another person about to take Hate Speech to the next level? A young man got out of the car —he was tall and seemed to be looking for an address. Nathaniel could see only the top of the head, not the face. Who was this? Fly on the Wall? The young man with the pen light? The list of suspects was growing daily.

The doorbell rang, and even Slacker jumped. "It's okay. It's okay," he said. Her eyes were alert as she stood up on the sofa. Maybe it's the wrong address, Nathaniel thought. The doorbell rang again, and the cat ran into the bedroom.

Nathaniel went down the stairs, not all the way, expecting to be able to see who it was through the window in the outside front door. Whoever it was was standing off to the side. "Who is it?" Nathaniel called.

It was his son.

"My God, you scared me!" he said, opening the door. "What are you doing here?"

"I'm the Satanist," Jim said.

It was a joke.

Nathaniel took a last look outside the condo, just to be sure that Jim wasn't part of a conspiracy. You never knew – "We'll get him through his son!"

Not quite eighteen, Jim looked even more like a man than the last time Nathaniel had seen him. This was despite the baggy cutoffs and tee-shirt, the uniform of his generation. He was six-four, brown hair cut short, his body muscular. He had a couple of scratches on one cheek. He seemed to be dragging one foot as he went up the stairs. He had just been a little boy five minutes ago. The time, the time, so soon gone.

"What happened to you?"

"Got hurt playing rugby last week."

Jim had stopped on the first landing and was watching him. "I have a couple of my bags in the car."

"Does this mean you intend to stay?"

Jim looked a little hurt. "You don't want me to?"

"Don't you usually call first?"

"You don't seem very happy to see me."

"I'm a little on edge these days."

They went inside the condo and Nathaniel got them both something to drink. He had some vodka, his third of the night. Jim just wanted water. "Whose car is that?" Nathaniel called from the kitchen.

"My mom's, but she lets me use it."

Jim was sitting where Slacker had been a few minutes earlier, sprawled, all legs, knees, a scar on his forearm.

"You got a cat?"

"She's hiding in the bedroom."

He scratched at his nose. "Got an allergy. Pet dander."

"Want me to close the bedroom door?"

"Naw, that's all right." He ran his hand over the sofa, testing for cat hair, then smelled his fingers.

"Do you take anything for it?"

"Naw."

Nathaniel pulled over a chair from the dining area. "You just happened to be in the neighborhood?"

"I needed to get away from up there."

"Is everything okay?"

"I'll tell you about it a little later, okay?"

" . . . Okay."

"How's Marty?"

The question took Nathaniel by surprise as much as the visit had. "I didn't tell you?"

Jim was halfway through the glass of water already. "Tell me what?"

Why hadn't he told him? They simply hadn't talked in months? He didn't want to expose his emotions? Because they were just the same old, same old father/son communicationless combo like everybody else?

"I'm afraid Marty's dead."

"Wo!"

"It's not a joke." Nathaniel bent his head and took a swallow of the vodka.

"What happened?"

"I'll tell you about it a little later, okay?"

" . . .Was it drugs?"

"Not exactly."

"Was it an accident?"

"No."

There was a pause.

"You're not going to tell me?"

"He killed himself."

"*Wo!*"

At least *Wo* was better than *Whatever*.

"Why would he do that?"

"He let life get to him." Nathaniel could hear the bitterness in his own voice. "He couldn't find any humor in it."

"I'm sorry to hear it. Are you all right?"

It was good to hear your son saying the Right Thing. Jim barely knew Marty and it was phony as hell and totally conventional, and yet it was a fragment of civilization you could hold in your hand. "I miss him very much," Nathaniel said. "I loved him more than I thought I did."

"You guys were together a long time."

Acknowledge our validity, just as I acknowledged all your girlfriends of the past and I will the ones in the future, and then your wife. "Yes, we were."

"Bummer," Jim said.

It wasn't Shakespeare, no. But at least he hadn't said, "It's, like, bummer."

Nathaniel wasn't exactly a "huggy" type, but it would have been nice to have his son get up and take him in his arms and comfort him, cry with him. Cry for Marty and cry for whatever it was that had brought him there. But of course that was too much to ask. Too faggy, no doubt.

They settled for re-fills on their drinks.

Slacker came back into the living room to see who the intruder was. She kept her distance. Cats were never sentimental. Never. "Is that the culprit?" Jim said, pointing at the cat.

"You should get some medication for that allergy."

"Yeah."

"Is my car all right down there?" Jim pointed at the window.

"You'll need to move it. And you need a parking decal on your dashboard. The lady upstairs might have you towed."

"I'm pooped." Jim stretched and yawned, didn't get up.

"It'll keep for a little while." Nathaniel went back into the kitchen to find the parking decal. He had an extra one in a basket on top of the refrigerator, but it was underneath some junk. "How long did you drive?"

"Twelve hours."

"Without stopping?"

"I stopped once."

"It wouldn't kill you to stop twice."

"What do you mean?"

Yes, it was good to be a man, but, Jesus, don't make it so hard on yourself! Nathaniel thought.

He came back and handed him the decal. "Leave it where it can be seen on the dashboard. And bring in your bags."

"Okay."

"So what happened up there?"

"Can't I just come for a visit?"

"You can, but I don't think that's what's going on here. Did you have a fight with your mother?"

"With Lana actually."

"Lana? Why her?"

Jim's eyes flared. "Because she's a dyke!"

Hmm. Nathaniel took a sip of his vodka. He was just beginning to feel the burn. "Your mother's a dyke too, as I recall."

"But she's a good dyke."

"Well, at least you're able to make that distinction. What was the fight about?"

"It was more than a fight."

"You didn't kill her, did you?"

"God, Dad, of course not!"

"Well, you never know." Having kids meant being relieved that they haven't done something worse! "Did you hit her?"

"She deserved to be hit."

"You hit a woman?" Oh, Christ. Something was grabbing at Nathaniel's gut, and it wasn't the vodka.

"I didn't hit her! I said she deserved it."

"No, she didn't deserve it."

"You weren't there. How would you know?"

"You're telling me you would hit a woman?"

"She hit me!"

"How big is she?"

"Five two."

"I rest my case."

"You don't want to know why she hit me?"

"Because you live together."

"What does that mean?"

"People who live together tend to hit each other."

And that's why you won't be moving in here permanently, my boy.

"I can't go back there."

"Tell me what happened — before I hit you!"

Jim smiled. Nathaniel was big, but Jim was bigger.

"Lana made my mom cry."

"How? Why?"

"My mom never cries."

"None of us does. Why this time?"

"Because of what Lana said to her."

"And that was?"

"I didn't hear it. Something in their bedroom. But I found my mom sitting on the back porch all red-eyed and sobbing."

"Is she going to leave Lana?"

"I don't think so. I wish she would."

About time for that Oedipus Complex to go, boy-o.

"It's just a fight, Jim. They'll get over it."

"It's the only time I ever saw my mom cry."

"Really?"

"She's strong."

"You can be strong and still cry." More P.C. bullshit, but what you gonna do.

"So I told Lana off — to leave my mom alone."

"Did you're mom ask you to?"

"No."

"Then you should have stayed out of it."

"I guess I should have. Now they're both mad at me."

"What did you say? Can you take it back?"

"I'm not taking it back! It's true!"

"That doesn't mean you had to say it."

"I'm not sorry."

"What was it?"

"It's sort of personal."

"I can't help you if you don't tell me what you actually said."

"I said she has a stinking cunt."

"Oh, great."

"Well, she does!"

"That may be, but you can't tell her that. What's the matter with you?"

"I thought we had free speech in this country."

Oh, dear. "Couldn't you go online and write her up on Dykesonparade?"

"What?"

"Never mind. Just a thought."

"I can say it if it's true! She smells very bad, and we have to share a bathroom!"

"I thought you fellows liked that kind of thing."

"What fellows?"

"You straight fellows."

"Not Lana's! Eeek! Yuck!"

"Okay, I get the point. Can she smell your ejaculate?"

"I beg your pardon!"

"No middle-class parlance now. Do you jack off in the bathroom?"

"No!"

"You probably do, and she can smell it. But she doesn't tell you you smell like cum! Which no doubt is a smell she doesn't especially favor."

"She can't smell it! I clean it up."

"The memory lingers sometimes."

Am I really having this conversation? Nathaniel wondered. . . . Why am I having this conversation? I made my bed, as my mother would say, and I must lie on it.

"Can I stay here?"

"For how long?"

"I don't know."

"Forever?"

"I don't know."

It would not be a good idea, Nathaniel could sense that. But he was missing Marty, and the boogie men were gathering in the twilight outside his condo, and his rugby-playing, macho son (who had cried as a boy) was there to lend his support and his strength . . . sort of.

"Does your mother know where you are?"

"I just up and left."

"No note?"

"No."

"She must be worried."

"I'm not apologizing!"

Nathaniel drank some more vodka. His face was beginning to flush, and that was good. "I doubt you can take it back anyway."

"Really?"

"Let me get this clear. Did you say she was a stinking cunt or she has a stinking cunt? There's probably a difference."

"She has one."

"Once you tell a woman such a thing, you can't retreat and say, 'I'm sorry, I don't really think you have a cunt that stinks. I just said that because I had to say something to get your attention.' Cripes."

"Well, she called me names too!"

"A stinking cunt?"

"No."

"Too bad. Maybe they'd cancel each other out. But I don't really think so. What did she say?"

"That I was a fucking prick."

"They should be the same, but they aren't. Anything else?"

"That I'm selfish and too macho."

"Her lawyer can beat up your lawyer."

"What?"

"Never mind. How are you doing in school?"

"Fine."

"Don't you imagine you should finish high school?"

"Can't I do that here?"

Nathaniel looked him in the eye. "Do you really want to do that?"

Jim looked off to the side and sighed. "I don't know what I want."

"A little more verbal restraint wouldn't have hurt."

Jim shrugged, half-heartedly.

"I'm fighting a lawsuit about the same thing, you realize. I'm trying to get people to be more responsible about what they spew."

"Well, you say things yourself!"

"I do . . . but I don't tell students their cunts stink."

"I've heard you complain about your students — a lot."

"It's all in *how* you say it. It's language! You can think it, but you can't always say it."

"What should I have said?"

"I don't know, Jim."

They sat and pretended to be interested in their drinks.

"You don't think I can take back what I said?"

"I don't know Lana that well. How forgiving is she?"

"She's a feminist."

"You're dead meat, kiddo!"

"Why can't I take it back?"

"In life there are some things you can never taken back, or if you can, they are never forgotten. This may very well be one of them."

"Really?"

"Really."

"But I can stay here, right?"

"What will you call me if I say no?"

"I wouldn't call you anything . . . honestly."

Nathaniel said nothing.

"I wouldn't!"

"That's what they all say."

"I'll be nice. I will!" Jim looked like he was wishing he was back in Oregon already.

"Ain't free speech grand!" Nathaniel said, toasting his son.

"I have a big mouth," Jim said. He let all the air blow out.

"I guess it runs in the family. I always thought people would appreciate it if you told them the truth — in my books, I mean. But I was so wrong. They'd much rather have lies. And you know what? *I'd* rather have them too."

"I guess I screwed up big time, didn't I?"

"It's not good, all this. I won't kid you . . . kid."

They sat there and didn't finish their drinks. The night was upon them.

"So what's going to happen to me now?" Jim said, wiping at the edge of one eye. "Damn this pet dander!" he said, to hide the fact that he was crying.

"Time will tell," Nathaniel the father said.

Jim was still sleeping, on the futon on the floor in the living room, a tangle of sheets and blankets. Slacker had placed herself between his legs, ever the opportunist. Nathaniel knew he should call Jim's mother while it was still early, before she and Lana went off to work. He tried not to wake his son and used the telephone in the bedroom.

"We don't want him back," Diana said.

"You're not serious."

"He was very mean to Lana."

"I agree, but still . . ."

"Did he tell you what he said to her?"

". . . No." Maybe they could get around this. "Whatever it was, I'm sure he didn't mean it."

"He meant it all right." Diana sounded haggard and angry.

"It was in the heat of the moment. What if he apologized?"

"I told him to apologize already, and he wouldn't. So I said to leave."

"I think he wants to come back."

"Why can't he stay there? We've done enough raising of him."

Nathaniel couldn't really quarrel with that.

"But shouldn't he finish high school in the same place?"

"You don't want him?" She sounded a little hard.

"It's not that I don't want him." Nathaniel moved toward the bedroom door, to make sure that Jim couldn't overhear. He was still sprawled, dreaming the dreams of a seventeen-year-old. His hair was sticking up on one side, the same way Nathaniel's did when he slept. "I just don't want this to separate you two permanently."

"He's not hurt or anything, is he?"

Maybe he should lie about that too.

"Jim's just tired." "Jim's just tired."

"I think this could escalate, his behavior, I mean."

"Maybe if he had his own bathroom that would help."

"We've talked about that."

"Maybe I could help you pay for it." How? His credit cards were maxed out already, and the Teacher Integrity Fund was dried up.

"I've got to go to work."

"Wait. How does Lana feel about this?"

"She said she'd leave it up to me."

"I'll have him call you — later tonight."

"I don't really want to talk to him." She hung up.

"Is that my mom?" Jim said, coming to the door of the bedroom in his underwear, clutching a blanket around him. "Doesn't she want to talk to me?"

"That wasn't her," Nathaniel lied. "It was a friend of mine named Karma."

"Oh. I thought it was my mom." Jim looked sheepish and ill-at-ease. "You sure it wasn't my mom?" There was still a lot of boy there.

So a week went by and the law was grinding its way to a conclusion, one way or the other, and Nathaniel's son was still living with him. It was a bit cramped and Nathaniel wasn't used to sharing a bathroom, not since Marty had died — and even that had been just once in a while. Now, since Jim wasn't going to school and Nathaniel had just one class to teach, they were around each other more than they had ever been.

It wasn't too bad. In fact, it was kind of nice.

Hell may be other people, but having no other people around can also be its own Hell. They went shopping at Pier 1 and got divider screen to create a sleeping area in the living room and a bigger futon so that Jim wouldn't hang over the side while he slept.

They even bought a smaller futon for Slacker so that she would sleep in her own spot. She wouldn't, of course. She preferred Jim's long legs, managing to dodge them although he tossed and turned and made stress noises in his sleep. Some allergy medication seemed to cut down on Jim's worst symptoms.

"Of course eventually you'll have to go back home, you realize," Nathaniel said.

"Can't this be my home now? I like it here."

"You can't just hang around the house all day."

"You do."

"Well, I'm trying not to. Once we win this goddamned lawsuit and the website is stopped from allowing the dirty tricks to go on, I'll be busier."

"I could find a high school here maybe."

"I don't think you can just walk into one. For one thing, you have to fit some racial profile."

"It looks like I might be a minority down here. It's so different from Oregon."

"Groups compete for dominance. It's called history." He didn't say more. He didn't want his son to be bigoted, just not a P.C. knee-jerk about everything. "Most people are simply mowed down by history and don't even know what hit them."

"I bet you can't live without me, right?" Jim joked.

"We'll see," Nathaniel's said. "But don't count on it now, all right?"

He didn't want to admit it, but he was sort of counting on Jim's staying too.

"From now on, I want every sentence to begin with 'Honored Father,'" Nathaniel said.

"Yeah, sure," Jim said.

"It's only Americans who think they've been told by God to rebel against their parents. Most cultures absolutely don't do that! There's a lot to be said for other cultures. Sometimes."

"Oh, really? Are you getting P.C.?"

"The bottom line here is do you want to keep your culture or change it for other people's and just how much."

"And which do you want?"

"I don't know. I can't control it anyway. That's the sad fact."

Yet no son of mine is going to play hooky, Professor Nathaniel swore –that I can control. They tried a little home schooling. They read some history books that Nathaniel had bought and never gotten around to reading, and he and Jim discussed them — even if they couldn't control history. "Maybe I can at least control my own history?" Jim said. "Hey, I like that!" Nathaniel said. There was even a quiz. He assigned an essay on superstitions of the past, and Jim's essay, written completely on his own, with only the assistance of Merriam-Webster, was better than most of those by Nathaniel's students at Shite. "I think you've got some writing skill," he wrote on the essay when he gave it back. God, it was nice to be sincere! "But *infer* is not a synonym for *imply*. See me!"

They went out to dinner sometimes and had some laughs and cooked together and watched TV and went to a rugby game at a college, and got to know each other more than they ever had before in their lives. The fed the ferals at school and argued quite a bit, especially about what was "music" and how loud it should be (par for the course), and Jim had a mouth on him that he had to learn to control. But he was trying. You could see him think something over more than he used to, before he said it, or he said it more carefully.

The odd part was that Nathaniel thought he might be doing the same. Being clever and controversial all the time wasn't everything. Sometimes you just wanted to be there and dull with somebody . . . like your son.

Nathaniel was up for some tests of his own. It was time for his peers in the English Department to observe him teach and write up their reports. Of Guy Mountain, Tadd Dryer, and Arlene Buboe-Pitsky, he thought he'd had the most confrontation and disagreement with Guy, so he is the one that he asked to be removed from the committee. Nona Dwibble was the replacement.

The *People* magazine article finally came out at that same time. It had a full-page picture of Nathaniel in the classroom, looking sad. It was ironic, because he was usually in his best public mode in the classroom. Maybe the photographer had captured Nathaniel's soul. The article itself, thank God, was favorable to him. Whether they admit it or not, lots of people read *People* magazine, and the reaction was substantial. A woman with her baby recognized him when he and Jim were out running on a track near the condo. "I hope you win your case!" she called. It was too much — exercise and fame and encouragement at the same time!

"Don't let it go to your head," Jim said, running alongside him. "Remember you're a mere mortal."

"Nice!" Nathaniel said, out of breath, pleased that Jim could allude to a general entering Rome in triumph. "Maybe you can test into some college early."

"What about Shite?"

"No, no, I wouldn't wish that on anyone, even Dude Lather. The ACLU should have to grade four thousand sets of papers, however."

Morgan of Morgan and Irene, his old friends, called and congratulated Nathaniel on the article, but it turned out that Irene was filing for a divorce — at eighty. After a little probing, it became clear why. Morgan had started using Viagra and Irene had developed a serious rash on her "parts." She wanted Morgan to stop the Viagra, and he didn't want to. Nathaniel didn't know how to advise them. Maybe he'd never see them as a couple again. Morgan also wanted a telephone number — Ludie Fauxville's, Nathaniel's transsexual friend's.

Spike Burns and other members of the English Department saw the article and congratulated him. "How's that lawsuit coming along?" several people wanted to know. "It's coming up soon for a determination by the judge," he answered. Some even gave him checks. Small checks, but it was more than the sentiment that counted. He was seriously in debt now. Lancet had done a great job, but he was asking for more money since they were finished with this phase.

"There's awful stuff on that website," Arlene Buboe-Pitsky said when she called to schedule her classroom visit. "Somebody accused me of condescending to my students because I say, 'Good morning, every one of you!' and somebody else said that I 'grade the papers by throwing them down a staircase.' Quote, unquote. How preposterous!"

She thought that was bad? She hadn't seen the real stuff then. At least she had finally looked at the website. He didn't say lots of things: Why didn't you look at it earlier when I asked you to? Maybe we could have hung together on this and gotten the faculty together and ended this lying tool of the monstrous before it got out of hand, as of course it was going to, and perhaps we wouldn't have had to go to a lawsuit at all if you and the rest of the faculty had pressured the Chancellor and the Board with even half the passionate but ignorant intensity of the Alliance of Students, to say nothing of one tenth one tenth of your brain power and factual knowledge. What are all your degrees and education for, assholes?!

No, he merely said he was looking forward to having her observe him. She would also administer the student evaluations — the real student evaluations, although he wouldn't get to see them until after the term was over.

Nona Dwibble called to make sure there was wheelchair access to his classroom and that the elevator was working. "I have been very disappointed with the accommodation that is mandated by the Americans with Disabilities Act," she complained.

"It was last working Saturday," he said, Mr. Agreeability. I guess no nun jokes when she's there.

Because she hadn't gotten back to him sooner, she'd have to attend the same Saturday morning class as Tadd Dryer, the Christian next door who hadn't talked to him in almost a year. Tadd had sent a cryptic note indicating that he would show up. *Brrr.*

Nathaniel had withstood mainstream journalists and their cameras and TV and radio shows and their callers and e-mailers. He could take on Tadd Dryer, hateful next-door office mate, and Nona Dwibble, former nun in her militantly disabled wheelchair — couldn't he? What doesn't kill you makes you strong, right?

He even asked his son if he wanted to come and observe his teaching with the rest of the crowd. At first Jim said yes, and then he backed out, to sleep in.

It was probably best. What if the class didn't go well? Maybe his son would write him up on Teachersonparade!

> Yo! I had Dr. Tack for a class and I couldn't stand him. He was too HARD and he pushes history and literature and crap like that on you. He made me write essays while on a visit and I had to sleep with his ugly old cat, who gave me allergies. Screw him!

> Jim, Tack's son REALLY!

But bring on the rest of the fuckers!

It didn't help — or did it? — that Nathaniel got this e-mail with attachment from Haywood Wire just as he left to teach the class that was to be observed by two of his English Department peers at the same time:

> Hi, Nathaniel.

> I see that you and the lawyer and Biff managed to get your legal work done without me. I knew you would! Maybe you can use the enclosed, which just came through on Teacherson-parade. I think it's from Fly on the Wall. — Your friend, Haywood

The enclosed was this:

> My fellow students,

> The Good Word has gotten out on sad, sad Professor Tack of recent *People* mag and other "fame." His classes are in s-h-a-m-b-l-e-s, with just one going this term, if that little bird has told me aright.

See, this site can do a lot of good if we just apply ourselves, as
our teachers always tell us to do. It takes "effort" and
"perseverance" to get the bastards of your choice, but at the
end of the day you win the trophy, and as you stand on the
face of your defeated opponent, you know an exhilaration
known by very few. Tack still is under the delusion that he is
about to win his frivolous lawsuit, but, oh, is he ever wrong! If
all goes well, the Tack Man may be out of our hair before the
spring term. With no classes and no lawsuit, he may have no
choice but to do what his "lover" did — put an ice pick into
his heart. Don't feel 'sorry' for the dread Professor. He brought
this on himself. What does it say that the person who 'loved'
Tack most killed himself rather than be around that man?
Shite will dump him, just the way his so-called 'lover' did. You
mark my words. I wish Tack would just shut up about the
'poor lover' instead of going on and on about it in class.

Nathaniel took a deep breath at the cruelty of Fly on the Wall, or whoever had
written it. He had never mentioned Marty's death in class, not once. I don't know that I
can compete with this kind of viciousness, he thought. I'm a piker compared to him. The
meek do not inherit the Internet.

The next thing he did was send a reply to Haywood Wire:

Haywood,

You are as despicable in your own way as Fly on the Wall is in
his. Never write or speak to me again. — Nathaniel

That burnt bridge smelled good, and yet side effects might include stomach pain,
nausea, and permanent bitterness in the brain and heart, similar to sugar pill.

The next thing after that was to teach his class, trying to be a professional. Tadd Dyer
was already in the classroom and didn't acknowledge Nathaniel when he entered. In fact,
he looked away. He had a sour look on his face. Must have been drinking his own pee
pee again. He was dressed in a stiff white shirt and tie with a Windsor knot, but that
didn't make him any taller. At least he hadn't brought the Bible along to read while
Nathaniel taught.

Nathaniel glanced at his notes and answered a question from a student. There were
eighteen people present, looking a little peaked, sleepy, most of them with day jobs, he
supposed, trying to squeeze in a class from 9:10 to 12:20 on a Saturday morning. Give
'em some credit, Nathaniel, he told himself. I give 'em credit. I just won't give them three
college credits unless they deserve them. I give nothing away. I am the Inspector Javert of
Shite College!

I need to perk them up with something — that was his next thought.

Where was Nona Dwibble? She was going to be late. Maybe he should shut the door
and tell her to come on time, the same way he told the students to. She'd probably sue

him under the Americans with Disabilities Act.

But then there she was, rolling out of the elevator across the hallway, using her hands on the wheels. She had never responded to Nathaniel's Committee on Truth inquiries about the accusations against her for making her and her wheelchair so "accessible" for her so-called sexual favors even when she'd sent the fifteen-dollar donation. Maybe she didn't think it was funny. Maybe she was right. Maybe I should teach this whole class without cracking a smile. And live the rest of my life doing the same. Life wasn't funny. Why did I ever believe it was?

Nona came in and at least waved at him. She motioned that she'd stay up in the front, and two students moved a desk to accommodate her wheelchair. She didn't look well, elderly, her face puckered up with wrinkles. She evidently didn't even try to touch up her hair. It just sat there on her head like gray seaweed. She was wearing a faded blue pantsuit long out of style. Her fingers looked crippled up with arthritis. So this was the woman mocked on Teachersonparade as a sexual plaything for her students. . . . ha. ha. Human voices call us and we drown.

He looked at the faces before him. They varied in age from late teens to fifties. They had *A Passage to India*, the text, on their desks, most of them anyway, ready to take notes, except for Ms. Steele, the dim bulb in the left back seat, who couldn't be bothered. He had a huge impulse just to walk from the room and never return. Or what if he cracked, went down, groveled and wept. "Please! Like me! Like me! Give me a good review! Please!" His hands in prayer, down on his knees right there in front of them all.

"Today we examine the novel," he began the class. "First, let's clear up some misconceptions about what a novel actually is. Ms. Steele back there, what would you say a novel is?"

"A bunch of lies?" she answered.

"Absolutely. But lies that tell the truth, no?"

Ms. Steele wrinkled up her nose. Paradox? Will that be on the final?

"Literature can actually do something besides pass the time," Nathaniel went on.

"But a good read is the most important part, don't you think?" Mr. Lange tossed out.

"Of course a 'good read' is necessary. Literature doesn't have to be dry or tedious or something dead from a long time ago. But I have the distinct feeling that many people today, including college students, have very little idea that fiction — and a novel is a book-length word of fiction, not just any book — that fiction is not just something you read and then leave behind on BART, or whatever rapid transit system you may use."

"It's supposed to be good for you too," Ms. Fang offered. "Right?"

Nathaniel screwed up his eyes. "It doesn't have to be that moralistic," he said. "At least in the West." He felt the chalk heavy in his hand, his arms weary, somewhat like Sisyphus with his rock. "Here's my sound bite about the novel." he went on. "It's truth, about life, about human beings, but not literal truth — and combined with craftsmanship. The literary novel is valuable because it allows a writer to dig deeper into human psychology, into human behavior than most things. Most things tell you lies — ads, friends, relatives, even most books, like diet books! Especially diet books."

They laughed.

"But not the novel, at least when it's not just a product made to sell — like toilet paper. And thus it allows a reader to delve. Sometimes fiction can even hurt, can stab us in the heart. We need literature. We must have it!" He heard his own voice, and he was glad it was excited.

"What's craftsmanship mean?" Ms. Steele asked.

He ignored her.

"Does anybody really want to be stabbed in the heart?" Mr. Lange said, tentatively.

"Maybe not." Nathaniel almost smiled. "Maybe not, Mr. Lange. Perhaps my metaphor was. . . not well chosen."

Arlene Buboe-Pitsky came the following week and gave out the student evaluations while he took a break. He thought his classes had gone well over all, but it was not up to him to judge. These are the summary comments from the evaluations:

> From Tadd Dryer:
>
> "Dr. Tack is a fully professional instructor. At times he could possibly try to be less frivolous."

> From Arlene Buboe-Pitsky:
>
> "Nathaniel Tack is the genuine thing. I had heard and read some disparaging remarks about him but had never visited any classes of his before. To judge from the hour and fifteen minutes that I observed him, he is insightful, witty, interested in his students' achievement, and a definite asset to our department."

> From Nona Dwibble:
>
> "Though controversial (and what's wrong with that?), Dr. Nathaniel Tack impressed me in his class (in which he discussed fiction) as being a man on top of his subject matter, a lively and thought-provoking college instructor, and a teacher who still cares. I have seen many, many who have given up and are burned out at our particular institution. That is not true of Nathaniel Tack. I envy him his commitment. (I even learned some things from him!)
>
> The entire college community should likewise forever be in his debt because of his fight to end the savage and uncivilized mistreatment of teachers by means of anonymous, deceitful, misleading, frequently libelous, criminal (and fake) reviews written on a website that is available on the Internet to one and

all around the world. I was, to be honest, not on his side when this controversy began, yet now I see that he was prescient when some of us were not. I wish him well in his pending lawsuit and hope that he remains for many more years at our beloved college. He is the kind of person who elevates us beyond ourselves."

Wow. Nona, I hardly knew ye.

"Beloved college" was a bit much, but it's always nice to be called "prescient." What does prescient mean, Ms. Steele? Look it up. Brighten your bulb.

Arlene said she wasn't supposed to let him see the student comments yet, but she said, "I can tell you this. They are quite favorable, with one or two exceptions."

For me, little old me? I wish to thank the Academy from the bottom of my heart. It was a triumph. The bastards had not ground him down. What do you mean one or two exceptions?

"You look pleased," his son said when Nathaniel came home with his copy of his peers' evaluations.

"I got a good report card," he joked. "Want to see it?" He had never seen one of Jim's report cards.

"Sure."

Jim was suitably impressed, peanut-butter-and-jelly sandwich half in his mouth or not. "Maybe this will help with your enrollment for next semester?"

"Probably not — unless you want to type them into Teachersonparade."

"You want me to?" He got the jug of milk out of the refrigerator and poured himself a big glass.

"No."

"I don't mind doing it."

"These are legitimate reviews. The rest are shit — somebody's crazed idea of progress. I will not play by their rules. Never."

"But you could make it seem like —"

"I could, but Fly on the Wall or some other psychopath can go on there right after you do and put in counter-reviews."

"Well, then I could come back again." Jim had a milk mustache.

"It's a futile battle, Jim. I'm a determined person, but people like Fly on the Wall and some of his cronies are relentless. He's truly sick. He makes me feel downright normal."

"But what if you can't stop him?"

"A very good question, class. To be honest, I don't know. I don't know what will happen. The judge is supposed to meet with all parties next week. We hope to get Discovery about who did what to whom."

"Then you'll kick his sick ass."

"One can hope."

Nathaniel got a glass of milk for himself instead of the vodka he wanted. "You're a good influence on me," he said.

"Hey, let's go sit on your patio," Jim said. "It's going to waste. What do you say? There's something I want to talk about."

Nathaniel's heart squeezed ever so slightly.

You had to go through the garage to get to the patio. Nathaniel didn't go there as much as he should have. It had ivy growing in too much profusion, covering the high walls between the units and all of the cement floor. They pulled up their chairs to the tiny, weathered table with old leaves and cobwebs on it, but it was a little too intimate, and Jim pulled his chair back, and they sat side by side, not looking at each other, sipping at the milk. The tree that Nathaniel had planted when he'd first met his son, ten years earlier, was sprouting up like a weed. "That's your tree," he said.

"Why mine?"

"I planted it after I got back from meeting you in Oregon. And look at it now." Indeed it was almost to the top of the condo's roof, branches sticking out, providing cover from the bigger units that had been built right next door since. "Do you remember the first time we met?"

"Not really, not too much."

"Sentimentalist."

"Yes, Honored Father," Jim said. "Why kind of tree?"

"It was on sale."

They smiled at each other. Life was good. "I have some of that meeting on videotape. We'll have to dig it out and watch it together. You want to?"

"Sure. Sometime."

Nathaniel shrugged. "It'll mean more to you when you're older. After you're not a virgin. By the way, are you still a virgin?"

"None of your business."

"Just asking."

"Yes, Honored Father."

"Shut up, Honored Son. What do you want to talk about?"

Slacker deigned to come out on the fire escape to look down at them. She could jump to the fence if she wanted to, but she wasn't sure. "Get down here!" Nathaniel commanded. "I've got some milk if you want some!" He waved his glass at her.

"Fuck you," she said and went back into the house.

"It's nice just to sit and do nothing, don't you think?" Nathaniel said, placing his hands behind his head, leaning back in the dirty white chair that had tree sap on it.

Jim paused, then said, "My mom called today."

"Oh?"

"We talked a long time."

"How did that go?"

"She wants me to come back."

"She's not mad anymore?"

"We worked it out."

"How about Lana?"

"I apologized. Hard." Jim gritted his teeth to show how hard.

'Did you? Good for you. And she accepted it?"

"Yes."

Nathaniel took a sip of his milk, hoping he wasn't making a milk mustache. "Women are better at that kind of thing than men are."

"Do you think I should go back?"

Their eyes met, but just for a brief moment, as men do. "Do you want to go back?"

"I like it here."

"Maybe it's just that you like not going to school."

"I'm going to school!"

"Yeah, well, where's that second essay I asked you to write?"

"It's coming. It's coming."

"Slacker ate your homework, no doubt."

"Can I stay here?" Jim seemed to be holding his breath too.

You don't want to send your only child away when it was good, like it was now. "Of course."

The pause.

"But maybe I should go back?"

"You think?" Nathaniel smiled. "I suppose you have more structure up there than you're getting here."

"My mom wants me to come home for my birthday."

"When's that?"

"You don't know when my birthday is?"

"Just teasing. Of course I know your birthday. It's two days from now."

"Were you planning a party?"

"Yep. Big party. All my friends are coming."

"What friends?"

"Touché."

"To tell the truth, I'm a little homesick."

"For the girls you left behind?"

"My mom said Amber Hatfield called and asked about me."

"And she's hot, right?"

"She's secretary of the yearbook."

Nathaniel smiled. "That's really hot."

"I can't help it. I like smart blondes."

"None of us can help what we find attractive. It's probably some kind of imprinting, like baby ducks."

"Thanks."

"You're welcome. That was going to be your next assignment — studying sexual imprinting. What about your school? Did it call too?"

"My mom took care of it. She told them I had scarlet fever."

"That's better than an enlarged prostate."

"What?!"

"Nothing." Nathaniel was 'experiencing frequent bladder control problems,' as the ads had it, the same thing his father had had. He'd probably have to have it operated on if the pills he'd gotten didn't work. Like father, like son. "Just always watch your prostate, my boy."

"You mean look up my ass?"

Nathaniel smiled at his boy. "Whatever." The milk was clogging his throat. Maybe he was developing an allergy. ". . . . I don't want you to go, Jim."

"And I don't want to go home, exactly."

Another pause, longer.

"Of course you have to finish school."

"I suppose I do."

"And Nature calls. I mean Amber Hatfield calls."

"You'd like Amber."

"I'm sure I would. You think you can get a grip on your mouth around Lana?"

"They're putting in a separate bathroom for me."

"Good idea."

"I don't really know anybody around here."

"I understand."

"It's not you! I actually like you. I mean —"

"Trust me, I understand. A boy's gotta do what a boy's gotta do."

"Will you be all right?"

"Sure."

"Not lonely or anything?"

"No, of course not."

"Maybe you could come up to visit."

"Maybe I could."

"At Christmas?"

"Sure. We'll be a Currier and Ives Christmas card, the bunch of us." He looked over at his son, trying not to lose it, not to well up too much, not at all. "You're going to be a good man, Jim."

"I am?"

"Yeah, any day now."

"Well, at least a man, huh? On my eighteen birthday," Jim said. "Self-sufficient? On his own?"

Nathaniel looked over. "I believe I may have a clever son."

"Naw, not me."

"Then maybe it's my other son."

"Must be."

"You've got a milk mustache," Nathaniel said, looking away.

"So do you," Jim said.

They both wiped them off. God, those goddamned allergies were something!

His son left the next day. If he drove straight through, he could get back in time for his birthday. "If it's your birthday, it'll probably be easier patching things up," Nathaniel said.

"That's what I thought too."

"Just don't drive if you're tired. It won't kill you to stop a few times. Have some coffee or orange juice. Do some push-ups against the car."

"Yes, Mom," Jim teased.

"Tell your mother and Lana I took good care of you — and hello."

"I will."

They shook hands through the car's window, somewhat awkwardly, and then Jim's car pulled out of the parking space at the condo and rolled toward Oregon.

Nathaniel called Biff and Karma and the lawyer and finalized the plans to meet at the court in two days, for Judge Garza's ruling. Karma said she'd be there. She'd take public transportation. Biff said he wanted to come, but he didn't know if he could make it. He and his wife were having "trouble." She was even talking about moving out.

"What's wrong?" Nathaniel asked.

"It's been building some time. The strain of the lawsuit has made it worse."

"I'm sorry to hear that."

"But I'll try to be there, if I can."

"You've been a great help, Biff. We'll carry on without you."

"If I'm not there, let me know what the judge says as soon as you can, okay?"

"Will do."

Nathaniel wrote some e-mails and returned some calls from media people. The new editor of the newspaper at Shite College had called and asked if he would do an interview. Nathaniel was somewhat gun-shy because the support that rag had given Teachersonparade before. But he thought he owed her the courtesy of a return call. Her name seemed somewhat familiar. Magdalena Isidro.

"I was your student in 101 several years ago," she said right off the bat.

"You were?"

Uh oh.

"I thought you were a first-rate teacher."

"Now I remember you!" It was true. A large Filipino woman. Unforgettably large. Big thighs. Juno the Journalist. "I gave you an A, yes?"

"No, just a B."

"Sorry."

"That's all I deserved. I was busy with other things than school that semester."

Good woman.

"I think what's on that site is pretty much an abomination," she went on. "That webmaster has had more than a year to get it functioning right, and it still has all this filth on it. I've talked to several other instructors who are stressed out by it, but they're afraid to speak up. They think they'll be targeted."

"They will be," Nathaniel said. "No question about it."

"Maybe I can run something that will discredit the site?"

"Really?"

"I think it's hurt more people than it's helped."

"An expose?"

"Something."

"Well, it can't hurt. Expose Dean Visigoth as the primary beneficiary of the fraud on the website."

"A dean? Might not I be accused of libel for that?" she said.

"I believe truth is an absolute defense against libel," Nathaniel said. "And isn't it sweet that the school paper has to worry about libel, but the website doesn't. See me laughing."

He talked to her for almost an hour as she took notes.

"I'll write an opinion piece too," she said, "definitely condemning the way the site is being used."

"Thank you. Can victory be far behind?" Nathaniel said.

The ACLU via Tether & Strafe at last came back with its Memorandum of Points and Authorities to present the other side's final legal arguments. Nathaniel's eyes swam as he tried to make his way through the legalese. It was like swimming in snot. There were nearly fifty pages, much of it repetitions from earlier legal positions. Assume the position, legal or not. Karma Sudra, born an Untouchable, was a gem and offered to write a gloss on the flaws of the opposing side's arguments. She had been so angered by the case that she was considering going back to school — to law school this time. "I fear this may take years to settle," she said. "However, someone has to do it!"

Touch her!

No wonder lawyers ruled the world. Most people hadn't a clue what was being said, or it was worded in the most constipated and arcane ways. People just threw up their hands in surrender. "I can't follow this. Have your way with me!"

He had no choice but to pay attention, close attention.

The heart of the case now seemed to rest on the good faith or bad faith of Dude Lather, illiterate, dog-brained, computer-gifted tech nerd and the words of Title 47 U.S.C., Article 230(c)2), which said — and, remember, you have been warned:

> No provider or user of an interactive computer service shall be held liable on account of —
>
> (A) any action voluntarily taken in good faith to restrict access to or availability of material that the provider or user considers to be obscene, lewd, lascivious, filthy, excessively violent, harassing, or otherwise objectionable, whether or not such material is constitutionally protected; or
>
> (B) any action taken to enable or make available to information content providers or others the technical means to restrict access to material described in paragraph (1).

The clear intent of this law, if "clear" could be applied in any way, was not to penalize people who tried to get rid of obscenity but perhaps didn't get it all. It was never meant to *protect* people who were spewing obscenities left and right at teachers or anyone else. The irony, for Nathaniel, was that he didn't give a damn about restricting pornography like the legislators who had fashioned this monstrosity did. He was a goddamn roaring liberal about that crap. But provide a loophole and slime will slide though it.

The main intention of Title 47 somehow had gotten obscured in all the verbiage. There it says "it is the policy of the United States to ensure vigorous enforcement of Federal criminal laws to deter and punish trafficking in obscenity, stalking, and harassment by means of computer." Hello! That's precisely what was happening – teachers being stalked and harassed and showered with obscenities.

He and Biff were even being vilified in the lawsuit as well, a copy of which was put up on the ACLU's website. Goddamn smarmy Gus Strappado was citing Biff's and Nathaniel's low grade point averages on Teachersonparade as though they were Gospel (based on "apparently authentic student reviews") and also saying "the Disclaimers on the website clearly indicate that the website is open to all." The "Disclaimers" consisted of one sentence in a tiny font buried at the bottom of Teachersonparade. Didn't these lawyers have any respect for the truth whatsoever? Was there no lie they wouldn't tell? All Nathaniel wanted was for Teachersonparade to make the people using it as accountable as they would be if they were running a newspaper or a magazine or any other comparable form of media. Mavis Spielberg, even with her favorable news story on Nathaniel, hadn't dared to quote the actual "reviews." The best she could do with such "filth" was to paraphrase it. Yet "crude" and "shocking" didn't quite carry the impact of the real words. Nor did the article point out that the majority of the "reviews" had not come from Nathaniel or Biff's actual students. Casual readers — in other words most people — would still think that these two men had upset their actual students and those students were saying possibly lamentable things about them but nevertheless things inspired by classroom interactions, when in fact they were way beyond that stage now and had been from the start.

A hobbyhorse that Gus Strappado and the Tether & Strafe gang couldn't seem to ride enough was "the automatic cloak of immunity" that supposedly put webmaster Dude Lather in the same camp with America Online and other true "service providers." Nathaniel could see why AOL shouldn't be held responsible for what every crackpot put online, any more than the telephone company should be held responsible for crank calls. Yet if the crank calls were sent, those that sent them should be uncovered and prosecuted. Even requiring the names of the "reviewers" to be attached to reviews most likely would have cut out ninety-nine percent of the libelous, toilet-wall dreck. Or was the ACLU about to defend that next? Remember, boys and girls — Thomas Paine wrote *Common Sense* with shit on a toilet wall!

And why in Heaven's name should Dude Lather be "immune" from prosecution when it was more than likely that he himself was writing bad reviews of those opposed to his website — in cahoots with Fly on the Wall, the First Amendment Club, probably Jake Trosky and the Alliance of Students, and you couldn't rule out Gorilla Woman and Dean Visigoth either — all provided a marvelous "cloak" to hide their "under-represented" deviltry.

So the judge owed Nathaniel and Biff some "Discovery" about the "Dude" webmaster and Fly on the Wall at the very least, and the very least is what Lancet had requested in the final Complaint. Both of these men were to be subpoenaed and their e-mails traced. And when they were "Discovered" they would be found guilty and pay a hefty penalty and be forced to stop what they were doing and allowing others to do!

But no — couldn't have that, the other side argued. The brave New World of Internet discourse must be saved from the likes of "failed educators" like the Plaintiffs. "Failed educators"!

He didn't actually know how good a teacher Biff was, though. Biff had told enough detail by now to make Nathaniel think he was a pushover when it came to grades. He said he gave mostly A's and B's and promised at least a passing grade if the students attended all the classes. Oh, Biff, what a falling off was there!

Strappado likewise argued that Dude Lather didn't "edit" the reviews. In fact he deleted or left in the ones he wanted to, lumped some together, put comments like "Tack is acting like an ass" and "Tack continues to spew his rantings" and made other similar "editorial" choices. Dude Lather was an EDITOR, just like the editor of the *National Inquirer* was an editor!

The Evil Ones were also now arguing that Nathaniel was a "public figure" because he had "willfully insinuated himself into the public spotlight." That was supposed to make it all right for any jackasses in Utah or anywhere else to write up evaluations of Nathaniel not as a media guest but as a teacher in a college even though the jackasses had no personal knowledge of Nathaniel as a teacher.

The Defendants also argued that the Plaintiffs showed "hypocrisy" in criticizing the site for having false reviews when "they themselves have submitted hundreds of false reviews." Nathaniel hadn't wanted to admit that he had sent in any false reviews — back at the very beginning of the website — but Lancet had included the admission in the final draft, and now it was being seized upon as though he and Biff "had submitted hundreds of false reviews" in an effort to "undermine a legitimate source of student information." Upside down and backwards, as usual. The invisible Haywood Wire had sent in the hundreds of reviews (and not very convincing ones at that), Biff had sent in forty or so, Nathaniel had sent in those few early ones — all to demonstrate the absurdity of the way the website was set up and operated.

Maybe they could get Judge Garza to submit some false reviews himself, from the comfort and security of his chambers. Would anything be more convincing than that? "Look, Your Honor, anyone can send in a review!" Maybe they could even do it in court — before the jury. But Lancet said, "If something goes wrong with the computer while the jury is watching, it could backfire. And we can't ask the judge to do anything unethical."

But, as Karma's notes said, "Almost everything about this website is unethical. There isn't one review on it that anyone can verify as coming from the source from which it claims to be!" Wait until they got Karma up there on the witness stand. She'd give Strappado his money's worth!

What really galled was when Nathaniel's objections to the site were labeled "efforts by self-appointed guardians of 'correct' thinking to squelch controversial topics" and to "harm the Bill of Rights." *What?*! It was Nathaniel's own 'incorrect' thinking that had led to some of his negative reviews by real students. All right, he would promise that if people were stopped from saying that he raped and murdered his students and went tooling for anus on Polk Street, he would work to see that the Bill of Rights didn't crumble into dust.

"We are going to win, aren't we?" he asked Lancet when he delivered his and Karma's final, final, final, final, final comments on the other side's final, final, final, final, final, final Legal Deceptions.

"It's up to the judge now" was all that Lancet would say.

"And what do you know about Judge Garza?"

"Just that he's an arrogant prick."

"And that's good, right?" Nathaniel said.

It was late that night that a call came. Nathaniel thought it might be his son calling to say he had gotten back to Oregon safe and sound.

It was Jim's mother. "I have some bad news," she said.

Nathaniel's heart jolted in his chest. "It's not Jim, is it?"

"I'm afraid so." She gathered her strength, though her voice was quivering. "He had an accident when he was driving back. He was tired and fell asleep apparently."

"I told him to take some rests. How bad is it?"

"I'm afraid Jim is in a coma. They fear brain damage."

There were no words, no sound he could make that would be loud enough.

"Are you there? . . . Nathaniel?" she asked.

"This can't be. Oh, please, no, tell me it can't be." He couldn't see the base of the telephone any longer, his eyes on fire.

"He was almost home." Her voice cracked, like her heart. "Just fifteen miles away. It was the day before his eighteen birthday."

He barely knew this woman. All they had in common was their son. And this is all that they had left to share now. Tears were stinging his eyes, snot running from his nose, the slimy, acrid taste on his tongue unbearable. "I was just getting to . . . know him!" he sobbed.

"I know. I know. He said he finally liked you, when we talked that last time."

Nathaniel wept. "We were learning to talk. We weren't just any old father and son." The snot was vile on his tongue. "We weren't!"

"He tried to get back too fast. Maybe he should just have stayed there. Maybe I should shouldn't have . . ."

"No, I shouldn't have let him go." Nathaniel wiped his face with the back of his hand.

Even Slacker seemed to know that something was wrong. She was watching him cry, her eyes big.

"His car was . . ."

"I don't want to know."

"It was my car. Maybe if I hadn't . . ."

"Diana, we can't do this. We can't do this to ourselves. We did the right thing."

She sobbed. "I know. That's what makes it so hard!"

They wept together. There were silences and dead echoes of his son's voice in Diana's voice, plus echoes of the conversations he and Nathaniel had had.

"Can you come up?" she asked.

"I have a lawsuit hearing tomorrow morning. I'll drive up right after that, okay? It's probably faster than flying, considering all the connections and . . . whatever."

"I think he'd like to know you're there. The doctors think he can still hear."

"I'll be there."

Oh, please, please!

Nathaniel did not sleep that night. He said no prayers. He drank no alcohol, either. He had no sex. Slacker was his one comfort, her sleeping, twitching body under his warm hand as the two lay in his bed as he stared at the ceiling. Not even sleep to fool the throbbing mind. This was the long night of the soul he'd heard about, not the first, but surely the longest in his life. Your lover dead by his own hand. Your only child lying in a coma in another state. Your body beginning its decline despite your best hopes to put off the inevitable. The teaching now deteriorated into the parody of education that it had largely become. The career in writing — a vast ocean of indifference ready to swallow you and all you'd spent your life creating. What did you tell yourself when it came down to this? What pretty tissue of lies and dreams could you fashion to make this all somehow mean something, anything, more than it clearly did when you took away all the sops?

None.

There were just you and the dark and the ceiling.

They were wrong — there *are* atheists in fox holes, and he was true to his principles.

The next morning the court hearing was held in a side room on the sixth floor. Biff didn't make it, but Lancet was there, dressed in a handsome suit. He was very reassuring as he shook Nathaniel's and Karma's hands. He had brought the final legal brief to present to the judge. Nathaniel said nothing to them about his son.

Gus Strappado, the lawyer for the other side, was there, looking like a million bucks in a thousand-dollar suit, big-faced, oily and competent, along with Dude Lather and some of his sup-porters. Nathaniel could make out Jake Trosky, Gorilla Woman, and Dean Visigoth, and some of the rest of the Alliance off to one side. There was also a man about thirty years of age with them. There was nothing distinctive about him — white, with dishwater-soap hair and ordinary features, dull eyes — but something in Nathaniel's gut told him that this was Fly-on-the-Wall. The banality of evil.

The judge was busy with some other matter in the back. But after half an hour he emerged and took his place on the bench. Garza was a young-looking fifty. He had thick, black eyebrows and narrow lips. He looked like he might be a runner, although it was difficult to tell because of the robe. He smiled at the assembled, and said, "Shall we?" Lancet was right. Judge Garza was an arrogant prick.

Each side was restricted to fifteen minutes to make its presentation of why the case should proceed or stop right there. Lancet was first, and spoke well, losing his place in his notes just once. Nathaniel and Karma kept looking at each other and at the judge trying to read his expressions. He seemed to lean on his right hand quite a bit. Did that mean anything?

Lancet was almost finished, making his final plea: that the reviews on Teachersonparade were often filthy and libelous and indefensible, and were "not in any way what the Founding Fathers had intended by the First Amendment" and the Internet should not be permitted "to facilitate the worse attributes of human beings," and that's exactly what was happening here, and the webmaster "could prevent this but wouldn't." Indeed he was using it, with the likely assistance of a few others, "to put himself in control of the lives of teachers, out of spite and revenge and hardly out of any pursuit of noble principles," and this was "the perfect case to re-interpret in a sane manner the law about the Internet and what was permitted on it and what was not." The Plaintiffs were asking for Discovery on just two people — the webmaster and one John Doe, tentatively identified as Fly on the Wall so that they could show, once and for all, how the site was a vicious fraud.

Strappado argued that the Chinese Communist Government and other "oppressive regimes" restricted the use of the Internet, and that's what was being attempted here. He said that Mr. Drew A. Lather was in no way an editor or a publisher, but merely "a service provider" and that meant he was fully protected by the law of the United States. The Plaintiffs were "rotten teachers" who were trying to silence their critics in "a clear violation of the express purpose of Title 47, Section 230." The Defendants had done nothing wrong despite the "libelous allegations" of the Plaintiffs and the case should be thrown out of court before it proceeded "one inch further" in "the destruction of what was finest about America."

He actually spoke a little better than Lancet, but that didn't make him right.

Judge Garza told the website's supporters to be quiet when they applauded too loud and too long after Strappado's words. That was good, wasn't it? Finally Judge Garza laced his fingers together. He had big hands. "I appreciate the arguments from counsel on both sides. Thank you."

"Thank you, Your Honor," Strappado said.

"Yes, absolutely, Your Honor," Lancet was quick to add.

Such obsequiousness. All through their presentations, both lawyers had kissed the judge's ass big time. There wasn't an eyebrow movement or a slight pause that didn't cause the lawyers to practically wet their pants in their eagerness to satisfy His Honor's vaguest whim. Teachers didn't begin to get this much "respect" from their students. Not even close. Surely the judge must know that he wouldn't be getting it either — if there were something called Judgesonparade.com — promoted with flyers in the corridors of Superior Court and via links from the Court's official webpage — if there were a place where lawyers and the sentenced and the idly vicious could go online and post anonymous reviews and "get" the judge of their choice:

> I have dealt with Judge Jesus Garza of Superior Court of Santa Francesca many times. He is an ARROGANT PRICK. Don't get him as your judge if you can possibly avoid him. Reschedule, postpone, hope for him to die, whatever it takes! He is a terrible, terrible judge!!!

> If he comes up for a vote, vote him OUT!!!

Or:

> Judge Garza takes bribes for his judicial judgments. He prefers money, but he'll settle for a blowjob under his bench if you don't get cum on his nice robe! I gave him one, even though he had a tiny, tiny dick that tasted like a bad Tootsie role, and I got off the charge. FUCK HIM UP HIS HONOR!!

"It seems to me," Judge Garza was saying, "that the U.S. Constitution is perfectly clear on this matter. You can't just yell 'Fire!' in a crowded theater and expect not to be punished. Further, libel does exist. I'm sure teachers have special problems, but they did choose that profession, did they not? I'm sure there are unfortunate things on the Internet as well. That's why I personally have avoided it. Perhaps more people should. But that's not really for me to say. I am sure that teachers don't like to hear unpleasant things said about them online, but maybe they need to develop thicker skins, the way we judges have."

Was he kidding? He hadn't heard an unkind word from anybody in his entire time on the bench! Nathaniel wanted to shout this out in the courtroom. But he bit his tongue.

"And I'm sure some quite unpleasant comments may have been made on the website in question."

Hadn't he read them? It didn't sound like it. Hadn't he read the endless Complaints that Lancet had so carefully written? Had he let his staff — students most likely! — read them for him and make recommendations? What was going on here?

"So it seems to me, Mr. Lancet," he said, looking solemn, "that you need to get together with your clients and Mr. Strappado and his client and work out some sort of settlement here."

Nathaniel saw Lancet's head sag. Oh, Christ!

"Let me just point out, to spur you on your way, that in similar cases in the past I have awarded judgments to the prevailing party in excess of $200,000. It would behoove you to act accordingly, would it not?"

"Yes, Your Honor," Lancet said, his hand at his forehead.

His Honor left the hearing room. What a sick, imperceptive fuck.

Nathaniel turned and looked at Strappado and his posse. They were bubbling over with happiness. "Oh, my God, we've lost!" Nathaniel whispered to Karma. "We've lost!" The lawyers gathered their folders and their integrity and prepared to vacant the hearing room.

He saw Fly on the Wall get up from his seat and smile at Nathaniel. He mouthed the words very slowly and carefully: "Who's ... got ... the ... last ... laugh ... now ... huh, Nathannyboy?" He spread his arms slightly and thrust his crotch hard toward Nathaniel, just once, just enough to "communicate" his message.

It rains in Oregon, they say. Nathaniel stayed in a motel because he didn't think he could bear to see Jim's room, the baseball hats, the toys. Any of it. He brought a copy of the essay Jim had written at the "home school" and showed it to his mother and Lana. They didn't read it. They couldn't bear to.

There was a nice picture of Jim on top of the closed casket. It said:

JAMES V. LAINE.

The kid didn't even have my name, Nathaniel thought.

Quite a few from Jim's high school attended the service at the Unitarian Center. Diana and Lana were Unitarians. The principal spoke. Didn't really seem to know much about Jim, but he tried. Lana spoke, told some little anecdotes about Jim — how they used to fight, but how "things were getting better, the older he got. He was a good kid," she said.

Nathaniel said a few words at the podium. His tic was hurting his cheek, but he spoke anyway. "Jim was my only son. He came down in California to visit me recently. . . . It was a nice visit. One of the nicest we ever had. We haven't had that many, to be honest." He was afraid he wasn't being very articulate. "I wish I had some funny stories to tell you, something charming to ease the pain here. But I don't really. Or at least ones I can say at a funeral. There's a time and a place for everything. Jim was learning that, I think. Not everyone is learning that, but my son was. He was a good kid. Every parent says the same, I suppose, but my Jim really was a good kid. . . ." Nathaniel turned his head to the side, toward the casket. "During his last visit, I told him he had to call me Honored Father." Nathaniel straightened his back. "Well, I want you to know that I am more than honored to have had such a son." He went to his seat in the first row and sat down.

"He's in Heaven now," one of the other speakers said.

Nathaniel wished he could believe in Heaven.

No, it was all a waste, such a waste.

Amber Hatfield, who had asked about Jim when he ran away from home, was at the funeral. She came up to Nathaniel afterwards and said, "I saw your picture in *People* magazine." She seemed impressed.

"Yes, we won the media battle. We only lost the war," he said.

Other people came around, and were nice. And then they left.

They buried James V. Laine in the local cemetery. Nathaniel inquired about other plots nearby his son. Diana and Lana were thinking about buying a couple for them-selves. Did Nathaniel want them to get him one too? They'd even buy it for him if he liked.

"I'll think about it," Nathaniel said. He did think about it, but he didn't make any decision. Because he had miles to go before he slept. Miles and miles and miles to go before he slept. Besides, he had Slacker and some under-represented ferals to look after.

One of these is the real ending of this story. But choose any one that amuses you:

Ending #1:

When Nathaniel got back home, he and Biff had to get together with Lancet to work out the settlement. The ACLU was demanding that all their expenses paid to Tether & Strafe be reimbursed — $150,000. Lancet got it down to $25,000 with a written apology from Nathaniel and Biff that they had been "morally wrong" and "legally reckless" to bring the lawsuit in the first place. Legally reckless perhaps, but hardly morally wrong. They wouldn't sign. Bring on the dogs! Lancet got it down to $10,000 and an acknowledgment that Biff and Nathaniel had "tampered with the integrity of Teachersonparade" and would "never do it again." Lancet said that was the best he could do, and they'd better take it. They signed and paid the money in installments over the next year. For being accused of various sins, including raping and murdering their students and being bad teachers, they were required to pay the *other* side and declare their own lack of integrity. Nathaniel also declared bankruptcy and thus got out of paying $2500 of it. The ACLU boasted in various press releases about "this great legal victory and precedent." With no lawsuit, the media coverage drained away to a trickle. Biff Thorgoode separated from his wife and retired from Shite College early. "I simply can't take this anymore," he said. Essentially, the Bad Guys won.

Guy Mountain won Teacher of the Year twice in a row. Karma Sudra was let go from the Shite College because her credentials weren't quite in order. She disappeared, as most people do. Haywood Wire was found dead in a hotel room of a gambling casino in Laughlin, Nevada, all very hush hush, but the cause of death was erotic auto-asphyxiation.

Nathaniel did not retire — he couldn't.

He tried to get the Bar Association to punish Modos & O'Harromog for the way they had mis-practiced law. The Bar Association did nothing. But Modos the older of the two lawyers, died. Perhaps it was the voodoo doll that Nathaniel used.

The webmaster virtually stopped enforcing his so-called code of what was acceptable or not on the site. The college revamped its website after the fact and stopped allowing flyers promoting Teachersonparade to be displayed on the campus, and and that helped a little. Nathaniel gradually made up his missed classes, and all his classes returned to normal enrollments, with the same old / same old problems — a Japanese American student told him that she should pass because there had been Japanese internment camps.

Nathaniel's facial tic faded as the stress lessened, as did all his vodka self-medication. Viagra, however, continued to prove useful. The sense of humor was the part of him that was most permanently affected. It died . . . or all but.

Fly on the Wall continued to post "reviews" as he chose, as did anyone else. Here is the last one Nathaniel bothered to read:

> Poor Nathannyboy. He most assuredly has had a run of bad luck this past year or so. He got his face rubbed in his own Legal Action, didn't you, bubie? My heart bleeds for you. Then he lost his 'lover,' though from what I hear there wasn't too much love lost between that pair. And then the poor sucker goes off and gets his own kid K-I-L-L-E-D by sending him home when he begged and begged to stay with his old dad. But, no, the Tack Man wasn't having that. It might interfere with your nighttime sex-capades, no? Why don't you pack it in, if you catch my drift, Fudge Packer!

KILL YOURSELF. KILL YOURSELF TOO!

Title 47, Article 230 of the U.S. Legal Code still stands.

Vicious lies, defamation, blackmail, bribery, and threats thus remain largely enabled by law in the USA. Fly on the Wall, by winning, became the Honored Father of Internet Trolls.

Educational standards continue to fall since many teachers fear online retaliation and losing their jobs for grading honestly.

Ending #2:

Nathaniel (AKA Daniel Curzon-Brown) resigned from Shite College and moved to San Francisco and got a job at City College of that fair city, which absolutely, positively bore no resemblance to Shite College of Santa Francesca.

Ending #3:

After Nathaniel did retire at age seventy-five, although he had been warned of the danger, on a sentimental return visit to the college where he had spent so many mercurial years, unfortunately he was sought out and assassinated by a certain Jake Trosky, late of the Alliance of Students, in a sympathy suicide bombing in solidarity with Oppressed Suicide Bombers Around the Globe. His ashes were sprinkled on the campus, where they are now used by feral cats as a litter box.

Ending #4:

Nathaniel Tack and Biff Thorgoode lost the case. But Nathaniel got his revenge by writing a book that was exceedingly kind and generous about all the people involved while still managing to make mad the guilty and appall the free. Alas, because of the double standard for books — but, oh, not the Internet — Nathaniel had to change some events and names to protect the bastards. He asked his friend Karma Sudra, the former Untouchable, who had been so supportive through it all, if she would proofread it for him. He printed out one copy of the lengthy manuscript and gave it to Karma — and not a moment too soon. The very next day a virus sent by unknown parties wiped out the entire contents of Nathaniel's hard-drive. Thus there was only one copy of his book in existence. When he and Karma met after she had proofread it (and failed to make a copy as she had promised), she insisted on going for a canoe ride in a city park, intending to explain to Nathaniel her feelings about his book in a pleasant, even bucolic, setting. He sensed that she had some criticisms that she wanted to give — but of course in person gently, like the kind soul she was. Just as she opened to page one, revealing her many red marks, and began her comments, the canoe accidentally tipped over. Both Karma Sudra and the manuscript — the only copy in existence, remember — fell into the water at the same time. It's very sad to say, but Nathaniel could save only one of the two.

You're reading it.

www.ingramcontent.com/pod-product-compliance
Lightning Source LLC
Chambersburg PA
CBHW030925020726

47498CB00001B/117